Penance: Book One
The Djinn of Aerlyn
JF Lingsch

Shadow Light Press

Contents

Dedication   VIII

Part One   1

1. The Sewers of Aerlyn   2

2. The Tutorial   9

3. Big Baby   16

4. The First Secret   21

5. It's a Trap!   27

6. Hidden Forest   34

7. The First Death   41

8. The Coronation Of 'Queen' Jamie.   51

9. Death Boons   57

10. Rigged Dice   67

11. One Rat, Two Rat   73

12. A Grim Stroke of Luck   82

13. Malice, Jamie Run 1, Part 1   90

14. Talkie Voice Thing   98

15. Consequences of Sin   103

16. A Devilish Idea   108

17. Out of Options   114

18. The Wizard   119

19. Why Would I Even Want Goblin Ears?   124

20. Minuscule Magical Menagerie   132

21. Did I Do Something Wrong?   137

22. Anger   142

23. The Second Floor   149

24. TREASURE. Jamie Run 1, Part 2   162

25. Penance Aflame   169

26. Will of the Heavens   176

27. First Time Seeing Your Corpse?   184

28. Forbidden By Penance.   194

29. Scan!   200

30. "Run, Rod, Run!"   211

31. "What Is a Kite?"   221

32. Whirling Vortex of Sludge   229

Part Two   237

33. Market Place Chase   238

34. Don't Panic   244

35. The Djinn   248

36. The Vault   253

37. Aunt Ersid   268

38. Textiles   274

39. Caution   279

40. Opulence of Objects   286

41. Lullaby   293

42. Aerlyntium   300

43. Zoo   307

44. The Best in the Business   313

45. Run Fatigue   320

46. Minion!   327

47. Thomas   340

48. Oasis   347

49. The Wall of Riddles   354

50. Glutyeknee   361

51. Horde   368

52. The Silver Mirage   376

53. I'm the Best. Jamie, Run 2, Part 2.   387

54. Fire!   396

55. Elemental Attacks   407

56. Squawk!   422

57. Nobble The Nasty   429

58. Lies! All Lies!   438

59. The Merchant's Luck   443

60. Awooo!   449

61. Overcharge   456

62. Marked By a God   462

63. The Great Will   471

64. The Red Death   477

65. Revenge   485

66. Get Better at Not Getting Stabbed   491

67. Sleep   497

68. Dumb Mistake   507

Part Three   516

69. Nice!   517

70. Grendelblin   523

71. Grendelkin   529

72. Unnecessarily Morbid   536

73. Prepare Yourselves!   542

74. Permanent Sacrifice   548

75. Kingsley   555

76. Whisperwind   563

77. Mini-Djinni   570

78. Jamie Run 2, Part 3   578

79. Run 7   585

80. Muridane   593

81. Trust   600

82. True Colors   606

83. Pain Of Death   614

84. Hyper Focus   621

85. A Meeting of the Gods   628

86. You Kill Them   634

87. Gore-Filled Things   640

88. The Lamp   645

89. Demon Bodies   651

90. Lightning Slam   657

91. A Slight Change of Plans   663

92. Never Done This Before   669

93. The Djinn of Aerlyn, Part 1 of 6   675

94. The Djinn of Aerlyn, Part 2 of 6   682

95. The Djinn of Aerlyn, Part 3 of 6   688

96. The Djinn of Aerlyn, Part 4 of 6   693

97. The Djinn of Aerlyn, Part 5 of 6   699

98. The Djinn of Aerlyn, Part 6 of 6   704

99. Jamie, Run 2, Part 4   710

Thank you   716

Acknowledgements   717

A Bit About The Author   719

You may also like...   720

Groups and Communities   722

To Dr. Hawkins:
Thank you for believing in me.
Rest in peace—the world is lesser without you.

Part One

Dice and Die

Chapter One

The Sewers of Aerlyn

{Rod. Wake up.}

I woke with a sharp inhale, choking on the stench of sewage. Darkness pressed against me like a suffocating shroud, its weight clawing at my chest. The air was heavy—thick with decay and rot—and every breath dragged the taste of filth across my tongue.

I squinted into the gloom, the faint outline of a murky corridor emerging from the black. *Where am I?* My pulse quickened, and my thoughts scattered like ash on the wind. Memories rose to the surface; fragmented and cruel.

I had died. An unbearable pain surged through me, then it was gone. Everything felt so foggy, and nothing made sense. Where was I? Had I died?

Penance, Prison of the Gods. The name echoed in my mind, dredged up from whispered warnings and half-forgotten tales. *A trial*, they said. A sentence worse than death. Vezwincourt's slums, where I grew up, were rife with stories—most dismissed them as myths, the kind of thing the Church used to keep the desperate in line. But the truth had teeth, and now they'd sunk into me.

Unbidden, memories flashed to my mind. My Father, dead. My best friend, dragged away from school. My gut twisted as the images flashed through my mind—too fast to grab hold of, too raw to forget. There'd been no trial, no chance to defend myself. Just chains and accusations. Then the void. And now this.

{Rod. Wake up.}

The voice from the abyss repeated itself, sharp and commanding, cutting through the haze. It wasn't my mother's voice. She'd whisper to me in the soft tones of bedtime stories and warm evenings by the fire. No, this voice was different—stripped of warmth, laced with urgency. A lifeline or a curse?

I pushed the panic down, grinding my teeth until my jaw ached. Survival first, questions later. The stories about Penance were clear enough: you didn't endure it—you escaped it. Or died—again, and again, and again.

I forced myself upright. My feet sank into something wet and foul, and a shiver ran up my spine as the almost sludge-like liquid clung to my boots. The stifling air burned my throat, each breath like inhaling hot ash. Somewhere in the blackness, a scroll materialized before me, its glow casting pale shadows on the crumbling walls.

{Would you like to undergo the Rite of Penance?}

A glowing 'yes' appeared on the scroll; the only option available.
Why would it ask if there wasn't even a choice?
The words hung there, carved into my mind even after the scroll dissolved into the dark. My stomach knotted, and I clenched my fists; nails biting into my palms. "I didn't want this," I rasped. My voice sounded foreign in the oppressive silence, hoarse and cracked.

The slime-covered walls oozed with decay, and rivulets of stagnant water traced sickly green patterns along the floor. Every step I took stirred the foul material, its chill seeping through my boots. I had to move though. The stories all agreed on one thing: staying still in the Rite was as good as a death sentence.

Mother once called the Rite a boogeyman—a tool for the Church to scare sinners into submission. *But if it was a legend, how did I end up here?*

I swallowed hard, bile burning the back of my throat. No answers were coming. Not here. Not now. The only truth that mattered was survival. And if the Church wanted me to atone, they'd have to watch me claw my way out of this cursed place first.

A scraping noise echoed behind me. My pulse jumped, a sharp spike of fear sent me stumbling forward, more of the sewage clinging to my feet attempting to drag me down. Questions swirled, clamoring for attention. *What if I found a dead end? What if something found me first?*

Ahead, a faint glow bled through the darkness, pale and flickering at the end of a narrow hallway. Light. It could mean escape—or something worse. I didn't care. I sloshed through now the knee-deep filth, gagging as the stench clawed its way into my lungs. A corroded metal door came into view, its surface pitted with rust. I grabbed the handle, grime slicking my fingers.

It didn't budge.

"No, no, no." The words spilled out, frantic, as I threw my weight against the door. Nothing. My chest heaved, each breath ragged and sour. My vision blurred, dizziness creeping in as the dark pressed closer. Memories hovered on the edge of my mind, sharp and unrelenting.

Think. This wasn't just a sewer. This was Penance. It wouldn't be easy. It wasn't meant to be. The Church thrived on fear, on agony. This was justice, they'd say. Punishment for sin.

A squeal broke through the silence. Something brushed against my leg, and I jerked back, bile rising in my throat. A rat. Its eyes glinted in the torchlight, twin embers sparking in the dark. It bared its teeth with a sharp, wet hiss.

"Back off," I muttered, voice low and shaky. My only weapon was the will keeping me upright—and it was already running thin. My eyes darted around, desperate. There—a torch, its flame faint but alive, wedged in a rusted sconce. I lunged, fingers closing around the handle, yanking it free.

The rat lunged first.

I swung the torch wide—clumsy and frantic. It dodged with a squeal, then darted closer, its teeth snapping at my face. Panic surged through me as I stumbled sideways, heart hammering in my chest. With a cry, I brought the torch down hard. The creature shrieked as the flaming end hit, its body twisting before it vanished into the muck.

My breathing came fast, ragged. I clutched the torch like a lifeline, its flickering glow casting twisted shadows on the walls. Faint shapes emerged, etched into the stone: murals, their scenes half-devoured by time. Figures in robes knelt before a blinding throne, their faces obscured by smears of mold and grime. A ritual? A prayer? Or something worse?

My head throbbed, the pain pulling me under as more memories surfaced.

My father, hunched in prayer, his face lined with worry. My best friend, wrists bound in chains, dragged screaming by the city guard. The Church's emblem, its sunburst cruel and unyielding, stamped on every wall of Vezwincourt.

The Rite of Penance. It had always been a ghost story, a whispered warning in the dark. But ghost stories didn't leave scars. And they didn't smell like death.

Another metallic clang echoed through the corridor, sharper this time. I whirled, torch raised, my back slamming against the corroded door. My breaths came quick and shallow, each one dragging the rancid air deeper into my lungs. Whatever made that sound, it was closer now.

Move. Flee. Survive.

I forced my legs into motion, the torchlight painting streaks of gold on the slick, grimy walls. The floor sloped downward, and with each step, the muck clung thicker, splashing cold filth onto my already soaked pants. My pulse thundered in my ears, louder with every distant clang, every unseen scuttle.

"Survive," I chanted, the word catching in my throat.

As I continued on, the corridor widened into a larger chamber. I froze, the torchlight flickering over three passageways ahead. Water dripped steadily from above, a sluggish rhythm that echoed too loudly in the silence.

Three paths. One surely had to be a way out.

I tested the first passage, stepping cautiously to peer inside. It stretched downward into darkness, no doors, no markers, just a tunnel descending deeper into whatever hell this was. My stomach churned at the thought of going farther underground.

The second route was worse—completely blocked by a wall of rubble. The remains of an iron gate jutted out, twisted and broken, half-consumed by the debris.

That left the third corridor.

A faint light flickered within its depths, barely perceptible through the murk. It could be another locked door, another dead end. Or worse. My fingers tightened around the torch as I pressed on, its feeble glow pushing the shadows back just enough to see.

Slime streaked the walls, glistening like oil in the torchlight. Beneath the muck, faint carvings emerged—circles within circles, with jagged lines radiating outward. They reminded me of the church's sunburst emblem, but twisted, almost feral. Older. More primal.

I swallowed hard. *This* was the Rite. It had to be.

The stories said that those overcoming the Rite would emerge purified, forgiven by the Church's mercy. But those were just stories. *I'd never heard of anyone making it out.* The torch trembled in my hand at the thought.

"I'm in danger." I chuckled, my voice high and nervous, teetering on the edge of a breakdown. I needed to escape, to survive. My head throbbed, and my thoughts were scattered, but the fire in my hands grounded me.

Focus.

I inched closer to the wall, watching in disgust as sewage oozed from the cracks and rolled upward. Impossible. The fluid slid toward the ceiling. A faded mural caught my eye beneath the filth, the drawings too smeared to make sense. Then I heard a sound, splashing through the muck.

My breath hitched. Something was out there, moving through the water.

Another rat waded through the filth, its eyes locked on me. It reared up, shrieking, bearing its sharp, yellowed teeth. I stumbled back, pressing myself against the wall. The torch flared in front of me, my only defense.

The rat lunged. I swung the torch down, but the rat dodged at the last second. Its fur smoldered as embers landed on its back, and it let out a screech of pain. It circled, ready to strike again.

Move. I threw myself to the side as it sprang at my face. I quickly sloshed through the muck; the rat missing me entirely.

The rat hesitated, confused, and I seized the moment. I swung the torch again, narrowly missing its head. My frustration boiled over, "Almost had you."

The rat snarled, and this time, it leaped. I raised the torch, but it used the torch body as a springboard, launching itself at my face. Instinct took over. I headbutted the rat, knocking it off balance. I grabbed it, slamming it down into the sewage, holding it under with all my strength. Its body convulsed, choking on the filth. I pressed harder, my heart racing. Finally, it stopped moving.

I survived. And until I found the true exit from this cursed place—*until I proved that Penance could be beaten*—I wouldn't stop fighting.I stood, panting, victorious.

Chapter Two
The Tutorial

My torch had gone out during the fight, leaving the room barely visible. Yet shadows still flickered on the sewage-stained walls. I looked around for a source of the light but I couldn't find one. Panic clawed at me, and my heart began to pound.

Focus, Rod. Get out of here.

The room shifted as a faint red glow permeated the air, its light staining the walls and sewage alike. The foul water glistened darkly, rippling as I moved. "What is that?" I muttered. The light brightened, pulsing like a heartbeat, and I began scanning the corridor.

Ahead, a rat's corpse bobbed in the sewage, half-submerged. Its body, torn and fresh, reflected the glow. I swallowed hard, my throat tight. The fight was still vivid in my mind—how I'd flailed uselessly, my torch failing to protect me. My chest tightened at the thought of Kandor, grinning as he teased, "Still the worst aim in Vezwincourt, Rod!" Kandor had always been there to patch me up, his laughter chasing away my fear. But now? Now I was alone.

The glow flashed brighter, dragging me from my thoughts. A crate sat near the far wall in a nearby room, illuminated as if by some sinister spotlight. Its warped boards and rusted nails looked fragile enough to snap apart under their own weight. My stomach twisted, but I stepped forward, ignoring the stench of sewage gushing around me. If there was something useful inside, I couldn't leave it behind.

The red light continued to flare, stabbing through the darkness like a blade. I squinted against it, prying the crate open with trembling hands. Splinters bit into my palms as the boards cracked and crumbled, raining debris onto the slick floor. My fingers brushed something solid inside.

Then it hit.

A sudden, crushing weight pressed down on me. It wasn't just the air—it was a presence, as if unseen eyes were boring into my very soul. My knees buckled, slamming into the muck with a splash. My breath hitched, shallow and panicked. The glow had grown overwhelming, twisting shadows into bizarre, shifting shapes.

And then, letters appeared.

They shimmered midair, scrawling across a translucent parchment that materialized out of nothing:

[Welcome, Rod, to Penance.]

"What...?" My voice cracked. My heart pounded against my ribs as a second parchment unfolded beneath the first, its swirling letters alive with unsettling energy.

[Greetings! I am your lifeline, your beating heart, the blood in your veins. As long as you have me, you shall not perish, and should you hold on to your sanity... well, we can get to that later. Would you like to view the tutorial?]

The words scrolled by on the page in front of me.

I stared, wide-eyed, the weight of the air pressing harder against my chest. Tutorial? What did that mean? Was this real? The text sounded equally sarcastic and amused. What did I know about Penance? Could I trust these floating papers? Or was this a part of the punishment?

A lump formed in my throat. My voice barely escaped as a whisper: "Y-yes."

[Great! I am your Life Crystal. I cannot be destroyed. I keep track of your stats, skills, quests, inventory, and more. Let me show you a basic overview.]

A translucent window unfurled before me, the text scrolling slower than I expected, as if savoring the reveal:

Rod
HP: 20/20
Stamina: 0/0
Mana: 0/0

[You haven't taken any damage from those rats, so you're still alive... or rather, not quite dead. You also have no stamina or mana available yet, so your skillset is limited. We'll get to the details soon.]

I swallowed hard. "Sure, thanks," I grumbled. "Good to know, I guess."

[Good. Now, shall I tell you about your inventory?]

Before I could reply, another window blinked into existence, the faint glow illuminating the grimy walls around me:

Inventory:
  • Torch (1)

  • Gold (0)

  • Death Boons (1)

[Torch: Deals minimal damage, with a small chance of causing burn.]

[Death Boons: A special currency for power. You'll need it to survive here, Rod.]

That last line hung in the air, the weight of it sinking into my chest. *Survive? I thought I was already dead.*

A sharp scraping noise echoed through the corridor, and I froze. My pulse quickened as the sound grew louder, reverberating off the damp walls. *Another rat? Or something worse?*

[Rod, while we talk, you should know creatures are drawn to your presence. Penance tests you. As such you might want to be prepared to defend yourself. That crate beside you could hold gear. Take a look.]

My gaze darted to the half-open crate. The shadows around it seemed to stretch and writhe in the flickering red light. Taking a deep breath, I reached inside, my hand trembling. My fingers brushed against something rough and leathery.

As I pulled it free, a small swirl of light danced around the item, its glow momentarily piercing the oppressive darkness.

[You have obtained: Leather Armor! You have earned 1 Death Boon for looting your first crate.]

Relief washed over me—actual armor, however modest. But as my fingers brushed the leathery material, a chilling thought pierced through my fleeting comfort: I was dead. Possibly trapped here forever. Every mistake, every regret, every crime had led me to this wretched place, the weight of it all sank deeper into my chest.

[Would you like to equip the armor? All you need to do is place it over your torso or imagine wearing it. Simple enough, yes?]

The patronizing tone of Crystal's words grated on me, but I complied, slipping the damp, battered armor over my soaked shirt. It fit snugly, the straps creaking as I tightened them. At least now, if something lunged at me, I might not die a second time... as fast.

A soft chime echoed in the corridor, followed by another glowing window of text that appeared before me, flooding the air with its faint red blue:

Rod
- **Level:** 1

- **Health:** 20/20

- **Stamina:** 0/0

- **Potency:** 0

- **Insight:** 0

- **Alacrity:** 0

- **Vitality:** 4

- **Defense:** 0

- **Magic Defense:** 0

- **Precision:** 5

- **Evasion:** 2

Equipped
Torch
  - **Damage:** 1–4

  - **+5% Burn**

Leather Armor
  - **Defense:** +1 if Condition > 5/10

I skimmed the list, only half-registering the details. The stats blurred together, a meaningless jumble of numbers and phrases. My father's voice echoed in my mind—*"Always pay attention, or the details will kill you."* Swallowing my frustration, I forced myself to focus.

"Hey, Crystal," I said aloud, my voice echoing faintly. "Why did that rat nearly kill me? I could barely land a hit."

[You lacked a class. Without a Class or Boon-based weapon proficiency, you have a -10 penalty to precision. In short: you can't hit squat with a torch.]

Crystal's bluntness stung, but it wasn't wrong. My grip on the torch tightened, the memory of my futile swings flashing through my mind.

[Would you like to unlock the Torchbearer Class? It costs 1 Death Boon.]

I froze, staring at the glowing words. A choice. My first real decision in this place. And then I laughed; it wasn't even a real choice.

"Fine," I muttered. "Yes."

[Congratulations! Torchbearer Class unlocked. Your penalty when using a torch is removed. Your precision will apply normally now.]

I waited for something—anything—to happen. A spark of insight, a rush of strength. But nothing. I swung the torch experimentally. It felt... the same. My mouth twitched in a wry half-smile. *Figures.*

The faint tapping noise reached my ears again, distant but deliberate. My body tensed as my eyes darted toward the corridor. Another rat? Or worse? I inched toward the exit, every step slushing through the foul water.

My breath shuddered. Dad wasn't here to bail me out of my mistakes.

"I've got to do this on my own," I whispered.

[Penance is a reflection of your soul, Rod. Whatever guilt brought you here, you must work through it or remain forever.]

I winced, my stomach twisting at the words. I'd stolen more than shoes. Run cons. Hustled marks. All to pay off Dad's debts, to save him—and us—from the edge of ruin. But in the end, I got caught. And disgraced. And... dead.

The memories clawed at me, sharp and relentless. My father's face hovered in my mind, blurry around the edges. I couldn't picture him clearly anymore—his voice, his laugh—they'd faded like fog in the sun. The thought stung more than I expected. *I hope I'm making you proud, Dad,* I thought bitterly.

Something scurried in the shadows behind me. My pulse spiked, and my instincts screamed.

"Crystal, can we continue this tutorial after I'm safe? Maybe after I'm out of these sewers?"

[You will never be safe in Penance. Be warned: your time here is limited only by your willingness to keep dying. And living. And dying again.]

A chill passed through me as I glanced over my shoulder. Were those eyes glinting in the dark? Or was it my imagination? Either way, I tightened my grip on the torch and turned toward the sloping corridor ahead. The faint outline of an opening loomed in the distance, shrouded in black.

"Guess there's only one way to go," I said, voice trembling but firm.

I stepped forward, ignoring the stench that clung to me and the echoes of my past clawing for attention. Dad's face flickered in my mind again, stern but hopeful.

The red glow behind me dimmed, and the silent parchment flickered out of existence. I inhaled, summoning the last shreds of courage. Whatever waited in the darkness, I wasn't going to die cowering in a corner. Not again.

I will see this through, Dad. I'll make sure none of your sacrifices were in vain.

With that silent promise burning in my chest, I took my first step toward the exit and left the room.

Chapter Three
Big Baby

[Oh, get over yourself, you big baby.]

A searing light pierced through my eyelids. The parchment appeared in my vision, even with my eyes closed. Somehow, the words on the page felt loud. Try as I might to ignore them, the words burned in my vision.

[You can't ignore me.]

I gulped, shutting my eyes tighter, my heart pounding in my chest and my hands trembling with a new fear playing in the back of my mind.

Why is this parchment berating me? I thought this thing was supposed to be on my side.

[You can't get rid of me. So buck up and act like an adult.]

I opened my eyes, and the text on the parchment continued scrolling, though it didn't seem to be screaming at me anymore.

[Everyone dies; it's not worth crying about. Get back to me after you die 100 times in here.]

I forced myself to remain still, focusing on calming the tremors running through my body by taking slow, deep breaths.

Everyone dies, the parchment had said, its cold indifference chilling me to the core. Gradually, the deep breaths helped me calm enough that the stabbing pain in my chest subsided, though the feeling that nothing would ever be alright again still lingered.

I shifted my attention to the crate beside me, slick with the green slime coating the room's bricks. I forced myself upright with a final deep breath, using the crate for support. My brown hair clung to my forehead, damp with sweat and slime. I wiped my hand on my thigh, staring at the sewage pooling on the ceiling like a dark omen. This place felt like a twisted nightmare, and the absurdity clawed at my sanity.

I really don't get this place. What kind of twisted nightmare had I been thrown into? The sheer absurdity of the situation makes me feel as if I am teetering on the edge of madness. As I struggled to comprehend the situation, another parchment appeared, covering my vision.

[Now, let us get back to business. Would you like to equip the leather armor?]

"Yes, of course. That sounds... great," I said, trying to muster enthusiasm despite the emotions smothering my soul.

I shivered, a sheen of slime covering my body, making the deep, dungeon cold harder to deal with. The numbness from the overwhelming emotions made it hard to summon the energy to care.

The leather armor materialized around my chest. Brown, supple, and form-fitting, the armor felt surprisingly comfortable. It didn't guard much, but it came with bracers and gloves, which made it easier to grip my torch.

[Congratulations, you have equipped your first-ever piece of armor. You have received a single Death Boon.]

"Can I use the Death Boons now?" I asked, my curiosity slowly overcoming the lingering fear as I wiped the green slime from my hands onto my leather bracers. *Oh, how easily my mind shifts gears.*

[No. With the exception of purchasing a new class, Death Boons may only be used in the entrance room.]

"Oh," I said, nodding. "I guess." I decided I would only be wasting time if I waited around in the room any longer.

As I approached the door, an unexpected calm washed over me, likely due to the leather armor now snug around my chest. For the first time since waking, I felt a glimmer of control over my destiny, a stark contrast to the overwhelming confusion that had plagued me moments before. Briefly, I allowed myself to believe that maybe, just maybe, I could survive this.

The door was a dull grey slab, functional but featureless, marked only by a simple iron bar. The bar, worn from countless uses and barely hanging onto the wall, clearly served as the handle. I pushed it in, and it creaked with age.

The door slid against the floor surprisingly smooth, revealing a room almost identical to the one I was still standing in. I leaned into the room to see better but did not enter.

A question spilled out of my mouth just as the next room came into view.

"Do you have a map?" As I crossed into the room, another parchment appeared, announcing the location I was entering.

~Run 1, Room 1L, Floor 1, Sewers of Aerlyn~

Before it, more words unfurled as Crystal 'spoke:'

[Unfortunately, not yet, Rod.]

I sighed and looked around. I could see the torch flickering in the distance. I gagged for a second, still not used to the awful smell of sewage. I forced myself to regain control, but it was too late. Before I knew what was happening, a rat the size of a dog screeched and jumped onto my arm, sinking its teeth into my flesh. Pain exploded from the bite, causing me to scream and flail my long arms in an attempt to dislodge the creature.

I hardly noticed the giant 4-sided die flying in the background. I would have laughed at how comical it seemed if it weren't happening to me.

[You take two damage.]

What, how did it deal so much damage? It's a rat! It landed just in front of me, and panicking, not knowing what else to do, I lunged forward, screaming, "Die!!" I swung my torch at the rat, hitting it on the head.

Another comically large four-sided die flew from nowhere and landed.

[You deal one damage. Congratulations on dealing your first-ever blow with a weapon in combat; you have gained 1 Death Boon.]

"Wait, what about the one I killed in the previous room?"

[You never struck that rat with the torch.]

"But I still struck it! And I choked it to death; shouldn't I have gotten more Death Boons?" Ultimately, it didn't matter; I was arguing with parchment while a giant rat tried to kill me. I felt like an idiot.

And worse, reading Crystal's messages and paying attention to the enemy was something that needed to mix better. I had no time to react as the rat jumped up to my arm again and took another bite of me.

I screamed again and, this time pushed the rat off my arm, the pain from the second bite nearly unbearable. Ignoring the message, I swung my torch at the rat, but the pain made it difficult to aim accurately. It scurried to find its footing, and I missed, my arm going wide.

I growled, "I thought you said I would be able to hit them now."

[No, I said without the class, you had a -10 penalty for your precision stat, not that you would always hit.]

Instead of attacking, the rat fled, putting space between us.

While the parchment text scrolled, I pressed the advantage, chasing the fleeing rat with a newfound sense of determination.

This is it. My first real chance to fight back.

The torch felt reassuringly solid in my grip as I chased after the rat. Before it could turn around, I swung the torch again; the die flew past as the torch connected. I heard a satisfying thunk noise, and the rat spun around.

It looked beaten to a pulp, blood flying from its mouth like spittle, one of its eyes wholly crushed. Another hit should be able to do it. I steadied myself, my heart pounding, and before the rat could react, I swung one last time. The torch connected with a solid thud, and the creature collapsed in a heap, dead.

I sank to the floor, exhausted. I hadn't had time to rest after fighting the first rat, and this fight had been even worse.

And what were with those messages? I can't believe Crystal made them appear like that. They completely blocked my view. I was going to need to say something about them.

Equipment

Torch

- **Effect:** Deals 1–4 physical damage. 5% chance of causing burn effect on target

- **Condition:** 10/10

Leather Armor

- **Effect:** +1 Defense

- **Condition:** 15/15

Chapter Four
The First Secret

[Congratulations, you have defeated the Giant Rat. For killing your first mob on the floor with a weapon, you have gained 1 Death Boon.]

"Hey, Crystal, your message thingies nearly killed me back there."

[Do you mean the notifications] A new one popped up mentioning something about a quest and escaping, but I shoved it aside for the parchment she actively talked to me on. [I am sorry, but it is a setting that must be changed separately by Death Boons.]

I sighed. Of course it wouldn't be that easy. As Crystal's indifferent response scrolled across the parchment, frustration bubbled up within me. Memories of waking in Penance flooded back.

Why me? Why had I been brought to Penance? The realization that I didn't have the force of will to leave this place weighed heavily on me.

Walking past the dead rat, I saw a sparkling cloud of dust rising from its corpse, almost like smoke from a flame. I kicked at the rat's remains, watching as they disintegrated into a sparkling cloud of gold dust. The surreal nature of this place struck me again.

[You loot five gold.]

Just when I thought this place couldn't get weirder. Corpses disappearing. Clothing that magically appeared around my body. Speaking, floating crystals. Giant Dice. Utterly bizarre.

Then, I saw it—a small orb descending from the ceiling. It pulsed with a bright blue light, casting odd, disjointed shadows. It moved slowly as if it knew I would wait for it to descend.

A part of me screamed not to touch it, warning that it was dangerous magic I didn't understand. But another part was mesmerized.

I had always loved magic, hadn't I?

I reached out to it.

Unexpectedly, more parchment appeared in my vision—comparable but not identical to the ones that woke me up. I shuddered as a ghost of pain flowed through me. This parchment was glowing with a similar but softer blue hue than the orb.

As I touched the orb, everything froze. The water flowing around my feet, my pounding heart, even the sound of water dripping—everything stopped.

~~~~~~{Memory Core 1/???}~~~~~~

{Would you like to view the memory?}
{Y/N}

Hesitantly, I said, "Yes." A sharp spike of adrenaline coursed through my body.

Memory Core? Is this why I can't remember anything? My heart pounded, and then, the sewer was gone.

~~~~~~{Memory Core 1 Start}~~~~~~

A serene garden gradually came into focus, the golden sunlight filtering through a canopy of leaves. I sat at a quaint table adorned with an array of delicious-looking meats, breads, and cheeses.

My hands and mouth moved on their own as if under a spell, mechanically lifting morsels of food to my lips. The taste was exquisite, yet I felt no pleasure, only a strange, detached calm as if I were merely a spectator in my own body. A jolt of electricity suddenly rushed through me, snapping me out of my detached state. I remembered. Our final lunch, though not our final meeting. Words tumbled out of my mouth before I could stop them:

"I'm going to kill your father."

I locked eyes with Queen Jamie, my gaze unwavering, challenging her to speak the question we both knew lingered in the air.

"I have to end it. There's no other way..."

Though only sixteen, Queen Jamie was the nominal ruler of the country. Yet, her father's shadow loomed over every decision, his influence palpable in every royal decree. Despite Jamie's proximity to power and our bizarre friendship, I still huddled in the cold confines of my parent's home every night while she slept in the warm fires of luxury. How much would it cost her to help me? To fix my broken life? Nothing.

Her response was as calm as the surface of a still pond, shattering my expectations of shock or indignation.

"My hands are tied," she said evenly. "Besides, killing him won't stop the pain. Killing him won't fix everything." She hesitated, but her voice remained steady.

"You know this; the Church of Rellum teaches us killing is wrong; all it will get you is a one-way ticket to an Eternity in Penance."

I clenched my fists under the table, my entire body tense with suppressed rage and frustration. I wanted her to yell at me, to call me rash and stupid. But there was no saving me now. I had made up my mind.

Even in this so-called Kingdom of Never-Ending Peace, people were still killed.

"That doesn't matter," I said, my voice unwavering. "I wouldn't end up there for this anyway. Only monsters end up there. Monsters like him."

He wasn't just a tyrant; he was an abomination who thrived on misery. My soul might be beyond saving, but at least I could save others from his cruelty.

Her eyes flickered with a shadow of something—regret?

"You think I haven't tried to stop him? He's my father, but every time I've opposed him, he's tightened his grip on the kingdom. On me. It's getting harder and harder to sneak out of the palace."

"Then help me before it's too late," I insisted. "You can do something. If you really cared about this kingdom, you'd stop him before he destroys everything. Look at me, Jamie. I'm what his rule has done. Do you want more people to suffer like this?"

I paused, waiting for a reaction. The queen looked down at her tea, little spirals of smoke wafting away into the air. She closed her eyes and frowned.

If you were really sad, you'd have your guard arrest him and take back control, I thought.

She hesitated, and then, in a tiny voice I struggled to hear, she said, "There's nothing I can do. I can't stop him."

I shook my head. *This isn't working.*

Instead, I changed tactics—subversion.

"Fine but at least give me your ring; it would help me get to him. I can stop him; I know that I can. That's why I need it." I didn't, truly. But a fast way into the palace would go a long way to helping my cause.

She pulled it off her finger and played with it. Sunlight reflected on its silver surface, catching my eye and making me squint. She held it up in the air and started talking.

"If I give this to you, I'll end up in Penance the same as you."

"I'm killing him with or without your help."

The wind rustled the leaves overhead, a small shower of foliage falling over us and settling into our cups. I picked up my tea, carefully removing the leaves, savoring the earthy aroma despite the tension. I wasn't so lucky I could throw away tea. However, the queen emptied her cup on the ground before picking up the carafe and refilling it.

But I was lucky, wasn't I? Somehow, I had met the Queen of the Realm, and here I was, throwing my chance away like she throws out afternoon tea. After my declaration, how could she bear to be around me? Especially now that her ring burned a hole in my pocket. The third rule of being a thief was to ask nicely but never take no for an answer.

The world turned grey as we kept talking, Jamie gracefully changing topics, and the subject of my imminent sin was forgotten. Leaves continued to fall from overhead, hopefully covering the evidence of my sin until I left.

If I learned one thing about her over our weekly meetings, it was this: the Queen didn't actually care. She was as broken as I was. She had seen the horrors of the world and given up on us all, content to let her father rule in her stead. The breeze came again, and this time, the tree shook violently. She stood, dusting the debris off her gown. We made our goodbyes. And—

~~~~~~{Memory Core 1 End}~~~~~~

The serene garden vanished as a horrific stench yanked me back to reality. I blinked a few times, struggling to acclimate to the sewage around me. What was that? I shook my head, a headache lingering, so I did what I always did when I was in pain: I distracted myself.

I walked toward the chest I had seen earlier. Placing my hand on the simple brown lid, I nudged it. It didn't budge. Realizing my error, I moved my hand to the metal latch securing the lid. I lifted it and opened the chest.

[You loot 25 Gold. You have received a Death Boon for opening your first chest.]

Great. Gold. A fat lot of good that would be. What could I even buy in Penance? There would be few people here, right? Or would there be a lot?

I didn't know what information I could trust. Ignoring my swirling thoughts, I left the room, determined to face whatever this twisted place threw at me next.

Quest Name: [Escape]
Type: Floor
Description:
Complete! Escape the sewers.
Reward:

- You can now start on the second floor

- You can also access the following new Boons:

  ◦ Waypoint

  ◦ Auto-Repair

  ◦ Vault Interest

  ◦ Potion Restore

  ◦ Upgrade System

- 5 Death Boons

Chapter Five
It's a Trap!

~Run 1, Room 2L, Floor 1, Sewers of Aerlyn~

The air in this room felt colder and heavier. Thankfully, my current path was linear, so I didn't bother asking for a map again. I took a quick glance around the room. There was a scary-looking black door, two giant rats, and a torch.

Walking into the next room, I heard a click and looked down. The floor was slightly discolored where I stood, a dark grey instead of the light grey, green-stained stone that filled the sewer floors. I realized too late that I had triggered a pressure plate. And, of course, I walked right onto it like an idiot.

My gaze shot up as a sharp sound pierced the silence. Before I could react, stings ravaged my body as a litany of arrows pierced my leather armor.

"Owww!" I shrieked before clapping my hand over my mouth, but it was too late.

[It's a Trap! You take 4 points of damage from the arrow volley. Your HP is now 12/20. Watch your step next time, Rod.]

The pain was intense, but I had no time to dwell on it. I was about to pull the arrows out of my chest when they vanished. Before I could react, the two rats let out ear-drum-rattling shrieks, snapping me back to the immediate danger. A frigid sensation crawled along my spine like a horde of frozen spiders.

They charged me together, but I was ready for it. As I avoided their blows, I swung the torch at the rat on the right. The dice rolled. I glanced at the notification quickly to see how much damage I had done. At the same time, I readied my torch and again evaded the attacks of the two rats. They were so easy to dodge; I couldn't believe I let the second one bite me so many times. I was learning, albeit slowly.

[You deal 3 damage.]

My muscles tensed in preparation, and I swung again at the first rat. The dice rolled.

[You deal 4 damage. Giant Rat 1 is defeated. Congratulations!]

The rat collapsed to the floor, a small spurt of blood fanning around it. A brief sense of triumph washed over me. Pushing aside early celebration, I swiftly turned to attack the second rat; my mind focused, torch ready for the attack. Except the rat wasn't there. Momentary though my pause may have been, it was enough for the rat to scuttle into my blind spot. I had no chance to react as the rat jumped on my back. The dice rolled.

[You take 3 damage.]

As my health dwindled to a mere nine points, Crystal's earlier warning echoed in my mind: I really was going to die. I yelled in anger and frustration; this wasn't fair! But now wasn't the time to give up. I couldn't afford to lose focus now. With a swift maneuver, I let gravity take over, crashing onto the ground, using my weight to crush the rat clinging to my back. The impact was satisfying, but I waited for the dice to roll.

[You deal 2 damage.]

The rat recoiled back, its movements becoming more frantic as the blow ebbed at its willpower. I quickly sidestepped its pathetic lunge, laughing at it, before swinging my slowly decaying torch. I swung at the rat in retaliation. The dice rolled.

[You deal 4 damage. Giant Rat 2 is defeated. Congratulations!]

The rat slunk to the floor, its eyes clouded in death. Exhausted but relieved, I took a moment to catch my breath, knowing this small victory was just the beginning of my journey through this treacherous place.

With the rats defeated, I allowed my gaze to drift across the room, taking in the usual reverse sewage and the shimmering golden stars rising from the giant rats. I looted them.

[You looted Rat Meat x1. You looted Rat Teeth x1.]

"What in the name of Malikap are these? Why would I even want rat meat?" I frowned and waited for Crystal to respond. Instead, my eyes caught a glimmer in the corner—a silver chest. My face brightened, eyes widening, rat parts forgotten.

Could this be my lucky break? Maybe I won't die after all. Take that, Crystal! Finally, something good amidst all this chaos. I dashed forward to the chest, heart hammering in anticipation, only to feel my hope shatter into a million pieces as my hand gripped the lock keeping the chest firmly in place.

[The chest is locked. You do not have the **Unlock** skill, nor do you have a chest key. Would you like to try bashing the lock?]

"Yes, of course." I struck the lock with my torch. A die rolled in my peripheral; I was starting to get annoyed by their appearance.

[You deliver a decisive strike, and the chest's lock gives way.]

The chest swung open.

[You've looted 3 items from the Uncommon Chest: You've obtained 10 gold coins, a Cloth Shirt, and Leather Greaves.]

A blue parchment appeared in front of me, showing the new items in my inventory.

My heart swelled with relief and excitement. Finally, some decent gear! I quickly equipped the cloth shirt and leather greaves, feeling a bit more protected and a lot more hopeful.

"What're my stats at now?"

[You have 2 defense, and 9 health now, Rod.]

"Wait, you didn't show me my full stats page."

[Well, yeah, it's not like you need the extra info at the moment. Can you imagine how exhausting it would be to read the entire page?]

I shook my head and then sat down on the floor cross-legged. I took a moment to pause and collect myself. While I wasn't in pain at the moment, I was worried—three-fifths of my health was gone, just like that. I shook my head; it was time to move on.

Feeling slightly more equipped, I approached the next door. This one radiated some sort of magical energy, absorbing the light from my torch and from Crystal. The area surrounding the door felt cold and wrong, as if standing near it would suck out all the happiness in the world and leave me helpless. The burnt facade of the stone looked mismatched against the gray of the sewers, like the wrong color skin grafted onto a hapless burn victim. The door handle was even more unsettling, resembling a cadaver's head more than anything else.

I could go back and try one of the other doors. But something in me knew I needed to press onward here. I closed my eyes, suppressing what little remained of my gag reflex as I pushed down on the corpse's head. The door opened with little fanfare or creaking.

My jaw dropped, hanging open, as I entered the next room. My eyes widened at the surreal scene before me.

I was no longer underground or in a sewer. The air shifted, a warm summer breeze filling my nose with the scent of flowers and the earthy aroma of a dark, forbidden forest. The room was full of trees and in the distance, I could make out a figure in a clearing. It was as if I had been whisked away to a midnight grove hidden deep within the dungeon. The walls were adorned with the massive, fearsome skull of a long dead dragon. In the room's eerie expanse, the dragon's skull loomed large, its hollow sockets casting an unnerving stare that seemed to follow my every move.

At the far end of the room was an altar, and what every dark and ominous altar needed was a no-good, rotten Necromancer. I shuddered. Every kid from Vezwincourt spent too much of their childhood learning about the Necromancer Wars. A thousand years ago, the neighboring Kingdom of Aerlyn had been wiped off the map; it was only recently that Aerlyn had started to be a thing again. Why anyone would want to build on the ruins of a dilapidated undead paradise? I didn't know.

Why do I remember that and not what my parents looked like?

The Necromancer laughed, a booming, dark laugh that made me shiver. It was at that moment I knew for sure I was going to die. A cacophonous noise filled the air as I turned to exit the room. The ground shook, and iron bars descended, locking me in the dungeon room with the Necromancer. My heart sank as I realized escape was not an option.

Health: 9/20
Defense: 2
   Inventory
   Death Boons: 5
   Gold: 40
   Arrows
   - **Amount:** 5

   - **Condition:** 4/5

   - **Effect:** Allows you to fire a bow

   - **Description:** A simple wooden arrow with a stone arrowhead

   Rat Teeth
   - **Amount:** 1

- **Condition:** N/A

- **Effect:** None

- **Description:** The incisor(s) of a Giant Rat. Who knows? If you collect a lot, something good may happen

Rat Meat

- **Amount:** 1

- **Condition:** N/A

- **Effect:** +5 Health, 80% chance of poison if consumed

- **Description:** Juicy, full of protein, and only tastes a little like sewage! Who knows? If you collect a lot, something good may happen
"Tastes like chicken!" – Photonius the Dead

Cloth Shirt

- **Amount:** 1

- **Condition:** 10/10

- **Effect:** +1 Defense

- **Description:** It's a shirt!
"My friend went to Penance, and all I got was this lousy T-shirt!"

Leather Greaves

- **Amount:** 1

- **Condition:** 15/15

- **Effect:** +1 Defense

- **Description:** A worked and treated pair of leather greaves covering the waist down to the ankles

Equipment
Torch

- **Effect:** Deals 1–4 physical damage, 5% chance of causing burn effect on target

- **Condition:** 4/10

Leather Armor

- **Effect:** +1 Defense

- **Condition:** 12/15

Leather Greaves

- **Effect:** +1 Defense

- **Condition:** 15/15

Chapter Six
Hidden Forest

The room's atmosphere grew even more tense as I realized my predicament.

The dragon's skull leered at me with a malevolent grin. A lump formed in my throat, and I swallowed hard, the metallic taste of fear lingering on my tongue. Across the room, the Necromancer watched my every move, his expression unchanged, as if he had anticipated this outcome.

My hands trembled, but I forced my feet forward, each step heavier than the last, until I stood before the powerful Necromancer. His glare intensified as I drew closer. The Necromancer's eyes bore into me, a sinister glint in his gaze making my skin crawl, yet there was a flicker of intrigue that suggested he was studying me as much as threatening me.

Silence hung in the air, thick and oppressive. "Who dares enter my domain?" The Necromancer's voice sounded loud through the room, shattering the silence.

I swallowed hard. "I–I mean no harm. I'm seeking my Penance. If you let me out, I'll leave you to your stargazing."

A cold smile tugged at his lips. "Seeking Penance, you say? This chamber is not meant for those who seek salvation. I am sorry to say you will not find it here."

He studied me for a moment, his expression unreadable. Then, with a sinister smirk, his demeanor shifted abruptly. Raising his hand, dark, crackling energy formed into a bolt of inky purple from his staff. With a flick of his wrist, he sent the bolt hurtling towards me.

I dodged to the side, just barely missing the deadly bolt. Not giving my enemy a chance to strike again, I rushed forward, swinging my torch down in an overhand swing, aiming for his right eye.

The Necromancer's eyes narrowed, his amusement fading as he moved closer. I struck right at his eye. The dice rolled.

[You deal 3 damage]

The Necromancer staggered back, momentarily blinded by the torch strike. His grip on his Necrotic Staff faltered. I pulled my arm back for another swing, aiming for his left eye. The die rolled again.

[You deal 4 damage.]

For a fleeting second, hope sparked in my chest, a tantalizing whisper that I might just have a chance. And then my torch crumbled to dust in my hands. I stared dumbfounded at the dust in my hands for just a moment too long. A die rolled, and a sickly black bolt flew towards me. I closed my eyes and ducked, knowing my death would come.

Somehow, the bolt missed again. I rushed forward without thinking, slamming my pitiful fists into the Necromancer's face. Anger surged inside of me. How dare this monster laugh at me. I would show him. Instead of a die, a giant coin flipped in the air.

[You deal 2 damage.]

The Necromancer's eyes widened, a flicker of fear mirroring my own as my fists made unexpected contact. His usual composure shattered momentarily. He pushed the staff point-blank range against me, and before I could react, the die rolled in the background.

[The Necromancer deals 7 damage.]

A scream tore its way from my lungs as agony surged like wildfire through my veins, my knees buckling under the searing pain. My vision grew red, but in the heat of battle, I barely noticed. I fell forward, grabbing the Necromancer's shoulder, preventing him from gaining any distance as I forced him down with me. I could swear I heard my heartbeat thunder in my ears.

The battle hung in the balance. This last move would determine if I could win or not. I steadied myself, and the coin flipped in the air as I reared my arm back for a punch. My fist connected with a satisfying crunch, but I didn't let up. I punched and punched and punched until there was nothing but blood under my hands. What's left of the bloody, beaten man collapsed to the ground, defeated. I screamed in victory.

[You deal 2 damage but take 1 point of damage from recoil. Congratulations! You have defeated the Necromancer.]

The Necromancer started to sparkle. I bent over his fallen form, fingers trembling as I rifled through his tattered robes. The familiar clatter of dice echoed in my mind, signaling the rewards of my grim victory.

[For killing a mob boss, you have received a Death Boon. You have looted Staff of the Necro Bolt, and a Chest Key.]

I did a little jig, feeling surprisingly spry and healthy despite my wounds from the battle; my vision remained red, and I could still hear my heart pounding. Which made me wonder how much damage I had taken. Was I that close to death?

"Crystal, how much health do I have left?"

[You have 1 health remaining.]

I blinked in shock. I really had been close to dying.

The Necromancer faded into the air as Crystal told me about my health. I sighed. The robe had looked so cool. But thoughts of the robe vanished as I spied the ornate gold chest with five rubies inlaid above the locked clasp. With no preamble, I opened the chest with the chest key. Multiple dice rolled around me. First, what looked like a 6-sided die and then eight giant 100-sided dice bounced around the room. I was starting to hate the things as I covered my ears to block the sounds of their rattling.

[You've obtained an Iron Short Sword. You've received an Iron Mace. You've received an Iron Helm. You've received a Potion of Health Regen.]

So much for dying quickly, I thought, laughing at Crystal. I had a health regen potion and actual weapons. I was out of the woods, at least for a little while.

I took the health regen potion from my inventory without a thought and immediately chugged it, not even asking how it worked.

"Wait," I said belatedly, "how does the regen potion even work?"

[The health regen potion recovers 2 points of health per room traveled. It recovers a maximum of 50 health. You did not have to consume all of the potion at once.]

I slapped my forehead and wrinkled my brow, but I set my grin and charged ahead. My eyes scanned the room, seeking anything else of value, but nothing else caught my eye within the red glow of Crystal's soothing light. I sighed. I did that a lot, sighing, but I was three rooms into this dungeon, and I was exhausted, mentally, at least. Physically, I felt better than I ever had, which really just made no sense to me.

After a battle like that, even with the potion, I need a break. I collapsed to the floor, resting on the grass floor of the Necromancer's room. In a rare quiet moment, I paused, sifting through my thoughts and feelings. Despite the recent violence, I felt fine. A strange calm settled over me, my mind clear, my body unburdened by pain or fatigue.

I had felt a calm like this before on the worst day of my life. That day was probably why I was here. It wasn't my fault, but I probably blamed myself even more than society did. I had been a wreck for a very long time after that, stealing more and more, harming my friends, and planning to kill a king.

But where did these thoughts come from? I couldn't even remember killing anyone, but I knew I had. This didn't even faze me. I could probably close my eyes and sleep just like a baby if I had been the least tired, but even after countless battles, I hadn't broken a sweat.

"Crystal, why don't I feel tired? Or hurt, for that matter? Or upset? I just killed someone."

[When Penance was built, it was decided that there should be no pain in the early runs of the dungeon. He decided it was better to slowly ease you into the horrors here. As for stamina...]

I ignored the rest of the message and interrupted her. "He who?" I paused, my mind reeling. "Who built this place? Malikap? Aurentum? Rellum?"

[The dungeon has always been here since before the gods stirred the primordial muck into existence. All of them had a hand in its creation, but...]

"But what? Why won't you tell me anything?"

[I am telling you what you need to know, and besides, you should dwell on why you are here, not on why Penance is here. Have you thought about why you are a Penitent yet?]

"And how am I supposed to do that? I can't remember a thing! I don't even know what kind of person I am other than that I stole a pair of shoes as a kid!" I screamed this last bit, more than a little frustrated at her suggestion. But it was true, though.

Not a second of my time in the dungeon had been spent on redeeming myself for what I had done or questioning why I was here. I honestly didn't even know how I died.

[You are right, Rod. I am sorry, you will recover your memories eventually, though I don't recall other Penitents taking as long as you to remember things. After all, how can you repent if you don't know what you did wrong?]

I shook my head, barely reading the words on the parchment. Perhaps if I made it to the next floor, I would start remembering things; it was worth a shot. I already knew I was in for a long journey. *I can be introspective later. A rat could sneeze on me, and I would keel over dead.*

For now, it was time to cheat a little. If the potion healed me by two health per room, I could travel back and forth between rooms to recover my health before moving further into the dungeon. Instead of wasting time, I asked Crystal if it would even work.

[You are currently locked out of the potential for a Death Boon for speed-running the first floor. However, there will be no penalties or consequences should you exploit that loophole.]

"Well, that's brilliant. Please equip my new iron helm, my iron sword in my left hand, and the mace in my right hand."

"Now we're talking," I said as I took a few test swings of the weapons, thinking about the 2 in Potency I now had. "Hey Crystal, what does Potency do?"

[Potency increases the damage you deal by 1 point. So if you roll a 1, you deal 2 damage; roll a 2, and you deal 3, and so on.]

"That's pretty amazing, thanks Crystal." I awkwardly waved my hand in a thanking gesture before realizing Crystal was above me. "Anyway, time to get to work."

I left the hidden forest that was the Necromancer's room. It blew my mind that such a place existed, but I guess it was the magic of the prison at work. I had heard that entire cities were hidden in its depths, so it wasn't too much of a stretch for there to be a forest, too.

I paced back and forth through the forest and a dungeon room for ten minutes, feeling the potion's magic slowly knitting my wounds, infusing me with renewed strength until my health was fully restored. The potion had already used up nine charges and would likely no longer be useful. But now, with my health restored, I felt a renewed determination to clear the floor.

I shoved the door open with enough force to break the rotten iron bar, which clattered to the floor with a dull thunk. Anticipation surged through me as I imagined the rats on the other side. They had no idea what was coming. Holding my new sword above my head, I ran in screaming.

Equipment

Iron Sword

- **Effect:** 1–6 physical damage, +1 Potency

- **Condition:** 20/20

Iron Mace

- **Effect:** 1–6 physical damage, 5% chance to stun, +1 Potency

- **Condition:** 20/20

Iron Helm

- **Effect:** +2 Defense

- **Condition:** 20/20

Leather Armor

- **Effect:** +1 Defense

- **Condition:** 12/15

Leather Greaves

- **Effect:** +1 Defense

- **Condition:** 15/15

Chapter Seven
The First Death

~Run 1, Room 1R, Floor 1, Sewers of Aerlyn~

Burning with a desire for revenge, I burst into the room with a battle cry, only to be met by an unsettling emptiness. The room was starkly barren, too: no torches, no chests, no monsters, and notably, no stench of rotten bodily waste. It felt like an afterthought, a forgotten corner of the dungeon, devoid of purpose or presence. Or was it? "Crystal? Are there secret rooms?"

[Yes, but there is not a hidden room here.]

"So it's got to be back in the Necromancer's room!" An orb the size of my head and pulsing white light descended from the center of the flooded ceiling. My eyes shone brightly for a second, and then I grabbed for the Memory Core that had crystallized in front of me.

{Memory Core 2/????}
{Would you like to view the memory?}
{Y/N}

~~~~~~{Memory Core 2 Start}~~~~~~

I was back in pauper's school, sitting at my broken desk that always leaned too far to the right. The cracked wooden surface wobbled precariously under my arms, making it a constant struggle to keep my papers and books from sliding off. Professor Perrod stood at the chalkboard, his back to the class, writing with his characteristic sharp, angular script.

"Little is known about Penance. Rumors and secrets hoarded like currency mean seldom few facts make their way to become everyday knowledge." His voice was a low, gravelly murmur, but it carried through the room with an eerie clarity. The dim light from the high, narrow windows made it difficult to see the board, but we all managed anyway.

I couldn't remember his face clearly—the magic of Penance had eroded those details—but his words rang in my ears as if he had spoken them just yesterday. "What we do know is that secrets in Penance are meant to remain just that. The more you uncover, the harder your time in Penance will become." The students around me sat in rapt silence, their eyes fixed on the professor, their expressions a mix of curiosity and unease.

As I listened, a chill ran down my spine. The secrets of Penance were tantalizing enigmas, forbidden fruits that promised both enlightenment and peril. Professor Perrod paused his writing, turning to face us, his eyes sweeping across the room. "Remember," he continued, his voice softer now, almost a whisper, "knowledge is power, but in Penance, it can also be a curse. Choose wisely what you seek to uncover, for some doors, once opened, can never be closed again."

~~~~~~{Memory Core 2 End}~~~~~~

I stumbled as I returned to reality—the image of the teacher fading, but the words lingering like tattoos. A cold shiver ran down my spine, and I felt an eerie sensation like an invisible hand tightening around my throat. With bravery I didn't know I had, I decided to look for a secret room anyway. I backtracked to the Necromancer's room, deciding that a room as large as that must have a secret or two.

For about a minute, I shuffled through the room, fingers brushing against the central altar's cold stone and the surrounding forest's rough bark; my eyes fruitlessly scanned the room for hidden mechanisms or clues. I kept looking for a trace of hope, for some secret to unveil itself. That hope reached a crescendo as my fingers depressed something on the underside of the altar. But the room remained silent. No hidden doors, no sudden monsters. Only a mystery to solve in the future. Frustration nipped at my resolve as I acknowledged the fruitlessness of my search.

With a crestfallen sigh, I returned to the empty room and through the same grey door with a rusty handle every other room held.

~Run 1, Room 2R, Floor 1, Sewers of Aerlyn~

Upon entering the next room, my hopes and fears were realized. In the dim light of a flickering torch, two rats scurried back and forth past a lone crate. The torch's flickering light cast elongated shadows of the rats, adding to the eerie effect of the sewage defying gravity.

I tightened my grip on my weapons and dashed forward, my weapons a blur as I swung them at the two rats. The dice clattered loudly against the stone floor.

[You deal 4 damage to Giant Rat 1 and 4 damage to Giant Rat 2.]

I grimaced at the damage numbers, thinking they'd be higher, noting it was a bit odd that they both dealt four damage. Maybe the Potency bonuses didn't stack with each other, or maybe they didn't do what I thought they did.

The rats, visibly weakened, moved slower, still attempting to attack. I couldn't help but laugh as their teeth failed to pierce my armor.

"Crystal, are you sure I'm going to die? That Necromancer was laughably easy, and now these rats can't even harm me. I'm going to clear this floor for sure." I laughed even as I read Crystal's comments:

[Hubris does not become you, Rod. These are but the weakest enemies in the dungeon, and the Necromancer took a third of your health in the only attack it got off. It will be challenging to clear that fight in the future especially if the Necromancer has summoned any Minions. Besides, you still need to make it to the boss on the floor. No one has ever cleared the first floor on the first try. Not even Elric when he was here.]

"You mean that story is real?" I said as I struck for both rats again. I missed the rat with my sword, but my mace connected with the first rat again.

[Yes, Elric the Founder was the first Penitent to clear the dungeon.] She paused and then, in a more monotone voice, said, [You deal 5 damage to Giant Rat 1.]

Under the crushing force of my mace, the first rat crumpled, its body collapsing like a deflating balloon, much to my grim satisfaction. The remaining rat launched at me but failed to overcome my defense. I brushed it off and laughed, then swung both weapons at it. The dice rolled. The rat tried to dodge, but my mace connected with a satisfying crunch.

[You deal 4 damage to Giant Rat 2.]

I noticed the telltale sparkle, signifying they had loot to drop. The dice rolled, and I got an additional 10 gold coins. I exited to the final room of the floor.

~Run 1, Room 3R, Floor 1, Sewers of Aerlyn~

As I entered the room, the oppressive stench of rot and decay hit me like a wall. The thick, putrid odor made my eyes water and my stomach churn. The air was damp and cold, carrying the faint sound of dripping water that practically boomed in the silence. I knew this was the final room because a set of stairs led down from beyond a metal grate.

Sewage defied gravity, flowing upward in a bizarre spectacle. Each droplet sparkled a sickly green in the torchlight, splattering against the ceiling and filling the room with an unnatural dance of toxic, shimmering rain. Even with the gravity askew, a lake surrounded the path I was standing on, which was somehow dry despite the sewage everywhere; in the center of a raised platform stood three goblins focused on casting a ritual around a putrid altar the same color as the sewage freely flowing around the room.

My gaze landed on the largest goblin, bile rising to my mouth as I noticed the slimy layer of sewage that seemed to flow freely from his pores. His hulking form was adorned with patches of worn cloth and a decaying iron armor and helm. His eyes gleamed with a twisted need to kill, and his long, matted hair was streaked with filth. He wielded a massive, crude club made from a piece of broken pipe, ready to swing it with brutal force.

The second goblin had a sinister grin permanently etched on his face. An odor so foul I could smell it over the rancid stench clinging to every surface of the dungeon wafted from his direction, and my eyes watered. His skin was coated in a grimy mixture of sewage and a black, tar-like oil. He wore an assortment of scavenged metal scraps and a wizard's robe, his fingers ended in sharp, elongated, blackened nails. This goblin clutched a gnarled staff adorned with leaking vials filled with toxic-looking liquids, hinting at his penchant for poisonous trickery.

The final goblin was the smallest and most agile-looking of the trio. His sinewy build allowed him to move quickly despite the slippery terrain. He was covered in tattered rags and clutched a pair of sharpened daggers, his eyes gleaming with cunning and malice. His movements were fluid and unpredictable, making him a dangerous adversary.

None of the goblins turned to face me despite the slam of the metal grate behind me, locking me into the fight. I facepalmed, realizing I had forgotten to loot the crate in the previous room. Hubris would be the death of me.

"Crystal, quick," I whispered urgently. "Equip my Necrotic Staff. I need to take potshots and run around the platform. It's my only chance at killing them."

[I am sorry, Rod, but you cannot equip a new weapon while in combat.] My face fell. I couldn't believe I unequipped the staff to dual-wield my weapons like an idiot. Crystal was right. I was going to die.

[Take heart, Rod. Even though you will die against these goblins now, you will reawaken as if nothing has happened; even better, whatever damage you deal before you are inevitably slain will stay through up to 5 runs before the boss encounter resets. Additionally, your loot corpse will stay through up to five runs, so unless you fail to reach this boss chamber, you will receive your rewards. Now, go forth, and die!] Crystal's words echoed in my mind, pushing me into a frenzy. With reckless abandon, born of a desperate need to stave off the pain of death, I lunged forward, my weapons slicing through the air. The dice rolled, and I let out a premature victory whoop. [You deal 4 damage to Gurgle. You deal 3 damage to Gurgle.]

I stared in horror as the goblin didn't even flinch. "How much HP do they have?" I blurted out. Then the attacks came. With a swift sidestep, I evaded the club's deadly arc, but my triumph was short-lived as I gasped, feeling the sharp sting of a dagger biting into my side. Blood began to seep from the wound, but it magically closed as the goblin pulled his dagger back. From point-blank range, the goblin I attacked fired a bolt of magic that looked like gravity-defying sewage into my face.

I sputtered and coughed the vile liquid out of my mouth, vomiting a little as I viewed the notification Crystal sent my way.

[Gurgle deals 4 damage. You are not poisoned. Drip deals 1 damage. You do not bleed.]

"Crystal, help me out here. What are their stats? What are these things even called?"

[I'm sorry, but the only information I can give you is their names and classes. Drip the assassin, Gurgle the mage, and Slikk the warrior.]

I glanced at Crystal's message, realizing I had no choice but to fight. Resolving myself to my fate, I charged at Gurgle again, aiming to make my future run a bit easier. The dice rolled.

[You deal 5 damage to Gurgle. You deal 3 damage to Gurgle.]

My attacks left me dangerously exposed, too close to Gurgle. Realizing my mistake a fraction too late, I braced myself as his attack blasted me squarely. I gritted my teeth as a wave of agony washed over me, and I fell backward into the muck below. The dice rolled. [Gurgle deals 3 damage. You are not poisoned.]

Miraculously, I dodged the daggers held by Drip, but I rolled right into the overhand swing of Slikk. He struck multiple times, each blow from his club pounding against me, a relentless drumming on my body. Panic clawed at my mind, a suffocating blanket of fear and pain threatening to knock me out. Knowing the next round would likely kill me; I attacked Gurgle with everything I had. The dice rolled.

[You deal 1 damage to Gurgle. You deal 2 damage to Gurgle.]

I let out a brief, nearly silent cry. A wave of despair threatened to overwhelm me; my attack felt like a feeble pebble in the vast ocean of this battle—three damage. I shook my head, trying to dodge the attacks I knew were coming, but Slikk was faster than I could hope to be. As Slikk slammed the club down on my head, everything went black.

~The Plane Of Torment~

I had no idea what to expect when I died, but it sure wasn't this. I could still see the scrolls that showed what the crystal was saying. I continued thinking despite my head caving in. Blessedly, I felt no physical pain, but emotions were a different story. I couldn't believe I had died so quickly. I wanted to rub my forehead, but whatever was going on, I no longer had a body. Before I could process anything else, Crystal spoke up again:

[You have died. You have earned 1 Death Boon. End of Run 1]

And then I felt nothing.

Inventory, equipment, and stats at the end of run 1.

Inventory

Death Boons: 7

Gold: 50

Items

Iron Helm

- **Amount:** 1

- **Condition:** 10/20

- **Effect:** +2 Defense

- **Description:** A well-crafted iron helm that offers solid protection for the head

Iron Short Sword

- **Amount:** 1

- **Condition:** 16/20

- **Effect:** Deals 1–6 damage

- **Description:** A sturdy iron short sword with a simple yet effective design

Quote: "Careful, it's sharp!" – 4 Fingers Lasalle

Iron Mace

- **Amount:** 1

- **Condition:** 14/20

- **Effect:** Deals 1–6 damage

- **Description:** A heavy iron mace with a solid, spiked head

Staff of the Necrobolt

- **Amount:** 1

- **Condition:** 17/20

- **Effect:** Deals 1–20 Necrotic damage. 10% chance to blind target

- **Description:** An ominous staff carved from dark wood and adorned with eerie runes that glow with an otherworldly light

Empty Bottle

- **Amount:** 1

- **Condition:** 0/0

- **Effect:** You can put potions in this

- **Description:** An empty bottle

Equipment
Iron Short Sword

- **Effect:** Deals 1–6 damage

- **Condition:** 16/20

Iron Mace
- **Effect:** Deals 1–6 damage

- **Condition:** 14/20

Iron Helm
- **Effect:** +2 Defense

- **Condition:** 10/20

Leather Armor
- **Effect:** +1 Defense

- **Condition:** 2/15

Leather Greaves
- **Effect:** +1 Defense

- **Condition:** 4/15

Rod's Stats
- **Health:** 0/20

- **Vitality:** 4

- **Precision:** 5

- **Evasion:** 2

- **Defense:** 4

Chapter Eight
The Coronation Of 'Queen' Jamie.

T he moment was finally here, and I was bored. Princess Jamie Regina Fellatrinx was bored. Everyone had always told me this would be my life's most exciting and wonderful day. The world would stop and revolve around me. I was being named the Monarch. I would carry on my mother's legacy as the next Queen in the grand experiment. But nobody ever asked me what I wanted. Though, to be fair, I didn't exactly know.

Light shined in from the outside; my maids had pulled back the curtains around twenty minutes ago but gave me privacy for my morning prayer. I hadn't done them since my mother died. As the heir, my belief wasn't about faith but was a matter of Royal Fact.

The royal family was privy to the Fundamental Knowledge, of course. What we knew wasn't just a belief in Penance but the proper understanding of the gateway to eternal life. In Penance, you couldn't die, but in the end, you earned your way to heaven or hell. Only 10% of people in Tragios made it to Penance, and what happened to those who didn't make it to Penance was unknown. At least, that was the story the Church and the Crown told everyone.

The Royal line always decreed that the truth was too terrifying. So we hid it from the Church. The Royal Scriptures were only read by members with Royal Blood. The Royal Family passed down the Book of Blood from generation to generation. In a few hours, it would be my turn to unlock the tome's clasp and recite the ancient readings. I would know the whole truth; everything kept from me, by my mother, by my father, finally revealed. He always said the truth would change me, destroy me.

Was I ready for such a thing? I could run away right now. I could hitch up my dress or steal a maid's outfit and sneak out with the morning rush. I could open up the window. I had an hour, well, fifty minutes, until my maids would be here to prep me for the naming ceremony. But this morning was far from the ideal time to run. No, the ideal time would be this evening before the ceremony was complete.

But I made my first mistake. Letting a stray thought about escaping wasn't right. If he found out about my journey's beyond the Gilded Gates, there would be Penance to pay. My father employed a mind thief, and if I wasn't careful, that would be it. Rod--- I shut the thought down immediately. It wouldn't due to dwell there. And it didn't matter anyway, I would still have to do my naming ceremony; however, there would be a ninety-minute window after Gifts: The Dignified Dramatica's presentation of The Liar and the Dove. It had been one of my mother's favorite plays, and we saw it every year of her reign; however, it hadn't been played since her death five years ago. I chose the play in her memory.

The time for prayer became a time to dream and hope. I imagined my flight away from my problems, and the realization brought out a sigh.

~The Presentation~

The crier posed upon the altar stood with over-rigid poise. "Presenting Her Royal Princess Jamie Marina Regina, Heir to the Fellatrinx throne, Lady of Venzwincourt, First of her Name, Forever shall she reign." The trumpet sounded loud and fast as if it wanted to leave the ceremony as quickly as possible. I didn't blame the trumpeter. I, too, wanted out of here.

I was led down the procession hall. Greeting duke and dame, one after the other, my keepers pressed me to take extra time with potential suitors. It wouldn't be prudent to present a sour face after all. The Duke of Pewertyn, Ferran; the Duchess of Merekka, Plaera; and the Duke of Aerlyn, Yorman, were all present with their heirs.

I smiled and curtsied at the men and moved on. Heirs weren't always known for their sex appeal. Poor decisions, political upheavals, and terrible luck cursed the heirs of my generation. I had not escaped the plight. I always tried to hide my heterochromia, especially after Duke Yorman Aerlyn said no one would ever marry a demon-eyed freak. I glanced back at the three human-troll hybrids and glared some daggers at Yorman for good measure. He didn't even look my way.

I was running out of reasons not to run away. As we left the hall, I glanced around at the Abbey. The relief of the Gods hung at the center of the hall: Rellum, the God of Purity; Aurentum, the God of Wealth; and Malikap, the God of Justice. It felt like I became judged under the weight of their stares.

~The Ceremony~

The thing about ceremonies is that you never know what kind of boredom you will face until you are stuck there, unable to move. The boredom came to a quick and sudden end when the sad trumpet from earlier made its final desperate plea for freedom. The band announced the Presentation of Gifts.

Suddenly, I was overcome with waves of grief and despair. I flashed back to my earliest memory at four years old. I was sitting in my mother's lap, playing with a bracelet on her arm. The bracelet that now rested on my arm.

"Jamie. Have I told you about my Aegis bracelet? I got this gift from my father on my naming day. This bracelet will protect your soul from evil. It will guarantee that your soul will find rest and ascend as long as you wear it. A father's role is to protect his children from evil, death, and Penance. And it is customary of the Fellatrinx royal family to bequeath upon its heirs an heirloom of protection. Your father and I are working on creating just such a gift for you."

My mother's words sang around in my head, and I wished time could freeze so I could just bask in her music, her warmth, and her love. The only reason I hadn't run away from my cruel and overbearing father. The only reason I hadn't escaped this cruel mockery of a life where my decisions weren't mine. The only reason I hadn't picked the lock and fled this gilded cage of lies built on the suffering of the people I was supposed to serve was the promise of my mother's final gift. All I knew was that it would be jewelry—my mother's last gift.

A cold liquid shocked me from my reverie as the priest anointed my head with oils. He waved the thurible in the air, and the room smelled dense with heavy perfume. And then he spoke. "In the name of Rellum, I bless you, Princess Jamie, *blah blah*, first of her name. *blah blah* Against all evils we anoint you to stand; stalwart in defense of the faith, do you renounce Malikap, all his works, and all his children?"

He droned on and on and I was still so bored, but it was my turn to speak. "I do renounce him."

"And when your failures count up through the decades, and you are found wanting, do you accept the wages of the Merchant of Death?"

"I accept the wages of sin." The priest froze, expectant, as if this moment was everything. I had always thought this moment would mean something: that I would suddenly rise to my station, that I would feel the world's weight on my shoulders, that everything would make sense, that I wouldn't want to run away anymore. Instead, I felt hollow, like this whole ordeal was wrong.

And it was wrong. Blasphemous, even. I said I didn't care about religion, and this was why. The hypocrisy of it all made me want to scream. The church had likely spent tens of thousands of gold on this single event. Money that was meant for the poor and hungry. Money wasted on someone who didn't even want the pomp and circumstance. Money wasted on someone who never wanted the power to begin with.

The moment passed, and the priest spoke. "Princess Jamie shall ascend. It is time for the presentation of gifts. King Turmeran, please step forward to present the Royal Heirloom."

I shuddered at the mention of my father. I wasn't happy that I would have to see him one last time before I ran away. It was unsettling seeing my father. He had always been a soft, gentle man. But his heart had calloused over the wound my mother left at her death had never healed. Ever since my mother died, he had changed. He never even hugged me. It was like his heart was a quivering mass of unfounded fears.

Yesterday morning, I prepared myself for a walk through the outer courtyard—something I had done dozens of times. However, my father accosted me at the gate of the inner courtyard. His rage was so visible, heat radiated from his face like from a fire stove.

"Daughter, you will not wander about the grounds this close to your naming day." He never yelled or screamed. The rage was in his piercing gaze, and his fanatical grin bit the air. "If you die before you produce an heir, our family, everything your mother and I built, will be for naught."

Trellis and Griesan, my father's guards, his first and second in command, grabbed me by the shoulder and practically dragged me back inside. I knew better than to cause a scene.

I felt stuck in these memories, these moments. I was unsure how to act or get my mind to move on. Back in the present, my father spoke. For the first time since my mother's death, he looked happy, serene even. His gruff stubble framed his face in a way that belied his years. He still looked manic, like a homeless man in his late thirties rather than the king of a nation, but his smile reached his eyes, and his once omnipresent kindness exuded once again from his frame. I wanted nothing more than to reach out and hug my father. To bask in what had been missing for so many years. But there was now a chasm between us I couldn't cross.

"Jamie, this gift, the Ring of Reditus, has a terrible but great power: it can recall the bearer of its twin, the Ring of Requiem, to any location the wearer resides in, ensuring you are always safe and never fear death, as it will bring you back to a marked place even if you are inches from death."

And then the light and gentleness were gone. A fire burned in his eyes, and darkness shadowed his face.

"Leave not this palace for beyond is a land of shadows and ill fate. Your only true shelter is within these walls."

He turned around and left the hall. The rest of the ceremony proceeded without him, King no longer, but still holding all of the power. My naming day marked my first ascent to power, but it would be years, decades even before I grabbed the reins, and who knew if I would still be myself? My mother always told me that power has an insidious way of eating away at the good of a person and leaving behind the bad. She never wanted me to lose sight of the woman she shaped me to be.

I felt the warmth of the ring on my finger. Little wisps of magic radiated from the ring like smoke from a flame.

I wish I had known then what I know now. I would have followed my father's advice and stayed in the castle.

Chapter Nine
Death Boons

~Run 2, Entrance, Floor 1, Sewers of Aerlyn~

I jolted awake, a rancid odor devastating my nose. Instinctively, I yanked my hand to my face and pinched my nose in a fruitless effort to block out the stench. Gone were the roses and vibrant blues of the sky where Jamie and I sat eating lunch today. The world had changed around me. Jamie? The pleasant thought of her faded, and I shook my head in desperation to recall her image in my mind. As the sweet memories melted away, I focused on figuring out where I was.

My feet squished in foul water, its cold, vicious touch sliding across my skin like frostbitten slugs, while the chill of the stone floor seeped into my feet as if I were walking on ice. Familiarity with this place sparked as I took in my surroundings. My heart ached at the thought of what brought me to this place. Ma always said Penance was a lie, a rumor the church started to keep us in line. A flash of light burst through my head as my brain tried to think. Ma, Jamie, who were they?

A torch flickered in front of me, and I moved forward to the light, each step a struggle as I battled against the fog of memories. I'd been here before. At this exact moment... I kept waiting for the synapses in my head to make the connections. Still, I didn't hesitate; I sloshed through the ankle-deep sludge, the sound echoing in the large chamber as droplets of muck reflected crystal light. Crystal, my spectral companion, hovered silently like a physical thought.

The suffocating darkness clung to every surface of the room, to my clothes, arms, and hands, smothering me despite the torch's feeble glow. My heart raced as I approached the torch and removed it from its sconce, the only lifeline in this abyss. With each step, I edged closer to the wall, hoping—desperately—for an exit. The flames of the torch flickered and merged with Crystal's light, casting eerie shadows and revealing the sewage seeping from the walls, unnervingly flowing in the wrong direction.

As I neared the exit, a sudden thought halted me in my tracks. A dark halo surrounded her, my Death Boons, physically shimmering like stardust. That had not been around her before.

[Hello Rod. How are you feeling?]

I blinked. And then I remembered. The rats. Those goblins. Death. I shuddered. I still felt a shadow of lingering sensation where the hammer had crashed into my head. At least I got Death Boons out of the deal. "Death Boons." I gasped out the word like a lifeline.

[Yes, you have 7 Death Boons to spend to get stronger. Would you like to do so?]

"Hey, Crystal. How do I spend my Death Boons?"

[That was an excellent first run, young one. Good work. As for your question, you spend Death Boons at the entrance to each floor, so thank you for not leaving the entrance yet. Your run starts once we leave this first room.]

[However, all in all, this was an impressive streak. Most Penitents die to the Necromancer on their first try. While indeed a challenge, we can earn our freedom together.]

"You're trapped here too, Crystal?"

[Of course, all creatures in Penance must seek redemption. Very few reach for or achieve it, but we are all governed by the same rules. It is why creatures, chests, crates, and even torches appear again. We are all just prisoners here. Before we get sidetracked again, let us discuss the Death

Boon store. Listed first are the stats. Death Boon Stat costs start at 1, then scale by 5, so 1 for 1, 5 for 2, 10 for 3, 15 for 4, etc.]

[Stat Boons....]

The text floated in the air on a canvas parchment that I could physically touch, making it much easier to read the large amounts of text suddenly before me. The lists showed me the different stats and what I had. But there was a lot of information, so my eyes glazed over. But Crystal wasn't done. More and more parchments kept appearing. So many I started having trouble keeping track.

Just when I felt like I would panic and give up, the clusters of parchment disappeared replaced by a single new parchment.

[Player classes. Base classes: Each base class costs 4 Death Boons to unlock. After death, class is unavailable for three runs. Therefore, the Torchbearer class is unavailable. After the first, classes are unlocked randomly. Clear the second floor for advanced classes.]

This was a lot more interesting. Mage, Fighter, Urchin. The famous Archetypes that Elric used to dominate the dungeon. But still, just like in school, I couldn't focus and the large amount of words flashed by in a blur. She had another list to show me. Something about dungeon benefits. I pinched my nose as the amount of information overwhelmed me.

[Are you alright, Rod? If you are upset at the lack of options, you will be able to unlock 10 more Dungeon Boons by purchasing all of the basic boons. And more categories and wider availability of Death Boons become available as you reach the other levels of Penance. I suggest you first spend your Death Boons to unlock a class, but you can purchase any Death Boon you see fit.]

"No, no, no. It's just all too much." I paused trying to collect my thoughts, and pretended I was stable. I breathed in and out, and when I felt okay, I continued. "Alright, let's use those points to purchase a class then. How does it work exactly?"

[It could be more convenient, but all Class boons are based on a die roll.]

My brow furrowed, heat rising in me. I buried the emotion immediately, fear taking its place. I didn't want to upset Crystal now that it was actually being helpful. "Is everything here left to chance? What if I end up with something lame like the barbarian or cleric classes?"

[Neither of those classes is lame. Your only other option would be to try a classless run, and I do not recommend that. Besides, a starting weapon is a huge benefit that makes the Torch Bearer class pale in comparison.]

"Well, I still hope I don't get either."

[Of course, Rod. Now, would you like to purchase a class?]

"Yes, let's roll the die." The die tumbled through the air; each bounce sending out waves of sewage.

Stat Boons

Potency

- **Cost:** 1

- **Current Stat:** 0

- **Effect:** Adds 1 point of damage to all physical attacks

Insight

- **Cost:** 1

- **Current Stat:** 0

- **Effect:** Adds 1 point of damage to all magical attacks

Alacrity

- **Cost:** 1

- **Current Stat:** 0

- **Effect:** Adds 1% to your movement speed every level

Vitality

- **Cost:** 1

- **Current Stat:** 4

- **Effect:** Adds 5 points of health per level

Finesse

- **Cost:** 1

- **Current Stat:** 0

- **Effect:** Adds 5 points of stamina per level

Arcanum

- **Cost:** 1

- **Current Stat:** 0

- **Effect:** Adds 5 points of mana per level

Defense

- **Cost:** 1

- **Current Stat:** 0

- **Effect:** Blocks 1 point of damage from all physical attacks

Magic Defense

- **Cost:** 1

- **Current Stat:** 0

- **Effect:** Blocks 1 point of damage from all magical attacks

Precision

- **Cost:** 1

- **Current Stat:** 5

- **Effect:** Precision is the likelihood of your attacks hitting your target

Evasion

- **Cost:** 1

- **Current Stat:** 2

- **Effect:** Evasion is the likelihood of your opponent's attacks missing

Player Classes Boons
Mage

- **Cost:** 4

- **Starting Equipment:** Mana bolt spell, Wooden Mage Staff

- **Stats:** Vitality 4, Finesse 2, Arcanum 8, Insight 5

- **Penalty:** Cannot equip physical weapons or iron armor

Fighter

- **Cost:** 4

- **Starting Equipment:** Iron sword, iron shield, skill Shield Bash

- **Stats:** Potency 3, Vitality 10, Finesse 6, Evasion 2

- **Penalty:** Cannot equip magic items

Cleric

- **Cost:** 4

- **Starting Equipment:** Iron mace, shield, the Smite spell, and a basic Heal spell

- **Stats:** Potency 2, Vitality 6, Finesse 4, Arcanum 6

- **Penalty:** Cannot equip bladed weapons

Urchin

- **Cost:** 4

- **Starting Equipment:** Two iron daggers, Unlock ability

- **Stats:** Potency 4, Vitality 2, Finesse 10, Precision 10, Evasion 10

- **Bonus:** Starts with the Unlock skill and the evade passive

Archer

- **Cost:** 4

- **Starting Equipment:** Wooden short bow, quiver with 20 arrows, and the skill Aim

- **Stats:** Potency 4, Vitality 4, Finesse 10, Precision 10, Evasion 8

- **Bonus:** Starts with innate ability Evade

Crusader

- **Cost:** 4

- **Starting Equipment:** Iron sword, iron shield, basic Heal spell

- **Stats:** Potency 4, Vitality 10, Finesse 4, Arcanum 4, Defense 2, Precision 4, Evasion 4

- **Bonus:** Has the Guiding Light spell

Barbarian

- **Cost:** 4

- **Starting Equipment:** Two-handed ax, skill Cleave

- **Stats:** Potency 4, Vitality 10, Finesse 6, Defense 2, Precision 6

- **Penalty:** Cannot equip shields, helms, or cuirasses

Conjurer

- **Cost:** 4

- **Starting Equipment:** Elemental Summon spell, Wooden Mage Staff

- **Stats:** Vitality 2, Finesse 2, Arcanum 8, Precision 2

- **Penalty:** ???

Dungeon Boons
Vault Access

- Gives you a place to store items and gold between runs. The vault can be accessed at the entrance of every floor

Audible Alerts

- Alerts are read audibly so you can hear them while fighting

- *Toggleable*

Turn-Based Combat
- Pauses combat so everything takes place in turns. Natural evasion becomes impossible, relying on the Evasion stat

- *Toggleable*

Enemy Stats Highlight
- Enemy stats are visible above enemies. Requires Scan Skill

- *Toggleable*

Stopwatch Timer
- Shows time in the upper-right corner of your vision. Essential for speed runs

- *Toggleable*

Disable Dice Rolls
- Disables dice rolls, preventing attack and skill randomness. Does not affect chest rolls. May weaken you

- *Toggleable*

Floor Map
- Displays a map of the current floor and shows secret rooms

- *Toggleable*

Hardcore Mode
- Enemies have triple stats and better weapons. Rewards include better loot and more Death Boons

- *Toggleable*

Quest Shop
Rat Teeth
- **Cost:** 1

- **Type:** Collection

- **Description:** Collect 5 rat teeth

- **Reward:** 5 Death Boons

Necromancer Eyes
- **Cost:** 5

- **Type:** Collection

- **Description:** Collect 20 Necromancer Eyes

- **Reward:** 25 Death Boons

Goblin Ears
- **Cost:** 10

- **Type:** Collection

- **Description:** Collect 50 Sewer Goblin ears

- **Reward:** 50 Death Boons

Chapter Ten
Rigged Dice

[You have rolled a 7. You have unlocked the Barbarian class. Would you like to use the Barbarian class?]

"Ugh, of course, it had to be barbarian. It's because I said something, isn't it? These dice are rigged." Why couldn't it have been magic? If my dad had been a wizard instead of a warrior, none of this would have ever happened. You can still be a mage with only one hand. *Where had that come from?*

I could swear I heard a tiny bit of stifled laughter coming from the crystal, but instead, the text just said, [Prepare yourself; the transformation can be a little intense.]

Suddenly, a swirl of blue and gold light engulfed me, lifting me into an ethereal embrace as my body began a surreal transformation. My muscles and bones stretched and contorted as my throat burned from the eardrum-shattering scream I let out. My mind flooded with red-hot pain as my body changed. Abruptly, I fell back to the sewage below, small waves cascading out from me as it splashed in all directions.

I could immediately feel the difference as I got to my feet with slow, careful movements. The pain was gone; instead, my body felt powerful, like I could leap and touch the ceiling, grab a crate, and lift it above my head with a single hand. *Did I get a boost to how strong I am?*

[How do you feel, Rod?]

"I feel fine, great actually," I exclaimed, a wave of energy rushing through. I wanted to sprint, jump, kill. A feral grin spread across my face. "This is amazing. I don't even remember why I was so disappointed. Let's get this party started." I then paused. I wanted nothing more than to test my new power out firsthand. Still, if my previous run taught me anything, I needed to think before rushing into battle. "Wait, Don't I still have three more boons? What do you think I should buy?"

[Oh. I would buy the audible Text boon or the map. If not those two, I would buy some stat boosts.] Crystal suggested.

"Hmm. The map is definitely useful, but I think I'm in need of stats, too, for now. I barely did anything to the bosses. Decisions, decisions. Oh, Crystal, couldn't you roll a die and decide for me that way?" I asked, looking up.

[I have no control over the dice.]

The parchment continued scrolling in response.

"Wait, what?"

[The dice are part of Penance and not something I have any control over.]

She was slow again, each word coming out a full second after the other.

"Alright, then I think I'll go for two stat boosts and the map. Is it random, like the classes? Or can I choose what stats improve?"

[It is only the classes that are random.]

"Alright, awesome. Then I would like to purchase a point of Potency and Vitality."

I glowed the same gold and blue light from earlier. I didn't feel any more powerful, but all the same, I knew something was different.

Barbarian

- **Cost:** 4

- **Starting Equipment:** Two-handed ax, skill Cleave

- **Stats:**

  - **Potency:** 4

  - **Vitality:** 10

  - **Finesse:** 6

  - **Defense:** 2

  - **Precision:** 6

- **Penalty:** Cannot equip shields, helms, or cuirasses

My eyebrows shot up in surprise. "Wait, so I can't equip a helm or chest piece as a barbarian?"

My voice came out unsteadily, and a tinge of heat crossed my tongue. That would be a considerable loss of defense. I took a deep breath and immediately regretted the action, gagging on the sewage. "This is outrageous! It's unfair! Did the description say all of that earlier?"

[Yes, and you would have noticed if you actually read the description of the class instead of just skipping over it. The barbarian has limited equipment due to your alignment restrictions.]

With a quick blink, I paused, memorizing that part about alignment restrictions. "What do you mean by alignment?"

[I don't know what you mean.] Crystal responded innocently.

"You just said I have restrictions due to my alignment. What does that mean?" I creased my brow, anger simmering in my throat.

[I cannot complete that request. Please try again later.]

"What the...?" I grabbed the bridge of my nose as unease trickled into my thoughts. Crystal's evasions sent a ripple of suspicion through me.

But pushing it didn't seem like a good idea. I shook my head and moved on. I left for the next room.

~Run 2, Room 1L, Floor 1, Sewers of Aerlyn~

This time, I was not at all afraid of what was coming. I knew that nothing posed a threat to me except the goblins and the Necromancer. The first room had a torch, a crate, and a single rat. I kid you not; the rat spun around on the crate like a ballerina. I stared dumbfounded at the rat. I was starting to get tired of this place and its bizarre antics.

I wished I could say otherwise, but my nose was starting to acclimate to the vomit-inducing smells of the reverse sewage. The flickering torch on the wall cast dancing shadows, including a giant one of the dancing rat.

The rat finally noticed me and leaped forward, ready to attack. The instincts of my new class kicked in as I gripped the sturdy handle of my Iron Great Axe. I swung. The dice rolled. I knew the ax would destroy these rats, and I was immediately proven correct as the ax cleaved the rat perfectly in two.

[You deal 16 damage. Overkill! You have killed Giant Rat. For your first kill this run, you have received 1 Death Boon. Overkill! You have received 1 Death Boon.]

The rat sparkled, and I looted it. The die rolled.

[You have received 1 rat meat.]

"Gross." I grimaced at the bloody chunk of rat meat in my grasp, already wary because of the vestiges of sewage on my hand and the stink in the air that clung to every surface. No way that's safe for human consumption. "Why on earth would I want this?"

[I assume you plan on eating and drinking at some point. However, I highly advise against drinking any liquids on this floor.]

I grimaced. I hadn't thought about food at all since entering the dungeon. It seemed like an afterthought while fighting to the death. And would food really matter if I just came back to life anyway? I thought about addressing my thoughts with Crystal but decided not to.

It was best to leave that loophole alone for now, in case asking would make me hungry or something. I put the rat meat away, noticing, as always, that it was banished into the nether space that was my inventory.

With my grip on the door handle, I was about to leave when Crystal broke the silence.

[Aren't you forgetting things? Namely, a crate and a torch?]

I didn't know where my head was with these crates. Merchant forbid I forget a boss corpse or a chest or something. I shook my head and returned to grab the torch off the wall before reaching into the crate. The dice rolled.

[You have received a cloth shirt. Congratulations.]

Sarcasm was hard to read through the text, but that certainly felt sarcastic.

"Stupid barbarian. Stupid not wearing a shirt. Stupid rigged dice." I put the shirt away, shivering, wishing I could at least put it on to protect myself from the cold air. I felt exposed.

[You have finished looting the room and may continue onward. There is no need to stand around wishing you could put on clothing.]

I left the room fuming. Crystal could do with a personality change. I liked it better when she only shared dice rolls and enemy names.

Rod

- **Rank:** 1

- **Class:** Barbarian

Stats:

- **Health:** 55/55

- **Stamina:** 30/30

- **Potency:** 5

- **Vitality:** 11

- **Finesse:** 6

- **Defense:** 2

- **Precision:** 6

Inventory

Right/Left Hand: Iron Great Axe

- **Effect:** Deals 1–12 damage

- **Condition:** 20/20

Chapter Eleven
One Rat, Two Rat

~Run 2, Room 2L, Floor 1, Sewers of Aerlyn~

A heavy breath escaped my lips, my shoulders drooping at the sight of two giant rats blocking my path. It was like the last run: one rat, two rat, red rat, blue rat. My vision blurred at the edges, light-headedness swirling through my thoughts, but I pushed it aside, ignoring the ever-constant dread of déjà vu that permeated the air like the constant sewage stank. The die rolled as I swung for the first rat. My axe cleaved through with unstoppable force, sending the rat's head soaring in a dramatic arc of blood and gore.

[You dealt 15 damage. You have killed Giant Rat 1. You have received an Overkill Death Boon.]

Before I can even react, the second rat leaps for my bare chest and attacks my stomach with a nasty bite. The die rolls.

[You took one damage.]

The rat had rolled a four but only dealt one damage. A snort of amusement burst forth as I struggled to maintain my composure at the pitiful attack.

Careful not to hit myself, I slash at the clinging rat with the ax. The blow connects. The die rolls.

[You dealt 17 damage. You have killed Giant Rat 2. You have received an Overkill Boon.]

I expected a sting or a mark where the rat's teeth had clamped down, but my fingers found nothing on my chest but unbroken skin. I was fine.

The way HP worked was confusing to me. Finally noticing the sparkles, I kicked both rats. The dice rolled.

[You have looted rat teeth x1. You have looted 5 gold coins. You have looted a Death Boon.]

I furrowed my brow, muttering, "Weird, I got a Death Boon from a rat." But I wasn't one to complain, and I wasn't going to complain about the multiple Death Boons. Crystal, though, heard me somehow and took it as a complaint.

[One shouldn't complain when given boons so easily, Rod. In future runs, this could be a viable strategy for you to collect as many as you need if you get stuck on a boss.]

I thought about it for a moment, and I guessed she was right. I almost sighed, but I caught myself and cleared my throat instead.

"Alright, you have a point, Crystal; I also take back what I said about this class being awful; so far, it's blowing my mind."

I could easily see myself getting 10-20 Death Boons with the axe easily one-shotting the small mobs, but I still needed to figure out how I was expected to collect 50 or even 200 for some of the more expensive boons.

I walked over to the center of the room where the green, slightly ornate, uncommon chest was. My hand hovered over the uncommon chest, a sigh escaping me. I grimaced, what was with that bad habit? It was frustrating, I felt Like Demaly Erickson, a girl from the paupers' school who always wore black, and talked about how horrible life was. It took my brain a moment to catch up and realize that a stray thought had brought back a twinge of memory. After the thrill of golden treasure chest in the last run, this felt like sifting through the sewage for copper.

The dice rolled as I lifted the lid of the chest.

[You've looted two items from the uncommon chest. You've obtained leather pants. You've got a leather helm.]

I sighed. The greaves were excellent, but yet again, I looted something useless. I had half a mind to toss the helm on the floor. But who knows, maybe I would find a use for it in future runs.

"Crystal. Please equip the leather pants. And are you sure you can't just equip the helm? I can place the thing on my head." To demonstrate, I lifted the helm onto my head, but it vanished as I placed it on my brown, cropped hair.

[No, you cannot equip the helm. The Merchant of Death has decreed it. I will, however, equip the leather pants, although you do know that you can just... put them on, right?]

I laughed as the pants materialized around my bare legs. "Of course I know that. But one of the coolest parts of this place is the magically appearing clothing."

I went through the next door. I almost forgot the room's torch, but thankfully, it was by this room's door, and I grabbed it as I swung by.

~Run 2, Room 3L, Floor 1, Sewers of Aerlyn~

Given the events of last time, I should have been on high alert. Yet, to my dismay, I blundered onto a hidden pressure plate. Instantly, a barrage of five arrows sprang forth like a swarm of angry hornets hurtling straight for my unprotected chest. This time, no die rolled. The arrows simply struck me.

[You take two damage]

Like last time, the five arrows vanished.

"I take back what I said about this class being lame. I'm one-shotting everything, and I've only taken three damage. Those goblins are dead for sure." I didn't wait for Crystal to respond before running across the room for the lone crate and reaching inside—the dice roll.

[You have received leather armor.]

I groaned. This entire run would be me picking up equipment I couldn't use. I put the armor away, grabbed the torch, and left the room.

~Run 2, Necromancer's Room, Floor 1, Sewers of Aerlyn~

I stepped back into the Necromancer's lair, only to find it empty. Gone were the Necromancer, the chest, and the altar. Strangely, not even a single torch flickered in the room. However, as before, the room was awash with natural light–its ceiling open to a starry night sky. The Dragon skull remained the one vestige of anything that came before. Above, the moon blazed like a celestial furnace, casting a surreal, almost daylight level of luminance over the abandoned lair. The air hung heavy and still, a sharp contrast to the former chill of the chamber, and somewhere in the shadows, something whispered, hinting at unseen mysteries.

I decided I had wasted enough time staring at the admittedly pretty trees and left the room through the next doorway.

~Run 2, Room 1R, Floor 1, Sewers of Aerlyn~

I paused, standing in the doorway, and turned around, scanning the Necromancer room, as something in my brain finally clicked. "Can you display the map for me?"

[Oh. I had forgotten we purchased that. One moment,] Crystal replied.

A parchment unfolded in front of me, expanding larger and larger until it was almost human-sized. The yellow fabric then turned black as ink splotches appeared all over it. Slowly, the ink faded, revealing nine black squares of equal size. Inside each square were other multi-colored squares: red for monsters, purple for pets and allies, blue for items like torches, green for crates and chests, white for doors, orange for stairs ascending upwards, and yellow for 'Other.' There was one more color on the legend off to the side, indicating a total of eight different colors. Pink, the final color listed, stood for secret walls. Apparently, there were two on the first floor.

In my first run, I had missed that there were secret rooms and treasure. The first of these rooms was off the Necromancer's room I had just cleared, so I turned around, and took off.

~Run 2, Necromancer's Room, Floor 1, Sewers of Aerlyn~

I was blown away by how different it seemed as I walked back into the room. Now that I knew there was a secret, I was hyper-aware of everything in the room. Trees shook with the wind that came from some far-off place. And the moon and stars shined too brightly in the sky. There was something off about the moon and how it sat in the sky. Almost as if it didn't belong in a random room in a sewer. "Stupid moon," I muttered. The room had always seemed bigger than it was, but as I tried to move through the trees where the wall would've been in any other room, I hit an invisible wall.

"Well, there goes that idea." I looked back at the map, and not surprisingly, I was nowhere near the pink dot on the map. I studied the map for a moment when it finally clicked. The Dragon!

The Dragon's head, maw, and sickeningly large teeth were open to the world like a cave. It threatened future pain, but the bones were static, unflinching. The Pink dot was in the center of the Dragon's maw, and I wanted to shake myself at how obvious of a secret it was. I approached the mouth of the beast and walked straight through an invisible doorway.

~Run 2, Treasure Room, Floor 1, Sewers of Aerlyn~

I clenched my fists, frustration bubbling up as I shook my head. This room had been here the entire time, after all that searching last run, I had never thought to run underneath the skull. The tiny, closet-sized space was crammed with four chests, each a different type, all miraculously unlocked, two crates, and a towering pile of gold coins. I took a deep breath, willing myself to stay calm. This was more wealth than I had ever seen in my life.

"Did you know about this?" I asked, glancing at Crystal while my eyes remained fixed on the glittering hoard.

[I knew of the existence of secret rooms but not of this particular one.]

I shook my head and walked forward, approaching the chests. As I opened all four chests and the two crates, dice clattered against each other, the sound echoing in the confined space. Some dice ricocheted off the walls, striking me in the head and knocking me down to all fours. I really need to get rid of those things... "Hey Crystal, is there a boon for getting rid of those stupid things?"

[Of course, Rod. Now, shh! Let me work.]

[You have looted the following items: Cloth sandals, copper mace, leather greaves, Iron Short Sword, 83 gold, The Dagger of Penetration, and a Lunar Staff of Tides.]

"Wow, this is worthless," I muttered, looking at the pile of junk. The staff and dagger were impressive, but both were locked behind classes I didn't even have yet. Everything else wasn't worth the space it would take to carry, at least given my class. *Ugh, what a waste of time.*

[You know, you complain a lot. Maybe you should work on that. You got over 500 gold worth of items here. And there's another 200 lying around.]

"You know," I mimicked her tone, "maybe you should work on—" I cut myself off, I didn't want to piss off the only friend I had. Building a good relationship with Crystal was crucial, but it felt like I took two steps forward and five steps back every time we talked.

[I know; at least you caught yourself this time. Imagine if you acted that way in the real world. You wouldn't get very far.]

"Hah, it's probably what got me killed."

I froze as a Memory Core descended from the ceiling.

{Memory Core 3/???}
{Would you like to view the memory?}
{Y/N}

"Yes?" I asked hesitantly. I was confused as to what triggered these. I thought it was battles, but this one came down in the middle of a conversation.

~~~~~~~{Memory Core 3 Start}~~~~~~~

My mind flashed back to a monsoon-like night: soldiers, a firing line of archers with bows, aimed arrows at me.

"Rod!" A woman screamed, restrained by a priest, barely visible in the storm. I couldn't make out who it was. My hands were tied behind my back, and I stood against a wall. A bolt of lightning cracked, and pain thundered through my brain as the memory ended in a flash.

~~~~~~~{Memory Core 3 End}~~~~~~~

I collapsed to the ground, clutching my head. Blood streamed from my nose as I rocked back and forth. My ears rang like cannons had fired nearby, and I could see Crystal's light frantically moving, but I couldn't hear her. The piercing rings reached a crescendo, and then—

[Rod! Are you okay?]

As suddenly as the pain came, it vanished, and my hearing returned.

"I think I remembered a glimpse of how I died. There was a firing squad. It was dark and storming, and I heard someone scream my name." It was an unsettling feeling. Knowing how I died. I couldn't find the energy to stand. It felt like every part of my body was weighed down by the memory of that storm.

[Did you recognize the voice?]

Crystal broke my reverie.

"No, I—maybe. It didn't sound like anyone I knew from my other memories. But... it was familiar," I whispered. I couldn't place the voice. My mind flashed to the memory of the Queen, but her voice was different. Besides, why would the queen care about me? Let alone be unable to stop my death. I shook my head to clear it. We had spent enough time on this floor.

I walked back into the Necromancer's room and headed for the next door, hoping that it wouldn't be the boss. After what I had witnessed, I needed time to recover, I think.

"The floor layout. It's different." I said, slowly pausing to look again at the empty room. "I don't remember how many rooms I went through before the Necromancer, but this layout is different for sure. And how come it's empty? Shouldn't there be a boss battle here?"

[Congratulations on your mastery of observational awareness. The layout is indeed different. And this room does not reset until you beat the level boss or die 5 times in a row.]

Two doorways flanked each other, touching in the room's corner. After hesitating, I gravitated towards the left, drawn by a slight hunch. I had been drawing a mental map based on the previous run, but I discarded it entirely with the layout being different this time. Somehow, talking with Crystal made me forget the awful memory, and instead of wanting a break, I hoped the next room would be the goblin lair.

I studied the door for a second. It was very similar to the others, with a grey slab and iron handle, but something was different. I pushed on the handle, and realization struck as it smoothly clicked instead of creaking and groaning. The door opened, and I walked through.

Chapter Twelve
A Grim Stroke of Luck

~Run 2, Boss Chamber, Floor 1, Sewers of Aerlyn~

The chamber was cloaked in a musty odor, its floor flooded by slowly drained sewage that seeped up the walls on all sides of the room in sinuous streams. In the center of the room, on a small, sewage-encircled platform, stood three grotesque goblins, absorbed in a ritual. Their gnarled fingers danced in the air as they chanted in a guttural tongue, focusing intently on a strange, pulsating artifact before them.

A jolt of recognition struck me as I noticed the object of their ritual: my corpse. A pit formed in my stomach as I stared into my own dead eyes. Blood covered my body like a sheen of sweat as the goblins dug away at the body for the ritual.

The sight of my corpse sent a surge of hot pain through my body, and I froze. The body was intimately connected to me yet alien in this sinister context. *What are they trying to do to me?* The realization that these creatures were toying with me sent shivers down my spine and made my heart race.

My initial bravado, fueled by a plan to charge in with a battle cry and an ax held high, dissipated, replaced by a gnawing, inexplicable dread that clawed at my mind like the goblins tearing into my corpse.

"What are they doing to me?" This time out loud to Crystal, keeping my voice as low as possible and hoping for a quick response. Instead, the chamber's silence deepened, and my hair stood on end as the goblins' attention shifted. Their glaring black eyes, void of discernable emotion, slowly turned to meet mine.

Time seemed to stand still. Neither the goblins nor I were ready to break the status quo. My fear was palpable now, a force that threatened to overwhelm my confidence in the barbarian class, but the momentary standstill ceased.

I pushed back my fear with adrenaline and rushed forward, ready to test the newly acquired **Cleave** skill. As I charged, it felt like fate itself had my back as three dice tumbled through the air. My ax swung with all the might I could muster, aiming to cleave through the goblin trio. With his unsettling agility, Drip ducked at the last second, evading the deadly arc of my weapon. But Gurgle and Slikk weren't as quick. The blade of the ax met its mark, slicing through their chests in a brutal, decisive motion.

[Drip has dodged your attack. You deal 3 damage to Slikk and 12 to Gurgle.]

The impact sent a shockwave up my arms, the visceral reality of the battle setting in.

For a fleeting moment, I reveled in the success of my strike and risked a glance at the notification to see I had dealt an excellent chunk to Gurgle and a pittance to Slikk. And while I couldn't see his health, I had a feeling the mage had to be almost dead, right?

The triumph was short-lived; however, Drip's eyes, now wide with fear and rage, locked onto mine. I steadied myself, ready for his counter-attack, the weight of the ax reassuring in my grip.

No sooner had my determination steeled than the goblins launched their coordinated assault. The dice rolled. Gurgle unleashed a beam of poison, which struck me squarely in the right cheek– a grim stroke of luck that it missed my eyes. At the exact moment, Slikk's club found my left shoulder, sending rivulets of pain up and down my arm. But it was the attack from Drip that broke my determination. Somehow, the demon of speed had circled behind me and slashed at my back with his daggers.

The pain from their attacks was sharp and immediate, flooding my brain so thoroughly I couldn't see. Then, as abruptly as it had come, the pain vanished, leaving me both relieved and bewildered. Why did this place even have pain if it just made it disappear instantly? My mind raced as I grappled with the surreal rules of this place. I didn't mind the pain disappearing, but I was as disoriented as I was distracted.

[Slikk deals 14 damage. You are stunned for 2 seconds. Gurgle deals 3 damage, and you are poisoned and will take damage every time you attack. Drip deals 5 damage.] I stumbled as my body locked up, and I fell face-first into the metal grate. Two seconds felt like an eternity in a battle, but they didn't attack, so I rolled to the side, planning as I did so.

Quickly, I did the math, I was around 25-30 hit points. I did not want to waste time and let them get another attack in by trying to ask Crystal, so without hesitation, I leaped back to my feet in front of them and activated **Cleave** again. The dice rolled.

[You deal 9 damage to Drip, 7 damage to Slikk, and 10 damage to Gurgle. Gurgle has died. You have gained a Death Boon. You take 6 points of Poison damage.]

Before they could attack again, I shouted. "Crystal, what's my health?"

The bosses attacked before I got the notification. Slikk bashed my stomach, knocking the wind out of me. And Drip once again teleported behind me with his daggers. A fiery lance of pain shot through my side, so sharp and sudden it felt like he must have hit my kidneys. My vision darkened as a symphony of agony crescendoed through my body—then abruptly and eerily, it faded into nothing. The pain vanished.

[Slikk deals 11 damage. You are stunned for five seconds. Drip deals 1 point of damage. You are not bleeding. You have 12 health remaining.]

I blinked. Twelve health? Stunned? I couldn't move a muscle. Panic clawed at my chest. Despite the raw power of this class, the relentless bosses had destroyed any advantage I held, causing a grim reality to set in. Blood pounded in my ears. I stared at the boss, waiting for him to attack, but it was like he knew I knew I was at his mercy. This next move would be decisive. If I could survive the next 5 seconds I could probably kill Slikk. I waited as the seconds counted down. They both attacked.

[Slikk deals 3 damage. Drip deals 2 damage. One second remaining on stun.]

With my health and stamina waning, I had just enough for one more strike with **Cleave** if only I could time it right. I jumped back as the stun faded, and I activated the ability.

[You deal 2 damage to Slikk. You take 4 points of poison damage.]

A primal scream tore from my throat, displaying my frustration at my lack of damage. Each swing of my weapon felt like a tree branch against steel. Just like last time, I was doing a pittance of damage. I gritted my teeth and waited for the attack. Before, wondering if I could use **Cleave** again without waiting, I did precisely that.

[Critical hit! Damage x 2 You deal 30 damage. You have killed Drip. You have gained a Death Boon. You deal 8 damage to Slikk. You have taken 1 point of poison damage.]

Before I could react, Slikk slammed his hammer down on my head.

[Slikk deals 13 damage. You are dead. You have earned a Death Boon.]

End of Run 2.

Rod
   • **Rank:** 1

- **Class:** Barbarian

Stats:

- **Health:** 0/55

- **Stamina:** 3/30

- **Potency:** 5

- **Vitality:** 11

- **Finesse:** 6

- **Defense:** 2

- **Precision:** 6

Inventory

Death Boons

- **Amount:** 8

- **Condition:** N/A

- **Effect:** Death Boons are power. Spend them wisely

- **Description:** A metaphysical currency provided by the Merchant of Death

Gold

- **Amount:** 288

- **Condition:** N/A

- **Effect:** The currency of Penance

- **Description:** A simple gold coin. On one side is the visage of the Merchant of Death, and on the other is a thumbs-up

Torch

- **Amount:** 3

- **Condition:** 10/10

- **Effect:** Deals 1–4 physical damage. 5% chance of causing burn effect on target

- **Description:** A simple wooden torch wrapped in oil-soaked rags

Dagger of Penetration

- **Amount:** 1

- **Condition:** 15/15

- **Effect:** Deals 3–7 damage. Ignores 2 points of defense

- **Description:** A sharp and durable iron dagger with a well-balanced design, perfect for quick and precise strikes
  Quote: "A very sharp dagger." — Photonius The Dead

Iron Great Axe

- **Amount:** 1

- **Condition:** 18/25

- **Effect:** Deals 4–14 damage

- **Description:** A massive iron great axe with a double-edged blade, designed for powerful and sweeping strikes

Copper Mace

- **Amount:** 1

- **Condition:** 15/15

- **Effect:** Deals 1–6 damage. 5% chance to stun

- **Description:** A robust copper mace with a heavy, rounded head

Arrows

- **Amount:** 5

- **Condition:** 4/5

- **Effect:** Allows you to fire a bow

- **Description:** A simple wooden arrow with a stone arrowhead

Rat Teeth

- **Amount:** 1

- **Condition:** N/A

- **Effect:** None

- **Description:** The incisor(s) of a Giant Rat. Who knows? If you collect a lot, something good may happen

Rat Meat

- **Amount:** 1

- **Condition:** N/A

- **Effect:** +5 health. 80% chance of poison if consumed

- **Description:** Juicy, full of protein, and only tastes a little like sewage! Who knows? If you collect a lot, something good may happen
  Quote: "Tastes like chicken!" – Photonius The Dead

Cloth Shirt

- **Amount:** 1

- **Condition:** 10/10

- **Effect:** +1 defense

- **Description:** It's a shirt! Made of cloth! Woah!
  Quote: "My friend went to Penance, and all I got was this lousy T-shirt!"

Leather Greaves

- **Amount:** 1

- **Condition:** 9/15

- **Effect:** +1 defense

- **Description:** A worked and treated pair of leather greaves covering the waist down to the ankles

Iron Great Axe

- **Effect:** Deals 1–12 damage

- **Condition:** 20/20

Chapter Thirteen

Malice, Jamie Run 1, Part 1

~Princess Suite, Palace of Venzwincourt, Floor 1~

W hen I woke, the world had changed. I was still in my plush bed, but the air was heavy, with ash and dust. I got up and looked for my attendants. Someone to help me dress in the ridiculous outfits expected of me. And that's when I heard the screams.

"Are we under attack? What's going on?" I searched the room for something light to wear in the sweltering heat, but all my clothes had disappeared. Fear flooded my mind, and I jumped back and forth, double-checking the dressers and closets. It was like I'd been robbed, so instead, I grabbed a linen sheet off my bed, the only material left in the room and wove it around myself for modesty. Then, I moved furniture around my room and barricaded the door.

Sure, I could see if people needed help, but I was wearing a sheet for Rellum's sake. I dropped down to the floor and plugged my ears with my fingers, trying to block out the nearly constant screaming.

The screams continued for what felt like hours, always different voices. I wondered if I would be next, so I got away from the door and searched for a weapon. There was nothing besides furniture. And then I saw my window. I had considered it a few times before. I would take a few linens from my bed, the curtains, and the posters and fashion a rope so I could climb down the castle wall and escape.

But as I looked out of the windows, I noticed something was very wrong.

The vibrant colors of the sky were replaced by a hell I never thought I would see. The grass and trees were all dead, and an inky purple haze permeated the sky as if night had come early. The sun's rays produced little light, and a rhythmic thumping against the castle gates replaced the typical midday chirping of birds. I expected to see my beautiful city as I looked past the castle gates. Instead, I was greeted by more of the inky purple mist, as if it had consumed the city.

I stared in horror, and my mind went to Rod—his smile, the glint in his eyes as we talked. And then, another scream, this time closer, shook me from the thought.

I gulped as I finally took in all the signs and realized where I was. I was in Penance. I died. And now my soul was being judged for the crimes I did on earth. I wept, tears flowing unbidden down my cheeks. I knew I should have fought my father harder on his wasteful whims—so much opulence and greed. So much money could have gone to help the people experiencing poverty. *Is that why I'm here? Rod, I'm sorry I didn't listen. I'm sorry I didn't protect you.*

I wanted to scream in frustration at how unfair it was that I was stuck here. I was stuck in a punishment that would never end for choices that I never even got to make.

I didn't want to risk going out the window now, but I also couldn't make it through without a weapon, and that's when I spotted it—the curtain rod I had taken down earlier. It was not the most powerful weapon in the world, but it had a little range. Whatever monsters were crawling around the Penance version of my palace, I needed something to keep them distant. I braced myself, hoping my toga-like dress would hold onto my body as I made my way through the palace halls. I moved the furniture aside and walked through the door.

Above my head, where it certainly hadn't been before, was an inky black crystal. It radiated darkness, scuffing out what light the sconce next to my door held, casting the hallway into obscurity. In front of me, a parchment declared:

~Royal Hall, Palace of Venzwincourt, 3rd Level, 1st Floor.~

"What the?"

[Hello... Queen Jamie.] A dark, angry voice intoned.

I could feel the hatred linger in the air as the voice spoke.

[My name is Malice, your Death Crystal. And I will be your companion throughout your trial in Penance.]

Death Crystal? Didn't only the worst of the worst in Penance get that? Was my family's greed really that bad?

"Alright, Malice. Your job is to guide me through this place, right? To at least help me make it to the end?"

The voice did not change tones. [Of course, I am here to assist you in whatever dark desires you request.]

He was testing me, feeling me out to see if I was as evil as my punishment required.

"All I desire is to leave this place," I said, not expecting a response.

[This level ends at sub-basement 3. I assume you know the way?] He pulled up a map and drew a line showing the direct path down to the sub-basement. For a malevolent-sounding crystal, he sure was being helpful.

Don't ask, Jamie. Don't ask, Jamie. Don't ask... "Why are you being so helpful? You don't exactly sound..."

[Like I should be helping you?] The crystal laughed, and its aggressive tone hurt my ears.

[I am stuck here, the same as you. And the longer you struggle, the longer I am stuck attached to a 16-year-old. So you'd better be worthy of my time. I expect us to finish this level in less than ten runs.]

Simple enough answer, but I had been trained in Theology School by the head Rellenter about Penance. Every time Penance appeared in the Book of Blood, Life and Death Crystals were mentioned. Penance, while ultimately mysterious, had a few known facts from Elric's "Foundations of Penance," which explored the nature of Penance. I knew better than just taking the word of my crystal.

We knew that Life and Death Crystals were of opposite attunements. Life Crystals were pulled from souls of another realm's Penance. People who needed extra chances to become whole. At the same time, the Death Crystals were pulled from Another's Realm of Torment. Evil and malicious people who were forever trapped in crystals were given one last shot at redemption. None ever earned it.

I wept as I started to accept my fate. I was not going to leave this place as I had been. I would either need to turn to the light or allow myself to turn to the darkness.

But those thoughts could wait. I shook my head. I had an eternity to ponder things, but I needed to find armor, clothes, or something other than a too-baggy sheet draped over my shoulder. Instead, I looked right and then left before making a decision. The hall to the right was wide open, and muted gray light streamed through curtained windows, showing an empty space. It was a lot better than the one to my left, which had three ambling people wandering down it. I quickly turned right and walked away from the others.

"Malice..." I whispered, keeping my voice down for fear of alerting them. "What are those people doing? How are there people here?"

[Those aren't people anymore. Feel free to kill them with impunity.]

I scoffed at his disregard for human life. "Alright, if they aren't people anymore, what are they?"

A parchment appeared in the air with an image of the zombie on it.

Enemy Entry 0001: Zombie Level 1 (Vezwincourt Horde)

It carries the Z-Virus, which, is totally not a rip-off of the T-virus. Not at all.

Warning: Don't get bitten!

Stats

- **Health:** 5/5

- **Vitality:** 1

Item Drops
Gold

- **Amount:** 1–10 coins

- **Chance to Drop:** 100%

"Zombies? Like people brought back to life by Necromancers?" I shuddered as my thoughts flashed back to my childhood tutor, Doctor Tot. His lectures on the Necromancer wars had given me nightmares for weeks.

[Most indubitably, my young queen. Exactly like that.]

I walked down the empty hallway. It was a brisk walk before the next suite, considering how my father had commandeered the biggest room on this wing; so big that the only way to enter it was from the grand hall.

I walked along wondering if I was making the wrong choice, avoiding the 'zombies', when I turned around. I needed to face them head-on. Everything I knew about Penance trained us to be proactive if we ever ended up there. And I had messed things up by wasting so much time in my bedroom cowering.

I ran forward, my curtain rod brandished as a weapon. I swung at the first zombie. As I did, numbers appeared above the heads of the zombies, though Malice also helpfully narrated the damage I dealt.

[You deal 3 damage. You deal 2 damage. Zombie 1 has died.]

Well, that was disconcerting. The numbers got smaller as I whacked at the enemies. My second strike killed the first zombie, its head snapping back with a sickening crack as it crumpled to the ground. The other lunged at me with a guttural snarl, rotting fingers outstretched. I stumbled out of the way, my heart pounding, and struck back in desperation.

[You deal 5 damage. Zombie 2 has died.]

I kept hacking away hard and fast, the wood splintering under the force of my blows. The third zombie reacted violently; its decayed visage twisted in rage as it launched at me. Its bony hands clamped onto my arm, and I felt the sharp pain of its teeth sinking into my flesh.

It snarled a sound that sent chills down my spine, and I had to consider the choices that had led up to this moment. How could I be here in Penance, being eaten by a zombie?

Blood trickled from the bite wound, warm and sticky, as panic surged through me. The stench of decay filled my nostrils, and the sound of my own ragged breathing drowned out everything else. I swung the curtain rod wildly, adrenaline giving me strength, and managed to knock the zombie off balance. It staggered, its grip loosening just enough for me to wrench my arm free. I retaliated quickly, swinging my weapon, over and over again. The force of the final blow must have been too much because the weapon disintegrated in my hands well before it should have.

[You deal three damage. Woohoo, you Negan'd that one.]

I wasn't sure if it was the pain or the virus working its way through my system, but I had no idea what he meant by that.

The zombie collapsed to dust as I recollected myself. "Hey, Malice. You said they inflict a virus? That was how you said it, right?"

[Yes, you have been infected with the Z-Virus. You have five minutes until your body succumbs. I suggest you use this time to search for a chest or crate and gather some items for your next run. They won't fade away if you leave them in your starting zone. You could also just pick up your corpse from where you die. Speaking of corpses, there are two perfectly good ones around you to loot.]

I looked at the zombies I had just killed and stared, unblinking. Above the heads of the two that hadn't dusted were sparkling little stars radiating up into the air before dissipating. I pressed my hand against the pockets of the corpse, looking for... well, I don't know. To be honest, I felt a bit silly.

[No. That's not how you loot; what are you a pickpocket?]

"Fine then, how do I loot them then? Oh, fount of all knowledge."

[Ohhh, I like the sound of that. I am a fountain of knowledge!] He cackled madly and then said, [Just kick the corpse with your foot; the items should automatically enter your inventory.]

I did so, and Malice spoke, [You have looted seven gold coins.]

"Oh wow, seven coins! I'm rich! I bet I could buy a whole banana."

[Yes, quite.] He paused for a second and then said, [Now, let's get some other treasure. I believe there is a room on our left if you would be kind.]

"What are you going to do with the treasure? Why do you even care? It's not like you have hands."

[It's fun. I always fancied myself a pirate when I was younger.]

I just stared up. There were zombies, and I was about to die, and this crystal was fantasizing about being a pirate.

[And while I can't precisely move arms and legs around, I imagined grand adventures on the high seas, going after the One Piece. Oh, wait. That's a manga, never mind.]

My mind raced as my heart beat furiously in my wound. Here I was dying, and this crystal-guy-whatever was rambling on about nonsense. Everything felt so sluggish. And my wound ached something awful.

I closed my eyes, took a deep breath, and recollected my thoughts. "Alright, I get it, you like treasure! Stop rambling and we will find some."

I walked down the hallway, stepping over the corpses of my downed foes, wondering why I even bothered to loot them. What need did I have for gold in hell?

Chapter Fourteen
Talkie Voice Thing

Jamie? The image in my brain grew fuzzy, so I shook my head. Ignoring the fading thoughts, I moved my body, trying to figure out where I was.

The memories came back quicker this time. The Necromancer's chilling presence in the first run, the way it felt as his face caved under my fist; then the grotesque goblins amid their ritual use of my first body, the pain of Drip stabbing me in the kidney; the adrenaline and joy as I cleaved enemy after enemy in two; and...

Then, how easily I slipped away. I scanned my surroundings, a sense of déjà vu washing over me. The same dank brick walls, the sewage that clung to every surface slowly rising to the ceiling—the same acrid air—I was back where I had started.

"No! I was so close this time," I groaned, my frustration boiling over. "How did I lose as a barbarian? I had so much health and a 2 in defense!" My voice echoed in the empty chamber, and I almost didn't expect a response. But as I grumbled about my defeat, a scroll materialized out of thin air, unfurling elegantly before me.

[I did tell you to watch out for your hubris. The first boss is always a difficult hurdle.]

The scroll, displayed in elegant, flowing script, seemed to chide me somehow.

"But I had the **Cleave** skill. It should've worked," I muttered, watching new words transform into text on the scroll.

[And now you are whining.]

I rolled my eyes and decided just to move on. "Alright, I have 8 Death Boons. How would you suggest I spend them?"

The words scrolled by slowly, which made my skin itch. Couldn't she hurry it up?

[My notifications always seem to get in your way. You should purchase the boon that allows me to speak physically. You are also locked out of the barbarian class for three runs, so it would potentially be a good idea to unlock another class. You have been lucky with your looting so far and always manage to get a weapon... but don't rely on that luck to continue.]

I sighed again, a habit that punctuated my thoughts lately. *Was I always this way?* I wondered, feeling a pang in my chest at my still fragmented memories. I desperately hoped I would 'unlock' more of them as I continued my way through this place.

Shaking off these thoughts, I focused on the task at hand. "Alright, first, I'd like to purchase a class."

[Very good, Rod. You spent 4 Death Boons. Rolling now.]

More text scrolled by on the page, and a die rolled past, splattering into the constantly draining muck. My anticipation was palpable as I watched it intently.

[You unlocked the Urchin class. This quick-footed class has the **Unlock** skill and the innate skill: **Evade**. This skill will slow down time on a successful dodge roll.]

I paused, absorbing this new information. *That seems broken. I can't believe I got a class this awesome.* Hopefully, it would lead to less pain and quicker fights. And chests! I didn't even need keys anymore. If lucky, I could probably start hoarding keys for future runs.

I was curious about how fights would go. Instead of defense, the Urchin class was focused on evading strikes. But if I did get hit, I was likely dead in the not-so-metaphorical sewage water.

"I don't think I ever asked how stats work. One to one. Do you mind explaining them?" I asked, hoping Crystal would finally tell me how this place worked.

[Can't you read? It literally explained it in the class chart!] Crystal brought the character sheet in front of my face. [Besides, we should finish your Death Boons before spending time retreading the tutorial.] The text appeared on the scroll, somehow suggesting impatience.

"But we never did the tutorial!" I said.

[And whose fault is that?] The scroll text flashed; this time, it seemed impatient, but I was getting frustrated trying to read and respond.

Wait, that's it!

"I want to buy that talkie voice thing for you," I said.

[You have spent 3 Death Boons. You have unlocked The Crystalline Voice Dungeon Boon.] Suddenly, there was a chiming sound.

"Did it work?" I asked, a bit unsure of what to expect.

[What do you think?] An angelic voice enveloped my consciousness before the words had fully materialized. It wasn't just a sound but an all-consuming presence resonating within me. The voice was so loud, overwhelmingly so, echoing through every fiber of my being. My head began to throb, the intensity of the voice manifesting as physical pain.

The sound wasn't just heard; it was felt, vibrating in my chest, reverberating in my skull. I clutched my head, struggling to adjust to this invasive, all-enveloping voice.

"Too loud," I gasped, wincing as each word seemed to amplify the pounding headache. It was so loud. Loud. **Loud. LOUD!**

"Ahh! Make it stop! Make it stop!" I cried out. The voice's intensity was unbearable. And then, as if in response to my plea, the overwhelming sensation ceased abruptly, just like all other pain in Penance. "What was that, Crystal? Why was it so loud?"

[I'm sorry, Rod. I had to adjust the volume. I believe it should be much more reasonable now,] Crystal said, now a soothing presence like gentle rain tapping against my consciousness.

Her voice resonated differently this time, stirring something within me. I felt an odd flutter in my chest, which warmed my cheeks with an unexplained blush. I looked down, trying to compose myself, but then an orb appeared in the air. I reached out and touched it.

{Memory Core 4/???}
{Would you like to view your memory?}
{Y/N}
"Yes," I said.

~~~~~~~{Memory Core 4 Start}~~~~~~~

Queen Jamie stood before me, her dark brown hair cascading in gentle waves as a dark mist pooled around her. As I clutched her ring in my pocket, her presence radiated warmth pushing back the mist, her bright heterochromatic eyes shining with kindness beneath long lashes. I shifted in my feet, uncomfortable under her piercing gaze that surely knew what I was hiding.

"Good morning, Rod." Her voice was eerily similar to Crystal's, though it tugged at something within me. I stared, unsure what to do. But then, as if I had no control, my body moved forward and grasped her in a hug.

"How's that ring treating you?" Her smile quirked up as she looked at my pocket where I kept the ring. Instead of the anger I had expected, warmth radiated out. Her high cheekbones accentuated a gentle smile. *Why did I want her? That first memory made it seem like I hated her.*

At that moment, my soul felt like a house engulfed in flames in the middle of a torrential downpour. The fire of my longing battled against the storm of guilt. I was going to use the ring to kill her father. But I couldn't do that to her, could I? She was still smiling as the memory faded away.

~~~~~~~{**Memory Core 4 End**}~~~~~~~

Chapter Fifteen

Consequences of Sin

The memory was so intense, so vivid, that it left me breathless, aching with a mix of longing and regret. I blinked, and the flash of memory vanished as quickly as it had appeared. Princess Jamie... Her name echoed in my thoughts. And then, my knees buckled as a searing pain rushed through my head, knocking me to the floor. When I awoke, the cold, damp floor pressed against my skin, leeching my body's warmth.

I slowly lifted myself to my feet, cradling my head with my hands. The pain is gone but not forgotten. *What was that? Will I be knocked to my feet every time I gain a memory?* Turning my thoughts outward, I said, "Crystal, do you know who Princess Jamie is? I just had my first memory, and it hurt. A lot." I managed not to cry as I spoke.

[I do not know the outside world, Rod, as I am from a different one. But it is a good sign you are recovering memories.] Crystal's voice responded, now a steady presence in my mind. [Do you know what triggered the Memory Core?]

Embarrassment washed over me at the thought of admitting the actual trigger of the memory. It wasn't love or anything, but Crystal's feminine voice had caught me off guard. I shook my head, trying to dispel the thought, and attempted a lie. "No-nothing triggered it, I just..." I trailed off as Crystal spoke over me.

[Do not try to lie again, Rod.] Crystal's voice was firm, almost scolding, like my mother's. I felt another memory start to trigger, but it faltered away as Crystal kept talking. [You do not want to face the consequences of sin here. And you would do well to avoid the Seven, especially.]

"So what? Is sinning forbidden here? I literally killed another human being. Doesn't that violate one of them?"

[Do you really not know of the seven deadly sins? Self-defense is not a sin, Rod.] She said, her words echoing in the hollow chamber. As she spoke, a fleeting vision surged within me. A glint of steel, the warmth and copper sting of spilled blood, and screams shattered the silence, but just as quickly, it vanished.

I grumbled under my breath. "Stupid Dungeon, Stupid Crystal."

[What was that?] I could hear the metaphorical eyebrow raise.

"Sorry, I was just grumbling," I replied, my fingers wrapping around the cold metal of the torch on the wall as I grabbed it off the sconce. Without another word, I stepped out of the shadowed room.

~Run 3, Room 1L, Floor 1, Sewers of Aerlyn~

As I stepped into the next chamber, my eyes quickly surveyed the surroundings. There, an unfamiliar chest caught my eye. Its intricate design a stark contrast to the murky sewer surroundings, a needed sight for my sore eyes. My gaze then fell upon a Giant Rat, its beady eyes attempting a menacing glare. A chuckle escaped my lips; after facing several of its kind, this one seemed more comical than threatening. Anticipation bubbled within me at the thought of testing my enhanced Evasion skill in battle.

Clutching my iron daggers tightly, I lunged towards the rat, blades dancing in swift arcs. As I struck, two dice tumbled through the air beside me, their face a blur of numbers.

[Your attack deals five damage to the Giant Rat. You have gained 1 Death Boon for killing your first monster of the run.] Crystal's voice echoed in my mind, as clear as the rat's death screech.

"Wow, that died quick. Didn't even get to test out my evasion." I laughed, my gaze skipping past the fallen rat as if it were mere background scenery. My steps were light, almost giddy, as I approached the chest. Its bronze surface gleamed under the dim light, the subtle hints of age only adding to its siren call. I marveled at the lock as I ran my fingers over the cool metal. A complex arrangement of gears and cogs was laid bare like the inner workings of a clock. My thoughts exploded like fireworks, excitement filling me as I traced the chest's robust wood and time-tested craftsmanship.

"Hey, Crystal," I began, curiosity in my tone. "How do I use **Unlock**? Is it similar to **Cleave**, where I..." My words halted abruptly as a sudden flash, obviously magical, erupted from my hands towards the chest. Crystal's voice filled the room, coinciding with a die materializing and ricocheting off the chest with a soft thud.

[You use your **Unlock** ability on the uncommon chest. You have unlocked the chest.]

The gears started whirring and clicking as the spell worked through the mechanism. With a final click, the lock disengaged, clattering to the ground before vanishing in a blue wisp of magic. I could feel my stamina drain away as the spell finished. I was curious why it used stamina instead of magic, *probably because it's a rogue-type spell.* A die flew around as I lifted the chest's lids, landing on a three.

As the three faded from view, six more dice took flight, zipping through the air in a chaotic dance.

[You looted a leather helmet, leather greaves, and cloth sandals.] Crystal said.

"Sweet! Please equip them for me." I called out. In an instant, the new gear wrapped around me, the leather helm snug against my head, the pants fitting perfectly, and the cloth sandals cradling my weary feet with much-needed support.

Eager to test the new armor, I broke into a series of quick sprints. The room, once slick with sludge, was now oddly clean, the muck having retreated to the ceiling in a bizarre defiance of gravity. My movements were unencumbered, the leather fitting like a second skin, flexing and moving with me. A nod of approval escaped me as I reached for the torch, ready to leave the room.

No sooner had I wrapped my fingers around the torch's handle than Crystal's voice pierced the silence.

[You didn't loot the rat corpse.]

A sigh of self-reproach slipped from me. "Right, of course," I muttered, returning to the fallen rat. Blue gold sparks flying into the air. *How could I keep forgetting?* With a swift motion, I kicked the creature.

[You have looted rat teeth.]

I left the room.

~Run 3, Necromancer's room, Floor 1, Sewers of Aerlyn~

A familiar emptiness greeted me as I stepped into the Necromancer's room. Above, the stars twinkled coldly; their light made my breath visible in the chilly forest air. My eyes settled on a lone wooden crate in the center near the empty ornate altar. Its aged yet resilient planks, worn smooth by time, bore testament to countless hands that had once moved it. Despite its years, the wood was rot-free, and the lid opened without a creak. A die rolled, and I reached inside.

[You have looted a Cloth Shirt.]

A jolt of surprise shot through me. With this, I had a complete set of armor. Granted, I was stretching the term 'complete, ' but I was no longer in danger of being called the dungeon streaker.

"Crystal, what's my defense now?"

[You have a defense of 4]

"Does that affect my **Evade** or anything?"

[No..? Why would it?]

"Well, You know, wearing a suit of plate armor would probably be pretty silly if I wanted to keep on avoiding things in combat."

[While logically sound, you are aware that everything here is magical in nature, right?]

I sighed, letting my head drop. I was tired of Crystal treating me like a toddler.

A flicker of worry had passed through me for a moment–the nagging thought that donning armor might reduce my evasion. I had a vague memory–even new ones struggled to form here–of something like that happening during my first run. But now, as I moved with ease, that concern evaporated. "Guess it doesn't matter now," I said aloud, the words getting lost in the quiet chirps of nature. My hand reached for the lone torch on the wall, its flame casting a warm, dancing light on the muted gray grass of the room. With a firm grip, I pulled it free and stepped through the doorway, leaving the mystery of the missing Necromancer, lost evasion, and my lingering doubts behind.

Chapter Sixteen
A Devilish Idea

~Run 3, Boss Chamber, Floor 1, Sewers of Aerlyn~

My heart hammered against my chest, a cold shiver racing down my spine as my eyes snapped open wide, fixated on what I knew would spell the end of my third run. I was already in the boss's room. Relief washed over me, though, when I noticed the third goblin was still alone. He was laboriously dragging my lifeless form onto the altar. Then, his fingers fumbled at the clasps of my worn armor. Giving up, he moved behind the altar, where the bodies of the two other goblin bosses lay. Their skin was pallid and unyielding to the touch of their still-living companion, who seemed confused by their state.

Before me, in the platform grate, was a square of rock, obviously mismatched from its surroundings—a telltale sign of an arrow trap lying in wait. Memories of the two previous runs flashed through my mind—each one a vision of me stupidly walking into the same trap and getting hurt. This time was different. A devilish idea entered my mind, and I stepped forward, triggering the trap.

The die rocketed across the ground, its roll echoing with ominous rattles as time halted. Each movement felt like a battle against an unseen current, my limbs pushing through an invisible, thickening resistance. My chest heaved as I struggled to draw in air, fighting the rising tide of panic that threatened to overwhelm me. I gaped for breath, but my lungs clenched against a suffocating emptiness as if the air had turned to vacuum around me.

Then, the world gradually lurched back into motion. Each second stretched out endlessly as the arrows crept closer. With a forced calm that belied my racing mind, I stepped out.

Crystal's voice chimed in as I cleared the trap, starkly contrasting my pounding heart: [You dodge the arrow trap.]

Relief washed over me, quickly replaced by annoyance at the movement of the remaining goblin. I thought for a moment he would dodge, but instead, the arrows sliced through the air with lethal intent, thudding into Slikk's armored chest. They betrayed their purpose as they clattered ineffectually to the ground. I stared, mouth agape. "What? Why didn't those arrows do anything to him?"

Crystal's voice cut through the chaos: [Slikk has a defense higher than five, making him invulnerable to your current attack methods. But I cannot say his stats until you unlock the bestiary Death Boon or **Scan** skill.]

I froze briefly, frustration mounting at my helplessness, even as Slikk charged ferociously. His battle cry tore through the air, a primal sound of rage as he hoisted his iron pipe like a warrior of old, the metal glinting ominously in the dim light. A die clattered across the cobblestone floor, echoing in the sudden stillness as time froze, trapping everything in a surreal tableau.

As time thawed, I sprang into action, sliding with calculated precision around Slikk's arc of attack, every muscle coiled and ready. "Crystal, please, I need help here! How do stats work?"

Crystal's voice, always so composed, held a note of mock exasperation: "Alright, here's the crash course, but couldn't you have just read the chart or asked earlier?"

"I did ask earlier!" I rolled my eyes, anger flickering despite the peril.

Crystal's voice, still slightly mocking, took on a tinge of concern: [Alright, I'll give you the quick version so you can focus. I can remember it being challenging to multitask when I was human.]

I frowned at Crystal's words, putting myself between Slikk, the altar, and the corpses. "What's that supposed to mean?"

Slikk bounded over the altar, swinging his pipe down in an overhand swing. As time ground to a halt, the world around me seemed to dip into a surreal stillness, muffling every sound as if I were underwater. A die tumbled through the air, its faces blurring before it landed, sealing my fate. But the fact that time hung suspended belied the result before I could see it, and I hurried back. Slikk roared in frustration as I dodged, his attack missing by inches. He then gestured rudely and spoke in his strange language.

[You dodge Slikk's attack.]

My daggers struck with a thud against Slikk's tough hide armor, the impact jarring my arms as if I'd struck solid stone.

I grunted in frustration as my daggers bounced off Slikk's back, disheartened to realize they hadn't even made a dent.[You deal no damage due to enemy defense.] Crystal announced.

Weaving around the sewer, I listened as Crystal finally made good on her promise.[Let's talk Def and Vit. Def is a one to one stat. One defense blocks one damage,] her voice was quick and urgent, trying to convey the info without distracting me. [Certain types of armor add a penalty per point of defense to Alacrity or Precision. This penalty does not apply to the Urchin class. Vit adds five health per point.]

As Crystal explained the stats, my mind raced, recalculating my strategy. Brute force wouldn't work—I needed a new angle. I eyed Slikk's hulking, rotten form, his front a canvas of scars and battle-worn cloth and leather armor. He was about to jump over the altar again. I dashed forward, eyeing my corpses.

"Can I loot corpses and crates mid-battle?" I asked Crystal as I ducked under Slikk's leap. The metallic scent of blood and rust filled my nostrils, overpowering the ever-present haze of sewage.

[Yes...] Crystal began, but her voice was drowned out by the rush of thoughts in my head. *The staff!* If I could loot it, I'd be able to kill this guy quickly. The world narrowed to just me and the potential treasure ahead; everything else, even Crystal's caution, faded into a blur.

As Slikk lunged, I braced for the familiar stillness of time freezing, but it never came. Confusion and panic clashed in my mind as his club came down on my head. I stumbled forward and kicked my corpse in the head.[You take seven damage. You are not stunned.]

A cold knot of fear clenched in my stomach as I pulled my foot away, its icy grip tightening with each heartbeat. I barely had time to process the grotesque reality of my actions—far surpassing the grave robbing of my past life. That memory flickered through my mind, a ghostly echo from a once-lived life, slipping away as quickly as it came.

A torrent of item notifications flooded my vision and ears as Crystal rattled off the list of items.[You have looted Corpse 1. For recovering your corpse you have earned 1 Death Boon...]

Distracted by the notifications, I barely noticed as Slikk swung his weapon. My heart pounded as time froze. I lunged aside, not wanting to experience the thundering pain again. Gasping for breath, I called out to Crystal. "Crystal, please equip the Staff of The Necro Bolt on my right hand."

[I'm sorry, Rod, but you can't equip weapons from your inventory during combat.]

I gulped. I was doomed.

Corpse – Run 1
  • **Gold:** 50

Items

Iron Helm

- **Amount:** 1

- **Condition:** 10/20

- **Effect:** +2 defense

- **Description:** A well-crafted iron helm that offers solid protection for the head. Its reinforced structure provides excellent defense against blunt and sharp attacks.

Iron Short Sword

- **Amount:** 1

- **Condition:** 16/20

- **Effect:** Deals 1–6 damage

- **Description:** A sturdy iron short sword with a simple yet effective design. The blade is sharp and well-balanced, perfect for quick strikes and precise cuts.
  Quote: "Careful, it's sharp!" – 4 Fingers Lasalle

Iron Mace

- **Amount:** 1

- **Condition:** 14/20

- **Effect:** Deals 1–6 damage

- **Description:** A heavy iron mace with a solid, spiked head. This weapon deals devastating blows, capable of crushing armor and bone alike.

Staff of the Necrobolt

- **Amount:** 1

- **Condition:** 17/20

- **Effect:** Deals 1–20 necrotic damage. 10% chance to blind target

- **Description:** An ominous staff carved from dark wood and adorned with eerie runes that glow with an otherworldly light.

Empty Bottle
- **Amount:** 1

- **Condition:** 0/0

- **Effect:** You can put potions in this

- **Description:** An empty bottle.

Chapter Seventeen
Out of Options

A raw, guttural scream tore from my throat, and my face flushed red. I felt like a weight pressed down on my chest, and I couldn't breathe. *How did I forget that?* As the pipe made contact with my head again, pain exploded, reopening the wound that magic had stitched up. Blood poured from the top of my head, forcing me to swipe at my eyes so I could see. I felt woozy, my feet unsteady, but I was determined to stay upright.

[Slikk deals two damage. You are not stunned.]

Squinting with one eye, I took in Slikk's towering form, which seemed to loom even larger as it cast a menacing shadow in the dim, flickering light of the room's lone torch. The realization hit me like a bucket of sewage to the face. *He's invincible. I'm going to die again, aren't I?*

A nervous chuckle escaped my lips, starkly contrasting the fear gnawing at my insides. As my health dwindled, my bruised and battered form shook. Luck had abandoned me just when I needed it most. My health was already at half. And somehow, the monster in front of me kept rolling numbers high enough for what should've been a 15% chance. Or something. I didn't know I wasn't a math guy.

My voice burst forth with desperation. "Crystal, you've got to help me. I'm out of options. What am I even supposed to do?"

[There's more than one way to crack an eggshell. Think about how stats work; the answer should come to you.] Her voice crackled with amusement, but mine did not. A slow-burning ember of resentment smoldered deep within me. *How dare she laugh at my expense?*

Her words hung in the air for a minute as I ran around the room to avoid the belligerent goblin. "But I don't know how anything works! You still haven't told me anything. You're so useless!" The ember grew so hot it ignited into a blazing fury, but instead of yelling more at Crystal, I turned around and lunged at Slikk. The dice rolled.

[You deal no damage.]

However, as my daggers sliced through Slikk, through the fiery haze, I noticed they were doing something, and I banished my anger as quickly as it had come. "Yes!" My shout echoed in the room. Small pieces of fabric flaked off of Slikk's armor. *He won't be invincible for long.*

[You dodge Slikk.]

As I narrowly avoided another of Slikk's blows, it struck me: I couldn't do this again. I couldn't fail against this boss. Amid the chaos, my mind was surprisingly clear, pieces of a plan clicking together like a puzzle, each move mapping out in my head.

Mechanics were made to be exploited by the Penitent; they had to be. And I would exploit the Penance out of this one.

My muscles tensed, and with a swift, fluid motion, I struck again at the goblin before retreating out of his reach. [You deal no damage.] As I struck blow after blow, a thought nagged at me—had my previous attacks as the Barbarian and the Torchbearer class affected the durability? I hadn't kept track, so there was no telling when it would actually break.

A triumphant grin spread across my face as another portion of the armor flaked off. My heart raced with exhilaration as I dodged another blow, each successful dodge and strike fueling my growing confidence.

My daggers were artist's brushes, painting a path of destruction across the frayed armor, each stroke Unraveling Slikk's defenses. And then, as the dice rolled, the masterpiece was unveiled. My daggers moved with a deadly grace, the first shredding the fabric of Slikk's armor as if it were mere paper. The other blade then danced along the goblin's skin, etching a slender, deep line across the goblin's chest, the stark red against his green skin like the final stroke of paint on canvas.

[You have destroyed Slikk's Armor. You deal four damage.]

Slikk staggered back, a guttural cry of pain escaping his lips as dark blood welled from his wound. He spat words in a harsh, throaty language like a rat trying to speak Common. Before Slikk had a moment to do anything, I attacked again. The dice tumbled in the air, their outcome hanging in the balance. In that brief pause, my heart raced, every sense sharpened for the next critical moment in our deadly dance. I breathed deeply and buried my daggers in Slikk's chest.

[You deal seven damage.]

My daggers found their mark with a satisfying thud. Yet, Slikk stood his ground, his resilience chillingly apparent. A flicker of surprise crossed my face as Slikk absorbed the blow without flinching, his endurance a stark reminder of my lack of information on the boss. In an alarming behavioral shift, Slikk wasted no time in retaliating. With a grunt, he hoisted his pipe, bringing it down with a force that threatened to crush everything in its path; however, a die rolled, and time seemed to halt, the air thickening around us.

[You dodge Slikk.]

With time frozen, I leaped back out of reach. As time resumed, I moved forward. With a swift, fluid motion, I yanked my daggers free and targeted his throat with a strike as sharp and deadly as a falcon's talons. The final strike was lightning-quick, lethal, and decisive. Blood poured from the wound like rain as the dice clattered toward the ground, a rolling, distant thunder heralding the end of the storm that was Slikk.

[Critical strike! You deal 16 damage. You have killed Slikk. You have earned 1 Death Boon.]

As I stood over Slikk, his life fading before me, a wave of conflicting emotions washed over me. I felt relief, triumph, and an unexpected twinge of pity at his disbelieving gaze—a stark reminder of the brutality of Penance. Slikk's eyes dimmed, slowly extinguishing the fierce light that had once burned there. His face, twisted in shock and resignation, seemed to question the loss silently.

A resounding, sonorous gong rang out, its resonating boom echoing through the chamber, a solemn note that marked the end of the first floor. Crystal then said, [Congratulations! You have defeated the Sewer Goblin Trio. You have earned 5 Death Boons. You have completed this floor in 37 minutes. You are ineligible for Speed Run Death Boons.]

I sighed, the adrenaline slowly ebbing away. *How fast did I have to be to get that Death Boon? And would it even be worth it?* I wondered as my gaze drifted from side to side with a calm I hadn't felt since waking in Penance. My eyes were drawn to the center of the raised platform where next to my one remaining corpse was an altar that looked to be made of destroyed sewer pipe, with a dais made of transparent glass held aloft in the broken pipes. There was something off from the first two times I had come through. But I couldn't connect the dots. On that altar, in the spot where the goblins had been messing around the previous run, was a ruby. The gem pulsed with an inner light, rich and deep as a drop of blood in clear water, a vivid beacon blaring red in the muted browns and greens.

[Enchanted Blood Ruby of the Sewage Goblin Tribes. This gem is a key. This gem is part of a set. While in your possession, you can speak Goblish. While in your possession, once per run, you can equip an item during combat. You can skip the normal rooms on the first floor and choose to fight only the Necromancer and the goblins. 1/7 floor keys.]

"Wow. What a mouthful. Could've just called it a blood ruby." I said, and then I heard a strange noise from the crystal, but she didn't say anything else, so I ignored it and pocketed the gem.

And then I saw it. An orb the size of my head and pulsing white light descended from the center of the flooded ceiling. It was just like the last one, but this time, it lowered so slowly I would likely have to jump if I wanted to grab it, so instead, I looted my remaining corpse and the three goblins.

Walking up to the corpse, I took a second to note what I looked like. And what greeted me was me... but also not me. The corpse was a warped mirror of life–showing bloated muscles, bulging and pronounced. My head hurt looking at myself, my brain not understanding my state. It was maybe a head taller. I noticed the familiar cascade of hair, matted with blood, falling just shy of a chin that was somehow the same but jutted out like a rocky cliff. I reached out, intending to close the lifeless eyes, but my fingers brushed against something unexpected–the Memory Core, forgotten in my shock– froze my fingers, shocking me with searing, brittle pain.

{Memory Core, 5}
{Would you like to view your memory?}
{Y/N}

"Yes," I trembled with a mix of fear and anticipation. The last memory had really thrown me for a loop. But I would get nowhere by ignoring these. The world around me warped and dissolved, colors and shapes blending as the memory flooded my mind.

Chapter Eighteen
The Wizard

~~~~~~{Memory Core 6 Start}~~~~~~

It was cold the day my parents died. The sun hid, a shy spectator behind a curtain of stubborn silver clouds, heavy with rain yet unwilling to cry. I had decided that night would be their end, even as my heart waged a silent war within. They wouldn't see another dawn.

Under my father's orders, I navigated the grimy market alleys for his usual–Whiskey and Blaze. The latter, a sinister red powder known for its fiery hallucinations, was a slow poison to the mind, but in our bleak corner of the world, even self-destruction had its allure. Technically, it was illegal for children to consume, but merchants didn't care. And my father certainly didn't either, but at least he didn't treat me like my mother. I could hear the shouting echo in my brain as I stepped into the decrepit shop, 'Lyric's ends and odds'–a play on words lost on most who frequented its dimly lit aisles.

'Gol' is gol,' Lerick the Merchant, said, as I handed him the silver and coppers. "But don't tell ta coppas ol' Lerick sold youse this." He gave me a brown bottle with a jagged cork. He then flashed a toothless grin, a defiant smirk that flaunted the gaps in his smile. That cork would be a pain to get out. Next, Lerick handed me a bulky wad of waxy, yellow paper–Blaze. Its warmth seeped into my palms as I cautiously cupped the dubious material. I left the store at a run, planning my next move.

I had turned watering down my father's whiskey into an art, subtly diluting it so he never caught on that the merchant wasn't to blame.

But the next cheapest merchant doubled the cost, and the other greedy merchants watered down their products, too. He never gave me enough money to afford the more expensive merchants, but I always left Lerick's with 6 or 7 pieces of copper in my pocket. I darted into Salio's Wholesale Bottletorium, bustling with transactions and boisterous laughter. I emerged with a small, refurbished bottle and five coppers lighter.

I had regularly pilfered a shot from my father's whiskey stash, siphoning just enough to avoid detection. But I never touched his Blaze—even the thought made me grimace. The idea of snorting that burning red powder, feeling it eat away at my senses, was a line I couldn't cross. Just the idea of ingesting something through my nose made my stomach churn.

It was the only thing that made the man happy, so I never begrudged him. I turned the corner from Salio's and went down the alley behind Juke and Jak's bar. My ears twitched at a particularly raucous turn of laughter. Despite the cheaper swill at Juke and Jak's, my father steered clear, preferring the solitude of his vice over communal inebriation. The alley snaked its way from 7th Avenue, a shadowy vein leading directly to the opulent palace gates.

There were 16 main roads in total that led straight to the city gates. You could see the Outer Wall from the palace in every direction because of this; it was a sight to see: Opulence screamed from the city in every direction as pillars, homes, shops, and warehouses created a unique circular skyline. The palace always boasted that King Turmeran Venzwincourt liked keeping an eye on his subjects from his palisades, though I could only guess whether he did it out of affection or suspicion.

In the secluded alley, the shadows cloaked my swift sleight of hand, shielding my actions from prying eyes. Carefully, I yanked the cork out of the whiskey and poured until the small beer bottle was full. Not a drop spilled. With a spare cork, I employed a nimble technique taught by my friend Peckolin, expertly securing it atop the beer bottle. I then took my water skin and poured some water into the whiskey bottle. However, I didn't replace all the water; that was a rookie mistake. I filled maybe ¾ of what was missing and then sealed the bottle. I shook it a few times and then put it in my satchel. My father knew it was watered down; why try hiding it? There was no need to perfect the ruse when his assumptions played in my favor.

As I exited the alley, I sighed in relief as I heard light snoring. Devars, the guard notorious for his dozing, was slumped against the wall of the local guard pavilion. His rusted iron helmet sat askew over a chainmail coif, and his breastplate and leggings had seen better days. Curiously, clenched in his hand was not a weapon but a fork, gripped as if it were his lifeline. The oddity nearly coaxed a snort of laughter from me, but I stifled it just in time. I wondered what culinary dream Devars was lost in, to hold onto a fork with such determination even in sleep.

The merchant didn't care about my age, but the guards sure would. On any given day, Blaze teetered on the edge of being contraband, its mere possession a risk that could attract the guards' unwanted attention. By this time, a little after lunch, the 7th Avenue Courtyard had emptied, and its morning energy dissipated as people retreated to their work or homes. A mid-day calm settled over the area, leaving it deserted and tranquil. There, sprawled on the courtyard steps, was Peckolin, lost to a drunken slumber. Like me, he found solace in 7th Avenue's overlooked corners, away from prying eyes. No one was ever watching, not even the guards.

Many shunned 7th Avenue for its proximity to the pungent main sewer entrance and because more convenient thoroughfares beckoned them elsewhere. The result was a lane often cloaked in an unwelcoming odor and deserted by those who preferred quicker, more pleasant paths.

I gently woke my friend up from his nap. I needed Peckolin alert, despite the assault on my senses his presence caused. There was information, magic, too, only he could provide. Before I did, I stuck a couple of wads of mint paper in my nose. Peckolin always reeked of an unbearable odor, a nauseating blend of stale alcohol, unwashed body, and the pungent rotten egg smell of the nearby sewers. It was a scent that, over time, I had come to associate with the bleakness of death. That thought percolated through my mind, making me think of Edoth, Peckolin's brother. But I shook away the sad, bitter thought and sighed. Even through the wads of paper, I got a hint of a whiff of his odor—a smell I never wanted to experience again.

"Huh... Whazzat? What time is it?" mumbled Peckolin, his voice groggy. He opened his gummed-up eyes slowly, resembling a heap of rotten garbage more than a man.

"Roddy! What a pleasant surprise. Is it that time of the week again? Whiskey, come to papa!" In an instant, as Peckolin leaped to his feet, the aura of neglect and filth vanished, replaced by an uncanny cleanliness. He now mirrored the palace steps in their pristine state–a testament to his wizardry. Peckolin was a wizard and the best kind of wizard. Peckolin wielded his magic with a moral code, never for harm, only for survival and the occasional harmless trickery. Though, if I'm being honest, those 'occasions' were more frequent than not. "What do you need from me today, my friend?" He put his arm around me; a gentle fragrance of roses wafted around him, penetrating even the wads of paper stuffed in my nostrils. Such was the subtle charm of his magic.

"Who said I needed anything? Can't a kid bring his favorite Magician a bottle of whiskey?" I said with a laugh.

"Shhh. Keep it down, Roddy," Peckolin hissed with a mischievous glint in his eye. "Mr. Sleepy over there is blissfully unaware that his precious sword is now part of my collection."

"Ah. I was wondering about the fork. Nice spell." I said, glancing back at Devars. The realization hit me–his rigid hold did resemble a swordsman's grip.

"Anyway, what's the real reason you woke me up?" With a snap of Peckolin's fingers, a door materialized out of thin air, its sudden appearance as nonchalant as his demeanor. He stepped into a cluttered storage room, a treasure trove of the bizarre and the mundane, packed to the rafters with items ranging from the peculiar, like a grandfather clock that moved in reverse and a candle that never melted, to the prosaic like his liquor collection or his Alchemy collection—I wasn't sure how he kept them separate given that they were right next to each other. It looked for a second like he put the whiskey on the Alchemy side, but I blinked, and he closed the door before I could get a better look. "And before you ask, I can't make you taller. Well, I could, but it might break your bones." He added with a grimace.

"Well, there goes my afternoon plans," I laughed. "I need a favor." I unfolded my plans to him, ones I had meticulously crafted over the years, each detail etched in my mind. Tonight, they would come to fruition. He frowned, nodding as I talked. After tonight, the screams that echoed through my house would be silenced, and the cycle of pain would finally be broken.

An uneasy laugh slipped out, the sound seeming out of place in the moment's gravity. Today would be the day that would change everything.

~~~~~~~{**End Memory Core 6}**~~~~~~~

Chapter Nineteen
Why Would I Even Want Goblin Ears?

As reality seeped back in, a hollow ache spread through my heart, the weight of the present moment pressing down on me. Seeing Peckolin so brimming with life, so effortlessly joyful, pierced me with a sharp pang. His carefree spirit was a stark reminder of what I once had. Overwhelmed by the ache in my heart, I found myself collapsing to the ground, a helpless heap unable to rise from the grip of my sorrow.

I lost track of time for a while, thoughts drifting back to my life and what little I could recall. I lay there helpless for a few minutes before I dried my eyes and got to my feet, determined. I would get that joy back. I would escape Penance.

As if she were waiting for me to calm down, Crystal had held the notification until I stood. [You have looted Corpse 2. For recovering your corpse, you have earned 1 Death Boon.]

I shuddered as my corpse exploded into stardust. I waved away the notifications, more interested in new loot than old loot.

As I approached Slikk's lifeless form, a sense of foreboding dampened my enthusiasm. For some reason, I knew I wouldn't get good loot from his corpse.

[You have looted 74 gold.]

I paused, letting an exhale of air escape my lips. *That was it? After all of the trouble that Monster gave me, I got 74 gold.* I rushed forward to kick the corpse in the head as a little revenge for the grief it gave me, but just as my foot would have made contact, the corpse vanished, causing me to stumble forward into the body of the next goblin: Drip. The dice rolled.

[You have looted a chest key.]

My face fell. All that work for something this class could do on its own. At least I would have it for a future run. My heart pounded with anticipation and fear as I moved my hand to the final corpse. *Surely, I'll get something better this time.* I looted the final goblin. The dice rolled.

[You have looted Gurgle's staff of noxious Fumes. You have looted a chest key. You have looted 47 gold. You have looted 2 Goblin Ears.]

Among the loot from the final goblin was Gurgle's staff, a twisted piece of wood that seemed to writhe with a life of its own, emitting a faint, eerie green smoke. Hanging from the top were five potion bottles I couldn't remove from the staff, bubbling multicolored concoctions swirling inside.

"Why would I even want goblin ears?" I spat in disgust as I looked up at Crystal.[Those trophies are as good as currency among certain unsavory types on the 2nd and 5th floors or as a quest item.]

"Hey Crystal, bring out the map. That second secret room was around here, wasn't it?"

[Your ability to recall information borders on clairvoyance,] Crystal said, mirth in her voice. I felt a surge of anger, but I did my best to ignore it and her comments and studied the map as it came into view. It was here in the boss chamber. Right next to the stairs. With all the fighting, it was obvious why I had never noticed the discolored bricks making up the boss chamber wall. The rest of the chamber was the standard gray-green of the rest of the sewers, but here by the path to the next floor the bricks weren't green at all. As if the slime had been moved away. I tapped on the bricks multiple times, and in different spots thinking that there was a hidden switch on the door itself. It wasn't invisible like the Dragon skull doorway, but nothing seemed to work. And then I remembered the switch on the underside of the Necromancer's Altar. Maybe there would be one here. I made my way up to the scorch-marked altar. I felt around the altar for a switch but couldn't find one. After a few minutes, I gave up, frustrated, before sitting on the altar and staring out at the room. I had to find the secret.

I stared around at the grey-green bricks.

Grey Grey Grey Green Green Green. Purple. Grey Grey Green Grey Green Grey. I sighed, hopped down off the altar. "Well, I guess that's that. You ready for the next floor."

Dejected, I walked forward to the stairs, when it finally clicked in my brain. Purple. There was no reason for there to be a purple brick if it didn't mean something, right?

I ran to the switch, excited, and slapped the brick. The room started shaking and then the wall slid upwards into the ceiling.

I raced forward and into the next room.

~Run 3, 2L, Floor 1, Sewers of Aerlyn~

The room was the smallest I'd come across so far—smaller than the previous treasure room, barely half as large as the entrance room. It had just two doors and a crate right in the way. I opened the crate and found a copper dagger inside. "Well, this might come in handy," I muttered, slipping it into my inventory. I stepped over the crate and headed for the door on the other side.

I stared uncomprehendingly at the door. It was completely different from the other doors on the level, inlaid with gold and full of intricate carvings of rats. I blinked a few times, trying to make sure I wasn't imagining things, but as I approached the door, I shrugged and pressed down on the handle, expecting the door to open. I slammed the door, having not stopped moving as I tried to open it.

It was a puzzle, of course. A secret within a secret. Just like the stories said, I felt a chill run down my spine as Professor Perrod's warning about leaving secrets buried flashed in my mind.

"There are some secrets in Penance that not even the gods know—the kinds of secrets they kill for. If you find yourself in Penance, run from every secret. Or soon you'll find yourself running from something far, far worse."

The voice faded as I studied the door. It was almost like a clock, 12 panels spaced out evenly each depicting a certain number of Rats. There was something off about the rats; I wasn't sure if it was the color of their eyes or something else. Like earlier in the dungeon, these rats showed signs of intelligence; one of the rats wore a ballerina outfit, another three swung from a trapeze, while 7 and 10 played different sports.

Yep, definitely something off about the rats here.

I noted briefly that Crystal was being silent but didn't say anything. After her earlier comments, I wasn't in the mood to talk with her.

Something else was off about the rats. I noticed that I could move the panels around on the door. But I was always terrible at puzzles and would probably be stuck here forever if I didn't get any help. There was nothing for it, so I had to say something.

"Hey, Crystal?"

[Oh, talking to me again, are we?]

Okay, weird. What does she have to be angry about?

"Any idea what I need to do here?"

[It's a clock. It's not that difficult of a puzzle to solve. Even someone like you can probably do it.]

Another dig. It was all she was doing now, and it was getting harder and harder to control my anger. I didn't think either of us would be happy with the end results. So I gritted my teeth and forced my thoughts down.

"A clock. Like the number of..." I trailed off and started counting the rats. *1, 2, 5, 3, 7, 4, 8, 9, 6, 12, 10, 11. The panels were out of order!*

Carefully, I pried the fifth panel off of the door, amazed at how easily it came loose. I stuck it back and place, and magically, a force made it cling to the door again. I took down the pieces and rearranged them in order. The door flashed, a lock clanged and clinked, and the door opened.

Corpse – Run 2
- **Gold:** 288

Items

Torch
- **Amount:** 3

- **Condition:** 10/10

- **Effect:** Deals 1–4 physical damage. 5% chance of causing burn effect on target

- **Description:** A simple wooden torch wrapped in oil-soaked rags.

Gold
- **Amount:** 288

- **Condition:** N/A

- **Effect:** The currency of Penance

- **Description:** A simple gold coin. On one side is the visage of the Merchant of Death, and on the other is a thumbs-up.

Dagger of Penetration

- **Amount:** 1

- **Condition:** 15/15

- **Effect:** Deals 3–7 damage. Ignores 2 points of defense

- **Description:** A sharp and durable iron dagger with a well-balanced design, perfect for quick and precise strikes.
  Quote: "A very sharp dagger." — Photonius The Dead

Iron Great Axe

- **Amount:** 1

- **Condition:** N/A

- **Effect:** Deals 4–14 damage

- **Description:** A massive iron great axe with a double-edged blade, designed for powerful and sweeping strikes.

Copper Mace

- **Amount:** 1

- **Condition:** 15/15

- **Effect:** Deals 1–6 damage. 5% chance to stun

- **Description:** A robust copper mace with a heavy, rounded head.

Arrows

- **Amount:** 5

- **Condition:** 4/5

- **Effect:** Allows you to fire a bow

- **Description:** A simple wooden arrow with a stone arrowhead.

Rat Teeth

- **Amount:** 1

- **Condition:** N/A

- **Effect:** None

- **Description:** The incisor(s) of a Giant Rat. Who knows? If you collect a lot, something good may happen.

Rat Meat

- **Amount:** 1

- **Condition:** N/A

- **Effect:** +5 health. 80% chance of poison if consumed

- **Description:** Juicy, full of protein, and only tastes a little like sewage! Who knows? If you collect a lot, something good may happen.
  Quote: "Tastes like chicken!" – Photonius The Dead

Cloth Shirt

- **Amount:** 1

- **Condition:** 10/10

- **Effect:** +1 defense

- **Description:** It's a shirt!
  Quote: "My friend went to Penance, and all I got was this lousy

T-shirt!"

Leather Greaves

- **Amount:** 1

- **Condition:** 15/15

- **Effect:** +1 defense

- **Description:** A worked and treated pair of leather greaves covering the waist down to the ankles.

Chapter Twenty
Minuscule Magical Menagerie

~Run 3, The Mischief Room, Floor 1, Sewers of Aerlyn~

In the room was a bizarre scene that I hadn't seen before. In the middle of the room was a full-blown three-ring circus. *You know, at this point, I really should have seen this coming.*

There was a ringmaster directing the rats through their acts, and a stand filled with dozens of smaller rats, all watching in rapt attention.

The creatures somersaulted through the air, their tiny bodies silhouetted against the dim light. A symphony of squeaks and the soft rustle of tiny feet filled the room as they swung from the rafters and twirled in delicate ballet routines. The minuscule magical menagerie was both enchanting and surreal.

My heart sank as I watched the rats' joyous performance. I hesitated at the door, my hand hovering on the handle, unsure if I should intervene. These rats clearly weren't a threat, and the idea of stopping their fun made me feel terrible. Or did I have to? Maybe if I approached with a friendly demeanor and showed no hostility, I could avoid a mess.

"Hey, Crystal," I whispered, glancing nervously at the performing rats. "Is there any way to show these rats I don't mean any harm?"

Crystal flared her light into the room and spoke, [How do you do, fellow creatures?]

I facepalmed, confident that she was trolling me since no one else could hear her. Then, the latest in a long line of off moments occurred. The ringmaster rat approached hat in hand, looking trite.

"Pardon me, sirs, madams, or others?" He paused looking at the crystal above my head. "We are but humble Ratses. We mean no harm. Justs having funs with our times in between the Penitents running. If you lets us clears outs we will have the two ratses ready for yous to kill."

"Oh, that's alright, no need to have another fight. I was coming through to find the secret room here. And Rod is fine, mister?"

"Rattigan Orvegicus, at your service." He did a little flourish with his hat and bowed. It was then that I finally noticed that, unlike his fellow rats, his legs and hands were slightly more humanoid in appearance.

"You're not like the other rats, are you, Mr. Orvegicus?"

"No sirs, I's am not," Rattigan said, shaking his head. "When this dungeon was created, I's was one of the firstsis to be put through its paceses. I's didn't wins, but I's mades it far enough downs that I's was rewardedes. I's was put here as the stewardess of rat kindses. Forever. Some would think it a punishment, but I's have been fondses of ratses my entire life. I's studieds them in schools. Rats flourish in the worst of places so in a way this is paradise for them. And when they die theys always comes backses."

"Wait, so the creatures here don't really die? That actually makes me feel a bit better," I said, wiping my forehead dramatically, trying to show guilt. It didn't pay to be rude to this guy, after all. "I have a couple of questions for you. Is that okay? what's with the circus stuff?"

"Of courses, of courses!." Rattigan replied, opening his mouth broadly in what I assumed was a smile. "As fors the circus, that be what I's do. I's a ringmaster. I'm head of the circus. Before the Penances claims me, I's be the head of mys own circus. Ratses be smarts. They alsos bored of waiting. Be needings to entertain for eternity. We plays cards, acrobasticses, readses bookses. Puts on showses, lots of things. Ratses not so smartses as humanses, but still smartses."

I leaned in, intrigued. "So you're really okay with the fact that I've killed a dozen of your rat friends?" I asked.

"Againses thatses whatses we're hereses fors." Rattigan said, his tone matter-of-fact. "Nows abouts the secretses. Theres actually two left, but ones won't be ons yours maps."

"Wait, really? I thought once I cleared a floor, the map was fully filled out," I said, frowning.

"There are always secretses lefts to uncovers. Especially the secretses of the floor Guardians. Each floor has one lurkings around somewheres, and ifs you completes our tasks, we gives you a special item. The item for this floor gives youses the ability to talks to all ratses, evens those on future floors," Rattigan explained.

"Alright, what do you need me to do for you?" I asked.

"Oh, this one's easy," Rattigan said with a wave of his hand. "The super bosses on the other sides of the door heres, he eats ratses and we don'ts come backes. Thankfully, ratses don't haves populations problems.'""

"So you'll reward me for doing something I was going to do anyway? Sweet!" I said.

"Of courses. Is always rewardses good deeds," Rattigan said, nodding. "In facts, if you ever wantses a challenge, I'd be happy to fightses you afters."

"Wait, really?" I asked, surprised.

"Of courses, I's don't die, but I's likes to battle. Be warned, you'll loses. I's haves 2250 healthses." Rattigan said with a grin. "If you win, I's award yous 800 Death Boons."

"Wait, if you're so powerful, why aren't you facing this super boss?" I asked.

"It will gain control of me," Rattigan said, shuddering. "Besides, I'm terrifieds, you'll sees why I's don't wants to fight."

I stepped onto the threshold of the next room, making sure that I didn't step further and trigger the fight.

~Run 3, Secret Boss room, The Plague Bearer, Floor 1, Sewers of Aerlyn~

From the doorway, I took in the sight before me and blinked. The secret room was massive, large enough to rival the castle from my earlier Memory Core. A wave of stench hit me, and I gagged, covering my nose with my sleeve. Rushing towards me like a stream of sewage was a gigantic monster composed of hundreds or even thousands of rats. It towered in an unrecognizable shape, ambling towards me on legs made of hundreds of rat corpses, eyes glowing with a sickly green light.

My heart pounded in my chest, and my breath quickened. A sound like an elephant's trumpet blasted through the room, and rat after rat was launched toward me. I exhaled sharply and slammed the door shut. A series of thuds hit the door in front of me.

~Run 3, The Mischief Room, Floor 1, Sewers of Aerlyn~

"How is that an enemy on the first floor?" I muttered, turning around to face an expectant-looking Rattigan. "I'm sorry, Rattigan, but I can't do it. That thing is way too powerful for me currently. It would wipe the floor with me."

Rattigan's whiskers twitched as he sighed. "I suppose thats its then. Ifs you ever kills it, it will not respawns strongers like others bosses and enemies do. This one gets strongers with times, yeses, but once clears, it should revertses to its naturals state before its consumeds hundreds of ratses. I will takes precautionses for now sos thatses it will not gets strongers. I will takes my Mischiefs withs me to the fifthes floors. Bewares the Ratses that will be lefts."

I shook my head, feeling a mixture of frustration and determination. "Well, that stinks," I said, more to myself than anyone else. But it didn't matter. I had already resolved myself to this goal. "Floor one or floor five, it doesn't matter. We will meet again."

Rattigan and his 'mischief' banished in the blink of an eye before I could say anything else. I looked around the plain, empty room. *What do I do now?* There was nothing for it. I left back to the boss's chamber.

Chapter Twenty-One
Did I Do Something Wrong?

As soon as I returned, my gaze flew towards the exit to the next floor. The second floor loomed as a more significant challenge, a test of skill and strategy that I couldn't afford to underestimate. I'd have to see which weapons I could use as a rogue and figure out how to make my way through it. I shook my head to clear my pointless rambling. It was highly likely clearing every mob on the floor would grant me a Death Boon or two, and a Death Boon was a permanent buff; it would always be worth it.

Upon entering, I spotted two giant rats nonchalantly lounging atop a crate as if they owned the place, seemingly unaware of the danger I posed to them. It almost seemed like they were relaxing, like they knew I had beat the floor boss and thought they were safe. I thought of Rattigan, and wondered if I should just say I came in peace, but before I could do anything to prevent it... The scene shifted dramatically; the once relaxed rats snapped to attention, their beady eyes locking onto me with newfound aggression. Without hesitation, I lunged forward, my right dagger arcing through the air in a swift slash aimed at the nearest rat. Inexplicably, my blade whistled past the rat, slicing nothing but air, a futile gesture at the start of the battle.

The rats, seizing their chance, lunged with startling speed. The dice rolled, clattering wildly on the hard stone floor. At that moment, time froze, and I dodged back while saying a prayer of thanks to the god of luck.[Giant Rat 1 has missed. Giant Rat 2 has missed.]With a swift, determined arc, my right arm sliced through the air, the dagger's blade whistling as it aimed for the rat. My muscles tensed in anticipation of impact. The die rolled.

[You deal two damage to Giant Rat]

"Gah! Die!" I screamed, frustration surging as my dagger merely wounded, rather than killed, the infuriating rat. I cursed under my breath. I kept getting bad rolls, likely using up all my luck with the dodges. I clenched and unclenched my jaw–my strategy to conserve my dagger's durability was teetering on the edge of failure. The rats snarled, and the first rat looked instead a lot like a carcass about to be spit-roasted. However, as one, the rats lunged again, and time froze. The dice rolled .[Giant rat 1 has missed, and Giant rat two has missed]

"Hey Crystal, I get it; they missed," I snapped, irritation lacing my voice. "Let's save the play-by-play for the real threats, like magic attacks, alright?"

As time returned to normal, I swung at the first rat again with my right dagger. The die rolled. The dagger met its mark unerringly, severing the rat's head with a gruesome efficiency as it rolled away, leaving a stark, crimson trail on the ground. The rat's corpse oozed blood into the already foul-smelling but ultimately thin layer of sewage that coated the ground, making the air even more pungent and the floor slippery be- neath my boots.My breathing slowed, and I allowed myself a moment's reprieve. I had been shocked more than scared when the rat landed on my back, but I shrugged the emotion off.

My right dagger, now teetering on the brink of uselessness, had a single point of health remaining. I had been hoping to kill both with the durability I had left from a single dagger, but that wouldn't be the case. Depending on how many enemies were left on the floor, I would have to dig into my bag for a different weapon.

I felt a sudden weight on my left shoulder, and a surge of panic gripped me as the rat's claws dug into my skin through the leather. Time hadn't slowed until it landed for some reason. Instinctively, I swung my dagger in a wide arc with my right hand, desperately attempting to dislodge the rat from my shoulder. The die rolled.

With a final, jarring snap, the iron dagger broke.

Not even waiting for a second to pass, I threw my left dagger into my right hand and slashed at the rat, which was still on its back. The die rolled—As the adrenaline rush faded, I crouched, taking a quick rest. I hadn't stopped to rest through any of my runs so far. I was going at a pretty non-stop pace, but only a few hours had passed since I 'woke up.' My eyes closed as I leaned back against the wall. I sighed, *Again? I really need to stop doing that.*

"Hey Crystal, any idea why I keep sighing so much?" I didn't bother opening my eyes while I waited for her response.

"Hey, Crystal?" I said, talking to the air. This time, I opened my eyes, glancing upwards at the red, pulsating light. It was starting to be a source of comfort, but something was wrong. "Are you there?"

[Yes, Rod?] The crystal's response was terse, and thinking back since the boss, she hadn't been talking much. Maybe I messed something up.

"Did I do something wrong? I asked you a question, and you didn't respond. In fact, you haven't been commenting on much of anything other than the battles lately. Whatever it was, I'm sorry."

[You have done nothing wrong.] Crystal didn't elaborate further.

"Okay, well, is there any way to fix this?"

[Nope] I sighed heavily, again, making my simmering frustration boil to a point as she abruptly ended the conversation. But I was determined not to let Crystal's capricious mood affect my dungeon run.

"Crystal, I've been meaning to ask. How do I–"

[No. You said I talk too much. So I'm being quiet.]

"What? You just told me it wasn't my fault. That's a lie!" I exclaimed, a mix of confusion and indignation in my voice. "After all the trouble you gave me for lying earlier…"

[I didn't lie. It wasn't what you did but what you said,] Crystal said, heat in her voice. I couldn't believe it; an inanimate object was trolling me.

"Alright, then. I'm sorry. Can you please get back to talking normally? We have a lot of things to discuss before moving onward," I said, trying to sound as apologetic as I felt. Some part of me worried that my tone might be too abrasive. *Is that who I am? Abrasive and rude? An angry, always boiling pot who sighs all the time?*

[Apology accepted,] Crystal said, her voice softening like thawing ice, a subtle shift from the sharp edges of her earlier words. [Now, choose your question wisely: health, food, sleep, or stats. Remember, you only get one here.] Her voice cracked like thin ice that was thawing too fast, each word laced with a stinging hurt. As she spoke, the red light radiating from her pulsed brighter, a visual echo of her pain, forcing me to shield my eyes from its intensity.

"What are you doing, Crystal? I said I was sorry." I stammered, confusion knotting my brow.

That's how apologies worked, didn't they? Just like Dad, constantly smoothed things over with Mom with those two words. A flash of a long-lost moment flickered in my mind, solidifying into another Memory Core. I didn't think they could form this late after a battle, but here we were. I reached out and touched the core. Argument forgotten.

{Memory Core 6/??? }
{Would you like to view the memory?}
{Y/N}

It was that same dark voice that I heard before I viewed my first-ever memory.

I hesitated. I hadn't heard that voice since, so I wasn't sure why I was hearing it now. But I needed to know more about who I was. I needed to know why I was executed.

"Yes, I'll view the memory."

Chapter Twenty-Two
Anger

~~~~~~~{Memory Core 7 Start}~~~~~~~

It was a stormy evening from when I was four in our cramped, two-room hovel we called home. A single small candle struggled to keep the room lit against the encroaching shadows of nightfall.

A home where my father had knocked mother's dinner off the rickety, wooden table, dust falling as the table shook. The leek and potato soup, smelling of warmth but not love, fell to the dirt floor, spilling in waves and generating mud in the sad excuse of a dirt floor. "I'm sorry, I'm sorry." My father said, his voice barely above a whisper. He didn't even budge from his seat. I swore I saw a ghost of a smile flicker at the corners of his mouth.

Mother was a flame, bursting with energy and heat, as she slammed a tiny fist against the table. More dust fell, her hand shook above the tabletop, and I covered my ears before the yelling started. Quick as a flash, an idea to stop the fight forming, I moved my hands to my wooden bowl. I was about to offer my mother my meager half-portion to stave off her anger when my father moved first.

He slid his bowl toward her, his smile fully formed now. As Mother ate, I took small spoonfuls, tasting the salty yet sweet taste of the leeks and the hearty flavor of the potatoes; she began to eat with vigor, ignoring my father's soft cry, "What about my dinner?"

After eating, she grabbed the bowls from the table and the bowl off the ground and put them in a basin with other dishes. Mother gave

Father the stink eye and pulled out the emergency rations of stale bread and moldy cheese from a dirty, grey cupboard hidden in a corner. Dinner was not so easily replaced.

My father had stood then, kicking back the chair. "I'm not eating that trash. Should have thrown it out weeks ago." His voice was quiet, barely above a whisper. Four-year-old me fell forward from my chair and quickly hid underneath the seat. I could feel a hot trickle down my cheeks; I started rocking back and forth, hoping my parent's fight wouldn't be a long one. I heard a crash, and—]

~~~~~~~{End Memory Core 7}~~~~~~~

As I came to, the room's darkness confused me. Crystal was as dim as I had ever seen her, and the torch was gone from my hands. I would've tried to fix the lighting situation, but the memory left me reeling as I focused instead on the sound of my father extending a fist against my mother. *What? What happened? A meek father like that wouldn't raise his fists, right?* And the way anger radiated off my mother like a hot stove, refusing my father dinner until after she had eaten. If my parents were really like that, it was no wonder I had ended up here. I was shaken from my thoughts as a loud noise filled the room. I covered my ears but to no avail.

Crystal screamed in rage, and I couldn't figure out what was wrong. I had forgotten that covering my ears didn't work because her sound was in my mind, not the room. She started letting out a deep glow that grew steadily brighter.

[I'm still hurt by the way you treated me. It's like you think I'm not even human.] The pain in her voice reached a crescendo, the light so bright I closed my eyes. The noise of her yell rose higher and higher and brought me to my knees.

The pain fought for control of my body drowning out all thoughts except a burning hatred for the cause of my pain. It was like an uncontrollable force wielding my body as a weapon, and I screamed back the worst thing I could have possibly said at that moment.

"What does it matter that you aren't human? You are a talking, floating crystal! Stop complaining about it; the yelling is killing me." I said these words with force and anger, digging my grave even deeper.

[Well, I never!] She spoke so loudly I could feel something burst, and I swear I felt a trickle of blood down my face. The next moment Crystal's light disappeared, and then she did, too, and I was shrouded in darkness. It felt like the world was closing in on me, constricting me, making everything hollow; I reached out in the darkness, trying to find a torch, Crystal, or anything. I hadn't realized how much I'd been relying on her and the benefits she gave me. If only I could see! That's right, a torch! In my panic, my anger disappeared like a looted corpse.

"Hey, Crystal. Can I equip a torch in my left hand, please?" I waited a couple of seconds but got no response from her. "Hello? Crystal? I'm sorry about what I said. Please don't do this. Crystal!" Fear and anger were trading places rapidly and I was uncertain what I should do. The battle ended though, as one emotion overtook the other.

I let out a scream, spittle flying, and my eyes flared so much I thought they would burst out of my skull. What was I supposed to do now? I couldn't access my weapons, and I couldn't see. "Crystal. Come on, I didn't mean anything by what I said. You are amazing. I can't survive without you." Nothing.

A deep anger welled within me, and I pictured my father with his hand raised about to strike my mother. My fist curled, and I banged my fist against the wall in frustration. I was going to be stuck here forever. I hit the wall again. The pain felt good. It hit the wall again, and again, and again.

The pain in my hand built to a throbbing, radiating orb of agony that beat like a drum in line with my heart. I became lost in the pain, my thoughts and fears eclipsed by the sensation of the strikes. I only stopped when I felt a pop in my left hand, and an overwhelming scream of pain made me rear back, cradling the hand. The throbbing continued to intensify as a slick wetness trickled down my busted, broken hand. It wasn't healing. The pain wasn't going away.

I needed Crystal back. I had died multiple times in three hours with her help; I wouldn't make it three minutes without her. I couldn't even equip the dagger I had found. I rocked back and forth like I did as a kid hiding under a chair; I couldn't handle this. I wished I was at home. Anywhere but here would be preferable. I wasn't supposed to be here in Penance. I was a thief. Thieves never got a shot at redemption. It was one of the seven deadly sins. Greed.

Who knew I had been this close to a panic attack for the entire time? Not sure what to do, I let myself fall to the ground. My body, both physically and emotionally spent, clattered to the ground with a rocky thud. I cradled my damaged arm, the instant healing gone with Crystal's disappearance. *This isn't fair. This isn't fair. This isn't...* I know I messed up. My few scattered memories filled me with guilt I had no frame of reference for. But did I truly deserve this?

The pressure in my eyes finally lessened, and I blinked them a few times as I tried to clear the tears. I had never felt this alone. How was I going to get myself out of this mess?

As my eyes adjusted to the lack of light, I saw them, the rats. Their corpses still sparkled, generating the only light in the room. Maybe I could still loot things. The small bit of hope lit a spark. Crystal may have abandoned me, and I probably deserved it. But I still had a chance to get as far as possible with this run. I could at least scout out the second floor for information and make headway for future runs. I didn't know my health, and I had no way to get to my stored weapons. And I had broken my left hand... However, I knew I could do something. I could make progress.

I could feel my heart beating faster, and my face started getting red from the heat. Even though my earlier memory of my parents made me question who I was, I had a partial answer ready. "I will not be like my father." I only had one image of him, but the emotion was so strong it could block out everything else. "I will not be my father." All that got me was shame and a broken hand.

Based on that single memory, and the one of my father tasking me with buying his escapes, both of my parents were awful, and if my only chance to do better was here in Penance, I would take it. I shook my head to clear the thoughts, set a grin on my face, and waved my hand through the rats. I felt my hand slide against something sharp. In the dim light, I could barely make out a glint of silver reflecting the dim light of the rats, and then it vanished.

The dice rolled, clattering against the stone floor as the light faded. They were still here, and I could still interact with everything except what Crystal did for me. Gold and rat meat fell from the sky like raindrops, tinkling as they fell. A small pile of gold coins clinked around my feet, and I hurried to pick them up. The coins felt slimy, covered in fresh blood from the sinewy rat meat.

Now what? What was I supposed to do with the coins and the rat meat? I had no way to carry them. *Think. Think. Think!* My left hand was ruined, my greaves didn't have pockets, and I couldn't even take off my shoes and use them to carry things as if they were sandals. *Wait. Shoes. Clothing. Helm.* The thoughts came to me rapid fire, less than a second passing between each word. I never knew how my thoughts jumped from A to B to Z, but I always surprised myself when they did. Shoes and pockets weren't the only clothing with space to carry stuff. Hats had plenty of space and what was a leather helmet but a skin-tight hat.

I sighed and took off the leather helm I was wearing. I could hold them in the helmet and leave them by the door whenever I entered a new room to have my working arm free from attacks. My left arm throbbed helpfully reminding me of its uselessness. It would make more sense to leave the stuff altogether, but a part of me felt that would be admitting defeat.

I left the room and immediately noticed something was off. No, Crystal reminding me that I should go back and pick things up. There was no title card announcing the location I was in. I should have realized that was Crystal's doing. Yet another way she was helping me, and I never even noticed. I wanted to kick myself. I had been so self-centered, so thoughtless, and for almost no reason other than Crystal didn't have a body. What a dumb thing to focus on.

I shook my head and finally took stock of the room; just like earlier, the Giant rats were doing bizarre things. There was an entire circus set up. Trapeze wires. A cannon. Flaming rings. The three giant rats were performing a circus routine. I closed my eyes and then blinked a few times, and then shut my eyes. I really needed to talk to Rattigan again, I get that it was their form of entertainment, but it was unsettling. When I opened them, everything was gone. And only two rats were remaining. And a crate.

My head started to hurt, which was odd because I hadn't had a headache since coming to the dungeon. Nothing here made sense, and it was all my fault. I could feel my frustration with my earlier actions rising, the consequences compounding, building to an explosive peak. And then I remembered the dagger. It was lost in the darkness in that previous room.

My tendency to forget things was going to get me killed. My father was like that, always forgetting things, making excuses, and always messing up. Even though I only had the two snippets of memory, I had so many details about the shame my father brought me. The shame I felt from being so much like him.

Using my rage as fuel, I decided to work it out on a productive target this time. I struck forward and slammed my non-broken fist down on the head of the rat, squishing its mouth against the stone-shattering its teeth. My right hand came away bloody as a dice bounced behind me.

I stared at the other soon-to-be victim, frozen in fear, the reflection of the lone torch in the room flickering in its eyes. A rage like no other I had felt before consumed me, worse even than the all-consuming fire that ruined my left arm.

I tried to focus on my thoughts about not being like my father, but the thoughts were soon eradicated. I couldn't see, I couldn't think. All my being focused on my rage. Before the other rat could glance at his dead friend, I started punching the last rat with my right fist without pausing as dice rolled behind me. And I didn't stop. As the rat squealed its last breath, I kept pounding and slamming my hand down. My hand was a bloody mess. I looked through the cracks in my finger and saw only a puddle where the rat had once been. My other arm hung loosely at my side, the hand still throbbing.

What is happening to me?

Chapter Twenty-Three
The Second Floor

I stared down at the bloody pulp that used to be my hand. Tears fell painfully from my eyes. I wanted to curl into a ball and just let myself cry, but where had that gotten me? Without the crystal here, it felt like I was devolving into a baser state. *What had Father Krastor always said about rage? Father Krastor. Where had that thought come from?* The mental image of the Father refused to form in my mind entirely. I shrugged and took stock of the room.

Two blood pools from the rats were precariously close to being washed away by the sewage that streamed from grates on the floor. The sewage spent some time crowding out the floor before ultimately flowing up the walls and toward the ceiling.

I looted the crate. The dice rolled. A small pile of gold coins clattered to the bottom of the crate. The shadow of the lip of the crate obscured the number of coins in the almost complete darkness. As I moved the coins from the crate to my helm, I looked at the crate. Unlike chests and monsters, the crate didn't disappear. It remained where it was.

Tentatively, I went to the crate and dumped out the gold and meat I had gathered. The loot didn't vanish.

Then came the moment of truth. If I couldn't move the crate, it wouldn't matter that things would stay inside. I wrapped my right arm around the crate, clutching it against my chest, and I heaved up as I lifted with my legs. The crate was as light as a feather. I could lift it against my chest and carry it one-handed without my useless hand.

I immediately dropped the crate in celebration. I whipped and cheered—the one good thing to happen since Crystal left. And then I made one of the best decisions I made in my entire time in the dungeon. I took off my necklace, the one I had gained from the boss, and placed it in the crate. I knew without Crystal that I was going to die pretty quickly on the second floor, and it just wouldn't do to have to fight these rats again on the off chance the floor dropped better loot.

I walked back to the entrance room and put my crate there. Crystal's silence hung over me like a shadow, her absence more palpable with each passing moment. I had no idea how long Crystal's tantrum would last; so much of the game behind the dungeon relied on her. Without access to the inventory, I had to carry everything, and with a broken hand, that just wasn't possible, so I needed a place to store all of my loot from however far I made it with this build.

Thankfully, everything stayed where you put it in the entrance room. With Crystal's absence, I had no access to weapons or a way to check my health. I could return for the dagger I left in that room, but it had a single strike left and didn't seem worth the effort. I wanted to get up to the second floor because the sooner I got there, the sooner my run and my pain would end.

But I was damned if I wasn't going to take this run as far as I possibly could. This wasn't just about surviving anymore; it was about proving to Crystal and myself that I didn't need her. I returned to the rooms where the other two crates were and carried them back to the entrance room one at a time.

I wasn't sure if I could keep the torch in the crate because the flame automatically lit, and I wasn't going to store a lit torch in a wooden crate, even with magic around. Who knew, the sewage around here was probably all flammable. It would be just my luck to end a run early because I blew up the entire sewer.

With no more preamble, I approached the ladder that led to the second floor; it was intimidatingly large, and I worried about climbing with my injured arm. I moved forward and grabbed a rung as high up as I could. As I moved up, I braced with my shoulder, cursing my earlier anger. Each rung creaked with an ominous sound as if the whole thing was about to collapse under my weight. The further I climbed, the more the air began to change. Slowly, the acrid scent of flowing sewage was replaced by sweet-smelling cinnamon, the lemony scent of cardamom, and the smokey scent of paprika. *Was there a market above my head?* I began to feel an oppressive, dry heat, a welcome reprieve from the damp, mildewy, and humid air of the sewers.

I pushed against the sewer grate and stepped out into a bustling city. There were people! Actual humans. No sooner had I stepped toward the city's heart than I glanced back only to see the sewer grate vanish like a mirage, sealing my retreat. I realized I had left the money in the first room. A scream tore from my still raw throat, turning several heads in the vicinity. I didn't care as the merchants and passersby stared at me. "Why do I keep forgetting things? Crystal? Why aren't you helping me?"

The questions hung in the air, unanswered as Crystal didn't return. I didn't care anymore. I was useless without her and couldn't make it on my own. Her silence was a chasm widening since her departure, each hardship—self-inflicted or otherwise—making the problem worse. Without her, my earlier resolve failed.

I didn't care anymore. I didn't care about the dungeon's danger, the dungeon, or the monsters trying to kill me. I didn't care about struggling to make something of the rest of my run. I just didn't care.

And then I smelled it *right before I died*—the heavenly smell of freshly baked bread and barbecuing meat. I almost cried as my stomach growled the loudest it ever had. It was so painful I took a step forward, anger forgotten. On a food stand in front of me, next to a baker whistling a jaunty tune while placing bread into the oven, was a mountain of freshly baked bread. As I approached the food, my head felt dizzy, my mouth slavering at the thought of food. If I had taken the time to slow down and think, I would have pondered that I hadn't felt hungry until I arrived on the second floor of the dungeon.

I grabbed a handful of bread. I took a bite, and an explosion of chewy, gooey bread and cheese melted in my mouth. It was filled with a cheese I couldn't Identify, but the sour flavor complimented the crust of the bread well. The food was terrific, but, as if by magic, I suddenly felt an overwhelming sense of dread and despair.

Suddenly, my earlier despair magnified tenfold. My mind shattered as I thought of the hopelessness of my situation. I knew I couldn't win this floor. I didn't deserve to win this floor after what I did.

As despair tightened its grip around my heart, the guard loomed closer, his movements not those of a determined warrior but a soulless automaton. Each step he took seemed laborious, as if the greatsword he carried was a burden far beyond its worth, dragging him down with its weight. There was something deeply unsettling about him; his armor appeared pieced together from a mismatch of scraps, each piece clinging to him as though by some unseen force. The only clean part of his outfit was a shining gold helm with a blue plume jutting out like a horn. The plates of armor, a dull clash of red against blue, resembled shards of broken pottery, jagged and ill-fitting, and were made worse in contrast to the majesty of the helm.

His eyes were the most haunting part; they shone with an unnatural glow, surrounded by a haze of inky smoke that swirled in shades of purple and black. There was an undeniable menace to it that rooted me to the spot. Anxiety wrapped around me like a cloak, adding to the weight of dread that kept me rooted to the spot. My body wouldn't respond to my frantic desire to escape. As he approached, brandishing a sword that heralded my end, a sudden insight cut through my fear...

A stark choice crystallized before me in the shadow of the looming guard. The despair, which had gnawed at my edges over the past minute, now devoured the little will to persevere I had left. *If I let this guard end me, everything resets.* The notion of resetting the run and granting myself a clean slate at the cost of my current one sparked a desperate kind of logic amidst the chaos of my thoughts. As I stood vulnerable, the resolve to let go and embrace whatever came next settled in, a decision born from the darkest depths of hopelessness.

Making the decision and experiencing the consequences were two completely different things. When the first swing made contact, it didn't just cut through flesh and bone—it severed my connection to a part of myself. There was a surreal moment where my mind couldn't accept the reality of my arm, now separate from me, lying on the ground. Shock buffered the initial wave of pain, a merciful dullness before the actual agony set in.

It felt like molten metal flowed through my veins, a scorching torrent that consumed all sense of time and space. In a brief moment of disorientation, as I disconnected myself from the extreme pain, I tried to wiggle my arm and hands. It was so odd. It still felt like I could, but of course, nothing happened to the severed limb. And then, as I looked up from the limb, the giant sword swung back around, and the all-consuming pain somehow magnified until all that I was became pain. My head plopped to the ground, and I heard a thunk as my body collapsed. I blinked once, twice, and—

~~~ The Plane Of Torment ~~~

[You big, dumb idiot. You don't steal on the second floor, or the floor guardians will execute you. Dear Rellum! I think I'm even angrier now!] I was dead, but somehow, I still heard her voice through the darkness.

[If they manage to strike you, they can deactivate all your class skills, leaving you only with weapons and armor for defense. And that's when you haven't destroyed an arm in a temper tantrum. We're so screwed you can't even begin to fathom it. We're going to have to figure out a way to kill it now without attracting further guard attention. It doesn't just reset like bosses do. This guard has your scent forever.]

[You have died. You have earned 3 Death Boons. End of Run 3]

Run 3 Corpse

- **Death Boons:** 13

- **Gold:** 338

Inventory
Iron Helm

- **Amount:** 1

- **Condition:** 10/20

- **Effect:** +2 defense

- **Description:** A well-crafted iron helm that offers solid protection for the head. Its reinforced structure provides excellent defense against blunt and sharp attacks.

Iron Short Sword

- **Amount:** 1

- **Condition:** 16/20

- **Effect:** Deals 1–6 damage

- **Description:** A sturdy iron short sword with a simple yet effective design. The blade is sharp and well-balanced, perfect for quick strikes and precise cuts.
  Quote: "Careful, it's sharp!" – 4 Fingers Lasalle

Iron Mace

- **Amount:** 1

- **Condition:** 14/20

- **Effect:** Deals 1–6 damage

- **Description:** A heavy iron mace with a solid, spiked head. This weapon deals devastating blows, capable of crushing armor and bone alike.

The Staff of the Necrobolt

- **Amount:** 1

- **Condition:** 17/20

- **Effect:** Deals 1–20 necrotic damage. Has a 10% chance to blind the target

- **Description:** An ominous staff carved from dark wood and adorned with eerie runes that glow with an otherworldly light. The Staff of the Necrobolt channels dark energies, unleashing powerful necrotic bolts that can wither flesh and bone.

Gurgle's Staff of Noxious Fumes

- **Amount:** 1

- **Condition:** 16/20

- **Effect:** Deals 1–20 poison damage. 20% chance to poison the target

- **Description:** A twisted piece of wood that seems to writhe with a life of its own, emitting a faint, eerie green smoke. Hanging from the top are five potion bottles that cannot be removed, each containing bubbling multicolored concoctions swirling inside.

Empty Bottle

- **Amount:** 1

- **Condition:** N/A

- **Effect:** You can put potions in this.

- **Description:** An empty bottle.

Torch

- **Amount:** 3

- **Condition:** 10/10

- **Effect:** Deals 1–4 physical damage. 5% chance of causing burn effect on target

- **Description:** A simple wooden torch wrapped in oil-soaked rags. When ignited, it produces a flickering flame that casts a warm, golden light in a small radius.

Gold

- **Amount:** 338

- **Condition:** N/A

- **Effect:** The currency of Penance

- **Description:** A simple gold coin. On one side is the visage of the Merchant of Death, and on the other is a thumbs-up.

Death Boons
- **Amount:** 13

- **Condition:** N/A

- **Effect:** Death Boons are power. Spend them wisely

- **Description:** A metaphysical currency provided by the Merchant of Death. The currency allows you to get progressively stronger as you face new threats in Penance.

Dagger of Penetration
- **Amount:** 1

- **Condition:** 15/15

- **Effect:** Deals 3–7 damage. Ignores 2 points of defense

- **Description:** A sharp and durable iron dagger with a well-balanced design, perfect for quick and precise strikes.
  Quote: "A very sharp dagger." — Photonius The Dead

Iron Great Axe
- **Amount:** 1

- **Condition:** N/A

- **Effect:** Deals 4–14 damage

- **Description:** A massive iron great axe with a double-edged blade, designed for powerful and sweeping strikes.

Copper Mace

- **Amount:** 1

- **Condition:** 15/15

- **Effect:** Deals 1–6 damage. 5% chance to stun

- **Description:** A robust copper mace with a heavy, rounded head. This weapon deals devastating blows, capable of stunning opponents.

Arrows

- **Amount:** 15

- **Condition:** 4/5

- **Effect:** Allows you to fire a bow.

- **Description:** A simple wooden arrow with a stone arrowhead. Stronger arrows provide additional effects.

Rat Teeth

- **Amount:** 1

- **Condition:** N/A

- **Effect:** None

- **Description:** The incisor(s) of a Giant Rat. Who knows? If you collect a lot, something good may happen.

Rat Meat

- **Amount:** 1

- **Condition:** N/A

- **Effect:** +5 health. 80% chance of poison if consumed

- **Description:** Juicy, full of protein, and only tastes a little like sewage! Who knows? If you collect a lot, something good may happen.
  Quote: "Tastes like chicken!" – Photonius The Dead

Goblin Ears

- **Amount:** 2

- **Condition:** N/A

- **Effect:** ???

- **Description:** Waxy, flaky, and oddly heavy, these ears are likely a waste of space! But who knows? If you collect a lot, something good may happen.

Cloth Shirt

- **Amount:** 2

- **Condition:** 10/10

- **Effect:** +1 defense

- **Description:** It's a shirt!
  Quote: "My friend went to Penance, and all I got was this lousy T-shirt!"

Leather Greaves

- **Amount:** 2

- **Condition:** 15/15

- **Effect:** +1 defense

- **Description:** A worked and treated pair of leather greaves covering the waist down to the ankles.

Leather Helm
- **Amount:** 1

- **Condition:** 15/15

- **Effect:** +1 defense

- **Description:** A sturdy leather helmet crafted to provide basic protection for the head.

Cloth Sandals
- **Amount:** 1

- **Condition:** 10/10

- **Effect:** +1 defense

- **Description:** Simple yet 'comfortable' cloth sandals that offer minimal protection but great mobility.
  Quote: "Don't worry, you'll miss the sewage under your toes after an hour with these!" – Photonius

Enchanted Blood Ruby of the Sewage Goblin Tribes
- **Amount:** 1

- **Condition:** N/A

- **Effect:**

  ○ You can speak Goblish

- Once per run, you can equip an item during combat

- You can skip the normal rooms on the first floor and choose to fight only the Necromancer and the goblins

- **Description:** A dark, gleaming ruby imbued with the ancient magic of the Sewage Goblin Tribes. The ruby is also one of seven keys needed to escape Penance.

Chest Key
- **Amount:** 1

- **Condition:** N/A

- **Effect:** Unlocks one chest of any rarity

- **Description:** A small, intricately crafted key that glows faintly with a magical aura.

Chapter Twenty-Four
TREASURE. Jamie Run 1, Part 2

A s I turned left into the room, I noticed how the doors seemed aged, as if the castle had been abandoned. It didn't make sense since I heard people screaming, but something about that detail nagged my brain.

~Head Maid Quarters.~

[TREASURE.]

The crystal oozed enthusiasm, or maybe it was black ink; it was hard to tell in the dim light. I stared at it, baffled by its sudden change in behavior. Its unpredictable nature was both intriguing and unnerving, leaving me unsure how to respond.

I was immediately struck by the mold and old wood smell as I walked into the room. It was starkly silent, in contrast to the earlier screams, except for the occasional drip of water from the ceiling. The discomfort was tangible, making me want to leave as soon as I entered. It took me a minute to find the treasure the crystal was talking about.

I was in a small room off the side of my bedroom. It belonged to Agatha, the head maid of the castle and quite possibly the bitterest old crone on the planet. She always treated me kindly, but the way she treated my other servants was atrocious. On the other side of the maid's bed was an honest-to-Rellum gold chest, but I didn't head for it yet.

I surveyed the room, gliding my hand along the wall and picking up a film of dust on my fingers. As I grabbed for the sconce to light up more of the room, the silence was shattered by a menacing growl. A zombie dog sprang from the darkness, its eyes wild with hunger. I recoiled in horror, barely managing to block its first attack with my injured arm. The pain was excruciating as its teeth tore through my skin, but I pushed through the agony, determined not to let this beast end my journey here.

In a desperate move, I slammed the zombie dog against the wall, hoping to weaken its hold on me. The dog loosened its grip, and I took advantage of the brief respite, crawling back using my uninjured arm, and I grabbed the torch off the floor. I swung vigorously, each strike a mix of fear and resolve, aiming to end the threat once and for all.

[Smash him in the head! Smash him in the head!] my crystal shouted, his voice grating. As he spoke, more inky smoke wafted out of him, making it even harder to see in the dim light.

I smashed the zombie dog over and over with the torch, hitting its eye with the first smack and its ear with the second one.

[Oh yeah! Damage baby! You dealt four and then two damage! Keep going, though it has about ten HP left. Don't let up!]

I kept hammering away, bringing the torch down repeatedly, not letting up for fear of the dog attacking me further. With a final powerful swing, I knocked the zombie dog to the ground, its body finally still. Exhausted and relieved, I let the remnants of the torch drop from my grasp. The room was mostly pitch black now, except for a small amount of flickering dark red light from the Crystal. The silence that followed was a stark contrast to the chaos of the fight, marking the end of the terrifying encounter. A moment later the silence was burst by Malice celebrating.

[Congratulations! You have killed the Zombie dog! Now loot its teeth and make a necklace!]

"What? No!" I shook my head as I tried to get off the ground.

[Aw, but think of how cute it would look on top of your toga. You'd look like some mythical warrior from ancient Aerlyn.]

That made me chuckle a bit through the pain and fog slowly spreading through my brain. "How much time do I have left?"

[I'm not sure. It was five minutes when we entered a minute and a half ago, but you got bit a second time. I'm unsure if the virus gets faster with more in the system. But have no fear! If you loot that beautiful iron chest over there, I can take all of the loot for you. Wouldn't want it to get lost.]

I nodded and walked to where I thought the lone iron chest was. I wasn't sure if I could find it without a light source, but I didn't want to give up. I groped through the darkness, kicking around with my feet.

[Cold! Colder!] Malice shouted.

I wasn't sure if he was taunting me or genuinely trying to help. I moved to my right blindly walking through the dark.

[Warm, warm. Hot, Hot, Hot! You should be able to open the chest.]

"How are you able to see? You don't have eyes?"

[How are you still breathing? You died?] Definitely mocking me.

I felt my way through the darkness again, each step uncertain but necessary. My hands reached out, hoping to brush against the iron chest I was searching for. The lack of light made every small noise seem louder, every moment stretched out in suspense. I banged my injured left arm against the edge of a table. I screamed from the pain and dropped to the floor, cradling my arm again.

[Warmer! But you're running out of time.]

My hand finally brushed against something cold and metallic—the chest. Relief flooded through me, releasing the tension built over the wasted minute spent searching. I knelt down, feeling the rough edges and the cool metal, anticipation building as I prepared to see what was inside. I had found the chest and was about to open it when a thought crossed my mind.

"If I loot this, will you return the treasure when I respawn?"

[No. Nu-uh. It's mine. My treasure.]

I eyed the crystal warily, knowing I needed its help but not fully trusting it. "How about we make a deal?" I proposed, my voice steady despite the uncertainty. I needed to sound confident and convince the crystal and myself that this was the right move.

[Yeeees? Deal? I like deals.]

"How about all of the treasure? It will be yours when we leave, but you let me use whatever I need while I am here."

I had no delusions of grandeur that I would be the one to make it through. Even with all of my training, even with all of my knowledge, I had been dealt a fatal blow within 3 minutes of my first run. Given the nature of my crystal, I suspected I fell under Malikap's domain. There were three greater and dozens, if not hundreds, of lesser domains. Domains determined how power worked for you in the dungeon. The classes, skills, stats, and even how money worked. It was a bad deal that I'm sure would return to hurt me.

"And you help guide me in here. No trickery. You don't have to tone down your mocking but remain helpful. I've heard horror stories."

[How? Nothing leaves Penance.]

"The royal family has its methods," I smirked.

[Deal. Deal I–No— Yes, I like the deal.]

The crystal began to glow with a faint grey light, casting more shadows than it dispelled. Yet, it also illuminated just enough of the area for me to see and open the chest. I picked up the rough, leather-sewn chest lid by a ragged metal corner and was shocked to see the bounty inside.

Five items practically spilled from the chest: a chainmail vest whose sleeve hung over the side, a polearm that couldn't fit jutted out opposite the chainmail, and a bounty of three different color potions. Staring at the potions with hungry eyes, I queried my crystal.

"Can you tell me the contents of these potions?"

[Yrd vutr Bryky Grynd Gomy, Klub Yrdo, and Byrnk Yrth Yrd.]

"What the what?"

[Yrd vutr Bryky Gomy, Klub Yrdo, and Byrnk Yrth Yrd.]

"In Aerlynthian, please."

[Oh, the first is a cure zombie potion, but it only works on dogs. I'm not even joking. It will turn our little zombie friend here, who would die otherwise, into a pet you can use whenever you need it. It will tattoo the pet onto your arm, and when you spawn, you simply tap the tattoo to summon the minion. You may want to hold off on using the pet until we leave this floor, though, as the dog is not immune to zombification after the potion leaves his system. The second is a fire resist potion, and the third heals 25 health.]

"How much longer do we have before the virus kills me?"

[Oh, I'd say less than a minute. Maybe book it back to the spawn room, so we can easily loot your corpse?]

"Oh, right."

I spun around too fast, and my world rocked. I stepped forward, and it felt like I was trying to run through water. I looked at my arm and saw green throbbing veins coursing up and down my arm towards my heart. My legs struggled to carry me forward as I moved past the doorway moving sluggishly.

My head throbbed with each step, my pulse quickened as I kept moving, pushing through. I had always heard that when you enter Penance, there is lots and lots of pain, but it disappears over time.

So... "Why am I still in pain?" I asked as my right hand and arm skidded across the silk-cherry wood of the hallway, where I leaned against the wall for support. As I kept walking, malice responded, [The effect is no longer removed. The gods decided it lessened fear of death, and no one learned their lessons.]

Another wave of nausea flushed through me, and my legs buckled under me as the infection took its toll. I crawled, each movement more laborious than the last, fighting for every second of life left. But as the cold floor met my cheek, the fight faded. I surrendered to the inevitable, my body too weak to continue the battle. The cold of the stone immediately soothed my face and my wounded arm.

[Twenty seconds to the room with yah, don't bleed out on the marble. So hard to clean.]

In my dying haze, I appreciated that Malice kept up his antics by wasting 5 seconds; however, it was just what I needed to motivate myself to move. I crawled forward, my arm reaching out to the edge of the doorway and feeling the solid silk-cherry door.

[Ten seconds.]

Everything ached as I inched myself to my feet, using the door for support. I grabbed the golden handle and fell into the room. Just as I thought I was going to die, my pain vanished.

I thought for a second it was the Euphoria we go through when we die; instead, on my bed was something out of a nightmare. It was like a tree of inky black smoke had sprouted up from my bed. Branches flowed beneath it for support, and two branches, like arms, grabbed onto the bed as one pointed at me. Its maw stretched open, showing an endless abyss that wanted nothing more than to swallow me but held back as if by common courtesy.

My pulse quickened again, and I glanced at my wound, worrying that the sickly green veins would pulse again, but they were gone. I swallowed, not sure if I should be elated or horrified.

[Malikap! Your highleyness! I'm so excited! We've had so much fun together, Jamie and I. We killed four zombies! She let me eat one!]

The gaping maw made a sound like branches snapping in a storm, and I felt myself back up until I hit the now-closed door, the jam digging into my back.

"I did not. Please do not take offense at his lies. Yeah, so, umm, There's a god on my bed. I think I'm going to go back into the hall." I reached behind with my right arm, feeling for the gold handle. It was gone.

We all stared at each other in silence. Malice and I were waiting for the god to speak up, but he continued holding his arm stretched out at me.

After a minute of unbearable awkwardness, I spoke again, "Is there? Umm. Something I can help you with? If you want the bedsheet, I would rather not be naked here."

The same grating noise exited his mouth, and I recoiled again, hitting my head against the door.

"You... are... my... last..."

And then he disappeared. As he did so, time unfroze, and I fell forward. My wounds returned as suddenly as they had vanished, a fierce, excoriating fireball of pain that seemed endless—until everything went black.

[Congratulations! You died! Woohoo! You've reached the end of your first run! Look at me; I'm so proud I'm practically shining! You killed four zombies (one zombie dog) and gained four Malice points! Go, team Jamie!]

End Run 1.

Chapter Twenty-Five
Penance Aflame

~Run 4, Entrance, Floor 1, Sewers of Aerlyn~

As I awoke in the sewers beneath Aerlyn's vibrant streets, the world above became a faded dream, and I found myself once again ensnared in a realm where daylight was but a distant memory. The gray brick walls of the sewer, usually slick with the moisture of neglect, now seemed dryer than the desert city above. As I looked at the walls in the dim torchlight, I could see something I thought I hadn't before: dozens of images on each wall illustrated in simple but beautiful art.

At first glance, the images on the wall were perplexing—simple, basic forms that depicted scenes with an almost charming innocence. There were figures armed with spears, animals in mid-flight, and indecipherable symbols whose meanings were as lost to me as the civilization that created them. One mural showed a gathering around a figure slightly larger than the rest. Was this a leader, a hero, or a figment of ancient imagination? The scenes shifted, with basic shapes and lines attempting to convey meanings I couldn't comprehend. Another portion of the wall was dominated by a dark blotch, encircled by lines that could be walls, mountains, or even waves.

My eyes widened, taken aback. Were these murals always here? I took a step closer. The texture, the faded colors, the rough scent of the sewer-stained walls. Except. The stains were gone. The wall was now pristine. I reached out a hand to the wall, and then I remembered My feud with Crystal could wait for later, though—Goblish! The ruby allows me to understand Goblish! I could finally get to the bottom of these stupid murals.

I rushed to the crate in the center of the room, happy that at least one mystery of this place would finally be answered. My heart pounded in anticipation of one of Penance's secrets being revealed as I lifted the ruby out of the crate and asked, "Crystal, how do I equip the ruby?" A pregnant pause came and went before I prompted Crystal again. A feeling of dread centered itself in the pit of my stomach. "Crystal?" I eyed her warily; afraid she might vanish on me again.

[I'm waiting.] Crystal's voice, tinged with impatience, echoed through the damp air.

A part of me was overjoyed that she was back, but the other, dumber part of me was angry, especially since she didn't want to help me decipher the strange murals.

My breath hitched painfully in my chest as words failed me. My hands clenched into fists at my sides, an unconscious reflection of the turmoil swirling within, all thoughts of the mural completely forgotten. "For what? An apology? You destroyed my last run—that was worse than what I did to you."

My shoulders slumped, my tone teetering on the abyss of anger. "I was doing great, and then you left me to die. We'll never get out of here if you keep that up." The chill in the room seemed to deepen with Crystal's silence, and I watched as my breath slowly faded into the dank air. I struggled to steady my breathing, each exhale a fight as I struggled to maintain control in the face of overwhelming emotion. I just wanted to hit a wall again, but I clenched my fists to stop myself—no need to ruin yet another run.

[Your last run was never going to make it past level two.] The room seemed to close in around me, the walls echoing her disdain, magnifying the isolation I felt at that moment.

"I was doing great," I repeated to myself. *Why wouldn't I have made it?* But the doubt nagged at me. I hadn't been doing great. I was crippled in a limb, and other than the evasion, the damage output of the class was outrageously bad. I felt useless in my previous role, even though speed and stealth came naturally to me. The only reason I won against the boss was sheer dumb luck.

A flicker in Crystal's radiance suggested the equivalent of a smirk, made evident by the tone of her voice. [Do you mean besides the fact that almost all of your weapons were shattered and that it took you three entire runs to kill the easiest boss room in the dungeon?]

My face twisted in a grimace, the sting of her words opening a fresh wound. *I knew I wouldn't make it that far, but still,* "You made me miss out on Death Boons. Who knows? There could have been more rare weapons like that Necrotic Staff I still could have used." Crystal's silence was heavy in the already oppressive and cold air.

"Look, I know I messed up, but you overreacted. You're stuck here with me, too, and the longer I take to leave, the longer you take. I didn't mean to insult you earlier." I let my words hang in the air, giving space for their weight to settle in the dim light she generated. My next words stumbled out of my mouth like a kid learning to apologize. "It's just, you're not... you know, human right now. That's all I meant. No insult intended. So if you took offense, I am sorry, I think." I hoped that wasn't a lie. I felt no guilt for bruising her ego; she needed to learn to grow up. But I was apologetic that my actions led to the past hour.

Crystal's dim light flickered above us, casting shadows that seemed to dance with the unsaid words hanging in the air, mirroring my uncertainty. And then she spoke, her voice softer, almost a whisper. [I already warned you about sins here. You need to be more careful. Stealing is a sin. And the guards on the second floor are beyond dangerous. I still don't know how we will get out of this one.] And then, as if she had never dimmed, Crystal brightened to full strength and said, [But you are right.

I overreacted *a little*. If I ever want to be a human or get home again, I need you to survive this place.]

"Where's home?" I asked, hoping to change the subject from our little lover's quarrel.

[Nowhere, you know. Nowhere I care to remember.] Her light flickered, and a wistful sigh escaped. [I'll equip your Ruby for you. It will take a second, but the words will automatically translate. Every floor has a language and a hidden quest to translate it. Sometimes, these messages will tell you the history of Penance; they also give power or reveal a secret boss or Ayleric.]

"What's an Ayleric?" I said, distracted by the word. It sounded old and powerful.

[Aylerics are items that unlock a permanent bonus. Unfortunately, they do not appear until you clear the second floor, and then they get added to all boss chests and sometimes to special static chests. Some Aylerics are situational like boots that allow you to double jump, or walk underwater. Some Aylerics will allow you to build items, and others still will stop you from dying. Unfortunately, they also have a cooldown like classes, but it is much less severe. Usually, only a one or two-run cooldown.]

Honestly, as cool as it all sounded, I lost interest halfway through her talking, my mind instead going back to the big reveal. I tried not to come across as a jerk when I said, "Wow, that was helpful. Thanks, Crystal. I can't wait to get one. That said, I'm going to see if I can read Goblish now."

I walked to the first mural and glanced at the alien letters below the mural before taking in the obtuse images. The 'hero' sat on his throne with eyes cast on a giant block. Square? Thing? The image still didn't make sense to me, but as the image bored into my soul, I stared back defiantly. And then I dropped my gaze to the still alien letters, confused that there was something I had missed about applying the language learning skill, but as I read the alien words, knowledge came unbidden in my mind like a whirlwind of understanding. As I looked at the Goblish, I read the words aloud in common:

"Sitting, lone guardian on throne, Penance oversees entirely, catches eye. Gaze frozen, connection to Penance conveyed."

I had to repeat it to myself a couple of times before I got used to the sensation of knowing a language I didn't speak. Even worse, my brain kept translating each individual word rather than understanding what was being said, so the sentence came out choppy and weird. But the images suddenly made more sense. It was the history of Penance. The being on the throne was mightily important. And he oversees Penance? Does that mean he's watching me? I felt a headache building as I glanced around, looking for secret portholes through which this guardian could watch me. I shuddered, but I moved on to the second mural.

The intensity of the pain was building, which was odd as I hadn't felt prolonged pain since coming here. I blinked a few times to clear the discomfort as I moved to the second wall. Like last time, the second mural had a wider variety of images. Simplistic depictions sprawled across the brickwork, and the accompanying text expanded to narrate these scenes. My eyes immediately shot to the Goblish text:

"Departing Penance, Elric established a great settlement, Oasis's Shore. Departure, mockery of silent expulsion. Sword high, leading great forces, Penance aflame falls to ash."

The headache grew as I stared at a series of enigmatic shapes and lines that seemed to pulse. Magic sparkled over the ancient, flaking paint of the wall.

The headache was now a light throbbing as I stared at the abstract imagery assaulting my senses. I cast my eyes down, hoping to avoid staring at the shapes. The pulsating was now like an all-consuming fire as I cradled my head in my hands; however, I couldn't turn away as I stood transfixed. This figure held aloft an object, possibly a weapon, pointing towards what could be the sky. Around them, smaller shapes clustered, perhaps allies or followers, their forms varying from basic outlines to slightly more detailed figures, all moving away from the turmoil behind.

The scene became even harder to identify as it turned from images to obscure figures—horizontal lines and rounded shapes that might have represented land and water. The central figure reappeared, this time with their object pointed downward. This act, set against a backdrop of other simplistic shapes, might represent structures and figures engaged in various activities.

Further along, the mural depicted a confrontation between two prominent figures, their forms tangled in a complex and abstract struggle. The space around them was a frenzy of lines and curves that made less and less sense as I stared at it. My headache had built to a peak, and I dropped to the ground, grunting in exhaustion. The wall was cooking my brain.

[You okay there, Rod?] She said from her new spot, just a couple of feet off the ground.

"No. What the heck is with these Murals? It's like someone jammed a spike into my head." I said as I wiped blood off my nose. I looked at the blood on my hand. My wounds weren't healing.

[Oh.] I had a thought that if she had been human, her eyes would have widened. [I am so sorry, Rod. I forgot. These are Magical Murals. I might have messed up.]

Magical Murals. The word shouted in my mind, like Crystal's volume was maxed out. It felt like my head was about to split in two. After a few seconds that felt like an eternity, the pain lessened, and the words faded. I took deep, calming breaths, but my heart was erratic. I didn't dare look at the words again, but they were all my mind focused on. A memory stuck like words on the tip of my tongue and clung there. I could tell this was something important. And then, the Memory Core formed in the air, which overwhelmed every thought, the pain, my actions, and everything else as I reached out for it. My hands moved of their own accord, desperate to escape the pain of the present.

{Memory Core 8/???}
{Would you like to view the memory?}
{Y/N}

"Yes." My hand made contact, and the world vanished into a dark, inky black and purple mist.

Chapter Twenty-Six
Will of the Heavens

~~~~~~~{Memory Core 8 Start}~~~~~~~

"In Penance, there are so many perils Elric had to watch out for." Professor Perrod said as he scrawled a list in white chalk upon the black slate of his board.

A student held up his hand, a snotty-nosed brat named Candar. He was the most annoying kid in the year, so naturally, we were friends. Without waiting for the teacher to call on him, he said, "This is boring. My brother, Peckolin *the Sage,* said Elric probably wasn't even real. And if he wasn't real, this isn't history." He inhaled with a deep sniff as he said this last part.

Professor Perrod's face grew red hot, and I could tell he was about to lose it, but it was like Candar didn't even care. But then the professor breathed out a sigh and started to answer the question seriously.

"Whether or not Elric was a real figure is not up for debate. We have scholarly accounts of his life from multiple different historical sources of the time, including a Magical Mural older than the three-thousand-year-old palace it is contained within." A quick series of rapid chalk strokes produced a series of illustrations on the board. But I barely listened as my mind wandered to a much more important topic: Magic. Anytime magic was mentioned, it was as if a fire was lit in my brain, and magic was water.

I consumed as much information as I could get my hands on, wanting to know more and wishing I could get my hands on it. I knew Magic was the way out of my personal Penance. You'd think that since he was talking about magic, I'd be able to focus, but my brain had other plans.

This was my escape from pain and poverty, and the pettiness of my awful parents. I waited for a pause in topics and raised my hand, shaking in anticipation as much as fear. I never asked questions. But unlike Candar, I waited for the Professor to nod so that I could speak.

"Si–prof—sorry, Professor Perrod, what is a Magical Mural?" My hand was still shaking as I lowered it, but I could see excitement in the faces of my classmates, so I knew it was the right call. He looked at me, confused momentarily, wondering where the change in topics came from. He muttered something under his breath before recollection hit his old, tired eyes, and he brightened.

"Magic Murals are a fascinating but also insidious bit of magic. They store more than just pictures, but also bits of the soul of history. The magical embodiment of history, if you will. And like all magic, it comes with a price that seldom few wish to pay. It takes a bit of your life force every time you look upon it. In exchange, reading the caption of the mural and looking at the art can confer great rewards. Knowledge, money, or even the ability to wield magic." Great Rewards. Wielding magic. This was it. Magical Murals. That was definitely the key to a better life. Piles of gold flashed in my eyes as Professor Perrod moved on to a different topic.

~~~~~~~{End Memory Core 8}~~~~~~~

I slunk down to the ground as the memory faded, my brain feeling diced to a thousand pieces by the past few minutes. Professor Perrod hadn't been joking about the loss of life force. I didn't dare look at my HP, let alone the next mural; my health was nearly gone, and I hadn't even killed an enemy. To make everything worse, the first two Mural walls didn't confer magic, money, or anything.

"Crystal? Do you know how I get the reward from the Magic Murals? I'm nearly dead, and I didn't get anything out of it." The pain had been like staring into the sun during an eclipse; a couple of years ago, Peckolin, Candar's older brother, convinced us that he got his magic powers by looking at an eclipse when he was our age. *Where had that come from?* It was continually confusing that some memories popped up as brief thoughts, and others created the cores. Hopefully, I would figure out what the difference was soon, so I could streamline unlocking the cores and fix my shattered mind. The magic binding the mural to the sewer walls harmed the eyes, yet I found myself having to force my eyes away.

"Crystal, I need a favor," I said, keeping my eyes closed. I wondered why it had hurt this time when I had stared at the murals just as long the first time through. "Can you read the last mural to me? Maybe I have to complete all of the murals to get the reward."

[It will not work like that, Rod. If you don't read it, you won't get the reward.]

Of course, it couldn't be that simple. I slowly rose to my feet, and I was shaking something awful. Seizure-like tremors wracked my body. I wasn't used to this level of pain. It was infuriating and confusing. But my mind was set. I was going to look at the last mural.

The second I turned to the last mural, my eyes poised to open, Crystal shouted, [Wait!] I paused, eyes still closed. [If you look at that last mural, you'll die and lose a life without having gained a single Death Boon.]

"Wait, what?" I said in shock before immediately turning around so I didn't risk it.

[In your current state, it will kill you.]

"That's so stupid! What's the point of the thing if it just kills you?"

[It is the will of the heavens; I would not deign to call them stupid.]

I wanted to scream and tantrum again, but I glanced down at my miraculously healed hand. I wouldn't do that again. Instead, I clenched my fist and forcibly stamped down the anger. But how was I going to get out of this situation?

"Then what do we do? I might as well give up if I'm already getting locked out of treasures." I said dejectedly.

Crystal sighed before saying, [You need to lighten up. There's an easy solution. Change your class, and you'll be fine. Haven't you noticed that your health is always full when you change classes? In fact, now is a good time to focus on your Death Boons.]

I blinked and then thought back. The memories were as foggy as everything else; I would have to take her word for it. She kept talking as my mind drifted.

As Crystal's voice wove through the air, my gaze drifted upwards to the mural, lured by a flash of light I wasn't expecting. I fell to my knees, banging so hard they hurt, but it felt like little more than an ant bite compared to the pain of the last bit of knowledge entering my head.

The final wall showed Malikap, The Merchant, and Rellum locked in an eternal battle within Penance, unable to escape. I knew for a fact that was what I saw with this one, as even the Goblish called them Malikap and Rellum, although The Merchant was called something different. I touched the words as I said them out loud, translating them into Aerlynian.

"Malikap, The Merchant, and Rellum, eternally bound, indeed, Penance crumbled, renewed to be strong."

As I finished talking, a flood of memories entered my mind—memories that weren't mine. The Memory Core formed above me, and I grabbed it, unsure what it would show me.

~~~~~~~[Elric Memory Core 1 Start]~~~~~~~

Being the first of anything is usually a noble goal. The first King, the first queen, the first guard, the first chef, the first to survive Penance, all noble, lofty attainments. But there are plenty of firsts that are not so lofty. The first to lie, the first murderer, the first prisoner, the first to be executed, the first Penitent. That's me, by the way, well, all of those things. The first victim of execution. The first prisoner of the gods. The first murderer.

They lopped my head straight off with an ax, which was surely meant to be the end; however, I awakened in Penance as the first Penitent. In those days, the dungeon was vastly different. Each floor had a few rooms and a boss, which is hardly the lofty multi-plex it is today. Still, the scars on my soul, forged in Penance, changed me forever—an experience that made me the king I am today.

As I watched it burn for the first time, I felt my power grow to new heights. I would reclaim my birthright. My older brother didn't know the cost of usurping my place. I would watch with joy as I led my army to slaughter him and his kingdom. My subjects would be behind me, of course. I beat Penance and freed the gods, after all—gods that the soon-to-be former king disavowed.

I left my mural here to show you a truth–a truth I want you to know. Penance is a lie. It's not what we've been told it is. But, before I tell you all of that, let this old man tell you a story, one that may illuminate that truth. Because this is important, without proper context, the truth is but words on the wind.

It's true that I escaped Penance and rebuilt society from the lawless-ness of the Wastes. While everything I told you is true, they are those very words on the wind. I was the first prisoner, the first executed, but I was not the first murderer. In fact, my only actual crime was a lack of foresight, a rippling anger that jerked my behavior around before I could rein in my thoughts. The first murderer, though– that lofty prize went to my brother; he poisoned our father and attempted to usurp the throne. I only did what was right for everyone. I killed my brother when he told me the truth. Of course, his wife saw the whole thing and got a bunch of hunters to trap me.

There wasn't even a tribunal–the concept hadn't been invented yet. I was found guilty by public assent, and I was speared through the head. I wasn't even allowed to defend myself. It was awful. My own people betrayed me after my father was murdered, and I wasn't allowed to say a thing in my defense.

A lot of my own people were confused when I took my oasis army and killed them all after I escaped Penance. That wasn't in the history books, of course, but why would it be? I am hailed as a hero outside of here, but that's because they don't know the truth anymore.At this point, I am probably rambling; Penance takes a toll, after all, and coming back for a third time has hampered me. There is something wrong with my memories. It didn't used to be this way. I could recall with clarity my entire life and both of my after-lives, but the second and third time through, I couldn't recall anything about how Penance worked. My mind was a broken sieve, leaving behind nothing.

But Penance has now fractured my mind, and I am scared it has finally won. It is only that I've clawed my way down to this sewer that I have some semblance of who I am again. The Memory Cores that have spawned are fascinating creations filled with power and hope. They inspired me to make this mural, and they are the reason why I have hope Penance can be destroyed. Perhaps He decided a full mind was too much, too overpowering? It matters not, for I am here with the Truth and not speculation. Penance can be defeated, but it cannot be killed.

~~~~~~~[Elric Memory Core 1 End]~~~~~~~

My mind became my own again, and I had to cradle my head in my hands as it felt like someone was cramming a second brain into my head. I couldn't hear, see or think. The memories overwhelmed everything that I was and replaced it with a man who was just rambling like crazy without any coherent meaning behind what he was saying. And then, I died as the Mural exacted its price.

~~~The Plane of Torment~~~

[You idiot! If you had waited five seconds you wouldn't have died! End of Run 4]

I floated aimlessly. The pain was gone, and for the first time this run, I felt clear-headed. *Does this still count as part of a run? Where am I, anyway?* I tried to look around, but all I could see was an inky purple and black darkness.

But before I had time to wonder about anything else, Crystal, in a completely different, chipper voice, said, [Congratulations! You have completed the first Magical Mural, and you have gained a permanent ability: **Scan**. This ability allows you to scan living targets for their stats, weaknesses, and loot tables. This ability costs 5 stamina. Enjoy!]

Rod – Run 4 Corpse
- **Death Boons:** 13

- **Gold:** 0

Items
Enchanted Blood Ruby of the Sewage Goblin Tribes
- **Amount:** 1

- **Condition:** N/A

- **Effect:**

  - While in your possession, you can speak Goblish.

  - Once per run, you can equip an item during combat.

  - You can skip the normal rooms on the first floor and choose to fight only the Necromancer and the goblins.

- **Description:** A dark, gleaming ruby imbued with the ancient magic of the Sewage Goblin Tribes. The ruby is also one of the seven keys needed to escape Penance.

Chapter Twenty-Seven
First Time Seeing Your Corpse?
Jamie, Run 2, Part 1

I awoke with a start. The cloth clinging to my frame was sticky with sweat, and my hair felt damp, too. For whatever reason, my pillows were gone, and then I remembered. Penance. Malice. Malikap. I threw up off the side of the bed, the disorientation of my situation making me sick, and then hid myself under the covers, hiding my sickness and the truth. If I closed my eyes, I would wake up, right? I couldn't be dead. I couldn't.

Despite my waking sweat, the room was cold, and a chill seeped into my bones as I shivered under the blanket. The walls, once a comforting shade of pale blue inlaid with gold leaf patterns, now seemed oppressive, closing in with each shallow breath I took. A thin layer of dust covered everything, undisturbed except for the eerie path from the door to my corpse. I closed my eyes quickly as if, by not seeing, it would all disappear.

A few minutes passed, and I was certain that if I opened them, I would return to my real room instead of this sick joke of a replacement. Malice finally spoke, shattering the illusion.

[Run 2! Run 2! Oh, this is so exciting! You have Malice Points! Together, we can Malice our enemies. I'm even going to give you a one-time discount. But only if you get out of bed. This is kinda sad.]

I pulled my arm against my face and rested my eyes in the crook of my elbow. I ignored the wetness but wallowed in my pain. I was a good person, right? I knew the things Father made me do weren't always good, but the decisions I could make were good: Rod, the orphans, refusing the royal bed chamber, and letting the head maid keep her job.

The screams echoed into the room and pierced my heart. Yet another selfish choice. I screamed, covering the noise and blocking everything out but the heavy beats of my heart.

[What a baby. C'mon, this is your second time dying; you didn't act this bad last time. I wanna go kill things... come on...] I shook my head and screamed louder, blocking out the noise. If I screamed loud enough, I would never have to face anything.

[Look, I get that I'm not so good at the touchy-feely stuff, but cowering in here and screaming so loud that all the zombies on the floor can hear you isn't exactly following Elric's survival plan.]

My mind left the pain momentarily and wandered to thoughts of Doctor Tot teaching me everything I needed to know about Penance. Doctor Tot had been my private tutor until the day before my naming day, when my father decided I no longer needed instruction. As if education truly stopped at 16, there was so much more I wanted to explore about the world and more I needed to see. And I would never get that chance. Wait, how could I remember him? Wasn't my memory supposed to be erased?

[You'll never get the chance to leave if you keep moping here, acting like the world has already ended for you. This is Penance. Strive to take a chance for yourself, to prove you have what it takes to do what only Elric, the Merchant, Rellum, and Malikap have done. Become a God.]

I laughed bitterly, "Winning Penance doesn't make you a god, and even if it did, why would I ever want to be one?"

[Because, if you left here, you could fix everything your father had broken: Rod's death, your death, even your mother's.]

At the mention of my mother, everything changed. My eyes widened, and I shot up in bed—or at least, that was what I pictured happening. Instead, I caught my arms in the blanket and tumbled out of bed.

[Classic Jamie move.] Malice barked a laugh. [Now, c'mon, we also have a deal to get back to. Treasure, treasure!] I imagined Malice as a little kid, pumping his arms up and down above his head as he ran back and forth shouting 'treasure.' [Oh wait. Malice points! I'm so excited. Each point does one of two things for you. It's great because the other systems are so complicated. Don't even get me started on how much there is to Death Boons.] If the crystal could shudder, then it did.

[Be glad Malikap is your patron; this could've taken an hour. For our purposes, it costs 2 points to unlock a class, with the half-off bonus, or you can increase every stat by 1 for 4 malice points. Exciting, right?]

"Stats, classes? What?" I shook my head, making sure I had heard him properly. *The Book of Blood had never covered this.*

[Hush, dear, it's simple. There are 8 stats; you'll learn them as we go. They make you stronger, healthier, quicker, blah, blah, blah. It's not important. Oh, and classes—there are so many, but Malikap lets you choose them. I think pirate should be the first class. Or maybe mage. Whichever you pick, it's going to be fun, though. Oh, I'm just so excited to eat another zombie.]

"Oh, I don't care; why don't you pick for me, Malice, since you are so excited."

[Oh really, you'd let me do that? Can I? Can I? Can I?]

I pinched the bridge of my nose, wanting to throw something at the crystal. Instead, I just picked myself up off the floor, draping the blanket over myself back into a makeshift toga... before remembering about my corpse.

I looked around the room, eyes darting everywhere but to the end of that trail of dust, my pulse threatening to dig a hole out of my neck. I couldn't put it off anymore; I had to look. It was surreal, with copper hair, blue eyes, a small button nose, a petite fit, and perfect, manicured nails. I was staring at myself. There was something hauntingly serene about the corpse's face as if it were in death; it had found the peace that eluded it in life. Yet, the slight furrow between the brows suggested a lingering worry, a final thought frozen forever on its pallid face. What had I been thinking at the end? The thought tormented me, an unanswered question hanging heavy in the stale air.

As I stood over the corpse—my corpse—a wave of nausea overtook me. The room seemed to tilt, the edges blurring into a tunnel vision centered on the still figure before me. My heart pounded loudly in my ears, a frantic drumbeat against the silence. I swallowed hard, fighting back the rising panic and the surreal horror of confronting my own mortality laid out before me. My stomach grumbled again, and I had to force down what was left... except there shouldn't be anything in it. I was dead; I hadn't eaten anything since before Rod...

[Oh, this is always fun! Is this your first time seeing your corpse?] My pallid complexion was a ghastly mirror of my own, but my wide eyes, frozen in death, were something else entirely, and I could swear they positively glowed, tiny little embers sparkling above them. My stomach growled again, and the horrid stench that wafted my way almost knocked me over. I regretted getting out of bed already.

I hesitated, my hand trembling as it hovered over the cold, stiff arm of my own corpse. This was me, yet it felt like touching a grotesque statue in my likeness. The reality of my death, my actual, tangible death right in front of me, was a truth I wasn't ready to confront. I froze, shocked at how rigor mortis had already set in; electricity shot up my arm, and a pit formed in my stomach. I had died. I was touching my corpse. I was smelling my own decay.

[Oh, I sure do love the smell of death in the morning. Ahhh.]

The urge to throw something at the crystal returned, and I didn't resist this time. I threw the blanket off myself and wrapped it around the crystal above my head, suffocating the little freak and ending his tyranny over my loot.

Okay, I didn't, but I definitely could have. Instead, I asked him a question and tried to ignore how much I was starting to hate him.

[Yes. Good. Let the hate flow through you.]

"Are you reading my thoughts?" I asked, hesitating. Had he heard my imagination running wild? "That wasn't a real thought. It didn't mean anything..."

[Relax. I know. Killing me was just a fun little fantasy. Besides, I can't die, sadly. Imagine how much fun it would be if I could die alongside you.] Malice sighed dreamily.

"So you're not mad?"

[I'm Malice. I'm never mad, but I am always thinking about how to hurt others and how to revel in pain and agony. It's oh so much fun once you give in! Oh, and if you want the chain mail, just kick your corpse with either foot, and I'll automatically loot it for you.] Malice laughed as if it was the funniest joke in the world. It was hard to understand the emotions coming from Malice. Their inflection changed, but there was no face to the voice, just pitch-black ink that absorbed all light.

I shook my head to clear it and then kicked the corpse.

Five items practically spilled off my corpse as it disintegrated against my foot: a chainmail vest whose sleeve hung over my shoe, a polearm that sliced against my bare skin, causing me to shout out in pain, and the same bounty of three different sizes and color potions.

I now had a weapon and something to cover a little of my modesty. "Okay, Malice, it's time to live up to your end of the bargain. Do you have someplace to hold these potions?"

[Oh yes! Treasure! I will gladly hold onto those potions. Won't be of much use to you this run? We need to be much quicker if we want to use the Yrd, Vutr, and Xombi potions. It doesn't work on the already turned. Thoughts about whether that would be cool if it did?]

"Oh, alright, well. I best be going."

[Wait, don't you want to know what I chose for you? I chose Paladin. Isn't that funny? It's a holy class, and here you are working for the father of sin and despair.]

"Oh yes, how clever." As soon as I finished speaking, golden light encased my body, and I was lifted into the air, my chainmail and halberd clattering to the floor.

The magic engulfed me, and I fell to the ground with a loud metallic thunk.

Wait, a thunk? I moved my hand to my chest, expecting soft skin, but instead, I met thick, sturdy metal armor. My hands, now covered in the same shiny metal, thunked against the breastplate covering me. My head, too, was now covered in a chainmail coif.

"Wait, where did the armor come from?" I gasped, my voice echoing slightly under the metal helm. The armor was cold and unyielding against my skin, its weight unfamiliar and oppressive. As I struggled to my feet, the metal plates clinked together. Each movement was a chore, and the armor fought against every flex and bend of my muscles.

[That's easy. Magic. Duh. So silly. And now you should be safe from the pesky zombies. Zombie teeth can't exactly pierce steel, you know?] Malice laughed, and I felt tempted to say thanks but shook my head, ignoring it.

"So, is the armor the only thing being a Paladin brings to me? Or do I get something else out of the deal?"

[Paladins are holy knights of the church of Rellum. You get the 'Turn Undead' spell and a minor healing spell; in addition, the class starts with a full suit of armor. Of all the base classes, it is the best one. Plus, you now have 20 hp. You are so welcome.]

"Spells, too?" I murmured, the idea of wielding magic sparking a flicker of excitement beneath the heavy layers of steel. That was one aspect of my life as a royal I had never experienced.

Why did my father always rob me of reality?

"How do those work?"

More laughter. Malice was enjoying himself too much. [Don't worry, It's magic. Don't even try wrapping your head around the rules. Just do it.]

"Awesome. Is there anything else I should know before I go kill some zombies?"

[Don't destroy the head, or the treasure will be destroyed.]

"But they're zombies. Don't I need to destroy the head?"

[No, not at all. This is Penance; everything has HP.] Malice laughed, and my goosebumps raised in protest. They did not like Malice at all.

I walked to the door, armor clanking loudly, before I struggled with it, generating even more noise for good measure. [Wait! Wait! Waity! Wait! We gotta give you stats!]

"What?" I said, my hand hesitant on the turned knob.

[You have Malice Points, which means stat boosts! So, did you want 2 potency, 2 vitality, or a plus 1 bonus to 3 different stats? Oh, this is so exciting.]

A blue thing, almost like a giant parchment roll, flooded my vision to the point where I couldn't see anything else. I swiped at it with my hands, but they passed right through it. "Malice, what are you doing? I can't see a thing!"

[What?] Innocence radiated from the crystal, almost making it seem like the shining beacon at every St. Rellum Church.

"The thing that popped up! I know it gives me stats, and I can raise them, but why is it so large? It's like it's just there to take up space." I waved a hand through it again, frustration evident in my movements and words.

[Fine.] Malice relented, making it smaller and easier to read. I had a lot of 0s. I glanced over everything, taking the time to memorize what everything did.

"We should go with the bonus to Vitality; I don't want a repeat of last time where I died too quickly."

My stats page updated, showing my vitality growing by two and my health increasing to thirty. I didn't feel particularly healthier, but I trusted Malice enough to know he wasn't lying about my stats.

I opened the door and walked into the hall only to find the three zombies from my previous run in front of the door, arms raised, faces scrunched in unending hunger.

I jumped back, an action slowed by the bulk of my armor, but swung the halberd forward at the same time to create space.

As the first zombie lunged, its gait awkward and desperate, I braced myself and thrust the halberd forward. The blade sank into its decaying flesh with a sickening squelch. I grimaced as I tried to pull the weapon free, the zombie's weight a dead anchor. Panic flickered through me as the other undead shambled closer, their groans a grotesque symphony in the cramped hallway. Making a decision, I pushed the halberd forward, throwing the first zombie back onto the ground, and charged forward with the momentum of the shove before rearing back my right arm into a curled fist.

My attack shattered zombie teeth as the momentum carried my blow forward.

The second zombie fell to the floor after losing its footing, so I turned my attention to the third zombie. Deciding to change tactics, I kicked the third zombie in the stomach.

"How am I looking on damage?" I asked as I ran forward, hoping to capitalize on my opening moves.

[Zombies 1 and 2 have four HP remaining, while Zombie 3 is sitting pretty at 8 hp.]

As I smashed my foot into the zombie's knee, the bone gave way with a grotesque crunch, a gruesomely satisfying sound in the silence of the corridor. I recoiled as the halberd, somehow upright, swung towards me, the staff end striking me sharply in the eye. Pain flashed through my head, bright and searing, blinding me momentarily and sending me to the floor in a clang of metal.

"How in the..." My hands instinctively reached for my eye, expecting blood, but found nothing—just the cold touch of my gauntlet. I quickly scrambled to my feet.

The metallic taste of fear was in my mouth as I pushed myself off the floor. My armor clanged loudly, a constant, cumbersome companion in this fight. I charged forward, shoulder first, using the heft of my steel-clad body to drive the remaining zombies against the wall. Their bodies hit with a thud, the impact echoing down the empty hall.

[Woohoo! We won! We won!] Malice's voice cut through the din, his glee starkly contrasting with my fatigue.

"What are you talking about? You didn't even help!" I gasped out, my breath heavy, each word punctuated by my panting.

"Nuh-uh. I told you how much HP they had, and my magic created the armor." His retort was smug, as if he had swung the halberd himself.

I leaned against the cool wall, letting its firmness support my tired body. The adrenaline was fading, leaving behind a deep, bone-weary exhaustion.

"Fighting in armor is hard."

Jamie

> **Stats**
> - **Health:** 20/20
>   *Health is burned as fuel to keep you from dying.*

- **Stamina:** 0/0
  Stamina is burned as fuel to make skills function.

- **Mana:** 30/30
  Mana is burned as fuel to make skills function.

- **Potency:** 0

- **Insight:** 0

- **Alacrity:** 0

- **Vitality:** 4

- **Finesse:** 3

- **Arcanum:** 6

- **Defense:** 4

- **Magic Defense:** 0

- **Precision:** 5

- **Evasion:** 0

Chapter Twenty-Eight
Forbidden By Penance.

~Run 5, Entrance, Floor 1, Sewers of Aerlyn~

As I awoke in the sewers beneath Aerlyn's vibrant streets, the world above became a faded dream, and then the pain came flooding back, knocking me to the floor. After a minute of agony, I propped myself up against the wall using my shaky, unsteady limbs.

I blinked. It was like the floor, ceiling, and walls were brand new, with silver, polished stones as unblemished as dawn. I tilted my head in all directions, marveling at the room around me. And then, Crystal's voice finally broke through my mental safari. [Hello? Rod? You in there?]

I blinked, "Yeah, sorry, that was really disorienting." I rubbed the back of my head. "What were we doing before I killed myself?"

[You were going to spend your boons. You have 13 boons, enough to purchase several stat boons and a new class. Would you like to do so? Or is there a dungeon boon you wish to purchase?]

I bristled at her deciding my choices for me, but making my stats higher was probably the right call. "Alright, Crystal, sounds like good reasoning. Can I get my class first and then spend points on the stat-ups?"

[It is not a good idea to build your stats based on a random class for a single run. I would advise you to build up your health and defense before considering other stats.]

"What? Why not? If I get mage, it would make sense to build up the attack stat for magic."

[And then on your next 3 runs when you get all offensive classes, and those stat ups sit wasted?]

"Oh." It was a good point, but I was still annoyed at her.

"I would like to spend three boons on a class first, still." I took a sharp inhale of breath, hoping for a magic class.

A moment of silence hung in the air, heavy with anticipation, before the die clattered on the stone floor, sealing my fate. I took a sharp inhale of breath, hoping for a magic class.

My heart pounded against my chest, a rhythmic drumbeat that I could hear in my head. "Oh, that's... interesting." I wasn't sure how I felt as a vision of my father holding a bow appeared. "My father was an archer," I said.

[Oh? Is that so? Do you think you'll actually be good at this class?]

Archer
- **Cost:** 4

Starting Equipment
- Wooden short bow

- Quiver with 20 arrows

Stats
- **Potency:** 4

- **Vitality:** 4

- **Finesse:** 10

- **Precision:** 10

- **Evasion:** 8

Bonus
- Starts with the innate ability *Evade* and the skill *Aim*.

I gripped the bow that had magically appeared in my hands and felt for an arrow. My hands took on a mind of their own as I pulled the arrow back into the nook. I had never been trained in archery, but it was like I had suddenly spent my whole life hunting in the woods. I was itching to kill something with the bow, but a question was burning through my mind. I was so tired of killing the same five rats over and over and over again.

"Hey Crystal, if I kill a couple of rats to test out this skill, can I still use the Blood Ruby I picked up to skip the floor?" I asked. Her light brightened momentarily as if she was thinking about how to phrase things.

[You haven't picked it up. It's on your corpse. By the crate. And it doesn't allow you to skip the floor; it takes you to the bosses on the floor. But yes, it will still work if you kill a few rats before coming back through. You need to use the amulet before you leave the room the first time, though.]

As if reading my mind, her words stopped me, hand already on the rusty bar to the first room. "That would probably be a good idea."

I headed for the crate and corpse and picked up my belongings. [You have received 47 gold, a leather helm, and an Enchanted Blood Ruby of the Sewage Goblin Tribes.]

The ruby pulsated in my hands, warmth radiating off of it. "How do I activa…" I started, but the words died on my lips as a burst of heat and light pulsed from the ruby, flooding the room and blinding me.

When my vision cleared, three new doors appeared along the stone sewer wall. They were of varying levels of ornateness. The first, a stone door with a skull in place of its door knob, led to the Necromancer. The second had a goblin head and was made of a brilliantly shining limestone, and the 3rd was a dark wood that felt malevolent somehow, like even coming close to the door would put me in danger. I tried not to let my thoughts linger on what I knew to be on the other end of the door.

With my future path forward assured, I walked back to the plain wooden door blocking my path to the first mobs of the floor.

I suddenly stopped, realizing something. "Before we move forward, I would like an explanation of skills and how they work. I keep asking you things, and I never find out. Please."

[You don't need to beg. It's not even complicated. Each class has 1-2 skills depending on alignment, each costing five stamina. **Aim** and **Scan** both cost five stamina.]

"Okay, great. What does alignment mean?"

[I can't say.]

"What do you mean you can't say? I'm sure it's not that hard to explain."

[I mean, I am literally forbidden by Penance.]

"That figures. I guess there's nothing to it, then. How about I spend my other boons?"

[Sure, what would you like to purchase?]

Rod *(Rank 1, Archer)*
Stats

- **Health:** 45/45

- **Stamina:** 50/50

- **Potency:** 1

- **Vitality:** 9

- **Finesse:** 10

- **Precision:** 15

- **Evasion:** 10

Inventory
- **Death Boons:** 9

- **Gold:** 47

Items
Gold
- **Amount:** 47

- **Condition:** N/A

- **Effect:** The currency of Penance

- **Description:** A simple gold coin. On one side is the visage of the Merchant of Death, and on the other is a thumbs-up.

Enchanted Blood Ruby of the Sewage Goblin Tribes
- **Amount:** 1

- **Condition:** N/A

- **Effect:**

  ○ While in your possession, you can speak Goblish.

  ○ Once per run, you can equip an item during combat.

  ○ You can skip the normal rooms on the first floor and choose to fight only the Necromancer and the goblins.

- **Description:** A dark, gleaming ruby imbued with the ancient magic of the Sewage Goblin Tribes. The ruby is also one of the seven keys needed to escape Penance.

Leather Helmet
- **Amount:** 1

- **Condition:** 13/15

- **Effect:** +1 defense

- **Description:** A sturdy leather helmet crafted to provide basic protection for the head.

Chapter Twenty-Nine
Scan!

With the number of Death Boons that I had left, I decided to purchase an additional point in vitality, which cost 5; I would also shore up my defense, magic defense, precision, and evasion. That zeroed me out on boons, but I would have better survivability, even if only just barely.

With the issues of Death Boons settled, I left the room through the only remaining non-boss door. I was in luck. I would get to test my new class right away.

~Run 5, L1, Floor 1, Sewers of Aerlyn~

Two Giant rats, greased with sewage, sat in the center of the room; they seemed oblivious to my entrance. A single torch illuminated the room, hanging above a normal crate. Loot was always welcome, even if the goal was only ours. I was once again naked, except for a bow slung around my shoulders and a quiver full of arrows. "I would like to use my **Scan** ability on one of the rats."

[Scanning target...]

Enemy Entry 0002: Giant Rat (1) [Level: 2 (Unaffiliated Horde)]

The Giant Rat is a common foe found in the dark and damp regions of the Sewers of Aerlyn. Despite its extremely low health, it can be quite a nuisance due to its Potency, which increases by 5 at each level.

Weaknesses: Target eyes for a critical hit guarantee.

The eyes of the giant rats glowed the same gold as the loot stars. Perfect pinpoints to aim at. "How does critical hit damage work?"

[A critical strike doubles the damage dealt after factoring in Strength, weapon bonuses, and the dice rolls.]

"How do I use my **Aim** skill?"

She paused as if my question was the dumbest thing she had ever heard. [*Just* aim at the target and say, whisper, or think the word '**Aim**'.]

I slung my bow around, and even though I had never used one before, it felt natural in my hands. I steadied my aim and whispered the word, aiming for the second rat's eye. The arrow loosed and flew straight through the air as if following an invisible current. The dice rolled. [Critical strike! 14 damage! You have killed Giant Rat 2 and have received an Overkill Boon.]

Before the other rat could react, I whispered '**Aim**' again. [Critical strike! Six damage! You have killed Giant Rat 1, and have received an Overkill Boon.]

Before the golden loot sparkles rose from their bodies, I swiped my hand over the corpses and looted them. [You have looted rat teeth x 2 and rat meat x 1.] As the corpses faded, my arrows clattered to the floor. I examined them, and they were still in seemingly pristine condition, so I put them back in my quiver.

With the demise of the last giant rat, dissolving into the murky waters below, silence reigned. I broke it immediately with a question.

"Hey Crystal, how do arrows work? These two I pulled out are fine."

[Stone arrow 1, durability 3/5, Stone arrow 2, durability 3/5. They degrade like any other item; however, using a skill like '**Aim**' uses up an additional point of durability. If you receive a weapon or loot your corpse, I recommend saving your arrows until the second floor.]

[You can only replace them on the third floor unless we're lucky with arrow traps or, better still, a merchant with arrows on the second floor.] I looked at the bow in my hands. I could speed through this floor and potentially be in danger on the next, or I could find a weapon and slowly make my way through. Of course, I would have to find a weapon first. There was no way I was resorting to using the torches again. That had been sheer desperation.

"Hey Crystal, can I use **Scan** on a crate? So I can see the loot table?"

[Unfortunately, not yet. There is a boon you can purchase on your next run, or a skill in the Urchin line of classes will eventually give you a chest/crate-specific **Scan** skill.]

"Wait, line of classes?"

[What did you think Rank 1 meant?]

"Oh, right, I guess I skimmed over that."

Crystal let out a loud and long-suffering sounding sigh. [You know I don't do any of this for my own benefit. It's designed to help you navigate Penance and survive.]

"Alright, alright, I'm sorry. What does it mean?"

[Starting when you beat the second floor, you gain access to more powerful classes; think of the difference between a leather helm and an iron helm. The next rank of classes will be a larger improvement, but it works similarly.]

I sighed, walked over to the crate, pushed the lid off, and reached in.

[You have received a copper short sword.]

"Huh. That's five less durability than iron," I mumbled to myself, a note of surprise lacing my words. Deciding it was time to strategize for the future, I stored my bow, hoisted the crate, and returned to the entrance room. Once there, I couldn't help thinking about leaving items at the entrance for the next run. If I got another sword, I could leave it there and have a fresh weapon at the start of a run.

Or I could have a Necrotic Staff or a whole set of armor. The possibilities were endless. "Crystal, can you confirm something for me? Everything left in the entrance room stays there, right? So I can leave these crates and maybe a couple of pieces of armor or weapons to make my next run easier?"

[Your crate from run 3 was still here, wasn't it?]

"Okay, true. Are there any other locations where I can leave a crate?"

[You may leave a crate in the first room of any floor; however, it is unnecessary, as upon entering the second floor, you gain access to the vault boon. You can purchase a vault where you can store any and all items and then access the vault on the first floor. As a bonus, the durability of all items will reset as well.]

"Why are you just telling me this now?" I said, frowning at the news.

[You couldn't afford the boon earlier and didn't ask.]

"How was I supposed to know to even ask for it?" Frustration was building, but I pinched my nose to try and tamp it down.

[You weren't.]

I seethed but decided it wasn't worth fighting over. I ignored Crystal and walked to the door to the Necromancer's room.

~Run 5, Necromancer's Room, Floor 1, Sewers of Aerlyn~

I stepped confidently into the Necromancer's lair, the air thick with the scent of a summer breeze and decay. I was expecting an empty room, but to my dismay, the Necromancer was back—hunched over an altar, ominously chanting as he hovered his hands over a corpse that was barely better than a skeleton, missing most of the skin and muscle from its legs, arms, and body.

A chest was on the floor, partially hidden behind the ritual altar. A sense of danger overwhelmed me before I could step into the room, and I quickly backed into the previous room. "Crystal, If I drop a weapon on the ground, can I use it in combat after using another weapon first?"

[Sure, anything not in your inventory is fair game. That even works with potions, rings, and armor; however, anything left on the ground is also fair game for bad guys. Especially if they are humanoid and/or intelligent.]

"So, If I could somehow wrestle a weapon away from a humanoid, I can pick it up?"

[You know, I have no idea. But do you really wanna be that close to a Necromancer's staff?]

"Probably not, but that's what evasion is for."

Clutching my bow tightly and gripping the worn handle of the copper short sword I had just looted, I steeled myself and stepped back into the Necromancer's dark domain. I didn't waste time; I threw my bow and arrows down and immediately cast "**Scan!**"

Enemy Entry 0003: Necromancer (Level: 6)

The Necromancer is a powerful and sinister caster who commands dark magic and manipulates the forces of death. Necromancers are often found in secluded, dark places where they perform their forbidden rituals.

Weaknesses: Target eyes for a critical hit guarantee.

I started salivating at the drop table. There were so many different things that you could get from this boss. I had a feeling I would need to come back here a few times to try and get some of the rewards if I wasn't lucky this time. And then I looked at the stats; I had a feeling that last time, its Insight hadn't been so high. With an eight in the stat, it would've killed me, and it would likely kill me now. But I had a plan that might work.

Stat Boons

- **Potency**

  - **Cost:** 5

  - **Current Stat:** 1

- **Vitality**

  - **Cost:** 10

  - **Current Stat:** 6

- **Defense**

  - **Cost:** 1

  - **Current Stat:** 1

- **Magic Defense**

  - **Cost:** 1

  - **Current Stat:** 1

- **Precision**

  - **Cost:** 5

  - **Current Stat:** 6

- **Evasion**

  - **Cost:** 5

  - **Current Stat:** 3

Inventory
- **Gold:** 47

Items
Leather Quiver
Stone Arrow
- **Amount:** 2

- **Condition:** 4/5

Stone Arrow
- **Amount:** 18

- **Condition:** 5/5

Copper Short Sword
- **Amount:** 1

- **Condition:** 10/10

- **Effect:** Deals 1–6 damage

- **Description:** A well-crafted copper short sword, perfect for close combat. It is less durable and reliable than Iron, but still a valuable tool for any adventurer.

Bestiary

Enemy Entry 0002: Giant Rat *(Level 2 – Unaffiliated Horde)*

The Giant Rat is a common foe found in the dark and damp regions of the Sewers of Aerlyn. Despite its extremely low health, it can be quite a nuisance due to its Potency, which increases by 5 at each level.

- **Weaknesses:** Target eyes for a critical hit guarantee.

Stats

- **Health:** 5/5

- **Potency:** 8

- **Vitality:** 1

- **Precision:** 5

Item Drops

- **Gold**

    ◦ **Amount:** 5

    ◦ **Chance to drop:** 33%

- **Rat Teeth**

    ◦ **Amount:** 1–2

    ◦ **Chance to drop:** 33%

- **Rat Meat**

    ◦ **Amount:** 1

    ◦ **Chance to drop:** 33%

- **Death Boon**

  - **Amount:** 1

  - **Chance to drop:** 1%

Enemy Entry 0003: Necromancer *(Level 6)*

The Necromancer is a powerful and sinister caster who commands dark magic and manipulates the forces of death. Necromancers are often found in secluded, dark places where they perform their forbidden rituals.

- **Weaknesses:** Target eyes for a critical hit guarantee.

Stats

- **Health:** 10/10

- **Mana:** 40/40

- **Insight:** 6

- **Arcanum:** 8

- **Vitality:** 2

- **Precision:** 10

Item Drops

- **Gold**

  - **Amount:** 15–25

  - **Chance to drop:** 25%

- **Necromancer Eyes**

- ○ **Amount:** 1–2

- ○ **Chance to drop:** 35%

- **Skull Amulet**

  - ○ **Amount:** 1

  - ○ **Chance to drop:** 15%

- **Apprentice's Grimoire**

  - ○ **Amount:** 1

  - ○ **Chance to drop:** 15%

- **Dark Leather Boots**

  - ○ **Amount:** 1

  - ○ **Chance to drop:** 4%

- **Necromancer Robes**

  - ○ **Amount:** 1

  - ○ **Chance to drop:** 4%

- **Lunar Amulet**

  - ○ **Amount:** 1

  - ○ **Chance to drop:** 1%

- **Solar Amulet**

  - ○ **Amount:** 1

- ○ **Chance to drop:** 1%

Chapter Thirty

"Run, Rod, Run!"

Before combat could start, I cast **Aim** and threw my short sword with as much might as my measly 1 strength would allow, aiming for the Necromancer's right eye.

[Critical hit! You have dealt 12 damage. You have killed the Necromancer.]

A lot of things happened all at once. My sword flew through the air magically as if pulled along by a string that originated behind the Necromancer's eye. It pierced through his eye and into his brain as the sword made a weird squelching noise. The Necromancer let out a gut-wrenching scream that echoed off the stone walls, marking the end of his dark deeds. He fell backward into a small pond of water behind his altar, his body disappearing into the murky lake. I was confused at how easily I had cleared the Necromancer boss again. It was laughably easy.

Then, as if brought to life by my thoughts on the room's difficulty, the Skeleton on the altar woke up and reached into the water. It picked up the Necromancer by the sword and held the dead man aloft. A snort escaped me despite the rising tension; the absurdity of a skeleton wielding a Necromancer like a hammer was too surreal. However, my laugh must have upset it as an unearthly screech emanated from the Skeleton as it charged forward.

I yelled, "**Scan**!" while backpedaling, only to slam into the dropped gate.

Enemy Entry 0004: Skeleton *(Level 4)*

Skeletons are the reanimated remains of fallen warriors brought back to life through dark magic.

Weaknesses: The joints in the arms and legs are natural weak points, but skeletons are naturally resistant to all physical damage types.

As the skeleton raised its 'club', the familiar sound of a dice rolling echoed in my mind, signaling an evasion check. As the result set in, time slowed.

[You have dodged Skeleton.]

I dashed to the side and took aim with the bow. Aiming for the elbow joint on its right arm. The die rolled.

[Critical strike! You have dealt 1 damage.]

I fired, the arrow striking the Skeleton and skidding away. I quickly circled the altar again to keep my distance. It took a second to spin and face me, so I knocked an arrow and pulled back, but I couldn't get a clear shot as it turned around. And that's when I noticed a tiny glow beneath the Necromancer's feet. Doubt filled me for a second before I shook my head. Right. Aim. Thank goodness for magical aiming, then. I cast **Aim**, and the arrow followed along another invisible string.

My **Aim**-guided arrow swerved and struck the Skeleton's ankle.

[Critical strike! You have dealt 3 damage.]

The ankle of the Skeleton shattered from the force of the arrow, and the Skeleton fell under the weight of his necro-hammer. This time, I couldn't help myself and laughed at the ridiculousness of the situation. The Skeleton shoved the hammer off of himself, and I took another shot with **Aim**.

[Critical strike! You have dealt 3 damage.]

The arrow obliterated the Skeleton's elbow, leaving it staggered and barely standing. I aimed again at one of the remaining two weak points.

[Critical strike! You have dealt 5 damage.]

The snap and shattering of the bone was cathartic, but I realized the problem I had found for myself. I still needed to deal about eight more damage, and only one weak point remained. It's not the end of the world, but it would be annoying to clear if I could only deal one damage at a time and only if I rolled 4s. I took aim.

[Critical strike! You have dealt 0 damage.]

The leg disintegrated into dust. *At least it can't attack anymore.* I dove out of the way as the skeleton opened its mouth and fired beam after beam of dark energy toward me. Thankfully, evasion kicked in on the last one as well. Otherwise, I would have been a goner, my health still sitting at one from the mural. I eyed my quiver, the few remaining arrows rattling against each other. A frown creased my brow as reality set in—this fight was burning through my resources faster than I'd thought it would; I might struggle against the goblins. Hopefully, I would still have arrows after this.

Ultimately, it took me thirteen more arrows to kill the Skeleton. Each arrow that failed to strike the killing blow added to a growing reservoir of frustration. Seventeen arrows damaged, just like that—*What a waste.* I slunk down to the floor, panting. I had been running around the room like crazy; my limbs felt heavy, fatigue rolling over me in waves. Each breath seemed harder to draw than the last, my body aching as I leaned against the cool stone of the altar, the dungeon's chill seeping into my bones. For the first time in the dungeon, I had no energy to move forward as I slunk back against the altar and closed my eyes. If my eyes had been open, I would have noticed the Memory Core descending from the ceiling and conking me on the head.

{Memory Core 9/???}
{Would you like to view the memory?}
{Y/N}

"Yes." I was answering the question automatically now.

~~~~~~~{Memory Core 9 Start}~~~~~~~

"Run, Rod, run!" Peckolins voice was filled with laughter and an almost childlike wonder. He stared at something behind me and kept laughing but turned around and started running. As soon as I glanced behind me, I started running.

Our guard was in the distance, trying and failing to chase us down. Peck cast some odd spell that made the armor and clothing the guard wore change in size. His helmet fell off as it shrunk to the size of an ant. His metal boots got comically large and slipped off his feet. His gloves started dragging on the ground as the fingers grew, but the cuff and palm shrunk. Peckolin's laughing became contagious as we turned a corner.

His breastplate clattered to the floor, and he had to climb out of the now house-sized suit of armor.

His clothing became the next thing to increase in size, though, and soon, he was wrapped up in a shirt blanket. I kept running until Peck held his hand up.

We were a few streets over. The shouting guard was now a faraway whisper, hidden in the hustle and bustle of our large city. As I came to a stop, Peck waved his hand and said, "Apertar arvex." Suddenly, a door appeared. It blended seamlessly into the wall as if it had always been there.

Peck opened the door without preamble and pulled me alongside him into the doorway. We exited out into another alleyway halfway across the city.

"I know, I know, I shouldn't use my magic that way, but he was just begging for it," Peck said, suddenly serious. "He destroyed Mag's shelter and took an entire week's worth of alms yesterday. He's a dirty rat." "He did what!?" I exclaimed. Mags had lost her entire family to the Blends, a horrifying magical plague that had swept through the world a couple of years earlier. The monstrous disease left what few living victims remained behind as cripples. Mags was left with a single solid leg she hobbled on with a cane. It was a grotesque sight to see.

I wanted to scream and let that guard have my thoughts, but it was not worth the trouble that would follow. Instead, I stared out into the wide expanse of the city. Dozens of stores and shops lay ahead of us.

The great thing about large cities is that you can always have places to be. I had just left a marketplace earlier that morning, and now I was in an entirely new one. Nothing like the tiny little cottage village I was born in. This was the big city.

There were rows and rows of shops selling meat, fresh fish, and mountains of spices. Merchants hawked their wares, and townsfolk shopped, laughed, and wandered. But none of these bounties had what I needed to die. Nothing here was worth months and months of stealing Alcohol to sell full bottles to Peckolin. Instead, Peckolin was taking me to his shop.

Lathaniel's Lovable Lions (and other assorted pets). The green and blue sign glittered with literal magic, vibrant against the market street's subdued browns, reds, and blacks. The mural would be mine, and Peckolin had just the animal to help me get it.

~~~~~~~{End Memory Core 9}~~~~~~~

My eyes refocused, and I was awake. I was also low on stamina. A large part of the battle had been running around, waiting minutes for my stamina to recover while avoiding those stupid shadow blasts. It was also the first time I had been bored in the dungeon. This class was overpowered, even more so than other classes had been. The **Aim** skill was ridiculous. But the stupid thing wouldn't die. It had been worse than trying to kill Slikk during the previous set of Runs.

I proceeded to loot everything in the room. Bronze stars hovered above the Skeleton, igniting a spark of excitement at the prospect of valuable loot. I eagerly tapped its cold remains, only to hear the familiar dice roll in my mind. A slight pang of disappointment washed over me as I realized the roll was terrible, and my face fell as Crystal said, [You have looted Bonemeal.]

I dropped it in disgust, grateful it had come to me inside a bag and that I hadn't touched actual ground bones. I shuddered. I was doubly grateful as the item disappeared into my inventory.

I moved on to the next lootable item only to kick it in frustration.

The chest had a lock, and I forgot that I had a key. Thankfully, I had figured out a loophole in the previous run, so I hefted the chest up to confirm that I could carry it. It was heavy, but thankfully, it came with an iron grip on either side of the chest. Gritting my teeth, I lifted the cumbersome chest, feeling the weight strain my muscles. The silverish metal gleamed as I slowly lugged it towards the entrance.

I then looted the Necromancer's staff since I had somehow disarmed him when I shot him through the eye. The weapon had been dropped and was considered lootable; no rolling required.

It was pristine, unlike the first one I had gathered.

I picked up all of my arrows and put them away. I wish there had been an easier way to pick them up after a battle, but at least they could be reused.

A weary exhale slipped through my lips as I reached out and cautiously prodded the Necromancer's still body. A die rolled, and I laughed and laughed. Absolute joy overtook me.

[You have received a Lunar Amulet.]

I equipped the newly obtained amulet and just sat basking in the moonlight for a minute.

[You have recovered 1 health.] I grinned. That would be extremely useful. I would definitely be resting soon, but I decided to take care of the rest of the loot first.

I picked the chest up from its spot and lugged it back to the entrance. I knew I only had the final boss room left and started worrying. So far, this run has been easier, but still no walk in the park. The **Scan** was by far the most overpowered of all my abilities. Guaranteed critical hits as long as I had enough stamina for **Aim**? I was no longer worried. The combo meant I had it in the bag. I stepped back into the Necromancer's room, ready to exploit my new item.

I sat on the altar and stared at the stars, unaware if they were real or not. I had been trapped in this dungeon for hours, and I already felt that time would never end and that I'd be stuck here for years and years to come. As I stared, I kept trying to think of the last time I had seen stars, willing a Memory Core to form, but it never did. It must be that wanting a memory to form prevented them from occurring. I dozed off, but Crystal didn't let me rest for real as it felt like moments later, Crystal chimed in and said, [Your health is now full.]

I headed to the boss's room. Round 2 was going to go differently. It had to.

Enemy Entry 0004: Skeleton *(Level 4)*

Skeletons are the reanimated remains of fallen warriors brought back to life through dark magic.

Weaknesses: The joints in the arms and legs are natural weak points, but skeletons are naturally resistant to all physical damage types.

Stats

- **Health:** 20/20

- **Mana:** 40/40

- **Potency:** 2

- **Insight:** 2

- **Arcanum:** 8

- **Vitality:** 4

- **Defense:** 6

- **Precision:** 10

Item Drops

- **Gold**

  - **Amount:** 15–25

  - **Chance to drop:** 30%

- **Bone Meal**

  - **Amount:** 15–25

  - **Chance to drop:** 30%

- **Ragged Cloth**

  - **Amount:** 1–5

  - **Chance to drop:** 30%

- **Ancient Scroll**

  - **Amount:** 1

  - **Chance to drop:** 5%

- **Enchanted Bone (Quest Item)**

  - **Amount:** 1

  - **Chance to drop:** 4%

- **Skeleton Key**

  - **Amount:** 1

  - **Chance to drop:** 1%

Inventory
- **Death Boons:** Not specified

- **Gold:** 47

Items
Lunar Amulet
- **Amount:** 1

- **Condition:** N/A

- **Effect:** Heals one health per minute under direct moonlight

- **Description:** This enchanting amulet shimmers with a faint, magical glow, resonating with the energy of the moon.

Chapter Thirty-One
"What Is a Kite?"

~Run 5, Boss room, Floor 1, Sewers of Aerlyn~

The moment I entered the room, I was wholly confused. The altar was still placed on a raised dais in the center of the room. But instead of draining out of the room through the ceiling, the sewage was coalescing in the ceiling and slowly filling the room. Three rough-hewn beams, each at a different height, were scattered across the room, their uneven placement adding to the chaos of the surroundings. And yet, the goblins weren't there. The Enchanted Blood Ruby of the Sewage Goblin Tribes sat in the center of the room on the altar, and I rushed forward, hoping to grab it before the enemies appeared. I could get the gate to open and not have to fight them.

As soon as I approached the altar, I reached for the Ruby. My hand phased through it as if it wasn't there.

[You already have the Ruby. You cannot gain a second. The goblins are...]

I didn't hear the rest of Crystal's words as the three goblins dropped from above simultaneously. I couldn't understand how I missed them since the skinny pillars they must have been hiding on were mostly visible from where I stood. Drip landed to my right, daggers slashing, as Slikk aimed a crushing blow at my head from above. As all this was occurring, Gurgle must have swung his staff with that gas attack toward me from behind. I wasn't too sure because I thankfully rolled something good, and time slowed.

I vaulted over the altar and turned to knock an arrow, but somehow, Drip was immediately there, ready with another swing. Time slowed, and I moved out of the way, falling off the platform as I misjudged my distance. Icy sewage splashed over my face, the foul water stinging my eyes and chilling me to the bone. I decided I was in for a penny and a pound. I dove into the swirling muck to get some distance from the goblins. All at once, I was inundated by the acrid soup filling my ears and nose. I didn't dare open my eyes, but I churned my arms through the thick muck, getting as much space as possible between myself and the raised platform. I rose from the muck and finally turned around, knocking an arrow.

Thankfully, the space I had created allowed me to glance around the room briefly. Gurgle and Slikk were still on the altar staring down at me, but Drip was getting ready to do something. I released the arrow, not bothering to cast **Aim** since I hadn't been able to **Scan** yet. Gurgle was also active and cast a spell. His aim was so off that a die didn't even roll. The spell exploded into necrotic waste, merging with the still-filling room. That hadn't been a thing last time, right?

Since the fight started, I had been on the defensive and hadn't even had a moment to use a **Scan**. Seeing a moment, I said, "Crystal just read off the health and weak points. Please save the other stuff for later! **Scan!**" But she didn't listen to me and pulled up three of the blue scrolls as she read them.

Enemy Entry 0005: Slikk the Sludger (Sewer Goblin)

Slikk the Sludger is the bodyguard of Gurgle; his job is to keep Gurgle alive so he can summon their god. With high health and constitution, Slikk can endure prolonged battles, making him a tough opponent to take down.

Weaknesses: The eyes. It's always the eyes!

Enemy Entry 0006: Gurgle the Gusher (Sewer Goblin)

Gurgle the Gusher is the leader of the Sewer Goblins blessed by their god with magical abilities. Despite his low physical health and strength, Gurgle compensates with his defensive capabilities and magical prowess. Beware the Vortex!

Weaknesses: The eyes. It's always the eyes!

Enemy Entry 0007: Drip the Drainer (Sewer Goblin)

Drip the Drainer is the personal court assassin of Gurgle; his job is to kill you. With a balance of decent health and high dexterity, Drip excels in dodging attacks and countering with precise strikes.

Weaknesses: The eyes. It's always the eyes!

I waved my hand through them and screamed.

"Ahh! That's still too much, maybe just the weak points!"

[The eyes man! Target the eyes!]

Before Crystal had finished, Drip jumped below and closed the gap between us. I wasn't going to give up the slight upper hand I had, so I wiped sewage out of my eyes and immediately shoved my hands into Drip's eyes before he could retaliate. The dice rolled, and I must have had the best luck in my entire run. The sewage completely blinded the goblin, and the force of my shove knocked his head into the metal grate.

[Critical environmental hit! 16 damage to Drip! Target is stunned.]

Trying to catch my breath momentarily, I barely realized that Slikk was about to bash my head in. I narrowly dodged the overhand swing the wind tousled my hair from the speed of the blow. It struck Drip's right foot crushing it. Blood seeped from the goblin's ruined extremity, and I took out my arrow for a well-timed **Aim** at Slikk and used the spell.

The arrow flew straight into Slik's right eye as if being pulled along by a string.

[Critical hit. You have dealt 6 damage to Slikk.]

"Ugh!" A scream of frustration escaped me, echoing off the damp sewer walls as yet another attack barely made a dent. It was the same ridiculousness as the previous fight. Slikk had 4 points of damage resistance due to his Defense, and I would either have to get lucky or whittle him down again, just like last time. I thought Drip was out for the count, but I felt a sharp jab in my leg and looked down to see a dagger making a glancing blow off my cloth boots. The poor right shoe was hanging on by a thread, and blood spilled from a wound near my ankle.

A thunderous boom reverberated through the cavernous sewers, a sinister reminder of Gurgle's power, as his spell lit up the murky depths with fearsome energy. The spell came towards me in slow motion. I tried to move but looked down to see Drip's slimy green fingers pinning my leg. I aimed at the goblin and fired an arrow at point-blank range, casting **Aim**. The spell hit me at the same time my arrow hit Drip.

[Close-range critical hit. 13 damage to Drip! You have killed Drip. Gurgle has dealt 6 damage.]

A triumphant grin spread across my face as Drip fell, but I immediately grimaced at the big chunk of damage. I didn't precisely have HP to spare.

Drip gurgled as he died, and I immediately yanked my leg out of his grasp and took off running. I jumped up and grabbed the platform, pulling myself back onto it. I didn't have time to catch my breath, so I immediately nocked an arrow and aimed for the rampaging Slikk. He was slow, and I knew I would have more time, so I took aim at the goblin.

[10 damage to Slikk!]

My third critical strike for 10 damage in a row. *Crazy, weird luck.* I laughed momentarily at the comical sight of an arrow sticking out of the goblin's eye. The crazy thing kept it in and tried casting another spell at me. I vaulted over the altar as Slikk came charging up the slanted path of the platform. I fired arrows in quick succession, then tried to backflip off the platform. My foot slipped, aborting the flip midway, sending a jolt of panic up my spine, and I landed on my stomach on the platform, knocking the air out of me. I rolled over just in time to barely miss Slikk's weapon swinging down. I hadn't needed the supernatural time freeze because it had been sheer coincidence that I moved out of Slikk's way when I did. I aimed another arrow point blank for the same eye I had hit moments before.

[Critical hit close range x2.5 damage. Natural crit! 17 damage.] Slikk let out a blood-curdling scream, and I rolled the rest of the way off of the platform.

Gurgle hadn't been idle, and another gas explosion landed at Slikk's feet, barely missing him as I dived away into the muck. When I landed, I quickly ran under the platform before speaking quickly. "Crystal, can you do me a favor and just say the damage? It's hard to pay attention while dodging these guys. Please. I'm trying hard to be nice to you. I promise."

And that's when I noticed something was off. The altar above me emitted a ghostly green glow, its eerie light casting long, sinister shadows that danced across the damp walls of the sewer; gas emanated from it as if casting its own spell.

I ran to the other side of the platform and took aim at Gurgle with my bow launching an arrow, and then readjusted my aim towards the platform. It probably wouldn't work, but I wanted to try multiple things to disrupt whatever Gurgle was planning with the altar. Slikk let off a scream and jumped down with a slam. A die rolled, and I successfully dodged the slam attack, moving away into a sprint. My arrows did nothing to stop the spell; I could tell it would go off soon. I focused my efforts on Gurgle and retook aim, and nothing happened.

[Unfortunately, you are out of stamina, Rod. You could grab a dagger from Dripp; I believe he dropped one of his weapons. Or you can try to kite them while you recover stamina.]

"What do you mean by kite? What is a kite?" Suddenly, a pulse went out from the altar as the temperature in the room lowered. The ever-flowing sewage seemed to flow faster, and I took a moment to realize the sewage ceiling was already startlingly low.

[Oh, just run around taking pot-shots with your bow. If you're always moving, they're less likely to land hits.]

I tried not to ignore Crystal—it was a great strategy— but I likely only had minutes left to finish the fight. I ran to where I saw Drip's corpse earlier and panicked. There was no dagger in sight. But an idea formed in my mind. I knew I couldn't successfully aim and fire an arrow without the supernatural help **Aim** provided, but I learned how to stab things. I ran forward like a raging bull mimicking the guttural cry that Slikk kept letting out and slammed an arrow right into the left eye of Gurgle without hesitation.

[You have dealt 8 damage to Gurgle! Great work, keep it up!]

The words distracted me as I struggled with Gurgle for his staff. Somehow, I was having trouble yanking it out of his hands, but slowly, our tug-of-war went in my favor, and his hands slipped from the staff. I could immediately feel magic thrumming through the staff and cast a bolt point-blank in his face.

[You're amazing Rod! You have dealt 12 damage to Gurgle. Keep it up!]

Gurgle collapsed, momentarily stunned, but the pulsating continued. I could feel my anger rising, I gritted my teeth, struggling to keep from yelling. I asked her to make the messages shorter, and now she was inundating me with platitudes.

I didn't have any time to complain, though, as suddenly, the sewage ceiling coalesced into a swirling vortex, spinning around the room.

Enemy Entry 0005: Slikk the Sludger *(Sewer Goblin)*

Slikk the Sludger is the bodyguard of Gurgle; his job is to keep Gurgle alive so he can summon their god. With high health and constitution, Slikk can endure prolonged battles, making him a tough opponent to take down.

Weaknesses: The eyes. It's always the eyes!

Stats

- **Health:** 50/50

- **Potency:** 5

- **Vitality:** 10

- **Precision:** 10

- **Defense:** 5

Enemy Entry 0006: Gurgle the Gusher *(Sewer Goblin)*

Gurgle the Gusher is the leader of the Sewer Goblins blessed by their god with magical abilities. Despite his low physical health and strength, Gurgle compensates with his defensive capabilities and magical prowess. *Beware the Vortex!*

- **Weaknesses:** The eyes. It's always the eyes!

Stats

- **Health:** 25/25

- **Mana:** 40/40

Mana is burned to fuel spells

- **Insight:** 3

- **Vitality:** 5

- **Arcanum:** 8

- **Precision:** 10

- **Defense:** 1

Enemy Entry 0007: Drip the Drainer *(Sewer Goblin)*

Drip the Drainer is the personal court assassin of Gurgle; his job is to kill you. With a balance of decent health and high dexterity, Drip excels in dodging attacks and countering with precise strikes.

- **Weaknesses:** The eyes. It's always the eyes!

Stats

- **Health:** 25/25

- **Stamina:** 65

- **Vitality:** 5

- **Finesse:** 13

- **Precision:** 10

- **Evasion:** 12

- **Defense:** 3

Chapter Thirty-Two
Whirling Vortex of Sludge

Time froze as a die rolled, and I dodged. Slikk rushed me, and I escaped again; using the momentum of the goblin against him, I stuck out my foot and tripped him. A dice rolled, but he took no damage.

Using the situation to my advantage, I fired a point-blank arrow into his back, then turned and fled to the still-pulsating altar.

[You deal 2 damage to Slikk.]

I had hoped using the staff would kill Gurgle, but at least he was essentially out of the fight. My stamina recovered at a measly 2 per minute, and I needed to run circles around these guys to recover stamina.

[I never answered your question, but you discovered what I meant. Kiting is a means of running around, avoiding attacks, and waiting for skills to be available. I suggest you use your superior speed to your advantage]

Slikk was once again barreling up to the platform like a rampaging bull, making it ridiculously easy to shove him down again and shoot another arrow into his back. I did no damage this time but was okay with a war of attrition. If I remember correctly, his armor only had ten durability, but I had quite a few arrows left to use.

With nothing left to do but run, I devised and enacted a plan.

Gurgle dug around in the sewage, looking for something, before jumping up with a triumphant goblin yell. He had found Drip's dagger.

The vortex came for me again, but it seemed to have a low hit chance because I kept on receiving my dodge chance. As I dodged out of the way, I realized I had been extra lucky as the vortex swept its erstwhile ally back into the muck. Still wanting to save my stamina, but knowing I needed to change and do something instead of running blindly, I shot two arrows at Gurgle. Of course, they both missed, but he ran at me with the dagger, enraged.

Gurgle was not built like Slikk. I took aim with my bow, but this time, I waited as Gurgle charged up the ramp closer and closer. I loosed my arrow, and a dice rolled.

[You deal 3 damage to Gurgle.]

I jumped off the platform, only to realize I could take another useless potshot at Slikk, and I took advantage of his broad back to make sure I hit him. I, of course, dealt no damage, but I thought I only needed 5 more hits to kill him. Gurgle jumped down to attack me with a leap attack, but I dodged at the last second, using the slow-down effect to climb back up to the altar. I had a dangerous idea this time to buy me some time.

Slikk, behaving somewhat like a brain-damaged animal, came galloping up the grate a third time, still expecting a different outcome. I readied my bow as I would shoot and waited for Slikk to slam his weapon down. The die rolled. And time froze. And I realized just how broken my dodge skill was as I slammed an arrow through the goblin's frozen right foot.

[You deal 1 damage to Slikk.]

His aim went wide as he tripped and flailed. His bleeding foot is now pinned to the grate. I took advantage of his prone state and stabbed him again, this time in the eye.

[You deal 13 damage to Slikk.]

I realized it was a waste with how close this battle was now to keep saving stamina; I leaped back and cast **Aim**, still relatively close range.

[You deal 12 damage. You have killed Slikk.]

I literally whooped into the air, cheering that I was done, and that was when everything went wrong. Just as I regained my footing, a menacing cyclone of sewage swirled around me, its vortex drawing in debris and echoing with the hollow sound of impending doom. Gurgle's shadow loomed over me, dagger poised for a deadly strike. We lifted into the air on the whirling vortex of sludge. We grappled for the dagger, flying through the air in a sickly, sweet-smelling river of sewage. I gagged as some of it got in my mouth before completely throwing up in the face of my attacker. Somehow, that stunned him, and I wrestled the dagger free. I then proceeded to stab him in his remaining good eye, forcing the dagger into his brain with as much force as possible.

[Devastating blow. Instant death.]

The magic supporting the vortex immediately ceased, and I fell to the ground. I had never been so thankful to touch sewage, even as I attempted to wipe the sick from my mouth with a soaked sleeve.

"I'm alright, thanks for asking, Crystal." I was still annoyed by her antics. That was the most intense fight of my time here so far, and it was different from the first time. "Crystal, why was this time so different? The goblins seemed a little smarter, and that mage had much more to his repertoire than his staff. And the Necromancer—he had a skeleton with him this time. There wasn't even one in the room last time."

[Well, Rod, each time you clear a floor, it gets harder and harder. There are five levels of difficulty without using Death Boons. If you die, it goes down one level of difficulty until you can clear it again. On the bright side, there are benefits. You receive a bonus to all Death Boon rewards if you clear the floor, and loot tables favor higher rarity drops.]

"Oh, that's a nice bonus." I climbed my way up to the altar and leaned against it. I'm sure I looked absolutely dreadful, but thankfully, I hadn't seen a mirror or reflective surface in the sewer.

After resting, I proceeded to loot the three goblins.

I received four goblin ears. My luck was all over the place, but at least I got Gurgle's staff, which begged a question.

"Hey Crystal, how come I was able to use the staff? I thought weapons were locked to classes like with the torch, or the barbarian not being able to use one-handed weapon?"

[Certain classes have weapon penalties, including classless and the barbarian. The archer doesn't have any penalties.]

"What, why not? I mean, not that I'm complaining."

[I already told you, it's because of your alignment.]

"Okay, and what is my alignment?"

[I already told you I can't answer that. Now, if you're done asking stupid questions...]

I was hoping for a chest key drop, but then I remembered the one I had forgotten in my inventory. Which was great because I needed it to unlock the rare chest I had left in the entrance room.

I returned to the entrance, unlocked and looted the chest.

[You have looted 125 gold, 1 iron chest piece, 1 copper dagger.]

I didn't know what was up with my luck that day, but I knew it wouldn't last for the next floor. The Lunar Amulet ended up being an insane boon. As long as I was under the moonlight, I regenerated health. And I knew a room with a view of the moon. Happiness washed over me as I clasped the new amulet. After surviving countless life-threatening moments in these dark, twisting sewers, I finally had a way of guaranteeing I would win.

I hadn't been a jewelry kind of guy before ending up here; I'm sure that I had mocked men with jewelry before, but I had a feeling I wouldn't take it off for the rest of the run.

I collected all of my things and approached the 2nd floor—this time, with Crystal floating above my head.

[Stop, don't go any further.] Crystal said as I crossed the threshold of the first floor to the second. I stopped immediately, my foot floating in the air.

[I really messed things up. And I'm sorry. This next floor is going to take a lot of work for you. You won't be able to access the vault because you've aggro'd the starting guard, and he will immediately cleave you in two.]

What? What does aggro'd mean?"

[I'm sorry, I keep forgetting we're from different worlds, and my terminology doesn't translate well into the common parlance here.]

"Wait, you're from a world different from the Equiem? How is that even possible?"

[Yes, I come from a planet called Earth. I lived quite a happy life there; it was much safer than your world, but I was pulled here by...]

My balance wavered for a second, but I managed to purposefully fall backward so that I didn't trigger the grate and my death. I took some fall damage, but a quick trek back to the moon room would fix that.

"You were opening up and explaining how you got here."

[That's not important right now. What is important is planning a way to beat a boss that is equivalent to a floor 7 monster on floor 2. We need to talk this through and come up with a strategy. You can access the vault at the entrance, but there's no way you can loot your previous corpse right by the guard... your arrows wouldn't do much, but maybe they could hit a weak spot. We need to **Scan** the guard and figure out what he's vulnerable to...]

Crystal started talking really fast and trailed off as she realized something.

[The sewage here is highly toxic to humans. I have a plan.]

Enemy Entry 0005: Slikk the Sludger
Item Drops

- **Goblin Ears**

  - **Amount:** 1–2

  - **Chance to drop:** 50%

- **Gold**

  - **Amount:** 10–100

  - **Chance to drop:** 25%

- **Chest Key**

  - **Amount:** 1–2

  - **Chance to drop:** 15%

- **Dripp's Dagger(s)**

  - **Amount:** 1–2

  - **Chance to drop:** 10%

Enemy Entry 0006: Gurgle the Gusher
Item Drops

- **Goblin Ears**

  - **Amount:** 1–2

  - **Chance to drop:** 50%

- **Gold**

- **Amount:** 10–100

- **Chance to drop:** 25%

- **Chest Key**

  - **Amount:** 1–2

  - **Chance to drop:** 15%

- **Slikk's Club**

  - **Amount:** 1

  - **Chance to drop:** 10%

Enemy Entry 0007: Drip the Drainer
Item Drops
- **Goblin Ears**

  - **Amount:** 1–2

  - **Chance to drop:** 50%

- **Gold**

  - **Amount:** 10–100

  - **Chance to drop:** 25%

- **Chest Key**

  - **Amount:** 1–2

  - **Chance to drop:** 15%

- **Gurgle's Staff of Noxious Fumes**

  - **Amount:** 1

  - **Chance to drop:** 10%

Part Two

The Djinn

Chapter Thirty-Three
Market Place Chase

From the second I entered the second floor, I was struck by how large the "room" was. Unlike the previous floor, this place was practically an entire city. The marketplace was a tapestry of colors, with stalls draped in vibrant cloths, beneath which giant hills of spices displayed a painter's palette—burnt sienna cinnamon, vibrant yellow turmeric, and deep red paprika, all sending up heady, pungent aromas that mingled into a perfume that seemed to color the air itself. Unlike anything I had ever witnessed, merchants clad in colorful garments stood before their stalls, peddling foodstuffs to eager throngs of customers and deftly scooping spices from towering heaps, which they then packed into satchels to exchange for gold.

There are real people! Actual people here on this floor, I had known a lot of people ended up in Penance, but this was crazy. Literally, dozens, if not hundreds, of humans lined the street, busy going about their day like we weren't all dead.

Further away on the other side of a building, I could just make out merchants selling what looked like clothing and other fabric-based wares. I was in awe. If this was just the second floor, what would future floors hold?

I hadn't taken the time to explore what the city looked like earlier because I had been too busy getting my arm chopped off. I definitely didn't have time now because as soon as I entered the level, time slowed down as the gate lowered. I already felt the pull of dread that meant the guard had noticed me.

I had no idea what had happened, but I moved anyway, hearing rather than seeing the dagger clatter to the ground as I dove away. I dashed toward a narrow gap between towering stacks of turmeric and cardamom. The sharp, earthy scents were heaven compared to the sewers, but I didn't have time to enjoy the new scents as I squeezed between them, hoping to use their bulk to shield me from the guard's view.

I gripped the torch I had equipped before entering, heat blazing away above my right hand. I had read somewhere that most bazaars closed their doors at night because they couldn't afford magical lighting, and torches were too dangerous to keep near the spices. It was probably a made-up factoid to make the author seem more intelligent, but there had to be some truth to it, right?

I kicked the table of cinnamon in front of me into the guard and started coughing as some of the powder got into my lungs. An overwhelmingly thick cloud of reddish-brown dust exploded into the air. I pulled my arm back, the torch's flame flickering wildly. With a sharp thrust, I hurled it into the air. It arced gracefully before landing in the heart of the cloud of cinnamon dust.

A bright red flame exploded outward, engulfing the nearby spice towers. The force of the explosion knocked me off my feet, and I scrambled backward as flames consumed the guard and the spice towers around him.

A burnt and sooty smell filled the air as the towers of spices around us raged. Flames licked at my clothes, catching them on fire. Panicking, I stumbled backward and fell into a mound of thick spices, which smoothed the flames. The giant mound of pink salt I had landed on was much thicker and managed to put out the flames.

I patted my head with my hand and turned to run. And then, of course, I immediately tripped and fell into another tower of spices.

Thankfully, the burning towers didn't reach the new cloud I had landed in. For something so easy to move and soft to the touch, it felt like landing in a pile of bricks. I picked myself off the ground, dusting off the little black rocks I had landed in.

[Critical hit! 50 damage to Bazaar Guard!]

I didn't hesitate and yelled, "**Scan**! Weak point only!"

[Bazaar Guard: Weak point: Eyes]

I was happy I didn't have to repeatedly remind Crystal to condense the notification. That was just part one of my plan, I sighed, gearing myself up for the chase that was about to ensue. The guard wasn't even stunned; he jumped to his feet in a second.

But I was faster; I took a sewage-coated arrow from my grossly wet quiver and aimed at the guard. The weak point was a tiny slit in his visor through which he could see, but my spell was supernaturally better than his helm.

[Critical hit! You have dealt 1 damage. Sewage inflicts Aerlynian Sepsis. The enemy takes 1 point of damage per 10 seconds.]

His previously clunky red and blue armor was now charred a reddish black. The cinnamon fire had stained the plates a new shade. His mail clanked loudly now as he moved forward.

I scrambled to my feet and started running, slipping between stacks of spices as a proprietor started yelling at me—real, actual humans, I think. I would've paused to see, but I knew I needed to keep running. "Crystal, What's his HP at now?"

[Bazaar Guard: 148/200]

He had more health than I had hoped, but I had done a significant chunk of damage. It was time to enact part 2 of the plan. Oh, who am I kidding? I was making it up as I went along, although I did have part of an actual plan for the running away bit.

I wasn't joking when I said this entire first room was like a city, and I slipped into an alleyway just past the end of the rows and rows of spices. There was an archway between the two buildings, almost creating a tunnel. I walked in and ran blindly through the darkened tunnel. Unfortunately, the guard saw me and gave chase, and I came out on the other end of the alleyway into another marketplace full of colorful displays of clothing and armor.

I stared in awe, stunned at the variety of wares on display, before immediately running again, only to slip and fall in shock as I stared at a second guard, almost a twin to the one chasing me, except he was wearing a different style of helm and had some sort of blue plume, probably denoting rank. Gasping for breath, I pushed myself to my feet. I glanced at the new guard, noting his distracted gaze.

Seizing the moment, I sprinted past him, ducking low to avoid his attention. He turned to look at me, but I kept running. I looked back, and my guard was hot on my heels, but the plumed guard just turned around and kept walking.

Shoppers pushed past, seemingly oblivious to my chase, a swirling current of bodies. A woman in a shimmering blue scarf laughed as she haggled with a stern-faced vendor, her hands animatedly gesturing to a pile of plush, embroidered rugs. A small child tugged on the hem of her skirt, his eyes wide at the towering stacks of exotic fruits next to a blacksmith vendor.

Scenes like this played out all around me as the guard made a beeline straight for me. My eyes flickered back to the blacksmith where a burly man in pitch-black clothing, gloves, and goggles lifted a red-hot iron sword above his head. I moved closer, planning my next move.

A breath escaped me, one I hadn't realized I'd been holding, heavy with the sharp tang of fear and adrenaline. I halted abruptly, resting my hand against the adobe of the blacksmith's workhouse. My heart pounded fiercely against my ribs. It would take the guard less than ten seconds to catch up, so I turned to face my attacker, jumping and kicking him before he could bring his sword down.

Aim was a magical ability. I just had to think about my weapon and mentally look or "**Aim**" for whatever I wanted. I usually used weak spots, but a well-timed **Aim**-kick knocked the guard back and almost sent him careening headfirst into the blacksmith's lit forge. The horrified merchant/blacksmith jumped up from his grindstone before taking one look at both of us and running for his life.

In my head, it was quite comical: A half-naked crazy man charred to a crisp and coated in a fine layer of different colored spices with a bow around his back attacking an also charred but fully armored guard who had almost fallen face first into a fire. I would have been freaked out, too.

I tried to kick him again to faceplant him into the forge fire, but he instantly moved around and swung with his sword. Time didn't freeze, so I did everything I could think of and grabbed a shield off a nearby counter. The blow shattered the shield into two, but it deflected the attack away from me.

Unsure of how much damage the poison had inflicted, I was tempted to cast a **Scan** or just shoot more arrows, but Crystal had told me the plan would only work if no other guards or 'NPCs,' whatever those were, saw me breaking the law. I ran, worried that the blacksmith would report me breaking his shield, but the man never took his gaze off the guard's sword.

Seeing a perfect moment ahead, I jumped up on a table where a multi-colored rug with a golden lion emblazoned hung from an open window sill. I grabbed onto the carpet and climbed up into the window.

The room was mostly empty except for a straw bed, a cupboard, and a few chairs. I turned around and glanced at the guard, who stared up at me with malevolence. His hatred rose in the form of little black, ink-like tendrils above his head. I pulled my bow off from around my shoulders and finally took **Aim**. My arrow flew through the air and pierced the guard through the tiny hole in his visor. So overpowered.

I grinned as the dice rolled and Crystal spoke [Critical hit! You have dealt 12 damage. 120 HP remaining.] Well. This was going to take a while...

Ultimately, it took 12 more arrows to bring him down. I was down to about 5 and had no way to get more If I couldn't get to my corpse.

[You have killed Bazaar Guard.]

I sighed in relief as the guard collapsed to the ground. I jumped down from the strange room and went to loot the guard.

Chapter Thirty-Four
Don't Panic

[Wait! Don't touch him. Your notoriety has fallen to neutral, and you are no longer a target for any guard, but it's illegal to kill or touch a guard. It is also illegal to loot a guard. The captain of the guard will likely be here in moments. He probably knows or at least thinks you did this since he saw you earlier, and if he has line of sight, you will never leave this zone again. Go back up to that room and hide!]

"But my arrows—"

[Now! Before that captain comes back.]

I scrambled back to the strange room without having to be told a third time. I crouched down below the window line and risked a glance down to see the blue plume poking above the crowd.

I considered my options; the guard captain had likely been told by now about a crazy half-naked man kicking a guard, and I knew Mr. Plume had seen me. If this were anything like the real world, he would likely see the open window and send a search party for me, so I did the only thing I could think to do. I climbed back out of the window, and I hesitated as my right foot slipped. I caught myself on the edge of the window pane with my right hand, struggling to maintain my balance. I let out a small gasp and, terrified, looked down, certain the guards had heard me.

No, I shook my head. *Focus.* I didn't see a way up, and my mind panicked. Focusing on the eventual reality where I would be forced to clear the first floor, only to die the second I set foot up here until I spotted it. There were ridges in the adobe material like someone had carved out a ladder, and I climbed up to the very top of the building. I rolled over, sighed in relief, and let my body relax, my breathing heavy and adrenaline still pumping through me.

I peeked over the side of the building at Mr. Plume. He was inspecting the corpse of his friend before he stood and clicked his fingers. Like magic, 15 guards appeared around Mr. Plume. He clicked his fingers again, and a smoky but lifelike image appeared. I could barely make it out. But I could see the faint outline of a bow and multiple colors on the man. It had to be me.

"Crystal," I whispered frantically. "What are we going to do?"

[Don't panic!] She said. [If we can return to your corpse at the entrance, you can equip armor and hide your bow, and you won't look anything like that shade he summoned. You should be free to explore the zone at that point.]

"Zone? Crystal, you keep using these terms I don't understand. At some point, we need to talk about where you are from and the strange, strange words you use."

[The guards won't recognize you if you can disguise your face and chest. Alternatively, you could move on to the next zo– room and clear the floor, but you won't survive without being better prepared. And it would be best if you put that amulet in storage. It's useless on this floor, as it is perpetually daytime. In fact, you should put a lot of your stuff in storage, and we should spend your Death Boons.]

I paused, looking at the building next to this one and then back at the guards below. "How much damage will I take if I fall from this height?"

[It will be a d20 minus your defense.]

"So really bad or not even noticeable. Well, I can't do anything about it either way."

I rolled up into a crouch, glancing over the roof again. From my vantage spot, I could see the entire city, and it was massive, and this was just the first 'zone.' Whatever that meant. I hated feeling like I was in the dark. I really wish Crystal could have a normal conversation now and then. I glanced through the rows and rows of purchasable wares, food, spices, and clothes. I couldn't make out most of the people from this high up. But I could spot Mr. Plume and his friends just fine. They were all gray blobs with red and blue feathers standing out in a sea of color. I was wondering how to return to the actual entrance from here. The sheer size of the place overwhelmed me. Navigating back to the entrance seemed like deciphering a maze without a map— "That's it, a map! Crystal, can you summon a map of the zone? Will it show fine detail?"

Looking to my right, the terra cotta buildings continued to be uneven in size. However, the jumps seemed manageable.

"Crystal, I know the map doesn't have fine detail, but can you, I don't know, lead me to my body?" I glanced over to the side again and noticed that the guard's corpse was still there. Plumey and his friends hadn't touched it. Not waiting for Crystal to respond, I followed up with, "And what about that corpse or mine, can anyone else loot them?"

[Only the Penitent may loot, or even touch, corpses in Penance, and only you can loot your own corpse. You'll be fine if you get back to the entrance. I can create a waypoint for you to follow... but only if you buy the perk while back at the entrance; you don't have access to it yet. All I can do to help you is suggest you look for the spice stands you knocked over; they were in the first part of the area.]

I had half a mind to jump down now and retrace the steps I ran, but I felt pretty safe from up here and didn't want to lose that.

I found myself sighing yet again, a habit that seemed to have become more frequent lately—Maybe that was something I used to do before? I shook my head. I had wasted enough time; I needed to go get my stuff, but short-lived as it was, this had been the first real break I'd had since entering the dungeon.

I got up from my crouch and started running; I leaped from the first rooftop to the second, and the dice rolled. I didn't even see the die as I rolled upon landing and, thankfully, didn't fall screaming to my death. Instead, I rolled and flailed as I kicked up dust and landed painfully on my stomach. I was like a deflating bellows. But a second later, I got to my feet and kept running. Dice rolled, rooftops passed before me, and soon, I was at the entrance again. I was panting and gasping, but I took note of everything below.

Chapter Thirty-Five
The Djinn

As I gazed out over the market, the pungent aroma of burnt spices and charred bread from a nearby vendor's stall enveloped me, while the sorrowful sounds of merchants and the creaking of old wooden tables conjured a pang of guilt in my chest. What did I do? And then that guilt was forgotten as I spotted a loaf of uncharred bread on a lone table. No one is around. I could easily hop down, and! No! Stop! As I eyed the lone, uncharred loaf on the table, a shadow flickered at the edge of the market—patrol guards.

Any move towards the bread could draw their attention, but my growling stomach urged me to risk it. I had almost jumped down. A brief shock of pain passed through my body as I relived my last death. I clenched my fists, willing myself to wait just a little longer. Once I had my gold, I could buy food.

I glanced down at the open window below, a mere ten-foot drop. With a deep breath, I swung off the ledge, my fingers finding quick purchase on the sill, and slipped inside with a thud that echoed in the empty room.

I walked further into the room, and the familiarity hit me like a punch to the gut. The arrangement of books, the lack of wardrobes, the stark absence of chairs – everything was identical to the previous room. Just as I was taking it all in, a floorboard creaked softly behind me.

"Hello. Can I help you?" A voice inquired gently. I spun around, my bowstring pulled tautly, and faced the intruder. Wait, I'm the intruder here. I immediately lowered my bow.

The green crystal hovering above the Penitent's head seemed to pulse with a soft, gentle light, and I felt a sense of wonder at the sight before saying, "Woah, you're a Penitent, too?" He was about six feet tall and had copperish hair cropped reasonably close to his head. His eyes had a warmth and humor that mine had lost since coming here. "I'm sorry, that was rude of me. I'm Rod. Guards are currently chasing me, and I need to change my armor so I can hide from them."

As we spoke, our voices echoed off the walls, and I couldn't help but feel a sense of desperation creeping in, my hunger pangs, and the guards' pursuit weighing heavily on my mind. I needed to get to my corpse.

"Hello Rod, quite the predicament you've found yourself in," Klericho chuckled, tapping his staff against the ground. "I remember my early days well. The guards? Always itching for a fight. Gave up trying to dodge them eventually. We have an understanding now." His fingers tapped a staccato beat on the worn wooden staff, his eyes glazing over as his gaze drifted away.

"Anyway, I'm Klericho. Been stuck here on the second floor for a while. What run are you on? I can tell you're running the Archer build. I could never get the hang of it. A lot of useless abilities like **Scan**."

My eyes froze on his face, and my mind momentarily blanked as I took in his words. Is this guy crazy or something? Frustration bubbled up inside me, my words laced with a touch of sarcasm. I couldn't hold back, "**Scan** useless? Just when I thought you might be worth talking to. I'm on my Fifth run, and I know more than you already." I turned to leave, headed away from this waste of my time.

"No! Wait, I promise you don't want to head out just yet. I know you're hungry, and it's not a good idea to be around food here when you are."

I paused, thinking back to how I had been unable to control myself when I exited the sewer. "That's why the guards are after you, isn't it? What'd you do, steal a loaf of bread?" The other man laughed, thinking he was back in control of the conversation. So, I changed topics for him, hoping to keep him off guard.

"If Archer is so bad, then which classes are worth using? Which one are you right now?"

A shadow of something, maybe anger, crossed the man's eyes, but he responded kindly.

"Cleric." I grimaced—the worst class. "I would be a Summoner, but it's on cooldown for me. It is the best class. Elemental coverage through these cute little summon things," He looked wistful as if he was imagining his past again. "And then the class comes with staff mastery, too."

I furrowed my brow, my eyes narrowing as I repeated, "Staff Mastery?"

"Oh, it's great; it means infinite staff casting without fear of the staff breaking. It's impressive with the goblin's poison staff, but it's way better if you can get that necrotic bolt staff from the Necromancer boss. It's almost impossible to die with that class. It's crazy powerful, especially against the lower-level goblins you'll be facing soon. You can easily clear a horde of 20 goblins."

My stomach growled loudly, and I noticed a glint in the other man's eyes. But I ignored my stomach, needing the information the other man was sharing. I knew it. I knew magic classes were the way to go here.

"What? If that's the case, why are you still stuck here?"

He sheepishly rubbed the back of his head. "Well, about that. The floor is currently broken. There's no way to beat it."

"What? That's ridiculous. How could a floor be broken?" I shook my head in disbelief, mouth agape and a pit burrowing in my stomach. Of course, my stomach took that as a sign it needed to grumble again.

"It's because of the Djinn," he said, pausing dramatically as though I should know the term.

"What's a Djinn?" I asked, feeling stupid.

"Well, you're just full of questions, aren't you? It's a demon, essentially."

"Oh wow. A demon. Very helpful." His dour face told me he did not appreciate my sarcasm.

"No one is sure how, but the Djinn, the secret boss of the floor, usurped control. He's practically invincible. And no matter how many times you clear the—"

"Look, I'm just tired. I feel like I've been in this place for a week without sleeping." I faked a yawn. It wasn't exactly true, but I was tired of the conversation.

Klericho raised an eyebrow, skepticism written all over his face, yet he continued. "Tell you what, 20 gold for the night, and I'll even throw in some bread for now and a warm meal for when you wake up."

I was about to protest and say I wasn't hungry when my stomach growled uncontrollably. "That obvious, huh?"

"You did say you were avoiding the guards. Wasn't that hard to put two and two together. Breakfast will be ready for you around 10 hours from now. And make sure you close the shutters. The sun never sets here."

"But I'm not sure I can afford it."

[You have plenty of gold, Rod].

"Crystal says I only have 15 gold."

[What did I say about lying, Rod, this isn't a good idea.]

"Now I know for a fact that is a lie. I've run through the first floor over 60 times; the lowest amount of gold I ever made out with is 25." His eyes narrowed.

I shifted nervously on my feet.

"It isn't a good idea to lie here. It attracts unwanted attention." His eyes flickered side to side as if looking for something.

I rubbed the back of my head sheepishly. "Yeah, Crystal has told me a couple of times." His anger faded swiftly. He sighed, "Just give me the gold, and we forget this happened. Cross me again, and we're done, though. I don't have time for the unrepentant."

I was so hungry I didn't even process what he had said until I was squared away in the bedroom holding a loaf of bread. I devoured it in seconds; the dry, hard dough tasted better than anything fresh from the oven.

When I was finished eating, a bare straw bed awaited me, its single pillow forlorn without a blanket. I hadn't felt tired, but the second I hit the pillow, I blacked out.

Chapter Thirty-Six
The Vault

[I can't believe you forgot why we rushed back in the first place.]
I rubbed my eyes as I woke up, trying to clear away the sleep. My mind was as foggy as ever, and I swung my legs around the bed. I sat there longer than necessary, trying to get my brain to work.

"I don't know... What... You..." My words halted as my memory flooded back in. The bread. The guards. The chase. "My corpse!" The words jolted me upright in a panic. I jumped off the bed and dashed towards the door. Mid-stride, I halted, suddenly aware of my undressed state. "Crystal, this isn't the time for jokes. Put my clothes back on." I snapped at her.

My hands immediately flew to my delicates, but thankfully, Klericho was nowhere to be seen. Within moments, my usual cloth pants and shirt wrapped around me, materializing out of thin air. Stepping into the kitchen, a wave of aromas hit me — cooking meat mingled with exotic spices. My urgency faded as my stomach growled loudly. Resigning momentarily to my hunger, I pulled out a chair and sat down to wait for the meal.

I started tapping my fingers against the table out of boredom. Then, I was leaning back in my chair. I closed my eyes, hoping the food would be done soon. [Rod? The corpse?] Crystal's reminder chimed in my ear, sharp and insistent.

"Right!" I exclaimed, the word bursting out as I sprang to my feet and bolted outside. Finally, I remembered why I had gotten out of bed in the first place. A shiver ran down my spine, the same cold dread I'd felt the last time I stood over my own lifeless body. I didn't stop to ponder the eerie déjà vu; there was no time for that now. Instead, I lightly kicked myself to loot my missing belongings.

[You have looted Player Corpse 3 and gained 2 Death Boons.] But instead of the parchment, I had come to love, Crystal said, [I'm not displaying the parchment for now, but everything is back in your inventory. I'll display everything in a bit after you buy the vault.]

I immediately equipped leather armor in all the slots, except for the sandals, feeling its familiar weight settle into place. I wouldn't risk wearing cloth again with the guards on the lookout, even if it was less sweaty.

"Crystal," I said, wanting to get back on track now that the crisis was avoided, "I know I have to buy the waypoint system from you, but is there anything else you can do to help guide me? Maybe you could help me find this vault you mentioned?" I said.

[Oh, that's easy.] She said smoothly. [Tell me everything you want me to transfer to it, and they'll be there. You can even buy upgrades now that you have it. It's definitely worth getting the auto-repair feature. Which should transfer everything you don't need to there before we leave the zone.]

"Zone?" I sighed in frustration. "Can you maybe say that again and this time in common?"

[So touchy.] Crystal replied with a huff. [A zone is just a term for a large area like the Necromancer room on the first floor.]

I paused, eyeing the gear strapped to my chest—burns and nicks from the previous run marring the armor. "And Auto-Repair means?"

[That the item will be... repaired... to full durability... automatical ly... after you die.] She took long pauses again like she was talking to a toddler. I hated it when she did that.

"That's... amazing. Does it work with everything? Weapons? Armor? Arrows?"

[Anything that has durability, as long as it's in the vault, will have been brought to full durability at the start of the next run. We also need to talk about the amulet you received. It is an amazing item, but it does you no good to wear it and die with it equipped.]

I thought I had gotten everything I wanted out of the first floor for now, but the second I had access to one of the magic classes, I was going to speed run the first floor. Sure, I hadn't done the quests, but the Death Boon rewards had seemed negligible. As good as equipping an item in combat was, being able to skip the first floor was probably better for the interim. *Wait a minute. Quests!*

"Hey Crystal! I never received the quest reward for finishing the first floor!" My blood pressure started rising. If Crystal hadn't blown up, we'd be fine. But I controlled my breathing and let the anger pass.

[Oh.] **Quest Name**: [Escape]

Type: Floor

Description: Complete! Escape the sewers.

Reward:

You can now start on the second floor.

You can also access the following new Boons: Waypoint, Auto-Repair, Vault Interest, Potion Restore, and Upgrade System.

5 Death Boons

"Woah, that's a good chunk of Death Boons, is there anything I can purchase now?"

[As we are in the entrance of the second floor, you can purchase whatever you wish. But I would buy the Auto-Repair, and the Waypoint. They are steep at 10 total, but that is all you should buy. In fact, I would advise against buying boons at any time other than a new run in order to ensure access to a new class. That should always be the priority.]

"Okay, let's buy those two, and worry about the rest later. Also, please store everything in the vault for now. I need a break from the first floor anyway. Moving back to my earlier question, how does this vault work? I want to put everything in there and keep only a few weapons, arrows, and gold."

[Sounds reasonable. This floor has a wider variety of growth opportunities. And if your friend's statement is correct, we must clear this within 96 runs. As for the vault, were you even listening? I told you how it works. You just ask me to deposit things when we are in this first room. And then, on future runs, you can grab whatever you need out of here.]

"That's insane. I bet I could've won on my second run if I'd had half the loot I got that first run. How much gold do I have anyway? Is it enough to buy anything?"

[It certainly should be. At the very least, you can buy a shower and another hot meal. If you didn't notice, everyone else can smell the stink on you, even if I thankfully can't.]

Twenty minutes later, back in Klericho's modest dwelling, the savory scent of stew filled the air, its warmth seeping into my body. As a fellow Penitent, he had been a gracious host to me, remembering his early days in the dungeon and how hard it was to find your footing on the second floor. Klericho appeared to have brushed aside my earlier lie, yet a cautious tension hung between us. It was clear he wanted something—his occasional, probing glances said as much—but he seemed hesitant to voice it just yet.

"So Klericho, how did you figure out the 100-run limit for the second floor? That seems a little arbitrary. I thought we were supposed to have infinite runs. That's what my crystal told me." I started tapping my feet as we talked, and my eyes glanced back and forth around the room.

"As far as I know, Penitents like Elric had infinite runs back in the day. But as he returned time and again, the rules of Penance changed. Not only do fewer and fewer people make their way here, but we spend less time here before being forced to move on. Honestly, it's been a while since I've seen anyone come through, and all of them have perished fighting the Djinn. He's invisible. Impossible to defeat."

"Wait, you've encountered other Penitents? As in multiple?" My surprise was genuine. Everything I knew about Penance claimed it was a solitary punishment.

"You aren't the only fellow Penitent I've met, not by a longshot. I've come across quite a few in my time here. What feels like years ago, I encountered a woman on my 15th or 20th run. Probably the most beautiful I've ever seen. She had hair that cascaded like a waterfall and legs that could stride through eternity. Honestly, I always pictured the two of us conquering Penance together..." His voice trailed off, his eyes again taking on that distant, faraway look. An emblem dangled from his neck—a gravestone necklace with a figure of a kneeling man embossed on it. It seemed familiar, stirring a vague memory. But no crystal formed. As the conversation died, I started playing with the Lunar Amulet around my neck. *I could end it here and go loot things...*

But instead, I shook us both from our stupor by asking, "What happened?"

"To make a sad story short, we teamed up and made it to the Goblin King, the boss at the end of the floor. We had him dead to rights—10 HP left—he unleashed a stunning attack that killed me outright. I died, but it only stunned her. When I made it back to this place, she was nowhere to be seen. I always assumed she made it to the third floor." He looked earnest and maybe a bit wistful.

"What if that was her last run, and she didn't make it?" I blurted, instantly regretting my words as I watched the color drain from Klericho's face. His shocked silence told me he'd never dared to consider that possibility.

I gave the man an appropriate amount of time to process my mistake before asking a bunch of questions rapid-fire. "So, besides her, how many people have you met? How did you team up with her anyway? Are they all as hopeless as you?" I laughed, but Klericho gave me a look, so I shut my mouth.

"Normally, these zones challenge one person. But bring an ally, and it adjusts to the party size. Tougher monsters but better rewards. We thought a big group might be able to clear the dungeon. None were ever successful, though. The Djinn is just too powerful, invincible even." I yawned. I just had a full night's rest, yet I was yawning. I moved to get up and stretch my legs. I needed to know more about Penance. I wanted to know more, but my mind was starting to drift to other things. Goblins, treasure, more food.

"...at least, that was the theory behind the Penitent groups of Rellum, The Merchant, and Malikap." He stared at me, and then a brief spark of anger crossed his eyes. "Hey, are you even listening to me?"

"Sorry," I shook my head. "I got distracted. How about we change topics? Why did you stop trying to make it through?" He glared at me, and I had a sinking feeling he was only talking to me because he was out of options.

"I had a few Penitent friends through my runs, but none I miss more than Thomas. The guy was built to be a warrior. It was like he instinctively knew how to wield a blade. He was like a brother to me."

"What does this have to do with my question?" I asked impatiently.

"He died, My 98th run, his 100th. And, well, it's a lot harder to want to run through this place by yourself, especially after so many fruitless attempts. I just decided to settle down and live out eternity here.

"If you knew you'd run out of lives, why would you go so close to the limit? Why not just stay here and keep doing what you've been doing now? Running your little inn? Wouldn't you eventually get enough death—" Mid-sentence, a sudden jolt electrified my body, cutting off my words. It was as if the world had slammed into slow motion, but this time, I was frozen, too. And then, picking the absolute worst timing, Crystal made a parchment appear. I would've laughed if I had been able to move my face.

Rod – Run 3 Corpse
- **Gold:** 459

Items

Enchanted Blood Ruby of the Sewage Goblin Tribes

- **Amount:** 1

- **Condition:** N/A

- **Effect:**

  ○ While in your possession, you can speak Goblish.

  ○ Once per run, you can equip an item during combat.

  ○ You can skip the normal rooms on the first floor and choose to fight only the Necromancer and the goblins.

- **Description:** A dark, gleaming ruby imbued with the ancient magic of the Sewage Goblin Tribes. The ruby is also one of the seven keys needed to escape Penance.

Iron Helm

- **Amount:** 1

- **Condition:** 10/20

- **Effect:** Def +2

- **Description:** A well-crafted iron helm that offers solid protection for the head. Its reinforced structure provides excellent defense against blunt and sharp attacks.

Iron Short Sword

- **Amount:** 1

- **Condition:** 16/20

- **Effect:** Deals 1–6 damage

- **Description:** A sturdy iron short sword with a simple yet effective design. The blade is sharp and well-balanced, perfect for quick strikes and precise cuts.
  Quote: "Careful, it's sharp!" – 4 Fingers Lasalle

Iron Mace

- **Amount:** 1

- **Condition:** 14/20

- **Effect:** Deals 1–6 damage

- **Description:** A heavy iron mace with a solid, spiked head. This weapon deals devastating blows, capable of crushing armor and bone alike.

The Staff of the Necrobolt

- **Amount:** 1

- **Condition:** 17/20

- **Effect:**

  - Deals 1–20 Necrotic damage

  - 10% chance to blind target

  - Casts the spell "Necro Bolt": Deals 1–8 necrotic damage, with a 5% chance of turning the target into a zombie minion

- **Description:** An ominous staff carved from dark wood and adorned with eerie runes that glow with an otherworldly light. The staff channels dark energies, unleashing powerful necrotic bolts that can wither flesh and bone.

Gurgle's Staff of Noxious Fumes

- **Amount:** 1

- **Condition:** 16/20

- **Effect:**

  - Deals 1–20 Poison damage

  - 20% chance to poison the target

  - Casts the spell "Noxious Fumes": Deals 5–12 poison damage. 5% chance to poison the target

- **Description:** A twisted piece of wood that seems to writhe with a life of its own, emitting a faint, eerie green smoke. Hanging from the top are five potion bottles that cannot be removed, each containing bubbling multicolored concoctions swirling inside.

Empty Bottle

- **Amount:** 1

- **Condition:** N/A

- **Effect:** You can put potions in this.

- **Description:** An empty bottle.

Torch

- **Amount:** 3

- **Condition:** 10/10

- **Effect:** Deals 1–4 physical damage. 5% chance of causing burn effect on target

- **Description:** A simple wooden torch wrapped in oil-soaked rags. When ignited, it produces a flickering flame that casts a warm, golden light in a small radius.

Gold

- **Amount:** 338

- **Condition:** N/A

- **Effect:** The currency of Penance

- **Description:** A simple gold coin. On one side is the visage of the Merchant of Death, and on the other is a thumbs-up.

Death Boons

- **Amount:** 8

- **Condition:** N/A

- **Effect:** Death Boons are power. Spend them wisely.

- **Description:** A metaphysical currency provided by the Merchant of Death. The currency allows you to get progressively stronger as you face new threats in Penance.

Dagger of Penetration

- **Amount:** 1

- **Condition:** 15/15

- **Effect:**

  - Deals 3–7 damage

  - Ignores 2 points of defense

- **Description:** A sharp and durable iron dagger with a well-balanced design, perfect for quick and precise strikes.
  Quote: "A very sharp dagger." — Photonius The Dead

Iron Great Axe

- **Amount:** 1

- **Condition:** /25

- **Effect:** Deals 4–14 damage

- **Description:** A massive iron great axe with a double-edged blade, designed for powerful and sweeping strikes.

Copper Mace

- **Amount:** 1

- **Condition:** 15/15

- **Effect:** Deals 1–6 damage. 5% chance to stun

- **Description:** A robust copper mace with a heavy, rounded head. This weapon deals devastating blows, capable of stunning opponents.

Arrows

- **Amount:** 15

- **Condition:** 4/5

- **Effect:** Allows you to fire a bow

- **Description:** A simple wooden arrow with a stone arrowhead. Stronger arrows provide additional effects.

Rat Teeth

- **Amount:** 1

- **Condition:** N/A

- **Effect:** None

- **Description:** The incisor(s) of a Giant Rat. Who knows? If you collect a lot, something good may happen.

Rat Meat

- **Amount:** 1

- **Condition:** N/A

- **Effect:** +5 health. 80% chance of poison if consumed

- **Description:** Juicy, full of protein, and only tastes a little like sewage! Who knows? If you collect a lot, something good may happen.
  Quote: "Tastes like chicken!" – Photonius The Dead

Goblin Ears

- **Amount:** 2

- **Condition:** N/A

- **Effect:** ???

- **Description:** Waxy, flaky, and oddly heavy. These ears are likely a waste of space! But who knows? If you collect a lot, something good may happen.

Cloth Shirt

- **Amount:** 2

- **Condition:** 10/10

- **Effect:** +1 defense

- **Description:** It's a shirt!
  Quote: "My friend went to Penance, and all I got was this lousy T-shirt!"

Leather Greaves

- **Amount:** 2

- **Condition:** 15/15

- **Effect:** +1 defense

- **Description:** A worked and treated pair of leather greaves covering the waist down to the ankles.

Leather Armor

- **Amount:** 1

- **Condition:** 13/15

- **Effect:** +1 defense

- **Description:** A worked and treated leather vest covering the chest and arms down to the wrist.

Leather Helm

- **Amount:** 2

- **Condition:** 15/15

- **Effect:** +1 defense

- **Description:** A sturdy leather helmet crafted to provide basic protection for the head.

Cloth Sandals

- **Amount:** 1

- **Condition:** 10/10

- **Effect:** +1 defense

- **Description:** Simple yet 'comfortable' cloth sandals that offer minimal protection but great mobility.

Quote: "Don't worry, you'll miss sewer feet after an hour with these!" – Photonius

Chest Key

- **Amount:** 1

- **Condition:** N/A

- **Effect:** Unlocks one chest of any rarity

- **Description:** A small, intricately crafted key that glows faintly with a magical aura.

Chapter Thirty-Seven
Aunt Ersid

{STOP.}

I stopped trying to laugh, and time unfroze. Somehow, I remembered I had been talking. I said something other than I had intended, though, which was weird. "Deaths to get armor and weapons that would allow you to beat the boss?" And then I forgot. Everything that had just occurred. My mind went sheer white as nothing made sense for a minute, and my body flailed around uncontrollably.

"That's just it. I got every weapon and armor piece from the first floor and this one and nothing worked. Even between all 100 of those runs, I never whittled his health down past 50%, and he has a **Heal** and a **Shield**! There's no way to beat him. It's just not worth it."

"Hey, why are you on the ground? Weren't you just standing?"

I took a moment to look down; I was in a genuflecting position. I stared at the dried blood on my hand in confusion and my scattered arrows. *What happened?* I picked myself off the ground and noticed a bunch of scribbles on the ground, like a bunch of children trying to write something in blood.

"Aunt Ersid" I said out loud. "There's writing here in blood." *And blood on my hand.* But I didn't say that part out loud. "Aunt Ersid." I repeated, looking at the words on the floor.

I started freaking out. Trying to wrack my broken and shattered brain to figure out what was happening to me. Was I losing my mind? Was I blacking out? Something odd was going on here. Klericho got up from the table and walked over to me. "Why can't I remember anything? Does that happen to you?"

"What do you mean? Like the brain fog when you die? Do you mean how Penitents forget every death?" *No, that's the only thing I remember clearly.*

"No, I mean like anything. I can't remember how I got here; I can't remember who I was before I got here." I started to hyperventilate as the world disappeared. I couldn't deal with this. I couldn't do this. Klericho moved forward then and pressed a hand against my chest. He glowed, my vision cleared, and the constricting breaths stopped. I inhaled a huge lungful of air and said, "What was that?" My mind was clear. Everything was okay.

"I healed you of your anxiety."

"You did what?" I said, shocked. Clerics could heal mental injuries? I sat, too stunned to move. And hadn't I dismissed the cleric as a class? *Man, when I'm wrong. I'm wrong.* What else could magic do? And then I stared down at my hand panic forgotten, the blood starting to cake on my hand.

The writing was illegible, but something inside me told me it was important. "Aunt Ersid." It was silly, but I had to have written those letters. I drew my small A's with a little curve above the circle and I didn't know anyone else who did that. But the message made no sense. My parents were both only children. I shook my head, letting the thoughts rattle around. "You know anyone named 'Aunt Ersid'"?

"Not a clue. Is that what that says?" He replied. "I'm about as lost as you seem to be."

And like that, my brain switched topics. Aunt Ersid forgotten.

"Oh, right, Klericho, you have got to tell me everything you know about this place..." A couple of hours later, I had finally convinced Klericho that I would figure out a way to clear the dungeon. He had been amazed that I had cleared the first floor on my 3rd run. Something that had taken him a couple dozen runs. He had plenty of advice for clearing mobs.

"Be careful; there are traps and puzzles everywhere, and if you mess up on either, you have to fight powerful enemies. And the goblins like to fight in groups. It's easier than the Sewer trio; they have less health but can swarm and overwhelm you easily! Oh, and every five attempts to kill the boss, everything resets. That's why it took me so long to clear the first floor. I kept dying to the Necromancer, so any damage I did to the goblins was always reset." And then he hesitated. His eyes looked around, slightly shifty. "So I might have misspoke earlier. There are other Penitent here."

"What? And after all that crap you gave me about lying?"

"I didn't lie, not exactly. The reason I have seen less and less Penitent around is I haven't been leaving my house."

I pushed aside my anger, more curious than upset at his stupid lie. "Why lie then?"

"You can't trust anyone. Anyone you meet could be loyal to Malikap or, worse, Aurentum. You can't trust these people. They lie, they cheat, they backstab."

"You lied."

"Again, I didn't lie. You have to be careful with that kind of thing here. But truthfully, the only people you can trust here are Rellum's faithful. The other gods are in it for themselves."

I laughed. I could almost feel a Memory Core forming as bile crept up my throat. Rellum had never done anything for me, so I wasn't going to start trusting him now. I needed to get myself away from this guy, and he was clearly a fanatic.

I had something a lot more essential to do first: Shopping! I had never been a fan back on Eqiuem, but this was different. I had around 400 gold to spend and needed to make the most of it. My main priority was potions or something to increase my longevity, like iron armor. Somehow, I only had a helmet, which was great, but I wanted a full suit of armor.

I would avoid food for now because Klericho was kind enough to open his home to me, and we had feasted. He eventually expected me to help him, which I was inclined to do just to have a place to rest if needed. From the sound of things, unlike the first floor, the second floor would take days to clear fully. I wondered how I would speed run the first floor, let alone this one.

As I stepped out, the market buzzed with activity. Merchants busily repaired their spice towers and served fresh food. Amidst the hustle, I scanned the crowd. Unlike Klericho, none had a crystal floating above their heads. Were these people even real?

I approached a stall with dried meat and fresh fish stinking up the surrounding area. A middle-aged and portly woman stood cutting off fish heads from the day's catch. She had a seemingly endless mound of fish in front of her. She looked human, and when she talked, she sounded human. "Whotchoo lookin at aye? T'is ain't no winno shoppe. Make ye purchase or leave, will ye?"

Her accent was strange. Clipped and butchered like the words were escaping through a sieve. She looked at me with a broken-toothed grin that looked more like a snarl than a smile.

"How are you here? You know you are in Penance, right?" I asked.

"Wot? Penance? What's 'at? Tis here's Aerlyn this is. Noy buy sometin or geddot."

I was tempted to **Scan** her and figure out what she was considering, but I didn't want to risk the guards attacking me again. Speaking of which, I had yet to see Mr. Plume and his friends recently. Which was odd, considering they had split off after me.

Leaving the vibrant colors and lively chatter of the food market behind, I entered the armor and weapons market. Here, the scene shifted dramatically to a display of gleaming metal and the methodical movements of artisans at work. Armorsmiths hammering plates into body shapes, weaponsmiths with swords in forges, even leather workers tanning hides in the hot, desert sun.

And then, I saw them. The Penitent were everywhere. People with different-sized and colored crystals moved about the market, haggling with merchants, dueling at dueling stations, and even a few seemed to be trying their hand at blacksmithing. It was an entire community of people trapped here, just like me. One group consisted of a mage, a warrior, and a cleric, which was a brilliant idea. I kept to myself that first day, but I knew this would be a great way to find fellow adventurers when I needed help clearing the floor.

At the end of row after row of merchants, a large crowd of Penitents milled about in front of a wooden sign. Klericho had mentioned there would be other Penitents, but I had yet to learn there were so many. He had given me a rough idea how the city worked, explaining that the local economy was, somehow, largely independent of us. Even when we flooded the merchants with coin and loot, it all seemed to disappear the next time we came through.

As I browsed through the stalls, my eyes lit up when I spied a complete set of iron armor, an awesome upgrade on my current set. My fingers traced the cold, hard surface of the iron leggings and matching armor. The merchant, noticing my lingering gaze on the expensive items, leaned over his cluttered counter with a sly grin. "For the complete set, I could part with it for just 3,000 gold," he offered, his eyes gleaming with the prospect of a big sale.

My heart skipped a beat and my mouth went dry when the merchant named his price. Unable to afford anything I wanted, I moved from stall to stall, but it was all the same. The vibrant wares that had sparked my greed now mocked me, leaving a sinking feeling that I'd never get my armor this way.

Aware of the guards' suspicious glances, I knew it was time to leave. Avoiding another hassle, I left the market stalls and wandered aimlessly, trying to find the next room. Just as I was about to seek Klericho's help when I spotted the exit—a raised portcullis near the blacksmith I ran past earlier. Crossing the empty moat, I shrugged and walked on through, relieved to have found my way.

Chapter Thirty-Eight
Textiles

~Run 5, Textiles Room, Floor 2, The Fallen Merchant City of Aerlyn~

I pushed open the door and stepped through the archway, completely taken aback by what I saw. "What is this place?" I whispered, my eyes wide in astonishment.

[You are in the textiles room. This used to be a place where citizens of Aerlyn would create, clean, and care for the textiles of the town. This city used to love color, but now it is a ghost of its former self.]

Fabrics of every color imaginable filled the room. Crystal's light barely pierced the pervasive gloom that clung to every surface, yet the tapestries glowed faintly, their colors just visible in the distance. The contrast was surreal, and the oppressive size of the room made me feel small and insignificant like a lone figure lost in an endless dream.

I stepped forward, and the gate slammed shut behind me with a deafening clang. I jumped, heart pounding. "Not cool," I muttered, shaking off the shock.

The room stretched out before me, a labyrinth of textiles. Rugs, carpets, and upholstery formed intricate pathways, while clotheslines hung overhead, draped with various fabrics that created makeshift tunnels and barriers. The sight was mesmerizing and daunting, each path seeming to pulse with a life of its own, beckoning and threatening simultaneously.

I could barely see my hand in front of my face, yet the kaleidoscope of colors on the quilts was clear. "Weird," I whispered, a shiver running down my spine. An intense mix of perfumes and soaps clashed violently in my nose, overwhelming and almost suffocating. A quiet murmur in the background made me feel watched. The disorientation made my skin crawl with unease.

Hoping it wasn't a trap, I scanned my options, heart pounding in my chest. Each path forward was lit up with a different color of glyph pattern on the textiles, casting an otherworldly glow. To the right, a tunnel of hanging fabrics swayed gently, the cloth forming a narrow passageway. The red circular glyph leading the way seemed to pulse with an almost hypnotic rhythm, making the path feel alive.

Straight ahead, a narrow path lined with discarded clothes led deeper into the room, the air thick with the musty scent of old fabric. At the end, a purple triangle glyph formed a compass, its sharp lines cutting through the gloom and drawing me forward with a sense of direction and purpose.

To the left, brocades glowed faintly, their intricate spiraled patterns illuminated by the faint green light they gave off. The gentle hum of the green spiral-shaped glyphs resonated in the air, giving the path an eerie, almost inviting warmth. Each path screamed at me to choose them, as if my choices were sentient and would disappear without my choosing them. Each path called out to me, but something about the red circles seemed promising.

"Okay, here goes nothing," I muttered, my voice trembling slightly. Just then, I heard a sharp, blood-curdling scream like something or someone had been murdered coming from down the red path. I gulped. I glanced down the other two paths, uncertain which was the path I should take especially now, but my gaze kept lingering on the red circles.

[Don't be a coward, Rod. Red is likely the proper path forward.]

Deciding to trust my instincts and needing no further insults from Crystal, I moved toward the tapestries on the right, feeling the soft brush of damp fabric against my arms as I entered the tunnel. The room's oppressive size made me feel small and insignificant like a lone figure lost in an endless dream.

As I ventured deeper, the maze became more complex. Rugs of varying sizes and patterns overlapped on the floor, creating uneven terrain. Occasionally, I had to step over or duck under fabric lines stretched taut between poles, forming barriers that forced me to change direction. Upholstered furniture, long forgotten and covered in dust, acted as walls, narrowing the paths and adding to the maze's claustrophobic feel.

I reached out to touch a quilt's slightly wet surface. Light clung to my fingers like tiny, reluctant flames. 'Gross,' I gagged at the chemical smell that now seemed to cling to me.

I shook my hands to remove the moisture, but then the fabric patterns caught my eye, everything else forgotten. It was a second magical mural. I didn't know they could form on a quilt, but there it was in front of me, words and all.

Just like last time, the mural told a story, except this one was much easier to understand. Silhouettes of differing colors depicted the Goblin King's rise to power. His kingdom started small—a village formed when he was kicked out for being too weak. The King raised a family and a tribe. They raided cautiously at first, but eventually, they overthrew most of Aerlyn's outskirts. All except for an area protected by the Guardsman—fifteen soldiers who struck down everything the Goblin King threw at them.

At least a dozen more murals spread among the quilts. Still, I was afraid of triggering another killer headache, so after a lingering glance at the language beneath and a brief pause while Crystal read the language, I moved on.

I rounded a corner and, lost in trying to figure out why a mural about the history of the Goblin Tribe wasn't in Goblish, tripped over two crates that had been stuck together. The impact sent a jolt of pain through my knee, and I bit back a curse, my frustration mingling with fear that the noise would attract unwanted attention.

After dusting myself off, I opened the crates. [You have received a basic health potion and 65 Gold.]

"Yes!" I fist-pumped, elation surging through me before slapping my hand on my mouth. I looked around, hesitant, looking into the darkness for a hint of light or movement. After my pulse lessened, I focused on the red bottle in my hand. Now, I could heal some damage whenever I got hurt next. Unless I encountered a room with moonlight at some point, I would probably be out of luck regarding healing on this floor, what with the marketplace never experiencing nighttime.

After my brief looting adventure, I rounded the corner. My eyes adjusted to the dark just as a blast of golden light hit me. "Whoa!" I shielded my eyes. The tapestries had transformed into brightly glowing, patterned quilts, shining like the sun in the darkness. The quilts led me forward, and it was probably the right way ahead, but the light was so bright I blindly turned left down a corridor that had formed a cut-up quilt that parted before me to escape the pain in my eyes. New and old glyphs and patterns appeared in a new three-way fork. The green spirals were back, as were the purple triangles, an energy emanating from those paths as if something was trying to suck me in, to force me down those paths. I could almost feel my feet moving forward without my consent.

The new glyphs' light was gentler, though, and the energy less demanding. An alternating yellow and blue pattern made up these new glyphs, almost looking like the sun and a snowflake back and forth, back and forth. Without realizing it, my feet surged forward, but instead of feeling forced, I felt invited to go down this path. It made me feel wanted—something I hadn't felt in a while. I smiled despite the clear danger, ignoring the pit in my stomach; the sensation felt so far away, I didn't have to try to ignore it; it was just gone.

As I walked down this new corridor, instead of an omnipresent and clinging darkness, it was obscured by a dense, frozen fog. Crystal hadn't said anything for a hot minute, so I said, "You still there, Crystal? I hope we're doing good?"

Just then, the air grew frigid, and I paused, confused by the sudden shift.

Chapter Thirty-Nine
Caution

I was thankful for my armor's barrier to the cold but still shivered. My breath hung in the air, mingling with the fog like dust in the wind, and I moved my torch closer to my face for warmth. The heat felt good against the frost, quickly nipping at my nose, but I moved it to a normal position to move forward again.

[I am fine, Rod, just not much to comment on now. The maze is not something I can help you with as it is different every time; a path that might work this time may not work the next time.]

I moved like this for what felt like hours, following the path of the new glyphs. I was beginning to get frustrated with this floor. There were no fights, utter darkness, and nothing but long corridors, which meant sheer, utter boredom. I resisted the urge to sigh, getting annoyed at myself for even having the urge. Thankfully, a new light appeared ahead, pushing back the fog and warming me.

"Finally, some heat," I sighed in relief. The cold had seeped into my bones, but this heat melted the ache away like the first warm day after winter. This golden light was refreshing, making my aches and pains disappear. I was drawn into it and then felt a deep, primal fear. Was this my own decision? Or was something compelling me? What if this had to do with that weird memory blip? *Who is Aunt Ersid?* I again tried to remember what had occurred, but nothing came to me. I tried to turn around, but my feet moved independently of my thoughts.

I gulped as my feet walked me through the light into the lush, gold-adorned room. It was like a palace that had thrown up all its carpets, clothes, and awnings. Without warning, I could control myself again, which, of course, caused me to fall flat on my face. I had half a mind to turn around and leave the room, go for the blindingly bright hallway, but an altar was in front of me.

Something I had come to associate with bosses in the dungeon, but there didn't seem to be one this time. And then, I did something that I knew would surprise Crystal. I moved forward with caution. Looking every way and whispering, "Crystal, any idea what this altar is for? Should I be on the lookout for something?" What can I say? Maybe I was the kind of person that liked being unpredictable.

[Wow, caution. That's... new.] She paused, maybe thinking or taking a second to look around. [This is a relic altar. Starting with this floor, there is a powerful floor item called a relic that grants you a powerful boon. Some allow you to jump a second time in mid-air, some allow you to push heavy objects you should not be able to push, and others still grant you one-time power boosts. As for this altar, no bosses are present if that is what you were worried about, but I still would—]

She kept talking, but I ignored her. It was probably important, but I was entranced when I spotted the object on the altar. The altar wasn't very grand, about three feet tall, and decorated with white ornamental cloth. But that wasn't what grabbed my attention. Instead, the golden object resting on the altar drew me like a moth to a mattress. It looked slightly like a flute or an ocarina but something about it was wrong. I held the object in my hands and finally realized my error. It wasn't an instrument at all.

[Spout of the Immortal. Second Floor: Relic 1 of 3. This relic is a key. This is a one use item. It can open any secret door on the Second Floor. Don't drop it, or it will break.]

The spout, crafted from solid gold and quite heavy, featured ridges at the other end, clearly designed to screw into something. There were tiny, illegible letters on the spout in a spiral pattern.

Before I had a chance to do anything else, I felt a searing pain in my back, like someone had grabbed onto my spine through my skin and was trying to pull it out. I screamed in terror and jumped forward, wrenching the serrated knife from the hand of the black-clothed, eyeless goblin that had been wielding it. His comically large ears fluttered towards the noise as the dagger clattered to the floor behind me as I fell, rolling away.

[Sneak Attack! 23 damage!]

I yelped in pain and scrambled quickly to my feet, found the dagger, and kicked it as far away as I could, quirking an eyebrow as it vanished. The monster growled at me, enraged that I had taken his weapon. In my panic, I hadn't noticed the second goblin wildly waving his weapon, trying to stab me. A die rolled in my mind, time paused, and I quickly sidestepped the flailing goblin as time resumed. Panting, holding my bow with an arrow raised, I backed away, creating space between the monsters and myself. I used that space to cast **SCAN**!

Enemy Entry 0008: Shadow Strike Goblin (The Third Tribe) (2)

The weak spot is their ears, particularly susceptible to auditory attacks.

Stats

Health: 10/10

I didn't have anything that could produce loud noises, but it would be good to know for future runs, especially once they were stronger. I was probably going to one-shot them. I took my bow and cast **Aim** at the goblin still holding their dagger. The goblin, busy shrieking at his friend, turned his ear, and my arrow flew straight through his eardrum.

[Critical Strike! 14 damage! You have slain Shadow Strike goblin 2.]

The other goblin shrieked in rage and started running away. Not worrying about critical hits, I used **Aim** and targeted the goblin's spine for some cathartic revenge. I launched arrow after arrow, exhausting my stamina. The arrows ripped from my bow like dogs let loose upon their dinner.

[5 damage, 3 damage, 6 damage! Congratulations, you have killed Shadow Strike goblins.]

"That was much better, Crystal, just saying the damage is much easier to follow, especially if we get into one of those horde fights Klericho mentioned.] I rubbed my back where the knife had cut me; unlike on the first floor, I still felt a lingering pain where the knife had gouged into my back. My hand came away slick with blood.

"Crystal, what's my health at?" I asked, feeling a knot of worry tightening in my chest.

[You have 2 of 45 health remaining, Rod.] I sighed in relief and then immediately grimaced. It was a hard habit to break. I must have been a weary soul to sigh so much at 16 years old.

"Did I clear all of the monsters for this room?"

[Yes, you cleared all of the monsters for the room. However, the final decision must still be made.]

"What do you mean by final decision?" I asked. Deciding to make the most of my time, I looted the two corpses.

[You have looted Shadow Cloak. You have looted 14 Gold.]

"Woah, Shadow Cloak, what's that? And what slot does that even go on?

[Weird, I haven't seen an item like that before. It looks like it goes into a cloak slot.]

"What do you mean you haven't seen an item like this before?"

[I mean that in my time in Penance, I have never seen a Cloak slot. But now it's in your equipment list.]

"Alright, go ahead and show me just the inventory updates, please." I paused and quickly added, "Oh, and then equip it!"

[You have looted Shadow Cloak and Serrated Shadow Strike Dagger.]

I glanced over the words, curious at first about the dagger but then disappointed because of its low durability. The cloak, though? That was amazing. I would need to be careful, though, and make sure I didn't let it break.

I felt it flow around my neck and billow downward, enshrouding me in a cloak of inky, black mist. The color of the mist looked familiar, but I ignored it. A much more nagging thought crowding my mind now that the excitement of post-battle loot was done with. "Crystal? What did you mean by the final decision."

[I can't elaborate on that. Please just continue forward. All will become clear.]

I shook my head at her ominousness and moved forward. The path split again; by this point, I had to be approaching the middle of the room and the wall, or further, given that I could not tell how large the room was. I could move left or forward. Provided that I was still reasonably close to the wall, I figured that the forward path would lead me to another room if it weren't a dead end. It felt like a fifty-fifty shot.

The darkness around me eased as I held the golden spout. It worked much like the torches I had seen in other rooms. Instead of the pitch-black void that previously clung to the walls, shadows now danced along the quilted surfaces. The faint glow of the fabric made the walls appear more distant than they actually were.

The tunnel seemed to trudge on and on, but eventually, I came to a flat terracotta wall with another altar in front of it. *What is with this dungeon and altars?* This altar was gray, almost my height, and a couple of feet wide, but it was bizarrely shaped. It was thin, too thin, barely a hand in depth. In the center, an indentation indicated the shape and size of my newly acquired golden "torch." Without thinking, I took the spout and slid it into the keylock ridge side first. It slid into place with an audible click, and the altar shrunk into the ground. The wall soon followed suit as it shifted downward. In its place was the same wooden doorway shaped like an arch. I opened the door and paused."Crystal? Come on! What was the final decision?" I said, my voice an octave higher than I'd intended.

[Oh ye of little faith, walk through the door, and you will find out.] I walked through the doorway.

Enemy Entry 0008: Shadow Strike Goblin *(Level 2 – The Third Tribe)*

The weak spot is their ears, particularly effective against auditory attacks.

Stats

- **Health:** 10/10

- **Potency:** 12

- **Vitality:** 2

- **Precision:** 12

- **Evasion:** 7

New Inventory
Shadow Cloak

- **Amount:** 1

- **Condition:** 12/15

- **Effect:** Plus 5 Evasion

- **Description:** This cloak has a shadowy, inky quality. It absorbs light and leaves behind a ghost-like afterimage as you move. *Quote:* "Now with added arrow holes!"

Serrated Shadow Strike Dagger

- **Amount:** 1

- **Condition:** 4/5

- **Effect:**

  - Deals 2–7 damage

  - Guaranteed to deal 7 damage on a critical strike through defenses

  - Deals additional damage for every point of durability lost

  - Low durability

- **Description:** This serrated dagger, a favorite of the Shadow Strike Goblins, is great at dealing killing blows on weaker enemies, but its low durability makes it difficult to use as a main weapon.

Chapter Forty
Opulence of Objects

~Run 5, Treasure Room, Floor 2, The Fallen Merchant City of Aerlyn~

I f the last room was a Splendor of Sheets, the next room was an Opulence of Objects. My eyes widened at the sheer volume of it. *Unreal. If I had even a quarter of this wealth, my family would have been fine.* I had entered a room half the size of the entrance room filled with barrels of spices, broken and worn-down merchant stalls, weapons, armor, crates, chests, and gems all scattered around in a chaotic junkyard mess. My mind raced. What happened here? Who left all this behind? The absence of guards or other adventurers, although expected, was unsettling, to say the least.

In the center, a red and brown orb floated in the air, emitting blue wisps of power. I held my breath as I moved forward anxiously, each step clanging loudly in the vast, opulent chamber. The stillness was eerie, amplifying my anticipation of an impending trap. But nothing happened, and maybe *this time, nothing would.*

"What is this place?" I asked, my voice filled with wonder as I looked around.

[This is a treasure room. And you made your final choice, by the way. You will not get another Spout on this run, and it is, therefore, impossible to destroy the Djinn. However, you made the right choice, as there are untold treasures available in this room. The bounty of spices alone will yield well over 10,000 Gold. I don't understand what's going on. There should be dozens of people here, guards, too. The last time a Penitent I was with found the second-floor secret room, it was not like this.]

My jaw dropped, and I felt my heart skip a beat. This was a treasure trove beyond my wildest dreams. My hands itched to touch everything, to claim the riches before me. I could barely breathe as I took in the vast array of wealth, each item more dazzling than the last. "How do I store them in my inventory?"

[How do you store anything else?]

"Oh," I said, distracted. As amazing as the obvious wealth was, I felt like a cat chasing string as I stared, transfixed by the orb. I approached the orb, the wisps of power lashing out, crackling the air, making me jump in alarm. "Is that thing safe?"

[I do not know what this is.] Crystal paused, clearly thinking of the safest way for me to get to the orb. [But I would advise you to steer clear of it. It could be dangerous. Run ending, even.]

I should listen to Crystal, but... the orb called to me. It wanted me. Needed me.

Part of the reason was that for the first time in a while, I felt calm and at peace with the world, and not as if a goblin had almost ripped out my spine 10 minutes earlier. The source was clearly the magic arcing back and forth around the ball. My hair raised as I got closer but didn't hesitate reaching out to grab it.

As I put my hand on the orb, my world expanded. A new awareness sprang to my mind—I was not alone here. Time froze, and then everything vanished. The wind howled through the now empty streets. I gasped in horror at all of the wealth that was just gone.

It was the exact same sensation I felt earlier, except now, my mind was racing, hoping against hope that I could remember every detail, remember everything that I was about to face. I couldn't lose anything more; I just couldn't.

The golden light enveloped me once more, but this time, it was different. A profound sense of peace washed over me, soothing the terror that had gripped my heart moments before. My muscles relaxed, and a serene smile spread across my face. It was as if every worry, every fear, had been swept away by the warm, radiant glow.

The horrors of the past seemed distant and insignificant, replaced by an overwhelming sense of contentment and joy. *What did it matter that the spices were gone? What did my wound matter? Ah, life is good.* A tiny spark of defiance spoke through the haze.

{*No! Everything is not good. You are being—*}, but then it faded as the joy flooded my mind again. A voice spoke into the brightness.

"Hello, dearest child." Rellum the Progenitor whispered, and the words burned themselves into my brain. Each word was like a chisel against my soul, sealing in something new. He stood stark against the world. Popping out like corn on a fire. Vibrant, too real.

Is that Rellum? How? How can he exist? A rage I had never experienced rushed through me, overpowering the abounding joy, darkening it, changing it into a wisp of its former self. If I had learned anything in the dungeon so far, it was how dangerous anger could be. But at that moment, I didn't care. I moved forward, ready to gouge his eyes out when, once again, ecstasy wracked my body in almost frustrating waves. Anger forgotten.

Rellum was plainly dressed for a being so powerful. His piercing yellow eyes shone like stars beneath a plain white hood. The rest of his robe was equally unadorned, just plain white fabric held together by a simple brown belt. Despite his modest attire, his intense gaze hinted at the immense power he possessed.

{*He's manipulating you!*} a voice spoke through the fog. A voice I didn't know.

How could he be manipulating me? Everything felt so good, so right. And it was Rellum. The Rellum. God of Light, God of everything that was pure.

And then the voice was gone. Its seed of doubt was banished from my mind as another wave of joy brought me weeping to my knees at the splendor of a god.

"I have a request of you, my child." He said. "The Pact of Three limits my powers in this realm, but I must do what I can to protect my flock of followers. Those who were unfairly bewitched and trapped here with no hope of escaping. These orbs are the only trace of magic I am allowed on this floor. I need you to repair the city of Aerlyn. This was once a mighty beacon of peace and prosperity in Penance. A place for those new to the realm to figure things out, gather treasure, and prepare for the hardships of the next floor. But now, the once vibrant streets, the once vibrant Penitent community is gone." He paused, the light of his eyes fading somewhat and, with it, the rapturous elation.

I felt exhausted, drained of my wits and my mind. But with it, I could see. I could think through the haze.

Rellum, the God of Purity. The god of hope. The only god I didn't, couldn't believe in. As he stood before me, I struggled to reconcile the tales of his benevolence with the harsh reality of the world outside Penance. Doubts gnawed at my mind. How could a god of light allow so much darkness?

Memories of my father's abuse, of going to bed hungry, of cowering under a chair flashed before my eyes, fueling my skepticism. I clenched my fists, my heart torn between awe and distrust. What was the point of a god of goodness when evil existed in the world? Rellum didn't realize I had an epiphany about my past and this situation. I kept my face awed, though. There was no reason to give a being as cruel as he any more power over me right now.

Rellum didn't notice my internal struggle and instead gestured at one of the orbs. "With these orbs, you can begin to repair the damage."

"What? How? Why me?"

"You are a rare thing, Rod—an *unclaimed* soul past the first floor. There is so much that your free status brings to the gods—things we can't do with our own soldiers. And so long as you remain unclaimed, I can gift you the power to unlock these orbs. They come at a great cost, which you will likely hate me for, but I promise the rewards will be worth it by the end."

"If I'm so free, then," *I had assumed I was claimed by The Merchant.* I had wanted to say all this, but instead, what came out of my mouth was, "Why haven't the other gods claimed me?"

The god laughed, but there was no joy in it.

But instead of his voice, I heard someone else. {*Why would you want someone to claim you? Don't you want to be free?*}

Doubt soured my mind. *Am I actually unclaimed? What does that even mean?*

"Oh, I am certain that both Malikap and Aurentum have their greedy roots in you already, but I am not claiming you, not in the least. You can do whatever you want with my gift, even if you refuse it. All I ask is that you open one orb before you do." Rellum held his hand aloft, and I could tell he was about to leave.

"Wait, wait. What if I don't want to do this? Can't you find someone else? What about that Klericho guy? I know he worships you."

"Klericho is on his last run; as valuable as he is to me, he is not the right one for the job. This is a chance to restore balance to Aerlyn and perhaps uncover the truth behind the city's fall." He paused, his eyes radiant now, the stars burning so brightly I had to look away. "Refusing could mean leaving the dungeon's curse unchecked, dooming countless future adventurers to the same peril. What Penitent could refuse such an opportunity to prove their worth?"

{Do you even want to prove your worth? People who end up here are worth less than nothing. But I know what you are worth. Do not trust Rellum.} That voice spoke again, insidious and resonating, making me doubt myself.

What do I want?

"Are you real?" I said, a thought jumping to my mind, and a sudden spark of anger unleashed itself from the depths of my shattered memories. "Are you actually real? I could wrap my head around the Merchant and Penance being real, but you? How is the world so broken if you're real?"

"You want a sophisticated answer, but that's a question best searched for on your own. If I handed you the answer now, what would be the point of your journey here in Penance? Now, tut-tut, you have your tasks." He paused, staring above me at Crystal.

"Elizabeth, be a dear and help our friend complete this quest. Perhaps he will find the answer he seeks while he does."

Quest Log

Quest Name: [Fix the Floor]

- **Type:** Floor

- **Description:** Use the <Aerlyntium> to restore the second floor to its original state

Reward:

- Access to the third floor

- Access to new Boons

- Access to new merchants

- ????

Rellum disappeared in a puff of silver smoke, the golden light fading. And then, everything returned to the room. A thousand questions flashed through my mind as the deity I had once believed did not exist vanished from my sight.

How could he be real with how horrid the world is? By what right did he stand with all his accolades of purity while his churches continued to crush the downtrodden and push up the affluent?

How could he exist when everything the church taught was wrong?

How much money did the royal court waste on Queen Jamie...

And then, as randomly as always, a Memory Core descended from the ceiling.

{Memory Core 10/???}
{Would you like to view the memory?}
{Y/N}

I stared at it, not really in the mood for a trip down a memory lane I didn't remember, but I wasn't about to test what would happen if I said no to one either.

Chapter Forty-One
Lullaby

The palace walls glistened in the mid-morning dew as I watched through the wrought-iron fence gating in the courtyard. The fence gates opened and closed like a slumbering dragon, with the grating sound of the iron gates crashing back and forth as couriers, merchants, and dignitaries left for their morning duties after the prior day's festivities. I sat on my bench, hoping for an easy mark. The booming laughter of aristocrats without a care in the world emanated from behind silken-covered tarps as their drivers and guards led them away from the stables. Some groups left on foot, unusual for high society affairs but almost common in the early morning rush to leave.

The gates would close for a few hours until lunchtime for morning patrol at the top of the hour. As the final group left the safety of the palace, and the iron gates clinked close with a finality befitting royalty, I saw my mark. A tiny waif of a woman, it was clear she did not belong to the group she was coupled with. Her robes were a shade off, and that low-born group of wealthy merchants carried themselves off with a false sense of superiority that the woman failed to match. She was a person of purpose. Someone who came into the world knowing that every moment of her life was on a collision course with destiny. Her hair sparkled with the sheen that only came from upper-class pampering. And the way she slunk off alone down an alleyway only spoke to her lack of knowledge in debauchery. In short, she was a rank amateur up against a primordial pro. Or so I thought.

As I slinked down the alleyway toward my hapless victim, I was caught up in the idea that I was more intelligent and more aware of the situation than my victim possibly could be, which was how she managed to get the drop on me.

"Why are you following me?" She looked up at me with powerfully bright brown eyes that sang like a song of innocence that belied the cunning she so clearly had. Still, with her eyes focused on my face and not my hands, I moved closer and swiped a few things from her hands and bags.

The first rule of deception is to keep them surprised and focused everywhere you aren't.

"Oh, just a bit of window shopping. Not many pretty travelers like yourself are heading into clandestine alleyways. Name's Rod, your Majesty." The shock on her face was worth blowing any advantage that knowledge would have gained me. But how the new queen had escaped her confines and handlers, I didn't know. Honestly, something about it didn't sit right with me.

"Shh, not so loud. No one can know I'm here, or they'll force me back into the palace." She placed her hand against my mouth. A faint blush was playing on her cheeks, hidden by the cowl. A scowl played on her lips despite it. She turned as if to walk away from me.

"Now hold on, I know your secret, and I haven't gone blabbing to the nearest guard... yet. What's in it for me to keep your secret?" I played with the ring I "found" in her possession. It tingled in my hands as if there was more to it than gold and precious gemstones. I could feel the ring urging me to place it on a finger. *Is that magic?* I took it out and stared through the hole. The new queen looked at me as if confused that I would brazenly parade around the item I stole from her. I laughed and put it in my pocket. "I wonder how much the queen's jewelry will fetch me on the black market. Thank you for such an excellent opportunity to enhance my wealth. I miss eating solid food. Now that you are queen, will taxes lessen or increase? Starving the peasants for money only works for so long, y'know?"

Panic set in as she stared at the pocket where I kept my ill-gotten goods. "Look," The Queen said," I don't know what you think you're doing, but that ring isn't as valuable as you think."

"Don't insult my intelligence. I'm destitute, not stupid."

"Fine, since you truly know who I am, return my property. It's dangerous in the wrong hands." She said, "I'd hate to see you get killed over something as trivial as money. She clicked her fingers as if it was an afterthought, and a bag of coins appeared, falling to the ground with a clink. Without even thinking, I dove for the bag of coins. It was more money than I had ever seen. 50 Aurums. Most gold coins flowing through the city weren't real gold, but an alloy made to be lighter and cheaper for everyday commerce. The palace, however, used magic to create sturdy pure gold coins called Aurums worth 1000 gold coins each. It was enough to buy medicine and solid food for a year. I was sure it would be gone by the end of the next day if my father found it, that is...

The queen pulled back her hood, but I spat and threw the coins back at her before she could do anything. "I don't want your blood money. We starve while you parade around with your fancy titles and waste an entire smaller kingdom's worth of gold for your ascension. " I spat again. I really should have taken the money, but I was angry now.

"If I had a say, we would've spent nothing on this. I didn't ask to be queen. "

"And yet you are, and instead of fixing things, you let your father remain in power and run away to the city pretending to be a merchant's daughter." I was disgusted by her. What kind of human flaunts the level of wealth she has around and then pretends to be the victim? "It's been a week. One week since you ascended, and nothing has changed. My parents-."

~~~~~~~{Memory Core 10 End}~~~~~~~

</div>

The memory faded, and I screamed in frustration. Why did it cut out in the middle of our argument? And yet, her blush froze in my mind, angelic and pleading. I was out of my mind. She was a queen, and I was daydreaming about her smile like a love-sick puppy waiting for her master to come home. It was like she was now branded indelibly to the membranes of my mind; I closed my eyes and saw nothing but her.

In the memory, I was angry at her. She was the new queen, the one primarily responsible for my predicament, and I hated her. But simultaneously, as much as I wanted to be angry, for once, I couldn't get angry again.

As if saving me from my inability to control my emotions, a new notification came in, but it wasn't Crystal.

{For unlocking 10 Memory Cores, you have received 2 Overcharge Rings. This allows you to Overcharge Magical spells for different, more powerful effects. 30/30 charges.}

"Wait, what?" I looked at the rings as they appeared in the palm of my hand. *Fat lot of good this will do me. I haven't even gotten a magical class yet.* I would need to put them in the vault if I could even remember.

As I stared at the rings, I asked Crystal a question, my conflicting emotions distracted. "Hey, Crystal, Elizabeth, whatever your name is. Any idea what these rings are, or why I got them from my Memory Cores?"

[Memory Cores?] She questioned.

"Yeah, those orbs that fall from the sky and make me relieve memories. I just got my tenth, and it gave me these rings. I can't even use them."

[I don't know what you are talking about, I haven't seen any.] I froze, my face contorting. *She hasn't seen any?*

"And let me guess, you haven't seen me pause for minutes at a time while I relieve my past?"

[To my knowledge, no such event has occurred. It's a little troubling, if I'm being honest.] She paused as if considering something. I was about to interrupt when she finally said, [Also, my name is Elizabeth, but it has been a very, very long time since anyone has referred to me by that name. I do not care which you use, just be consistent.]

I paused, considering my words carefully. "Why would you keep that from me? It would have probably stopped me from going on that stupid tirade." I felt a pit forming in my stomach. *Am I the baddie?* "I'm so sorry. I was a jerk earlier. You had every right to vanish on me."

Crystal, or Elizabeth, flashed the angry red that told me she was mad, but then it passed. [Yes, you were a jerk but thank you for the apology. We have much to discuss now that Rellum has made his move. What do you know about the Creation of Penance?]

I blinked. "To be honest, apart from what the Magical Mural said about Penance, all I know is the nursery rhyme." And then, for the second time that day, a Memory Core formed, taking me back, further back than I had gone before.

{Memory Core 11/???}
{Would you like to view the memory?}
{Y/N}

~~~~~~{Memory Core 11 Start}~~~~~~

I was a little kid, maybe 3 or 4, and my mother had tucked me into bed. As my eyes closed, she began to croon.

"Two aurums, two aurums, you leave for the Merchant.

Two aurums, two aurums, you leave for the soul.

In Penance, the lost are a servant.

In Penance, in Penance, they all seek control.

The Penitent, the Penitent, no choice but to change;

The Penitent, the Penitent, they want to enrage

Rellum, Rellum, he wants to defame,

Rellum, Rellum, he wants to inflame.

Aurentum, Aurentum, all trapped in a cage.

Aurentum, Aurentum, the dungeon he must engage.

The Penitent, the Penitent, they want to enrage

The Penitent, the Penitent, no choice but to change;

In Penance, in Penance, Aurentum will control.

In Penance, In Penance, the lost are a servant.

Two aurums, two aurums, you leave for the soul.

Two aurums, two aurums, you leave for the Merchant."

As her singing faded, I drifted off to sleep, but instead of dreaming, I found myself standing beneath Elizabeth.

~~~~~~~{Memory Core 11 End}~~~~~~~

[He is trapped here, too. But by climbing the levels, there is every risk he can find his way to you and attempt to establish control of you. That must not happen. If he gains a foothold, there is no telling how insidious his power over you will be. If we hope to leave here, we need to...] I stood shocked as the memory of my mother faded. My memories and emotions disappeared through my hands as if they were a sieve for sifting sand at the beach.

[Were you even paying attention?] Elizabeth said to me. I shook my head no.

"You saw the Memory Core form; you even told me it was number eleven. Why are you even mad at me? It's not like I can control them."

[I don't know what you are talking about.]

"The Memory Cores. I just mentioned them! Those orbs descend from the ceiling and allow me to relive my memory. I've found 11 of them?"

"I don't remember you mentioning them at all." *What? What is going on here?*

Chapter Forty-Two
Aerlyntium

"Elizabeth. We were just talking. We just had the same conversation twice. You don't remember?"

[I am sorry, I do not recall.] Her light then blinked out, for a long, long moment. Then, her light came back, and she spoke again. [You must claim the Aerlyntium as soon as possible. Once you do, we can repair this floor to its original state.]

"Wait, what?" I said, feeling stupid and out of my depth. "Elizabeth, The Memory Cores. This is like the third time we are—"

{STOP.}

The voice was deep and resonant, and as it spoke, a spike of pain stabbed in my brain. I blacked out.

The second I awoke again, Crystal started talking, our previous conversation, forgotten. It was as if she hadn't even noticed me passing out.

[The orb in front of you is called an Aerlyntium. It is where the city of Aerlyn took its name from. These magical orbs keep souls, materials, and even whole buildings intact in magical stasis. They cannot free themselves or be used by anyone other than those Penitent Rellum gifted it to. And now that you have been gifted it, we must fulfill the request.]

"And if I choose not to?" *Rellum, the 'hero of the world,' had brushed me off immediately. Why shouldn't I brush off his request?*

[Then you are condemning people to a fate worse than Penance. They face non-existence. And besides, there are rewards for finishing Rellum's quests. Death Boons, weapons, items. It's definitely worth doing what Rellum asked, if only for yourself.]

I nodded. I had a veritable fortune waiting for me in this treasure room, but more power and treasure couldn't hurt, could it? "Alright, what do I have to do?"

[Easy, touch the Aerlyntium. It will open, and we can start the tutorial when we return to the entrance.]

I walked forward to the floating orb and gently touched it. The orb slowly split into two, and the halves spun around, forming a vortex. The vortex spun and spun and spun. Until the two halves moved away from each other and started devouring the room's contents. I let out a frustrated yell. "Hey, no, cut that out!" I screamed. "Crystal, what are they doing? I needed that stuff!" I rushed forward and started picking up barrels of spices left and right. I tried to get to a few unclaimed weapons or crates, but as soon as I approached, the orb would swoop in and devour the items before me. Eventually, they had their fill of the treasure room, burped contentedly, and flew towards me. The item landed in my hand and then disappeared into my inventory.

I spent the next 30 minutes combing through the dimly lit remnants of the treasure room. Dust hung heavy in the air, settling over the scattered debris. There were about six weapons left, each one dulled and tarnished by neglect. I sifted through the remnants, the cold iron rough and gritty under my fingers. The weapons lay among scraps of rusted metal and crumbling leather, remnants of whatever the Aerlyntium had done to everything.

Don't get me wrong, I was happy about the arrows and the armor, but there had been so much loot for the taking, and I was left with a measly six items. I felt cheated by Rellum and betrayed by Crystal-Elizabeth, whatever her name was. I was beyond frustrated, not just with the situation but with myself. How could I have let this happen? All that money, gone. I should have just said no.

[I am so sorry. I didn't know it would do that. I wanted us to get the loot. That money would have funded our next 20 runs, let alone geared us up for the challenges ahead. At least now we know for the future. It will take a minimum of 5 more runs to get the Aerlyntium for this room, let alone any more we need to claim for other rooms.]

My face fell. "Other rooms?" I asked, feeling a new wave of exhaustion wash over me.

[Yes, didn't you hear Rellum? This dungeon floor is supposed to be smaller than it is.] Crystal explained.

"Oh, right. The 20 rooms thing. So there's potentially one of these for each room? That's like over 100 Aerlyntiums we would need to claim. Are they guaranteed to spawn each run?" I asked, trying to wrap my head around the monumental task ahead.

[There won't be over 100; it will likely be around 50. Only 10 of the rooms need to be reclaimed.] she clarified.

"Oh, that's a little better, I guess." I sighed, feeling the weight of the information. I was completely worn out. Every muscle in my body ached, and my legs felt like they could give out at any moment. The relentless pace of this Penance was draining my energy fast, leaving me feeling weak and on edge. The exhaustion ran deeper than just physical tiredness; it was an emotional and mental drain that sapped my spirit. Memories of past failures haunted me, while fears of future challenges loomed large. I felt trapped in a relentless loop, with no clear way out. It was hard to stay hopeful when every step forward seemed to bring two steps back.

"Crystal, what's my health right now?" I asked, trying to distract myself from my spiraling thoughts.

[Your health is currently 02/45. I would advise you to take your health potion.] she replied.

"Alright then, get me the potion. How much does it heal again? I don't wanna waste it like I did that regen potion," I said, feeling a bit more in control with a plan in place.

[It recovers 10 health.] Crystal instructed.

"So, no reason not to drink it all?" I asked, not waiting for a response. I pulled the cork stopper off and drank the entire potion. I glanced despondently as yet another Memory Core descended from the sky.

{Memory Core 12/???}
{Would you like to view the memory?}
{Y/N}

"No." I was tired of these orbs and more than a little mad at whatever it had done to Crystal. I was finally going to deny them.

{Would you like to view the memory?}
{Y/N}

"I said no." My temper rising. Why ask if I couldn't say no?

{Let me rephrase: You will view the memory.}

Everything faded away.

Treasure Room Aerlyn 1 of 6

Alice
- **Amount:** 1

- **Effect:** This is a merchant

- **Description:** This is Alice. She fell down a rabbit hole one day and ended up here.

Lanterns

- **Amount:** 5

- **Effect:** It's a lantern... What do you think it does?

- **Description:** A small metal and glass lantern with a circular bail at the top.

Merchant's Stall

- **Amount:** 1

- **Effect:** This will allow Alice to sell her wares

- **Description:** An unstocked Merchant's stall.

River

- **Amount:** 5

- **Effect:** Do I need to explain rivers to you, too? It's like a lake, but the water flows in a direction. Like, c'mon, man, it's water!

- **Description:** It's a plot of water. Connect multiple, and you've got a river.

Item Barrel

- **Amount:** 1

- **Effect:** Allows a Merchant to sell items at their shop

- **Description:** A barrel full of random items useful for the random adventurer.

Inventory

Items

Arrows

- **Amount:** 20

- **Condition:** 1/5

- **Effect:** Allows you to fire a bow

- **Description:** A simple wooden arrow with a stone arrowhead. Stronger arrows provide additional effects.

Iron Short Sword

- **Amount:** 1

- **Condition:** 4/20

- **Effect:** Deals 1–6 damage

- **Description:** A sturdy iron short sword with a simple yet effective design. The blade is sharp and well-balanced, perfect for quick strikes and precise cuts.
  Quote: "Careful, it's sharp!" – Four Fingers Lasalle

Iron Dagger

- **Amount:** 1

- **Condition:** 1/15

- **Effect:** Deals 1–4 damage. 5% chance to cause bleed

- **Description:** An inscription on the hilt reads, "Point towards the enemy".

Iron Great Axe

- **Amount:** 1

- **Condition:** 4/25

- **Effect:** Deals 4–14 damage

- **Description:** A massive iron great axe with a double-edged blade designed for powerful and sweeping strikes.

Iron Greaves

- **Amount:** 1

- **Condition:** 3/20

- **Effect:** Def +2

- **Description:** Sturdy and well-crafted iron greaves that provide excellent protection for the legs. These greaves are ideal for Penitents who engage in close combat.

Iron Plate Armor

- **Amount:** 1

- **Condition:** 3/20

- **Effect:** Def +2

- **Description:** Heavy and robust iron plate armor that offers superior protection for the entire body. Its reinforced plates and solid construction ensure that the wearer can withstand the harshest of blows.

Chapter Forty-Three
Zoo

~~~~~~{Memory Core 12 Start}~~~~~~

The day I met Peckolin, my life changed forever. Candar and I had been friends for a few months when, out of the blue, he asked me if I believed in magic. Even in the bustling capital city of Venzwincourt, where the air buzzed with the sounds of merchants and the scent of exotic spices, magic was a rare and whispered-about phenomenon. Those few who had witnessed it spoke in hushed, reverent tones, their eyes wide with a mix of awe and fear. There were few independent sages, alchemists, and witches outside of the royal army, and of those, fewer still displayed their magic openly for others to see.

Candar invited me to meet his older brother, Peckolin, who was returning that day with his Sagecraft degree from the Repository of Sagecraft and Doorways. Peckolin was somewhat of a legend in our circles, known for his mischievous antics during his time at the pauper's school. The excitement in Candar's voice was infectious.

He met us in his favorite alleyway, just off King's Avenue. The narrow street was alive with the clamor of vendors calling out their wares, the rich aroma of freshly baked bread mingling with the musty smell of damp cobblestone. A cool breeze brushed past, carrying with it the scent of that bread. My stomach growled; I hadn't had breakfast, and a pauper's school lunch was never filling.

Candar led me to Jim and Butchers Ale and Meatery, an overpriced liquor and butcher shop—an odd combination if I had ever seen one. We arrived just in time. A man matching Candar's description of Peckolin stood there: tall, with piercing red eyes that seemed to glow behind square glasses. His purple cloak, adorned with embroidered planets and stars, shimmered in the afternoon light. He wore a stupid grin on his face, and a liquor bottle dangled from his fingers as he whistled a jaunty, carefree tune. There was, oddly enough, a towel wrapped around his shoulders.

When Peckolin saw us, his eyes went wide. He snapped his fingers, and with a sharp crack, a shimmering door materialized out of thin air, the air around it humming with a strange energy. A faint scent of ozone lingered as if a lightning strike had just occurred. Without missing a beat, he walked through it and vanished.

Candar sputtered before he shouted, "Brother! You said you would meet my friend and show off! Show us some magic!" His voice grew hoarse with frustration, and I began to feel stomach pains again. This time, it wasn't hunger; my father would be angry if I got home late.

"Candar, I appreciate you offering to..." My excuse died on my lips as a man, dressed in a completely different outfit but with the same piercing red eyes, appeared running up the alleyway behind us.

"Quiet, you want me to get in trouble?" Peckolin said as he approached, before reaching to lay a hand on his younger brother's shoulder. "I'm not old enough to buy liquor yet, so I can't be seen with you in my official graduate gear."

"Oh," Candar said, deflating a bit. "So you're still going to show us?"

Peckolin nodded. "I said I would, didn't I? How would the two of you like a private tour of the zoo?"

Before we could respond, Peckolin got a twinkle in his eye. "The first rule of magic, boys, is that every spell requires a catalyst—something from which to create the magic," Peckolin explained, his voice resonating with authority. He held up his fingers, dusted with a sparkling powder that looked almost like glowing sand.

"This door spell is great because the catalyst is very small." As he snapped his fingers, a bright spark ignited, and a door shimmered into existence, radiating a soft, otherworldly glow. "A bit of Portal Powder™ on my fingertips, and then a snap of the fingers causes the door to appear. My portal takes me to my lair, where I keep anything and everything I need."

"Come inside, my minions!" He did an over-the-top bow as he held the door aloft for us to enter. The inside was a chaotic treasure trove cluttered with bizarre artifacts. The air was thick with the scent of aged liquor and musty books. A shelf lined with dusty bottles glinted in the dim light, and another shelf held what looked suspiciously like Red Dust, its crimson grains catching the light eerily. My eyes widened in awe and a bit of apprehension as I took in the room's strange contents. I must have been staring at the room and its contents because Peckolin was a bit upset when he said, "Hello? I asked what do you think?"

"What do I think about what?" I replied, snapping back to attention.

"My plan," Peckolin said, his grin widening.

"Which is?" I asked, feeling both curious and apprehensive.

"I'm not saying it again if you failed to listen. If you're in, you'll get to see more magic. If you're out, there's the door."

I hesitated, but then the thought of seeing more magic overcame any doubts. "Sure," I said.

Peckolin grinned and snapped his fingers. Another door opened on its own, and we were no longer in his lair. We were whisked away to a zoo, of all places. The air was filled with the earthy scent of damp soil and the distant roar of animals. The rustle of leaves and the chirping of insects created a surreal backdrop. I could see the dark outlines of enclosures and the glint of watchful eyes peering through the foliage.

The three of us were huddled in the dark brush underneath a gnarled tree by the Walrus-Bear exhibit, the growls from the nearby enclosure resonating in the stillness of the late afternoon.

"What are we even here for?" I whispered, my voice trembling with a mix of fear and curiosity, my mind racing to make sense of our sudden relocation.

"Remember how I said all magic needs a catalyst? Well, I need one for a spell, and it just so happens that the catalyst is the egg of a dragon-mane," Peckolin said, inspecting his fingernails for dirt.

I stared at him in shock for a long moment before his brother beat me to respond. "That's what you want? Are you insane? Those things are so poisonous our dead parents will feel it!" Candar exclaimed.

Peckolin glanced at his younger brother and then at me. "What about you? Are you going to complain too?" he asked, his gaze intense.

I shrank back under his glare, still uncertain about the man. "No, but I assume you have a plan to get the egg."

"Yes, and it requires three people," he said, shrugging his shoulders. "Here's the plan..."

I half expected the memory to end, but instead, I blinked, and it was a couple of hours later. I was extremely grateful I didn't have to wait through the two hours it took for everything to get dark.

We left the Walrus-Bear enclosure, which had finally woken up from its nap, and looked at us with uncertain eyes. The zoo had already closed half an hour before, the night guard not even bothering to look at the bushes we had hidden behind. Why we hadn't just waited out in Peckolin's storage room or somewhere else, I didn't know, other than his excitement at playing "professional hide and seek," as he called it.

Now that everything was ready, Peck put his plan into motion. Using magic, he turned two rocks into keys and handed one to each of us. "It's important that this goes off without a hitch. You take this key, Candar, and you unlock the lion exhibits—all of them. And you, um, what's your name again? Roderick? Roadster? Roddy?"

I gave him a confused look, trying to hide my discomfort at the name Roddy. I hated that name.

"And you, you go to the west side to the tiger displays. Make sure you release the ant-tiger. If it sees the dragon-mane, they might fight. I'm counting on it."

I gulped. An ant-tiger was a terrifying beast with orange and green fur, deadly pincers, and a highly territorial nature. Even getting close, it might decide to chase me instead of the dragon-mane, and then where would I be?

It took me a few minutes to jog to the west enclosure, stopping to glance at the liger exhibit. I tripped in excitement upon finally reaching the first of the tigers. As I climbed to my feet, I ripped my school uniform on a sharp rock that jutted out from the liger enclosure. The tug of the rock almost sent me sprawling again, but I managed to steady myself. I looked down at the tear, certain my father would be ripping me a new one later.

The poor beast looked lonely and despondent. It was old, maybe over 20 years of age, and had been the first creature Baron Jonelle had created for his "Monstrique" Zoo. I wasn't sure what Peckolin's game was here, but I had a feeling it wasn't just about a catalyst.

I unlocked the cage for the liger, but the creature didn't even bother to leave the area. I sighed, feeling a pang of sympathy for the old animal.

It took about 20 minutes to unlock every animal's cage in the menagerie's west wing. I hadn't heard or seen the signal that Peckolin said was the key to his plan. In fact, I was starting to get fidgety, and I doubted that he would even do anything at all to help us leave. But he wouldn't leave his younger brother, right?

Just as my anxiety peaked, chaos erupted. A deafening blast like a gong from the depths exploded above the zoo, a brilliant flash of light searing my vision. The shockwave hit me with such force that I was thrown off my feet, the heat scorching my skin. My ears rang, and my head spun as I lay on the ground, struggling to process what had just happened.

My vision blurred and darkened at the edges as the world spun around me. I felt my consciousness slipping away; the last thing I heard was the distant, panicked cries of animals before everything went black.

~~~~~~{**Memory Core 12 End**}~~~~~~

Chapter Forty-Four
The Best in the Business

[Rod, are you okay?]

"Yeah, I think so." But I didn't move, my body felt heavy, and my mind swirled like a drain, my thoughts fading faster than I could form them. My hands clenched and unclenched reflexively as if trying to grasp the fleeting fragments of the memory. Of all the memories so far, this one had made the least sense. My mind raced, trying to piece together the fragments of what I had seen. Sure, it was when I met Peckolin, but the memory had barely shown me anything. I didn't feel like I knew myself better or knew any more about what kind of person Candar or Peckolin were.

[Then perhaps,] Crystal said. [Now that you are back from your little break, we can go back to the task at hand?]

I shook my head one last time, trying to clear the lingering haze. The air felt cooler, tinged with the faint scent of iron and earth from the terracotta walls around me. I could hear the distant echo of dripping water, adding to the mysterious ambiance of the room. "Alright, how does this work?"

[It's straightforward; now that we've cleared this room, you've un- locked a new interface. An interface is like my parchments that float around, allowing you to see what I say. This new one creates a pattern of lines, and the Aerlyntium items will pop into place along the lines. Currently, you only have 20% of the room space cleared to build in.]

"Okay, let's experiment then. Take out the merchant stall and place it here against the wall."

[Sure thing, but you have to place it. I can't do that for you.]

Suddenly, a merchant stall, ten feet tall and twice as wide, shimmered into a ghostly existence. The wood looked worn and aged, its surface etched with countless scratches. The faint scent of old spices and weathered wood filled the air, evoking memories of the bustling marketplace at the second floor entrance. I ran my fingers over the stall's surface, feeling the grooves and indentations left by years of use, the rough texture grounding me in the surreal moment. Like Crystal said, it moved along these green lines that formed boxes. I could mentally move it from one line to another quickly. I mentally shifted the stall in line with the wall closest to me. A tiny wisp of paper scroll appeared near the stall, fluttering gently in the air like the ones Crystal generated. My fingers itched to examine it, but I forced myself to focus on the task at hand.

The wall was nearly 100 feet high and made of the same terracotta material as the rest of the city. An iron grate was embedded in the terracotta wall, rusty and ancient. Below it, a dry river bed stretched out, its stones smooth and polished from long-gone water flow. My mind immediately went to the "river" item I had picked up.

"Crystal, I'd like to place an item down: the river item."

[Sure thing.]

The most surreal experience of my life happened in the next moment. I was immediately enveloped by a block of water, maybe 20 feet long and 5 feet wide. The water was cool to the touch, its surface shimmering with an ethereal glow. I gasped, expecting the icy rush to fill my lungs, but instead, I breathed in fresh, crisp air. My heart raced with the surreal sensation of being submerged yet completely dry. It was even more translucent than normal water but moved quickly without dispersing. I fell over from the shock and involuntarily gasped for breath; instead of the deluge of water flooding my lungs I was expecting, I was met with fresh, breathable air.

I took a moment to collect myself after the shock of not drowning. And then moved the water into place. The strangest part was how the water remained solid, almost like solid ice, staying perfectly in place. I ran my fingers along its surface, feeling the chilly, smooth texture that paradoxically felt both solid and fluid.

It was as if the water had frozen in time. I decided to lay down the river spots, except after the second one, I reached the end of the space I had cleared.

"Okay, let's put the river back for now, thank you." I walked over to the merchant's stall, which was too big, and finally looked at the paper scroll. I was about to reach out to the scroll when it suddenly unfurled on its own with a soft rustling sound.

The parchment was yellowed with age, and faint glyphs glowed along its edges. As I reached out, a tingling sensation ran up my arm as if the scroll itself was alive with ancient energy. I hesitated, a mix of curiosity and caution warring within me. As it opened, a faint, musty smell wafted up, like old books in a forgotten library.

Next to each item in the list was a grayed-out image that looked quite similar to each item. At this point, it was clear what I needed to do.

"Crystal, Elizabeth, gah, whatever you want to be called. Can you summon Alice for me?"

[Sure thing.]

And there she was, a matronly-looking woman with a big smile and fierce eyes. She appeared translucent at first, her form shimmering like a heat haze. I placed her next to the merchant stall, and with a soft pop, she solidified into a matronly woman with a warm, inviting smile and eyes that sparkled with fierce intelligence. My heart skipped a beat at the sheer magic of it, marveling at the seamless transition from thought to reality.

She stumbled momentarily, her feet finding purchase on the ground, then blinked rapidly as if adjusting to the sudden light. Her expression shifted from confusion to recognition, a warm smile spreading across her face as she took in her surroundings. Her sharp and observant eyes settled on me with a curious, almost appraising look. Then, a crystal popped up above her head.

Alice's eyes darted around wildly, her voice rising in pitch. "What, what's happening? How am I not dead? I ran out of runs... Wait, is that my stall? Where's my banner? Hey, who are you? What's going on?" Her panic was contagious, making my heart pound. I put my hands up in a placating gesture, trying to calm her.

"Hey, it's okay. I'm a Penitent like you. I'm not exactly sure how you are here except that it involved that Rellum guy." I scratched the back of my head, feeling the weight of her confusion mirrored in my own. "I got a quest to activate something called an Aerlyntium. And that Aerlyntium contained... well... you."

"But I died. The Goblin King grabbed my heart out of my chest and crushed it in front of me as I died." Her eyes glistened with tears, and I blanched at the vivid, horrifying description. "It was my 100th run. Rellum, brought me back?" I rubbed my hands together, my eyes lighting up with a brilliant, albeit greedy, idea forming. The thought of saving these people and having them indebted to me filled me with a mix of excitement and ambition.

I could save all of these people, and they would be beholden to and grateful to me: discounts, free money, an extra hand for making my way through the dungeon. My eyes shined with tears as I imagined an easy future.

"'What's past is breakfast,' my dad always says. Let's move on from that existential stuff. You got a new lease on life, and I plan on breaking through this floor to the third. Maybe I can score everyone an exit off this floor, get y'all back on track to finishing or moving on from here." I said.

"What's your name, lad?" She said.

"Rod. Rod Argent, at your service. As soon as I get more of these Aerlyntium things, I'll get your shop set up nice and proper-like." I said.

"Well, Rod, if you're serious about this, I have a couple of special requests." She said and then continued after I nodded assent.

"I would like to claim the center aisle spot. It always gets the most traffic and would benefit my business." She glanced around, her eyes calculating, as if she could already see the bustling market in her mind's eye.

"And what exactly is your business?"

"Goblin steaks! The best in the business. I actually started the fad. We hunted them so much; it's part of the reason I lost so many lives. I'd clear the dungeon floor, kill all the goblins, butcher their bodies, prepare the meat for storage, and then sell them here in the Hero's Market. And then, when I ran out of material, I'd let the floor reset, go get more, rinse, and repeat. Of course, I had only realized near the end that I was digging a hole for myself."

I grimaced, the idea of goblin steaks turning my stomach, but I nodded. "I only have access to about 20% of the room. I'll have to clear multiple floors before I can meet your requests, but I'll get there eventually."

"Oh, okay then," she said, her voice tinged with desperation. "Do you have any money? My inventory is gone, so I will have to find my corpse in the boss's room, which will take a while."

I grimaced. "How much do you need?"

"Not much, maybe 50, should be enough before I can get with some of my old contacts if there are any around." She sighed. "There is no way I could get back into the dungeon without any gear. At least they gave me my shop apron." She held her hand expectantly, and I tried to hide my grimace.

"Here you go."

"Don't you worry, this is a kindness I won't forget. I'll be able to scrounge some food and return here within an hour."

[I'm glad to see you learn from your mistakes. You didn't even lie and say you didn't have any gold. You aren't even complaining anymore. Still, what's your angle? This isn't like you.]

I wasn't even worried about telling the truth here. My plan benefitted me, and it benefited others. "A little bit of it is greed," I admitted to her. "This will help me greatly, but I should've realized a while ago that listening to you was a good idea." The realization felt like a turning point, a small step towards something better.

[My last host didn't make it past the 3rd floor because he made the same mistakes. And wasted all 100 of his attempts. And after he got through this floor in record time. He was stubborn until the end. Now stop dawdling, and let's store everything in the vault and sell some stuff.]

You would think I would be angry that I had a limit to the number of runs, the fact that Crystal had kept this from me, or even that Crystal wasted one of those runs on a tantrum. But I wasn't mad; the new opportunity was everything I had wanted it to be.

Our trek back to the entrance was tedious. The maze's twists and turns were familiar yet no less frustrating in the dark. The air was damp and cold, and the faint rustle of unseen creatures set my nerves on edge. Even with the torchlight flickering, I felt like I was groping through a thick fog. After 10 minutes of stumbling around, I returned to the entrance.

I yawned as I returned to the entrance. I really was tired. I felt like I could sleep a week, but I didn't know how much it would cost me this time. I decided to pay Klericho a visit, as he was the only friendly face I knew. Hopefully, he could help me figure out why I was so tired or at least help me figure out what to do about it.

Merchant's Stall 1 of ???

- **Progress:** 0% Complete

Slots

- **Alice:** 0/1

- **Lantern:** 0/1

- **Banner:** 0/1

- **Barrel:** 0/1

- **Butcher's Knife:** 0/1

Quest Name: [Alice's Request]

- **Type:** Aerlyntium

- **Description:** Complete Alice's request.

Reward:

- A merchant will like you

- 10 Death Boons

- *I'm Rod Argent, and this is my favorite store in Aerlyn!*

Chapter Forty-Five
Run Fatigue

Ten minutes later, I sat at a run-down wooden table In Klericho's brightly lit kitchen. The smell of fresh bread and tea permeated the small, cozy kitchen, bringing a wave of comfort. The warm, golden light from a hanging lamp bathed the room in a homely glow, and my stomach grumbled loudly, reminding me of how long it had been since my last meal. Stumbling around in that maze took everything I had.

I took a long, deep breath, and my stomach grumbled. "It's called run fatigue," Klericho said, waving his hands dramatically. His eyes twinkled with the satisfaction of sharing knowledge. I leaned in, eager for any information that could help me survive longer.

He put a piece of bread in his mouth, chewed, and then spoke again. "There's a limit to how many rooms you can explore without sleeping or dying. Depending on the class, it's two rooms for twenty-five points of stamina. It's too bad we can't just choose classes. It always bothered me that I'd get a different one every run. Some have next to nothing for stamina." He paused, then leaned in as if he was sharing a secret. "That's why I bought this house, figuring it was cheaper than spending 100 gold coins every night." My eyes widened as I stared at the other man. My mind raced as I worried about how I would make it through this next floor, let alone future ones.

"Wait, 100 gold? A night? That's insane; how can I afford that? I barely got 500 from 4 runs through the first floor. That's insane. I can't afford that."

"Again, buy a house. It took me about 50 runs, but it was definitely worth it. I can't help you for free, but I can let you shack up here for, say, 50 coins a night. That's the best deal you will get on this floor. I'll throw in a hot breakfast, too. I gotta keep myself fed after all."

The coins were barely out of my inventory before I jumped onto the spare bed he pointed out, and I fell asleep.

<p style="text-align:center">~~~~~~~Morning~~~~~~~</p>

The following day, I yawned, stretched, and rolled out of the rough cot in the dimly lit, stone-walled room. I hadn't slept that well in years. "Death has been good to me," I laughed at my joke and, almost automatically, walked to leave the building.

"Hey, where ya going? You gotta eat breakfast." Klericho was right where I left him, head cradled in one arm while he lazily ate some bread. He pushed a plate of warm, crumbly cornbread and a steaming cup of Grezling tea towards me, the sweet aroma filling the air. He then gestured to the seat I had sat in last night.

"I stayed up late last night, and I can help you more than I have. Honestly, I felt bad about how much I waved off your abilities. Just because I failed doesn't mean you will. These crystals have a lot more power than they let on. When crystals meld together, we can form what's called a Chrysalis."

I gave the man a blank look. "It's like the adventuring parties of old before the king banned them."

His eyes searched mine for a glimmer of excitement, but I just stared back, unflinching.

I threw up my hands sarcastically. "Adventuring parties, woo!" I exclaimed, my voice dripping with sarcasm. "Seriously, though, what's the point?" I raised an eyebrow skeptically, struggling to hide my disbelief. "I just don't see what you can bring to the table."

"You know, I'm trying to be helpful. You don't have to be such a jerk about it. As I was going to say," Klericho's eyes lit up with enthusiasm. "Evans, my crystal, can share all the floor information with us," he said eagerly as if revealing a secret weapon. "We'll know what's coming, which items to go after, and how to quickly kill everything. The only thing I can't give you is how to beat that Djinn." That was huge. Knowing what each run had would make this a lot easier for me.

I sighed, crossing my arms. "Fine, I'll bite," I said, my curiosity tinged with suspicion. "What's in it for you?"

"Oh, lots of things, but most importantly, I'm coming with you when you figure out how to kill the Djinn. It should probably be on a fresh run, though."

We sat for around an hour at the wooden table in the dusty, candle-lit kitchen, talking about various strategies. Thankfully, the first room I encountered was universally seen as the most complicated of the rooms, but there would be at least three more of the same scope and size. Apparently, I had gotten lucky with how easily I solved it. Klericho recounted the harrowing tale of wandering for days on his first visit to that room, unable to find his way out until hunger and exhaustion claimed him. I didn't say it, but I thought Klericho's failure stemmed more from his intelligence than anything else.

I finally ate the meager breakfast, and my mouth watered. The tea, by comparison, was just, well, tea. Honestly, it was disappointing after how good the cornbread was.

I waved at Klericho as I left, rejecting his attempt to continue the conversation. I never liked long discussions, and an hour was pushing it. I needed to get out of there and do something active.

I wound my way through the bustling market streets, dodging vendors and navigating through the throngs of townsfolk, not bothering to stop at any merchants; I did, however, ask Crystal to store everything I had gained in the first few rooms on this floor, especially the Overcharge rings. With the information fresh in my head, I figured it was best to strike while the iron was hot.

Twenty minutes later, I was on the other side of the maze-like textile district, surrounded by the smell of dye and the sight of colorful fabrics hanging from the stalls. My hunch was correct, and I was back on track for clearing another room.

~Run 5, Merchant's Alleyway, Floor 2, The Fallen Merchant city of Aerlyn~

The moment I stepped into the new quarters, beads of sweat began to trickle down my brow. The stifling darkness of the previous room was now replaced by an equally suffocating sense of constriction as if the very walls were closing in on me.

The world seemed to cave in with every step I took. My throat felt parched and tightened, as though an invisible hand was drawing a scarf around my neck, making it harder to breathe.

The tunnel ahead appeared to narrow with each passing step, its walls crowded with a chaotic jumble of obstacles. Debris from shattered crates and broken weapons littered the path, making it look as if a tornado had wreaked havoc there. Hundreds of destroyed crates, stalls, and weapons lined the hallway.

As I ventured deeper, my mind began to play tricks on me. My breath grew shallow, and my heart pounded like a drum in my chest. Anxiety clawed at my insides, making every step feel heavier. My hands trembled as I reached out to steady myself against the wall of broken and discarded wood. The rough, splintered surface bit into my palms, grounding me in the unsettling reality of this place. I carefully navigated through a large gap in the debris, only to come face-to-face with a sight that made the circus-performing rats seem almost tame in comparison.

A gray-skinned goblin was digging through the debris for something. It was muttering to itself, oddly enough in common, and screeched every time the weapon it pulled out was broken.

"No, no, not here. Not here. Kingsley mad. Kingsley most mad at Thumbs. Thumbs need to find it. Find it." He screeched again as he pulled a sword from the debris. It was plain and silver with a black flourish on the pommel. It was a complete sword and looked impressive. 'Thumbs' then chunked it at the wall, and it shattered into a million tiny pieces. My jaw dropped. He kept digging, and I had half a mind to shoot it while its back was turned, but my mother had instilled in me the idea that anything with a brain that wasn't outwardly hostile, you didn't strike first. *Where had that thought come from?*

Dumb rule, especially in a dungeon, but this one time, I figured it couldn't hurt.

"Thumbs, is that you?" I called out, trying to strike a balance between intimidation and politeness. My voice was loud in the slightly confined space, and I braced myself for the goblin's reaction.

The goblin shrieked in surprise, leaping high into the air. It landed awkwardly, then quickly scrambled to its feet, brandishing a tiny dagger in my direction. I stifled a laugh at the little guy and then made the most critical decision of my entire dungeon career. I asked the goblin if we could be of help.

"Thumbs, yes! Thumbs help by strang-urr. Need Kingsley red sword. Have much magic. Help Thumbs!" The goblin's eyes widened with fervor, and it gestured frantically with its hands. I lacked the magical ability to find things quickly, but I hoped that filling my inventory with as many items as possible would ease my claustrophobia and uncover some valuable treasures hidden in the debris. The sound of clinking metal and the rough texture of splintered wood filled my senses as I swept my hands through the mess.

"Hey Crystal, do me a favor; keep the notifications clear until I've finished looting everything. Oh, and **Scan** Thumbs here."

I began frantically sweeping my hands through the debris, scooping up anything that seemed remotely valuable. As each item vanished into my inventory, Thumbs' excitement grew, and he started hopping up and down, his screeches echoing through the tunnel.

"Thumbs thinks Bowman has many powers. Fast fast. Items poof." I had to admit; even I was impressed by how fast my claustrophobic environs disappeared down to something much easier to manage.

"I'm sorry, Thumbs, but I don't think the sword is in this area," I said, disappointment weighing down my voice as I picked up the last broken sword. Thumbs' hopeful expression faltered, and I felt a pang of guilt.

Enemy Entry 0009: Thumbs! the Goblin Hoarder [Level 2 (The Third Tribe)]

Goblin Hoarders are amiable and nice. All they care about is hoarding all the loot they can. They'll go for anything, but they like the shiniest things best.

Skill Has the **Unlock** Skill.

Weaknesses

Put a gold coin down, then smash their head in while they are distracted, you absolute monster.

Stats

- **Health:** 5/5

- **Vitality:** 1

Item Drops

Thumbs' Dagger

- **Amount:** 1

- **Chance to drop:** 100%

Chapter Forty-Six
Minion!

A s if to confirm my words, Crystal made a chart appear:

"Yup, no blue sword. Tell me, Thumbs, why did you want a blue sword anyway?"

[Red sword, Rod.]

"Right, the red sword. But you don't seem like the fighting type, Thumbs. Why is this sword so important to you?" I asked, genuinely curious about the goblin's motives.

His three pointy hairs were sticking every which way, but they jostled in the wind as he threw a temper tantrum, wildly jumping into the air.

Thumbs squealed in horror, his eyes wide with panic. "Bow guy not scare. Not find. No, no, no, no, no, no. This bad. Thumbs bad. Bad, bad, bad, bad." His voice was high-pitched and frantic, each word a desperate plea.

"Woah, Thumbs, it's okay," I said, trying to calm the frantic goblin. "What's so bad? Why do you need the sword so much?" My voice was gentle, hoping to ease his panic. The truth was, I didn't want to help this goblin much; they were monsters, after all, but if I could find this red sword, it would probably be worth some amount of money. Maybe.

"Thumbs not know. Kingsley says red sword here. Appear after Gregory dies. Gregory lives then dies then red sword. But Gregory is not here today. Here yesterday, or maybe last week? No. Bad, bad, bad, bad. Kingsley lead Thumbs here. Say stay until red sword. Kingsley hoard all treasure."

"This Kingsley fellow took your treasure? You poor thing," I said, reaching out to comfort him. As I did, I whispered to Crystal, "Hey, what's going on with this goblin? None of the other monsters have talked. Sure, he's odd, but he doesn't seem hostile."As if in response, a quest appeared.

Quest Log
    Quest Name: [Thumbs!]
    Type: Minion
    Description: Help Thumbs!
    Reward: Your first minion!

[I was never a fan of goblin hoarders. But if the dungeon is handing you a minion quest this easy, I would pay attention to it, even if it is screaming nonsense. Maybe if you pull out a gold coin, you can get it to stop screaming.]

At this point, the goblin had descended into inaudible wailing, punctuating each silent yell with angry back-and-forth arm waving. I pulled a single gold coin, tossed it at the goblin, and said, "Do you like gold?" The goblin's eyes widened like ripples in a pond, and he nodded, catching the coin.

"Bowman has gold. Must help. Help. Maybe I can buy safety? Yes, yes. Thumbs be okay. Kingsley lots gold. Take Thumbs's 4 gold.. Sad. but now new gold. Not let Kinglsey take new coin." As he said this, he kept petting the gold coin with a reverence that bordered on obsession. If this was how the goblin reacted to a single coin, I could only imagine what he would do with more. I sighed, sensing the complications ahead.

"I'm gonna regret this," I said under my breath before asking Crystal something. "Crystal, can you create a little baggie, like the ones the coins sometimes come in? I want a bag of 25 coins."

[Sure thing.] The bag magically plopped into my hand, a soft leather pouch with a drawstring. I could feel the weight of the coins through the material as I tossed it to the goblin.

"Here, catch."

Thumbs' eyes widened in sheer delight. 'Joy! Joy, Joy! Kingley, no king. Thumbs rich. Rich, rich! Golds, golds, golds!' He danced around, clutching the pouch to his chest as if it were his most prized possession. The goblin approached me then and peered up at me with his comically oversized eyes on his too-tiny face. "Thumbs is me." He gestured at himself with his right thumb. "Me minion of yous." A magical light glowed around the goblin and me.

Quest Complete

I probably should have felt something at getting a minion, but all I could focus on was the fact that Thumbs kept changing the way he pronounced Kingsley? Kingley? Kinglesley? Whatever it was, it was probably the floor mini-boss. A mini-boss goblin, considering he had an actual name. *Couldn't there be more variety? I was getting a little tired of goblins. It couldn't be the real Goblin King, right?* I was interrupted from my thoughts by Crystal chiming in.

[Congratulations. You have unlocked Minions! Each floor has an unlockable minion, but there are also monsters that can be turned into temporary minions through certain means. Collect them all, or don't! I couldn't care less.] Seemed like Crystal was back in her sarcastic streak. I was trying to figure out what the deal was with the floating thing. Some days, she was quiet; some days, she was sarcastic; and others, she was monotone. It was like the Merchant was sitting at a desk writing with a quill and parchment, uncertain what lines to give her every time she talked. I shook my head to clear my rambling thoughts.

"Wait, there's minions on every floor? What's the minion for the first floor?" I asked.

Quest Log

Quest Name: [Thumbs!]

- **Status:** Complete!

- **Type:** Minion

- **Description:** Help Thumbs!

Reward:

- You have received your first minion

- They follow similar rules to Penitents

- They have a limited number of lives and respawn when you do

[Shhh, it's a secret to everybody.] I rolled my eyes at her antics and turned my attention to my gold-obsessed minion. He was making a stack on the ground, counting his gold coins. I don't know why I gave him my gold, but he was cute and could unlock chests. I'd been lucky so far, but who would know if future runs could guarantee me keys? "So, Thumbs, what do you like most about gold?" The goblin jumped as if forgetting I existed.

"Shiny Shiny Shineeeeey." The goblin threw the gold coins into the air, jumping up and down underneath it. "Miney, miney, Miney! I have the gold! Gold! Gold!" The goblin was already starting to annoy me with its sing-songy voice and repetitive words. But at least it would be easy to control. I grabbed the goblin by the hand and picked him up. He didn't even try to fight me, but he held a single coin and put it in his mouth. "Mine," He snarled through the coin. "Mine."

"Woah, okay there, Thumbs, we gotta discuss some ground rules if you're to be my minion. First," I said as I gathered up all his coins and returned them to the bag. "We need to talk about gold. It's yours, fair and square. Consider it your starting pay. But if you want future gold, you must do what I say. Do you understand?" The goblin nodded in my grip. "Second, you need to be careful; if you lose your gold again, I'm not replacing it. You'll earn new gold every time you pick a lock or loot an item for me, but that's it. And third, you stay behind me at all times. I'm not letting you get yourself killed and waste my money. Wait..." I paused and thought for a second. "Crystal. How do minions work?"

[Am I wasting my time? Why do I even bother with describing these things in the charts if you never even read them?]

"It's just there's always so much to do. And there's so many I lose track!"

[Fine. It's so simple a toddler could understand. You get the creature to follow you, and then it becomes your minion. It dies when it dies and respawns when you respawn. Each minion is based on a different one of the classes. Though obviously much, much weaker. Now that you've unlocked a minion, you can spend your Death Boons on making them more powerful, too] I could hear the frustration in her voice.

"Alright, alright. I'm sorry. I'll try to do better about reading them... but one more thing.

I had been so focused on the events at the start of the second floor that I hadn't been paying attention; in fact, I don't think Crystal had even mentioned how many Death Boons I had been gaining. "Hey, Crystal, how many Death Boons have I gained on this floor? With everything that's happened—the guard, the god—I must have earned some extras, right?" The long, suffering sigh that she let out made me want to tear out my hair. "Sorry."

[Please. I'm begging you, Rod. Read the charts. You have accrued 15 Death Boons since the last time you spent them.] I nodded frantically, worried she would flare the light again, but instead, she said, [Would you like to see the list again? There are several new options.]

"Yes, that would be great," I replied, feeling a surge of adrenaline at the prospect of new power.

Inventory

- **Death Boons:** 15

- **Gold:** 114

Items
Wooden Scrap

- **Amount:** 800

- **Condition:** 1/1

- **Effect:** ???

- **Description:** It's a scrap of wood. Little more than trash.

Broken Sword

- **Amount:** 20

- **Condition:** 1/1

- **Effect:** ???

- **Description:** Assorted broken sword parts. Hilts, blades, doohickeys. You name it, you got it.

Broken Shield
- **Amount:** 7

- **Condition:** 1/1

- **Effect:** ???

- **Description:** A bunch of broken shields. What are you collecting trash for? Are you the dungeon janitor now?

Destroyed Book
- **Amount:** 50

- **Condition:** 1/1

- **Effect:** ???

- **Description:** It's a bunch of scraps of paper. Literal trash. *Quote:* "Uh-oh! Someone burned a book!"

Decayed Spices
- **Amount:** 300

- **Condition:** 1/1

- **Effect:** ???

- **Description:** The sewer smelled better.

Stat Boons
- **Potency**

- Cost: 5

- Current Stat: 1

- **Insight**

  - Cost: 1

  - Current Stat: 0

- **Alacrity**

  - Cost: 1

  - Current Stat: 0

- **Vitality**

  - Cost: 10

  - Current Stat: 6

- **Finesse**

  - Cost: 1

  - Current Stat: 0

- **Arcanum**

  - Cost: 1

  - Current Stat: 0

- **Defense**

  - Cost: 5

- ○ **Current Stat:** 1

- **Magic Defense**

  - ○ **Cost:** 5

  - ○ **Current Stat:** 1

- **Precision**

  - ○ **Cost:** 5

  - ○ **Current Stat:** 6

- **Evasion**

  - ○ **Cost:** 5

  - ○ **Current Stat:** 3

Minion Stat Boons (Thumbs)

- **Potency**

  - ○ **Cost:** 1

  - ○ **Current Stat:** 0

- **Alacrity**

  - ○ **Cost:** 1

  - ○ **Current Stat:** 0

- **Vitality**

- ○ **Cost:** 1

  - ○ **Current Stat:** 1

- **Finesse**

  - ○ **Cost:** 1

  - ○ **Current Stat:** 0

- **Defense**

  - ○ **Cost:** 1

  - ○ **Current Stat:** 0

- **Magic Defense**

  - ○ **Cost:** 1

  - ○ **Current Stat:** 0

Player Classes

Mage

- **Cost:** 4

- **Starting Equipment:** Mana bolt spell, Wooden Mage Staff

- **Stats:** Vitality: 4, Finesse: 2, Arcanum: 8, Insight: 5

- **Penalty:** Cannot equip physical weapons, cannot equip iron armor.

Fighter

- **Cost:** 4

- **Starting Equipment:** Iron sword, Iron shield, Skill: Shield Bash

- **Stats:** Potency: 3, Vitality: 10, Finesse: 6, Evasion: 2

- **Penalty:** Cannot equip magic items.

Cleric

- **Cost:** 4

- **Starting Equipment:** Iron mace, Shield, Basic Heal spell

- **Stats:** Potency: 2, Vitality: 6, Finesse: 4, Arcanum: 6

- **Penalty:** Cannot equip bladed weapons.

Crusader

- **Cost:** 4

- **Starting Equipment:** Iron sword, Iron shield, Basic Heal spell

- **Stats:** Potency: 4, Vitality: 10, Finesse: 4, Arcanum: 4, Defense: 2, Precision: 4, Evasion: 4

- **Bonus:** Has the Guiding Light spell.

Conjurer

- **Cost:** 4

- **Starting Equipment:** Elemental summon spell, Wooden Mage Staff

- **Stats:** Vitality: 2, Finesse: 2, Arcanum: 8, Precision: 2

- **Penalty:** ???

Dungeon Boons
Turn-Based Combat
- **Cost:** 20

- **Toggle Active:** N/A

- **Effect:** Pauses combat so that everything takes place in turns, making natural evasion impossible. You must rely on the actual evasion stat. It can be toggled on and off.

Identify Enemy
- **Cost:** 20

- **Toggle Active:** N/A

- **Effect:** Enemy stats are highlighted and visible above enemies. Requires the Scan Skill to use. It can be toggled on and off.

Time Keeper
- **Cost:** 2

- **Toggle Active:** N/A

- **Effect:** A stopwatch shows the time in the upper right corner of your vision. Essential for speed runs. It can be toggled on and off.

Challenge Mode
- **Cost:** 200

- **Toggle Active:** N/A

- **Effect:** Enemies have triple stats and better weapons but drop better loot and more Death Boons. It can be toggled on and off.

Quote: "Challenge Accepted!" – Photonius The Dead

Chapter Forty-Seven
Thomas

"Hey! Why'd you get rid of the effects?" I said, looking at the smaller-than-usual parchment for stats.

[I removed them a long time ago, and besides would you have read them anyway?]

"Point," I said, conceding to her. However, I had been planning on reading them this time. Maybe. The stats and other things scrolled by and I mostly ignored them until I saw one that saw something about Goblin Ears.

I had forgotten about the quests, and a wave of uncertainty washed over me. How could I tackle these when each quest seemed so time-consuming? I had a lot of time spent and very few ears to show for it. Almost all the quests would take multiple runs, which was not worth it, right? Unless I was missing something crucial, but I decided to let future me handle that. Right now, I had to focus on what I could control.

The Bazaar Goblin Ears quest was potentially rewarding, but it wasn't a sure thing. I thought back to the goblins I had fought, recalling the gritty texture of their rough, leathery skin and the shrill, ear-piercing sound of their screams. The memories were vivid and unsettling. I facepalmed as it dawned on me that I could simply take a dagger and slice the ears off the goblins myself. The thought was gruesome but necessary if I wanted to complete the quest. I suddenly felt a lot better about them.

"Crystal, is there something I'm missing with these quests?"

[Yes, there is. Each quest is a quest line. The base rewards aren't good, but by the end, the rewards can be worth multiple runs of Death Boons. I would advise you to start taking them seriously when you can. In fact, you should take the goblin one right now.]

I nodded, grabbed the quest. And then I looked back at the stats screen, and then a thought came to me. "Hey, Thumbs, want to feel more powerful?" I asked, watching the goblin's eyes light up with eager anticipation.

"Thumbs like pow pow. Make kill. Make kill!" Thumbs hopped from foot to foot with boundless energy, miming slashing enemies with his tiny dagger. A manic grin spread across his face, revealing sharp, uneven teeth. The tiny thing would most definitely get itself killed, but I could give it a slight boost.

"Crystal, is it okay to level up Thumbs now? You said I should wait until the beginning of a run to spend Death Boons."

[Maybe give him some defense or health. You'll be fine. You should be able to pick up a few Death Boons between now and your inevitable death.] I soured as she proclaimed my death was inevitable. "I would like to purchase two level-ups for Mr. Thumbs in those stats, then." Thumbs now had ten health and a single point of defense. He was a lot better off but would probably still die quickly.

"Okay, Crystal, thank you. That was great," I said. I needed to remember to thank her more. Crystal seemed to appreciate kindness, and I desperately wanted to avoid another second-run scenario. "Thumbs, what can you tell me about Kingsley?"

"Oh, Kingsley is scary. Large. Large, large! He uses spears. Much size. Much size! Squash Thumbs, squash, squash, squash."

"Do you know where he is?"

"Oh yes. Follow, follow, follow." Thumbs took off like a rat spooked out of a kitchen by a broom.

I took off after the surprisingly agile goblin. He moved so fast through the debris that he seemed to be swimming through it. I crawled to the next open space and saw Thumbs standing beneath an Aerlyn orb, his eyes wide with fascination. The swirling colors seemed to hypnotize him, and before I could react, he reached out and touched it.

"[Your minion, Thumbs Goblin Hoarder level 2, has been captured by an Aerlyn orb. You must power up and use the Aerlyn orb to reclaim your minion.]"

I grimaced, realizing that Thumbs might be more of a liability than an asset. His unpredictable behavior was a problem I couldn't afford right now, with so many other challenges ahead. I grabbed the orb. Just like before, the Aerlyn orb shot around the room, creating a roaring whirlwind of energy. The vortex howled as it sucked in every item in sight, the sound echoing off the walls. Dust and debris swirled around me, and I squinted against the powerful gusts.

Soon, the orb floated in front of my face, and I reached out to grab it again.

Merchant's Alleyway Aerlyn 1 of 6

Thomas
- **Amount:** 1

- **Effect:** This is a guard.

- **Description:** This is Thomas.

Alleyway Torch
- **Amount:** 5

- **Effect:** It's a torch... What do you think it does?

- **Description:** If I need to describe a torch to you, we have bigger problems.

Guard Post
- **Amount:** 1

- **Effect:** This will allow Thomas to better defend the hallway.

- **Description:** An unremarkable wooden guard post.

Thumbs
- **Amount:** 1

- **Effect:** It's a goblin!

- **Description:** He's your minion, remember?

Doorway
- **Amount:** 2

- **Effect:** It's a door. When you open it, it magically teleports you to another room.

- **Description:** It's a white door with a metal handle. The pattern is cool, but since you don't even read these, ROD, I'm not going to describe it.

"Why are you being so passive-aggressive with your messages? I've been trying to be nice, and I read them this time—at least the Aerlyn ones," I said defensively.

[Oh yeah, then what's Thomas's job?]

I tried to look back at the parchment, but Crystal had made it vanish. "I forgot... But I read it!" I shook my head and ignored her antics, deciding it was time to place everything.

I placed the torches along the long corridor, and as the warm light spread, the space transformed. It felt more open and inviting without the clutter of trash, the shadows receding to reveal smooth, stone walls instead of the typical terracotta. The flickering torchlight added a touch of warmth to the once gloomy passage.

After going back and forth several times, I picked out a good location for the guard post, only for Crystal to stop me.

[You have only claimed 33% of this room's Aerlyn Space. Please claim more Aerlyn orbs to claim more space.]

I shook my head and headed back to the door to the "treasure room." I placed the guard post down and then put Thomas in the open slot for the stall.

The guard materialized, wearing the same clothing and armor as the other guards. He opened his eyes and said, "Halt! In the name of the Magistrate!" The man thrust his sword point first at me.

I raised my hands in a pacifying gesture. "Easy there," I said calmly. But Thomas wasn't having it; he stepped forward, the tip of his sword glinting menacingly in the torchlight, his eyes hard with suspicion.

"State your business, Mongrel. This is a private hallway for merchant use only, and you are not a merchant."

I considered casting a **Scan**, but the floating crystal above his head gave me pause. Why was he acting like the other guards? His rigid movements and bizarre dialogue seemed eerie. This wasn't the behavior of a living, breathing person; it was unsettling.

"Can't you tell from my crystal? I'm a Penitent like you."

Thomas looked up at the crystal above my head, his eyes narrowing. "Having that crystal is not an automatic rite of passage. You glory seekers are all the same."

"What are you talking about? I summoned you from an Aerlyntium orb. Look around—this hallway is deserted. There's nothing here! You're guarding empty space."

The guard's eyes widened in sheer shock as he took in his surroundings for the first time. His metal armor clanged against the wall as he stumbled back, disbelief and confusion etched across his face.

"Oh. I died." He paused for a long moment. His eyes were wide, and his breathing heavy. "I lost my final run. How am I back here? "

"It's a gift from Rellum, apparently," I explained. "He created these orbs called Aerlyntiums that allow me to recreate things as they were before the Djinn. These powerful orbs can restore everything that was destroyed, though it will take me multiple runs to complete the restoration fully."

"Rellum still saved me? I'm not worthy," Thomas murmured, his voice tinged with awe and disbelief.

"Hey man, no one is worthy; it's why we are all here," I replied, my voice carrying a hint of bitterness. "Not everyone even gets a chance to come here. We all have to prove ourselves, right?"

I paused, sizing him up. "So, what do you say? Interested in teaming up? I assume you're a warrior class, right? As an archer, I can't take any hits, but with a strong meat shield like you, things would be much easier."

For whatever reason, it was much easier to ask this anonymous guard I had just met to join me than to ask Klericho. But this would be more beneficial; I could stand to play it less defensively. I might make actual progress on this run now.

I watched as Thomas wrestled with his thoughts. His eyes flickered with uncertainty, but then, as if finding resolve, his shoulders squared, and his posture straightened with newfound confidence. "I don't understand how I ended up in this hallway. I haven't been a guard for over a dozen runs." Thomas said, a note of hesitation in his voice. "Have you seen my companion, Klericho?"

"Oh, yeah, I know him. He's running an inn back at the entrance."

"Lead on. I can handle most monsters here, but you can deal way more damage unless you're like that idiot. I've never understood his hatred of bows."

Sensing the conversation was finally over, I walked past Thomas and placed one of the two doors. Power radiated out of the room, and it was likely the way back on track to finishing the floor.

[And what about your new minion? Are you just going to leave him hanging out in your inventory like your third pair of cloth pants?] I didn't want to free him. All of the treasure in this room had been destroyed.

I shook my head and reluctantly released the goblin from my inventory, knowing he would be more trouble than he was worth.

"Thumbs was scared. Dark, dark, dark. No warm. No air. So Thumbs sleep," Thumbs said, his voice trembling with fear. I couldn't help but feel a pang of sympathy for the little goblin. Maybe I wouldn't do that to him again. It reminded me of the Plane of Torment. What had the little guy done to deserve going there? I smiled at him reassuringly and opened the door forward into the next room.

Chapter Forty-Eight
Oasis

~Run 5, Opulent Oasis, Floor 2, The Fallen Merchant City of Aerlyn~

I entered the room and was immediately caught off guard as I lost my balance and fell onto the ground. My starting spot started shaking, the corners of it collapsing and fading away. I scrambled quickly to my feet and backed away. The floor continued to collapse, so I yelled at Thomas. "Look out, the floor's collapsing." But I was too slow, or he didn't hear me because the man stumbled over the same spot I did but fell backward into the abyss. "Thomas! No!" The man screamed as he fell, and my pulse started thundering in my chest. "Oh no, oh no."

On the other hand, my goblin must have gained intelligence when I resummoned him because he jumped across the gap and immediately ran up to me and clung to my back in fear.

The floor collapsed under me, so I scrambled to my feet and ran. I had yet to look at my surroundings and wasn't given much time as my feet pounded underneath me. Even with the lack of time, I tried to spy an exit from the room. Thankfully, the floor seemed stable until I walked upon it, so I could change directions as soon as I hit my first wall. I turned right around and ran much the same space I did before.

As I was making my back towards the entrance, everything went from bad to worse. A dice rolled, and time slowed as I slid across the stone floor, avoiding the dagger thrown above my head.

I finally took a risk and glanced around at my surroundings—something I should've done much earlier. The room was large, much larger than the previous hallway, but still more akin to the treasure room than the entrance. A vast open expanse of the same crumbling tile made a crisscross pattern across the room. In the center of the room, shining like a beacon, was an oasis, a shining tree covered in gems and jewels on a tiny desert island surrounded by water. Between the island and me, a goblin threw daggers at me and fifty soon-to-crumble platforms.

I continued running in the same direction I had been and grabbed my bow from my back. I looked left again and cast **Scan** at the new goblin. The scan confirmed it was just like the other goblins though with a different name. The Goblin Trickster had 10 HP and its weak point was the ears, which were a blackish red, and its body stood too tall in the room, casting an ominous shadow. As soon as I hit the next wall, I had my bow ready. I turned around and immediately used **Aim**, targeting the Goblin Trickster's ears. As soon as the arrow left my bow, I continued my run, not waiting to see if the arrow hit the goblin.

I ran a few steps ahead of the collapsing floor but didn't risk changing my pace or path. For all I knew, doing something different would make even more tiles fall. When the next pair of dice rolled, I was prepared and used the time slow-down effect to fire off two more arrows at the goblin; this time, I knew for sure the arrows had connected properly because Crystal chimed in [Critical strike! You have dealt 18 damage. You have killed Goblin Trickster. You have received an Overkill Death Boon..]

"Crystal, a little help here. Do I just keep running? Do I head for the center? What do I do?" I screamed as I hit the wall again and turned. I was honestly afraid that if I let the floor collapse by the time I got to the oasis, the water would fall away, too.

[Do I have to explain everything to you? Just jump. You know how to do that, right?]

I felt a mighty need to facepalm, but I controlled my impulses. Instead, I took a running jump to test it out, and what do you know, it worked. There were three or four tiny tiles of space behind me held aloft as if by magic. I kept running and tried to judge the distance I could successfully jump.

I did a few more test jumps to gauge if I was right before I turned toward the oasis. I gathered up as much space as I could and jumped and...

Dived into the surprisingly cool oasis water. Thumbs shrieked and flailed as we landed in the water, and I had to grab the goblin to keep him from drowning. I hefted the lightweight goblin onto the island, water flying off him like a dog. He landed face-first in the sand and sputtered before lifting himself up. He then ran face-first into an Aerlyntium Orb for what wouldn't be the last time.

[Your minion, Thumbs Goblin Hoarder level 4, has been captured by an Aerlyntium Orb. You must use the Aerlyntium Orb to reclaim your minion.]

This was a blessing in disguise as a dagger flew through the air where Thumbs' head had been half a second after he vanished. There were dozens of Goblin Tricksters running towards me. I had no idea what to do with the most enemies I had ever seen at once. I started blindly firing with **Aim**, expending mana faster than I could recoup it. The enemies came forward as a horde, but the floor did not. I noticed that only the floor underneath one of the goblins was vanishing. What had the scan said? Illusions? I started using **Aim** and ran out of mana, so I kept firing arrow after arrow at the goblin, but it was futile. As the arrow that killed the goblin landed, the final brick between the oasis and the nothingness below disappeared. The water rushed out of the vacuum quickly, flowing much faster than I had expected. Running out of time, I grabbed the Aerlyntium Orb.

The orb worked up a frenzy greater than the previous one. It sucked up the water, tiles, tree, and even the sand I was standing upon until all that was left in the room was the singularly solid tile I was standing on.

Opulent Oasis Aerlyn 1 of 6

Thomas
- **Amount:** 1

- **Effect:** This is a guard.

- **Description:** This is Thomas.

Carl
- **Amount:** 1

- **Effect:** He's a merchant.

- **Description:** He has a weird tattoo of a cat that he won't shut up about.

Desert Island
- **Amount:** 1

- **Effect:** It takes up about 30x30 Oasis Tile spaces. To make it an authentic oasis, you can place a water tile in the center.

- **Description:** It's an Island. Duh.

Oasis Tiles
- **Amount:** 250

- **Effect:** This will allow Thomas to stay alive next time y'all come through the room.

- **Description:** It's a 1x1 foot square tile with a spiral pattern.

Thumbs
- **Amount:** 1

- **Effect:** It's a goblin!

- **Description:** He's your minion, remember?

I immediately placed three tiles down so I had more space to stand. I was worried about losing my balance and falling into the abyss below.

I tried placing the desert island, but Crystal said, [You have insufficient Oasis Tile to place the island. Please place down more Oasis Tiles in order to establish Oasis Island.]

As tempted as I was, clearly I didn't have enough materials to place the island and escape, so I started placing down the Oasis Tiles, two by two, until I reached the next door. I still had around 100 left, so I placed down a ten-by-ten grid. Then I glanced at the last two things on the Aerlyntium list, and I realized something amazing.

I was so excited that I broke down everything and built a bridge back to the exit. I booked it back to the entrance and pounded heavily on Klerichos's door. He opened it rubbing his eyes as if he had been asleep.

"Hey Klericho, awesome, awesome news. You won't believe it, but you gotta trust me, it's incredible. I've cleared the first four rooms! You've gotta come with me.

"Woah, slow down a little man. You want me to go where? I told you, I ain't setting foot in there ever again." He said.

"What if I could promise you a way to get more runs? I promise I can help you. Please trust me, if it doesn't work, I'll give you 400 gold, I promise. We will leave it here in the house. That way, you know you can trust me."

Klericho followed me, cowering in fear the whole way. When we got back to the Oasis Room, I stopped him. "Be extremely careful here; Thomas tripped and fell to his death here."

His eyes got as wide as saucers, and he turned to flee.

"Wait! Stop! This is what I meant. I can bring Thomas back. Wait!" Thankfully, my words didn't fall on deaf ears. The man slowed his run to a walk and slowly turned around. He stood in front of me.

"Don't lie to me. What did you say?"

"I said, Rellum gave me the ability to bring people back. My companion, Thomas, fell to his death in the next room. But when I grabbed the Aerlyntium for the room, those things I told you about, one of the items I looted was Thomas. I'm sure of it. If you perish on this floor, I can bring you back."

Enemy Entry 0010: Goblin Trickster [Level: 2 (The Third Tribe)]

The Goblin Trickster is a cunning and elusive adversary who specializes in illusion magic. Known for playing mind games with its enemies, the Trickster creates illusions to confuse and disorient, making it difficult to distinguish reality from deception.

Weaknesses

The ears.

Stats

- **Health:** 10/10

- **Mana:** 0/0

- **Vitality:** 1

- **Arcanum:** 10

Item Drops
Gold
- **Amount:** 40–77

- **Chance to drop:** 85%

Throwing Dagger
- **Amount:** 5

- **Chance to drop:** 15%

Chapter Forty-Nine
The Wall of Riddles

With the revelation over, I placed the Oasis Tiles so my companions and I could safely stand in the room. The tiles shimmered with a faint, otherworldly glow as I carefully arranged them, creating a stable platform. Each tile, smooth and cool to the touch, felt reassuringly solid underfoot. The surface of the tiles bore intricate patterns reminiscent of the Magical Murals, which seemed to pulse gently with a life of their own. It freaked me out for a second as I stared at them, afraid I'd trigger that awful headache. I was tempted to revive Carl, too, but I figured it was best to handle one person at a time. I decided to start with Thomas.

I placed Thomas down on the grid, and the plate-clad soldier burst into existence in a poof of golden smoke. His appearance was dramatic, to say the least. "What... What happened? One minute, you were in front of me, and..." He backed away, his armor clattering against the tiles in a symphony of clanks and clangs. The fear in his eyes was unmistakable; his usually stern expression now shadowed with confusion and panic.

"Thomas, it's okay. I know you're scared, but it's okay. We're all friends here." I spoke gently, hoping to calm him down. The dim light from the torches cast flickering shadows on the walls, adding to the surreal atmosphere. Thankfully, he backed up towards the door rather than the abyss. I would hate for the poor guy to go through that ordeal again. "Thomas, you're alive again. Those Aerlyntiums I mentioned are amazing. I can get all of us out of this floor. Anyone who dies in a room while I'm in it gets transported into the Aerlyntium of that room. If you touch an Aerlyntium without the power Rellum gave me, it also places you inside the orb, but that's beside the point. I think Rellum gave me this power so that we could all make it past this floor."

Thomas finally stopped shaking long enough to notice Klericho. He stomped forward with what he probably thought was an ominous and domineering attitude. "Who are you?" he demanded, spittle flying from his mouth towards Klericho. His voice reverberated in the large room, amplifying his anger and uncertainty.

What was with my companions? It was like they were all determined to make my journey as difficult as possible. Klericho answered, "C'mon, Thomas, don't you recognize me? It's me, Klericho." I glanced at Klericho, who was fiddling nervously with the pendant around his neck, the tiny silver chain glinting in the torchlight.

Thomas squinted and then said gruffly, "Why are you a cleric? I thought you hated that class. You look weird, and fat."

Thomas finally calmed down. He was a hothead, the opposite of Klericho's cowardice. But with the two of us focused on ranged firing at enemies and Thomas keeping aggro, we would make quick work of more than a few foes. His armor, now slightly scuffed from the earlier fall, still looked imposing. Klericho, on the other hand, looked out of place in his simple robes.

"Here's my plan..." I spent the next hour planning our route for the rest of the floor. I would've shared the details, but the meeting got tedious. Thomas kept insisting we were overcomplicating things, and, well, he was right. Klericho tended to overcomplicate everything. His constant adjustments and hypothetical scenarios made the discussion drag on. We finally settled on a straightforward solution. Thomas would lead the way and get the attention of any monsters. I would kill them, and Klericho would help us up afterward. The torches flickered as we talked, casting dancing shadows that made the room feel alive with ancient spirits.

I had my companions leave the room, and I constructed the world's most precarious bridge. Each tile clicked into place with a soft, reassuring sound. I had to leave an empty tile at quite a few spots, creating a snaking path design. The gaps between the tiles were unnerving, the dark void below a constant reminder of the dangers we faced. Thankfully, my slowly forming dungeon party was smart enough to shuffle their way through the room without falling. Thomas's armor clinked with each careful step while Klericho muttered nervously. I held my breath as they navigated the perilous path, only exhaling in relief when Thomas finally walked through the door. The sense of accomplishment was palpable, a small victory in our ongoing struggle to survive this cursed place.

~Run 5, The Wall of Riddles, Floor 2, The Fallen Merchant City of Aerlyn~

[Aren't you forgetting something?] Crystal said, voice dripping with sarcasm.

I facepalmed. "Of course," I muttered, feeling a surge of frustration. I turned around and retraced my steps, the weight of my forgetfulness pressing on my shoulders. *Why am I always forgetting things? C'mon, Rod, get it together.*

~Run 5, Opulent Oasis, Floor 2, The Fallen Merchant City of Aerlyn~

The room was as I had left it, bathed in the eerie, shimmering light of the Oasis Tiles. The calm, reflective surface of the oasis water stood in stark contrast to the random holes in the world that led to the abyss. The radiant tree, adorned with glittering gems and jewels, still stood tall on its tiny desert island, casting a kaleidoscope of colors around the darkness of the room.

I summoned Thumbs, the familiar poof of golden smoke marking his appearance. The goblin materialized with a wide-eyed look, his hands already reaching for the unseen treasure that led to his former doom. His eyes, glinting with greed, locked onto the imagined loot just beyond the edge of the abyss.

"Thumbs, no!" I yelled, lunging forward. I grabbed him by the hand just in time, feeling his tiny, clawed fingers wrap around mine. He was light, almost weightless, yet his strength was surprising as he pulled towards the edge, driven by an insatiable urge to chase after what wasn't there.

The abyss loomed dark and menacing, a void that threatened to swallow us both. Thumbs wriggled in my grip, his eyes darting back and forth as if seeing treasures only he could perceive. His tiny body trembled with excitement and fear.

I tightened my hold on him, pulling him back from the brink. "You need to stay with me, Thumbs. There's no treasure down there. It's gone."

He whimpered, a high-pitched sound echoing off the oasis walls, but he stopped struggling. Instead, he clung to me, his eyes wide. The phantom treasure no longer lured him; instead, the certain death of the abyss stilled his eagerness.

With Thumbs secured, I took a moment to catch my breath, feeling the weight of everything I had just gone through.

As I was about to leave the room, Crystal said, [You are still forgetting Carl. I don't think leaving him sitting in the Aerlyntium is a good idea.]

I wanted to scream. *What is wrong with me?* I even considered helping him but decided it was better to help Thomas first. I shook my head, sighed, and then placed the man down. A burst of gold light and dust later, Carl stood before me. He was in his boxers and a black shirt-like thing that was open in the front.

[It's called a jacket, Rod. Have you never seen one before?] Her light glowed softly in the face of the man before he stepped forward. He was covered in markings, including a spider web on his elbow, and several others covered his bulky frame. His face got angry for a second before he took off running. Not even bothering to say thanks. I shook my head at yet another bizarre occurrence in this place and went back to my companions.

~Run 5, The Wall of Riddles, Floor 2, The Fallen Merchant City of Aerlyn~

Of course, the first room I encountered after assembling a party was one where no extra help was needed. The theme of most of these additional rooms so far had been magical or puzzle-based, and this room was no different. An elegant wall of various colors, ancient languages, and intricate pictures loomed before us, its grandeur both intimidating and mesmerizing. The wall was divided into seven sections, each presenting a riddle we would have to solve. The symbols and patterns seemed to dance in the torchlight, casting strange shadows that played tricks on my mind.

My heart pounded in my chest, a tight knot of anxiety forming in my stomach. Crystal chimed in, breaking the uneasy silence.

[This language is Djinnian. I can translate the riddles for all of us, but I cannot give you the answers,] she said, her tone dripping with condescension. [They all seem easy to solve, though, so I'll let the four of you struggle. It should be entertaining.]

Crystal's smirk and mocking tone showed off just how much of a jerk she could be. It was a small mercy she couldn't be heard by the others. Instead, I had to repeat her words back word for word.

"Riddle one: I am often seen in the mirror's gaze, higher than mountains, yet lighter than air. I soar without wings; I conquer without arms. When kings and kingdoms fall, it's at my beck and call. What am I?"

"Riddle two: I peer at others with a voracious eye, always wanting what's not mine. In hearts, I reside, silent yet strong. What am I?"

"Riddle three: I am a fire that burns within, flaring up at the slightest spin. I am often a guest in hearts and minds, leaving ashes and regret behind. What am I?"

"Riddle four: I am the king of procrastination, lover of rest. I avoid every task, preferring my nest. Time is my friend, for in it, I spend hours never moving until the end. What am I?"

"Riddle five: More and more, I always cry, never satisfied, no matter how I try. In the hearts of kings and beggars alike, I reside. What am I?"

"Riddle six: I devour all, never whole, always craving more; a bottomless pit, an endless chore. In feasts and banquets, I am king but leave nothing but emptiness within. What am I?"

"Riddle seven: I am the fire of desire, burning without a flame. In whispers and glances, I am called by name. I chase after flesh without caring for the heart, leaving a trail of longing and art. What am I?"

Crystal had me finish reading all seven riddles without giving us time to answer in between. They floated in the air, their words composed of giant, looping letters that shimmered and twirled, making them easy to read and hard to forget.

I turned to my group, my voice trembling despite my efforts to stay calm. "Anyone here good at riddles?" I asked, my eyes darting between them. Riddles and puzzles had always been my weakest point, and the idea of being thwarted by a wall of words filled me with dread.

Thankfully, Thumbs, despite his goblin nature and lack of intelligence, seemed to have the answer. His eyes lit up with excitement as he stared at the middle riddle banister, which contained the following riddle:

"I devour all, never whole, always craving more; a bottomless pit, an endless chore. In feasts and banquets, I am king but leave nothing but emptiness within. What am I?"

"Thumbs know. Kinglesy says. Say, say. Glutyeknee! Riddle is Glutyeknee!" Thumbs shouted into the air, his voice echoing off the ancient walls. He looked up expectantly, waiting for the riddle to be solved.

Unfortunately, his bizarre pronunciation was not accepted as the correct answer. The wall remained unchanged, and an ominous rumbling sound began to fill the room. The temperature seemed to drop, and the air grew thick with tension. I glanced nervously at my companions, their faces reflecting my own fear and uncertainty.

Chapter Fifty
Glutyeknee

A giant monstrous goblin, the largest I had ever seen, dropped into the room, nearly crushing us. Thankfully, time froze, allowing me to grab Thumbs and push everyone out of the way. Its bulbous weight jiggled as it landed with a thunderous crash. It roared, massive piles of spittle flying into the air and coming down like hailstones.

We dodged again, and I took a moment to cast **Scan**. "Health and weak point only!

Enemy Entry 0011: Glutyeknee *(Level 20 – The Third Tribe)*
   Weaknesses: Does not currently have a weak point.
   Stats
   Health: 150/150

We scattered like bugs, which was challenging in a room that felt much smaller now. Thumbs and I ended up on one side, Thomas and Klericho on the other. I nocked an arrow and let it fly.

[You have dealt 1 damage.]

I blinked in disbelief. There was no mathematical possibility that we could kill this thing. This was going to be the end of the run. It wasn't smooth, but it was my best run so far. A wave of sadness washed over me. But I shouldn't have accepted my death before it even came because of the armor-wearing guard with a helmet. Somehow, he had access to **Cleave**, and that was when the magic happened.

"**Cleave!**" Thomas shouted, his voice piercing with desperation. He waved his one-handed sword, slashing across the belly of the giant beast. Its stomach split open, and its intestines spilled out like glowing spaghetti. Which meant I had a weak point to target.

"**Scan** again!" I yelled, my voice breaking with urgency.

[Target the intestine with your attacks. They'll deal double damage!]

Glutyeknee's back was to me, but the intestinal trail it left behind as it lumbered away was unmistakable, a sickly green line shimmering in the moonlight. My breath hitched as I drew back my bowstring, the tension in my arm a familiar burn. This had to count. Every muscle protested, but I couldn't afford to miss. I released the arrow, a quick shout of "**Aim**" on my lips. My hand cramped, my arm ached, but it didn't matter—the arrow flew true, slicing through the night air and striking its mark with a satisfying thud. For a heartbeat, time stood still, and then the beast let out a low, guttural howl.

[Critical hit x 4! You have dealt 42 damage!]

In a few short seconds, I had dealt more than a third of the boss's life. This class was truly overpowered. *Man, I hope I never lose this class.*

The giant goblin roared in fury, its guttural cry painful in the cramped room. It tried to turn its massive bulk sideways to get at me, its rough, leathery skin scraping against the walls and ceiling. I held my breath, hoping it would get stuck or fall, but it finished the turn, revealing a gigantic open wound—a perfect target for my **Aim**. Seizing the opportunity, I sprinted to the back of the hallway, my boots pounding against the stone floor, putting as much distance as possible between myself and the thrashing goblin.

Around me, my comrades were equally proactive. Klericho relentlessly smacked at the goblin's heel with his mace, each strike a brutal crunch that slowed the beast's movements. Thomas, sweat glistening on his brow, aimed another **Cleave** near its kidneys, his sword cutting through the air with precision. Their combined efforts dealt 20 damage, a respectable amount for people who had recently died or avoided the dungeon altogether.

Without delay, I pulled back and fired, and fired, and fired until I ran out of arrows.

[Critical hit x 3! You have dealt 36 damage.]

I frowned, pausing in frustration. I reached again for an arrow in my quiver and hit only air. "Where are my arrows?"

[Arrows have to be equipped, Young Archer. And if you do not have them, you did not equip them. Ergo, you have left them in the inventory space.]

"Well, crap. What do I do now?"

[I suggest finding a way past his bulk so that he doesn't grab or eat you. Luck might be on your side, and time will freeze, or you could try to dash in and grab an arrow or two or three. The monster has 6 of them lining his intestinal wall like a clew of worms staked into the earth. Either is likely to end in your death, but it should be fairly entertaining for anyone paying attention.]

I gulped. The goblin was getting closer and closer, and all I could do to keep from hyperventilating was focus on the things I could control. I ran. I ran straight into danger. The goblin leaned forward, jaw unhinging, ready to swallow me whole. And then, the most beautiful sight in the world came into view: a comically large dice bounded around, bouncing every which way.

Time froze. I avoided the jaw-unhinging attack and slid underneath its legs, getting tangled in its steadily disintegrating innards. It roared and started moving away from me. Instead of panicking, I immediately grabbed as many arrows as possible and started using **Aim** with the rest of my mana.

[Critical hit close range x3. You have dealt 41 damage.]

By the time Crystal was done yammering, I was about to die, my eyes wide, staring, as the goblin leaned down with its giant face, ready to crush my body with its fists. I closed my eyes, not wanting to see how this run ended, but when no immediate pain came, I saw a golden shield covering me from head to toe. But that was all I could see as I had been swallowed whole by the giant goblin. The shield must have kept the goblin from biting me in half. I started freaking out as the claustrophobic feeling overtook me. My heartbeat raced, and my breathing grew shallower. Shallower. Shallower. I closed my eyes again, hoping the feeling would vanish, and then it did as I slid out of the monster's gullet.

Thomas had jumped and used **Cleave** on the Goblin's throat. Somehow, the carotid artery didn't get cut, but the esophagus did. The shield protecting me finally shattered, and I scrambled quickly to my feet, avoiding another swiping grab from the boss ogre.

The goblin roared, sending blood and saliva flying everywhere in the room. "You just saved my life. Thank you, man!" I shouted to Thomas. Cursing my stupidity and potential self-sacrifice, which wasn't my thing, I rushed forward and dove into the mess of intestines again. I grabbed for the arrows, careful not to break their brittle forms. They were guaranteed to be on their last breath. If I had a dagger, I could have just cut the intestines to pieces, but as it was, I was fairly happy with what I had done so far. Deciding to risk it, I scrambled, turned, and recast the **Scan**.

I grinned like a maniac. This boss had to give a great Death Boon reward. With the three remaining arrows, I pulled back and aimed three times in quick succession.

[Critical hit x 3! You have dealt 16 damage.]

My grin turned into a frown as my arrows turned to dust upon contact, striking the monster's intestines. I was out of options for damage. But I wasn't alone; just as I was worried about dying again, right before the shrill pain of panic set in, Thomas once again used **Cleave**, this time on the pile of intestines at the feet of Glutyeknee.

[Congratulations! Your party has slain Glutyeknee. You have received 4 Death Boons for killing a secret boss.]

I looted Glutyeknee and received a bag of coins. I shook my head. All of that effort, and I only got 30 measly coins. The loot stars were still shadowy above their heads, and they didn't vanish. "Hey, are you guys gonna loot the monster?" I asked.

"Yeah, on it," Thomas replied.

A large tooth-shaped dagger plopped out of thin air onto the ground. "Hey, Archer-dude, come grab this dagger. You were practically dead weight there when you ran out of arrows. We can't have that happen again. Besides, it's the least I owe you for bringing me back to life."

"I know, I forgot to equip my arrows out of inventory space. I should start doing that again."

[You have received a shark tooth dagger.]

Klericho, overhearing us as he came to loot the figure, asked, "What's an inventory space?" As he looted, a bag of coins jingled onto the ground. He picked up the pouch. "Nice! 100 coins. That's a good bit of change." He tied the strings attached to the pouch to his belt.

I wondered why they had so much stuff with them and realized I should have said something earlier. Man, I needed to be careful.

{Stop. Don't go revealing all of your secrets.}

Where had I heard that before? I wanted to share that I had them with this group, to say more about inventory space, but I couldn't form the words. Whenever I tried, it was like my tongue was glued to the roof of my mouth. Instead, as if my voice had a mind of its own, a lie slipped out. "Rellum gave me a magical item. I place all my belongings there so I don't have to carry them around. It's so convenient after how horrid lugging around crates was on the first floor."

"Yeah, at least here, if you own a space, you can stash your items there and return to whatever room you are in to move on. Still gotta lug stuff around, but it's safe, for the most part, when you own a place. That skill is mighty handy. In the future, we should just have you carry everything, and we won't have to worry about the extra weight," Klericho said, his face completely genuine.

"Okay, we've spent enough post-battle time chatting. Let's solve this room. As soon as I read the second puzzle, I knew without a doubt what all the answers would be. Crystal, repeat the next clue."

The words of the Glutyekneey puzzle lit up in a bluish-green color that radiated warmth. I felt secure in thinking beating the boss counted as a win.

"I am often seen in the mirror's gaze, higher than mountains, yet lighter than air. I soar without wings; I conquer without arms. When kings and kingdoms fall, it's at my beck and call. What am I?"

"The answer is the seven deadly sins: Pride, Glutyekneey, Lust, Wrath, Envy, Greed, Sloth!" I said all of the names one after the other. The parchments furled into scrolls and vanished. The writing and pictures on the walls lit up in the blue-green color from earlier. Then, a door appeared. I was suspicious of the fact that there was no Aerlyntium, but I could figure that mystery out later.

"Woohoo, we solved it! Go us!" I said, jumping up and down with alacrity.

Thomas and Klericho looked at me like I had grown an extra head. "What?" I asked, feeling a bit embarrassed but still exhilarated by our victory.

Enemy Entry 0011: Glutyeknee *(Level 20 – The Third Tribe)*

Glutyeknee is a fearsome Goblin-Ogre hybrid that will feast on your bones, your armor, and even your weapons. This beast is a devourer of all things. Do not let it eat you. Seriously.

Weaknesses: Attacking its stomach reveals its soft, gooey inside. All things are weak to evisceration.

Stats

- **Health:** 150/150

- **Vitality:** 30

- **Potency:** 10

- **Defense:** 5

Item Drops
Gold

- **Amount:** 30–100

- **Chance to drop:** 85%

Random Digested Item

- **Amount:** ?

- **Chance to drop:** 15%

Chapter Fifty-One
Horde

~Run 5, Goblin Gauntlet, Floor 2, The Fallen Merchant City of Aerlyn~

T he next room loomed ahead, a stark contrast to the previous one. Shadows danced on the elongated walls under the dim, flickering light of the Aerlyn orb, casting eerie silhouettes that seemed to stretch endlessly. The air was heavy with the metallic scent of impending danger, tinged with the acrid smell of goblin sweat. At the far end, the ominous dungeon door stood as a grim sentinel, its iron surface cool and foreboding to the touch. My heart hammered against my chest like a trapped bird beating against its cage. Cold sweat trickled down my back, and a shiver ran through me, but the sight of my friends steeled my nerves. We had faced worse before, and we would again. *But there are just so many.*

Quickly, I pulled out my arrows from inventory space and placed the dagger at my feet. Glancing around, I saw no natural avenue for victory apart from my friends. Fourteen goblins of varying shapes and sizes were bearing down on us—mages with staves already collecting mana, archers with arrows primed and ready, thieves blending into the shadows, bulky tanks prepared to take damage, and worst of all, the brutes—unstoppable wrecking balls of power. Then, all Penance broke loose.

The warriors and brutes charged, their war cries reverberating off the stone walls. The red beady eyes glowed above their cohort's crooked noses. Oddly enough, the brutes all looked identical, down to the gleaming bronze armor they wore. I took a deep breath, nocked an arrow, and let it fly. One. Two. Three. Four. Each arrow found its mark, yet the horde surged forward, unfazed. I readied my bow and cast **Scan**.

Enemy Entry 0012: Goblin Brute *(Level 3 – The Third Tribe)*
   Weaknesses: The eye. What are you, new here?
   Stats
   Health: 25/25

It was unlikely I'd get Overkill Boons killing these guys with a perfect shot, but I let off four arrows quickly, one for each brute, aiming for their eyes. The magical **Aim** shot true, and each goblin collapsed, though only two died.

[Critical hit x 4! You have dealt 84 total damage between targets. You have gained Overkill Boon x 2.] I stared in shock. *Klericho is insane if he still thinks this class is weak after that.*

The rushing horde of goblins stampeded over their fallen comrades. I took another claw grip of arrows and fired again. Four more fell, staggering but not stopping. The relentless tide pressed on.

[Critical hit x 4! You have dealt 56 damage. You have gained an Overkill Boon x 2.]

The goblins moved forward as one. Like soldiers marching towards the enemy line, these monsters knew their orders. Each one was ready to die for their seemingly inevitable goal—our death. The horde was upon us, but my teammates were not inactive.

Thomas grinned fiercely, "Keep them off me!" he shouted, his sword a blur of steel.

"On it!" I replied, releasing another volley of arrows. He was a force of nature, his weapon slashing back and forth with a precision I had yet to see from him. With fantastic speed, he used **Cleave** repeatedly with his giant two-handed sword, shearing through goblin after goblin. The initial wave of brutes was over, so Thomas was cleaving through the dagger-wielding goblins that failed to reach him before their head was cleaved clean through. Their heads rolled away as their bodies dropped limply to the ground. Klericho was perfect with his timing, deflecting enemy arrows that could have stopped Thomas with gold shields that popped in and out of place around Thomas.

His spells seemed to warp around Thomas's body, keeping him safe even as droplets of blood from their victims rebounded off the spell and onto the ground, leaving him pristine and dry.

I stood there dumbstruck as my team cleared the most overwhelming force I had seen in the dungeon. *How were you supposed to clear this room solo?*

"Yo, Rod, we could use some support!" Thomas shouted as he cleaved off another round of goblin heads. "They just keep coming. Those goblins in the back are doing this."

I pulled my bow back, aiming for the source of our problem. *How hadn't I realized that before?*

In the back were two mages, similar in size and build to Gurgle, repeatedly casting an overly complicated spell. Each time the spell finished, a new wave of goblin fodder formed. I cast **Scan**.

Enemy Entry 0013: Goblin Warmage Summoner *(Level 10 – The Third Tribe)*

Weaknesses: Their eyes. However, they wear hardened glass goggles to protect against critical hits.

Stats
Health: 60/60

I had relied heavily on my **Aim** and **Scan** skills to the point that I was paralyzed, unsure how to proceed, when I remembered my new item. I hadn't even bothered to ask Crystal about it, but I had, thankfully, placed it at my feet.

I took off down the hallway during a lull between a wave of mobs and Thomas using **Cleave**. I had my bow ready and used **Aim** as quickly as I could to kill two goblins on the right side of the hall.

[Critical hit x 2! You have dealt 36 damage. You have gained an Overkill Boon x 2.]

I didn't bother grabbing the arrows. I still had 18 in my quiver to use against other incoming mobs. I jumped over the corpses and readied my bow for the next group of goblins to spawn. I knew something was up when they didn't, but I didn't back up. The mages began a long cast, aiming the inevitably destructive spell my way. I felt the golden shield cover my body as I moved forward. I still needed to learn how the shield worked since I had yet to get to try the class.

A giant fireball as large in diameter as the hallway was wide bore down on me like I was an ant beneath a boot. The heat was oppressive, and I wanted nothing more than to curl up and protect my face, but my actual health wasn't dropping, so I urged myself forward one step at a time. When I was finally up close, I could see the goblin underneath his cloak and hood. He would be the stereotypical wizard of any other race, but his face looked like a hammer had squashed it, and his beard was singed in ten different places. His pockmarked face bulged with open sores, festering with comically gross ooze.

He channeled his magic through a staff twice his size and cast another fireball. This time, I was so close the fireball affected him and his friend. While Klericho's shield broke and my health started to plummet, I didn't let it faze me. I pressed forward, determined to end this.

Gritting my teeth in concentration, as soon as I was in range, I dove forward onto the first of the two goblins, knocking him to the floor. His staff clattered away and disappeared. Straddling him, I ripped off his goggles and started stabbing at his eyes with relentless precision, shouting **Aim** with each thrust of my dagger. A sickening pop through the air as I demolished the goblin's eyes and brain. Dice fell from the sky like boulders off a cliff as I decimated the still-struggling creature.

[Critical hit x 5! You have dealt 60 damage.]

I knew I had wasted more than half my stamina on just the one goblin, but I ignored my fear of running out and leaped onto the next one, using my weight to bring him down. I ran out of stamina after the third strike, and it took three more strikes to finally kill him. Gasping for breath, I began the grim task of gathering as many goblin ears as possible. We had to have killed over thirty goblins, which would net me at least sixty ears.

When I finished with my two goblins, I went over to Klericho and Thomas, who were slumped against a wall, exhausted. Thomas's usually steady hands were trembling, and Klericho's face was flushed, his breathing ragged.

"Good work, guys," I said, bending down to collect goblin ears. "Lots of loot to collect. Is this how you bought your house, Klericho? I must've found over four hundred coins here. We could camp out with three people using **Cleave** and a cleric, farming wave after wave."

Klericho nodded but didn't elaborate, his eyes distant. His face was red, and it looked like casting spells had drained him completely. I didn't say it aloud, but he was struggling even though Thomas and I did most of the physical work so to speak.

A few minutes later, I had gathered all of the goblin ears, totaling thirty-four in my inventory. Eventually, I dumped my entire inventory of collected items out in the room for Klericho and Thomas to see. They looked at the items, but they didn't find anything they wanted. So we decided to let me keep the loot, and they'd keep the gold. It sucked, but I was feeling guilty that I hadn't shown them the Summoner's Staff. I couldn't use it, but a future run probably could.

I finally approached the Aerlyntium, eager to see what this level would spawn.

[Error! Aerlyn orb does not detect enough material to spawn items. Please provide a source of the following material: Wood 0/25, Metal 0/25, Organic material 0/300]

I sighed. Nothing was ever easy with this dungeon. Frustrated, I spent ten minutes trying different combinations of items to trigger the activation.

Enemy Entry 0012: Goblin Brute *(Level 3 – The Third Tribe)*

Bulky and a hit taker. Don't let him get in front of allies, as they take half damage when he is guarding them from attacks.

Weaknesses: The eye. What are you, new here?

Stats

- **Health:** 25/25

- **Vitality:** 5

- **Defense:** 4 *(8 when guarding)*

Item Drops
Gold

- **Amount:** 15–55

- **Chance to drop:** 75%

Bronze Shield
- **Amount:** 1

- **Chance to drop:** 15%

Bronze Cudgel
- **Amount:** 1

- **Chance to drop:** 10%

Enemy Entry 0013: Goblin Warmage Summoner *(Level 10 – The Third Tribe)*

The most important mage in a goblin army, the Warmage Summoner, was always lonely growing up, so he started dabbling in friendship magic. He summoned a friend, and then one day, a dirty, horrible, evil, no-good, rotten human child killed his friend. He went berserk and joined the goblin military for revenge. As always in society, the problems come down to children being raised to be monsters, creating other monsters.

Weaknesses: Their eyes. They wear hardened glass goggles to protect against critical hits.

Stats
- **Health:** 60/60

- **Vitality:** 12

- **Defense:** 5

Item Drops
Gold

- **Amount:** 30–100

- **Chance to drop:** 85%

Mana Ring

- **Amount:** 1

- **Chance to drop:** 14%

Summoner's Staff

- **Amount:** 1

- **Chance to drop:** 1%

Chapter Fifty-Two
The Silver Mirage

Before we moved forward, I took a second to look at my inventory. I was out of the Aerlyntium supplies, which probably wasn't a good thing, but I had gained over 20 Death Boons from the previous room alone for a total of twenty-four. I needed to figure out how to get there quickly with a group willing to stay and fight for an extended period.

The next room we entered was surreal. Light shone from an undetectable source amid floor-to-ceiling mirrors. Everything was visible but reflected ten, a hundred, no, a thousand times over. The mirrors reverberated back and forth, creating an illusion of infinite depth. According to Klericho, the room was another maze-type challenge. Seeing my reflection in the mirror was unsettling; the new me looked gaunt and disordered, almost like I wasn't me anymore.

I was trying to figure out how to navigate the maze since every inch was covered in a never-ending series of reflective surfaces. It looked like there were twenty Aerlyntiums in the room, though I knew there was only one. "What was this place, Thomas?"

"The old room was nothing like this," Thomas replied, shaking his head. "There was a ballerina studio with floor-to-ceiling mirrors and a clothing store, but that was it. There used to be a door in the entrance that would take you straight here, but the Djinn's magic destroyed it."

He sounded bewildered, which was odd to me. It shouldn't have been his first time through, right?

Squinting, I realized we needed a plan. "Any bright ideas for making our way through this room? I'm tapped out."

"I say we just smash the mirrors until we find a path," Thomas suggested.

"Yeah, we're already in Penance. It's not like seven years of bad luck could make things any worse," Klericho chimed in, a hint of sarcasm in his voice.

I stared at my companions, unsure if they were serious. Their images multiplied endlessly in the mirrors. Then I spotted it: the real Aerlyntium. I could tell it was the real deal because it called to me through whatever power granted me the ability to interact with them. Given the room, it had to absorb mirror essence, right? Once again, it was up to me to solve everything. You'd think, with their dozens of runs worth of experience, they'd be able to handle the floors and know what to expect. But it was like their time in the dungeon had run through a sieve, leaving them bumbling through the dark.

"Wait here," I instructed my companions. I approached the nearest mirror and placed a steadying hand on it. "Crystal, I'm going to do something reckless. Can you be my eyes if an enemy appears?"

[Sure thing, Rod. If I had eyes, I would be happy to assist you. But as a floating crystal, I do not have standard senses to help you.]

I rolled my eyes. "I know you don't have eyes, but you can detect when there are enemies nearby. Just keep an eye out."

[Again, I am a floating crystal construct. I'm not human, by your words, and do not have eyes.]

"Are you ever going to let that go?" I muttered, more to myself than to Crystal.

[Nope,] Crystal said cheerfully. I shook my head, deciding to ignore her. Closing my eyes, I traced my hand along the smooth glass. Instead of letting the mirrors disorient me, I would let them guide me. As I moved, my hand slid along the panes, bumping off the glass at the joints. I hadn't done something like this since I was a kid. It felt meditative, almost like channeling my inner child—a desperately needed respite. A Memory Core descended from the sky. It had been so long, that the new light source shocked me, and I stumbled backward. I recovered and grabbed for the core, before stopping myself, hesitating. I gave the core a sidelong glance; maybe if I didn't touch it, whatever was behind forcing the memories on me wouldn't be able to...

As if it were reading my thoughts, the prompt came in anyway.

{Memory Core 13/???}

{Would you like to view the memory?}

{Y/N}

~~~~~~~{Memory Core 13 Start}~~~~~~~

I was a little kid again, transported back to a darker time. The small, dimly lit kitchen seemed foreboding and angry. The chair I had knocked over earlier lay sprawled on the rough, uneven floor, a silent testament to my scared movements. Neither of my parents bothered to fix it, their indifference a familiar sting. At four years old, I lacked the strength and coordination to lift it on my own, so it remained.

Bored and with nothing to do, I began tracing designs on the house's walls with my fingers, leaving faint trails in the thin layer of dust that had settled there. The walls were made of sturdy mud brick, their rough texture a comfort under my fingertips. This material was common in the lower-class hovels that crowded the city, a patchwork of despair and poverty. The coarse, earthy scent of the mud bricks and the faint aroma of the stew simmering on the stove for dinner, a blend of home and hardship.

As I traced the shapes, my mind wandered, imagining elaborate patterns and stories within the cracks and crevices of the walls. The cool, slightly damp surface of the bricks felt grounding, a stark contrast to the instability that seemed to permeate our lives. In that small act of creation, I found a fleeting escape, a momentary refuge from the weight of the world I was too young to understand fully.

I don't know how long I spent like that, circling the room. But I do know when I stopped. "Rod!" My mother screamed from behind me. She grabbed my wrist, jostling my arm hard. "Look at the wall! You've destroyed it!"

I turned to see the wall, covered in finger marks and grooves in the thin layer of dust my parents never bothered to clean. She lifted me into the air and dragged me to the bedroom, reaching for the club she always used to punish me with.

My mother's grip was tight, her bony fingers digging into my skin as she dragged me through the dimly lit doorway. Her long brown hair, the same shade as mine, whipped around her face as she moved, and her blue eyes flashed angrily. We both shared the same frail, skinny frame, a constant reminder of the poverty that shadowed our lives.

In the bedroom, the sparse furniture stood as silent witnesses to what was about to happen. The small bed, covered in a threadbare blanket, and the rickety dresser with peeling paint seemed to shrink back into the shadows. My mother reached for the club, her go-to instrument of discipline, lying ominously on the dresser. The air was thick with dust and the scent of my fear, mingling with the faint smell of mildew that permeated our rundown home.

As she raised the club, I couldn't help but glance at the window, its glass cloudy with grime. Outside, the world seemed so distant, so unattainable. The laughter of other children playing in the street starkly contrasted with the harsh reality inside our home. My heart pounded in my chest, and I squeezed my eyes shut, bracing for the inevitable pain.

~~~~~~{Memory Core 13 End}~~~~~~

Unlike after most of my memories, the emotions didn't fade. My hands felt clammy, and I struggled to breathe as I crouched in the dimly lit room. The memory replayed in my mind—Mom's face, a flash of anger, the club, and then darkness. *What was that? Had my mom really...?*

Crystal's shout jolted me back to the present. [Watch out!] Time seemed to slow as I dodged, just in time to avoid a dagger-wielding ninja in full black garb who slashed the air where I had been. "**Scan**!" I shouted.

Enemy Entry 0014: Goblin Ninja

Weaknesses

Eyes or ears. Some enjoy one weakness or the other, but this one has both.

Stats

Health: 15/15

As Crystal blathered on, the ninja goblin vanished. One second, there was one ninja and a small crowd of reflections; the next, an overwhelming force was bearing down on me. I started shooting arrows using **Aim** until I was out of stamina. Eight different arrows flew from my bow. Thankfully, the magic of the skill made them hit real targets and not the reflected duplicates. The shadow clones dissipated into smoke as the arrows hit home. None of the targets were the real goblin, so I slung my bow around my back and pulled out my dagger just in time to deflect a dagger strike from the real goblin.

Time hadn't slowed, but luck had been on my side. I could feel the poison radiating heat as it came close to striking my flesh. I shoved the goblin away with my superior size and strength, trying to repeat the same body move I used on the mages. But the ninja was too fast, dodging my lunge. I rolled onto the ground helplessly, sure I would feel the sting of the dagger in my back, when I suddenly heard a loud roar. Thomas came barreling down the hallway of mirrors, sword held aloft. He jumped, aiming for the goblin, but smacked straight into a mirror.

The distraction was enough. I turned over and kicked the feet out from under the ninja goblin. Leaning over it, I attempted to pin it down, but it struck out with its dagger. Time didn't freeze, and it slashed at me. Though my defenses took no damage from the strike, the poison attack stuck. In retaliation, I plunged my dagger into its eyes over and over until the loot stars appeared above its head.

My head started to fog as the poison worked its way through my body. My arms felt sluggish, and a fire erupted in my chest, radiating outward from where I was attacked. It was like someone had poured alcohol over my body and lit me on fire. My vision blurred, and I couldn't see. I knew this was the end of the run, but I wanted to loot the Aerlyntium, at least before I died. "Thomas, I can't see! Guide me to the orb. I think the poison is going to kill me."

A golden light radiated warmth, starting on my wound and pulsing outward. I could feel Klericho's magic battling the poison, but it was insidious. As soon as the magic faded, the poison rushed back, filling the void. I spasmed in pain, collapsing to the floor as the poison attacked my heart. It felt like I was breathing through a straw.

Each pulse of light brought a fleeting promise of relief, only to be snatched away by the relentless poison. My mind was a whirlwind of fear and pain, but somewhere deep down, a stubborn flicker of hope clung on. I felt rather than saw Thomas drag me through the maze of mirrors. Every movement sent waves of agony through my body. The fire inside me reached new heights, consuming all rational thought. "End it, please, god, end it," I cried, my voice raw with desperation. My skin scraped against the floor, as the fire scraped against my soul.

The reflections in the mirrors showed a distorted, pain-wracked version of myself. I could barely process the sights around me, but the surreal images added to my torment. Barely cognizant, I sensed Thomas grabbing my wrist and pulling my hand out to touch the orb.

[Error! Aerlyntium does not detect enough material to spawn items. Please provide a source of the following material: Wood 0/25, Metal 200/250, Glass 1000/1000, Organic material 50/300]

I screamed in frustration as my body shut down. The last thing I heard was Crystal's cold notification:

[You have died! End of run 5.]

Enemy Entry 0014: Goblin Ninja *(Level 5 – The Third Tribe)*

The Poisonous Twin of the Goblin Trickster. Don't get hit unless you enjoy fire spreading through your veins while your organs shut down and you suffer incontinence. What fun! Oh, and he can make copies of himself.

Weaknesses

Eyes or ears. Some enjoy one weakness or the other, but this one has both.

Stats

- **Health:** 15/15

- **Vitality:** 5

- **Defense:** 4 *(8 when guarding)*

Item Drops

Gold

- **Amount:** 15–55

- **Chance to drop:** 75%

Poison Daggers

- **Amount:** 1–2

- **Chance to drop:** 24%

Antidote

- **Amount:** 1

- **Chance to drop:** 1%

Leather Quiver
Stone Arrow

- **Amount:** 26/26

- **Condition:** 1/5

Rod – Run 5 Corpse

- **Gold:** 89

- **Death Boons:** 24

Items
Wooden Bow

- **Amount:** 1

- **Condition:** N/A

- **Effect:** 1–4 damage

- **Description:** A simple piece of rounded wood held together with a sturdy string.

Leather Greaves

- **Amount:** 1

- **Condition:** 15/15

- **Effect:** +1 defense

- **Description:** A worked and treated pair of leather greaves covering the waist down to the ankles.

Leather Armor

- **Amount:** 1

- **Condition:** 15/15

- **Effect:** +1 defense

- **Description:** A worked and treated leather vest covering the chest and arms down to the wrist.

Iron Helm

- **Amount:** 1

- **Condition:** 20/20

- **Effect:** +2 defense

- **Description:** A well-crafted iron helm that offers solid protection for the head.

Cloth Sandals

- **Amount:** 1

- **Condition:** 10/10

- **Effect:** +1 defense

- **Description:** Simple yet 'comfortable' cloth sandals that offer minimal protection but great mobility.
  Quote: "Don't worry, you'll miss sewer feet after an hour with these!" – Photonius

Throwing Dagger

- **Amount:** 1

- **Condition:** 5/5

- **Effect:** Deals 5–10 damage

- **Description:** A dagger designed to be thrown through the air.

Shark Tooth Dagger

- **Amount:** 1

- **Condition:** 20/20

- **Effect:** Deals 2–8 damage; 10% chance to bleed

- **Description:** A serrated dagger made out of the teeth of a giant shark.

Summoner's Staff

- **Amount:** 1

- **Condition:** 15/15

- **Effect:** Funnels magical attacks through the staff, changing them into different magical creature-based attacks.

- **Description:** This staff has two emeralds at the top, forming an animal head - I wanna be the very best!"

Chapter Fifty-Three
I'm the Best. Jamie, Run 2, Part 2.

Sweat flicked off the chain coif attached to my helm as I took it off my head and leaned back against the wall. My hair was matted against my forehead, and I wanted nothing more than to wipe the sweaty hair away, but I didn't even take the gauntlets off. Instead, I rested my head against the cool metal of the cleaner gauntlet.

"Man, no one ever told me combat would be so exhausting and gross." I groaned, slumping against the wall. " I don't know how the Kingsguard did it every day."

I didn't want to whine, but I already smelled, and bits of blood were stuck to the bottom of my boots and to my right gauntlet, where I had clocked a zombie in the face.

[It smells like success to me. And treasure. Loot the zombies, please!] Malice exclaimed, his crystal shining brightly despite the dark color.

I closed my eyes and took a deep breath, forcing myself to ignore the stench as I worked to steady my racing heart. After a minute, I felt okay to continue and got to my feet.

I would have liked nothing more than to go past the zombies and collapse onto my bed. Instead, I did as asked and got to my feet before trudging over and kicking each zombie in the arms or legs.

[You have received ten gold coins and one slightly used halberd, zombie not included.]

After I finished looting, I finally took a good look at the hallway, and my brow furrowed. My room had the same layout I was used to. It had a king-sized bed, five wardrobes, and giant glass windows to see the city. But outside my room was the east wing second hall, just off the servant's hall. In an act of defiance against my father for all the extravagant decisions that had torn our country apart, I had purposefully chosen the smallest royal suite. It was my quiet rebellion, a way to reject the opulence he valued.

And, somehow, he had agreed. He had let me use the relatively diminutive room.

I walked out, expecting the creak of old wood underfoot to be warm, familiar, and comforting. Instead, my boots met polished marble that resounded with each step, casting cold, unfamiliar, and discomforting sounds in the air.

Where the cramped, shadowed passageway of the east wing should have been, a grand corridor stretched out instead, bathed in white and silver. This was not the east wing's second hall. It made no sense; even if a giant playing dollhouse had picked up my room, they wouldn't have so seamlessly moved it.

Walking out into what had to be the west wing, I looked around the hall, wondering why the same number of zombies were in two different hallways. I turned right, heading for the main foyer. As I walked past the pristine white wood and silver chandeliers, their delicate tinkle mingled with the eerie groan of the expansive hall. Each step I took echoed ominously down the long, empty corridor, punctuated by the occasional distant crash of something unseen falling apart.

It did not take me long to figure out why there was a breeze. A musty, damp smell assaulted my nostrils as I entered the foyer. The air was heavy with the scent of mold and the iron tang of fresh cannonball wounds on ancient stone walls.

I stood, stunned into inaction, as I stared. My childhood home had been destroyed.

The palace creaked ominously as the wind continued to whistle through the holes. "What– What happened here?" I stammered, my gaze darting around the ruined foyer as I struggled to comprehend the damage.

[This is the future of your home, Jamie,] Malice said, taking on an unusually serious tone. His light grew brighter, elongating my shadow across the room past the shattered remains of my home. [That's what Penance is showing you. Your sins lead to this. Or rather, they could lead to this.] His voice dropped to a whisper, laden with threat. [*If you manage to leave one day*, you can fix it. You can change the outcome.]

I wanted to scream that he was wrong. That my home could never be attacked. That the city, the people would be destroyed first... My thoughts flickered back to my first view of Penance out of the window.

I spotted a bolt of fabric flying in the wind before me, caught by a few strands against a piece of splintered wood. I moved to the hole and grabbed for it. As I lifted the fabric free, I was struck by its unexpected weight. Each thread was soaked with regret and blood, sticking slightly to my fingers as if reluctant to let go of the tragedy that had been wrought upon it. The symbol, a dragon eating a Necromancer, was beyond recognition. A single wing remained, and the rest of the pennant burned beyond recognition.

I may not have cared for my father's choices, but my people... their plight gripped my heart as I clutched the pennant in my hand. *Had my poor choices, the waste of money, and my refusal to stand up to my father led to this? Then, only one choice remained.* No longer would I allow circumstances to dictate my actions. This choice—to stand and fight—was *mine*. I would break out of Penance and free my people.

[Are you done with the internal monologuing? So lame. It's way less cool than when I do it. Watch: Oh yes! Treasure! Killing zombies! Oh yeah! I'm the best.]

I fish-hooked my right eye at Malice. He had been weird so far, but that moment pushed it.

"Right, I'm the lame one." I scoffed, rolling my eyes." You just called yourself the best."

[Nothing wrong with stating the truth.] Malice responded with a tone that conveyed a scoff before continuing with his usual fervor.

[Treasure, treasure, treasure! Let's go kill zombies!] Wherever that serious Malice had come from, he was gone.

"Fine, fine," I conceded, my voice tinged with reluctant humor as I shook my head at his undampened enthusiasm. "But we need to figure out where everything has moved. I have a feeling the basement is no longer through that door." I added.

I pointed toward the massive oak doors that sprouted from the ground like the trees they were made from. Silver handles formed the shape of crescent moons, and the floor was slightly scuffed from repeated use.

As I pulled the door open, a loud creak carried through the hallway, seeming never to cease. If there were any nearby zombies, the element of surprise would have been entirely lost, not that I would have kept it long with my clanking armor.

I thought I had found my resolve, but thoughts fought at the back of my mind as I walked down the new hallway.

What am I doing? I was a terrible princess, an even worse queen, and now I want to play hero?

Though the door had been for the east hall of the silver wing, the one my room was supposed to be in, the one I walked into was not the silver wing. Instead, ornate gold chandeliers threw light to the floor, almost as if trying to replace sunlight entirely.

The opulence before me sparked a wave of fierce anger. Each golden chandelier, hanging with ceaseless care, each tapestry depicting the glories of past kings, and the gilded statues of saints and warriors screamed of the 100,000 aurums squandered here. This was wealth that could have sustained the pauper quarter for a decade.

The floors, inlaid with colored marbles from distant lands, shone underfoot, reflecting their new suns. The extravagance of it all contributed to the mocking parallel of the destruction outside. As rage boiled over me, this untouched royal excess, despite the destroyed outer wall, symbolized everything I vowed to change. I wanted to scream at Malice that I wasn't the problem—merely a product of my circumstances. It was my father who made those choices. Why, then, was I the one being punished? But I stopped myself; screaming would solve nothing.

I walked down the corridor, listening for moans, screams, or other signs that the undead were nearby. Nothing. I moved forward, Malice whistling some mad tune. "Hey, Malice, there are three doors in this hall. You pick two, and I'll go looking in one for treasure."

[Oh, umm, 2 and 3... no 1!]

I rolled my eyes but headed for the first door. The flowery pattern on the door reminded me of Agatha's room.

But it didn't make sense—her room was from the missing silver wing, right next to mine. Nothing was right here; all the rooms, everything about this place, was wrong.

I placed my hand on the crystal doorknob, marking it as a maid's room, and pushed the door open. *What was it Doctor Tot had told me? Gold for kings and queens, silver for royalty and guests, crystal for maids, and diamond for guards? That would probably be important to remember. —Or would it?* The layout had changed; surely the door handle system had, too? The door to the basement had been none of these, so I was sure to be on the lookout.

[Are you sure you only want to clear one room? There could be treasure!]

I was sure. For now, I needed to get the lay of the land and figure out how this place worked. Not horde resources like royalty always did. There would be plenty of time for that later.

The door swung open, letting light from the hallway spill into the darkened room beyond. Although lamps lined the walls, I could tell from the doorway they would never be lit again.

"Hey, Malice," I whispered into the oppressive darkness, "Can you do that thing where you generate light?"

He muttered something about a torch, and then a dark purple—but surprisingly bright—glow radiated from him. Stepping inside, I was overwhelmed by the stench of rotting flesh that overpowered the musty, long-unused air. The acrid smell of blood hung heavily, almost tangible.

On the ground lay a corpse, being gruesomely devoured by a limbless torso and head—a creature that had somehow managed to kill Agatha. The ghastly sight revolted me, and I vomited; the bile splashed against the inside of my helm and slid into my plate armor.

I immediately gagged again, unable to bear the sickening situation.

Driven by grim determination, I charged, my boots thudding against the hard floor, and plunged my spear deep into the zombie's ear. The sickening squelch of decay pierced the silence of the room.

And then, I felt the tug on my boot, afraid for half a second that it would be followed by a sharp pain as a zombie bit into me. Instead, I heard a rasping sound as the 'corpse' spoke.

The words were a hoarse whisper, filled with pain, "Jamie. Kill... me... please... kill me."

Nasty green veins ran up and down the woman in the purple light. I backed up until I stumbled against her dresser.

"Oh, Rellum, she's still alive. Malice, is there anything I can do?"

[Oh, sweet! Murder her, murder her now!]

"I— I can't do that."

[If you don't, she'll turn. And you'll still have to kill her. Besides, can you imagine how much pain she's in? Unlike you, Penance doesn't limit what she feels. Some people believe that it even enhances sensations.] His serious tone was back, and I eyed him suspiciously.

A moment later, he continued. [Oh man, I miss pain. So much fun.]

"Jamie, please..." The woman's eyes closed, and she started to convulse as she coughed and hacked blood from her mouth. Horrified and without thinking, I slammed my halberd straight through her heart. Her convulsions ceased abruptly, her eyes flaring open in shock.

The zombie moved forward on the halberd, reaching for me. I tried to back up, forgetting I was between my maid and a cabinet. I pushed against the halberd, trapping her against the bed. I knew what I had to do. It was the only thing that truly killed them so far. I clenched my armor-plated fists, pounding her head repeatedly. Each blow resonated through my gauntlet with a sickening thud. I thought the metal would dent or break apart until I realized that the only item that had broken so far had been the curtain rod.

I was about to talk, grateful for the distracting thought, but I was beaten to the punch by Malice exclaiming, [Baby's first murder, oh it brings a tear to my eye. I am so proud of you. I think that deserves 10 malice points.]

I heard a sniff as if he were crying, but my own shock numbed me to anything else.

"No, I–What? I didn't murder her; she turned, so it was..."

[No, she didn't turn until after you attacked her,] he said, his voice dripping with true malice. [This was a good thing. The more you kill humans, the easier it gets. Just let the rage flow through you; before you know it, Penance will be ours.]

The inky mist that always pervaded Malice's crystalline body seemed more tangible in the purple light of the maid's quarter.

I stared out in pain at the corpse of the Matron. A woman who was practically a second mother to me. *What have I done?*

[Oh! This was a matricide, was it?] Malice's voice reverberated tauntingly around the somber maid's quarters. [Now I'm even more proud! 40 Malice points!]

Now his voice was slightly higher pitched and *genuine*. [I will cherish this memory forever. They grow up so fast.]

Malice's words cut deeper than any blade could. How could he find joy in such horrifying and devastating circumstances? I slunk down to the ground again, staring at the corpse. Tears dripped against the metal of my helm, mingling with the earlier mess. I blinked hard, trying to stave off the overwhelming grief.

As I stared down at her still body, the reality of my actions settled like a cold weight in my chest. Was this mercy, or had I crossed a line from which there was no return? *What was I going to do now?* I had committed one of the seven deadly sins in Penance. The scripture lingered in my mind, a stark reminder of the sin I had just committed.

There are seven sins, the most foul, untenable vices that change the soul. Murder, the domain of beasts, the first and last of all the sins. But was this really murder? It was a mercy, right?

[C'mon, pick yourself off of the floor; we gotta go celebrate! This changes everything.] His chipper voice echoed around the room like a little kid on Rellum day.

Malice was right; this changed everything. I had ended her pain. This was a good thing, right? I decided to ignore Malice and work through my emotions on my own, but his commentary never ended.

[Ignore me all you want, mother-*killer*. I'll never forget this moment. Now, don't forget to loot her as you leave this place.] He almost sounded bitter at first, but his chipper voice was more exuberant than normal by the end.

I pulled the halberd out of her corpse. It wasn't a very effective weapon against these monsters, but at least it kept them at bay long enough for me to crush them with my fists.

I didn't loot her corpse. That seemed like one step too far. Instead, I knelt beside her, the cold floor numbing my knees, as I gently closed her eyes. Drawing a sheet from the bed, I covered her with care, a silent vow forming in my mind. I was determined that I wouldn't let this moment change things. After all, it had barely been murder, right? She turned into a zombie immediately after I stabbed her. The more I thought about it, the less guilty I felt.

Yes, Everything would be fine. This wouldn't affect me at all. I left the room.

[Wait! Where are you going? The loot! Nooooooooo!]

Chapter Fifty-Four
Fire!

~Run 6, Entrance, Floor 1, Sewers of Aerlyn~

I jolted awake with a start, my hand flying to my nose to block out a smell so foul it made me gag. I moved my body, trying to figure out where I was. As I moved, my feet squelched in the foul water, its cold, vicious touch crawling over my skin like slugs. The chill of the stone floor beneath seeped into my feet, making it feel like I was walking on ice. I knew where I was. Memories flooded my brain as I fell to my knees in the muck.

A ninja had poisoned me, and my veins felt like they were on fire, every nerve ending screaming in agony. It was the most excruciatingly painful moment of my entire life—something I never wanted to repeat. I was also mad because my last class was so overpowered that it wasn't funny. **Aim** and **Scan** were the best possible skills. Without that combo, there would be no way to make it through the rest of the dungeon, right? *Oh c'mon, don't be like that.*

"Hey, Crystal, what a rough one, huh?" I said, trying to shake off the lingering pain, my voice strained.

[You should have heeded my advice and not run off without your tank. It was a very foolish decision,] Crystal said, her voice as calm and unruffled as ever.

"Yeah, yeah, I don't think I'll ever do that again," I grumbled, rubbing my aching arm. "Not a big fan of pain, to be honest." I sighed and sat down on the ground. The familiar smooth stone of the entrance was cold against my bare skin. "How much should I spend?"

[Amazingly, you have twenty-four. It's enough to buy your next class and some stat-ups or quests,] Crystal replied.

"Are you reading my mind? If so, please stop.," I said, narrowing my eyes.

[No, I don't think I will,] Crystal replied with a hint of amusement in her tone.

I shook my head, feeling a mix of frustration and reluctant humor.

[You should also turn in the Goblin Ears quest,] Crystal added.

"What Goblin Ears Quest?" I asked, surprised.

[The quest you took before you leveled up Thumbs? You finished the quest when you cut off all those ears. Wait, why am I even surprised?] Crystal said.

"Oh, c'mon, they were hard to keep track of when you're covered in green blood and your friends are staring at you. I had to tell them I wanted to collect them in case they were worth money," I said, rolling my eyes.

"All right, show me the Death Boons again," I requested.

"Hey, Crystal? Is it a one-time-only thing? The quests? Or can I buy the Goblin Ear quest multiple times?" I asked, curiosity piqued by the mechanics.

[You can purchase the quest and turn it in once per run; however, once you finish the first tier, better versions of the quests become available,] Crystal explained.

"Well, that's alright then. I'd like turn in the Goblin Ears quest," I decided, feeling a surge of adrenaline as I jumped for joy. *50 Death Boons. What a boon!*

[You have earned 50 Death Boons for completing your quest! Would you like to spend your Death Boons?] Crystal asked.

"Yes. I would like to buy quite a few things. I want all of the classes. I want the loot table. Then, get all of my stats upgraded by 1," I replied eagerly, excitement building inside me. My heart pounded as I reviewed my options. This was it—the moment I'd been working towards.

[Congratulations! You have unlocked Mage, Cleric, Fighter, Crusader, and Conjuror. You have also unlocked the map, and loot tables. Additionally, all your stats have been boosted by 1,] Crystal announced.

Crystal's words echoed in my mind as a surge of power enveloped me. One by one, the classes and abilities unlocked, each announcement a step closer to my dream.

"Sweet! Okay, I'd like my class this run to be the Conjuror, please," I said, my voice trembling with excitement.

My body transformed. I was smaller and a little chubbier, but I felt something new coursing through my veins—unfathomable and uncontrolled—magic. As the magic flowed through my veins, I felt a tingling warmth spread from my core to my fingertips. The air around me crackled with energy, and the faint scent of ozone filled the room.

"Magic!" I shouted, jumping up and down with joy. "I have magic. Real magic!" I could feel a Memory Core about to form, and then, for some reason, it just didn't.

Without even thinking, I cast **Elemental Summon**. The uncontrolled magic swelled in my belly like I had eaten too much, flowing up and out through my arms and fingertips.

A living fire rolled out of my fingertips and onto the ground. The flame bubbled up like a liquid and burst into life. It took the form of a dog. "Fire!" The flame dog barked, running around the room, leaving a trail of flames in its wake. "Fire!" It yapped again before sitting expectantly in front of me.

Tentatively, I reached out to pet it, half-expecting to get burned. Instead, it felt like real fur, tickling my fingers as they moved through the flames. The dog barked happily as I petted him.

"You're a good boy, aren't you? A pet like you needs a name," I said, thinking aloud.

"Fire!" the dog yipped, jumping up to lick my face. I expected to feel heat, but instead, I was soaked in slobber.

I laughed as the dog bowled me over, licking my face. "What a good boy," I said, still laughing.

"What should I name you?" I looked into the coal-black eyes of the little flame dog. Inspiration struck. "How about I name you Coal?"

Coal yipped and barked, "Fire!" again. He ran to the first door of the first floor, chased his tail, and finally settled down to sleep.

[Don't leave yet. We have plenty to discuss,] Crystal said, her tone suddenly serious.

[Here in the first room of the first floor, your privacy is sacrosanct. Nothing can violate it. There are forces at work here that are beyond everything you've encountered, and you are stuck in the middle. Rellum has gifted you power over the soul. You can bring people back from the beyond. That isn't a power gifted lightly. And I am sure you have noticed that you are the only one with Death Boons,] Crystal explained.

Crystal paused, and I interjected. "Why did he do that anyway? I'm nobody special. I still have no idea who I was other than a common thief. I don't think I'll ever be a good person; I almost got rid of you just because I couldn't deal with the fact that you might have been human."

[I do not begin to understand the machinations of gods, but there is more at play here. Death Boons are not Rellum's doing. I talked with the other crystals, and they had no idea what they were. However, I have an innate knowledge of them, as if they have always been part of this dungeon, and I only just noticed the veil being lifted. You aren't supposed to have a tool like this. And things like this usually come at a price,] Crystal said.

"Wait, you can talk to the other crystals? Since when? And you've mentioned past Penitents? Didn't they have Death Boons?" I asked, feeling more confused.

[Yes, I talked with Thomas's crystal and with Klericho's. That's just it. I don't think they did, but in my recollections, they did. Whatever gave us this power edited my memories. Just like yours,] Crystal replied.

My mind returned to the indecipherable words I had scratched into the dirt. "Remember that weird message scratched in the dirt? I think it's related to this. I'm pretty sure I had been about to mention Death Boons to Klericho, and then it was like everything froze for a moment and unfroze. I'm pretty sure it was one of the gods. And then, on the ground, I had somehow written out the words Aunt Ersid. And then I kept trying to tell you about something, and it was like your memory was being erased before my mind."

[It's not like many options exist for who is doing this. The only ones powerful enough are Rellum, Malikap, and Aurentum. But none of them are known to mess around with memory.]

Aunt Ersid. Aunt Ersid. What did it mean? My mind raced. If the gods were involved, it had to be a clue about one of them. Aunt... Ersid... Erased! That's it! Aurentum erases minds.

"I think it means that Aurentum erases minds," I explained, feeling a chill run down my spine. "To what end, I don't know, but he seems determined to prevent people from finding out about the fact that I have access to Death Boons."

[Maybe it has to do with what Rellum said about you being unclaimed,] Crystal said, her tone grave.

"Rellum said he would contact us again. Maybe once we finish the Aerlyn quest for him, we can let him know that the Death Merchant is using us somehow," I suggested, clinging to a sliver of hope.

[And tell him what? That the Merchant of Death is erasing our minds but giving us superpowers?] Crystal questioned, skepticism in her voice.

"Superpowers? I like how that sounds. I don't know, but I would rather be under the protection of the one that's supposed to be good than under the auspices of someone who keeps erasing my mind," I said, trying to sound resolute.

[Fair enough, Rod,] Crystal agreed.

"So what should we do?" I asked, seeking guidance. There was so much more to talk about, but I was confused, and more than a little exhausted from fighting and dying, and speaking.

[I suggest you focus on clearing the first floor again. This new class has a bit of a difficulty curve. But once you learn it, it is overwhelmingly powerful,] Crystal advised.

"Alright then, how does it work?" I inquired, eager to get started.

[I believe you once commented that the Death Boon for turn-based combat sounded boring and dull. Well, the class you selected was made for that boon,] Crystal explained.

"Oh. Should I have bought it?" I asked, suddenly uncertain.

[Not necessarily,] Crystal replied. [I can't guarantee you will get the best results without it, but this is the first floor. With your current stats and general knowledge about the strengths and weaknesses of mobs, you will easily overwhelm this floor without that boon. Floor 2, however, you will need it.]

"Alrighty then, how many boons do I have left after my spending spree?" I asked, eager to know my remaining resources.

[You currently possess 12 boons. You need 20 to purchase the turn-based combat boon,] Crystal informed me.

I did a quick calculation. I could gather eight boons between now and the next floor; I just needed to get Overkill Boons, and I would be fine. Determined, I turned my focus back to the task at hand.

"Crystal, does the time we've spent talking count against speed runs?" I asked, hoping for some leniency.

[Unfortunately, yes, it does,] Crystal replied, her tone unwavering.

"Drat," I muttered under my breath—no time to waste. The torches flickered as I squared my shoulders, ready to forge ahead.

Stat Boons

- **Potency:** Cost 5 | Current Stat: 1

- **Insight:** Cost 1 | Current Stat: 0

- **Alacrity:** Cost 1 | Current Stat: 0

- **Vitality:** Cost 10 | Current Stat: 6

- **Finesse:** Cost 1 | Current Stat: 0

- **Arcanum:** Cost 1 | Current Stat: 0

- **Defense:** Cost 5 | Current Stat: 1

- **Magic Defense:** Cost 5 | Current Stat: 1

- **Precision:** Cost 5 | Current Stat: 6

- **Evasion:** Cost 5 | Current Stat: 3

Player Classes
Mage

- **Cost:** 4

- **Starting Equipment:** Mana bolt spell, Wooden Mage Staff

- **Stats:** Vitality: 4, Finesse: 2, Arcanum: 8, Insight: 5

- **Penalty:** Cannot equip physical weapons, cannot equip iron armor.

Fighter

- **Cost:** 4

- **Starting Equipment:** Iron sword, Iron shield, Skill: Shield Bash

- **Stats:** Potency: 3, Vitality: 10, Finesse: 6, Evasion: 2

- **Penalty:** Cannot equip magic items.

Cleric

- **Cost:** 4

- **Starting Equipment:** Iron mace, Shield, Basic Heal spell

- **Stats:** Potency: 2, Vitality: 6, Finesse: 4, Arcanum: 6

- **Penalty:** Cannot equip bladed weapons.

Crusader

- **Cost:** 4

- **Starting Equipment:** Iron sword, Iron shield, Basic Heal spell

- **Stats:** Potency: 4, Vitality: 10, Finesse: 4, Arcanum: 4, Defense: 2, Precision: 4, Evasion: 4

- **Bonus:** Has the Guiding Light spell.

Conjurer

- **Cost:** 4

- **Starting Equipment:** Elemental summon spell, Wooden Mage Staff

- **Stats:** Vitality: 2, Finesse: 2, Arcanum: 8, Precision: 2

- **Penalty:** ???

Dungeon Boons
Turn-Based Combat

- **Cost:** 20

- **Effect:** Pauses combat so that everything takes place in turns, making natural evasion impossible. You must rely on the actual evasion stat. It can be toggled on and off.

Identify Enemy

- **Cost:** 20

- **Effect:** Enemy stats are highlighted and visible above enemies. Requires the Scan Skill to use. It can be toggled on and off.

Loot Table

- **Cost:** 20

- **Effect:** Allows you to scan chests and crates to see their potential contents.

Time Keeper

- **Cost:** 2

- **Effect:** A stopwatch shows the time in the upper right corner of your vision. Essential for speed runs. It can be toggled on and off.

Challenge Mode

- **Cost:** 200

- **Effect:** Enemies have triple stats and better weapons but drop better loot and more Death Boons. It can be toggled on and off.

  - *Quote:* "Challenge Accepted!" – Photonius The Dead

Quest Shop
Rat Teeth

- **Cost:** 1

- **Type:** Collection

- **Description:** Collect 5 rat teeth

- **Reward:** 5 Death Boons

Necromancer Eyes

- **Cost:** 5

- **Type:** Collection

- **Description:** Collect 20 Necromancer Eyes

- **Reward:** 25 Death Boons

Goblin Ears

- **Cost:** 25

- **Type:** Collection

- **Description:** Collect 100 Goblin ears

- **Reward:** 100 Death Boons

Aerlyntium Shop
- **Wood**

  - **Cost:** 5

  - **Amount:** 1000

- **Metal**

  - **Cost:** 5

  - **Amount:** 1000

- **Organic**

  - **Cost:** 5

  - **Amount:** 1000

- **Glass**

  - **Cost:** 5

  - **Amount:** 100

Chapter Fifty-Five
Elemental Attacks

"How does this class work? You said it is unique," I asked, curiosity piqued.

[You have to give commands to your pets. You can have all eight elemental pets out at once, but it can be hectic controlling many beings without the forced turn-based combat. However, you can cheat through the first three floors with that perk. The fourth floor is an entirely different beast that we will get to eventually] Crystal explained.

"What's on the fourth floor?"

[It's called the Tournament of the Gods, but there isn't much we can do about it right now. Let's get back to the new class.] *Really? She's going to tell me something like that and expect me to move on?*

"Fine, but we're going to talk about that later. What about the attacks? I know you said I give them commands, but what skills do the pets have? What about their stats?" I pressed, eager to understand the mechanics.

[Their stats are dependent on your stats. They are one to one with yours.] Crystal replied.

"And what about their dice rolls?" I asked, trying to wrap my head around it.

[Each pet has 4 different attacks. Two physical and two magical. Each type has a non-elemental and an elemental attack. The elemental attacks do critical damage to enemies that are weak to their element,] Crystal continued.

"Oh, so like water beats fire, fire beats plants?" I guessed.

[Yes, except you have it entirely wrong, as usual,] Crystal said sarcastically. [There are three sets of elemental rock-paper-scissors and the two mirror elements.]

"Mirror elements?" I echoed, puzzled.

[I'll get to it; let me explain,] Crystal said, pausing. I nodded, and she continued, [Fire, water, and ice are the first trilogy of elemental powers. Ice freezes water. Water extinguishes fire. Fire melts ice. But that's just with elements versus elements. Some monsters are straight-up weak to fire, ice, or both. The second set of elements is electricity, earth, and wind. Earth grounds electricity, electricity is carried on the wind, and wind buffets the earth. The third set is ailments. Poison, necrotic, and stun. They don't traditionally stop each other; their effects tend to compound each other, which can be a hassle for most people. Getting stun-locked and poisoned is how you just died. It was quite brutal.]

"I'm aware of how I died. I don't plan on repeating that death ever again," I said, wincing at the memory.

[We can't always get what we want,] Crystal started in a sing-song fashion. [But if you try sometimes...] She trailed off, realizing I had no idea what she was singing. [The final two elements are the mirror elements. Shadow and light. You can't have one without the other, but both can overpower each other if given the chance.]

"Alright, so my pets are these different elements? Am I able to summon more than one at a time?" I asked, trying to piece it all together.

[Yes, that is the beauty of this class. You can have all eight pets out at the same time. However, it costs a full bar of mana for each pet summon, no matter your intellect, so you have to sit idly and wait for the mana to recharge. That was one of the things I wanted to talk with you about.] She paused dramatically as if what she said held great power over my life.

[It's time to take out the Lunar Amulet, and the staves. You must go through this floor without any magic regen until you reach the Necromancer's chamber, but you should be fine with Coal. His skills are going to make a difference,] Crystal explained.

Without further preamble, two of Crystal's pages appeared in front of me. They showed the pets stats in full, but it was a little confusing.

Coal: Level 1 Fire Elemental

Stats
- **HP:** 30/30

- **Stamina:** 20/20

- **Mana:** 20/20

Skills
Slash
- **Effect:** 1–6 damage

- **Description:** Coal swipes with his claws. Uses 2 stamina.

Fire Slash
- **Effect:** 1–6 damage, 10% chance to burn target

- **Description:** Coal swipes with his claws. Fire element. Uses 5 stamina.

Mana Bolt
- **Effect:** 1–4 damage

- **Description:** Coal sends out a non-elemental bolt of magic. Uses 2 mana.

Fire Bolt

- **Effect:** 1–4 damage, 20% chance to burn target

- **Description:** Coal sends out a bolt of fire magic. Uses 5 mana.

Cauterize

- **Effect:** End any bleed effect by cauterizing the wound.

- **Description:** If you burn a wound, it stops bleeding? I mean, it's magic—don't overthink it.

The attacks sounded impressive, but I needed more details. "Can you describe them in more detail? The chart doesn't do much to describe it?"

[**Slash** and **Fire Slash** are claw-based attacks where Coal uses his claws to attack the target. These are valuable because they cost stamina to use instead of mana. Each pet has a supply of stamina and mana based on your stats. So you have to manage those resources as you fight. Unlike your personal stats, pet stats recover upon resting after a battle; pets will usually curl up and sleep until a room is cleared out and the team is ready to move on to the next room,]

"How many elemental pets can I access right now?" I asked, eager to know my options.

[Again, Rod, you can have up to eight, but it will take you killing the Necromancer boss to summon more. Are you even listening to me? Stop being a dunderhead and pay attention. The Necromancer's Den is the only place on this floor with moonlight. And your MP regen is pitiful without the Lunar Amulet equipped,] Crystal replied bluntly.

"Alright then, let's go," I said, feeling a surge of determination.

I walked over to where Coal was sleeping and gently nudged the fire dog awake. He looked around, confused, until he sat down and stared intently at the door. I smiled at his focus and patted his head.

"Time to move, buddy. We've got work to do," I said, feeling a mix of anticipation and excitement.

~Run 6, Room 1R, Floor 1, Sewers of Aerlyn~

The room was the same boring sewage system I had been in a dozen times. Broken pipes hung from the ceiling, and sewage defied gravity again for no discernible reason other than to confuse the newly Penitent. Three rats were playing a game of cards on the single crate in the center of the room.

Before they could react, I cast **Scan**.

Enemy Entry 0002: Giant Rat *(Level 3)*

Weaknesses

Susceptible to fire, lightning, and dark-based attacks but immune to water, ice, and ground attacks.

Stats

Health: 5/5

Potency: 13

I did a double take at the insane increase in potency but then glanced at the 5 health. Unless I was stupid in how I handled them, they weren't a threat at all.

"Coal, do you see the three rats? I want you to use **Firebolt** on the first one." I took the Necrostaff I had off its sling and held it in front of me in a combat stance.

Coal barked in understanding, and I cast Necrobolt at a different rat simultaneously. Dice rolled, and Coal barked as fire shot out of his mouth in a quick and fast as a bolt of lightning. The bolt traveled quickly through the air before exploding into the first rat.

[Critical hit! Weakness: Fire. Your pet has dealt 36 damage. You have received an Overkill Boon.]

The rat evaporated into a pile of smoke as the bolt of necrotic energy from my staff flew straight and true. It collided with a second rat, engulfing it in a puff of dark energy.

[Critical hit! Weakness: Shadow. You have dealt 10 damage. You have received an Overkill Boon.]

Before the third rat could react, I shouted, "Coal, as quick as you can, use **Fire Slash** on the final rat."

Coal moved into close range, his fiery claws slashing down on the slow-moving rat. It was over in an instant.

[Critical hit! The target is weak to fire and shadow. You have dealt 30 damage. You have received an Overkill Boon.]

I let out a breath I hadn't realized I'd been holding. "Great job, Coal," I said, patting his head as he wagged his tail. The adrenaline from the fight left me feeling both exhilarated and exhausted. We had won this battle, but the dungeon still held many challenges.

Three down, twelve to go. I was on a roll, and the level had barely started. I would also still get boons from the Necromancer and the goblin trio. This class packed a punch. I loved how much power it had. I was hitting 30 damage per hit. Crazy good. And the fact that **Slash** hit three times. *Oh baby, where was this class my first few runs?*

[It was just the luck of the draw, Rod. There are other powerful classes, especially once you unlock the advanced classes. You have so much ahead of you that you don't know what's coming. But first, we have to beat the second floor,] Crystal said.

"Wait, I unlock advanced classes on the third floor?" I said, puzzled.

[Honestly, I can't wait; I'm bored of these rats and the Necromancer. I wish you would go straight to the boss,] Crystal replied, a hint of impatience in her voice.

"You're the one who said I needed to learn how this class worked," I pointed out.

[Yes, and you are taking your sweet time. Now hurry up and finish looting,] Crystal urged.

I sighed and kicked the three rat corpses to get my loot.

[1 Rat Teeth and Rat Meat each]

"Gee, thanks," I muttered.

I threw the Rat Meat to Coal, who devoured it in a single gulp, then curled up into a ball and went to sleep. I then opened the crate, reached in, and pulled out a pile of gold. Twenty-five coins. I wished I was back on the second floor fighting the horde. *I bet this class can handle that room all on its own.*

When I approached the exit door, Coal was back on his feet, and we went through.

~Run 5, Necromancer's Room, Floor 1, Sewers of Aerlyn~

"Yes!" I shouted as I walked into the room, my excitement mounting as my mana started refilling automatically. It was slow, but definitely worth waiting for.

"Who dares invade my ritual chamber?" The Necromancer's voice was all bark and no bite.

I quickly cast **Scan**. "Coal, let's smoke this jerk. Cast **Firebolt**," I commanded.

Enemy Entry 0003: Necromancer (Level: 7)
Weaknesses

Light, shadow, ground, fire, ice, and lightning.

Stats
Health: 15/15
Mana: 40/40

Coal's mouth glowed as a fireball coalesced, and a die rolled. The fireball flew like an arrow, colliding with the Necromancer's head, which promptly exploded in a burst of flame.

[Critical hit! Weakness: Fire. You have dealt 20 damage. You have received an Overkill Boon.]

The Necromancer dropped dead just as a skeleton rose to its feet. It shambled forward, and I cast **Scan** again.

"Coal, use **Fire Slash!**" I ordered.

Coal moved in, his fiery claws slashing down on the skeleton. It was over in an instant.

[Critical hit x 4! Weakness: fire. You have dealt 106 damage. You have dealt 5 times an enemy's maximum health. You have received 5 Overkill Boons.]

What was up with my luck lately? I wasn't complaining, but there had to be another force at play here. Other than the ninja, I had been killing this faster and getting higher rolls. Something was up.

[I thought the same thing, too, but we can discuss it later,] Crystal interjected.

Sometimes, it was unsettling that Crystal could read my mind, but it was probably for the best that I didn't voice my previous thoughts out loud. I kicked the necro corpse and the skeleton corpse to loot them. The dice rolled.

[Due to the nature of the Necromancer's death, the loot table has changed. You have looted the Amulet of Skulls from the Necromancer. You have looted Ragged Cloth from the Skeleton.]

"Great! A useless piece of cloth and another amulet. I bet it's use-less, too," I muttered, frustrated but curious.

[Neither item is useless... In fact, you are quite lucky to have re-ceived that Skull Amulet. It could allow you to take the skeleton as a minion in a future run. It could also work on future skeletons, but they isn't a mob you'll encounter until the third floor,] Crystal explained.

"And this tiny rag masquerading as a pocket square isn't useless?" I asked, holding up the rag skeptically.

[Nope. It's a quest item back in the marketplace. Now that you have one, I will point out how to turn in the quest for you once we get to the second floor. Now, it's time for us to cheat again,] Crystal replied.

I sat on the altar, staring up at the sky. As soon as my mana re-generated to full, I started my long-winded summoning spell. These summons were not the kind of magic I could easily recast in battle. The die rolled.

Just like the earlier cast, the mana pulled out from my belly. It swelled inside me like I was about to lose my nonexistent lunch. I was just as giddy as when I cast my first spell earlier. Sure, it was the same spell, but magic is magic. It flowed through my channels and out of my arms as it coalesced into a blue shape. At first, it was formless, like a blob, before it started to shake. Suddenly, water flew everywhere as it shaped into a supine feline. Its tail flicked back and forth, sending water in all directions with each flick. Its whiskers mirrored the tail, flicking water back and forth with every movement.

Coal saw my new companion and started yapping incessantly. "Fire!" he growled at the cat. The cat gave Coal one look, licked its paw, and then curled up and went to sleep. Its sleeping form was a giant pearl of water, which seemed like the perfect name for the orb-like cat. I went up to the creature and petted it. She hissed, backed up, and walked away.

Coal approached me, barked "fire," happier this time, and sat pa-tiently waiting for me to pet him.

I stood there for several minutes petting the dog; as my magic slowly recovered, I prepared to cast the spell again. I liked how the magic felt. It was an addicting rush that I couldn't get enough of. The mana pulled from my body, swelling inside me like a balloon about to burst, and then rushed out of my hands. The die rolled.

Pearl: Level 1 Water Elemental

Stats
- **HP:** 30/30

- **Stamina:** 20/20

- **Mana:** 20/20

Skills
Claw
- **Effect:** 1–6 damage

- **Description:** Pearl scratches with his claws. Uses 2 stamina.

Water Claw
- **Effect:** 1–6 damage, 10% chance to slow target

- **Description:** Pearl scratches with his claws. Water element. Uses 5 stamina.

Mana Bolt
- **Effect:** 1–4 damage

- **Description:** Pearl sends out a non-elemental bolt of magic.

Uses 2 mana.

Water Bolt

- **Effect:** 1–4 damage, 20% chance to slow target

- **Description:** Pearl sends out a bolt of water magic. Uses 5 mana.

Bestiary

Enemy Entry 0002: Giant Rat *(Level 3 – Unaffiliated Horde)*

The Giant Rat is a common foe found in the dark and damp regions of the Sewers of Aerlyn. Despite its extremely low health, it can be quite a nuisance due to its Potency, which increases by 5 at each level.

- **Weaknesses:** Susceptible to fire, lightning, and dark-based attacks but immune to water, ice, and ground attacks.

Stats

- **Health:** 5/5

- **Potency:** 13

- **Vitality:** 1

- **Precision:** 5

Item Drops

Gold

- **Amount:** 5

- **Chance to drop:** 33%

Rat Teeth

- **Amount:** 1–2

- **Chance to drop:** 33%

Rat Meat
- **Amount:** 1

- **Chance to drop:** 33%

Death Boon
- **Amount:** 1

- **Chance to drop:** 1%

Enemy Entry 0003: Necromancer *(Level 7 – Malikap)*

The Necromancer is a powerful and sinister caster who commands dark magic and manipulates the forces of death. Necromancers are often found in secluded, dark places where they perform their forbidden rituals.

- **Weaknesses:** Light, shadow, ground, fire, ice, and lightning.

Stats
- **Health:** 15/15

- **Mana:** 40/40

- **Insight:** 8

- **Arcanum:** 8

- **Vitality:** 3

- **Precision:** 12

Item Drops

Gold

- **Amount:** 15–25

- **Chance to drop:** 25%

Necromancer Eyes

- **Amount:** 1–2

- **Chance to drop:** 35%

Skull Amulet

- **Amount:** 1

- **Chance to drop:** 15%

Apprentice's Grimoire

- **Amount:** 1

- **Chance to drop:** 15%

Dark Leather Boots

- **Amount:** 1

- **Chance to drop:** 4%

Necromancer Robes

- **Amount:** 1

- **Chance to drop:** 4%

Lunar Amulet

- **Amount:** 1

- **Chance to drop:** 1%

Solar Amulet
- **Amount:** 1

- **Chance to drop:** 1%

Enemy Entry 0004: Skeleton *(Level 4 – Malikap)*
Skeletons are the reanimated remains of fallen warriors brought back to life through dark magic.
- **Weaknesses:** Fire, Light, Shadow.

Stats
- **Health:** 20/20

- **Mana:** 40/40

- **Potency:** 2

- **Insight:** 2

- **Arcanum:** 8

- **Vitality:** 4

- **Defense:** 6

- **Magic Defense:** 2

- **Precision:** 10

Item Drops
Gold

- **Amount:** 15–25

- **Chance to drop:** 30%

Bone Meal
- **Amount:** 15–25

- **Chance to drop:** 30%

Ragged Cloth
- **Amount:** 1–5

- **Chance to drop:** 30%

Ancient Scroll
- **Amount:** 1

- **Chance to drop:** 5%

Enchanted Bone *(Quest Item)*
- **Amount:** 1

- **Chance to drop:** 4%

Skeleton Key
- **Amount:** 1

- **Chance to drop:** 1%

Chapter Fifty-Six
Squawk!

Bolts of electricity swarmed out of my hands, forming a second orb, smaller and more concentrated than the water. The orb then exploded into a lightning bolt, leaving scorch marks on the ground and ceiling. Left in its wake was a tiny bird, flapping its wings and trying to stay airborne. It fell to the ground, shuffled over to Pearl, and looked at its reflection. It squawked in indignation before flapping its wings and casting a lightning bolt on itself.

The small beast absorbed the electricity, growing into a medium-sized bird. I could now tell it was a parrot—the squawking should have given it away. This gave me the perfect name for my new friend: Squawk. Squawk flew around the room a few times before perching next to me on the altar the Necromancer had left behind. As my magic refilled, I absent-mindedly petted my new bird. He was soft and fuzzy, almost like the sensation of constantly touching static.

"Squawk! Hello. What are we doing? What are we doing? Squawk!" the bird chattered.

"Hello, Squawk. I am waiting for my magic to regen so that I can summon some more companions," I replied.

"*Squawk*! My name is Squawk. *Squawk*!" The bird covered its face with its wing as if embarrassed by my name choice. I shrugged. Names weren't my forte even before coming to the dungeon.

My mana refilled, so I cast the spell a fourth time. The rush was still there, as was the feeling of being inflated. But something was different this time. My mana didn't flow out of my body so smoothly; it rushed out and exploded into smoke. The spell failed, and I sat staring dumbly at the bloody stumps that were my fingertips before screaming bloody murder.

"Crystal! Why didn't you warn me?" I shouted, shaking my hands to ease the pain. It was so intense that nothing I could think of would help. My fingers cramped as blood poured over my hands, so I curled them into fists. "Cloth shirt! Hurry!" My cloth shirt appeared, and I wrapped my hands in it, trying to staunch the blood flow. Thankfully, I hadn't lost the fingertips; it would have made for an awkwardly painful trip through the dungeon.

[Magical failure can occur when the same spell has been cast too many times or its effects have taken up too much of the ambient magic. I didn't think this would occur, but you likely can only cast this spell three times on this floor. You might be able to cast the spell more on the next floor, but I'm not sure. It could also be tied to twice your INT stat. For whatever reason, there is a gap in my knowledge here that I don't understand,] Crystal explained.

I shook my head, and said, "Alright. Should I go back to the entrance and purchase the turn-based skill? How does it work exactly?"

[It's a bit wonky, to be honest,] Crystal replied. [It's similar to your time freeze skill. Time freezes for everything in the room, whoever's turn it is. Turn order or initiative, is decided by a dice roll equal to the number of individuals in a room. I promise this will greatly benefit you and your pets.]

"Is there a limit to the number of attacks per turn or something? I recall you saying something about dodging being different, too," I asked, trying to wrap my head around it.

[Stats are much more important with turn-based combat turned on. Evasion, for example, is 100% dependent on the stat. No more kiting monsters around or outrunning goblin attacks. You should be able to dodge everything on this floor, but the next may prove more dangerous if you do not consistently raise your stats.] Crystal explained.

"Are you sure my stats are enough?" I asked.

[Hold on, you keep adding questions before I answer the previous one,] Crystal tutted. [The number of attacks is based on the skill in question and the stat it is based on. For example, your Finesse is high enough that Coal can attack three times with his Fire Slash. Your Insight and Arcanum need one more point each for the Fire Bolt skill to be cast twice. It's the same thing for your other pets.]

"Let's head back to the entrance then. I think it's time we purchase this Death Boon," I decided, feeling a mix of anticipation and wariness.

[One last bit of forewarning: it can take some getting used to, so hopefully, you don't run into the Boss room in the next room,] Crystal cautioned.

"Why would you go and phrase it that way? Now that's what the next room will be; you just don't test fate like that," I muttered, shaking my head.

[I make my own fate, Rod. I suggest you do the same,] Crystal retorted.

"Bold words for a crystal stuck in a dungeon," I shot back, a smirk tugging at my lips.

[Shut up,] Crystal snapped, but I could almost sense a hint of amusement in her tone.

~Run 5, Entrance, Floor 1, Sewers of Aerlyn~

As I stepped back into the room, I focused on something vital to my future survival. *Crystal, since you can read my mind, should I even bother talking out loud?*

[No one else can hear me, so it is entirely your choice.]

Well, then, can we talk about private things without worrying about where we are or who is nearby?

[No, that is not quite right, Rod. Even your inner thoughts are not always yours. I can read them anywhere, at any time. And in the grand scheme of things, I am not that powerful. If anything, you shouldn't even think thoughts hinting at that.]

I thought we were safe here.

[Only when we first revive from our death. And even then, the timeframe is quite fluid. Minutes, if that.]

"Okay, then let's get that Death Boon," I said out loud, a sense of urgency causing me to blurt it out quickly.

[The turn-based Death Boon is not guaranteed to—oh, never mind, you are quite the smart adventurer. You already bought everything cheaper, so it's the only option. Now remember, everything is impacted by this combat, even movement. Once a battle starts, save your limited movement for sitting, crouching, diving, or anything. All movement is limited per turn based on your Finesse stat.]

"It feels like everything is changing. Is it really worth it? What does it bring me?"

[Remember how Coal one-shot the rats before they could do anything. Could you work that quickly with three pets? What about six? Ten? What if 100 enemies were barreling down at you? Like in the Goblin Horde room? You can easily sit there for a long time killing goblins on your own now.]

"Alright, I see your point. Let's buy it," I said, steeling myself for the change.

[You have bought the Death Boon: Turn-Based Combat. You are activating turn-based combat. Once active, this setting can only be changed once you have arrived on the next floor,] Crystal announced, her tone carrying an unusual gravity.

Her tone was different, and there was something off about it that I just couldn't place. "Yes, I am sure. Why do you always double-check with me after I ask for things?"

[It's part of the system. Some crystals are much less... sane... than I am, so the triumvirate stepped in. These restraints are automatic responses that I have no control over.]

"Ah. I, for one, am glad I got an emotionally responsible crystal that definitely hasn't overreacted to any situation we've been through."

[For someone who is supposed to be Penitent, you sure are a jerk.]

"So I've been told. I'll work on it. And you're right; I shouldn't have said that. I'm noticing more and more how I need to think before I say the first thing that comes to my mind. Not that it matters since you can... Sorry."

[As long as we work on it, it's okay. I am sorry for my part, too,] Crystal replied, pausing momentarily. [Let's go ahead and get back to the task at hand.] She paused again, and her light pulsed once. When she spoke again, her tone was different.

[Activating turn-based combat. On every floor, you will be asked to confirm this setting. Please be aware that this setting cannot be turned off in the middle of a floor. Some floors may not be well suited to this kind of combat.]

"Alright, let's hop to it. I think if we... Wait." I paused and facepalmed. "Maybe I should start making lists to help me keep track of things. Didn't I have the amulet? Instead of fighting my way through the rest of this floor I can just teleport to the boss's room, right?

[There is no reason not to Rod. Why don't you do it now?] I put the Lunar Amulet into the vault and withdrew the goblin ruby thing.

As soon as it made contact with my hands, the room morphed as two new doors appeared. I had already cleared the Necromancer room, so I moved straight to the boss chamber.

Squawk: Level 1 Lightning Elemental

Stats
- **HP:** 30/30

- **Stamina:** 20/20

- **Mana:** 20/20

Skills
Claw
- **Effect:** Deals 1–6 damage

- **Description:** A physical attack that uses 2 stamina.

Thunder Peck
- **Effect:** Deals 7 damage

- **Description:** A physical elemental attack.

Mana Bolt
- **Effect:** Deals 1–4 damage

- **Description:** A non-elemental magical attack that uses 2 mana.

Electric Bolt
- **Effect:** Deals 1–4 damage, 20% chance to stun the target

- **Description:** A lightning-based magical attack that uses 5 mana.

Fly

- **Effect:** Uses magic to lift you into the air for a brief period of time

- **Description:** He lifts, you fly.
  Quote: "A five-ounce bird could not carry a one-pound coconut."

Explode

- **Effect:** Deals 18 damage to you and 27 damage to an enemy at close range

- **Description:** This skill is triggered when Squawk dies.

Chapter Fifty-Seven
Nobble The Nasty

~Run 6, Goblin Boss room, Floor 1, Sewers of Aerlyn~

It was so convenient that the amulet worked the way it did. I was getting tired of killing rats, and I definitely didn't want to get near Slikk again. I switched my noxious staff out for Gurgles, since I had a feeling it would allow me to control the sewage like it had for Gurgle, and I had no intention of taking another mouthful of sewer water.

When we stepped inside, the door slammed shut, trapping my companions and me. The turn-based battle system seized control, and I was not ready. And to make things worse, Slikk, Gurgle, and Drip had a new friend in tow.

Parchments burst into the room like a flurry of pages from an exploding book. Each one shot towards a goblin, my pets, or me, glowing bright red with the numbers we rolled. Eight dice tumbled through the air, ricocheting off walls and landing haphazardly. I couldn't keep track; the deluge of information overwhelmed me, and once the battle began, turn order became a chaotic blur.

Despite Crystal's best attempts to explain, the turn-based combat was a misnomer. It was something called the Active Paradigm window. The parchments were transformed into small clocks, each with a 5-second timer for movement and a 10-second timer for actions. Each team had a 30-second 'Paradigm' to act. Turns could overlap, and if you finished quickly, you could reduce your wait time to a two-to-one ratio. The overlapping turns created a hectic mess that still gives me a headache.

[Active Paradigm Battle. At the start of your Paradigm battle, assign a role to each of your pets or assume manual control. Time will not stop while you are making decisions, so beware,] Crystal instructed.

"Wait, what? I thought the point was to give me pinpoint control over the battle? You said it was turn-based! Like Gods and Kings!" I exclaimed, frustration creeping into my voice.

[APB gives you pinpoint control if you choose to use it, and in many scenarios, it's worth it. But with this many enemies, including a new boss, I would advise against it,] Crystal explained calmly.

"Then what do I do?" I asked, my voice rising in panic.

[**Scan** the goblins on your turn, then before ending your turn, set the Paradigm for your pets to target weaknesses. You should have about 8 seconds left to do this,] Crystal replied, urgency in her tone.

"**Scan**, as in multiple?" I asked, trying to process the instructions despite my panic.

[Hurry now; time is of the essence!] Crystal urged.

"**Scan** them all!" I shouted, hoping it would be enough.

Enemy Entry 0005: Slikk the Sludger

Weaknesses

Lightning, Water, Shadow, Light, and Fire.

Strengths

Resistances to Ice, Ground.

Health: 60/60

Enemy Entry 0006: Gurgle the Gusher

Weaknesses

Lightning, Water, Shadow, Light, and Fire.

Strengths

Resistances to Ice, Ground.

Health: 35/35

Mana: 50/50

Enemy Entry 0007: Drip the Drainer
Weaknesses
Lightning, Water, Shadow, Light, and Fire.
Strengths
Resistances to Ice, Ground.
Health: 45/45

Enemy Entry 0015: Nobble The Nasty
Weaknesses
Lightning, Water, Shadow, Light, and Fire.
Strengths
Resistances to Ice, Ground.
Health: 45/45
Mana: 50/50

[And your Paradigm?] Crystal prompted urgently, her voice tinged with anxiety.

"Weaknesses!" I shouted, my voice echoing off the stone walls as the chaos erupted. I set the paradigms just as the timer ticked to one second. Gripping my Lunar Staff, I summoned a wave of sewage that surged forward, blocking the path between us and the goblins. My pets remained composed, seizing their moments with precision.

Coal launched himself into the air, flames flickering around his form as he cast **Firebolt** at Slikk. Squawk flapped its wings, rising with a burst of energy to cast **Electric Bolt** at Drip. Pearl, glowing a radiant golden hue, must have activated **Elemental Dodge**, transforming into a shimmering golden-blue orb. Then it was the goblins' turn.

Nobble, the newest goblin, waved his staff with a sinister grin, causing the sewage shield to waver and falter, leaving my team vulnerable.

Slikk rushed forward, swinging his club in a wide arc aimed at Coal's head. A die rolled, but I didn't have time to see the result as a blast of noxious energy from Gurgle streaked toward me. My feet felt rooted to the ground. I saw the die land on a 3 just as the blast slammed into my chest, an explosion of pain spreading through my body.

[You have taken 5 damage.]

Reeling from the miasmic blast, I watched as Nobble directed a stream of putrid sewage at Pearl. She dodged effortlessly, her movements fluid and precise, but Squawk's Electric Bolt went wide. Drip teleported behind Squawk, daggers gleaming as he slashed at the parrot's wings. SQUAWK! The parrot screeched, feathers scattering as it plummeted to the ground.

[TURN 2. 30... 29... 28... 27...]

I shook my head, trying to clear the toxic fog clouding my vision. Gritting my teeth, I wielded my staff again. The power surged through me, wild and unsteady like a bucking horse. I managed to control the torrent of sewage, sending it crashing into Nobble. He was bowled over by the onslaught, unable to retaliate since his turn hadn't come up yet.

My turn ended, and I shifted my focus to my pets, who moved with a will of their own. Coal lunged forward, claws glinting, and slashed at Slikk as three dice rolled overhead.

[Critical hit! Weakness: Fire. 16 damage.]

Squawk, recovering from his earlier attack, dove at the sewage-coated Nobble. His **Electric Bolt** struck true, the conductivity amplifying the effect. Nobble began to smoke from the damage, barely holding on.

[Critical hit! Weakness: Lightning. 33 damage.]

Pearl, nimble as ever, darted forward with her aquamarine claws gleaming. She aimed for Drip's eyes, but without magical enhancement, her slashes were less effective.

[4 damage to Drip.]

And that's when things started to unravel.

Nobble manipulated the sewage with practiced ease, conjuring tornadoes that whirled through the room. He directed them at me, but I leaped aside just as a die rolled and time unfroze. Before I could retaliate, time froze again.

Coal, within range of Slikk, took a solid hit from the goblin's club. The club seemed to pass through Coal's fiery head, diminishing his flames but not his resolve.

Drip, with a swift flick, hurled a poisoned dagger at Squawk. It nicked the bird, and my heart sank.

[Drip threw a poison dagger at Squawk. 3 damage. Squawk is poisoned.]

Squawk plummeted to the ground, triggering flashbacks to my painful demise on the previous floor. I shuddered, dread creeping in.

Just like before, sewage began to flood the room, rising steadily toward the ceiling.

[Turn 3 start.]

Immediately, I cast **Noxious Bolt**, aiming for Drip. I couldn't risk leaving the poisonous assassin alive. The bolt shot through the air, trailing sickly green and black light before striking Drip.

[You deal 4 damage!]

Despite his poisoned state, Squawk swooped down, his beak crackling with electric energy. He targeted Drip's eyes with precision.

[Critical hit! Weakness: Lightning. You dealt 27 damage.]

Sensing danger, Coal retreated to our defensive line and cast Firebolt at Slikk.

[Critical hit! Weakness: Fire. 16 damage.]

Still, under the illusion spell, Pearl showed no fear. She rushed into the fray, focusing on the bleeding Drip. The assassin, barely standing, was a mess of wounds. Pearl seized the moment, her claws charged with water elemental magic. With a powerful slash, she aimed for his eyes, determined to bring him down.

[Critical hit! Weakness: Fire. You attacked a weak point! Natural crit! You dealt 48 damage. You obliterated Drip.]

[Turn End. Enemy turn starts.]

As I froze again, uncertainty gnawed at me. The paradigm system's timing mechanic made me feel rushed and insecure, and being a sitting duck during enemy turns was frustrating.

"Crystal, what's the point of this again? So far, it feels like I'm a sitting duck," I complained, irritation bubbling up.

Time unfroze for me, and I dodged out of the way of Slikk's club. I tried to ready my staff for a counterattack, but my complaints to Crystal had distracted me. The sight was almost comical—Slikk frozen mid-swing, his club pointed downwards, while my noxious staff hovered inches from his face, ready to cast.

Pearl faced Gurgle, but the bolt of noxious energy passed harmlessly through her intangible form. The cat lazily flicked her tail, appearing almost bored.

Nobble sent a deluge of sewage at Squawk. The poor bird fell to the ground again. For some reason, Squawk seemed weaker than my other pets. Just as I thought that the electrified bird vanished in a burst of electricity at my feet. A die rolled, and the burst struck both me and Slikk.

[Your pet, Squawk, has perished. Squawk used **Explode**. **Explode** hits at close range. Explode deals 18 damage to you. Critical hit, Explode deals 29 damage to Slikk. Slikk has perished.]

Enemy Entry 0005: Slikk the Sludger *(Sewer Goblin)*

Slikk the Sludger is the bodyguard of Gurgle; his job is to keep Gurgle alive so he can summon their god. With high health and constitution, Slikk can endure prolonged battles, making him a tough opponent to take down.

- **Weaknesses:** The eyes. It's always the eyes!

Stats
- **Health:** 60/60

- **Potency:** 5

- **Vitality:** 10

- **Precision:** 10

- **Defense:** 5

Enemy Entry 0006: Gurgle the Gusher *(Sewer Goblin)*

Gurgle the Gusher is the leader of the Sewer Goblins, blessed by their god with magical abilities. Despite his low physical health and strength, Gurgle compensates with his defensive capabilities and magical prowess. Beware the Vortex!

- **Weaknesses:** The eyes. It's always the eyes!

Stats
- **Health:** 35/35

- **Mana:** 40/40 *(Mana is burned to fuel spells)*

- **Insight:** 3

- **Vitality:** 5

- **Arcanum:** 8

- **Precision:** 10

- **Defense:** 1

Enemy Entry 0007: Drip the Drainer *(Sewer Goblin)*

Drip the Drainer is the personal court assassin of Gurgle; his job is to kill you. With a balance of decent health and high dexterity, Drip excels in dodging attacks and countering with precise strikes.

- **Weaknesses:** The eyes. It's always the eyes!

Stats

- **Health:** 45/45

- **Stamina:** 65

- **Vitality:** 5

- **Finesse:** 13

- **Precision:** 10

- **Evasion:** 12

- **Defense:** 3

Enemy Entry 0015: Nobble the Nasty *(Sewer Goblin Mage)*

Nobble the Nasty is a vile and cunning sewer goblin mage blessed by his god with the ability to summon and manipulate sewage. Known for his cruel humor and devastating area-control magic, Nobble is a critical threat in the goblin ranks. His spells slow, debilitate, and trap his enemies in hazardous sludge, while his allies take advantage of the chaos.

- **Weaknesses:** Lightning, Water, Shadow, Light, and Fire

- **Strengths:** Resistances to Ice, Ground

Stats

- **Health:** 45/45

- **Mana:** 50/50

Item Drops
Gold
- **Amount:** 30–100

- **Chance to drop:** 85%

Nobble's Nasty Staff
- **Amount:** 1

- **Chance to drop:** 10%

- **Effect:** Allows the user to cast "Sludge Wave"

Nobble's Amulet
- **Amount:** 1

- **Chance to drop:** 5%

- **Effect:** Increases resistance to poison effects and slows

Chapter Fifty-Eight
Lies! All Lies!

[Turn 4 Start.]

I staggered back as my turn started, the blast's pain still fresh. Anger flared as I turned to where Squawk had just been killed by Nobble. It was my first pet loss, and it had caused me significant damage. I cast my sewage spell, knocking Nobble off the platform and into the muck below.

[You dealt 7 damage to Nobble.]

Coal rushed forward to where Gurgle was, slashing with his claws.

[Critical hit! Natural crit! You dealt x3 damage. You dealt 39 damage. Gurgle has perished.]

Pearl leaped to the platform's edge and shot a mana bolt at the fallen Nobble. His HP had to be hanging by a thread, so I wasn't surprised to hear Crystal's voice announcing victory.

[You dealt 10 damage. Nobble has perished. Congratulations, you have received 5 Death Boons.]

I slumped to the ground, exhausted. Technically, the battle had been easier than previous ones with three pets to soak up damage and attack the enemies for me. During the first couple of runs, I felt highly underwhelmed in terms of power. The Torchbearer class was utterly useless, and the Barbarian, while strong, was not worth using, in my opinion, unless I was just using it wrong. And something was off about the fact that all these other classes got two skills and seemingly no penalties, while that class couldn't even equip chest armor or a helmet. None of the other classes had penalties, and two were so overpowered compared to the others that they weren't even fair comparisons. **Aim** was outright busted. Automatic critical hits? Who designs something that way?

The summoner class—able to hit a variety of enemy weaknesses with exceptional damage capabilities and having three physical bodies fighting alongside me—seemed unbeatable. The only drawback was the time limit Crystal mentioned. I still had three more classes to try, but maybe I had gotten lucky with Archer and Summoner being the best ones.

I shook my head to clear my thoughts and began looting the room. I sat on the side of the raised platform, kicked at a fallen goblin, and then moved to loot the three other corpses. Immediately, four dice bounced around the platform, splashing into the sewage below. A fifth die joined them shortly after.

[You have rolled a 64 and a 52. You have looted 52 gold from Drip. You have rolled a 22 and received a Goblin Ear from Gurgle. You have rolled a 77 and looted a rare chest key from Nobble. You have rolled a 93 and received Slikk's Sewer Pipe of Stun.]

There was still an ornate golden chest by the altar, which was, of course, locked. I immediately used my new chest key to unlock it. As soon as I looted the chest, four dice rolled. I had forgotten that boss chests gave extra loot. I felt a surge of excitement at the possibilities.

[You have received a Lunar Amulet. You have received two Astral Scrolls. You have received a potion of health regeneration.]

"Astral Scroll. What does that do?" I asked aloud, curiosity piqued.

[Oh, it's very useful,] Crystal explained. [It will turn a room from day to night and night to day for the duration of a run. So, if you use it at the entrance to the second floor, that entire giant area will be nighttime, potentially providing different quests and options. Just try not to let the temptation to steal get to you. There will be quite a few opportunities, but besides the fact that stealing is wrong, guards will still know it is being used, and we need to avoid a repeat of the previous run. You are very, very lucky you managed to kill that guard. He easily could have aggro'd the other guards and taken dozens of your runs from you.]

"Yes, you've told me. I definitely don't want that to happen. Again," I muttered, the memory still fresh and unpleasant. The Memory Core fell so fast I couldn't have dodged it if I wanted to. In an instant, I was whisked away. Whatever force was sending these to me, was clearly done asking.

{Memory Core 14/???}

~~~~~{Memory Core 14 Start}~~~~~

The flashback hit me suddenly. One moment, I was talking casually with Crystal, and the next, I was back in my house in the real world. Unlike my other memories, which played out like dreams where I had no control, I was fully aware in this one.

I moved into the kitchen and grabbed a knife. Why? Because I knew what was coming, and if I could stop it, maybe I wouldn't die. The kitchen was bare and dirty. Plates with caked food debris lay scattered around the room, and our food cupboard was empty from the fight earlier that morning.

"I've apologized ten times already. I don't know what else you want," I heard my father's voice, strained with frustration.

"I want the food back! That was a week's worth of vegetables. Now they're not even good as scraps for a dog," my mother shouted, her voice edged with desperation.

"It was an accident! I know I messed up! I tripped, and the food fell into the waste bucket. I got distracted and placed it in the kitchen before throwing it out. Again, I'm sorry. I'll go down first thing tomorrow," he pleaded.

My parents walked into the kitchen, and that's when I moved. I thrust the knife straight into my father's eye, knocking him to the floor, dead.

My mother screamed a blood-curdling scream. Then my father exploded. He had been addicted to this drug for years. It was mostly harmless, except for two significant side effects. The first was the typical drug-seeking behavior. The second? The corpse exploded on death. A layer of blood and viscera covered the room, and I retched as I caught a mouthful.

Why had I killed my father? I didn't know how the original memory played out, but it involved Peckolin and the plan he helped me with. Now, I preemptively killed him to save my mother. Except, I stared in horror at the knife jutting out of my mother's stomach as she bled to death. The force of the explosion had caused the knife to bury itself in her stomach.

"Rod? W-Why did you do this? Was I a bad mother? It's so..." Her voice faded as the life left her eyes. I fixated on the blood on my hands. Then the memory reset.

I was back in the kitchen, with empty plates. I grabbed the knife in self-defense. But this time, when my father and mother came into the room, I talked.

"Dad, that's not what happened this morning, and you know it," I said, my voice shaking.

"What are you talking about? The waste got all over my clothes and everything. I already put them in to soak," he replied, confusion and guilt flashing across his face.

"You sold our food for red-essence that you always make me buy."

"Gerald," my mother said, aghast, "is this true?"

"I—no. Yes, it's true. I'm so sorry. I promise tomorrow I'll—" he began, but my mother screamed in rage like a banshee. She charged forward, pushing my father to the ground, and started mercilessly kicking him in the stomach and head until we both heard his neck snap.

I stood still, paralyzed with terror at the scene because I knew this wasn't how my father died. *I remembered what I had planned with Peckolin. It didn't happen this way, right? These memories were a lie. All lies! And if these memories couldn't be trusted, which could I trust?*

And that's when I flashed back to the present.

~~~~~~{Memory Core 14 End}~~~~~

Chapter Fifty-Nine
The Merchant's Luck

[And it won't happen again if we don't risk stealing.]
Crystal paused, clearly waiting for a response from me. But I couldn't focus.

I slumped down, not caring, as my arm banged heavily against the altar. What had I just seen? Four different loops of myself and my parents killing each other in horrifying ways. I couldn't understand what had really happened. Did my parents kill each other? Did I kill my father in self-defense? Did they drop dead of food poisoning? The memories all contradicted each other and made no sense.

I put my head in my hands, tears streaming down my face as the pressure built in my skull like a rodent trying to force its way out of a trap. I sniffled and leaned my head back against the smooth, cold stone.

How long had it been since I entered the dungeon? Though I knew it had only been a few days, it felt like an eternity. Time was a blur here. It couldn't have been much longer because of how long it took to clear each room. These memories were tearing me apart.

I wanted to be done with this place. I wanted to be back home, even with my parents' constant arguing. I wanted to be with my friend, experimenting with magic and annoying the guards around town. I wanted my life back.

[Unfortunately, Rod, there is no going back. Dead is dead,] Crystal reminded me, her tone gentle yet firm.

"You people always say that, but what about Elric, the founder? He found a way back home," I retorted, desperation creeping into my voice.

[And like all rules, this one was made to be broken,] Crystal replied.

"Why can't I be the one to break the rules? The Triumvirate is already messing with me. Who's to say we won't make it?" I argued. A flash of anger sparked briefly as I thought of Rellum forcing me to do his task.

[Look, all I am saying is don't expect it. That makes things more challenging in the long run,] Crystal cautioned.

I sighed and ran a hand through my hair. Slowly, I picked myself up off the ground, using the altar for support. "Whatever. We should stop wasting time. I'm determined and won't let anyone determine my fate again. Rellum, Aurentum, Malikap—they built Penance for a reason. We were taught growing up that it was a test to determine who should lead the world. That we get a final wish at the end. If there's a chance, I will take it, and no amount of negativity or fear on your part will prevent me."

If Crystal still had a body, I could imagine her shaking her head, but I ignored my mental image. There were two exits to the room, and there was still a second secret to find. I had figured it would be here in the boss chamber, but a quick glance at the map parchment showed it was two rooms away, in the furthest room from the entrance. Before moving any further, though, I had to detour to the Necromancer room to recover my mana and summon a new pet.

~Run 6, Necromancer's Room, Floor 1, Sewers of Aerlyn~

I sat on the altar, the premier place in the dungeon. From my vantage point, I cast an **Elemental Summon**. The uncontrolled magic swelled in my belly as if I had overeaten, then flowed up and through my arms and fingertips. A die rolled.

A fire, a living fire, rolled out of my fingertips and onto the ground. The flame bubbled up like a liquid and came alive in an explosive burst. A mouth and nose formed on the flame, elongating as it morphed from a bubble-like blob into an all too familiar shape: a dog. Another fire elemental.

"Fire!" the flame dog barked, running around the room and leaving a trail of flames in its steps. "Fire!" the dog kept yapping before it came up to me and sat down expectantly. Coal came running and pushed the imposter out before barking happily at me. "Fire!" Coal said. The new dog pushed back against Coal, barked, and growled.

"There are two of them!" I exclaimed, eyes wide in disbelief. "Did you know that could happen?"

[It was always in the realm of possibility, yes,] Crystal responded calmly. I was blown away. I was also stuck; what would I name a second fire dog? Should I dismiss the dog and try for a third element? A brilliant plan for making this dungeon even easier came to mind.

"Crystal, **Scan** works from doorways, right? Before the gate slams down?" I asked, excitement building in my voice.

[You have done so a couple of times by this point,] Crystal replied.

"Brilliant. Let's go; come on, Pearl, Coal, Coal 2," I said, gathering my companions.

[Did you seriously name your second fire dog Coal 2?] Crystal asked, sounding slightly incredulous.

"Yes," I said innocently, smiling to myself.

In my mind, I imagined a humanized version of Crystal shaking her head.

[I don't look like that!] Crystal interjected, catching my thoughts.

"Oh, did I touch a nerve? I know you can create images with these parchment things. What did you look like on E-arth?" I asked, curious.

[It's pronounced Earth. And no, I'm not going to show you what I look like, you pervert!] Crystal snapped.

"What, no? I—never mind," I said, giving up on the line of questioning. It was time I left for the second floor.

I stepped through, leaving the first floor behind. Coals 1 and 2 flanked me on either side while Pearl dozed at the top of the stairs. The fresh air, crisp and cool, was a balm for my frayed nerves, the stress of merely glimpsing that super boss lingering like a bad dream.

Emerging from the dank, oppressive sewers into the open air of Aerlyn was a relief. The city was a beautiful sight, especially in contrast to the horrors I had just left. I made a beeline for Klericho's house, the cobblestones clicking under my feet with every step.

When I pushed open the door, the familiar creak of his door announced my arrival. Thomas and Klericho were seated at a table, and there, unsettlingly, was my unlooted corpse.

"Hey guys!" I called out, trying to ignore the sight of my own lifeless body.

"Rod! How'd you get back so fast? That was barely an hour. You must have set a new record," Klericho exclaimed, eyes widening in surprise.

"Haha, hardly. But it was easy with the class I just unlocked. It's called Conjurer, and it—"

"You don't find that class hard to use? It was powerful, but getting the pets to attack immediately was difficult," Thomas interrupted, shaking his head. "I pretty much gave up every run I had with that class."

"Didn't you say the same thing about the Archer class, Klericho? That it was too difficult to use properly?" I teased, raising an eyebrow.

"I did, too; keeping track of arrows was annoying and didn't always lend itself to feasible battles," Thomas replied with a sigh. "Especially when the enemy was resistant to arrows. I always had to skip the Necromancer room when I got the archer class."

"How do you skip a room?" Klericho asked, looking puzzled.

"You just go the other way. Hadn't you noticed that the first floor was a giant circle?" Thomas said, gesturing in a circular motion.

"I guess not," Klericho responded, scratching his head. "We got your corpse for you, but now that you're back on the floor, everything will have respawned."

"How were you all able to get my corpse? Crystal said non-Penitents couldn't touch corpses," I asked, curiosity piqued.

"What are we? Chopped liver?" Thomas laughed pointing above his head as I kicked my corpse, sighing in relief as my items re-entered my inventory.

Ignoring my innatention to their crystals, I continued. "Thanks for that. This should be easier now," I said, enthusiasm creeping into my voice. "I figured out a way I could easily switch out my pets because I looted that Astral Scroll and the Lunar Amulet. I got two of both, so now we must discuss strategy."

"What are those?" Thomas leaned forward, eyes gleaming with interest.

"The scroll makes it nighttime in a single room for the duration of the run, and the amulet creates a slow but steady mana and health regeneration under the moonlight," I explained, pulling out the items to show them.

"And you have two? Of each? You have the merchant's luck," Thomas remarked, shaking his head in amazement.

"You're not the first to say that. I've been oddly lucky," I replied with a shrug.

"I think we can give Klericho my second amulet and heal up between fights, but where should we make it nighttime? I don't want to inconvenience anyone, but how would people react if it was suddenly perpetually night here?" I wondered aloud, looking between Thomas and Klericho.

"You don't know about the curse, do you?" Thomas's voice dropped to a whisper, eyes darting nervously.

"What are you on about? This is Penance. There are no curses here because we are all already cursed," I scoffed, rolling my eyes. "What's the worst that could happen? We die? We already know I can bring you back. Everybody else respawns when I restart my run. We need a room for the night."

"The Djinn cursed this city so it would never be night again. If his curse were to fall... horrible monsters would attack," Thomas said, his voice trembling slightly.

Klericho snorted before I could respond. "What a load of malarkey. There are no curses in Penance. Who even told you about this curse?" he asked, crossing his arms.

"Jackiel. Remember him? He managed to get the level bypass to spawn off the King and left the floor that way," Thomas replied defensively.

"Level bypass?" I echoed, intrigued.

"Like the Blood Ruby from the goblins on the first floor drop," Thomas explained.

"If there's a level bypass, why are you both still stuck here?" I asked, frowning.

"Look, this conversation is getting off track. We need the moonlight to—" Klericho began.

"Then let's clear the textiles room and make it nighttime there. I'm telling you this is a bad idea," Thomas said, looking genuinely scared.

"It's two against one, Thomas; we're going to do it," Klericho said with an air of finality.

Chapter Sixty

Awooo!

~~~~~Later~~~~~

I should have listened. But after the ninja killed me, Thomas and Klericho ran for their lives, terrified of dying the same way. They said it felt like the only choice left to them. Since we were in a group, the increased difficulty of the goblins made it even more challenging to use the textiles room as a base, and the fact that goblins respawned in that room at night made the room a lousy choice for base launching.

Kericho's second floor had an exposed open-air window for creating cooling drafts in the hot climate. And now, it would expose us to moonlight and allow us to recover.

Klericho and I equipped the amulets, and I equipped my overcharge ring, something both Crystal and I had forgotten about, and I finally cast my Astral Scroll. Watching the skyline was surreal —it was like the world blinked. One moment, it was a hot and windy desert day; the next, it was a cold and windy desert night. At first, we thought everything was okay. Thomas was still stressed, so we talked while Klericho's mana finished regening.

Our conversation went on for another twenty minutes or so. We talked about our favorite moments or runs in the dungeon. Thomas had an entire run as a rogue, and he didn't take a single hit until he got to the boss fight on the second floor. Klericho said his favorite run was his first. Just the craziness of it had him feeling so powerful. Of course, that ended when Slikk caved his head in. It had taken Klericho fifteen runs to clear the first floor, and Thomas only took nine. I was the fastest at three runs. They still didn't believe me, especially after my poor showing in our second group battle had led to my death. But that didn't matter, as long as they trusted me to... My thoughts immediately left me as an unearthly howl filled the area.

"Oh, no. I was right." Thomas said, his voice heavy with the cadence of fear. "It's the curse." The pale moonlight illuminated the burly man's face. His eyes were wide, and his breaths were heavy as he talked.

"We don't know for sure that..." I cut myself off as all-too-human screams replaced the unearthly howls. "Okay, fine. I might have been wrong."

Klericho and Thomas both looked at me.

"Alright, fine. I shouldn't have used the scroll here. We need a game plan to get past this," I said.

"You and your plans. Can't we rush headlong into whatever this threat is?" Thomas asked.

"Yeah, because that worked so well for us last time."

Klericho chimed in, "We need to be more careful. I'm hesitant to let myself get killed here. We haven't seen any of those Aerlyntiums here. Besides, we don't know what we are facing yet, and none of us have a class with **Scan**."

"About that..." I said, directing their attention back to me. "When Rellum gave me the ability to loot the Aerlyntiums, he also gave me the ability to use **Scan** with every class. And it even gives me class-dependent info." Whatever force wouldn't let me tell them about the Death Boons, wouldn't let me mention how I got **Scan**, either, so I lied, again. Anyone keeping count?

"That's a load of goblin bung," Thomas said, anger lacing his voice. " Why are you so special? Klericho and I have been kicking it here longer than you have. What have you got that we don't?"

"Thomas, I suggest you stop." Klericho had an intensity in his gaze. "Whatever is going on here is nothing you want to be at the center of."

I nodded thanks at Klericho, grateful that at least one of my floor companions wouldn't want me dead with the revelation. "Look, we can put this conversation aside for now. Instead, we need to figure out how these monsters work. I have a plan, so please listen..."

A few minutes later, we were back downstairs, ready at the doorway to the outside world. We moved away from our barricades and stepped into a war zone.

Everything was frantic and chaotic. Long limbs and mismatched fur, skin, scales, and metals clashed in a hoard of mis-sharpened monstrosities. Like the stories I had heard growing up, the werewolf curse was all-consuming. The guards had been transformed but so had their armor. Their bodies had fused with the hauberks and surcoats. Fur took on a metallic sheen, and blues and reds clashed in tufts of fur like chainmail ringlets.

Yet even more werewolves flooded in to form a concentric circle against our group. What I could only assume were spice mongers, were the most malformed of the lot. Large bulbs of spices formed mounds like camel humps on the backs of rainbow-colored wolves. They were not metallic like the former guards but seemed powerful and intimidating.

And then the battle started. I had been worried about how paradigm battles would conflict with my companions and their fighting ability, but I had already spoken privately with Crystal about how that worked. The time-based mechanics were purely for my benefit. Time didn't slow down for anyone or anything else, only for my pets and me. It was to give me some increased time to focus and ensure I used the correct skills for myself and my pets.

I had three staves I could use in my battle: 2 already out, one in each hand, and the third tied to my back. Between the staves, I had necrotic, poison, and water elements. I tried resummoning my other pets, but a new one popped up. A beautiful violet colored moth with a 2 foot wing span and a terrifying face hovered above me.

Depending on my luck, I knew it could hit for around 25-40 damage, so I would wait for the werewolves to be in range of a death shot. My job was the damage dealer in my group; Klericho only there to heal, with Thomas planning to use his bulk to keep the werewolves from attacking us. The big problem was that they were not tiny monsters. At a towering eight feet, I was wondering if Thomas could match their bulk. But as time froze, I stopped worrying and got to work.

[Turn 1 Start]

I used **Scan**. Multiple times. For whatever reason, it didn't count as using my move for the turn, and each multicolored werewolf was considered a different monster.

Enemy Entry 0016: Werewolf Soldier *(Type: Aerlyntium Guard)*
Remember that guard you 'accidentally' got the attention of? Yeah, well, this is what happens when you steal his bread instead of a merchant's.

- **Weaknesses:** Fire, Shadow

- **Strengths:** Resistance to Ice, Ground

Stats
- **Health:** 200/200

- **Mana:** 50/50

Item Drops
Gold
- **Amount:** 5

- **Chance to drop:** 33%

Enemy Entry 0017: Werewolf Captain *(Type: Aerlyntium Guard)*

Erik, the guard captain, was the kindest person in the dungeon. It wasn't even his fault he ended up there. It's not my story to tell, but it sure is horrible that you did this to him.

- **Weaknesses:**

    ◦ Fire: 1.5x damage

    ◦ Shadow: 3.0x damage

- **Strengths:**

    ◦ Resistances to Ice, Ground

Stats
- **Health:** 200/200

- **Mana:** 50/50

Item Drops
Gold
- **Amount:** 5

- **Chance to drop:** 33%

Enemy Entry 0018: Werewolf Merchant *(Type: Innocent Victim)*

The merchant you stole from? That was his last loaf of bread, and now he and his children are out on the streets because he couldn't afford his taxes. What a great hero you are.

- **Weaknesses:**

  ○ Fire: 1.5x damage

  ○ Shadow: 3.0x damage

- **Strengths:**

  ○ Resistances to Ice, Ground

Stats

- **Health:** 200/200

- **Mana:** 50/50

Item Drops
Gold

- **Amount:** 5

- **Chance to drop:** 33%

Enemy Entry 0019: Werewolf Swordsman *(Type: Innocent Victim)*

These merchant bodyguards were once Penitent. Now, they are forever a part of the city of Aerlyn. If you want the absolute truth about what this dungeon entails, these are the people you want to talk to.

- **Weaknesses:**

  ○ Fire: 1.5x damage

- ○ Shadow: 3.0x damage

- **Strengths:**

  - ○ Resistances to Ice, Ground

Stats
- **Health:** 200/200

- **Mana:** 50/50

Item Drops
Gold
- **Amount:** 5

- **Chance to drop:** 33%

Chapter Sixty-One
Overcharge

I was overwhelmed by the flood of information, so I mostly skimmed it while saying to Crystal, "Hey, mute the messages, please, I need to focus." The stats still poured onto the parchments, and I had to wave them away to focus. The whole interaction had taken 20 seconds, so in a panic, I said to Crystal, "Please set my pets to ranged magic and weakness only." While I did this, I angled myself to the right of Thomas going for the nearest target.

I used my Necrotic Staff to attack the guard captain, figuring he would take the longest to take out.

[You have dealt 4 damage to Werewolf Captain.]

As I froze, I surveyed the battlefield. Thomas was frozen with his sword extended to his right and his other splayed to the left. A golden magical shield radiated around him, Klericho clearly having successfully cast his shield.

And then, the werewolves attacked. For monsters, they were extremely well coordinated. The guard captain focused on Thomas but directed his allies to try to flank around. Thankfully, time froze for them right as they approached Klericho.

I hadn't had time to focus on my pets, but now they moved before I did. Coal launched a flame missile at the werewolf attacking Klericho, and then Pearl jumped in front and used her claws to slash at the two werewolves.Dust, my poisonous moth, which I totally didn't forget to tell you the name of, hovered above the crowded field and used an area-of-effect poison spell.It only did 3 damage, but it had a 60% chance of inflicting poison. Even if I rolled a 1, that was better than any poison I had seen so far.

I didn't want to waste my turn, so seconds before Crystal updated me on my pets, I again aimed my staff at the guard captain. [You have dealt 2 damage to Werewolf Captain.]

[Calculating poison chances.] I had been afraid of that. The poisonous cloud that erupted was not what I had expected. Acrid red smoke that looked similar in color to the crushed remains of a dead body burst from around my purple familiar in a ball shape, which overtook everything. My other two familiars, Klericho and the Werewolves, all breathed in the thick smoke.

[Congrats! You have successfully poisoned your other pets!] Now wasn't the time for Crystal's antics, so I looked around trying to figure out who had been poisoned.

I wasn't sure how the results were assigned, but I hoped the critical failure would go to Klericho so that he at least would be spared the poison. As if my prayer had been heard, the poison cloud parted around Klericho and one of the wolves. Both my non-moth familiars were poisoned. Coal took on a deeper red color, and the smoke that poured off his tail had changed to match the color of the smoke from the moth's attack. On the other hand, Pearl had taken on a deep purple hue. Little motes of red swirled around her hydric body.

[**Poison Cloud** has poisoned the Werewolf Soldier, Captain and Merchant as well as Coal and Pearl. Klericho and Werewolf Swordsman are not affected. Poison has enchanted the elemental bodies of Coal and Pearl. Ability unlocked: **Elemental Fusion**: By casting one elemental's attacks on another elemental, you can combine elements to create unique elemental beings. Elements discovered:

Noxiflume: Poison-inflicting flames and smoke. Take on a dark red hue that makes it almost look like blood. Inflict a fire elemental with poison.

Blightbrine: Poisonous water. Takes on a byzantium hue, the murky waters as deadly as they look.]

I blinked and then glanced at the time. The third turn was almost upon us, and I hadn't paid enough attention to combat because of being inundated with information. I had no idea where anything was, the entire area was still covered in red smoke. But the nice thing about this paradigm battle was how it functioned, something I was overjoyed to finally figure out.

Each thirty-second turn was 6 seconds of real time; each second slowed to five seconds for my advantage. It was a more extended version of the freezing time that occurred when I evaded. Time passed normally for everyone else, even if it didn't seem like that way for the monsters. It was why their attacks and movements seemed so slow. The only real downside was that I was frozen for 30 seconds, but the fact that my teammates moved during that time was like a boon to me.I would have to figure out ways to make this work to my advantage, and I also needed to figure out ways to ensure this didn't seem suspicious to my teammates.

I had already figured out that I could move around during the enemy's turn, but I had no idea how lucky I would be for my companions. My plan was to cast a spell at the end of my turn, trapping myself in the two-second cast animation—which would actually stretch longer from my perspective. Then, depending on whether any enemies were attacking, I could throw myself or roll away. But, as with all plans, this one only got a little bit past thinking it out loud.

My muscles felt like lead as I gripped my staff and cast the spell; time stretched to infinity as the spell collected energy. I had thought ten seconds would go by quickly, but as I mentally tallied seconds, fifteen turned to twenty, turned to twenty-five, and suddenly it was my turn again, and I was still frozen. The world around me zoomed chaotically.

[What are you doing?] I heard Crystal's voice super-fast, so I couldn't understand her. But I could still read her parchment notes. [You can't cast spells during downtime.... Oh, wait. Your Overcharge Ring. You'll be fine.]

As my count approached north of 200 seconds, it finally happened; my spell had been charging for 10-fold the time it had typically taken to cast. I was not surprised when the spell launched off like a missile from a cannon. It exploded into the Captain, who was already down by more than three-quarters his health. A giant 100-sided die rolled by as time returned to normal, and my spell launched.

[You have successfully used the Ring of Overcharge. You have dealt 65 damage to Werewolf Captain. Overkill! You have killed a progenitor with Overkill damage. Combat ended.]

And just like that, combat was over. And I did not expect it at all. We had killed the werewolves, their corpses sprawled out in the entrance foyer, loot stars shining above their heads. I wish I had known I could do that earlier. Four people I could have saved, but at least they would respawn when I came through on my next run.

I tapped the corpses for my share, and Crystal inundated me with loot messages. The wall of loot messages confused me as Crystal changed the loot again for what had to be the sixth time. At least she was consistent in her lack of consistency.

[You have looted: Swordsman's Hide, Assorted Gems, Gold Coin x 76, Wolf Pelt, Canine Tooth, Enchanted Ring of Vitality]

I then turned to look at the eight villagers who survived the ordeal of the curse. The clothes they had been wearing were damaged or frayed beyond saving in a couple of cases. They huddled together as we all surveyed the ruins of the city. The werewolf charge destroyed the spice tables, and spice piles clumped together on the ground into unrecognizable mounds. Buildings were damaged or outright destroyed, and we could see the blacksmith section in the distance through what remained of a four-story apartment building.

All this horror and damage was my fault. This wouldn't have happened if I hadn't insisted on using the scroll. The only good thing that we got out of the deal was the loot, and several of the items seemed intriguing to my mind, but everything was forgotten as a flash of light blanketed the room, and then an Aerlyntium Orb lowered from the ceiling and appeared in the middle of the foyer.

I groaned, realizing that even if we came back to this place in a future run, it would be a while before all of the shops, people, spices, and items were back. As I stared at the Aerlyntium, a second, smaller orb descended from the sky.

I approached the Memory Core, cursing my horrible choices as I flashed back to another memory.

{Memory Core 15/???}

~~~~~{Memory Core 15 Start}~~~~~

The daily life of a citizen of Vezwincourt. That thought burned through my mind as I experienced the city's glory. I was six years old, and my father had a rare day off from the royal court. My father was a guard, one of the best. His position was low, but his value was in his dedication and his service. 6pm to 6am. The night duty was essential, even if it wasn't considered respectable.

His father always told him that assassination attempts were most likely to occur in the night. It paid to be alert, and my father had the Eyes of Gold. A rare magical gift that allowed him to see everything. Enchantments, illnesses, lies. His magic was seen as inferior to the training of the elite members of the guard. Magic was seen as broken, a curse of Aurentum's touch on Equiem. Of course, the royal family all had magic powers; no one seemed to care that they had them; they were just ordinary people. Wizards were hunted or forced to hide; my father was fine as a member of the royal guard because his innate trait was allowed to exist.

I was six when I first saw the signs of stress my father dealt with due to this magic. During the day, he had to shield his eyes from the sun's light. His wide-brimmed hat dipped low over his hazel eyes. I saw the light in my father then, half magic, half joy at the world around him.

"Never forget, Roddy, my boy, the world is full of wonder; we just have to choose to see it."

~~~~~{Memory Core 15 End}~~~~~

Chapter Sixty-Two
Marked By a God

As I flashed back to reality, I was increasingly concerned about my parents. Every memory made less sense than the one before it. *Had my father, really, once been kind to me? Or was it a manipulated memory just like the one of their deaths? I knew he had been an Archer once. What had happened to him?*

I stared at my dust-covered feet, not wanting to face reality, not wanting to know the truth, just wanting one more moment with that version of my father. Come on, *keep it together.*

[Rod, are you okay?] Elizabeth asked me, breaking me from my reverie. [You should loot the Aerlyntium. It's just standing there, menacingly.]

I wiped my eyes and looked up. Thomas and Klericho were idly chatting, keeping one wary eye on me and one on the Aerlyntium as if it would do something harmful if I approached it.

As my hand touched the pulsating blue of the Aerlyntium, the orb floated up and started to consume the entire wasteland that used to be the entrance bazaar. The blue spiral of a tornado sucked up spices, clay, metal, and wood, and even the corpses of people caught in the battle against the werewolves.

[You have received:]
- **Entrance, Night Aerlyntium 1 of 6**

- **Spice Merchant** x 4

- **Entrance Light** x 5

- **Guard Post**

- **Spices (mixed)** x 5

- **Doorway** x 2

- **Spice Table** x 3

- **Merchants Shack** x 2

- **Consumer** x 10

- **Butcher** x 2

- **Fletcher** x 1

- **Food Depot** x 1

You have received the following raw materials:
- **Gold** x 150,000

- **Wood** x 60,000

- **Silk Fabrics** x 20 bolts

- **Wool Rugs** x 10

- **Copper Utensils Set** x 3

You have received:

- **Tim** x 1

- **Tim's pet hamster-dog, Timothy the Second** x 1

- **Tim's House** x 1

"Stop, okay? Woah, I get it, Elizabeth. I picked up an absurd amount of wealth here." I said, staring at the parchment in front of me with a level of disbelief unmatched by anything I had encountered, and I had seen a rat circus. Even though she stopped talking, the parchment continued to list item after item after item that the Aerlyntium had picked up. "Did I just plunder the entire city? Does this mean it will be empty when I return? Because that's not good." Sweat covered my forehead as I furrowed my brow. "I just messed up big time, didn't I, Elizabeth?"

[Well, you didn't make it easier. That's for sure. But I have a sense Rellum knew this would happen at some point. Why else would an Aerlyntium appear here?]

"So you think that Rellum knew this would happen? And he still let all of those people suffer and everything?"

[Even Thomas knew this would happen, and he's practically married to the idiot ball. If you think about it, this was almost guaranteed to happen.]

"It's going to be a pain replacing the whole city," I groaned, hiding my growing furor over Rellum and the things he let happen. I imagined pulling up the building frame and placing items individually. It would take me days, if not weeks, to fix this entire zone. Elizabeth spoke up just as I was about to give up and curl into a ball at the unimaginable boredom my life would soon become.

[Stop being such a drama queen. Even if we had all 6 Aerlyntiums right now, this wouldn't take nearly as long as you are panicking about. There are mass-placement settings and a repeat action setting, though I wouldn't use that immediately. You can shape this area, all areas, to meet your needs. Or to meet the needs of the people living here.]

"But what if I place something in the wrong location? Won't they get mad?"

[Sure, but how on Penance would they realize it was your fault?]

"Oh. They won't, but how will I ask them their preferences?"

[There's this magical tool that you should consider. It's more powerful than any tool in the dungeon. It will get you all of the answers you seek here and then some.]

"What? What is it?"

[Talking.]

<p style="text-align:center">~~~~~Later~~~~~</p>

It took us half an hour to place down all the locations I had received and the people to whom they belonged.

When I placed the spice merchants, I spotted three big problems. First, there were only three shacks for four merchants and three tables.

"What do you mean my shack was destroyed?"

"It's okay. It will be fixed eventually. You just need to be patient." Thomas glanced towards me, but I nudged his foot to encourage him to keep going.

"Just be glad you survived. The other people won't return until the reset, and who knows how long that will be." He stared at the man's faded, pink crystal. It was sad how some people gave up on their quest to learn what happened to them.

"Oh goodness, you saved me? Yous a real one. You is." The shifty-looking merchant was relieved, and I was happy we didn't have to spill my secrets. I had always had secrets on Equiem. Perks of the Trade. Thievery was a very introverted and secretive trade.

It didn't surprise me that the train of thought led to a Memory Core descending from the sky. I grabbed it and didn't even bother waiting for a prompt before I said, "Yes."

{Memory Core 16/???}

~~~~~{Memory Core 16 Start}~~~~~

It was an hour after leaving my bizarre meeting with the princess. I had no idea why royalty wanted to talk to me, and I felt exposed. I held my cloak against myself, trying to blend into the shadows and away from this unsettling feeling. I rattled down the hallway and slipped the ring onto my finger. For some reason, it was a lustrous gold scuffed in a single spot like it had been scraped against rough castle walls. There was an inscription around the inside of the ring, but it had to be in a different language because the letters made no sense to me.

The ring was magically warm on my finger, and I was tempted to take it off. The ring was probably cursed, knowing royalty the way I did. My father had once worked for the royal guard, but in the wrong place, at the wrong time, and fell from grace after he lost his ability to use a bow. Things had been great for the first few years of my life. Always taking, never giving. Always wanting more and more.

~~~~~{Memory Core 15 End}~~~~~

I wasn't sure how long I had spent staring off into space as a memory overtook me, but the merchant had walked away, and Thomas and Klericho were looking at me expectantly.

"What?" I asked, their sly grins making me uneasy. Thomas opened his mouth as if to speak, and then his crystal pulsed, and I heard its voice instead.

[Good day, lad. I am Maximillian Bonaparte the fourth. It is time we have a talk.]

"W–What, How am I hearing you?"

[That's a long story, but it isn't important right now. Let's get to somewhere private before we start divulging the god's truths in broad daylight.]

~~~~~Klericho's House~~~~~

"It's that simple? Why make a big show then? Surely you can't be serious?" I said, staring at the crystal. The big secret was that Rellum had decided his Life Crystals would be able to talk to anyone that Rellum trusted. That was it. I felt like he was trying to pull one on me.

[I am serious, and don't call me Shirley.] Elizabeth chimed in. I looked at her funny, trying to hide my confusion.

We were in Klericho's shack again. It was one of the few buildings that had survived the battle unscathed. Primarily because we were preventing it from taking damage, but still.

"Are the wards up?" Thomas asked, sounding sharp, alert, and completely different from the dimwitted idiot he'd been since I met him. Now if only Klericho could sharpen up, too.

"Enough that Aurentum could still see through but likely won't come searching. The fact that it uses Malikap's signature instead of Rellum and is designed to keep Rellum out should mask our conversation."

Klericho had changed, too. Gone was the soft, gentle smile, replaced by a grim and stern expression.

"Anyone mind telling me what's going on?"

[Allow me, gentlemen. It is me, Maximilian. I am the leader of this Penitent group. Rellum himself left me in charge. Your Aerlyntium was specifically given to save us. We have an important task after all.]

"And what task is that?"

[Stopping you from freeing Aurentum, The Merchant of Death.]

"Wh-what? Why would I free Aurentum? Is he even real? I mean, I know this place exists, and I've seen Rellum, but that doesn't mean..." I stopped talking as I thought about the strange moment when I woke up in the fetal position. And the words were written down. Had it really been? Elizabeth had been strangely silent through everything so far, so I sent a thought through our link, asking her if we should trust them or just play along.

[I think they are telling the truth.] Crystal said, [There is no need to be wary here. I tested the wards, and it is essentially the same protection in place as when in the first floor Entrance Room.

"Oh. That's good."

Thomas looked at me expectantly. And then Maximillian spoke, [We are at a critical point in the structure of this dungeon floor. And thankfully, you are here, Rod. The fate of the dungeon rests in your hands.]

"What? What are you talking about?"

Klericho chimed in, responding to my question, "You are marked. You have to be. Just like Thomas and I are marked by Rellum. You must have some sort of power that we don't have, just like we have power that you don't. The final nail in the coffin was the battle we just had. You had way more power than I've ever seen a Summoner have." He paused, staring at me intently. "The eight base classes are balanced based on the powers of the three gods. Rellum influences the healer and fighter classes, specifically Cleric, Paladin, Fighter, and Barbarian. Aurentum controls the magic and rogue classes, specifically Urchin, Archer, Summoner, and Mage."

[No one knows what classes Malikap influences] Max, the crystal, said, taking over the conversation. [Additionally, each god directly influences the dungeon in specific ways. Aurentum has the Death Market—]

I cut him off, "Death Market?"

[Yes, what is Death Market called? Where and how you spend your Death Boons. Rellum's Penitents gain access to the Life Market, and we can spend Life Boons.]

"What, how do you know about them? Every time I try to talk about them, weird stuff happens." I glanced around the room, my pulse racing, waiting for everything to freeze. But nothing happened. *Wards. That had to be why. I guess they did work.* "If you are aligned with Rellum, and I'm supposedly aligned with Aurentum, why are you telling me all this?"

[Because of the Aerlyntiums. They shouldn't exist. Once you are marked by a god, the others can't touch you.]

"Rellum said I was never marked."

Klericho and Thomas shared a glance with each other. "There's no way that's right, maybe you misheard him?" Klericho said, his face souring into a frown.

"I didn't mishear him. He said the only reason I can have access to the Aerlyntiums is because I am not marked."

We argued for a few more minutes before I stood, heat radiating off of me as I paced the room to try and calm down. "This doesn't matter. What do I need to know? Stop wasting time." Max spoke up again, [Penance is part of the spiritual realm. It is the path between life and death. Heaven and Hell. It is called different things in different places. Penance. Purgatory. Barzakh. The Astral. Gehinnom. The Medium Place. All interpretations of the same idea exist, though no one gets it right. But unlike the others, this place has become a prison designed to keep existence safe from Aurentum and Malikap. Here, their presence is held firm. Stable. But out there in the realm of the living, their power would be catastrophic.] He paused, his scrolls unfurling with a neat black script.

[We all know the story of Elric, the founder. But he never actually escaped Penance. Instead, a friend of his stopped him at the peak and took his place. A man named Malikap.]

"Wait... What now? Malikap? As in the father of evil? The man behind the curtain of all monsters, big and small? He was the founder?"

[Yes, and then he built the grand cities of Equiem. He shaped the waterfalls of Rynerath. Plucked the World Seed from the Flower of the Heavens and created the Ever-Forest. At the crucible of existence, he met The One True God, the father of all things who built Penance and gained the Breath of a God. Malikap had never been meant to leave, but he was granted the ability and was allowed to shepherd humanity]

"Okay, that's equal parts fascinating and terrifying, especially that he shepherded humanity... but what does Malikap have to do with Aurentum."

[I'm getting there. Just be patient.]

Chapter Sixty-Three
The Great Will

I was getting annoyed at this. The information was valuable, but I was getting antsy and bored. I had never been one to sit still. I always preferred to be in motion, to be doing something. I enjoyed learning, but after a certain point, my mind would drift. My thoughts always wanting to focus on something else.

All I wanted to do now was hop back into the dungeon. I had thought up some new strategies now that I knew the overcharge skill was a thing. I wanted to see if I could overcharge my summons.

[Due to this, Malikap... Are you even paying attention?]

I had started staring off into the distance, lost in my thoughts. But I shook my head and focused on the red pulsating crystal. "I'm sorry, I'm trying. I've just never been good at this kind of thing."

[What kind of thing? Listening?]

"Yes...?"

[How did you survive school? The teachers at my school would have throttled me if I had as bad a focus as you.]

"I'm sorry, I'm trying my best, but I wanna get back to clearing the dungeons. While we are sitting here talking, those Aerlyntiums are floating there. Real people are stuck in a quasi-state of death when they could be here and alive again."

[I understand that. But I am explaining some important things here. Information that you will eventually want to know.]

"Is this information going to help me clear the monsters fast or move to another floor?"

[No, but...]

"But nothing. Give me one good reason why I should continue listening to you. You started by talking about Aurentum, and then you took a segue to ramble on about Malikap and that Elric was killed and Malikap took his place. It's a crazy revelation, but why is it important? Why must I know about him or Aurentum to survive in this place? I think I proved my competence in fighting, so what does the knowledge part matter?"

If crystals could breathe, Maximillian would have let out an insufferable sigh.

[This is important because you've been pulled into the middle of events. You now have to decide if you will be a part of the solution or a part of the problem. We want you to be a part of the solution. I know this information doesn't feel important, but I promise it will only help you clear this place. I'm not trying to bore you or stall you. There is a reason we are speaking, so please. Listen.]

People didn't tend to like me. I knew my wizard friend liked me, and maybe that girl I kept having memories of did, too, but I had a feeling that I was an outcast and not someone many people wanted to be around. It was strange not knowing who I was. Or was it weird? Maybe my experience here was perfectly normal. I hadn't opened up to these people at all. If I listened, they would listen, too, right?

I rested my arms on the table before me, clasped my hands around my elbows, and put on my serious face.

"Alright, I'm sorry I haven't been attentive. I'll try a little harder."

[To fix our problem here, I'll refocus what I'm saying to be quicker. Malikap broke out of this dungeon and, in so doing, created a hole. Everyone always thinks Aurentum created this place, but he didn't. This place is a bridge—a bridge between two realms, life and death. And when we are here, we are neither. When Malikap broke out, the realm of the living could not accommodate him, so God created magic. To fix that hole.]

"And that hole is where Aurentum comes in?" I started feeling bored again, but I was determined to fight against this quasi-fatigue plaguing me. What was wrong with my mind?

[Yes and no. We are almost there. When God created magic, he created what are called Aspects. These are beings that are in control of how existence works. Beings that manage weather, rivers, erosion, earth, growth, and wealth. Beings like Rellum, Aurentum, and Malikap.]

[To imbue people with free will, he gave us the Choice. Good and Evil. Sin and Virtue. Yin and Yang. But Aspects, the lesser gods, were not given free will. As a result, Aurentum is a victim of his circumstances. As an Aspect, he was given power and influence over wealth. He controlled the ebb and flow of markets, money, and greed but grew tired of never having his own say. And one day, he refused The Great Will.]

"What's The Great Will?"

[It's nature. It's order. It would be like grass refusing to grow green. Rain refusing to fall. The sun refusing to rise and set. Rivers refusing to flow. Refusing The Great Will is disorder, chaos, and death. It's going against the greater nature of existence.]

"And that's bad because?"

[Is he serious?] The crystal took on a strange tone as if it disbelieved my words were real. I had a feeling that if the crystal had a human body, he would turn around and raise his eyebrows at his friends. I didn't like people questioning my intelligence. It wasn't my fault I knew little about the world religion.

When my father was disgraced, my family stopped attending sermons. So, even though the will to learn had always been there, I never had the opportunity to learn my own religion. It was part of why I fell to thievery. It was an easy skill to learn and I didn't have to listen a lot. I could almost feel the memory form, but something stopped it. Almost unbidden, words I didn't even want to say, came out of my mouth.

"Look, I'm not defending Aurentum; I think I get how evil he is, but what is wrong about betraying 'The Great Will.' Everyone does. You're both speaking with me, and I'm not one of Rellum's chosen. You're using Malikap's ward instead of Rellum. You're cavorting with an enemy and going against the right way of doing things."

[We have permission, and it's not like you weren't chosen by Rellum anyway.]

"So he didn't ask his dad's permission before sneaking out of the house, and now he is locked in a prison for all time? Isn't that a tad harsh? And aren't Rellum and Malikap stuck here too?"

[It is more complicated than you are making it seem.]

"How?"

[It's more like he broke out of his dad's house after destroying the kitchen table, stealing the family coffers, breaking the front door, and absconding with all the family pets. To break the metaphor, he destroyed what trust he had in the Father, destroyed innocent lives in the process, and tried to play the role of the victim.]

"Alright, but I thought Rellum's thing was forgiveness. Why can't Aurentum be given a chance at forgiveness?"

[He's too bitter. He sees it as capitulating. He won't let himself because he feels too much pride.]

"So, why exactly did I need to know this information?"

"You need to know that you can't trust them," Thomas spoke up for the first time in the whole conversation.

"Well, duh! That was obvious. We're in a prison, I wasn't born yesterday." I shook my head and then looked at Thomas. "Let me see if I've got this straight. Malikap, Rellum, and Aurentum have specific natures to follow. The reason why Aurentum was jailed here was because he betrayed his nature. And now Malikap has betrayed his nature, too, and now it's up to myself and two other Penitents to climb the tower and find out why?"

[Essentially, but there are others of us on future floors. The problem with this place is in its structure. Once we leave this floor, we lose access to the shops and Klericho's base of operations. We have been here for at least a year trying to move on to the other floors, but we got stuck. And then we ran out of runs.]

"Alright, say I help you with this stuff. What is in it for me?"

[Teammates that will stick with you throughout the entire dungeon.]

I tilted my head and shrugged. That was probably a good thing to have. I lost on my previous run because I got impatient with the assassin. I was going to need to be more careful with this build. "Alright, I'll bite, what's the plan? How are we going to make it past the Djinn boss? Isn't that the wall that stopped you both?"

"You have 94 more runs, right? We have already discovered that you can bring us back each run, or if you die but we don't, we can high-tail it back to here."

"I'd prefer not to use up all of my runs."

[We know, but how else would you make it through this floor?]

"Brute force?" I laughed, hesitant in my answer. As soon as I said it, I knew how silly it sounded.

[There are still several things we can try, including plenty of methods for overcoming the challenges of this floor. With your new pet fusion skill, we can try nuking the boss down; maybe that will bring enough damage.]

"Okay, that sounds like a good plan to start with. It will take a plethora of runs before we finish them all. Unless there is a way to get multiple Aerlyntiums per room per run..." I facepalmed as I realized an easy test we could do. My eyes lit brightly as I said, "How does grouping work? Is it the first one through the door? What happens if Thomas goes through first?"

"No, nothing like that, but I think we have wasted enough time."

I nodded. "Alright, let's do this."

As a group, we walked over to the door to the dungeon. Thomas and I held Klericho's shoulder as he walked through the dungeon door.

Chapter Sixty-Four
The Red Death

~Run 6, Merchant's Alleyway, Floor 2, The Fallen Merchant City of Aerlyn~

I grimaced as I looked at the room. *Why did the first room have to be the worst one?*

I hated small spaces and did not want to go through this place again. Chairs, tables, knickknacks, and assorted obstacles formed an increasingly small tunnel. This was nerve-wracking and wasn't any better the second time through. I climbed through the mess as a desk chair dug into my side, and a sword tip poked through my shoe between my toes.

"Ahh!" I yelled, grabbing my food and falling to the other side where I had met Thumbs. This time, there was a new goblin trickster to fight. I had already discussed my plan to supercharge my summoning spell with my companions. As soon as I caught sight of the goblin, Crystal interrupted my screaming and flailing:

[Turn 1 start. Thirty seconds remain.]

I cast **Scan**. Staring down the goblin. He was tall for a goblin, maybe around four and a half feet, and wielded a red sword with black lines in a spiral going from the blade's tip to the hilt. Oddly enough, it also glowed purple.

Enemy Entry 0020: GregOre! the Goblin Hoarder
- **Weaknesses:** Put a gold coin down to distract him, then smash his head in while he's enchanted. You absolute monster.

Stats

- **Health:** 20/20

And then I cast a single bolt from my staff. The necrotic bolt slipped lazily through the air and blasted into GregOre.

[You have dealt four damage to GregOre.]

[Turn 1 end]

Time froze me, allowing my hands to move slowly through the molasses-like air.

And then I cast summon, hoping overcharge would allow me to produce something powerful. GregOre shrieked and started running towards me. He seemed to move with the speed of lightning, barreling down on me. As I slowly cast, I thought the goblin would attack me, but before he could, Thomas appeared in front of me just like we planned. He brought his giant sword down on the head of the goblin in a cleaving motion, instantly killing the goblin. Time still didn't unfreeze, as I was stuck in the overcharge casting. Unfathomable, uncontrolled power coursed through my veins, filling my body until I thought I would burst. I felt my mana drain away, as did my health and stamina. It swelled in my belly, filling me until I was about to burst.

Just when I thought I couldn't survive any more of it, the mana exploded out of my fingertips, coalesced in dark, black motes of magic, and took the form of three ambling skeletons. One was wielding a sword that shined as bright as starlight, one a normal bow, and one a staff. By the time I was done admiring my pets, Klericho and Thomas had already kicked in the goblin's head.

"Bones one, two, and three; glad you are all here," I said, christening my new pets. The bones of the skeletons radiated the dark purple and black mist from earlier. The mist dispersed around my hand as I waved it through the skeleton's forearm before the bone reformed.

"Cool. Shadow Skeletons. Hey Crystal, any chance these guys resist physical damage or something?"

[That would be awesome, but if you notice, these skeletons don't have HP. Instead, they have double the normal MP of other pets. Anything that disperses their mist causes MP damage. And unlike other mobs, they do not have MP regen. They are exceedingly fragile but powerful. Also, unlike other pets, they do not have both melee and ranged attacks. Only whatever their weapon provides them. And since you overcharged the spell, they only took up one pet spot. So you can still summon three more pets.]

"Wait, I thought it was three max?"

[It's based on the floor you are on. You can summon an extra pet per floor. But this overcharge mechanic seems to overwrite the rule and could potentially allow you to summon up to 12 pets right now.]

"That's crazy. This class is overpowered. Let's hurry onto the next room."

[Don't forget to loot all of the random stuff here. It will be needed when we start placing all of the Aerlyntium items.]

"Right." Thomas, Klericho, and I spent the next 15 minutes looting every item we could from the room. Ultimately, I received the same amount of loot I did from the previous time through the room, which was nice. I wondered if I could sell the excess broken swords to a forge for gold. Even broken, the iron could be salvaged, right?

We made our way through the empty hallway before I noticed the new sword hanging in the scabbard on Thomas's back. The hilt was now glowing a pulsing black, the same color as my skeleton.

It gave me an idea I didn't know how to ask. But without even prompting, Thomas threw the sword to me. "But I get the next sword, no matter what."

I grimaced; I didn't want to bet against future loot, but whatever this sword was, it looked like a huge boon for my pet. Crystal shared its stats without prompting.

The Red Death (*Unique*)

- **Amount:** 1

- **Condition:** 35/35

- **Effect:**

  ◦ +3 Potency

  ◦ −10 Constitution (minimum of 1 Constitution)

  ◦ Every successful hit adds +1 Potency.

  ◦ Every kill regenerates 1 point of durability (can overcharge).

Description

The sword reeks of death, its aura palpable to all who dare to wield it. The blade is a deep crimson, with sparkling black tendrils running up and down its shaft. It pulses with an eerie purple light, resonating with a hunger for blood and power.

Flavor Text

"There can only be one."

I gasped at the Potency bonus. With my base Potency of three, my pet would have a Potency of 6. That meant every hit with this sword equipped would one-shot monsters on the first floor. I wondered, "Hey, Bonesword." I had decided to rename my pet "Come Here." My wispy skeleton waddled over to me. "Take this sword in your left hand, but don't use it in battle. Only use your normal sword for now."

My skeleton's teeth clacked against each other in an unsettling clang as he nodded at me. My other skeletons looked upset that they weren't receiving buffs. I pulled the Staff of Lunar Tides and handed it to the mage skeleton, and then I pulled out my quiver of arrows and gave it to the archer skeleton. My pets were ultra-stacked now, and I could see us making it far. But hubris had been the death of me too many times so far, so I decided to be cautious this run.

"Okay, guys. We need to talk." I said, putting my hand on the door to the next room. "In this next room, please; nobody does any tricks, shortcuts, or walks off alone. I know there is a scary assassin that one-shot my last run but don't interfere until I start casting the big spell. "Bonesword, you're on defense. Please jump in front of me as soon as you are able. Thomas, same deal. Klericho, cast that bubble shield thing on all 3 of us as soon as you can. Start with Thomas, then me, and then the skeleton. I don't want to lose him already, but a pet is better than one of us. Mana is a concern, but as soon as my big spell is cast, we can all rush the Assassin. We're bound to hit him down quickly, given our numbers."

Thomas grinned and said, "There's no problem here. One swing of my sword, and he died last time. Our real problem will be the speed with which we take it down. If it dies before you cast your big spell, what?"

"Then we try something else in the next room."

~Run 6, The Opulent Oasis, Floor 2, The Fallen Merchant City of Aerlyn.~

"Wait, this isn't the assassin room," I said, raising my arm to stop my companions from triggering the trap. "Why are the rooms out of order?"

"We didn't want to say anything, but we wondered why you were talking about the assassin. The room order changes every time. Didn't you know that? It's less obvious on the first floor where there are only three rooms."

A question floated through my mind, and I hesitated. Thomas and Klericho were supposed to have comprehensive knowledge of the second floor. Yet, last time, Thomas had tripped and fallen to his death. Was I supposed to believe he was indeed that clumsy? "Don't forget the floor collapses, so we need to be careful." But apparently, I shouldn't have bothered because almost immediately, Thomas tripped into Klericho, and they both fell to their deaths. That answered that question.

I sighed and started running. The second time around, the dangers of the oasis were different. As I turned the first corner, a stalactite fell from the ceiling. Then, a nightmare occurred.

The entire platform I was on started shaking, and then, radiating out in diamond-like patterns, half of the floor fell away. I blinked, and suddenly, the room resembled a broken chessboard. Thankfully, the platforms stopped falling. Taking a minute to calm my heart rate, I caught my breath and examined the tiles.

Tentatively, I stepped onto the next platform. As soon as my right foot was on the new tile, the one under my left started to collapse. I cursed under my breath. That's when I finally remembered my companions. I looked back at the entrance and sighed with relief. All three of my skeletons were hanging out on the barest platform of wood at the edge of the room.

The new trick to the room was clear: I had to jump or walk between platforms, but as soon as my feet left one for more than a second, it vanished. I had to leap into the air, lurching for another platform just as the one I had been standing on disappeared. To complicate things further, four legendary chests were scattered around the room. If I triggered the Aerlyntium Orb in the center, it would consume the chests.

I decided to play it cautiously. I would move between the chests slowly, activating them within range. My hands shook with anticipation as I jumped toward the first chest. This would be my first chest with an upgraded loot table.

Previously, Klericho or Thomas had claimed all the chests. Now, these four were ripe for the picking, and their contents would be mine. It felt good to adventure alone again, even if only for a brief respite of solitude.

And then, a Memory Core appeared, of course.

Enemy Entry 0020: GregOre! the Goblin Hoarder *(Level 4 Goblin Hoarder – The Third Tribe)*

Goblin Hoarders are amiable and nice. All they care about is hoarding all the loot they can. They'll go for anything, but they like the shiniest things best. GregOre! is a minion of Kingsley, known for his insatiable greed and a knack for finding treasure. Despite his endearing personality, GregOre! is not to be underestimated—especially when he uses his Unlock Skill to gain access to hidden treasures.

- **Weaknesses:** Put a gold coin down to distract him, then smash his head in while he's mesmerized. You absolute monster. Bet you didn't even notice I changed the wording.

Stats
- **Health:** 20/20

- **Vitality:** 4

Item Drops

The Red Death

- **Amount:** 1

- **Chance to drop:** 100%

Chapter Sixty-Five
Revenge

{Memory Core 17/???}

~~~~~{Memory Core 17 Start}~~~~~

I was back in the alleyway where Jamie and I were arguing. I held the ring I had taken from her in between my thumb and my forefinger, studying it. I was about to speak, but Jamie beat me to it.

"I've never understood thievery. All that time, energy, and patience, all to take what could easily be gained legitimately."

I remarked, "Well, excuse me, princess! Of course, you don't understand it; you've never lacked for anything. For breakfast, lunch, and dinner, the world is brought to its knees for you while we hunger and thirst for two meals a day, let alone one." I had raised my voice, that vein in my head throbbing in a cruel echo of my father, and Princess Jamie shrunk back like I was about to hit her.

"How much money was spent to craft that ridiculous outfit you're wearing? You don't even look like a peasant, let alone nobility." I paused, taking a deep breath and trying to soothe myself.

"You haven't been caught this morning because my friend Peckolin bought me this little guy here." I pulled out my Glass Narwhal out of my pocket. He was so tiny and invisible that I wouldn't know he was there if I didn't feel his weight in my hand. Jamie stared at me like I had grown a second head, but I grabbed her hand and placed Invisible into her hand. "This is my Glass Narwhal, Invisible. He creates a barrier around himself that can hide people. We are still physically here, but people will pass us, assuming we stay out of their way."

"You named your invisible pet Invisible?" She just stared, but I laughed before scratching my head.

"I'm bad at names, okay? And don't go changing the topic."

"I-I didn't, you did. I–" I cut her off, and my anger rose again.

"Everyone looks down on thieves when it is the wealthy that should be looked down on. Think about your coronation in two weeks. How much money are they spending on that ceremony to say you're the queen?" My fists clenched, and my breath quickened,

Princess Jamie put her hands up defensively, but I wasn't done unleashing my rage. I felt a heat rising like a pillar out of the ground, consuming everything I was; my brain stuttered, and I couldn't think of what else to say. "And, and..."

I paused, my anger still hot but words failing me. Jamie looked at me with an expression I couldn't read. We just stood there for a moment, the silence heavy between us. Princess Jamie did something so arresting that the tirade stopped on my tongue. She leaned forward and grabbed me, a commoner, in a hug. She was so close I could feel her breath upon my ear as she whispered, "I'm sorry, Rod. You're right... It's my fault, but I don't know how to stop it."

~~~~~{Memory Core 17 End}~~~~~

The memory ended abruptly mid-sentence again, and I fell to the platform. I grabbed the ledge frantically, trying to keep myself from falling off. I don't know why, but the memory of Jamie made me pause. *Okay, maybe it wasn't worth it to be so greedy.* My past self hadn't known how the greed of the kingdom had destroyed my family, so why would

I succumb to the same greed just because no one would be the wiser? I shook my head and left the room.

~Run 6, The Silver Mirage, Floor 2, The Fallen Merchant City of Aerlyn~

As I walked into the room, I was shocked to see Thumbs on top of the assassin's corpse; our job was already finished. The diminutive goblin was trying to yank a gigantic red sword out of the assassin's corpse but was struggling because the sword was twice as big as he was.

"Thumbs Kill! Thumbs Kill." Thumbs screeched in his goblin speak. He struggled still to pull the sword out of the goblin corpse until I walked over and yanked it out. Thumbs stared up at the sword, tears forming in his eyes as he realized he would lose it.

"Thumbs, come here, buddy," I told the goblin as kindly as possible. I pulled 50 gold coins out of my inventory. The magic of the inventory space created a bag for the coins. I gave the pouch to him and said, "In exchange for the sword. Anytime you find awesome weapons or items like this, I'll give you gold in exchange. That way, you don't hurt yourself."

Thumbs grabbed the bag greedily, and then the bag's weight made him fall to the ground. He stared up at me with wide eyes.

"Bag, Bag, Gold! Heavy! Lots of gold, gold!" He picked up the bag, opened it, and sat on the ground to count his coins. I laughed.

[Rod, must I always have to remind you? You left 4 treasure chests and your companions in the previous room.]

I facepalmed, turned to Thumbs, and said, "Stay here," before returning to the other room.

~Run 6, The Opulent Oasis, Floor 2, The Fallen Merchant City of Aerlyn.~

"Alright, that was anticlimactic." The Aerlyntium only contained tiles this time. But Klericho and Thomas reappeared in one piece each. "Hey guys, look at what I found: four treasure chests!" I said, pointing to the chests. "I bet there's a lot of good treasure there. If we work together, we can easily get all four." I turned and began to head for the nearest one but stopped in my tracks as something unexpected hit my ears. Laughter.

I turned around, and Klericho and Thomas were laughing. "Those aren't real chests," Thomas said between breaths. They're level 100 mimics. Instant run enders and corpse takers."

I didn't believe them, so I did what I always did when faced with a new enemy and shouted **Scan!**

~Run 6, The Silver Mirage, Floor 2, The Fallen Merchant City of Aerlyn~

We walked through the maze of mirrors, our reflections ungainly and confusing in the bizarrely shaped mirrors. It felt like an unbearable presence was holding us down to the ground and keeping us from moving forward. I was frustrated because even using the right-hand wall trick, it still took us fifteen minutes to locate the Aerlyntium. There were three colored hallways. Red, blue, and yellow. The strange tint of the mirrors affected the way we looked and the way I felt. Just when I thought I had figured out the pattern to explore the hallways, I would hit a dead end or end up back at the entrance. I started marking the hallways with coins, but then I discovered Thumbs kept picking them up when my back turned. I could tell Thomas and Klericho were laughing at me behind my back. I knew I was a terrible leader, but I didn't see either stepping up to lead the way. My anger started to boil in my heart unbidden.

When I had died on my last run, Thomas had been able to drag me to it so quickly, but now the maze felt like an exercise in nihilism. "Thomas, how could you navigate the maze so quickly on the last run?" I had to bite my tongue as I spoke so as not to scream at the guy. My words sounded funny, and I could hear my pulse in my ears.

"See those red, blue, and yellow markings. It took so long because you needed to follow the blue path. You kept switching paths. Red is a dead end. Blue is forward. Yellow is back."

"And why didn't you share this with me?"

"Felt more fun to see if you could figure it out. But you just got angrier and angrier. It wasn't as funny to watch as I thought it would be. I'm sorry."

Like a pressure valve had been released, I sighed long and suffering. "You know what? It's fine. In the future, let's pool our knowledge and resources. I know that's a bit hypocritical, given that I tried to hide my knowledge from you, but going forward, we all need to do better. You guys have already been through this dungeon almost a hundred times. We need to figure out how to get through here as quickly and as painlessly as possible."

"I get that, but why are you acting like I killed your dog, man?"

I took a few breaths to calm myself. This was as good an opening to explode as any, but I had finally learned my first lesson in Penance. Anger didn't solve problems. It created them. My anger with Crystal destroyed our earlier run. My anger with Thumbs only ended with me getting hurt by the assassin. If I truly wanted to grow and show I was capable of the change Penance required to escape, it would start here. The Memory Core forming didn't surprise me, but what I saw did surprise me.

Enemy Entry 0021: Mimic *(Level 100 Mimic)*

Tales of Mimics date back to the founding of Aerlyn, with origins in the infamous mistake of Gerald Arneson, who accidentally cast a necromantic spell on an empty chest. Since then, Mimics have plagued adventurers, turning their greed into a deadly trap. These ancient entities are unmatched in strength and resilience, representing a challenge few can overcome.

- **Weaknesses:** Lightning, Water, Shadow, Light, and Fire

- **Strengths:** Resistance to Ice, Ground

Stats

- **Health:** 500/500

- **Mana:** 500/500

- **All Stats:** 100

Item Drops
Gold

- **Amount:** 50,000

- **Chance to drop:** 90%

Death Boons

- **Amount:** 10,000

- **Chance to drop:** 10%

Chapter Sixty-Six
Get Better at Not Getting Stabbed

{Memory Core 18/???}

~~~~~{Memory Core 18 Start}~~~~~

The classroom was a maze of wooden desks and dusty chalkboards, the walls adorned with ancient maps and magical charts. Sunlight filtered through tall windows, casting long shadows across the room. Professor Perrod stood at the front and announced today's debate topic. "Theories on the recent zoo bombing." It was all anyone had been discussing and was sure to engender a furious debate.

Ten minutes in, however, I was bored out of my skull. I knew the real culprits and couldn't even share it. I still didn't know what Peckolin had been trying to accomplish, and that's when everything went downhill. A pigeon-dove flew into the classroom and dropped a note off with Professor Perrod, who read it with great haste.

Candar raised his hand. Ever since we destroyed that zoo, Candar had been snootier than ever. Two days had passed, and he acted like he had become a king. Peckolin's influence had turned him into a pompous know-it-all, and it grated on everyone's nerves. Nobody did anything, though, because who would want to risk facing Peckolin's wrath?

"Actually, my brother Peckolin said the zoo attack couldn't have been the Aerlyntians. They don't have magic cores ever since the last of the Djinni-bloods were eradicated."

I stared in shock. Candar, what are you doing, buddy? Please don't give away that you were involved.

I tried to get his attention, but he continued on and said, "He thinks there's a new magical faction on the rise. This is eerily similar to how the Necromancer Wars got their start."

Multiple classmates gasped in horror. One did not simply mention the Necromancer Wars. While based on historical events, it was a cultural taboo to mention the near collapse of our country.

Professor Perrod took charge and, after giving Candar an odd look, started talking.

"Children, children, settle down. There is no need to fuss over this incident, though I will remind certain students not to mention the taboo in my classroom. In fact, now is a good a time as any to mention the news. The debate is now over."

There were groans from some of the more active participants.

"This missive pertains to everyone, so listen up. A school uniform badge was found near one of the exhibits in the rubble." The classroom erupted in chattering and the walls seemed to close in around me. I felt for my emblem, forgetting that I had left my uniform in the lockers during morning trash duty.

"After lunch today, the authorities will come by to check your uniforms for your badges. How fortunate for them that each student only has a single uniform. And don't worry; the saboteur will be swinging from the gallows soon." Perrod chuckled darkly, a horrible grin consuming his formerly friendly face.

It felt like the whole world stopped. I reached over to my left breast again. How could I have been so careless? The realization hit me like a punch to the gut—cold, sharp, and unyielding. I felt equal parts horror and anger at the realization that I would get caught.

~~~~~{Memory Core 18 End}~~~~~

Was that how I died? Killed because of that stupid zoo? I blinked, tears blurring my vision and streaking down my cheeks.

It was just so stupid. I tripped and lost my student emblem, then I died. That's why I'm here? Because I'm occasionally clumsy? I wanted to scream in rage at such a pointless, stupid death. My tenuous grasp on my anger was slipping. A hand rested on my shoulder, and I reflexively struck out.

Thomas jumped back, eyes wide, hands raised in self-defense. "Hey! What the—" he exclaimed, shocked.

I took a step back, breathing deeply to soothe my frayed nerves. "I'm sorry, Thomas. I shouldn't have done that," I said, my voice trembling.

"Whatever," he muttered, lowering his hands. "Let's just get that Aerlyntium."

[Error! Aerlyntium does not detect enough material to spawn items. Please provide a source of the following material: Wood 25/25, Metal 250/250, Glass 1000/1000, Organic material 100/300]

I groaned and turned back to the team. "I guess the goblin is giving us 50 organic materials per run. That's frustrating," I explained, feeling the weight of our task. "I guess this room will be one of the last we'll clear. Because, of course, the dangerous assassin that can one-shot me is a totally fair fight."

[Perhaps you just need to get better at not getting stabbed,] Crystal chimed in.

I laughed despite myself. "Thanks for the encouragement, Crystal," I replied, sarcasm lacing my voice. I turned and opened the door to the next room.

[You have received a Death Boon for progressing past your previous location.]

~Run 6, Magic Carpet Ride, Floor 2, The Fallen Merchant City of Aerlyn~

"What happens if we fall in?" I asked, peering into the chasm in front of me. "What did it feel like when the two of you fell in that other room?" The space was vast like a canyon, but there was thick, black emptiness instead of a river or mountainous terrain. Vertigo washed over me, and I stumbled. Thomas's outstretched arm saved me from falling in.

"Pain, soul-deep pain," Thomas shuddered. "And then nothingness until you revived us. It was quick, though."

I had no intention of feeling "soul-deep pain."

Above the chasm was an unbelievable sight I couldn't have imagined last week, but here I was. Carpets of various shapes, sizes, and movements glowed, piercing the omnipresent darkness. A few carpets descended deep into the chasm, fading out of sight.

The magic of this place was unfathomable. Where the sewers had been claustrophobic and cramped, these rooms were wide open and endless. This expanse eclipsed even the capital city of Vezwincourt. Awestruck, I paused to take in the wonder.

"So what's the shtick here?" I asked, turning to Klericho.

"Honestly, I wish you had stayed in the Archer class; it would have made this much easier," Klericho sighed, pointing at two elevated carpets before us. I spent a minute absorbing the ebb and flow of the carpets as they passed each other.

"I think I get it," I said. "Do I have to time my jumps between the carpets so that I land and the motion doesn't knock me off?"

"Pretty much. Which can be hard with a build with zero stamina." I was about to say it would be fine when my words died, and time froze.

Suddenly, he appeared. Aurentum, the Merchant of Death. His resplendent robes of silken blue had gold lace trim swirling in patterns that flowed like waves. A wreath of delicate gold framed his head in a crown that was somehow see-through but visibly solid. With each step, little mounds of gold formed as if his wealth were trying to escape him. He radiated a sickly aura, which increased in intensity with each step as I felt my mana and stamina being sucked away.

"Hmm," the robed man mused, his pale face almost skeletal. "Rellum's favorite losers. It's a pity these are the companions you're saddled with. No matter, I will help you solve this room without their interference or them learning anything I want to be kept secret. But remember, you owe me now."

With his robed hand, Aurentum reached out for Thomas and Klericho, transforming my companions into pillars of coins.

"What!" I yelled, rushing to inspect the pile of coins. Greed tugged at my heart, urging me to take the coins, but I pushed those thoughts aside. "What did you do to them?"

"Remember how I helped you when it comes time to betray them. Do not test my patience." With a flourish and a burst of gold light, Aurentum vanished.

"This wasn't even helpful!" I shouted, feeling hopeless and helpless against the cruel deity's idea of 'help.'

Did that just happen? Why would one of Penance's deities just zap my friends into piles of coins? It made no sense. Maybe I'm hallucinating?

"Crystal, was that Aurentum? He seemed unstable."

[That was indeed him, but I can't say I'm surprised. His screws are a bit loose.]

"Is there anything I can do?"

[He's a god. There is nothing to be done. He could decide you are a rat and make you spend the rest of your time in Penance with Ratigan at the circus. Who knows why they act the way they do?]

There had to be around 7,000 coins, but the money didn't matter as much as finding the Aerlyntium to bring back my companions did.

Hey, was that personal growth again?

I sighed, looking one last time at the pile of coins before taking them and turning to the moving carpet platform. "Crystal, what do you think my chances are? I managed the Oasis Room, somehow."

I spent the next little while running and jumping by the door, but no matter what I did, I couldn't seem to jump as far as I would need.

Finally, Crystal said, [I believe we will be here for a very long time, but I do not fear you ending this run prem—] Crystal stopped her speech short, and I swear I heard something suspiciously like a facepalm.

"Did you just realize something stupidly obvious that will make the past ten minutes seem like a colossal exercise in abject stupidity?" I asked.

[Yep.]

"Lay it on me."

[Summon Squawk.] My facepalm reverberated throughout the room.

Chapter Sixty-Seven
Sleep

I t took an hour to get the bird summoned, running back and forth between the first room, regenerating, and summoning other pets. I summoned one new pet I hadn't seen before, a thrilling experience for sure.

[What is that thing?] Crystal said when the turtle-like oddity appeared in front of us. It was a diminutive, turtle-like being with green, textured skin and hands clasped as though in meditation or prayer.

"I was going to ask the same thing. Isn't it your job to tell me? Can't you make one of those status boxes appear?"

[I'm too lazy. You've already summoned 10 pets, and doing all your work for you gets exhausting.] She whined.

My favorite pet started simmering in my mind, but I bit my tongue before the anger overflowed. And asked nicely, "Can you please give me a chart for the turtle?"

[...Fine.]

??? - Level 1 Holy Elemental

Stats
- **HP:** 30/30

- **Stamina:** 10/10

- **Mana:** 40/40

Skills
Pray

- **Effect:** Restores 1–6 health.

- **Description:** ??? prays for healing, channeling divine energy to restore life.

- **Mana Cost:** 4

Cure

- **Effect:** Cures poison, burns, or stuns.

- **Description:** ??? prays for purification, removing harmful effects from allies.

- **Mana Cost:** 10

Holy Bolt

- **Effect:** Deals 1–4 damage to undead targets only.

- **Description:** ??? unleashes a divine bolt of holy energy, smiting the undead with radiant light.

- **Mana Cost:** 2

Bark

- **Effect:** Confuses and terrifies opponents.

- **Description:** ??? releases a fearsome bark, shaking enemies to their core and breaking their concentration.

- **Note:** Ever seen a turtle bark? It's terrifying.

"It can bark? What?"

[Don't ask.]

"Alright then, guess there's only one thing to do. Name it Dog."

[I hate you.]

On the twelfth summon, I finally had my little Squawky boy back. I looked at his yellow feathers and stroked his frame, feeling relief and affection. The one thing I didn't like about this class was that every time one of the pets died, it felt like losing a piece of myself. These creatures weren't just tools; they were companions, each with their own quirks and personalities.

"Squawk, I'm so glad to have you back. You're going to my permanent collection. I can't wait until I get the option to choose which pets I get," I said warmly.

Squawk squawked in response, and with a smile, I headed back to the Magic Carpet Ride room, a vast chamber filled with floating carpets that shimmered in the dim light. The room was both enchanting and intimidating, a place where the rules of reality seemed to bend and twist. I had already tested it, and Squawk couldn't support my total weight, but he could help offset some of my weight as I jumped between carpets.

Then, the creature Crystal informed me was something called a 'giraffe' did something I didn't expect. He picked me up with his mouth and gently placed me onto the first carpet. As I found myself almost 15 feet up in the air, a mix of excitement and anxiety washed over me. This new vantage point was breathtaking, and I could see more glowing carpets in the shrouded-in-darkness room. It was a vast expanse of moving, floating carpets, almost like a river moving in a chaotic symphony, but I could now see that there were also more treasures than I first thought. I knew I would discover something if I rode those carpets down into the depths.

The uncertainty gnawed at me—whether it would be a treasure or a trap, I couldn't tell. But my curiosity, that relentless drive to uncover the unknown, was impossible to resist. I had to find out, no matter the cost. After Giraffey had lifted me into the air, Squawky landed on my shoulder. He pecked at my hair briefly and then flapped his wings a few times.

"Hey, Squawk, can you do me a favor and dive down where that carpet keeps flying?" I asked.

"Squawk! In a hole! Squawk in a hole!"

While waiting for Squawk, I focused on memorizing the patterns of each carpet. The carpet I stood on followed a distinct pattern. It rose, paused for five seconds, descended over ten seconds, then waited another five seconds before rising again. Each movement was predictable yet disorienting, a dance that demanded my full attention. While every rising carpet adhered to this sequence, the horizontal movements were so varied that I couldn't keep track of them all. I would have to make my decisions after every couple of jumps.

Just as I started worrying about Squawk, I saw a bright halo of electricity. In a flash, the bird burst from the depths, surrounded by yellow sparks of magic.

"Squawk, you're okay!" I said as my bird returned to my shoulder.

He squawked again, and I realized the major flaw in my plan of sending the bird down as reconnaissance. While I knew he could kinda talk, it wasn't real language, more like a kind of mimicry.

"Okay, Squawk. I'm going to ask you a bunch of questions about what you saw down there. Squawk once for yes and twice for no. Is that alright?" I asked, hoping for clarity.

"Squawk! There's stuff! Squawk!"

"Alright then. Did you see anything dangerous down there?"

"Squawk, danger! Squawk!"

"Oh, good. Did you see anything down there?"

"Squawk! See!"

"Was there a floor to land on?"

"Squawk, no floor, no floor! Squawk!"

"Okay, so it was all just carpets?"

"Squawk!"

"Were there any chests?"

"Squawk! Shiny, shiny!"

"Is there anything else I should know about down there?"

"Squawk! Down there!"

I turned to Crystal, raising an eyebrow. "Crystal, any chance you're able to speak bird?"

[Oh yeah, sure, I speak beaver. I speak bird. I speak about every language there is.] I could feel her metaphorical eyes rolling.

I sighed, pinching the bridge of my nose. "When we get down there, will I notice what I need to know?"

"Squawk, Squawk!"

"Okay, will you be able to show me?"

"Squawk!"

I smiled, feeling a bit more confident. "Alright then, let's try to escape this death trap."

I inched to the back edge of the carpet I had been standing on. It was only around six feet long and two feet wide. With a death grip on Squawk's talons, I waited twelve seconds for the arc to be correct, then dashed forward. Heart pounding, I rushed ahead, one foot in front of the other, and took a leap of faith. Midway through the jump, Squawk stretched up in the air, making it feel like we had jumped again. My left foot found purchase, and I stumbled safely onto the next carpet, landing on my stomach and knocking the air out of me.

"Good job, Squawk! You saved my life there," I praised, catching my breath.

"Squawk!" The bird squawked cheerfully.

Ahead, the next carpets were a series of horizontally moving platforms, each with a different speed but much closer than the previous gap. I counted seconds, watching the first carpet, then the second, and finally, the third complete a full lap past my position.

The first carpet was the slowest, taking thirty-five seconds to move back and forth. If I timed it right, I could step down onto it, using my downward momentum to carry me forward. The second and third carpets would be more difficult. At slightly different elevations, with the center one lower and the third higher, I'd have to time my movements perfectly. To make matters worse, they moved at entirely different speeds—carpet two in around fourteen seconds and the third in twenty-eight, moving twice as slowly.

I decided to get closer before figuring out a plan. I looked at the center carpet, counting out its approach once more. "Twenty-two, twenty-three, twenty-four, twenty-five," I muttered, then took off on a running sprint, gripping onto Squawk but hoping I wouldn't need him. If I didn't make this jump, the others had no hope. At the last possible moment, I put all my energy into my feet and leapt the three-foot gap, landing on my stomach once again. I was beginning to think I liked having the air knocked out of me.

I rolled into a sitting position, catching my breath as I studied the carpets. Heights had always made me uneasy, especially after a friend broke his leg in a fall. I shook my head, rejecting the memory. Now was not the time to lose focus.

The advantage of the faster-moving carpet was that it gave me momentum when jumping and pulling myself up onto the next one. Even though I hadn't moved in a few minutes, my heart pounded in my chest.

I'd already died four different ways that I could remember and a fifth that I couldn't. I wasn't eager to add a sixth to my collection.

I counted the seconds and took a sideways running jump with four seconds left between the carpets. Squawk used his magic to elevate us again, and I managed to grab a fistful of shag material with my right hand. Letting go of Squawk, I grabbed the carpet with my left hand as my momentum threatened to pull me away. Had I still been alive, I wouldn't have possessed the athleticism to grip the carpet and make the jump. As it was, my muscles strained against my weight as I pulled myself up. On the first attempt, I couldn't get my leg onto the carpet and swung back down, panting. I was running out of energy fast.

Knowing that my death hung in the balance did crazy things to my body. Even though every muscle screamed in pain, I changed my grip and tugged myself up with the last of my energy. I cried in relief as I lay back against the plush carpet, immediately closing my eyes. When I opened them, what felt like seconds later, Crystal spoke up.

[Did you know you snore in your sleep? You should get that checked out.]

I shook my head to clear the fog of sleep away and sat up. I must have been exhausted to fall asleep instantly. Suddenly, I heard a shriek and looked over to see Giraffey fall over, dead.

"Uhh, Crystal, what is that?" I asked, my voice trembling. Hundreds of feet away, floating off the ground, was a dark, black cloak wielding a reaping scythe. Black skeletal fingers grasped the scythe while the other hand absorbed what was left of my turtle named Dog..

[I don't know everything! Use **Scan**!] Crystal's genuine fear was evident in her voice. Even though I was ridiculously far away, **Scan** still worked.

Enemy Entry 0022: Room ReaperI don't know what this is, and *Scan* doesn't tell me anything. All I know is that it's terrifying, and you should run. Seriously. Run, idiot, run!

Stats: ALL STATS UNKNOWN. RUN!

I didn't wait much longer; I took off running, leaping between carpets without bothering to figure out how they worked. The fear of death loomed over me, and the memories of my past demises flashed through my mind. I knew I was missing out on multiple treasures and whatever Squawk had wanted to tell me, but I had one goal left: the Aerlyntium. It was at the top of the room on a carpet that moved from the top to the bottom of the room.

My heart pounded as I jumped from carpet to carpet, my muscles burning and my breath coming in ragged gasps. The Room Reaper's dark presence was a constant threat; every moment felt like it could be my last. I focused on the orb, my one chance at getting out of this mess, and pushed myself to keep moving despite the dark thoughts saying this was the end.

At first, I worried that the Reaper might fly, but in an almost comical twist of luck, it could only hover a few feet off the ground. It floated up, then landed on a carpet, moving steadily toward me. I realized I wouldn't make it to the Aerlyntium before the Reaper caught up... but maybe I could fight it. The idea was reckless, possibly the dumbest thing I'd done in the dungeon so far, but the Reaper needed a surface to keep floating, right?

I turned around immediately, feeling a physical pain as I headed back toward the monster. My body was beyond screaming at me to stop, my muscles past the point of exhaustion and into new realms of tiredness. I didn't even feel the pain anymore. Instead, the weariness fueled me. The sooner the Reaper was gone, the sooner I could sleep again.

The moment of truth came as we met on the plush carpet where I had slept. I timed my move and ran toward the Reaper as it leaped onto the carpet. Using my elbow to focus my momentum, I jumped and elbowed the Reaper in the face. It stumbled back over the side of the plush and started to fall. Something slowed its descent, and I feared it might rise again. Then, I received the notification.

[You have killed a Room Reaper. You have received a one-time-only bonus of 100 Death Boons for killing this mob.]

I collapsed onto the plush carpet but didn't let myself fall asleep. "What? Are you joking? 100 Death Boons? I'm rich! How long was I out earlier?" I asked.

[You slept for around eleven hours. The time limit per room appears to be twelve hours. That wasn't the only Room Reaper that would be sent after us if we didn't move forward faster.]

"But why is it here? And why doesn't one come after everyone at the entrance?" I questioned.

[If we recover your companions, perhaps one of them can enlighten us.]

"Right." I sat there for about twenty minutes, soothing my aching feet and arms. The memory of Dog's death and the fear of another Reaper gnawed at the back of my mind. As soon as my stamina was full again, I felt fine—as if I had never run at all.

I picked myself up and looked around at my options. While it would be quicker to get the chests first without sharing the loot with my companions, I now knew how dangerous it was to travel on this floor alone.

I worked my way up to the Aerlyntium. It was ridiculous how tired I got just jumping between a few carpets. Each jump cost five stamina, and I only had twenty. I didn't stop, though. In the back of my mind, I was constantly afraid that another Reaper would come for me. The sickening crack as it killed Giraffey still echoed in my ears. It had been sheer luck that my gamble had worked, and the Reaper fell to its death.

With each leap, I pushed past my limits, driven by the need to survive and the hope that the Aerlyntium would offer some respite. Finally, I saw the orb within reach, its glow a promise of hope in the dim, dangerous room.

Chapter Sixty-Eight
Dumb Mistake

As I approached the Aerlyntium, I finally let myself take a break. I sat cross-legged and pulled out a water skin and some bread from my inventory. While the bread was bland and stale, the water felt refreshing after my acrobatics display. When my stamina was restored, and I felt refreshed, I reached out to touch the orb. As soon as I did, I realized my mistake.

The orb started spinning and zooming around the room. It began guzzling carpets, and I ran as fast I could, jumping and flying down them quicker than I ever could have believed.

I was in the center of the room, and the exit was on the far left side. Thankfully, the orb was starting with the carpets closest to the entrance, but time was still of the essence.

I can't let a dumb mistake be the end of this run. Well, it wasn't a dumb mistake, per se. I would have had to open the orb to save my companions, but this entire run had been a mess. I just wish everyone would stop meddling and that companions would stop getting themselves killed, even if there was no way to prevent this one.

It was surreal that I had encountered two of the three gods by now. Something was nagging at my head, though; I just couldn't figure it out. I'd have time for that later; for now, I jumped from carpet to carpet, all caution sent to the wind.

The orb was closer now, having devoured half of the room, and I had only made it about two-thirds of the way to the exit. I was far beyond out of stamina—it felt like I was burning my own blood for fuel. I made a particularly long jump between two horizontal carpets and fell against the carpet, knocking the wind out of me.

This is it; I'm going to lose the run and be without my companions yet again.

I let out a cry, my voice hoarse and ragged, my muscles screaming in protest. This whole thing was frustrating and stupid. Just then, a voice broke through my despair, one I was not expecting to hear.

[You have looted Aerlyntium 1/7. Magic Carpet Ride. You have received the Proprietor. You have received the Proprietor's shack. You have received Thomas. You have received Klericho. You have received Thumbs. You have received Magic carpet x 25. You have received a wooden deck plank x 25. You have received basin floor x2. You have received water x 10.]

I let out a groan and sat up. I had to be blessed by some god of luck because the Aerlyntium had stopped devouring items right before the carpet I was currently resting on. Around a quarter of the carpets were gone, but there was still a path to and from the entrance. I lay there for almost an hour, not moving. I knew I needed to worry about the Reaper and bring my companions back, but I was just so tired.

It had been one thing after another after another. I had always read about these great heroes in stories that toiled and toiled without resting. But here I was in a dungeon with infinite lives and recovery, and I was sick of it after just a few days. *What does that say about me?*

Whatever it said, I couldn't let it get to me, so after my too long break, I finally picked myself up, waited a moment, and jumped to the next carpet. I immediately stumbled and fell, barely hanging onto the carpet. I pulled myself back up and wiped the sweat off my forehead before resetting my position.

In all my earlier hustle and bustle, I hadn't worried about the timing of the jumps or the placements. The momentum I had carried, or perhaps even a bit of Lady Luck, had allowed me easier passage through the room. I took a position at the edge of the carpet and tried again. This time, I flew over the carpet and landed in a crouch.

"Just three more, Crystal," I muttered, catching my breath before launching myself at the final elevating carpet. I managed to land running, kept my momentum, and launched myself at the last carpet. It was horizontal and moving away, but I caught the corner of the rug and used my momentum to swing up and onto the carpet.

My stamina was now at 5, and I could feel the burning in my legs intensify, but I pushed on. I stumbled off the carpet, legs trembling, and collapsed onto the landing dock, gasping for breath. It was time to bring my group back. With a deep breath, I activated the Aerlyntium Placement Grid. There was a lot I could do with the APG, but it made more sense to start placing things when I had more stuff on my next run. So, instead of placing the deck, carpets, or Proprietor down, I put Thomas, Klericho, and Thumbs.

"Hey guys," I said, looking at my companions' angered expressions. They remembered what had happened. "I'm sorry. I had no idea that was going to happen. It's not like I can control Aurentum. At all."

"You accepted his bargain. I can feel the taint on you now," Klericho spat with a fury I had yet to see in him. He had always been so relaxed, calm, and rational, but now his eyes were icy with fire, and he left little room for compassion or explanation.

"What bargain?" *What is he talking about?* I thought, panic rising.

"When you picked up the coins he dropped, you made a bargain with him. You're tainted," Klericho continued, his voice dripping with anger.

"Look, I didn't know anything like that would happen; I'm sorry."

Thomas put a hand on Klericho, calming him.

"Fighting now won't fix the problem, and we need to continue onward if we hope to make it to the next floor."

~Run 6, Textiles Room, Floor 2, The Fallen Merchant City of Aerlyn~

"Oh right, this place," I said as I walked into the room, following behind Klericho. "It smells so gross and musty here, like week-old socks that haven't been changed."

"Yes, fortunately, we won't be here long," Thomas replied.

"What are you talking about? It took me about an hour to get through here by myself," I said incredulously.

Thomas took on a self-satisfied smirk as if he knew something I didn't. He grabbed torches out of his inventory and started throwing them at the carpet maze. As he threw his tenth torch, the magic happened. The rising heat and thick, feasting flames of the torch pile gathered near the wall, finally started blazing at the base of the carpets. Later, an explosive tidal wave of heat rocketed into the room, making me fall to the ground as the dust in the carpets created a bomb of heat and fire.

The fire spread like a plague among the carpets, a devouring beast claiming the rich silks and woolen fabrics as fast as possible. When the flame, thick and fat with its feast, reached the other end of the room, I received a notification.

[All devouring flames has killed trickster goblins 1 and 2. You have dealt Overkill damage. You have received Death Boon x 2]

"Well, alright then. That was easy," I remarked.

"Only works on this room, but it makes good use of all of the torches you probably picked up on the first floor," Thomas spoke this time. "It destroys the loot of the goblins, though."

A horrifying thought entered my mind, and I paused before asking, "Did it destroy the key?"

"What key?" Thomas asked genuine confusion in his voice.

"The key to the treasury room. There's an Aerlyntium in there," I explained.

"Wait? No one told me about another room," Thomas replied, surprised.

"Did you even try solving this room alone, or have you always destroyed the carpets with fire?" I asked, my irritation mounting.

"Um, the first one?" Klericho admitted sheepishly.

I shook my head, anger welling up in my chest. Their solution was quick, but we'd lost out on loot from the two goblins, the Aerlyntium, and an entire 'treasure' room worth of loot. The anger boiled over, and I couldn't control it.

"You complete idiots! Have you ever considered that maybe that key is somehow needed to beat the Djinn or that collecting all of the Aerlyntium might do it? What is with you?"

Thomas grimaced, but Klericho was done with me. He screamed back, getting in my face and grabbing me by my leather armor.

"Thomas, I believe I am done with this miscreant. Once the Merchant has his claws this deep in someone, there is nothing to be-"

Just then, an ethereal light, full of silver and purple hues, descended on the wooden platform. The heavens had opened up, and Rellum appeared. He spoke with little preamble: "Klericho Ardentia. Did I not command thee?"

"Yes, my lord, but..."

"Did I not command that you forgive all and forsake none?"

"Yes, my lord, but..."

"Did I not command that those under the clutches of the Merchant of Death and Malikap were of equal value? They are creatures one and all in need of grace, compassion, and mercy. Your decency and patience mean naught if you only afford them when you feel they are deserved."

"Be careful, young one," he said. "Penance is seldom awarded to Aurentum's chosen. And of those in the dungeon, they are currently most valuable," Rellum said, not quite glaring but keeping all three of us held aloft in his gaze. "The work we are all doing here is essential. One may not be one of my Flock, but their future is in their hands." He turned and addressed me specifically. "I know you never believed, but Aurentum must not be allowed to leave this realm. His influence will re-corrupt the world, reintroducing evils once thought lost to time. If you work hard, we can prevent him from exiting."

"Why do I have to do the hard work? You are the saint. The will of God on earth. Why me?" I asked, frustration and fatigue evident in my voice.

"My powers, like Aurentum's, are limited here. I can only work directly through boons or through my devotees. Unfortunately, a large number of my devotees have been corrupted through the schemes of Malikap. This weakens my power and ultimately strengthens Aurentum's power here. That, however, is a worry for another time."

"Alright, I can understand that, but why me? There are so many other Penitents wandering around. Surely, they are better choices than me. I was a thief. I was a murderer." I hesitated, unsure about that last bit. The glimpses I had caught of the worst day ever hinted that I had done something terribly wrong. And then those two strange memories where I had controlled the events? I kept killing my father. There had to be something to that. Was that indeed the person I had been?

"If I only chose the most pure people, then I would've ascended alone. What I truly seek out in the Penitent and the devoted are a set of qualities that stand above everyone else—qualities that you have."

"And what qualities are those?"

"You are persistent. You are good-natured and friendly. And most of all, you believe that you can change. That was the part that filled most people with uncertainty. People come here, knowing what Penance is, and do not show any initiative to figure out what they need to fix about themselves." He paused, a look of gentle pride on his face.

"But from the beginning, you have been fixated on it. Couple your nature with your status as a mercenary in Aurentum's army, and we have a foot in the door towards fixing everything. That is if you want to do this. I am all about choices."

I asked, "What does it mean that I'm a mercenary? I don't even remember signing up. Did I even get a say? I'm certain he's been messing with my mind. Is he the one responsible for why I forgot everything?"

"No, I do not suspect that you had a real choice. However, we now live in the world of that decision or rather lack thereof. As a mercenary, you are not considered a true Penitent. While you can still ascend the tower freely, you cannot leave. Instead, Aurentum intends to leave in your place when you reach the peak. Just like what happened with Elric."

"So everything I've been doing is a waste? Some jerk of a deity is just going to swoop in, claim my hard work, and leave me here for eternity?" I sighed heavily as wrath filled my heart.

I struggled to stand under the force of anger. It felt more substantial and amplified than it ever had. I don't know what he did to me, but I despised Aurentum. He had caused every problem I had in the past few runs.

"Not necessarily. That's why I'm here. I plan to fix things, but I need your help."

"Alright, what do I need to do?"

Magic Carpet Ride *(Aerlyntium 1/7)*

The Proprietor
- **Amount:** 1

- **Effect:** This is a specialty merchant who sells magic carpets.

- **Description:** I don't know his name. But he has one of those swirly villain mustaches.

- **Quote:** "What's His Name, What's His Name, We Threw Out His Name!"

Proprietor's Shack

- **Amount:** 1

- **Effect:** It's a tiny one-bedroom shack.

- **Description:** See effect.

Thomas

- **Amount:** 1

- **Effect:** It's Thomas! Exciting!

- **Description:** Ever notice how he dies a lot?

Klericho

- **Amount:** 1

- **Effect:** It's Klericho! *jazz hands*

- **Description:** He dies a lot, too, so it's no wonder they never beat this floor.

Thumbs

- **Amount:** 1

- **Effect:** It's your minion!

- **Description:** He finds stuff!

Magic Carpet
- **Amount:** 25

- **Effect:** It's a magic flying carpet.

- **Description:** You can use these carpets to fly around. Requires mana to use. I can show you the world, shining, shimmering, splendid.

River
- **Amount:** 10

- **Effect:** -

- **Description:** Do I need to explain rivers to you, too? It's like a lake, but the water flows in a direction. Like, come on, man, it's water!

Wooden Plank
- **Amount:** 25

- **Effect:** Basic building material.

- **Description:** Helpful in constructing bridges, walkways, or repairs.

Basin Floor
- **Amount:** 2

- **Effect:** Durable flooring.

- **Description:** A sturdy surface for setting up camp or placing structures.

Part Three

The Game of the Gods

Chapter Sixty-Nine

Nice!

~Run 6, Treacherous Treasury, Floor 2, The Fallen Merchant City of Aerlyn~

As soon as I stepped into the room, I took a giant breath and sighed in relief. I had begun to think I would never leave. Rellum, his minions, and I had spent a good hour sketching out the basis of a plan. It stank to high heavens and frustrated me, but we couldn't win this run.

Beating the Djinn required a series of relics, and their 'shortcut' was why they had never come close to winning. Self-sabotaging in the worst way. An exercise in abject failure. But Rellum didn't let an ounce of contempt leak through his demeanor. He was kind and gentle with his charges, optimistic that we could handle the boss of the floor on my next run. Additionally, we planned out the skeleton of a plan to address Aurentum by accepting his help and agreeing to assist him.

My mercenary tag had changed to something called a "Reformed." Apparently, it happened to all people who changed their allegiance to a different deity once they moved on through Penance. Rellum even had the means to obscure my new status from Aurentum until we were ready to reveal the truth to him. I was not the first, nor even the only active mercenary Aurentum employed in the dungeon. And here I was, thinking I was special. I was a little worried that I would lose access to my Death Boons and the extreme power-up of 100 boons I had earned from my suicidal rush in the previous room. I was on board with helping, but I'd be dead in the water if I lost the Death Boons.

Rellum assured me that I wouldn't lose my Death Boons. Buffs, once given out, could not be taken away.

The room was practically a repeat of the first treasure room I stepped into. Mountains of gold, weapons, and treasures filled the room to the point of bursting. I gave a wary glance at the room banner as I continued forward. I looked down and sighed. I had been about to step on a pressure plate and sidestepped at the last second before falling over and landing hard on a mountain of gold coins.

[Yay! Character development! I'm so proud of you, Roddy.]

My companions followed me a few moments later, content to let me take the lead. I scrambled to my feet and pushed them out of the trap.

"Watch your feet as we move through here; traps are everywhere."

"We know. You didn't have to shove us; we were about to walk around," Klericho said, an odd tone in his voice. I don't imagine he enjoyed being dressed down by his boss or my helpful shove.

"Oh." I looked at my companion for a second, thinking about how to respond to his tone before thinking better of it. "Alright, have you two been here before? I assume we just have to avoid the traps and fight any enemies that might appear."

"There's a couple of goblins? No big deal, really," Thomas said, glancing at his partner as if asking for permission to talk to me. It was as if, even after the god practically scolded them, they still wanted to mistreat me.

I felt a pressure building behind my eyes. I didn't want any of this. I didn't want their anger. I didn't want their god's attention or any other god's focus, for that matter. I just wanted to scream in anger and frustration, but I couldn't let myself be the villain they accused me of being.

"Alright, let's hop to it," I said, walking forward. My hands twitched at my side as I took in the treasure troves around me. I squeezed my palm, letting my nails dig in deep as I took a deep breath. I recentered myself and looked away from the obvious traps. The fleeting gold was scarcely worth the time it would take to pick it all up.

"Hey, I know you're new, but we must pick up the pace. The treasure here isn't even real. It's marked as treacherous when you pick it up. It even infects other treasures. Best just to ignore it." Thomas informed.

"Infects other treasures?" I asked, eyebrows raising in surprise.

"If you pick up even one coin, you'll have to throw out all the gold you have. It all becomes infected and rots away outside of this room."

"Well, that's all kinds of insidious. I figure that's happened to you at least once?" I said, trying to lighten the mood.

Instead of replying, Thomas nodded and took off with a charge as time froze. It felt like days since the last time I'd been in real combat. I still wasn't sure how my charge got past the turn-based battles, but I just chalked it up to yet another oddity. The more time I spent in the dungeon, the more I felt like someone was making up the rules as I went along.

The goblin trickster was diminutive for an already small race. He stood just over three feet tall and held some sort of potion or something in his hands. Instead of drinking the potion, he lobbed it through the air, splashing it on top of Thomas. I had already cast a long summon as I'd started calling this overpowered spell.

Only this time, something was different. It was still the same spell, but the energy felt infested and darker, somehow. I bit down on my cheek to keep from stressing.

Dark tendrils like octopus tentacles reached out of my hands as the spell unleashed itself. And it seemed my simile was apt as several limbed and shadowy octopuses slinked into existence through my hands and out into the open.

The battle had already ended as my three new pets squelched onto the ground with horrifying wet sounds. As their suckers attached to and detached from the ground, my stomach felt queasy. The octopus was inky purple and black with dark blue spots. While torch light was almost always a poor illumination source, the flickering flames showcased the Ottos (my new name for the pets) spots, which barely contrasted against the pitch black of his skin.

The Ottos approached me, and then I almost lost my lunch as they jumped onto me in three different positions. Each one weighed at least 10 pounds, but I soon relaxed as their weight felt quite comfortable.

"What are those? I was okay with your other pets..." Klericho shuddered. "But octopi? Really?"

"You know I have no control over what's summoned, right? It's just like everything else in this place: It's summoned through a roll of a die. Anyway, what's the deal with this room? Is there anything I should know besides the traps? Or was that the only fight here?"

"Oh, this room is a cakewalk. That was it. Just avoid the colored tiles; gray tiles are safe. It's kind of silly how easy this room is compared to the previous one."

[It's a breather room,] Thomas's crystal broke in. He hadn't talked in a while, so having a new voice participate in the conversations was nice! [When Penance was constructed, The designer built this prison to punish, teach, and heal. And nonstop torture is not suitable for any soul. Even the Penitent need to rest.]

The crystal went dark and ceased talking.

I shrugged my shoulders and felt myself relaxing for the first time this run. I needed a pause after the absolute marathon of the previous room. I needed to rest my head from the headache I had been nursing, so I looked down instead of staring at the gold and the temptation it brought. And I was so thrilled that I did.

They were right that there were a bunch of gray tiles mixed with colored ones, but they weren't right about the traps.

I felt a weird sense of déjà vu as I looked at the colors. The patterns were the same as those lit up in the textiles room: red, blue, blue. Red, green, green. Green, blue, green. "Crystal, do you remember the pattern of the carpet colors from back in the textiles room? Is that something you can keep track of?"

[What do you take me for? If we have the exact guess, you're looking for the fourteenth pattern. Green, purple, red.]

I moved happily along the rows until I came upon the fourteenth pattern. It was the first purple tile I'd seen, and I didn't hesitate to press the plate. As I expected, it wasn't a trap. Instead, a sound much like grates falling reverberated throughout the room. Some of the piles of gold shifted, and I worried for half a second about an avalanche—err, well, coinvalanche? But the coins settled, and they tried looking around for the noise source. Klericho reacted before Thomas did, his question sounding accusatory rather than curious.

"What did you do?"

He turned around from his vantage point a few rows of tiles ahead of me.

"I pressed the purple tile here. The patterns are set up just like the carpets in the textiles room..." I paused for a second as realization hit me. Squawk had been trying to tell me the entire time that a secret key was hidden below. I had already destroyed everything by grabbing the Aerlyntium orb when I did, so there was no way to backtrack and find out if my hunch was correct. I would have to backtrack one more time to clear the floor. No matter, I shook my head, "Did anybody see a door that opened? The key to removing the floor is inside—or at least part of it is."

"You idiots destroyed the first one with your fireball stunt, and I bet I accidentally destroyed the path to the other one when I revived y'all with the Aerlyn Orb."

"We were stupid when we destroyed one, but it's an accident for you? How charitable." Klericho irritably commented.

"Of course," I said, owning my words with no shame. He reeked of hypocrisy. He dared to get mad at me in front of his god, and now he was taking that anger out on me after his god had rebuked him. I wanted to scream, but again, I held my tongue and bit my cheek to keep from crying; the wound was already an ulcer, but it didn't make me any less mad.

I walked forward and climbed a gold mountain for the height. From my new vantage point, I could make out the whole room. And because of that, I could see the exit easily from my perspective.

There were two exits, but one had been closed, I assumed because of hitting the treasure lock. I assumed it was there to funnel you to the right place, but it would also be a sick twist if, instead of leading to the key to exit this place, it led to a dead end, and we couldn't progress any further.

Chapter Seventy
Grendelblin

~Run 6, The Perfumed Prison, Floor 2, The Fallen Merchant City of Aerlyn~

The room smelled of wine and cheap perfume, with vibrant incense visible in the air. Cells lined both sides of the wall, stretching into the distance. As my companions entered, I stopped and turned to them.

"We already know we can't win on this run, but we can figure out a plan for the next one. This room might hold an item that allows the boss to take damage. Let's try and find it!" I suggested to the others.

"How did you find this place? Fifty runs in, and we never discovered it," Thomas asked, his voice a mix of amazement and frustration.

"I'm guessing once you discovered each room's trick, you stopped exploring," I replied, raising an eyebrow.

"We might have... but it's not our fault. The other devotees here before us 'showed us the ropes.' Rellum said we could trust them," Thomas spat bitterly, his right fist clenched at his side.

"Well, spread out. For all we know, there's treasure here, too." I took off at a brisk jog, glancing into each cell as I passed. They were all unlocked but closed, obscured by a thick fog of different-colored perfume. Despite their emptiness, something nagged at me. Each cell's colorful smoke—reds, blues, greens, and purples—had to be hiding something.

After the fifteenth empty cell, frustration crept in. I called out to my companions, "Every cell is empty, but there has to be more to this.

Almost every room on this floor has been a puzzle. Let's go back to the beginning."

They grimaced but followed. As we reset at the start, I took note of the colors. Red and green had adverse effects—arrow traps and poison, if my memory served. Blue and purple seemed safer.

"We should only enter the purple and blue cells. I'll test the first one on my side. Leave red and green alone."

"Why? What if there are items or treasures? I'm going to open this first one," Klericho declared, stepping towards the red cell.

"No! What are you doing?" I screamed in frustration, feeling fire flood my veins. My anger had seemed to have reached a peak again, ever since the revelation that Aurentum had claimed my hard work for himself.

Klericho opened the first red jail cell, and like a line of dominoes, each red cell clanked open, one after another.

With bated breath, I watched as horrifying monstrosities climbed out of each cell.

"**Scan!**" I shouted, not wasting any time.

I stared in horror. Not since the horde room had we faced such numbers. Instead of weak trash we could quickly push aside, these monstrosities would likely take hit after hit, given their high health.

As turn-based combat started, my one solace was that I had nine pets under my control—it was about time I began to use them to their full worth. I had been itching for a real battle.

The first Grendelblin was to my immediate right. I jumped forward, swinging a bolt from my staff down on its head.

"All on me!" I shouted, commanding my pets to focus on the beast before me.

[You have dealt 5 damage.]

Time froze as my three skeletons ambled forward. Bones 2 shot an arrow aimed at the eyes, Bones 1 slashed with his red, pulsating sword, and Bones 3 made clicking, cutting moves at the Grendelblin's back.

[Critical strike, Bones 1, 2, and 3 deal 40 damage.]

Then, the three Squawks came charging in with their ranged lightning bolts.

[Squawk 1, 2, and 3 have dealt 35 damage.]

The final points of damage were claimed by Otto 1, as the tiny octopus flew through the air and bowled the beast to the ground.

Otto 1 proceeded to slurp and squelch as it devoured the head of the beast, which then exploded in a burst of blood and skull fragments. Unsurprisingly, there was no remaining brain matter.

[Otto 1 has used **Brain Slurp**. Otto 1 has dealt 83 damage. Otto 1 has Overkilled Grendelblin 1. You have received an Overkill Death Boon.]

I couldn't move as the enemy turn came up. The next Grendelblin crouched, its muscular, sinewy limbs tensing beneath dark, leathery skin, each limb ending in a sharp, claw-like point. Large, pointed ears jutted from the sides of its head, framing a face twisted into a snarl that revealed jagged, razor-sharp teeth. It pounced for me, but suddenly, Thomas was there blocking the blow like a teleporting giant.

As my next turn came up, I faced a crowd of three Grendelblins. I knew our tactic of rushing them down with targeted damage wouldn't work, so I needed to apply some tactics. Otto's special ability only worked on mobs with less than 10% health, almost always dealing a critical blow with damage up to 100—a crazy good skill to have in my bag.

I decided to send my pet 2s and 3s after Grendelblin 2, calling them Group A, and my 1s after Grendelblin 3, calling them Group B. I hoped Thomas was smart enough to focus on Grendelblin 4 so no group would get overwhelmed.

With the remaining ten seconds of my turn, I shouted orders and decided to avoid getting within damage range, opting to cast spells from my staff. I focused on the third target, relying on my pets to mitigate possible damage from the enemies. This plan would only work if I could count on Thomas and Klericho to perform well in combat, and thankfully, neither man had been a slouch so far.

As the seconds ticked, I cast **Necrotic Bolt** at Grendelblin 4 and closed my eyes, fearing retaliation.

[You have dealt seven damage.]

I heard the clash of Thomas's sword against the Grendelblin's flesh. I popped open an eye to confirm my thoughts and waited for their turn to tick away.

Team A focused on Grendelblin 2, functioning like a well-oiled machine. Six missiles of varying types charged down on the unsuspecting mob in a cavalcade of colors.

[Group A has dealt 31 damage]

Thirty-one damage wasn't too bad, but I was very concerned about the damage my pets were about to take. Suddenly, Thomas was there, deflecting the Grendelblin's blow with his sword. Meanwhile, Bones 1 stepped up to attack Grendelblin 3. The Red Death absorbed light, casting a dark aura as he swung at his target. Two missiles backed him up: a golden bolt of electricity from the sky and a purple wreath of magic encircling the monster's head.

[Bones 1 has made a second consecutive hit without taking damage. The Red Death has recovered 1 point of durability damage. Potency increases +1. Group B has dealt 18 damage.]

The Grendelblin reared back with a roar, charging at Bones 1, but Klericho was faster, his golden sheen of magical light surrounding Bones 1 just in time.

[Grendelblin has used **Rear** on Bones 1. The attack does no damage due to **Shield of Light**.]

I fist-pumped the air as the shield faded, then almost facepalmed as Grendelblin 4 prepared to strike Bones 1. But Thomas was there again. I had played Barbarian before, and the class was never as fast as Thomas seemed. It could have been due to the Devoted buffs or some sort of warp spell. Then it hit me. That was exactly what was going on. They had told me as much, and now I realized the implications. The power of these classes was due to the perks that came with being a mercenary for the Merchant of Death.

And if they got those perks while being devoted, I got mine from being a mercenary. Rellum had said I would keep all my perks if I 'switched' sides, but could I afford to listen? I didn't like physically oriented classes and had spent an eternity toiling away. The extreme fatigue seemed the most off-putting. I decided not to dwell on the thought; it felt like bad form to focus on anything other than the battle in front of me.

I moved forward from my vantage point and cast a poison bolt from Gurgle's staff. The greenish glow of the bolt streaked through the air and struck true. I jumped in the air in a small victory. With a five in one-hundred chance, it was crazy that I had seen poison take effect twice in under twenty casts. I froze as my turn ended, watching the results of my pets' attacks unfold.

Group A moved precisely, and another six blasts exploded into Grendelblin 2. I let out a cheer as the coordinated assault continued.

[Group A has dealt 36 damage.]

Thomas wasn't idle; he swung his giant sword and cleaved the monster in two. It was a gruesome sight, with blood and viscera spilling to the floor like my father's spilled soup. I gagged at the errant thought.

And then the real magic happened.

Enemy Entry 0023: Grendelblin

These beasts are the discarded, often jailed progeny of the great mythological beast Grendel. It is claimed that once upon a time, he was happy and in love with the Goblin Queen. They married and had all sorts of horrifying offspring. They lived a happy life until one day, Grendel's mother came looking. She slaughtered the Goblin Queen coldly and lured Grendel back through magical control. These Grendelblins were left creating chaos in their parents' wake. The oldest, a boy named Hob, on the cusp of adulthood, corralled his disorderly siblings and threw them all in here. And you crazy idiots just freed them. All 20 of them. Good luck.

Weaknesses: Shadow, fire, water
Strengths: Nothing

Stats

- **Level:** ???

- **Health:** 100/100

- **Potency:** 5

Item Drops
Gold

- **Amount:** 5

- **Chance to drop:** 75%

Prison Rags

- **Amount:** 1

- **Chance to drop:** 25%

Chapter Seventy-One
Grendelkin

Bones 1 was on fire—or at least it looked like fire, but it was tinged with black and gray instead of yellow and red. Standing in the heart of the ancient dungeon, shadows danced ominously around him. Since he had attacked multiple times with his sword without being hit, the sword now dealt triple damage, affecting his outward appearance. He attacked.

[Bones 1 has dealt a third consecutive hit without taking damage. The Red Death has recovered 2 points of durability damage. Potency increase +2, total: +3. Group B has dealt 87 damage.]

There was still one target left near us, ready to attack Bones 1, but again, Klericho cast his golden shield, and Bones 1 was fine. As my turn rolled around, I looked past the remaining Grendelblin with horror as the rest were devouring each other. Fewer enemies would have been great, but as they killed each other, the winning Grendelblin would stretch, morph, and become bigger. Much bigger.

I wanted to run forward and attack, get in the middle of the fray, and stop them from getting worse, but I had no idea if that would work or not. Besides, I still had the smaller one in front of me. I wasn't a fighter class, but I was charged. I had a feeling our only real chance was letting Bones get his dice rolls absurdly high, so I let myself get in the way of potential damage. I swung my staff, which I had obtained from Gurgle during our last perilous quest. The staff, imbued with toxic sludge, bonked the Grendelblin on the head, dealing 10 damage. The creature shuddered as the poison seeped into its veins, taking an additional 4 points of poison damage.

And then groups A and B were upon him.

[Group A has dealt 21 damage.] A pause, and then a new parchment. [Bones 1 has dealt a fourth consecutive hit without taking damage. The Red Death has recovered 1 point of durability damage. Potency increase +3, total: +6. Group A has dealt 237 damage. Otto has absorbed the opponent. You have dealt a double Overkill. You have received 5 Death Boons.]

Then Otto did something gross again. He rolled a 100, an insane stroke of luck. Apparently, there was a hidden feature of the **Brain Leech** skill triggered by critical success. As he absorbed the Grendelblin, Otto sprouted a full head of coarse, green hair. The sight of a miniature octopus sporting human-like hair was both hilarious and oddly terrifying.

I couldn't help but chuckle despite the ongoing battle. But there was no time for fun. The battle was far from over, and the remaining Grendelblins were still a threat.

"Keep it up, everyone! Focus on the next target!" I shouted, rallying my team.

As we regrouped, I noticed the remaining Grendelblins still engaged in their gruesome feast, growing larger and larger. One had spikes larger than my head now. We needed to act fast. I steeled myself for the next wave, ready to unleash everything we had.

"Group B, get ready for the big ones. We need to take them down before they get any stronger," I commanded, my mind racing with strategies.

Bones 1, now glowing with an eerie dark fire covering not just the sword but his entire frame, took his place at the front. This was our chance to turn the tide.

I swung my staff, feeling a surge of energy as the bolt left before it connected with the nearest Grendelblin. The poison took hold, dealing additional damage. The creature staggered, but it wasn't enough to bring it down.

"Now, Group A!" I yelled.

The combined force of our attacks descended upon the Grendelblin, and I watched as its health dwindled. We were making progress, but the real test was yet to come.

My mind sparkled at the possibilities. I recalled a boon that promised a rigged roll per floor. I could rig the roll to summon Otto as soon as I got to the first floor and then get Otto to absorb every monster on the floor. His stats would get jacked up so fast that he'd be invincible. I cackled, getting strange looks from everyone but the Ottos, who happily jumped back on top of me.

With the first four Grendelblins out of the way, we turned to face the other 16. Except they were gone. Standing in the middle was an even more grotesque version of them. All jagged, sharp angles and spiky protrusions. It looked more like a dragon than either a goblin or whatever a Grendel was. It was twice again as big and a little wider than the other Grendelblins, its spikes sharper and deadlier. I cast **Scan**. My face paled as Crystal relayed the information..

"What is that thing?"

"It's a Grendelkin. While we were busy fighting these," I paused, gesturing at the corpses, "it was busy eating its siblings. It has 600 health and 10 potency."

Thomas audibly gulped. "The stats are insane. Even with my armor and the cleric's shield, we're screwed. A lucky hit could take half of my HP."

A million scenarios went through my mind faster than I could usually process, and then one solidified.

"I've got a plan, but most likely, everyone but me, Bones 1, and Otto are going to die. Are you all okay with that?"

Thomas looked determined. "As long as we win, you have my sword."

"You have my shield," Klericho said firmly.

"You have my squawk!" Squawk cawed.

I could swear I heard Crystal laughing, but I didn't have time to react as the battle started, so I put my plan into action.

I rushed forward and cast a poison bolt. I knew it wouldn't inflict poison, but I needed to do something. Bones 1 moved into the flank while my other pets cast their missiles at the giant target. The monster had 600 health and it would take an avalanche of critical hits to ensure we killed it quickly unless we took advantage of my pet weapon.

Thomas jumped forward and swung his axe overhead at the monster. It immediately retaliated with a backhand swing, and Thomas went flying. Bones 1 used the moment to attack and then froze.

[Bones 1 has dealt a fifth consecutive hit without taking damage. The Red Death has recovered 4 points of durability damage. Potency increase +4 total: +10. Groups A and B have dealt 91 damage.]

Unfortunately, Crystal never updated me on what Thomas or Klericho contributed. I had forgotten for a second that the turn-based constraints did not bind Thomas and Klericho, so I was surprised to see a gold light shimmer as Thomas ran forward while Klericho healed him.

Thomas got in front of Bones and deflected a strike with his axe just as the Grendelkin was about to strike Bones. The strike still clipped Thomas, and he grunted in pain. Then, the Grendelkin froze as round two started.

[Bones 1 has dealt a sixth consecutive hit without taking damage. The Red Death has recovered 4 points of durability damage. Potency increase +5, total: +15. Groups A and B have dealt 79 damage.]

The attacks all happened in an instant—a flurry of magical spells and arrows. The light blinded me for a moment, and then we all froze as the Grendelkin retaliated. The Grendelkin bore down on Thomas, and he glowed gold one final time. I thought for a second the blow had taken him down, but he grinned and brought his axe down on the Grendelkin's head.

It froze, and another round started up. Before anything else, I cast **Scan** to check how much HP it had left.

[Grendelkin, HP 430] As if she had read my mind, Crystal only displayed the HP amount.

In just a couple of rounds, we had whittled down a couple hundred damage. I was excited about that, but I was still wary. Thomas was on his last legs. We had some backup plans but needed to deal more damage faster. We had to get it down to 150 HP before the Ottos could triple-team their finishing move, and that was if we were lucky enough that they were still alive when he was in range.

[Bones 1 has dealt a seventh consecutive hit without taking damage. The Red Death has recovered 6 points of durability damage. Potency increase +6, total: +21. Groups A and B have dealt 90 damage.]

The flames covering Bones 1 were now unbelievably large and hot. I could feel the hairs on my arm starting to burn from the heat.

We were nearing halfway down on the Grendelkin's health when Thomas finally kicked the bucket. The claw swiped at his face, and he was gone. My heart sank, but there was no time to mourn. This next part was going to be tricky, but I spoke my directions out loud and hoped for the best.

"Squawks, Guardian formation around Bones 2 and 3. Flank Bones 1. Ottos, protect any hole in the defense. Remember, the goal is to keep Bones from taking damage. Klericho, if you can, get in front. I think you could successfully block two rounds of attacks. It's probably not enough, but if we can get at least four more rounds in, I think the Ottos can clear this."

I cast the poison bolt again and sighed in frustration as the bolt failed to poison the boss.

Such a useless weapon, I thought. Then Grendelkin grunted in pain before launching right for me, and I knew my run was at its end.

Enemy Entry 0024: Grendelkin, Enhanced

Grendelkin, the evolved form of the Grendelblins. This is an almost perfected form of the Grendelblins. The winner has devoured his siblings and has grown considerably more powerful for it.

Weaknesses

- Shadow, fire

Strengths

- Nothing

Stats

- **Level:** Not specified

- **Health:** 600/600

- **Potency:** 10

- **Defense:** 2

- **Magic Defense:** 1

Item Drops
Gold

- **Amount:** 5

- **Chance to drop:** 75%

Prison Rags

- **Amount:** 1

- **Chance to drop:** 25%

Chapter Seventy-Two
Unnecessarily Morbid

Bones 1 executed his eighth consecutive hit, his Red Death gleaming as it restored its durability. The blade shimmered with an eerie, dark red light that overwhelmed his body and the area around him. Each strike was more precise and deadly than the last. Each swing carved through the air with a whisper of death, culminating in a devastating critical strike that dealt significant damage.

Squawk followed up with a swift, agile attack, his feathers ruffling as he darted in to deal additional damage. Otto, their eyes glowing with intense concentration, unleashed **Brain Blast** after **Brain Blast**, the psychic energy crackling around them as they added to the tally.

Bone 2, calm and focused, cast **Aim** on the enhanced Grendelkin, the spell wrapping around his target like an invisible net. He delivered a critical hit with precision. Bone 3's **Necrotic Bolt** shot forth like a dark comet, and Squawk's **Lightning Strike** followed, the air sizzling with energy. Squawk's critical hit caused a spectacular explosion of light

[Bones 1 has dealt an eighth consecutive hit without taking damage. The Red Death has recovered 2 points of durability damage. Potency increase +8, total: +36. Both groups deal a combined 148 damage.]

The Grendelkin morphed again, its muscles bulging grotesquely through its skin, veins pulsing visibly. Its claws grew sharper, glinting menacingly under the dim light, and its fangs elongated into razor-sharp points. With a brutal, swift swipe, Klericho vanished in a spray of red mist, the cleric's form disintegrating into nothingness. My heart pounded in my chest, a frantic drumbeat of fear and adrenaline. We were just under 200 HP. Just two more rounds of attacks, and we could take it down. I prayed our defensive line, battered but resolute, would hold against the relentless onslaught.

Bones 1 executed his ninth consecutive hit without taking damage. The Red Death restored its durability, the blade humming with renewed vigor. Each swing moving faster than before leaving streaks of read like a tear in the fabric of reality behind as it move. The sword terrified me the more it was used.

Squawk, feathers flaring with electricity, darted in to deal additional damage. Otto, eyes blazing with psychic energy, unleashed a **Brain Blast**, adding to the tally. Bone 2, with unwavering focus, cast **Aim** on the Grendelkin, delivering a precise critical hit. Bone 3's **Necrotic Bolt** hit its mark with dark, shimmering force, followed by Squawk's **Lightning Strike**, which caused a burst of electrifying damage. Squawk cast another **Lightning Strike** with unyielding determination, while Otto, her psychic powers surging, unleashed **Mind Blasts** that added to the total damage inflicted on the Grendelkin. Repetitive though it may have been, the attacks were extremely affective. [Bones 1 has dealt a ninth consecutive hit without taking damage. The Red Death has recovered 2 points of durability damage. Potency increase +9, total: +46. Both groups deal a combined 137 damage.]

The Grendelkin was a frenzied whirlwind of rage and power. It spun its massive arms around, claws tearing through the air in a wild attempt to hit everything within reach. Its furry hands, now soaked in blood, left trails of crimson as its bulging muscles strained and split its skin. Thankfully, Bones 1 remained unharmed, narrowly dodging the chaotic swipes as one of the Squawks vanished in a burst of electricity, a casualty of the fierce battle. Then, arms spread wide in the middle of its erratic spin. The Grendelkin froze. Luck was on our side as Bones managed a final critical strike. With his damage alone, the group cleared 65 damage, and the three Ottos surged forward, their combined psychic energy like a swarm of bloodthirsty mosquitoes.

Blood and gore rained down in tiny droplets while chunks of bone and muscle fell like hailstones. I cackled in victory, collapsing to the ground, mentally and physically exhausted. The air was thick with the metallic scent of blood and the acrid tang of burnt flesh.

Despite not engaging directly, it felt as though I had run a marathon. My limbs ached, muscles screaming for rest, but the haunting memory of the Room Reaper pushed me to keep moving. The weight of survival bore down on me, a relentless reminder of the high stakes of our quest.

I was alone, save for my five loyal pets, each a testament to the battles fought and companions lost. Their presence was a bittersweet comfort, a stark reminder of the price of this relentless journey. We could only handle another battle without regrouping. In future run-throughs, I would avoid the red cells like the plague. Losing momentum to an overpowered beast was not an option.

I looted the corpses, the task mechanical and detached, my mind racing with calculations and strategies. The theme of the second floor seemed to be puzzles and absurdly powerful bosses with equally powerful rewards. I came away with my third-ever necklace and immediately traded it for my current one. The new necklace, Grendel's Blessing, significantly boosted my highest and lowest stats, granting me 2 points in constitution and 4 points in wisdom. The power surge was palpable, a brief moment of triumph amidst the chaos.

I looked at my remaining pets; they looked rough around the edges, their forms battered and worn, a reflection of the battles they had endured. I had 1 Bones, 3 Ottos, and 1 Squawk remaining. Tentatively, with a tremor of fear in my steps, I approached the first blue gate and slid the door open. I sighed in relief as a single crate was in front of me.

[You have received iron great sword.] The sword was bigger than the crate it came out of.

I proceeded to open every single one of the blue gates, each one creaking open to reveal its hidden contents. I looted four more crates: two normal rarities, three rare, and one legendary chest. The thrill of discovery was tempered by the fatigue weighing on my shoulders. I also found the room's Aerlyntium orb, but I was still a little annoyed at how cavalier Klericho had been in drawing the attention of the mobs. I told them to do it, but did they listen? Nooooo. I sighed, the frustration a brief distraction from the weariness.

I left the final blue cell and went looking for the purple cells. Earlier, I thought there were six purple rooms, but I had to be mistaken, as there were only three of them when I went looking.

The first room was life-changing—or, well, changing. I thought the only way to boost stats and runs was with Death Boons and necklaces, but this room added a new item to my ever-growing list of items to keep track of in the dungeon. I had found a relic—two of them.

The first relic was fantastic, but it made me facepalm in frustration. [Merchant's Coffers: Increases the chance of rare or legendary item drops by 10% and 5%, respectively, while decreasing common and uncommon drops by 5% and 10%.] If only I had found this before looting the chests. The 250 gold from the crates seemed insignificant now. The second relic, however, was much more intriguing—it was an old, dusty...

[The Merchant's Timepiece: This relic allows you to take two back-to-back turns in exchange for your opponent doing the same or move twice or attack twice per turn.] How amazingly useful would that have been. Bones could have attacked twice per turn and fled while our team formed a wall to protect him.

With that goal accomplished, I looked around the room. The reward for killing the boss had been excellent, but I wasn't sure if clearing the green-colored rooms would be worth it. What kind of prize would traps bring except pain and potential death?

Instead, I walked forward toward the Aerlyn Orb and pressed my hand against it. In an instant, it flew around the room, absorbing all of the smoke, the iron gates, the discarded crates and chests, and the four monster corpses I failed to loot.

[Insufficient material found. Please provide]

Well, that's not good. Thomas and Klericho were stuck in the Aerlyn Orb, and I had to find a way to get the missing organic matter. It was a horrible idea, but I immediately wondered if it could absorb my pets. I could quickly summon them back with magic.

"Bones, wait in the previous room; Ottos, sorry in advance."

As soon as my skeleton pets left the room, I asked Crystal my question, "Hey Crystal, can I ask you a question?"

[Did you finally realize I was still here? Why do you keep forgetting me?]

"I remember; I've just been too busy to talk unless you didn't notice the run almost ended twice in the past three rooms. Look, anyway, I need to know if I can summon my pets over and over to meet the organic material needs of this Aerlyn Orb. Yes or no?"

[As if it were that easy. They don't count as they are made of magical essence and not organic matter. Your best bet is to hope we encounter the horde room next. Managing without Klericho and Thomas might be challenging, but you can. Especially with that two-turn thing, you can quickly clear a couple of waves before they even meet up with you. I recommend summoning. Even a single extra pet will help when you only have five.]

"I know, but I don't want to be forced into an underpowered situation because I can't unsummon my pet."

[Why do you think you can't unsummon them?]

I stared at the crystal floating above my head, its light pulsing gently.

[Didn't you unsummon them earlier?]

"No, I had them kill themselves."

[That's unnecessarily morbid.]

"Weren't you there?"

[Sometimes, I just pretend I got attached to someone with a brain. It's nice in my imagination. And I'll imagine I'm back on earth playing a video game instead of living in one.]

"What's a video game?"

Crystal ignored me and went silent, so I shrugged and left the room.

~Run 6, The Horde Room, Floor 2, The Fallen Merchant City of Aerlyn~

As I walked forward into the next one, I blinked in surprise. It was indeed the horde room, the air thick with tension and the scent of impending battle. I planned to get around the fact that I'd be stuck unmoving until I summoned my third group of pets. I knew I could summon one pet, but the horde came in waves, and I could handle a single wave with just the five I had.

As soon as the battle started, five diminutive goblins came running towards us, their snarls echoing off the walls. Time seemed to freeze as they prepared to receive the first attack, their eyes gleaming with malicious intent.

Chapter Seventy-Three
Prepare Yourselves!

The goblins froze in unison; their crude weapons halted mid-swing. Bones 1 deftly sidestepped, his skeletal frame moving with uncanny agility.

"Strike now, Bones 1!" I commanded, and the Red Death ignited in his hands, a blazing red flame enveloping the weapon. With a swift motion, Bones 1 sliced through a goblin, blood spraying into the air as the creature crumpled to the ground.

[Bones 1 has dealt a ninth consecutive hit without taking damage. The Red Death has recovered 2 points of durability damage. Potency increase +9, total: +45. Bones 1 deals 51 damage. Double Overkill. +2 Death Boons.]

As Bones 1 froze, my other minions unleashed a coordinated barrage of spells. Otto initiated with his **Brain Blast**, a surge of psychic energy that staggered Goblin Warrior 1, dealing 3 points of damage.

Bone 2 aimed at Goblin Warrior 2, his attack a critical hit, dealing a devastating 10 points. Bones 3 followed with a **Necrotic Bolt**, dark energy crackling from his fingertips. The bolt struck Goblin Warrior 2, adding 6 points of necrotic damage.

Squawk, our avian storm mage, cast **Lightning Strike**, the air around him crackling with electricity. The bolt of lightning struck Goblin Warrior 2 with a critical hit, dealing a massive 16 points of damage and reducing him to ashes.

PREPARE YOURSELVES!   543

Squawk 3 immediately followed with another **Lightning Strike**, this time targeting Goblin Warrior 3. The lightning hit with slightly less force but still dealt a solid 6 points of damage.

Otto 2, undeterred, cast another **Mind Blast**, his psychic powers overwhelming Goblin Warrior 1's defenses. The attack was a critical hit, and the sheer mental force inflicted 8 points of damage. Otto 3 joined in, her **Mind Blast** dealing an additional 3 points of damage, bringing Goblin Warrior 1 to its knees and finishing him off.

With Goblin Warriors 1 and 2 eliminated, our focus shifted entirely to Goblin Warrior 3. Bones 1, recovering from his momentary freeze, lunged forward with the Red Death, the weapon's necrotic energy flaring to life. His strikes, fueled by the flames of the Red Death, sliced through the goblin's armor, reducing him to a lifeless heap in seconds.

The battlefield was silent, the goblin threat entirely eradicated by the relentless fury of our combined efforts. But the respite was brief as the second wave approached. The summoner goblins were out of range of my pets, but we didn't attack them anyway as I needed organic material to summon the Aerlyntium.

Even though the next wave got their turn, they froze within inches of us, failing to attack. I grinned. There were six monsters this round, increasing by one monster each round. My summoning spell finished just in time, and I had three bulky flame dogs ready to take aggro and kill indiscriminately.

The second round went even smoother than the first. Bones 1 unleashed his physical elemental attack, the Red Death, obliterating another goblin in a single, devastating swing. The sheer power of the Red Death was astonishing, leaving nothing but a charred husk in its wake.

[Bones 1 has dealt a tenth consecutive hit without taking damage. The Red Death has recovered 2 points of durability damage. Potency increase +10 total: +55. Bones 1 deals 64 damage. Triple Overkill. +3 Death Boons.]

As Bones 1 froze in place, the rest of our party unleashed a new set of spells. Otto initiated with his elemental ranged attack, **Mind Flare**. A wave of psychic fire engulfed Goblin Warrior 3, dealing 4 points of damage.

Bones 2 followed with his physical normal damage attack, **Skeletal Smash**. The powerful blow dealt 8 points of damage to Goblin Warrior 4. Bones 3 then cast a non-elemental ranged magic attack, Dark Spike. The piercing Coal dealt 5 points of damage to Goblin Warrior 4.

Squawk, not to be outdone, cast a physical elemental attack, **Thunder Peck**. His beak crackled with electricity as he struck Goblin Warrior 3, dealing 7 points of damage. Squawk 3 followed with his non-elemental ranged magic attack, **Air Slash**, dealing 4 points of damage to Goblin Warrior 3.

Otto 2, undeterred, cast a physical elemental attack, **Psi-Blade**. His psychic blade struck Goblin Warrior 3, dealing 6 points of damage. Otto 3 then cast a ranged elemental attack, **Soul Burn**. The ethereal fire dealt 5 points of damage to Goblin Warrior 3, finishing it off.

The combined assault left Goblin Warriors 3 and 4 eliminated. Our focus shifted entirely to Goblin Warrior 5. Bones 1, recovering from his momentary freeze, lunged forward with the Red Death, the weapon's necrotic energy flaring to life. His strikes, fueled by the flames of the Red Death, sliced through the goblin's armor, reducing him to a lifeless heap in seconds.

As the battlefield quieted, we prepared for the third wave of goblins. Time froze as my flame dogs formed a protective circle around Bones 1. The wave of seven goblins froze in front of us, unable to attack.

With my flame dogs ready, I no longer worried about Bones 1 taking damage. Coal 1 guarded Bones 1 while the rest of the group took out the mobs. Group B dispatched one mob, Group C another, and I used my staff twice on a goblin, killing it.

As the fourth wave approached, I noticed something different. Goblin archers were now protected by a frontline of goblin warriors. The archers nocked their arrows, their eyes gleaming with malevolent intelligence. This round was going to be tougher.

"Prepare yourselves!" I shouted, my voice steady despite the rising tension. The archers had the advantage of range, and the warriors were well-armored, forming an effective shield for their allies.

Bones 1, ever the stalwart, took position at the front, ready to engage. My three flame dogs, Coal 1, Coal 2, and Coal 3, growled in anticipation, their fiery forms flickering with contained energy.

The battle commenced with the goblin warriors charging forward. Bones 1 swung the Red Death, its flames cutting through the air. His strike connected, dealing a heavy blow to the leading warrior.

[Bones 1 has dealt an eleventh consecutive hit without taking damage. The Red Death has recovered 2 points of durability damage. Potency increase +11, total: +66. Bones 1 deals 64 damage. Triple Overkill. +3 Death Boons.]

But the goblin warriors held their ground, and the archers took their shot. Arrows flew through the air, aimed directly at Bones 1.

"Coal 1, intercept!" I commanded, and Coal 1 leaped into the arrow's path. The impact was devastating, and despite his bravery, Coal 1 could not withstand the onslaught. He disintegrated in a burst of flames, his sacrifice not in vain.

The loss of Coal 1 was a blow, but there was no time to mourn. Coal 2 and Coal 3 charged forward, their fiery attacks directed at the goblin warriors. Coal 2 managed to land a hit, dealing 12 points of fire damage to a warrior. However, the second wave of arrows came swiftly.

"Coal 2, look out!" I cried, but it was too late. Another volley of arrows pierced through the air, and Coal 2, too, fell, his flames extinguishing in a final, desperate flare.

I gritted my teeth, frustration mounting. "Squawk, Otto, we need to break through those warriors and take out the archers!"

Otto responded first, casting **Mind Flare**. The psychic fire engulfed a goblin warrior, dealing 4 points of damage. It wasn't enough to take him down, but it weakened him. Squawk followed up with **Thunder Peck**, electricity crackling as he struck the same warrior for 7 points of damage.

Bones 2 and Bones 3 joined the fray. Bones 2 used his bow to attack from range dealing 8 points of damage and killing a warrior.

Bones 3 cast **Dark Spike**, a non-elemental magic attack that pierced through the warriors' defenses, adding 5 points of damage to an archer as well as the warrior it struck first.

The goblin warriors were weakening, but the archers remained a deadly threat. Another volley of arrows flew, this time aimed at Otto. Otto 2 cast **Psi-Blade**, deflecting one of the arrows and striking a goblin warrior for 6 points of damage, but taking half his health in damage. Otto 3 followed with **Soul Burn**, her ethereal fire dealing 5 points of damage and finally taking down one of the warriors.

With a gap in their defense, Squawk 2 seized the opportunity to cast **Lightning Strike**. The bolt of electricity struck an archer, dealing 10 points of damage. The archer staggered but remained standing.

Bones 1, seeing an opening, lunged forward with the Red Death. His strike, infused with necrotic energy, cleaved through the air and struck a goblin warrior. The warrior fell, reduced to a lifeless heap.

"Keep pushing!" I urged. "Go, Coal 3, take down those archers!"

Coal 3 darted forward, leaping over the warrior blockade, its dark form a blur. It landed on an archer, its fangs sinking into the goblin's flesh. The archer shrieked, and the attack dealt 9 points of damage and disrupted their aim.

The remaining warriors tried to regroup, but our coordinated assault was relentless. Squawk 3 cast **Air Slash**, the sharp gust cutting through the air and dealing 4 points of damage to an archer. Otto 2 followed with another **Mind Blast**, the psychic energy overwhelming another archer for 6 points of damage.

Finally, Bones 1 swung the Red Death one last time. The necrotic flames flared brilliantly as he struck down the last goblin warrior, clearing a path to the archers.

The archers, now exposed and without their protectors, faltered. Coal 3, Squawk, and Otto launched a final coordinated attack. Coal 3 pounced, Squawk cast **Lightning Strike**, and Otto unleashed a **Brain Blast**. The combined force obliterated the remaining archers, leaving their lifeless bodies scattered across the battlefield.

As the dust settled, I took a deep breath, surveying the aftermath. We had lost Coal 1 and Coal 2, but we had prevailed. Bones 1 stood tall, his skeletal form untouched, a testament to the sacrifices made. But I was also starting to feel the early stages of run fatigue. It was probably a bad idea, maybe, but I also trusted my pets to clear the rest of the room, especially since Bones 1 could easily slaughter every goblin.

"Okay guys, listen up." I said, speaking to my pets. I gave them a battle plan and let them go. As long as they killed the archers quickly, the fight would be over soon. "I'm going to take a nap. You all got this."

Instead of participating, I did just that. I saddled up against the wall and rested my eyes. About five minutes later, Bones 1 nudged me with his skeletal foot.

It took another couple of rounds for the mobs to be successfully cleared out. I figured this out as I went around lugging the corpses into my inventory. I ended up with around 60 corpses. Hopefully, it was enough organic material to summon back my friends.

Chapter Seventy-Four
Permanent Sacrifice

"Crystal, can you stack the corpses for me?"

[Of course,] Crystal's voice echoed in my mind, and the corpses magically piled around me into a neat pyramid shape. The stench of death and decay was thick in the air, a nauseating blend that clung to my clothes and filled my nostrils reminding me of our time in the sewer. The faint, echoing drips of water from the dungeon's ceiling punctuated that feeling, amplifying the oppressive atmosphere.

I approached the Aerlyn orb, pleasantly surprised that I had gathered enough materials. The orb, a powerful artifact capable of amplifying magic tenfold, was crucial for my goal of escaping this cursed dungeon.

I breathed a sigh of relief as Thomas and Klericho appeared in a heap. I hadn't even noticed when Thumbs died during the chaos of the previous room's battle. Thumbs, the little goblin appeared, waving his tiny dagger about before he put it away to chase after the remaining Coal.

My contentment wouldn't last, but I was glad to have a little piece of it. Now that Thomas and Klericho were awake, it was, unfortunately, time to start planning the next run and end this one. I didn't like that it had to be this way, but I was wasting time.

The relentless battles, the endless strategizing—each step forward felt like dragging my feet through mud. Sure, I was gaining Death Boons and loot, but I had a stockpile of over a hundred. There was no discernible reason to keep up with this run other than getting a feel for the rooms.

Thomas must have seen the look on my face, so he approached me, his tone light and friendly. "What's on your mind there?"

"The loot on this floor has been impressive, but I am concerned about the value of trying to clear more rooms, knowing that no matter what happens, I can't kill the boss this run. It seems like I may be better off ending things prematurely here and—"

"No, stop your train of thought now. The dungeon has ears."

"Well, I know that, but—"

"No, lazy trains of thought like that lead to negative consequences."

"And me giving up on a run is so bad? I'm just taking a shortcut to get ahead."

"If that was your real reason for doing it, that might be okay. But no, you are just being lazy, wanting to get out of doing something difficult. Therein lies the sin of sloth. Rest is necessary, and laziness is a good thing when the body and mind need rest, but when you shortcut that rest—when you shortcut doing what you need to do to be healthy—"

"Very wise, Thomas," Klericho cut him off with a sarcastic lilt to his voice. "If the kid wants to kill his chances at leaving this place, let him. He's already ruined Rellum's plans."

Klericho's constant badmouthing was wearing thin. Our rivalry stemmed from me getting marked by Aurentum, an event I had no real control over. I could see the resentment in his eyes, a constant reminder of the price we all paid. "I didn't—" I started speaking, but I was cut off as a member of the big three casually strolled into my day. This time, it was one I hadn't met.

Then, time froze. Malikap, one of the big three, materialized before us, his presence warping reality. His grotesque form split the very fabric of reality. He stood on his broken tripod; limbs splayed like gnarled tree branches. His torso sprang upward in two halves, split by a weave of solid darkness. His face radiated malice, so much so that it physically pained me to look at him. I averted my eyes.

"Anger. It is such a beautiful thing, especially when it is righteous. The anger of those justified in spilling blood and spewing hatred always tastes so delicious, like burned grease or melted fat on bread." He smacked his mandibles in his grotesque, misshapen jaw, and I had to look away again to stop from gagging. For a god of justice, he never seemed very just to me. Evil sometimes came in awful packages, and clearly, he fit that perfectly. Everyone new Malikap was the worst of the gods.

He clicked his mandibles again and tsked. "You were warned again and again, boy, not to trifle with me or my domain, and yet here you sit under my watchful thumb. Like grapes so fresh and plump for the picking. Your head so full of misplaced rage I could pop it right now." To emphasize his point, he pinched his thumb and forefinger together. I felt my whole world condense in pain and agony, my vision shrinking as if he had actually pinched my head like a grape.

I grasped at my staff poking out from behind my back. I knew it would do me no good here, but all the same, it brought me a bit of comfort.

"Relax. If I was here to end your run, there are easier ways than freezing your teammates. In fact, I'm here to help you. The other gods think they are so crafty. But leaving you unclaimed for so long will be their undoing." His offer was like the blaze my father was always taking. I could feel the temptation to wield it, to swallow it, and its empty lies of pleasure, but as soon as I did, I knew that its tort would never end. Malikap started laughing. A mad, barking laugh that was loud and made me feel small. His mandibles clicked, punctuating every part of it.

"I don't want anything from you."

"This isn't an offer, boy. It is a gift. You can never refuse a gift from a god. Especially not in here." He snapped his fingers, and time unfroze. At that moment, his mandibles unhinged from his jaw, his head swelled, and he enveloped Bones 1, crunching down in one solid gulp. As Bones 1 died, the other two faded away.

I blinked, and Malikap vanished, too; confusion overwhelmed me, and I dropped to my knees. Twice in one run, a god's promise of help had only plunged me deeper into peril.

I could easily re-summon Bones if I tried hard enough, but the amount of work getting the sword strikes to be that powerful again would take a conscious effort.

"What was that?" Klericho asked, his voice tiny and quiet. Blood had drained from his face, leaving him looking rather corpse-like.

"It was Malikap," Thomas spoke before I could respond, and we were both taken aback by his rather bland delivery. "Rod here has hit the first threshold of Wrath. Look at the mark on his arm."

I looked down, and there was a tattoo on my forearm. It was a curved, serrated dagger surrounded by spiraling flames from the center. In tiny pinprick letters, the word wrath was spelled in blood-red letters along the flat of the hilt.

The clumsy man's observation startled me. He had always seemed so goofy, but now, I saw a glimmer of faded intelligence in his eyes. "Well, go ahead and **Scan** yourself. See what kind of 'reward' you got from him." He spat out the word reward like rotten food he had somehow taken a bite of.

I cast **Scan**, immediately taken aback by what I saw. Then, a grin crept across my face. Deep down, I knew I should be purging these sins to survive the dungeon, but so far, the perk seemed worth it—despite a god killing my best pet.

[Malikap's Domain of Wrath. Generates a domain around the user. Allies within the domain get 5 points of potency or insight per permanent sacrifice to Malikap. For every attack made while this domain is active, a 5% health drain is applied. Permanent sacrifices made: 2.]

My grin at the 10-point stat boost quickly faded as the realization hit—I had permanently lost Bones 1 and another of my pets. I looked around, my heart sinking.

Squawk, Otto, Coal 3. All were fine. The only one missing was...

"He killed Thumbs!" The small goblin had been clinging to Bones 1. Now, both were gone, victims of the monster's ruthless hunger.

I froze. Poor, sweet, innocent Thumbs was gone. Forever. Instead of rage, a hollow, cold emptiness settled within me, as if something was irrevocably wrong with the world and my place in it. Like nothing would ever be alright again.

I slunk down to the floor and cradled my head. I hadn't had the minion for long, but he was a part of my team. How could Malikap be so cruel? And Bones 1 had been my main damage dealer. I had no idea how I would deal damage now. I walked over to where the sword lay on the ground. Tears welled at my eyes, but I shook my head. I wouldn't let the gods and their petty games stop me.

"All right, if idleness spells danger, let's clear the rest of this floor, amass a trove of loot, and return stronger in the next run."

Opulent Oasis Aerlyn 1 of 6

Gail the Gaoler
- **Amount:** 1

- **Effect:** This is a gaoler. She keeps prisoners in line.

- **Description:** A stern and formidable guard who oversees the prisoners.

Thomas
- **Amount:** 1

- **Effect:** It's Thomas! Exciting!

- **Description:** Ever notice how he dies a lot?

Klericho

- **Amount:** 1

- **Effect:** It's Klericho! *jazz hands*

- **Description:** He dies a lot, too, so it's no wonder they never beat this floor.

Thumbs

- **Amount:** 1

- **Effect:** It's a goblin!

- **Description:** He finds stuff! He's your minion, remember?

Thurible

- **Amount:** 10

- **Effect:** Releases fragrant smoke creating a calming effect on the prisoners.

- **Description:** A censer used to burn incense.

Gaol Key

- **Amount:** 25

- **Effect:** Opens a cell in the gaol.

- **Description:** It's a key. Do I really need to explain keys?

Pot

- **Amount:** 10

- **Effect:** Stores various items.

- **Description:** This is a clay pot used for storage.
  Quote: ~Keep away from Link.

Chapter Seventy-Five
Kingsley

I blinked as we entered the next room. The stark contrast to the previous room left me momentarily disoriented, and the sudden silence was jarring. A faint antiseptic smell lingered in the air, and the white walls gleamed almost blindingly under the harsh overhead sunlight.

In the center, on a prayer rug, sat a stout, overweight Grendelkin with a name floating on a parchment above his crowned head. Hob. He was the son of Grendel, who was mentioned in the description of the Grendelkins in the prison room. As Kingsley spoke, snippets of the prison room's descriptions flashed through my mind—'Son of Grendel, a survivor of his grandmother's wrath.' It all clicked into place just as Elizabeth's bestiary entry popped up.

"Ah, hello. I have been expecting you." His gravelly voice sounded like he was talking through shattered glass but with a deep, velvet bass in the background. A scar ran from his face to his stomach as if someone had tried and failed to gut him. Kingsley's hand absently traced the scar down his chest. "This?" he asked, catching my eye. "A reminder of the price I paid for my father's sins." His furry, clawed hands were held up in a defensive position as he stared at me. I somehow took on the role of leader yet again.

"I know what you are. Why should I give you even a moment's hesitation?"

"Look around you. Does this look like a kingdom? It's my fault; I know it. That Djinn ruined everything and then trapped me here.

I should never have made the wish. It gave me room to expand my kingdom, but what kingdom? My followers are enslaved or mindless. My brothers and sisters are in jail, driven insane. And here I sit in the blandest prison of them all. A room I can never leave."

He paused, gesturing at the walls.

"And with no food, water, or sleep, I slowly go insane. Day in, day out. The same, the same, the same!" He screamed this last word and pounded his feet with thunderous power. I couldn't understand what he was trying to convey, but Klericho was quicker on the uptake.

"If you are honest in your words, then unlock the door and step away. We want as much as you do for this stupid Djinn to be behind us. The sooner we kill it, the sooner we leave this floor behind."

"I can't do that. You are too weak. You only have one of the relics necessary to defeat the king of magicks." I grimaced. "Without those relics, the Djinn cannot be resealed." He paused again, looking at Klericho and Thomas with an undisguised fury.

"I am here to ask you to end your run; it is the least you can do after your companions destroyed the Djinn's lamp. To let me win a victory against you. Rellum wishes to have you all die here and use this place to launch your assault against the Djinn in your next run. I can even make all my minions docile against you for your next run only. It won't help you on the previous floor but will make things easier as you return. I can even stop floor guardians from assaulting you. But you have to die. All of you. To reset the floor completely."

As Kingsley pleaded, I felt a tug-of-war within me. I looked at my companions, trying to gauge how they were feeling.

Can we really trust him? Every instinct screamed caution, yet was it right to condemn him without hearing him out? Everything in me demanded quick decisions, but my conscience urged me to consider his plight. I couldn't shake the feeling that we were all pawns in a larger game.

I sighed, frustration bubbling beneath my calm exterior. This wasn't how I envisioned the end of this run. The thought of abandoning our progress gnawed at me, but the logic in Kingsley's plea was undeniable. I turned to my companions.

"I know it's what I wanted earlier, but I can't help but feel a little cheated now that I actually wanted to go through with clearing the rest of the floor."

"I still think we should do it. Time doesn't matter here, so long as we stay away from the Djinn's room."

"If Rellum wants us to stop now, we should."

"How about we ask our crystals for further input?"

[Clearing more of the dungeon is the wisest course of action.]

[If we do not clear the floor, we will have a more challenging time on the next run. We need every advantage to clear out the Djinn promptly and safely.]

"Your Majesty," I said, trying to keep my impatience in check, "how about we move past, clear the rest of the floor, and you stay here? Your plan is solid, but we need to explore more for loot if possible. Every little bit will help in the final battle."

The king nodded, his expression stern. "If that is your wish, so be it. I will neither hinder nor aid you in this. However, if you confront the Djinn with the lamp, the Djinn will win. He must not know you hold the key to his defeat. Now begone. I wish to nap before my magic is required."

[Congratulations! Kingsley is now a temporary ally until you leave the second floor!]

As we left the room, a sense of unease washed over me. It felt like we'd stumbled into a secret boss fight that hadn't quite materialized. The Goblin King and the Djinn seemed out of place, like puzzle pieces that didn't fit.

I let out a sigh, shaking off the lingering oddness. We needed something more thrilling. These endless conversations were wearing thin, and I longed for the exhilaration of battle. I pushed open the door to the next room.

~Run 6, The Jeweler's Jumble, Floor 2, Sewers of Aerlyn~

The sight that greeted me was overwhelming. The room was a riot of color and sparkle, with towering piles of rubies, sapphires, and emeralds reflecting the flickering torchlight. Gold coins cascaded like waterfalls over ornate goblets and chalices, forming glittering mounds. It was like stepping into a dragon's hoard.

But there was no time to marvel. The gemstone piles shifted, revealing goblin Treasuremancers within. I felt a thrill of excitement. This was more like it. Gripping my staff, I prepared for the fight, the earlier boredom forgotten.

[You have dealt 22 necrotic damage.]

I couldn't help but laugh. It didn't kill him, but the damage was impressive. "**Scan!**" I shouted at Crystal.

[The Hobbit? Mark Zuckerberg?] I shook my head at Crystal's antics and launched another necrotic bolt. The +10 insight boost was insane. Despite being a mage build, I was dealing damage like a seasoned warrior. Maybe I'd go Berserker in my next run.

Several Treasuremancers advanced, their greed-fueled eyes glinting with malice. I fired another necrotic bolt, watching it sear through a goblin's chest. Thomas, the Barbarian, let out a war cry and charged, his massive two-handed sword cleaving through two goblins with a single swing. Goblin parts flew, painting the floor with dark blood.

Klericho, our cleric, raised his hands and summoned a localized golden shield. Arrows and daggers bounced harmlessly off its radiant surface, protecting us from harm. Suddenly, two more goblins appeared from behind the gemstone piles and rushed towards me. Before I could react, they slashed at me, reducing my health to a dangerously low level.

Staggering back, clutching my wounds, I summoned my pets for support. The Ottos used their **Brain Blast** spell and leech attack to overwhelm the goblins. Coal, my flame dog, charged forward, biting and burning a goblin.

Klericho, seeing me in peril, raised his hands and summoned a golden shield to protect me. He followed up with a healing spell, enveloping me in a warm, golden glow that healed my wounds. Rejuvenated, I targeted a Treasuremancer and fired three rapid **Necrotic Bolts**. Total damage: 49. The Treasuremancer was left with just one point of health. One of the Ottos leaped and used a **Brain Blast** spell to finish off the weakened Treasuremancer.

The remaining pets swarmed Thomas's target, pinning it down. Thomas, unfrozen from a previous pause, attacked twice with his sword, finishing off his target. One goblin mob decided to flee, but I sprinted forward, closing the distance quickly. Using my full turn, I unleashed a barrage of **Necrotic Bolts** at the fleeing goblin. On the final hit, my staff hummed with energy, and the goblin disintegrated into black ash.

We stared in horror as all the gold, treasure, and items turned to decrepit black ash. Kicking a boot through the pile, I realized everything was wasted. We left the room and moved on, the thrill of victory marred by the hollow feeling of loss.

~Run 6, Willow Whispers, Floor 2, Sewers of Aerlyn~

Like the Necromancer room on the previous floor, I was transported to a realm that defied logic. The walls were now clawing bark and wood, with branches and leaves reaching down to the floor. The vision was surreal and oddly calming, but I stayed alert, ready for anything.

Enemy Entry 0025: Hob "Kingsley" GrendelKing

King of the goblins and son of Grendel, this monstrosity shouldn't even be alive. Yet it outlived its grandmother's wrath and now commands the goblins of the Third Tribe. These outcast scallywags are blissfully unaware that their kind has been set free beneath their feet in the sewers. Hob "Kingsley" GrendelKing harbors an extreme hatred for humans. And now he knows you're here. You really should have gone back to regen mana after that last fight. At least you had the presence of mind to put up the overcharge rings and the mana regen amulet.

Weaknesses: Shadow, fire, ice

Strengths: Lightning, holy, earth, poison

Stats

- **Level:** Not specified

- **Health:** 1000/1000

- **Potency:** 25

- **Defense:** 7

- **Magic Defense:** 3

Item Drops
Gold

- **Amount:** 500

- **Chance to drop:** 40%

Ring of Grendel's Strength

- **Amount:** 1

- **Chance to drop:** 20%

Cloak of Shifting Shadows

- **Amount:** 1

- **Chance to drop:** 20%

Amulet of Abyssal Wisdom

- **Amount:** 1

- **Chance to drop:** 10%

GrendelKing's Battle Axe

- **Amount:** 1

- **Chance to drop:** 10%

Enemy Entry 0026: Treasuremancer

The ultimate sin of greed lies not in amassing wealth but in denying others the chance to do the same. When you become so evil that you deny basic needs to others, it truly becomes the worst sin. These Treasuremancers are like if Mark Zuckerberg and the dragon from *The Hobbit* had a baby. Kill them and burn their tainted gold.

Weaknesses: Lightning, ice
Strengths: Fire, shadow, earth, poison

Stats

- **Level:** ???

- **Health:** 100/100

- **Potency:** 25

- **Defense:** 7

- **Magic Defense:** 3

Item Drops
Tainted Gold
- **Amount:** 50

- **Chance to drop:** 100%

Chapter Seventy-Six
Whisperwind

[Willow trees? They don't belong on this planet. How did they get here? Watch out!]

Time seemed to freeze, but I couldn't duck in time. A wad of green mana, almost like vomit but not as sickly, flew towards me. It smacked into my chest, a jarring force that drove all the air from my lungs in a painful rush. I gasped, a sharp cry escaping my lips as I collapsed backwards, my heavy frame hitting the dirt with a dull thud.

Swinging from the willow branches, almost like monkeys, were diminutive goblins. Poor Thumbs, sacrificed in an earlier encounter with Malikap, could have lifted one in each hand. I cast a quick **Scan**, my vision blurring at the edges as exhaustion weighed down my limbs. I tried to take stock of myself, but the truth was I was spent.

It might sound like I'm complaining or lazy, but back-to-back runs with barely a little bit of sleep? My eyelids drooped like leaden weights, each blink a herculean effort. My legs wobbled under me, as heavy and uncooperative as sacks of flour, while my arms dangled at my sides, imprisoned by the unyielding stiffness of my sweat-soaked clothes.

Despite my exhaustion, a stubborn resolve pushed me to focus. Crystal's voice cut through my fatigue like a lifeline, anchoring me in the chaotic present.

[You have been affected by stamina rot. Stamina was lowered to 50%, and stamina recovery was also halved. Yeah, don't let anything throw their snot at you. Gross, didn't you just escape a sewer? Do you have a fetish for this stuff?]

Crystal's sarcastic remark made me shake my head with a faint smile. As her words lingered, I couldn't help but remember the smell of the sewer and shuddered.

I shook my head at her antics and refocused on the swinging goblins ahead. Several of them were frozen in midair, suspended by the turn-based system. I wondered if I could remove the branches they were hanging from instead of killing them outright.

My hesitation was brief; I needed to act quickly, so I turned to my pets and began formulating a plan. If only I still had the skill **Aim**. I had a bow, but I remembered all too well how poorly aiming had gone without that essential skill.

Determined to shake off the fatigue, I refocused on the swinging goblins ahead. With my plan hastily shared with my pets, I leaned back against the rough vine-covered wall, praying it would work. The cold stone bit into my back, a stark reminder of the reality I was in. My flame dog sprang into action, spitting four fireballs in random directions, transforming my strategy into reality.

The room erupted into a chaotic symphony of smoke, lights, and sound. As chaos erupted around me, a pang of guilt twisted in my gut. The screaming willow trees and the helpless, burning goblins stirred an uncomfortable remorse within me.

The branches from which the whisper goblins hung quickly succumbed to the fire, but the goblins themselves remained suspended in the air as if time had yet to decide their fate. Their small forms dangled high above the ground, and I anticipated some magical occurrence once the system unfroze them.

When time resumed, four goblins dropped simultaneously, splattering onto the ground with a satisfying crunch. As the blood and guts exploded outward, I scanned the room to assess the damage.

If I found the room on my next run-through, I would have to try to solve it without using a shortcut. Cheating my way out of rooms wasn't the path to victory, and I already knew there were consequences, but it was almost like the room had wanted me to take the easy way out. That I had been compelled to kill the goblins this way.

It took another half hour for the trees to finish burning out, leaving us with a pile of ashes and burnt, unlootable corpses. As I stood amidst the ashes, a heavy guilt washed over me, seeping into my bones like a winter's chill.

"I'm sorry," I murmured, addressing no one in particular but everyone all the same. "I got mad at both of you when I just cleared a room in the same cheap way that you both did. I kept letting my anger get the best of me earlier, and I'll do my best not to do it again."

The ensuing silence felt like a weight pressing down on me, a stark reminder of the loneliness that often shadowed these battles.

"It's too late."

"What?"

"It's too late for apologies," Klericho repeated. "You are beyond the realm of redemption now. I wouldn't be surprised if your next gate descends instead of ascends. You broke the seal of wrath and got blessed by Malikap the worst of them all." He spat at me.

"Rellum will surely end his parlance with you as soon as we finish this floor. Until then, we are allies by necessity, but that is it." Klericho turned his face and sneered.

"Alright then. I'm still sorry for what I did, even if you won't accept it," I said, trying to keep the bitterness from my voice. "Let's just move on. We probably have a handful more rooms to go through, and then I'll reset against the King."

We trudged through the ash-ridden room, waving away the lingering smoke with our hands.

~Run 6, The Blacksmith's Foundry, Floor 2, Sewers of Aerlyn~

The moment I stepped into the next room, a wave of heat hit me, making the heart of one of coal's fireball spells seem like a mere flicker. The relentless, overbearing heat was like the midday sun of summer—consistent, painful, consuming. I almost stepped back into the previous room, but Klericho and Thomas pushed past me with their bulks, and I stumbled forward.

The room was lined with lit forge after lit forge; smoke and heat billowing into the air before slowly settling back to earth. A goblin was hammering away at a red-hot sword, molding it into the perfect shape. Every forge had a similar setup: some with armor, others with halberds, and some even with piles of coins.

But the telltale signs of the black plague had settled over most of the materials in the room. The goblins' skin, once a vibrant green, had turned an almost black viridian hue that pulsed ominously, in sync with the infected coins, armor, and weapons.

I did a head count of my pets. Otto and one Coal were still there, but I was hoping for a good pull to summon either my water cats or thunderbirds. I was about to suggest that we sneak up on the nearest goblin when Thomas tripped for the sixth time on this floor, clattering to the ground in a heap.

Time froze.

As soon as the battle started, I overcast my summoning spell and readied myself for the possibility of taking damage. There were eight of the goblin forgemasters, as I had taken to calling them. Truth be told, I had yet to **Scan** them, so I had no real idea if that was even their proper title.

Regardless, I wasn't going to take a shortcut in this room. I hadn't gotten a single Death Boon from the last fight, and even if it would be a drop in the ocean compared to the 130 I had banked, a Death Boon was still a Death Boon. It wasn't about being greedy; in fact, it was the opposite. I was doing this to ensure I could make it through the next round for the benefit of others, even if they hated my guts.

My Flameys and Ottos launched their missiles at the first group of approaching goblins.

[Your pets have dealt 15 damage.]

The first forgemaster nearly went down, but before I could breathe a sigh of relief, he hurled a flaming hammer through the air. The weapon flew and flew, eventually crushing an Otto against the wall, killing the tiny octopus instantly.

[Goblin Forgemaster 1 has dealt 10 physical damage to Otto. Otto has been defeated.]

I gulped. Sure, Ottos were weak, but that one had died in a single hit.

My cast continued as the forgemasters took their turn, the magic bubbling up and out of the pit of my stomach, forming a robust and impenetrable ball of mana. It burst forth, and I blinked as a new summon appeared. Only one. I stared hard at the creature.

"Why aren't there three of you?" I muttered. The creature, a boxy, ox-like beast with curled horns and a wisp of icy mist flowing from its hooves, reared its head as if to say, "Are you serious?" Then, it charged forward in a bull rush, knocking over the entire group of goblins and freezing them in place. It was the coolest thing I had seen in the dungeon.

[You have frozen the goblin forgemasters.]

I grinned before running forward and swinging a spell at the face of the first goblin. With my new bonus to insight, my spell either had a lot of force behind it, or the mobs were frozen solid because the goblin shattered into thousands of tiny ice cubes.

[You have dealt 25 ice damage. Goblin forgemaster 1 has been defeated.]

My companions fared just as well. Thomas, wielding the super sword, swung again and again, hacking away at another goblin.

[Thomas has dealt 25 physical damage. Goblin forgemaster 2 has been defeated.]

Klericho didn't even bother casting a **Heal** or **Shield**; instead, he brought his mace down repeatedly, shattering a third goblin.

[Klericho has dealt 25 physical damage. Goblin forgemaster 3 has been defeated.]

My pets ganged up on two other goblins, sending spell after spell into their torsos. Magic wasn't as practical for shattering the goblins, so for the second round of attacks, Otto used the mind skill, netting an Overkill Boon.

[Otto has dealt 50 mind damage. Goblin forgemaster 4 has been defeated. You have gained an Overkill Boon.]

The rest of my companions charged forward and switched to physical attacks. Icyox, as I decided to call my new pet, wasn't idle either. With the last two moves of his expanded turn, he gored a goblin in the head, ripped it off, and threw it like a cannonball into the next prone goblin.

[Icyox has dealt 25 physical damage. Goblin forgemaster 5 has been defeated.]

The head shattered, but the other goblin seemed relatively unharmed.

[Icyox has dealt 10 physical damage. Goblin forgemaster 6 has 15 health remaining.]

Then, my new pet dissolved into a wisp of icy smoke, disappearing.

I was simultaneously happy and angry. Although my new pet only lasted two turns, it was clearly an insane boost over my previous level of summons.

It escaped my mind until then that I hadn't even tried casting **Scan**.

Enemy Entry 0027: Whisperwind Goblins

These small goblins spend their lives flying through the thick branches of forests, ready at a moment's notice to take their anger out on the world.

Weaknesses: Fire

Strengths: None

Stats

- **Level:** Not specified

- **Health:** 25/25

- **Potency:** 2

- **Insight:** 4

- **Defense:** 2

Item Drops

Gold

- **Amount:** 5–25

- **Chance to drop:** 75%

Monkey's Paw

- **Amount:** 1–2

- **Chance to drop:** 25%

Chapter Seventy-Seven
Mini-Djinni

"Hey... Crystal? Do you have any idea what happened with that new summon? I thought the class only had eight summons," I asked, looking up at a crystal's red, beating heart. The crystal's surface was faceted, catching the dim light and refracting it into a dance of crimson glimmers that filled the room.

Crystal pulsed faintly, almost as if considering.

[I'm... not sure. It could be due to Malikap's boon pushing you past an insight threshold. You could also have somehow channeled a spell from an advanced class early. You aren't supposed to be able to use them until you unlock them with Death Boons.]

My eyebrows shot up in surprise. "Oh, huh. Advanced classes. That's neat, I suppose." I shook my head, trying to push the confusion aside. Now wasn't the time for mysteries. With renewed determination, I tightened my grip on my Necrotic Staff and charged forward. The staff was a gnarled piece of dark wood, twisted as if grown in the shadow of something ancient and evil, its tip crackling with faint, greenish energy.

The system just skipped the turns of the frozen goblins. In a blur of motion, my staff swung through the air, its necrotic energy shattering the neck of the goblin I struck. Its flesh withered instantly, and its life drained away in a sickly green light. Beside me, my companions turned the other into a frozen pyramid of red and green ice cubes. I panted, the cold air stinging my lungs, grateful it was over.

"Well, that was the easiest fight we've ever had," I said between breaths, eyes scanning the room. Once bright and bustling, the forges were now lifeless and cold, the metal surfaces slick with corruption. "Too bad everything here is corrupted. Except..."

My gaze fell on a chest in the center of the eight forges on a pile of corrupted ingots. The chest was an anomaly of pure, untainted wood, its surface unmarred by the creeping blackness. The corruption was alive, slowly inching toward the chest, moving through the ingots like rotten molasses, thick and foul. Heart pounding, I ran forward, yanked the chest off the pile of evil, and flung it toward the group, careful not to get any black liquid on myself or the chest.

It was only rare, but the entire point of the exercise was to gain loot, and this was our only chance to get all of the metal and items destroyed by the Djinn's curse. Thomas was the first to approach the chest, kicking it open with the tip of his right boot. The chest creaked open, revealing its treasure as dice rolled around us. I was again grateful that everyone got their loot from the chest.

[You have received four items.]

From the chest, I retrieved a potion and three weapons. Relief washed over me as I realized this was the first chest in a while that an Aerlyntium hadn't eaten. I gave the weapons to Thomas and Klericho, including a steel greatsword, a steel mace, and a steel great axe. All these were items I couldn't use on this run, and I had no plans of being in a physical class anytime soon. I kept the mana potion, though; who knew that would probably come in handy.

"Do you guys think we've cleared enough? The gold plague is spreading, and we probably won't get much from the last few rooms," Thomas said, his voice tinged with rare uncertainty. The usual confidence in his voice was replaced with a shadow of doubt.

I eyed the tall man warily before responding. "You're the one who has been pushing us to loot these rooms and to clear everything except the Djinn."

Thomas's expression turned serious as he pointed to the only exit from the forge. "I feel that the room on the other side of that door is the Djinn. Look at the molding on the door. See the intricate patterns there?"

We all turned to the ornate doorway, which starkly contrasted the plain, wood-paneled archways that separated most rooms on the second floor. Someone had spent hours, if not days, intricately carving a design all over the door. The design was maze-like, with twists and turns, and it pulsed briefly with the ever-present sign of mana. A collective shiver ran through us as we realized we did not want to enter that room.

"I don't want the run to be over," I confessed, stroking the flame dog's fiery mane. The flames flickered under my touch, surprisingly warm and soft, like silk threads ablaze. The thought of ending it now felt like a loss, a missed opportunity to see what else I could achieve. My heart ached at leaving my pets behind, their loyal eyes looking up at me as if understanding my thoughts. Uncertain if I'd ever feel this sense of purpose again, I struggled to hold back a wave of sadness.

"Every run has to end sometime," Thomas said, his tone as firm as the hard line set in his jaw. His weathered face, marked by countless battles and narrow escapes, showed no hint of doubt. "You've been on this run for days. Don't feel bad; you've probably gone further than anyone expected. Several of these bosses should have ended your run. They barely needed to lay a finger on you, and you'd keel over. It's almost like you're following the goddess of luck instead of Rellum and Aurentum."

"Hah, there's no such thing as the goddess of luck," Klericho interjected, rolling his eyes. His sarcasm was evident in the smirk playing at the corners of his lips, his skepticism as deep as the creases on his brow.

"Either way," Thomas continued, undeterred. "We should return to the Goblin King and see what he thinks about ending this now."

Reluctantly, I followed them back to the Goblin King, my mind wrestling with the prospect of leaving this adventure unfinished. Each step felt heavier, the silence between us growing more oppressive. The corridor's dim torchlight cast long shadows that seemed to cling to us, reflecting my inner turmoil. Just as we neared the king's chamber, a sudden roar echoed through the hall, and chaos erupted.

Dozens of creatures I'd never seen before swarmed the room, flapping tiny bat-like wings. They had furry faces in a variety of colors with large, expressive eyes that reflected the dim torchlight like obsidian mirrors and curled ram horns that added to their otherworldly appearance.

I quickly cast a **Scan** at the largest, which had an orange coat and four tiny little legs.

The orange mini-Djinni locked eyes with me. Despite the ominous description from the scan, I couldn't help but find it strangely adorable. Its round face and childlike features were disarming, starkly contrasting the ferocity described. My heart raced as it flew towards me, but not out of fear. Its large, black eyes seemed to pull me in, and for a moment, I was lost in their depths. I wanted– no, I needed to pet it.

"Hiiiiiiiiiiiiii, I'm Frannie. What's your name?" The creature circled my head energetically, its tiny wings buzzing like an overzealous hummingbird. "I think I'm gonna adopt you. I've been needing a new human. Wanna go overthrow my dad?"

It glanced at Thomas and Klericho with a look of disdain. "I don't like them. After this floor, you have to ditch them. Or we could ditch them now."

"I need their help," I replied, torn between amusement and apprehension. "I still need to return and gather the materials to kill the Djinn. Without them, I won't stand a chance."

"Oh, my father can't be killed. He can only be overthrown and trapped like in those Aerlyntium's. Or like how my brethren and I have been trapped here and can't leave. It's annoying. I've heard the 3rd floor has books, and I've always wanted to eat one."

"Don't you mean read a book?" I asked the flying orange-thing, raising an eyebrow.

"That's what I said. Oh, look, they killed the Goblin King. No, come on, don't eat it. You're supposed to cook goblin first."

I sighed. "Frannie, focus. How do we trap your father?"

Before I could react, Frannie lunged at Otto, its jaw unhinging grotesquely. In an instant, Otto was gone, swallowed whole. My stomach churned at the creature's body, expanding unnaturally to accommodate him.

"Hey, what the hell? Why'd you just eat Otto?" I yelled, my voice shaking with a mixture of shock and anger.

"Oh, stop whining," Frannie said nonchalantly. "It tasted like mana-fried shrimp. It was pretty good."

My anger flared, the vein in my forehead throbbing. Why did I keep attracting these utterly insane things that could kill me with just a thought?

Thomas's face contorted with rage as he swung his sword at Frannie. "Get away, demon!" he shouted.

"Hey, watch it!" I dodged, pulling Frannie with me.

"These Djinni are the cause of the whole problem," Thomas growled, his eyes wild. "They freed the Djinn. And now they've killed the Goblin King and ruined our chance at a truce. It's their fault we're stuck here."

"Thomas, chill," Klericho said, placing a steadying hand on Thomas's shoulder. "You don't want to trigger any milestones."

Thomas's eyes lost some wildness, and he took a deep breath. "I'm sorry. That was uncouth of me. I don't know how Rod will make to this room on the next run with the king dead. Unless he has another ace up his sleeve, he can't get through without us."

"And why don't the two of you just head back and wait at the entrance?" They looked at me like I had grown a second head.

"Right, we should probably do that. Wouldn't want you to fail five seconds after stepping onto the second floor."

"No, silly, it'll only take him one try. That boon is insane." Frannie interjected, seemingly unfazed by the tension. "I can see the power coursing through him, and it's wonderful. And it's the kind of power that wins, unlike yours. You think your god is so mighty and unassailable, but the truth is she's just another coward, another cog in the machine of this place. No matter what you two do, he will make it to the end, even if I must drag him myself because I will be leaving this floor."

With that, the puffball roared, unhinged its jaw, and swallowed us all whole.

[You have died. You have earned 1 Death Boon. End of Run 6]

Rod - Run 6 Corpse *(destroyed)*

Gold
- **Amount:** 873

Death Boons
- **Amount:** 132

Items
Spout of the Immortal: 2 of 3
- **Amount:** 1

- **Condition:** Temporary

- **Effect:** Opens doors

- **Description:** This relic is a key. It can open a secret door or serve another purpose yet to be discovered. Handle it with care, as it is fragile.

Iron Great Sword
- **Amount:** 1

- **Condition:** 25/25

- **Effect:** It's a sword

- **Description:** This class couldn't even use this.

Mana Potion
- **Amount:** 1

- **Condition:** 20/20

- **Effect:** It's a potion

- **Description:** Use this to recover 20 mana.

[Rod, did you never pick the Red Death back up? You absolute moron! That would have been our ticket to escaping Penance, but who knows if it will ever spawn again? And was that all you got? Those Aerlyntiums cheated you out of loot, didn't they?]

Enemy Entry 0028: Mini-Djinni

The bastard children of an all-powerful Djinn. Throw the rules of reality out the window when dealing with Djinn and their offspring. These demons will eat the skin off your bones while you're still alive—or pull out paper and teach you advanced calculus. Each Mini-Djinni is unique. Perhaps one might even adopt you and make you its minion.

Weaknesses: None

Strengths: Everything

Stats

- **Level:** Not specified

- **Health:** 100/100

- **Potency:** 15

- **Defense:** 15

- **Magic Defense:** 15

Item Drops

Gold

- **Amount:** 50

- **Chance to drop:** 40%

Djinni Wings

- **Amount:** 2

- **Chance to drop:** 60%

Chapter Seventy-Eight
Jamie Run 2, Part 3

Malice was still a belligerent, howling mess as I rushed down the hallway. I did my best to ignore him, but you would think I had murdered a kitten with how upset he was.

[But you promised me all of the loot. Jamie.... Nooooo, please go back. I'll do anything!]

"Rellum, save me," I sighed, staring up at him. "Are you really not going to let this go?"

[You promised me all of the loot. Are you really going back to your word? What a good queen you are. Reliable. Trustworthy.] He said this with a mocking tone, which just made me want to continue ignoring him.

"I'm uncomfortable watching someone I love turn to dust."

[Then close your eyes. I'm a completionist, and it's hard enough that you're skipping rooms on me, but skipping actual loot, too? What did I do to get cursed with such a waste of a partner? Oh, woe is me!]

"Laying it on a little thick there, aren't you?"

[Shame. Shame. Shaaaaame.]

This is getting me nowhere, and if it doesn't stop soon, I'll kill myself just to end the stupidity.

I turned around.

"Fine." Every fiber of my being was yelling at me not to do this. It felt like an even worse betrayal than killing her had been, but I just couldn't deal with this guy.

What an absolute menace. That should have been his name, not Malice.

I opened the door to the previous room. The heavy wooden door creaked on its hinges, revealing a space filled with dust and cobwebs. The air was thick and musty, carrying the scent of forgotten memories and decay. A single, flickering candle cast eerie shadows across the worn stone walls. I stared long and hard at the Matron, my mind flashing back to the last hug she had given me, the morning, everything went wrong.

~Flashback~

The Matron was wearing the house uniform. A frilly black and gold maid's outfit covered every inch of her skin, exposing nothing and causing quite a bit of overheated maids. But it was what the King wanted and what the King got.

"Matron, I need to tell you something. But you can't get mad."

She eyed me warily, uncertain. The sunlight streaming through the tall windows highlighted the fine lines of worry etched on her face. But I stood my ground.

"I think I've fallen in love."

"Oh, oh no. Is this with that pauper boy you have been meeting with?"

My eyes widened.

How does she know about that?

"The palace employs mind mages. You think there are any secrets here?"

"That doesn't matter; I am the Queen. My word is law."

"Tell that to your father then, young lady, and act your age. It is unbecoming of an adult to act the way that you do. Sneaking around with a pauper of all things. It'll be the death of our country. What's next? A commoner owning land? A nobleman working the fields?"

The room around us felt like it was closing in; the heavy drapes and ornate furniture suddenly felt like weights tying me down. Better a penniless pauper than the incestuous creeps Father insists I meet with.

"I am the queen. You will mind your tongue."

She silenced herself, but I could see an unreleased rage simmering behind her eyes.

~Flashback End~

I snapped back to the present, the cold reality of the room pressing down on me. The flickering candle seemed dimmer, casting longer shadows. The Matron's figure was still, lifeless, like a statue trapped in time. The weight of my decision bore down on my shoulders, a tangible pressure that made it hard to breathe.

Alright, maybe I remembered her wrong. Had she really been that hateful, and had I really said that?

As I got closer to the Matron, I questioned my life choices—the decisions that had led me to this moment, about to kick the corpse of my Matron. For loot. Because a talking, floating crystal wouldn't shut up. The once warm and comforting scent of lavender now mixed with the stench of decay, a cruel reminder of how far I had fallen.

If I was in Torment, I couldn't imagine the punishment being any worse.

I kicked her corpse. She vanished in a poof of ash and decay, the air around me thickening with the residue of her disintegration.

[Congratulations. You have received the Matron's key. You now have access to all locked doors in the palace.]

I blinked away the tears that had formed and laughed bitterly. Oh yeah, sure. She had a key to every room. Now, no excuse could get me out of helping Malice achieve his goal of looting everything. The amount of power he held over me was terrifying.

There were five doors down that hallway; I ended up looting 200 gold and a copper sword and shield. The shield was adorned with intricate engravings of ancient battles and added a single point of defense. I equipped it and got on with the show. Now that we had the key, I took us back to the original hallway, netting us a couple more weapons. Malice was quiet, which was odd, barely talking other than to tell me about damage and loot.

But I ignored his antics, much more concerned with how the rest of the floor would go. The armor made me practically invincible, and at first, I had been concerned about durability, like the upholstery, but Malice said higher-quality items didn't degrade when you were part of Malikap's unbreakable legion. Justice is iron-clad and unbreakable, after all.

Zombies really hadn't been an issue. I cleared another five, wandering aimlessly around the halls, clearing room after room and making Malice happy, when I finally stumbled upon a unique room that I knew for a fact hadn't been there previously. The door stood starkly against the palace's magical mural, its black hues contrasting sharply with the vibrant artwork.

I hadn't wanted to approach the mural. Father had told me never to approach them, but I found myself mesmerized by the calming blues of the ocean depicted in the painting. The guardian light of Rellum shone through the mural, and I tried to absorb the knowledge—the magic within—but all I got was Malice saying:

[Error! Cannot use Magical Mural. Alignment Error.]

This confused me, given that I was aligned with Malikap and no other god, and this was Malikap's path, home of his domain and alignment.

I shook my head and walked through the new doorway, only to find a large, empty room with a blank canvas for the wall and very little sound. The silence was almost oppressive, the air thick with an unsettling stillness.

"Hey Malice, you okay up there?"

[I am quite satisfied with my haul of loot. I'm rich. Haha, it's the best deal I've ever made. Thank you, my dear.]

I stared up at the lunatic crystal. He was happy?

Whatever.

As soon as the door closed behind me, chaos erupted. Lights blared from every corner of the room, and Malice made excited chittering noises like a squirrel that had found a nut. It was the chapel. The door certainly hadn't led there back in Equiem, but there it was. The rows of pews. The stained glass window depicting the gods. The place where I doomed my soul.

In the center of the room were two people I knew, but they looked off somehow, their eyes glazed and movements stiff.

"Hello, Trellis and Griesan," I greeted them with a strained smile. "Funny finding you here."

They opened their mouths to speak, but instead of words, an awful noise reminiscent of two cats being boiled alive came out. They spoke in unison, their voices merging into a distorted symphony of horror.

"Who dares approach the sacred sanctum?" The sound was inhuman, chilling me to the bone.

I shuddered before I said, "I get the whole creepy zombie motif, but I can't give you the raise you wanted if you're going around treating my father like he's the king when I'm the one in charge."

I sounded bold and confident, which was a complete lie. My knobby knees were bumping into each other like clattering bones.

"Punishment. Imposter to the throne."

I sighed. That gambit had been a long shot, and now it was time for battle.

I charged forward, halberd raised high over my head, and screamed. These men had been a pain for decades, and now, here, I was scheduled to end it.

I entered the cathedral cautiously, my halberd at the ready. The air was thick with the stench of decay, and every step echoed ominously off the stone walls. Suddenly, two zombies emerged from the shadows, their eyes glowing with a sickly, unnatural light. They hissed and snarled, their rotting flesh hanging in tatters from their skeletal frames.

Heart pounding, I charged at the first zombie, swinging my halberd in a wide arc. It moved with unnerving speed, ducking under my swing and clawing at my legs. I felt its nails scrape against my armor, a chilling reminder of how close it came to breaking through.

Before I could recover, the second zombie lunged at me from the side. I pivoted just in time, thrusting the spear tip into its chest. The force of the blow sent it staggering back, and I grunted with the effort, feeling the strain in my muscles.

The first zombie wasn't finished. It leaped onto my back, trying to bite through my armor. I stumbled, my breath hitching in panic, but then I slammed backward into a broken pillar. The impact crushed the zombie against the stone, and it slid to the ground with a grotesque gurgle.

I barely had time to catch my breath before the second zombie, now recovered, rushed at me with a rusty sword. I parried with the halberd's shaft, then spun the weapon to deliver a powerful slash to its midsection. The zombie's guts spilled out, yet it still tried to reach me, driven by some unholy force.

As I fought, the first zombie clambered back to its feet and grabbed my shoulder plate, yanking it off with a growl. I gasped, feeling the cold air on my exposed skin. Fear surged through me, and I desperately tried to avoid its snapping jaws. I brought the halberd up just in time to block its next attack, then jabbed the butt of the weapon into its face, breaking its jaw with a sickening crunch.

Backing up, I kept a wary eye on both opponents, moving towards a pile of debris that might give me an advantage. I kicked a broken pew toward the first zombie, tripping it momentarily. Seizing the opportunity, I swung the halberd in a downward arc, splitting the zombie's skull. Black ichor splattered across the floor.

[Nooo! The loot!] Malice howled.

The second zombie, despite its injuries, let out a guttural roar and charged at me. Planting the halberd in the ground, I braced for impact. As it reached me, I stepped aside and used the halberd's hooked end to catch its leg, pulling it off balance. It crashed to the ground, but not before grabbing my leg and pulling me down with it.

We struggled on the ground, its foul breath hot on my face. I kicked furiously, freeing myself just in time to roll away from its snapping jaws. Scrambling to my feet, I gripped the halberd tightly, both of us rising for a final confrontation. We circled each other warily, the tension almost unbearable.

I feinted with the halberd, then swiftly reversed my grip and thrust the spear tip into the zombie's throat, piercing through its spine. It shuddered violently before collapsing in a heap.

Breathing heavily, I scanned the room for more threats. My halberd dripped with black ichor, and the silence of the cathedral was deafening.

Chapter Seventy-Nine
Run 7

~Run 7, Entrance, Floor 1, Sewers of Aerlyn~

I jolted awake, my hand flying to my nose to block out a stench so vile it made bile rise in my throat. The world had changed. The image blurred, and I shook my head, trying to hold onto it. Ignoring the fading thoughts, I moved, trying to figure out where I was.

My feet squelched in the foul water, its icy, viscous touch crawling over my skin like slugs. The chill of the stone floor beneath seeped into my feet, making it feel like I was walking on ice. Memories flooded my brain as I fell to my knees in the muck. My companions were dead. My minion was gone for good. I shook my head, trying to clear the revival fog.

"Hey Crystal, what do you think we should do?" I asked, frustration edging my voice.

The crystal above my head pulsed with a soft red glow, flickering in time with her response. [About?] Her voice echoed in my mind, its resonance sending a faint vibration through the air.

"Everything?" I paused, annoyed at her unhelpfulness. Despite her earlier obstinance, I had hoped for more by now. My fingers tapped impatiently against the rough stone floor, sending small ripples through the stagnant water. It was nice lying down again. That run had beyond exhausted me.

[It's best that you buy an advanced class. I know you wanted to play mage again, but an advanced class will give us the power boost we need to clear the second floor.] Elizabeth's light grew steadier, almost as if it were emphasizing her point.

"Okay, and that would cost me?" I stood up, the cold water sloshing around my ankles with a sickening squelch.

[100 Death Boons. You have well over a hundred and thirty, so you can still level up a few stats. How would you like to use them?] The crystal brightened momentarily, casting eerie reflections on the damp walls.

"Show me the stat boon list again, please." I raised my hand, and the crystal projected a shimmering holographic list in front of me.

I scanned the list. "Alright, I have about 30 points before I need to buy the class. Let's get another point of vitality, insight, and alacrity. That should balance me out." I made selections with a few quick taps, each choice causing a faint chiming sound.

[Of course, Rod. Now let me show you the advanced classes.] Elizabeth's glow intensified, and another scroll appeared, this one detailing the advanced classes.

[Advanced classes: Each advanced class costs 100 Death Boons to unlock. After death, the class is unavailable for 3 runs. This affects basic and advanced forms of all classes.]

The chart for the advanced classes started to form, but I waved it away.

"Don't even show me what's available. Just buy one of the advanced classes for me." I closed my eyes, not wanting to see the results.

Please be something good. Please be something good. The die rattled against the wall; the sound amplified in the small room.

Even with my eyes closed, I sensed the best possible outcome. She flared brightly once again, and I felt a surge of energy coursing through me.

[You have unlocked the Wizard class. The advanced version of the class: Mage.] The crystal's light settled into a steady glow, signaling a successful upgrade.

Wizard

Starting Equipment: Sage Ring, Enchanted Mage Staff, Mana Robe

Stats

- **Vitality:** 6

- **Finesse:** 4

- **Arcanum:** 12

- **Insight:** 8

- **Magic Defense:** 5

Penalty

- Cannot equip physical weapons

- Cannot equip iron or steel armor

Bonus

- Starts with innate ability *Malikaps*

There was something odd about the bonus ability, but I paid it no mind. A surge of adrenaline and joy rushed through me as a dream I never thought would come to fruition came true. I was going to be a Wizard. This run, I knew, would be legendary now, regardless of whether I beat the Djinn or not.

I took a deep breath and commanded, "Crystal, make me a Wizard."

As the energy enveloped me, memories of my Conjuror's devastating spells flashed through my mind. If the Conjuror was powerful, the Wizard would surely unleash even greater arcane might. The transformation rippled through me, yet my body remained unchanged in height and weight.

The new energy coursed through my veins, urging me forward. I stepped into the next room, anticipation prickling my skin. I felt invincible like nothing could stand in my way now.

The room revealed a lone rat perched on a chest, coins spinning through its tiny claws. I sighed, shaking my head.

This little rodent is the first test of my newfound power? Couldn't even be two rats?

It seemed almost laughable. As time froze and the turn-based battle initiated, I smacked my forehead. "Really? Forgot to disable it,"

Whoops.

But then I smiled. I got two chances to kill every enemy I encountered before the battle even started. My mind raced with possibilities. I lifted my hand into the air, made a little gesture, and my first spell came out. The gesture wasn't needed, but it felt cool.

The spell welled in my stomach just like the summoning spell did. I felt the fire building, burning away at something inside me before it surged up my veins and out of my hand. The fireball that formed was bigger than the rat and the chest, and I felt the heat radiate out, burning the hairs on my hands and fingers. A thrill of power coursed through me. This was it. This was what I had been longing for.

The fire was magical and crisp. It spun through the air on as direct a course as the **Aim** spell always managed. Before I could do anything else, it utterly consumed the rat and the chest. The fire was a devouring maw, opened wide.

As soon as it hit the creature and treasure, like wood in a pile, burst forth in fire and flame. Both evaporated into a pile of smoking ash as the spell dissipated. The smell of burnt wood and singed fur filled the room.

My heart pounded with exhilaration. This was just the beginning. If a simple fireball could do this, what could I achieve with even more powerful spells? My mind buzzed with the possibilities. I couldn't wait to see what lay ahead. The doubts and fears that had plagued me were gone, replaced by a fierce determination. This run would be legendary, and I would carve my name into the annals of this world.

[You have killed Giant Rat. You have dealt 137 damage. You have gained 5 Overkill Boons.]

I blinked in disbelief. "Say that again?"

[You have gained 5 Overkill Boons.]

"No, not that—the first part."

[You have killed a Giant Rat.]

"Gahh! No, how much damage did I do?"

[You have dealt 137 damage. Now hurry; you can most definitely claim your first speed run boons if you don't dawdle.]

137 damage. That was more than I had ever dealt before, evens Bones had barely approached that amount. The numbers danced in my mind. I felt like electricity ready to explode. Without hesitation, I dusted off my feet and rushed through the door into the next room, my mind racing with possibilities.

I had four spells to choose from, but the fire spell was the one that most readily came to mind. The thrill of casting it was still fresh. I wanted to experiment or keep spamming the OP fire spell, but the temptation was too great, so I asked Crystal to tell me how the other spells worked.

[The spells are as follows, each one magically entering my mind unbidden:

Fireball: A swirling ball of fire consumes all it touches. 10 mana, 5-15 damage per point of insight.

Winter's Breath: This is a close-range attack. Inhale air and exhale wintry ice to freeze any foes in range. 4-8 damage per point of insight. 25% Chance to freeze the target.15 mana.

Mana Drain: Siphons life force from foes and converts it to the mana. 10 mana, 2d10 + Int, converts half of the damage dealt into mana recovery.

But as Crystal got to the fourth spell, something weird happened. Her voice distorted, and the words on the scroll twisted into nonsensical scribbles.

Malikap's Shadow: ~~~"~'"~~~~~~~'>]

Her voice was garbled, and the spell description was a jumble of gibberish. I stared at the scroll, my brow furrowing in confusion. If I was genuinely interested in using it, I would have to try the spell without knowing what it did. But for now, it was a mystery I didn't have time to solve, especially if I wanted the speed run Death Boon.

As I stepped into the next room, I saw three rats scurrying in the dim light. The room was clear of crates but dripping with a monotony of sewage. The sight was disgusting, but my mind was focused on one thing: testing my spells. Without hesitation, I lifted my hand, feeling the familiar surge of power as I cast my spells.

The fireball spell welled up inside me, a comforting warmth that quickly turned into a searing heat. I could feel the mana coursing through my veins, gathering in my palm before erupting in a blaze. The fireball shot out, bigger and brighter than before, consuming one rat instantly. The heat singed the air, leaving a trail of smoke and the acrid smell of burnt fur.

The other two rats somehow avoided the fireball, either getting a lucky roll and dodging, or being just out of range, and I decided to try Winter's Breath.

Stat Boons

Potency
- **Cost:** 10

- **Current Stat:** 2 + 10

Insight
- **Cost:** 5

- **Current Stat:** 1 + 10

Alacrity
- **Cost:** 5

- **Current Stat:** 1

Vitality
- **Cost:** 20

- **Current Stat:** 7

Finesse
- **Cost:** 5

- **Current Stat:** 1

Arcanum
- **Cost:** 5

- **Current Stat:** 1

Defense

- **Cost:** 10

- **Current Stat:** 2

Magic Defense

- **Cost:** 10

- **Current Stat:** 2

Precision

- **Cost:** 10

- **Current Stat:** 7

Evasion

- **Cost:** 10

- **Current Stat:** 4

Chapter Eighty
Muridane

Since everything was frozen due to the turn-based system, I didn't need to worry about the rats getting a sneak attack. I moved directly into the range of one of the rats and cast **Winter's Breath**. The mana bubbled up inside me. Unlike the warm mana from the Fireball spell, this one felt fantastic yet nauseating.

It slithered like a snake up my body, cold and unnerving. I shivered involuntarily. Instead of turning right, it continued rising and escaped through my mouth. My teeth chilled painfully as wintry fog escaped my mouth like breath on a cold winter's day. The fog kept coming, billowing out until it merged into a cloud that moved forward and engulfed the rat, freezing it solid. Watching the rat turn into an ice sculpture, I couldn't help but marvel at the power I wielded, even as my body ached from the effort.

The other rat's eyes darted around fearfully in its tiny frame. It knew what was coming, making it all the more satisfying. I held out my left hand and cast Mana Drain. Instead of forming a ball or bubbling like a cauldron, the spell formed a knot around my source of mana. The knot loosened, and a rope launched out of my hand like a cannon, coiling around the rat and squeezing until the rat popped like a balloon.

Instead of blood and guts, a crystalline blue orb formed in its place. The rope wrapped around the orb and yanked it back into me. The sudden rush of mana into my body was exhilarating but left me momentarily dizzy.

[You have killed Giant Rat 1. You have killed Giant Rat 2. You received 2 mana, rounded down from 2.5. You have received Overkill Boons.]

"Gahh, why so little mana?" I grumbled, frustration tinging my voice. "I did like 45 damage."

[The mana amount is determined by the health the target loses, not by how much damage you deal. As we delve deeper into the 3rd floor, you will want to start using that every turn, especially as you learn to properly modulate mana usage and your spells.]

Elizabeth's explanation made sense, but it didn't make it any less annoying. The next room was the Necromancer's lair. I didn't hesitate; as soon as time froze, I blasted two **Fireballs**. One at the Necromancer, the ball burbling in my chest and arm, leaving little pinpricks like sunburns all along my arm. I used my left arm to launch the second fireball at the skeleton.

I was sure there was more to the fight, given that the whole floor got stronger the last few times I came through, but I wanted to see if the speed run boon reward was worth it or if I should just skip this entire floor on future runs. It was overstaying its welcome to an extreme degree; even the second floor was getting a little boring, and I still needed to finish that one.

The second fireball was nowhere near as annoying as the first, but I still took a single point of damage as it left my hand. The fingertips on both hands were charred black, and I had to fight back the urge to suck on them. After all, I was in the sewers. Who knew what kind of infections lurked down here?

The map crystal showed four more rooms, not including the secret rooms, which I decided to skip on this run. As powerful as I was, I didn't have a chance against the super boss yet. I sighed, a mix of determination and fatigue settling in. Instead, I just blew through the rooms. The next room was new, and I had to pause to take it all in. What now?

Four rats stood in room 2, significantly larger than the usual Giant Rats, with human-like limbs reminiscent of Ratigan's. They had claws on their hands and torsos covered in fur, making them look more monstrous. Their faces retained intelligent eyes but still had a rat-like structure.

As they turned to attack, I felt a surge of anticipation, and time froze. These were no ordinary pests. I cast a **Scan**, thankful that this skill didn't consume one of my actions.

25 HP. That's it? All that build-up, and they barely compare to the weakest mob on the second floor.

I shook my head, disappointment mingling with amusement.

I cast my spells. The mana surged through me, a familiar warmth spreading from my core to my fingertips. With my stat boosts, I had around 35 HP. As long as I kept killing efficiently, I'd clear the floor before needing to heal.

The fireballs disintegrated the corpses instantly, leaving nothing but ash. "Good riddance," I said aloud, appreciating the efficiency. There was no need to waste time looting. I ran forward, vaulting the altar and ignoring the lone container in the room. It was a rare chest, but it was useless to me without a key.

The next room was empty, though I glanced at the spot where the secret door was hidden. *It was always tempting, but not today.*

Before I knew it, I was in the goblin room. Four goblins stood resolute around the boss altar, the familiar glowing orb floating above it. Time froze as the goblins sized me up. Why were they standing here instead of trying to ambush me? No time to ponder.

I cast two **Fireballs** in quick succession, feeling the sharp pain as the charring spread to the second knuckle of each finger. My HP dropped to 29. I hissed, ignoring the pain. Speed was crucial; I couldn't let a little pain phase me.

I knew how quickly things could spiral downward if I played this wrong. Although I didn't have the timer Death Boon, I knew how little time I had left. My options: get in close and hope **Winter's Breath** would take out multiple goblins, or use two **Fireballs** and pray neither missed, or I could use Malikap's spell...

The spell sensed my thoughts before I could finalize my decision and cast itself. I was yanked forward in a rush of red and black. Smoke flooded my nostrils as mana coursed through my entire body, not just the pool in my stomach. It filled me, thick as ice but warm as fire. Black electricity tingled up and down my body like static, and then I exploded.

Laughter echoed around me, but I could no longer see as the room filled with black, oily smoke. Panic surged, but I forced myself to stay calm. What now?

"I knew it," a voice sneered, dripping with smug satisfaction. "I knew my corrupting power would be too much for you. You couldn't resist my spell."

"Who are you? What's going on?" I demanded, trying to peer through the darkness.

Please leave me alone.

"So, let's discuss your rewards," the voice continued, ignoring my question. "I have consumed the bosses for you, so worry not about them. Your pitiful 'speed run' is paused, too. Now, let's discuss the real rewards. I am now forever a part of you."

The oily smoke dissipated, revealing a twisted shadow of a tree-like man. Multiple tree-branch limbs sprouted from his torso, which ended in a constantly moving tornado of branches. He approached, grabbing my chin with his wooden, branch-like hand. I cringed at the cold, rough texture.

"How did you describe me? Oily smoke?" he mused, his voice a sinister whisper. "Yes, from now on, my oily shadow will follow you. You will be at my mercy and live at my discretion, but I will also bless you.

That **Fireball** spell? Let's make it double-cast. And that ice breath? Far too weak."

"What have you done to me?" I asked, my voice trembling with a mix of anger and fear.

He smiled a cruel, twisted grin. "You'll see. In time, you'll see."

I tried to speak, to defy the monster before me. But he released more smoke. This time, it flew into my mouth and nose, choking me. I spluttered, falling to my knees, helpless. My lungs burned, and panic gripped my chest.

[You have lost **Fireball**. You have gained Malikap's Fireball. You have lost **Wintry Breath** and gained **Malikap's Breath**. You have lost **Mana Drain** and gained **Mana Battery**.]

I couldn't help but notice the power immediately. Malikap's spells were far superior to the ones I had before. Why would anyone choose Aurentum's deal?

Malikap sneered, "I am done with you. I will summon you when you are needed next." His voice was cold, final. The smoke vanished, leaving a sour taste in my mouth. I gagged, realizing I had fallen and what had caused the sour taste.

"Every time," I muttered, spitting out the foul liquid. My body trembled as I scrambled and rushed to the ladder. I was so close I could feel it. I climbed one leg after the other, each step a struggle, my muscles aching with every movement.

[Congratulations! You have set a new speed record. You have completed the silver-level speed run and have received 75 Death Boons.]

I nodded, impressed.

So much for skipping the first floor.

The quests and this speed run were the way to go when I needed to farm Death Boons. Still, I was shocked to have access to Death Boons after what just happened.

Was I just supposed to stand there and take the abuse from these so-called gods? The more I got embroiled in their machinations, the less I felt like I learned about who I was. Each god had their dirty, grimy claws in me to the point that I no longer felt like myself. And I didn't understand why each one was heaping power and more power onto me. I felt like a pawn in a game and was too stupid to understand. In fact, I felt like I didn't understand anything about this place even after all of the time I had spent here.

Memory Cores, my one method of finding out who I was before Penance, were something I couldn't trust, yet every time they appeared, I was powerless against them. As if summoned by my thoughts, a Memory Core descended from the sky.

Enemy Entry 0029: Muridane
Upon reaching adulthood, a giant rat gains a slight level of sapience and develops a humanoid body. These Muridane are the initial wave of Ratigan's latest mischief. If adventurers stopped killing them while they were young, more would reach this adult stage.

Weaknesses: Fire, Ice, and Lightning
Strengths: None

Stats
- **Level:** Not specified

- **Health:** 25/25

- **Potency:** 10

- **Defense:** 5

- **Magic Defense:** 5

Item Drops
Gold
- **Amount:** 5

- **Chance to drop:** 33%

Rat Teeth
- **Amount:** 1–2

- **Chance to drop:** 33%

Rat Meat
- **Amount:** 1

- **Chance to drop:** 33%

Death Boon
- **Amount:** 1

- **Chance to drop:** 1%

Chapter Eighty-One
Trust

It was early the morning after my parents died. Princess Jamie's coronation had been the day before, and the city was alight with activity. I couldn't believe someone so wonderful and genuine could do something so evil and wasteful. But who was I to judge, given the horrors I had committed the previous day?

I went to our spot, a mini garden on the edge of a rich residential area bordering the palace. I wasn't expecting to see her, but I wanted to glimpse her one last time before the guards came for me.

Murder was a heinous crime, to say nothing of killing your parents. I would be lucky if the gallows were the only fate in store for me. I kicked at a puff of dirt that had formed in front of the bench I was sitting at. The circle had grown more extensive in the *weeks* of meeting with Princess Jamie.

How could I be so evil, so stupid? A numbness had settled over me, a cold emptiness that refused to thaw. My eyes stared blankly ahead, unseeing, as if all the color and feeling had been drained from the world, leaving only a void where my heart used to be.

Just empty, as if I were covered in an inky-black mist of nothingness. The chaos my parents sowed in my life had brought nothing but pain to me, and here I was, not even bothered by their deaths.

That was wrong, I knew, but they were monsters. Cruel, abusive monsters. Right?

I could justify their deaths all I wanted, but as I looked down at my 'pristine hands,' all I saw was red—red that hadn't come out when I jumped in the river earlier, red that hadn't come out when I smeared my hands in the dirt earlier or poured my waterskin over them.

"Hello," the timid voice sounded small and frail as it shook me out of my reverie. I looked up from my dirt circle to stare at the most beautiful sight I had ever seen. Long brown hair curled into ringlets around her shoulders. Piercing eyes—one brown and one green — seemed severe yet soft. A cute button nose that highlighted her kind smile betrayed the seriousness of her eyes. The face of a princess—no, a queen.

"Hello," I said back sullenly, but I did not look up. My gaze remained fixed on the ground, the weight of her scrutiny a palpable force. I could almost feel her eyes piercing through me, searching for the truths I desperately wanted to keep hidden. Of course, she could immediately tell something was wrong.

"Are you okay, Rod?" She sidled up next to me, and I felt heat radiate down my arm as she brushed against me. I sighed and cradled my head in my hands.

"No. I ruined everything."

Jamie sat in silence. Not expectant, just companionable. She didn't even ask anything but grabbed one of my hands and gripped it gently but firmly. If I was going to make it out of this, I had to tell her the truth, but my voice trembled, and I hesitated.

A sharp intake of air and then I said, "My parents are dead." *I wanted to tell her the truth, but I couldn't have those eyes look at me with hatred. Come on, Rod. Say the truth. Maybe she will know what to do.* "I— I killed my father after he killed my mother."

Her eyes widened, and she dropped my hand from hers. Then, she quickly grabbed my hand back.

"What happened?" I could feel her stress and fear as she stroked her thumb against the pad of my right hand. She was wary and uncertain but pushing herself forward.

"My dad was drunk, and my mother was angry. Dad ruined dinner so that he could buy more drugs, and mother threw a knife at him. But then... It was like magic... the knife redirected itself at her, and then she was dead."

"My father came rushing forward to attack me. I put my arms up to defend myself, and another blast of magic came out of nowhere. And then he was dead. So I didn't kill them."

I paused, tears finally falling. *I hated them, so why did it hurt so much?*

"But the thing is, I don't have magic. They died only because I asked my friend Peckolin for help, and he gave me this. I pulled out the amulet that had brought me so much misfortune and death. I took it off and threw it to the floor.

"If I had never asked him for it, if I had never..." The onslaught of emotion was heavier now, tears falling across my cheeks like streams. The emotions that hadn't come earlier were now entirely on display in front of the only person I didn't want to see them. "I'm a murderer. You should leave me alone, Jamie, before I murder you, too."

Jamie picked up the amulet and held it before her as if trying to identify what it did. She let out a hearty, throaty laugh, and I just kept on sobbing. My emotions were no longer mine to control. The mists at the edges of my vision were heavier now, punctuating the heaviness of my emotions.

"This amulet doesn't murder. It only defends. Your parents both had murderous intentions for you. You've always defended them, said they both weren't abusive, but this amulet only kills as a last result when to do otherwise would end with your death."

She held out the amulet for me to take it back, but I put it in her hands.

"I don't want it anymore. If it does what you say, then you should take it. Keep the queen safe, keep the kingdom safer."

Jamie leaned forward. She was so close to me that I could feel her breath on my face and see the opposite color flecks in both eyes. And then, we kissed.

It was long, soft, and confusing. I had never allowed myself to dwell on my feelings for her, not just because they could never be reciprocated but because I never imagined they would be. I leaned further into the kiss, the soft flavor of honey butter on her lips.

When we broke the kiss, I saw a light red flush on her cheeks.

"You are not a monster, Rod. Your parents were monsters. They mistreated you. Never called you by your name. They attempted to kill you. Most of your life, you've spent rooting around in the trash and begging for food because they would rather spend the pittances they had on themselves instead of their only child."

"You've been my friend for almost a month, and I know the real you. You are kind, gentle, always wanting to do what is right. You are strong and worthy, not just of me but the whole kingdom." She kissed me again, but this time, she was hesitant. She leaned back almost immediately after our lips touched, and now she was the one who was crying.

"I want to be with you. I am queen—supposedly, I rule the kingdom, make the laws, and decide how everything works." Tears rolled down her cheeks, and my hands, almost as if they had a will of their own, moved to wipe away. I made to talk, but she shook her hand and continued.

"But no matter what I say or do, nothing I command happens. I didn't want the coronation to go the way that it did. I don't want my father to still have the power that he does. I want to lift you and take you into the palace with me. I want you to be my suitor, but..."

The tears came faster now. "In a way, you're free now, Rod." I looked at her questioning but immediately schooled my features.

"You're free to move about to go wherever, do whatever, but the only freedom I have is this garden, and were it discovered, I would lose even that. I'm a queen of my kingdom but a prisoner of my palace. What I am saying is I need your help to escape. I'm going to abdicate my throne, flee this country, and then we can go somewhere else together." Hope radiated on her face as her eyes took on a far-away, dreamy quality. I couldn't help but share her enthusiasm. If I could get away, I would never be in trouble.

"To flee, though, I need your help." She pulled out a ring from her pouch and handed it to me. "As long as this ring is on my person, the King and his mage know where I am at all times. I can immediately be pulled back to where I 'belong'. And to make it even worse, I can only leave this ring with someone I trust; otherwise, it will reappear in my person. I can't leave the castle grounds as long as this ring is on me. But if we can leave the castle and the city, the ring will be rendered useless." I should've listened better because it would fail as soon as she said the plan. If the ring could be detected no matter where it was, it wouldn't matter where I was; I would be found with it. Her plan would fail. I grabbed the ring, and the memory faded.

~~~~~{Memory Core 19 End}~~~~~

It didn't make sense. At all. Hadn't I met her after she became queen? And here she was saying we had been friends since a month before. My head hurt as I tried to reconcile all of the conflicting memories. I didn't know what was real. I didn't know what I could trust.

I closed my eyes, trying to piece together the fragmented images in my mind. I remembered the argument after she had snuck out of the palace, the way she had looked at me with those piercing eyes when I first approached her.

Was any of it even real to begin with?

Chapter Eighty-Two
True Colors

I had thought there would be a pause before the next memory, given that I had never experienced any in quick succession. But as the core descended from the ceiling, I braced myself for the next memory. This one, however, took me by surprise.

{Memory Core 20/???}

~~~~~{Memory Core 20 Start}~~~~~

I thought the next memory would be of what happened after I put on the ring, but I was wrong. Instead, I was back in the alleyway where Peckolin and I had stopped the guard with the ridiculous armor, and things had gotten weird. A dark hazy mist suffused the memory and flooded my mind.

As I stared into the distance, the guard stopped and fell asleep, and then he was in front of me. I reached out my arm, and I killed him. I stabbed him over and over. Each thrust was fueled by a misplaced rage, a desperate attempt to silence the laughter of Malikap. The knife in my hand felt foreign yet disturbingly familiar, its blade slick with blood. My breaths came in ragged gasps, each one echoing with the ghostly laughter that filled my head.

And then, it wasn't the guard. It was someone else. Peckolin's face was twisted in agony, his eyes wide with shock and betrayal. The guard's ridiculous armor, which once seemed so laughable, now lay in pieces, revealing the vulnerable flesh beneath. Blood seeped from Peckolin's wounds, pooling around his body and staining the cobblestones. His lips moved, but no sound came out, his final attempt to communicate lost in the chaos of the moment. The light in his eyes dimmed, replaced by a hollow emptiness that mirrored the void growing inside me.

I was so confused because it felt real and seemed like something that could have happened, but instead of betrayal in his eyes, I heard the same laughter I heard from Malikap as he overtook my spells. The laughter echoed in my mind, a twisted reminder of my own helplessness. It wasn't just the guard I was stabbing; it was every failure, every moment of weakness. The world around me felt tilted off-kilter, as if reality itself was slipping away.

The sky turned a yellowish gray, casting an eerie pallor over the scene. A specter rose from my friend's corpse, its form wreathed in shadows and dripping with spectral blood. Its eyes, hollow and accusing, locked onto mine. "Traitor!" it yelled, blood falling from its ghostly lips like an accusation. Each drop of blood was an attack against the last vestiges of my innocence, a physical manifestation of my guilt and shame.

My heart pounded in my chest, a wild drumbeat of fear and confusion. The weight of the knife in my hand became unbearable, and I dropped it, my fingers slick with blood. I wanted to scream, to deny the reality of what I had done, but no words came out. The specter's taunts echoed in my ears, mingling with Malikap's laughter, creating a cacophony of torment that threatened to shatter my mind.

~~~~~{Memory Core 20 End}~~~~~

[For unlocking 20 Memory Cores, you received 5 Library Checkpoint Tickets. This allows you to set a respawn point on the 3rd floor.

One-time use. You will also receive The Ring of Lifting. This will allow you feats of incredible strength at a 4-point penalty to vitality while the ring is equipped.]

I awoke with a shout; the ghostly specter of my now-dead friend haunted me and my thoughts. I had been certain that when I arrived on the second floor, there was something wrong with the memories. And not just the one where I had managed to kill my friend. There was something off about the one with Jamie, too. But dwelling on the memories never brought more clarity, so instead, I thought about my new items. I was certain the tickets would be valuable later, but that ring could come in handy on this floor, especially if I had to collect a bunch of corpses again. As my thoughts wandered, my feet did too, and before I knew it, I was in the market square.

The city had respawned anew, pristine and untouched by the item or the chaos of the battle with the werewolves. The clean slate felt surreal, a stark contrast to the turmoil inside me. I needed to pull my item out of the bank and get a hold of the bonuses that nighttime would bring me, but I hesitated. I knew how powerful this class was, especially with the new buffs that Malikap had brought me, but did I really want to use the provisions of this class? Did I really want to cause so much pain and horror for these people who just wanted to live out their meager existence?

What was the point of Penance if I wasn't actually getting better? I made my choice. As I walked to the vault, a sense of foreboding settled over me. The air seemed to grow thicker, charged with an unspoken tension. When I reached the vault, my hands trembled as I put the amulets away. Everything in me screamed that I was making the wrong choice, but every choice I had been making lately had led me down a sinister path that I knew I did not want. No, while I had to use the power of the class to succeed, I would not use other powers that only brought more harm.

As if my choice wasn't hard enough, time froze, and suddenly, two figures materialized before me. Aurentum and Rellum stood side by side, their presence both awe-inspiring and terrifying. Aurentum's form shimmered with an unnatural light that made my skin crawl, his voice undercut with greed and frivolity. My ears shook from just being near him. Rellum, in contrast, exuded a calm, divine aura, his eyes filled with a wisdom that seemed to see through me.

"We have come to an understanding," Aurentum started, his voice echoing with a hint of malevolence.

"We need you to continue on your current path, though I am proud of the choices you are making. Harming innocents for our own expediency is never the right course of action," Rellum said, his voice imbued with sagely wisdom and divine calm.

"Then what are you here to do except harm me for your expediency?" I demanded, frustration and fear boiling over.

"Though you see yourself as an innocent, nothing you have done here has been the act of an innocent. Demanding an item that would go better with an ally. Letting your allies be killed. Turning the whole city into night and unleashing that devilish plague are all things you could have made better choices with. Now, it is simply the consequences of your actions. You don't get to choose the right thing at the last second and think it absolves you of everything."

"What do you even want me to do?" I asked, feeling cornered and desperate.

"You are going to relinquish your pact with Aurentum and fully enter into your pact with Malikap. If you choose to do so, we will allow you to continue your runs in this dungeon so that we may track Malikap. As dangerous as Aurentum's escaping would be, Malikap's escaping would be the end of all existence. That is his very goal. And he does need an icon/minion/lackey in order to leave. That would be you."

"And if I refuse?"

"Then I crush your skull, and we take away any remaining runs that you have."

"So I would lose my Death Boons? Why would I choose to do such a thing? Why would you," I paused, putting a finger in Rellum's face, "want me to do the wrong thing? I thought your shtick was that you never led people astray?"

"I am not leading you astray; you have already led yourself astray and become irredeemable."

The words were like a sword to my heart; in fact, it felt very similar to when Drip stabbed me, and I bled to death. My mind flashed back to the memory of Jamie. Where she said I wasn't at fault. Where she said I was innocent. Where she said I was not lost.

"I am my own person. I don't have to do what any so-called god tells me I must do, and besides, I know the truth now. So no, I won't relinquish my pact, but I also won't be serving you—either of you. You have no power here. You are all prisoners in the same cell, squabbling over the only pillow."

I walked past them not certain my gamble would work. Two gods now had killed or claimed people under my control or near me, but they had yet to touch me, and I think I finally knew why.

Aurentum had taken Elric's place. I'd known that, of course. But what I hadn't realized was the significance. I hadn't become his when I picked up the coins—I had already been his, for the entire time I was in Penance. That's why I had immediate access to Death Boons.

The gods' powers, I now understand, could only directly affect their opposing opponent. Like in the game Ozball: Red beats both, Green beats Red, and Red beats Blue. But if Green and Blue team up, they can overcome Red. The pieces aren't free to attack each other individually.

Malikap could help me grow stronger and hurt Rellum's minions. But Rellum and Malikap could not harm me; because neither teamed up against Aurentum. I was hedging a bet that Rellum was testing me.

He wanted me not to accept but to force myself to see who I was, not just the magically enhanced anger.

I walked and walked. I passed by the spice tables and then down an alleyway. As I exited, they appeared again in front of me. The pile of coins was smaller than before, and I filed that away for later. But I just walked past them again, their complaints falling on deaf ears.

I followed the map, and they appeared again. This time, Aurentum struck with a lantern, but it phased through me, and I almost cackled. However, after Malikap's laughter kept echoing in my ears, I shuddered and ignored the temptation.

As I passed the merchants, I was tempted by the displayed potions and armor. In my rush to clear the first floor and now to avoid literal gods, I hadn't grabbed a single piece of armor. Sure, my defense was now at 7, and I was probably good for this floor, but all of my spells, not just **Fireball**, took HP to cast now, and I knew there were bigger threats lurking on this floor that I still hadn't tested.

I ignored the stalls and marched forward into the second room.

~Run 7, The Wall of Riddles, Floor 2, The Fallen Merchant City of Aerlyn~

Somehow, the first room had been textiles in the past two runs. So far, my luck had exceeded all possibilities. The last time I had run through and got the gluttony question wrong, I was rewarded with a difficult fight for three people. But now, I had spells on my side, one of which I was excited to test out. It was no longer called **Mana Drain**; it was called **Mana Battery**. It had a 1d4 chance to turn an enemy into a "mana battery," a mindless mob that I could consume for mana or, you know, hide behind if I needed to avoid attacks because I ran out of moves.

I went through all seven puzzles looking for my target. It was the same as before; depicting the engorged glutinous goblin that I would fight. I repeated Thumb's cry of "Glutyeknee" and ran away as fast as I could before time froze.

I grinned.

"**Mana Battery**," I shouted. The spell, this time, was closer to the shadow spell, except it started in my head. A ball of static invaded my mind, and I saw stars as I fell backward to the ground with a splitting headache. I feared I had gone blind as the mana escaped through my eyes. I heard rather than saw the dice roll. And then the monster screamed. Was I really that lucky? Afraid the timer would run out, I asked, "Did it work? I can't see." My vision finally started to clear as Crystal said-

[No, Rod, hurry!]

I had almost no way to aim the spell, as the blurry shapes of the room and the monster all blended together. So, instead of wasting a cast, I ran forward, and while my vision didn't clear, I could tell the monster was in front of me. I didn't have the luxury of waiting or trying to figure out how to clear my vision. Making a snap judgment, I picked an object that looked close enough like the goblin and cast.

The pain was worse than before, and this time, I felt blood drip down my face as my eyes bled from the mana toll. The dice clattered on top of my fallen form, but the blast connected. As I passed out, I heard Crystal say-

[Congratulations, you have turned gluttony into a mana glutton. This unique minion will devour creatures for you and turn their life force into mana.]

"HUNGRY!!!!" the voice screamed, and I jolted awake. My eyes wouldn't open, and I remembered how badly the spell had damaged me.

"Crystal, I think I messed up. I still can't see."

[You're fine; stop being so dramatic.] Crystal punctuated the statement by dropping a canteen of water on my head. It hit so hard that I felt like I blacked out again, but I instead grabbed the container of water and opened it. After a refreshing sip, Crystal prompted me again.

[Are you going to try and summon another floor guardian? It won't get you any more boons.]

"What? No, I just can't see."

[I gave you the stupid canteen so you could flush the dried blood out of your eyes. How obtuse can you be?]

"Oh."

"HUNGRY!!!" The giant goblin smashed the floor with his hammer, and I jumped.

I started flushing my eyes with the water and then grabbed a handful of cloth. I rubbed my eyes clean and blinked them clear a few times. It's nice to see that I can actually see again.

I got up off the ground and patted Glutyeknee, which I named "GluttyKnee" on the back. I left the room, not bothering with the other tents. Something I'm sure won't come back to bite me in the butt later.

Chapter Eighty-Three
Pain Of Death

~Run 7, The Perfumed Prison, Floor 2, The Fallen Merchant City of Aerlyn~

I blinked a couple of times as I stepped into the perfumed prison, my face full of confusion. The room was filled with an intoxicating mix of scents that clung to the air, making it hard to focus. At least I knew how to solve the room without triggering hordes of Grendelblin or, worse, the Grendelkin.

A thought stuck in my head as I walked past the red, blue, green, and purple smoke-filled jail cells. I knew this Djinn was nigh unbeatable, and while I could certainly pack a punch, I couldn't fight a horde of angry beasts or a giant with over 500 HP. But maybe Glutyeknee could.

"Glutyeknee, come here, and you'll get to eat your fill, I promise."

I had yet to try one thing with this class, and that was overcharging a spell. I was thankful that Klericho gave me back the ring after we found out it didn't work for his healing spells. Doing so with the different spells would lead to some exciting results, so that was what I did.

Leaving Glutyeknee to soak up the first horde, I opened the red cell. The cell door creaked open, releasing a dense, acrid smoke that made my eyes water and my throat burn. I knew for a fact that it would take a couple of turns for the Grendelkin to form, so I wasted time, one turn at a time, by casting **Scan**.

By moving around behind my pet and not letting any of the mobs get close, my giant monster didn't need my help, even though I could have easily cast a few spells at the Grendelblins. The ground shook as my giant monster swiped with his oversized arm, grabbing all five of the Grendelblins surrounding him and swallowing them whole. The monster let out a burp and fell to the ground, satisfied.

I was grateful I wouldn't have to command him to stop. Instead, I focused on the sight in the background. The loud growls of the Grendelblins were almost cute, sounding more like distressed puppies than terrifying man-eaters. I kept pacing to end my turn, and it took around five turns for the Grendelkin to emerge victorious over his now-eaten siblings.

As soon as only two monsters were left, I implemented my plan. I moved around, ended my turn, and overcast my **Mana Battery**. My mana drained to 0 immediately, and I started taking damage as an excruciating pain overwhelmed my body.

It's said that when someone dies, their nerve endings cut out and the body releases something called endorphins, making them feel excellent and gets rid of the nasty pain of death. I still didn't know how I died, but as the memory of my death finally came to me, I could only remember thinking how much of a rotten lie it had been that the pain of death wasn't felt. A ball of pain had formed in the core of my being, and it radiated outward, growing bigger and bigger.

A Memory Core descended from the sky, and I jumped for a chance to escape the pain, but it only got worse as the memory didn't appear. The pain was no longer a ball but a spike driven through both of my eyes and out every single part of my skull simultaneously. I grasped my head and screamed my lungs out before fading away into the memory.

{Memory Core 21/???}

~~~~{Memory Core 21 Start}~~~~

The rain's icy needles pierced my cheeks and scalded my bound hands, each drop a tiny blade. Forced to kneel, I awaited my sentence, the cold dampness creeping through my clothes and settling into my bones. A shiver rippled through me, more from the dread twisting inside than the chill.

I kept my face a mask, my eyes locked on the queen. She stood before her father and the judge, pleas for my release written in the tears mixing with the rain on her cheeks. Desperation widened her eyes, a silent scream for mercy.

A sudden crack split the air as her father's slap echoed louder than the downpour. Jamie's cry was a dagger in my heart. I strained against my bonds, a useless gesture to reach her, to comfort her, but I was powerless. Condemned to watch.

"Insolent girl," her father roared, his voice a thunderclap. "This is exactly what I warned you about. This boy could have killed you at any time. He was found with a warder's amulet and two bloodstained knives. It's clear he already killed and planned to kill you. You may bear the crown, but you cannot bear the leadership." He seized her hands, dragging her to her feet.

"Father! That isn't what it looks like. Rod is my—" Her protest ended with another slap, leaving a red welt on her face. "Guard, take her away."

"No, wait. At least let me stay. I'll be quiet," she pleaded, her voice breaking. But the guards and the judge answered to no one but him.

I masked the turmoil, pain, and rage battling for dominance. I knew this was the end. Life had held so much promise, magic, and wonder. Now I'd never see the ocean or escape the city's muck.

Tears mingled with the rain on my face. For a fleeting moment, I'd known love—the only love I'd ever felt. Jamie mouthed something to me, her lips forming the words I knew without hearing: "I–I love you."

I blinked away the rain and tears, my composure finally cracking. Then, the judge's voice cut through the storm.

"Rod Argent. You stand accused of High Treason. Of kidnapping the queen and plotting to assassinate her. How do you plead?"

"That's what I'm accused of?" I spat, my voice raw. The judge's smirk stoked my fury. "I didn't do anything of the sort. I would never harm Jamie."

"Let the official record reflect his claim of innocence. However, the royal advisor—the former king—has declared him guilty. There shall be no trial. You are sentenced to death. Ready the royal executioner." The man spoke with detachment as if the entire proceeding were a waste of his time.

The Royal Executioner stepped forward, a grim silhouette in the rain. Panic surged within me, and something within me broke.

"You're as useless as my parents were! You're the queen! Do something!" I shouted at Jamie, my voice cracking with desperation.

I closed my eyes, not wanting to face my death. I heard the whoosh of the sword, expecting sharp pain and nothingness, except when I opened them again, I was caught by a sight that would haunt me for the rest of my existence and beyond Penance. The scream that my mind's eye conjured every time I closed my natural eyes. The scream etched forever in my thoughts, never to go away.

On the ground, a sword caught deep into her side, perforating her kidneys and liver, was Queen Jamie. She reached out to me. "Rod, I—" The light left her eyes, and she collapsed to the ground, broken and hollow.

I did this. I killed a queen. I destroyed the world.

The king rushed me, and as I looked into the hatred burning in his coal-like eyes, I saw rather than felt his powerful hands grip my neck. It felt like I was floating outside my body, staring as life began to leave my body. His grip tightened, and I felt the raw strength behind his fury. All at once, I snapped back to my body as the sensation worsened.

"Jamie! What have you done?" he bellowed, his voice filled with rage and betrayal. The pain of his choking me was overwhelmed by the euphoria of a lack of air and the absolute despair that permeated my being. My vision blurred, darkening at the edges. Jamie... As my vision faded to black, I stared at Jamie one final time, willing whatever afterlife exists to give me one more chance with her—a chance I never should have gotten and never deserved here on Equiem.

~~~~~{Memory Core 21 End}~~~~~

"HUNGRY!" The loud noise startled me to the present. Had it just been the one Glutyeknee, I'm not sure it would have awakened me, but standing before me, chanting in unison, were my two mana batteries. One was a giant overstuffed Goblin, and the other was a Grendelkin. It felt surreal being able to control monsters from the floor.

I reached up to my face, which was heavy with tears. What had I just witnessed? Was that the end?I wanted to believe it was false, but something about the memory felt right—as if it had to have gone down that way. I curled up into a ball, letting the world fade away as I focused on the image of a queen dying for me.

"HUNGRY!"

"Okay, let's go get y'all fed."

Just like with the summons, overcasting broke the rules regarding pet limits. I could feel the hunger radiating from the two batteries. They craved mana, and I needed to provide it before they got the idea to eat me. I was just about to leave the room when Crystal said something that made me pause.

[You did all that work, and then you're just going to leave an Aerlyntium and the key to defeating the Djinn?] I facepalmed.

I walked back and touched the Aerlyntium, but like last time, it said, [Insufficient resources acquired.]

I then laid my hands on the real treasure.

[Spout of the Immortal. 3 of 3. This relic is a key. It can open a secret door or for some other purpose, you have already figured out. Please don't drop it, or it will break.]

Ironically, unlike the rest of the relic, the body of the lamp was a plain gold, as if its intricate patterns had all been rubbed away.

I put the Lamp away, understanding its fragility. It would be my luck to go through all this and fail because I dropped an item. I moved forward and left the room, my lumbering oafs following behind me... and then groaned as I entered the worst possible room.

Enemy Entry 0023: Grendelblin

These beasts are the discarded, often jailed progeny of the great mythological beast Grendel. It is claimed that once upon a time, he was happy and in love with the Goblin Queen. They married and had all sorts of horrifying offspring. They lived a happy life until Grendel's mother came looking one day. She slaughtered the Goblin Queen coldly and lured Grendel back through magical control. These Grendelblins were left creating chaos in their parents' wake. The oldest, a boy named Hob, on the cusp of adulthood, corralled his disorderly siblings and threw them all in here.

Weaknesses: Shadow, Fire, Water
Strengths: Nothing

Stats

- **Health:** 100/100

- **Potency:** 5

Item Drops
Gold

- **Amount:** 5

- **Chance to drop:** 75%

Prison Rags

- **Amount:** 1

- **Chance to drop:** 25%

Chapter Eighty-Four
Hyper Focus

~Run 7, Magic Carpet Ride, Floor 2, The Fallen Merchant City of Aerlyn~

It was in the carpet room that my plan hit a snag. GluttyKnee and Grendelkin were powerful and could do many things but couldn't jump. Thankfully, it was about then that I finally decided to look at the map. There was a door I had missed back in the entrance room. Apparently, because there had only been one exit the previous three times didn't mean that was always the case. But I still needed to grab the relic that was in this room. I was certain that if I didn't feed the two lumbering oafs soon, they would collapse to the ground and waste all the effort I put into spawning them.

So, I did what any sane person would do in this instance. Using my 17 in strength, I tried to pick up GluttyKnee, and wouldn't you know it... I was strong enough to lift the giant collection of whale blubber. I grinned. I wouldn't be able to see if he was in front of me, but I had the solution to that, too.

From my infinite container of useless junk, I summoned rope and a bunch of wooden planks I had found in the previous run. These rooms full of random junk were starting to pay off.

Using the rope and planks, I fashioned a device that would allow me to hoist the oversized goblin onto my back or to drag him from carpet to carpet, and then I would do the same for the Grendelkin. It was absurd and ridiculous, but this entire place was both. Having my friends for whatever battle lay on the other side of that door or even down below in the depths was worth any amount of embarrassment.

I chuckled, imagining the sight I presented, and then jumped. For example, last time, I had to take the time to figure out when I would need to jump between.

This was the dumbest thing I had ever done in the dungeon, but I had to do something to get them over. But as soon as he was on my back, I tried to jump, and my feet wouldn't budge. I tried different angles and different moves, but as strong as I was now, I couldn't jump. I let myself fall to the floor while the mana battery yelled, "HUNGRY! HURT!" I sighed. I had to think of something. I started pulling out all the wood and metal I had gathered over the past few runs. The pile was much larger than I thought, and an idea formed.

I pulled out the ropes I had gathered, worried I wouldn't have enough for my plan, but I had plenty on hand. So much, in fact, the pile started to dwarf the small hills of wood and metal that had formed beside me.

I started shaping the wood into platforms and then placed the metal into sheets on top of the wood. It was wonky like a child had cobbled it together from sticks and rocks. I used the ropes to tie the makeshift bridge together. And then came the moment of truth. I leaned the bridge against the first carpet, grateful it was stable.

I was now testing whether the carpets could hold my new friends or if I had to abandon my plan altogether. I grabbed GluttyKnee by the wooden straps and pulled him onto my back. I was unable to jump, but I could carry him around. It was much like running around on the carpets without any stamina.

I successfully walked him up to the first carpet, grateful it had enough room for us both. I dropped him off and went to receive our other friend. He was much heavier but broader overall, and balancing his lighter weight was awkward after getting used to GluttyKnee.

I placed them on the carpet and then tried to devise a plan to move them to the next carpet.

It was moving horizontally, so I couldn't lay the bridge down onto it, but I could do something different.

When balancing items at the store for my mage friend, I knew I could easily use heavier things to keep an unbalanced item from falling over a ledge. So, if I kept GluttyKnee on this carpet as a balance, I could make two bridges that overlap.

[What are you even doing? This seems like it needs to be clarified.]

"I know what I'm doing. I will make alternating platforms extending the carpet length to transport my pets.

[Alright, but why are you doing it now? What if the room on the other end is a dead end? Wouldn't it make sense to go check that other room first?]

My hyperfocus faltered, and I stumbled.

"Oh." My brain shut down briefly as I looked around at the pile of wood, metal, and ropes and my half-starved mana batteries. What was I doing?

I shook my head and slowly extricated my pets and myself from the first carpet.

I shook my head, slowly awakening from the mind fog I had been stuck in. This wasn't the first time I had done something stupid and convoluted...

I then recalled a memory without a memory core:

~Flashback~

The day I first met Jamie, I pulled off a heist, stole from the palace, and almost got myself executed that first day. Father had spent our breakfast money on Blaze—as always—and I had missed dinner the previous night because I had been hanging out with friends.

It had been a fruitless endeavor. The palace was crowded with political guests and guards, and security was heightened because the next week would be the queen's naming ceremony. I shrugged my shoulders as I hid underneath a table in the hallway. Thankfully, it had a skirt hanging down to protect the edges, so the only thing visible would be my shoes, and only if they looked down.

As soon as the guards' voices died down, I snuck back around the corner and followed them carefully. If I could find a kitchen or a dining room, I could steal the gold and silverware that was sure to be there. If I had been careful with my pilfering, I would have been able to hide my theft altogether.

I tried the first door I came to down the hallway and found exactly what I was looking for.

I could get 1000 Aurums from just a handful of plates, spoons, and forks. They were thankfully easy to carry. I did a quick glance around the room. There was a dusty-looking cupboard that was likely decorative next to two tall-looking plants. My fingers itched as I spied gold and silver cutlery set up for midafternoon tea. And then I heard the voices.

The plan was already settled, so I jumped into the cupboard. Dust piled up and floored me in a cloud, and I had to bite my lip to prevent myself from coughing.

I could feel the tickle in my throat as I hid. I bit down hard and felt the blood trickle out of the tiny wound.

As the voices died, I pushed the doors slightly ajar, light filtering through the crack. Whoever had come in was gone, so I immediately grabbed a few items. I never grabbed from the same plate; instead, I randomly grabbed to ensure that someone would think it was just speedy employees making mistakes.

I had just finished grabbing my fifth item when voices returned. I nearly tripped over myself, rushing back to the cupboard. I had been worried that I would be caught, and in my haste, I knocked over the vase that had been precariously placed on top of the cupboard.

"What was that?"

I thought I was caught, but I quickly shuffled the shards into the cupboard and pulled them closed.

"It came from the dining hall."

"Spread out. Today's luncheon is crucial to the king. He is meeting with the ambassador from Aerlyn."

If 'past me' had known what I do now, my eyes would have widened. How could Aerlyn be a real place? It was the kingdom of Penance. Wasn't it?"

~Flashback End~

I flashed back to the present.

"Crystal, is Aerlyn a real place?"

[Yes, we are standing in it now.]

I shook my head. "You know what I meant. Not in Penance but in real, living life."

[Aerlyn is the kingdom that Elric, the founder, first established. It is a real place. And this vision of it in Penance is based on the real one. Some say the effects of Penance are felt even in reality.]

I was reeling from the implications. If Aerlyn was real, what did it mean?

Ultimately, it meant nothing to me *now*. I would never see the real world ever again.

I backtracked through the rooms to the prison, and my hunger giants continued screaming. And there, in the middle of the jail cells, was the door I had somehow skipped.

I pushed the door open and stepped into,

~Goblin Gauntlet~

And lucked into the best possible room to feed two hungry beasts that kept screaming for food.

I wanted to test out my new spells since I barely used them even in the previous rooms, but I was hesitant with the drawbacks that mana drain had brought.

Instead, I just sat back and kept ending my turn. It was a slaughterhouse.

As the first wave of goblins approached, Grendelkin reached back on their hind legs and grabbed a goblin with each hand before rearing back and biting them in half. GluttyKnee rolled into the room and crushed the two goblins under his bulk. He peeled them off the ground before rolling them up. He then shoved one after the other into his cavernous, unhinged mouth.

He crunched down and swallowed the goblins whole without chewing. "MORE FOOD!"

I wasn't sure which started the chant, but the two mana batteries echoed each other repeatedly as the next wave of goblins spawned.

"There you go, boys, more food."

MM, YUMMY." GluttyKnee rolled forward until he stopped, his turn ending and halting him mid-roll. Five goblins rolled forward and started swinging at the giant blob.

"Hurt. Stop." GluttyKnee roared, and then our turn came back, and the rolling continued at the same speed as if it had never stopped. He only crushed three goblins, but it didn't matter as Grendelkin grabbed the remaining two between his paws, pushing them against each other before biting their heads off like he had.

This all occurred over the course of a minute. There was more carnage than I had seen than in any previous thing I had done, and it wasn't even a true minion spell—it was a **Mana Battery**. What the?

As soon as the turn ended. Both of my pets froze bits of gore on their mouths and hands. And a shadowy figure slithered up from the ground.

Chapter Eighty-Five
A Meeting of the Gods

"I see you are enjoying my gifts," Malikap's voice oozed malice, sending a shiver down my spine. My fingers twitched as he traced his bony, blackened wood finger against the blob-like goblin. I sighed, tensing in anticipation of him killing another assistant. I knew he would sacrifice them for me, though I had never asked for it. He didn't care.

"Relax. I am not here to collect my due... yet. That will come, boy, that will come." His smile twisted his face, a predatory gleam in his eyes. "Instead, I am here to ask you something. I know you have fallen victim to my glory like so many others. But are you sure this is the path you want? Are you on my side or theirs?" He gestured behind me. Over my shoulder, Aurentum and Rellum stood close, watching and whispering.

I stole a glance at the two gods behind me. Aurentum, the God of Wealth, and Rellum, the God of Purity, their eyes boring into me with an intensity that made my skin crawl. Their presence felt like a judgment, a constant reminder of the precarious tightrope I was walking.

"Have they been there the whole time? Don't you have anything better to do than watch me struggle? This is beyond absurd... it's ludicrous. Why me?" My eyes widened as I took in the insanity of it all. My heart pounded in my chest, and I could feel the walls closing in. Three gods, several dead pets. Two giant monsters turned into quasi-magical battery/murder demons. I just wanted it to stop!

A memory rushed in, unbidden, dragging me back to a time I wished I could forget. I was at home. My parents were screaming at each other. Dad threw a pot of food, and Mom shattered the kitchen table trying to get at him. They were despicable. Wrong. I couldn't take it anymore. I just wanted it to stop! The idea formed then. Money was the problem. If I could steal enough, I could fix everything. I knew it.

I took a moment to listen to my parents. "I've had it with this, Gerrick. Every day, you ruin the food we should be eating with your drunken stupor. I don't care that you drink or take Blaze; just don't do it before we need to eat! It's not that difficult." Another crash, this time, a shelf or a chair. My heart broke as what was left of my innocence shattered like the water mug thrown harshly to the floor. Not caring about the noise, I slammed the door to our house, its hinges rattling, and took off. My parents deserved each other; that much was certain.

[Rod... Say something,] Crystal urged, her voice barely a whisper, like she was trying to speak without a mouth.

"I'm sorry, what?"

[Are you joining Malikap, or staying with Rellum? It's your final test for the second floor. The test of morals. Are you ascending or descending the tower?]

"I get a choice?" I shook my head, stunned. I had assumed that once my anger took hold, my fate was sealed. I glanced at Malikap, then at Aurentum and Rellum. Truth be told, I hated all of them. They were using me, manipulating me for their own ends. I just wanted to scream, but that was precisely how I got into the Malikap test in the first place.

I could feel the anger simmering, ready to burst out in self-righteous fury. But I bit my lip, like in the memory, willing myself to calm down and think critically. These gods, with all their power and influence, had turned my life into a game. I was a pawn, a tool in their hands. They didn't care about me—they cared about what I could do for them.

Sure, the absolute power Malikap offered was tempting. His spells, the sacrificial power boosts—everything was easily within reach compared to the immense effort required with Aurentum. But Malikap was a villain. No matter what I did, it felt like I was being forced to rely on evil to advance. All the teachings from school and church said this place was meant to cleanse us of sin, to guide us away from it. Instead, it was pushing me deeper into wrath, greed, and sloth. The other sins were almost laughably easy to ignore, but why was this place designed this way? It was as if they didn't want people to get better; they didn't want anyone to win.

My mind flashed back to all the times I had been thwarted from making easy progress in the dungeon. The countless traps, the deceptive allies, the relentless challenges—it was as if every step forward was designed to pull me two steps back. I know I'm slow on the uptake, but once I learn a lesson, it sticks. Penance was not about repentance; it was about growth. It was about recognizing our sins and gaining the tools to face them head-on. Rellum, duplicitous as he was, led me to this realization. Just because the source of power was evil didn't mean its use had to be. It was the way it was used that mattered. Here was my chance to grow beyond the influence of the most evil god and prove that I deserved my place here, to become the man I needed to be.

"It's a rather generous offer, but a deal is a deal," I said through gritted teeth. There was no need to show my hand too soon. "I promised something to Aurentum, and while I can't seem to remember it, I know I made it. I need to keep my word before I become something I don't want to be."

As I walked toward the blue robes and kneeled before the Gilded God, a wave of uncertainty washed over me. Could I trust Aurentum? Would he betray me as Malikap surely would? The gods were fickle, their favor fleeting. But I had to make a choice. "I am here to serve, Aurentum," I lied.

A smile curled Aurentum's lips. "Finally, you see the light of reason. After this run, I can restore you to the glory of the gilded ones." He waved his lantern, sending magical sparks flying in my direction.

Crystal's whisper broke through my thoughts again. [Rod, are you sure about this?]

I nodded slightly, not wanting to give away any hesitation. "For now," I whispered back, barely moving my lips. "One step at a time."

As the sparks enveloped me, I felt a strange mixture of dread and determination. This wasn't just about surviving the dungeon anymore. It was about shaping my destiny, one difficult decision at a time. I had to stay vigilant, had to keep my wits about me. And as much as I hated the gods, their trials, and their manipulations, I knew I had to play their game to find my way out.

Malikap's eyes narrowed, a sinister smile playing on his lips. "Interesting choice, boy. But remember, every path has its consequences."

I didn't stare at Aurentum; instead, I watched Rellum, gauging his reaction. The duplicitous god's expression was inscrutable, a mask of mild interest. Why were all three gods so focused on my journey? What did they stand to gain from my struggles? I needed to stop playing into their hands.

Summoning a flicker of defiance, I winked at Rellum while Aurentum was turned away to address Malikap.

"You know the rules, Malikap. Rod is mine to do with as I please. You may not interfere with his journey any further."

"Fine, then I shall take my leave and remove my gifts. No harm, no foul."

I sighed, knowing what was coming. Here comes the god to ruin my run and make things awful.

"Stop." Rellum voice echoed through the room, freezing everything—not just in a turn-based pause or time freeze, but more. My eyes couldn't move, the blood in my veins halted, and a trickle of sweat down my neck stopped mid-fall.

The sensation was suffocating. Panic surged within me, but I couldn't even twitch a muscle. Rellum's power was terrifying, a reminder that the gods were far beyond my comprehension or control.

"Do not make me repeat the rules, Malikap. You do not want to increase my power today of all days."

"I do not understand why you give them so many chances; they never improve."

"This one might, and that is what matters."

Malikap's disdain was palpable, a heavy weight pressing down on me. His words cut deep, fueling the frustration and helplessness simmering inside me. I hated that he saw us as nothing more than pawns; disposable and insignificant.

"Fine. He may keep his powers for this run only, but when he dies, he shall never taste of my powers again."

The shadows and gods vanished. I collapsed to the ground, frustration boiling over. I struck the ground with my fists and screamed, unable to contain my anger.

[Wrath 2/7]

By the time I calmed down, the third wave was nearly finished. I had thought the reason I never experienced memories on previous runs was due to the Memory Tokens being divided among us or not being earned as easily with a group clearing the dungeon. But as I stared at the notification, I noticed a glaring and obvious change.

It was the damn emotions. Losing my cool, relaxing too much, being lazy or greedy—it all hindered my growth. The things that helped us grow were opposed by falling into old patterns, relying on old behaviors, and deliberately doing wrong.

The system's strictness almost made me want to give up and lose points, but I picked myself up and moved forward. It was time to blow off some steam.

I rushed forward using one of my movements and launched two **Fireballs** from a single spell. The magic welled up and burned both of my hands, damaging me as it came out, but the result was definitely worth it.

The two spells split off into four **Fireballs** as promised, cruising through the air like I had used **Aim** and burning through goblins, which each fell over dead. The wounds on their chests were cauterized by the flame, leaving behind no gore.

I shook my hands from the pain, my anger abated, and I waited for my minions to clear the last three mobs. It took a little time.

The mini-boss rush was swiftly handled as well, and I honestly think it would have been handled better were it not for the interruption or my time spent trying to reinvent the wheel.

Grendelkin chomped his food in two, and GluttyKnee ate his rolled goblin candy. And I ran right into the face of the Goblin Knight and breathed all over him. Err, um, I mean, I used my ice spell. It fueled up from my stomach, coming out as mist through my mouth as if an angry dragon was propelling icy fire from my mouth.

The ice burned through the Goblin Knight, breaking his shield and freezing him to the spot. I jumped in the air, cheering.

[Fight complete!]

Crystal made a little musical trill that was pretty catchy as I patted my minions on the back.

Chapter Eighty-Six
You Kill Them

I approached the Aerlyntium, my hand hovering over it. Doubts gnawed at me. Did I even have time for this? My team—if I deserved to call them that—was waiting on me, and organic matter was scarce. Batteries had downsides, but mana was essential, reminding me that I was running low.

"Elizabeth, how do I gain mana from my batteries?" I asked, my voice barely steady.

[Oh, that's easy. You kill them,] she replied, her tone deceptively casual.

"What?" I froze, my heart skipping a beat, and a chill running down my spine.

[I kid, I kid,] she added with her trademark chuckle. [Just place your hand on it and say, '**Mana Drain.**']

I exhaled in relief, the tension easing from my shoulders. "So, I won't harm them?"

[You will drain out however much mana you need,] Elizabeth explained. [These fellows should be fine, but if you ever get the **Mana Battery** spell back, be careful not to drain them to 0 health]

I nodded, confident I *wouldn't* forget. "Got it."

With a deep breath, I approached GluttyKnee and commanded, "**Mana Drain!**"

My fingers tingled as mana flowed through my pet and into my hands. The sensation was almost electric, sending chills creeping up my arm and spreading through my body. I shivered as the cool mana surged into my veins, flowing towards my heart.

[Mana recovered to full,] Elizabeth announced, her voice too loud in my mind.

With my mana replenished, I turned towards the door, racing about what lay ahead. Thoroughly planning on running through to whatever gauntlet was next, I hesitated as Elizabeth interrupted my thoughts.

[Aren't you forgetting something?] she inquired, a hint of amusement in her tone.

"Oh, right," I muttered, glancing back at the orb. "It's best to leave the orb, although I should gather the corpses. Who knows how much material I'll need."

I sighed, the weight of responsibility heavy on my shoulders. I moved to the fallen bodies, my steps clicking loudly in the silence. With a reluctant kick, I sent the five remaining corpses to Elizabeth for storage. They vanished, one by one, leaving a stark emptiness in their place.

As I left the room, I looked at the Aerlyntium, its faint glow casting eerie shadows. I just hoped neglecting them wouldn't come back to haunt me.

~Run 7, The Silver Mirage, Floor 2, The Fallen Merchant City of Aerlyn~

The door creaked open, revealing the dimly lit maze beyond. I steeled myself, ready to face whatever lay ahead. I stepped into the room and bit back an exclamation of anger. Feeding my struggles with Wrath wouldn't be wise, nor did I want to alert the assassin to my presence. Despite the shield of turn-based combat, I couldn't risk the monster getting the drop on me and one-shotting me.

Instead, I stepped aside and ordered, "GluttyKnee, roll forward and take the lead."

With him at the front, I felt a semblance of security against ambush. No monster, however smart, could resist such an easy target. My hunch was confirmed moments later when the assassin froze and lunged to backstab the giant blob. Its dagger sank deep into GluttyKnee's flesh, eliciting a roar of pain.

Then, GluttyKnee died.

I stared, dumbfounded, realizing my horrible mistake. I had drained GluttyKnee, leaving him without a chance to recover any health. I resisted the urge to facepalm or scream in frustration. My jaw clenched as the weight of my error sank in. Time froze for the assassin, and I decided it was time for payback.

Despite my low health, I knew some point-blank **Fireballs** to the head and hands would end anyone. I approached, glaring at the mob that had ended such a powerful ally. Its gross face, covered in snot and pus, had a recessed mound of acne slowly oozing yellow liquid.

Determined, I muttered, "You're going to regret that."

My left hand reared up a second later, and I launched the **Fireball** point-blank. The spell's energy was too much; my fingers cracked and crumbled to ash as the blast exited. I screamed in agony, clutching the stump of my hand.

I yelled, my voice echoing off the dungeon walls.

I stared at the clump in my hand as the pain faded from my mind. No matter how many times it happened, I would never get used to the dungeon turning on my pain receptors. My breaths came in ragged gasps, and I kept staring at the useless hunk in my hand that didn't return.

"No matter how powerful Malikap made me, it wasn't worth this cost," I whispered. "I'm done casting **Fireball**, that's for certain."

I wandered around the maze, the adrenaline slowly ebbing away. My heart jumped when I almost scared myself silly, thinking Grendelkin was another mob.

Thankfully, he screamed, "HUNGRY."

Given my lack of a hand, I laughed a shaky sound that seemed out of place.

"Glad it's just you, Grendelkin," I said, patting his head.

Somehow, I'm taking this surprisingly well. I'd better get this back on my next run, or there will only be two gods running around.

I continued my search, my eyes scanning every corner. Finally, I found it hidden in an alcove behind a two-way mirror that reflected wrong angles. The chest wasn't locked and was somehow rare.

"Thank the gods," I muttered, kneeling to open it.

The room's oppressive silence seemed to lift slightly as I opened the chest, its hinges creaking. The die rolled across the dusty floor, and I held my breath, hoping for a potion. My luck had been amazing, but I needed a potion—the market! How could I be so stupid? I had nearly 2500 gold, probably more since I stopped counting. I could just go back to the market and buy potions. I still couldn't cast the **Fireball** spell, but at least I wouldn't have to worry about dying in a single hit from whatever absurdity tried to stop me next.

No dice on the potion, but the Scroll of Mana Regen I received was an excellent find. It would likely help once I inevitably lost my Grendelkin.

I looked at Grendelkin, who eyed me expectantly. I pulled a goblin corpse out of my inventory with a small sigh. "Eat. Stay," I instructed, hoping the simple-minded mana battery could follow such basic instructions. I watched as he tore into the corpse, then booked it back through the rooms to the entrance.

"Hello, fine merchant," I greeted awkwardly, feeling out of place.

The merchant, a wizened old man, looked up from his wares. "What do you want?" he croaked, eyes narrowing suspiciously.

"Do you have any health potions?" I asked, trying to keep my voice steady.

He grunted, scratching his chin. "Can't regrow hands, nothing that powerful. But I have health potions. Got the gold?"

"How much do they cost?" I asked, my stomach tightening in anticipation.

"100 gold each, 450 for five," he replied, his grin showing a row of crooked teeth.

I swallowed hard. It was a lot of money, and I felt he was ripping me off. But being able to heal fully was a godsend and something I needed without access to Klericho's spells. I weighed my options, and the metaphorical sack of gold at my side suddenly felt lighter.

"Alright, I'll take it," I said firmly. But I'm sampling the merchandise after I pay for the first one. If it doesn't work as you claim, I'm taking my business elsewhere."

The merchant chuckled, a raspy sound that grated on my nerves. "Alright, alright. It works, it works," he assured me, holding up his hands in mock surrender.

I handed over the gold, my heart pounding as he passed me the first potion. I uncorked it, the smell of herbs and something faintly metallic hitting my nostrils. Taking a deep breath, I drank the potion, feeling its warmth spread through my body. I looked up at the merchant, who was watching me closely.

"Seems to work," I admitted, my tension easing. "I'll take the rest."

He nodded, his eyes glinting with satisfaction as he handed over the remaining potions. I secured them in my pack, feeling a sense of relief. This would give me a fighting chance.

As I turned to leave, I caught the merchant's eye.

"Thanks," I said, surprising myself with my sincerity.

"Good luck out there," he replied, his voice softer than before. "You'll need it."

I nodded, heading back into the maze, feeling more prepared for whatever awaited me next.

I almost swallowed the yellow-orange liquid in a single gulp, but before making that mistake again, I asked Elizabeth, "Can I drink it all in one go, or is it like the regen potion?"

"You can drink it in one gulp," Elizabeth replied slowly, using her talking to children voice. "It will heal you completely whether you drink a sip or all of it. It's a lovely potion, but you already drank one and don't need to drink a second. How do you dress yourself in the morning with how often you forget things?

Chapter Eighty-Seven
Gore-Filled Things

I slowly returned to Grendelkin, thankful that the giant fur ball was still there.

As I approached, he screamed, "HUNGRY!" again, his voice echoing through the dim corridor. I threw him one of the corpses from my inventory, watching as he munched happily on the remains. His contented chewing was oddly reassuring as I moved us to the next room.

I opened the door, two wooden slabs creaking between an archway. As I entered the room, I was completely taken aback. In every direction, every color imaginable adorned tapestries, brocades, and clothes. I was struck with a debilitating sense of déjà vu.

I stepped forward, and the room gate slammed shut loudly. Already jumpy from the unnatural darkness, I shook myself, my nerves frazzled. My heart jumped into my throat as I approached the fabrics on display. The room was a maze; the materials formed their paths. And then the fog lifted. I avoided directing my gaze at the Magical Murals responsible for my fugue state.

I sighed as the memory of my first time in the room faded. I knew where I was and what to do. It was immediately clear that the room had changed, but I charged forward anyway. Instead of going right, I went down the left path, ready to face the goblin thieves if needed.

Once I got this piece, I just had to navigate the carpet room. I was a little worried because I had already wasted a lot of time there this run, but I would cross that rug when I came to it.

The carpets hung limply, letting off the same faint glow as before. I pulled out a torch and waved it before me to see my feet. The flickering light cast eerie shadows on the walls, and I hoped I wouldn't have to spend an hour navigating the maze-like last time. The exhaustion weighed heavily on me. I should have made time for a nap in the entrance room, but I worried about Grendelkin hurting himself or running out of HP if I left him alone too long.

The oppressive atmosphere pressed down on me as I moved through the maze. Each step felt heavier, the weight of my decisions bearing down. The glow from the carpets provided minimal guidance, and I relied on the torch's light to guide my way. The memory of Klericho's endless lectures about brocades and fabrics seemed almost comforting now, a small piece of familiarity in this twisted place.

I continued forward, my senses on high alert. Every rustle of fabric and distant sound kept me on edge. My mind raced with thoughts of what lay ahead, but I steeled myself and focused on the task. I couldn't afford any more mistakes.

We shuffled forward and came to the first turn. It was easier to see in the alcove here, the torchlight carrying a little more in the broader expanse. Then I stared at a scene I wished I had never seen. Two goblins were engaged in a private activity, their grunts and movements unmistakable.

My face flushed with embarrassment. "Oh, gods," I muttered, quickly turning around. "Grendelkin, charge forward for your snack!"

As soon as time unfroze, Grendelkin lunged at the goblins, his ferocious growl echoing through the hall. I moved past the blood-stained goblins, their lifeless bodies now strewn across the floor, each with a sizable chunk taken out, looted what was left of them, and took the first left.

I remembered the rule I had always been told about mazes: take the same direction every time you move down a hallway. Consistency will eventually help you arrive at the end. I tried it the first time with eventual results, so I stuck to the same routine again.

For a while, there were no enemy encounters. The silence was almost eerie; the only sound was our footsteps echoing against the cold stone walls. I kept taking left turns, not feeling like I was approaching the center, but not hitting dead ends.

It had maybe been thirty minutes before I came to a familiar clearing—the same one I had encountered the last time I ran through here. In the center was a raised altar, its surface gleaming faintly in the torchlight. My heart began to pound in anticipation.

On the altar was what I now knew to be the oil well of a Djinn lamp. As I picked it up, my heart raced with anticipation, the cool metal smooth under my fingers. Happy that after three or four failed runs, I was finally making progress; I held the lamp above my head.

Crystal made a weird musical trill and then laughed. I glanced at her, puzzled. "What's so funny, Crystal?"

[Nothing. You have received Djinn Well. This is an artifact. This artifact is part of a set. Artifacts found two thirds. Complete the set for a full description.] Crystal announced, her voice filled with a rare note of excitement.

I breathed a breath of relief, the tension melting from my shoulders.

I immediately hightailed it back through the way I came, aiming for the front entrance. The corridors seemed less oppressive now, the way lit by the lamp's soft glow. My steps were lighter, each one bringing me closer to safety. I glanced back at Grendelkin, who was happily trotting along, his fur matted with goblin blood.

As we approached the exit, a sense of accomplishment washed over me. This was just one step, but it was a significant one. I knew there would be more challenges ahead, but I allowed myself a moment of victory for now.

The entrance loomed ahead, a gateway to temporary safety. As I stepped through, the familiar, musty air of the dungeon gave way to the slightly fresher scent of the upper levels. I leaned against the cool stone wall, catching my breath.

"Crystal," I said, my voice echoing softly, "What do you think our chances are if we keep this up? Can I beat the Djinn this time?"

Crystal replied, her tone thoughtful. [If you continue to apply what you've learned *and listen*, your chances of success increase significantly.]

I nodded, feeling a renewed sense of resolve. "Then let's keep pushing forward," I said, determination hardening my voice. "We have a set to complete and a dungeon to conquer."

Grendelkin growled softly in agreement, his eyes gleaming with an eagerness that matched mine. We would face whatever came next, one step at a time.

I shook my head. It didn't matter. I gathered torches from my inventory and started throwing them one after another.

The fires burned bright for the next fifteen minutes, smoke rising high into the air, visible due to the flames permeating the room. I didn't sleep but closed my eyes as I leaned against Grendelkin. He was a surprisingly soft pillow. I was afraid I was going to summon another room demon, but I was awakened before I could by a rumbling voice shouting, "HUNGRY."

I swear that Malikap gave me this power to annoy me.

I shook my head and ran forward over the ashes of the carpet kingdom. I hesitated on the threshold as I walked through the next door. I had a mental tally of rooms, and fewer than five were left. I needed to ensure I went to the right place with the right things. It wouldn't do to go forward without the whole Djinn lamp in place. But it also wouldn't do to leave me without my pet, and I could already tell he was fading fast.

As soon as I had the thought, I knew I needed to go forward.

I stepped into what used to be the Goblin King's domain, and I gulped. Dozens of Mini-Djinni were flying around.

I was unsure if I could fight the Mini Djinni Army by myself, considering how quickly they had eaten me last time. But I wasn't here to fight. I had a hunch that I wouldn't need to.

"Oh my god! Hi Rod!" Frannie, the Mini Djinni, screamed as he flew toward me. His friends were in the center of the room... doing things... to the Goblin King's corpse. I stared, horrified, for a second before Frannie started talking again.

"I hope you haven't forgotten how useless it is to try and fight me. I am so powerful. Look at me; I'm positively radiating power and elegance." The demon propelled itself on its wings in a loop-de-loop that crackled with electricity. I cringed, afraid that the demon was going to electrocute me. However, it did nothing of the sort. Instead, it floated there, hovering menacingly.

"No, no. I haven't forgotten. I just want to make a deal. I know you plan on getting out of here, and I can help you. All I want is for you to babysit my Grendelkin here. Maybe provide him with some nice and tasty food while I get the handle of the Djinn's lamp. It's hard to keep him fed while I'm busy playing jump the carpet, y'know?"

"Yes, yes. And we all need that lamp. But, bring it to me first before you use it."

"I'll think about it."

"Alright, deal." the demon closed its left eye and flapped its wings. A few of his demon friends came flying toward us. They dropped dead on the floor in front of Grendelkin. It was like a slaughterhouse, and the furry guy started chewing into the surprisingly gore-filled things.

Before I got sick, I turned around and high-tailed it to the flying carpet room.

Chapter Eighty-Eight
The Lamp

~Run 7, Magic Carpet Ride, Floor 2, The Fallen Merchant City of Aerlyn~

I was wary as I stepped into the room. The last time I went through here, while I earned a fantastic reward—quite possibly the best I had ever earned—I also endured the most exhaustingly painful experience yet in the dungeon. The way the carpets moved was nauseating to my senses as I stared at them, waiting for the reaper to jump out at any moment. Goosebumps rose on my skin as I looked into dark corners, wary but determined to find the carpet that descended far below instead of just going up and down a few feet.

I started jumping between carpets, catching my breath as I did so, waiting and watching my step. "It wouldn't do," I muttered to myself, "to go through all this trouble and end up with a new run with much less power to dominate this floor."

The carpets were farther apart than I remembered, but my determination and the fact that I had already done this before meant I was no longer stumbling when I landed on a carpet.

After jumping through fifteen carpets, I finally saw the one that lowered into the depths. As it approached, I aimed my jump to land on level ground. Once it was in sight, I pulled out a torch, wary of previously unseen enemies or a trap that could still end this run. The flickering torchlight spread through the abyss, casting eerie shadows on the walls.

I could make out three shapes in the distance, and a broad smile came unbidden to my face.

I'm not sure what to do. I thought, adrenaline coursing. "Elizabeth, I don't see a platform to land on. Getting back-up here would be a pain. What do you think?"

[I'm certain that is where you need to go. You have plenty of supplies in your inventory, maybe there is something you could use to make your way back up.]

My inventory! That is exactly what I needed to hear. A plan had already formed in my mind.

Thinking quickly, I threw the torch in my hand, aiming for the handle but hoping I'd miss just enough not to send it flying off the platform. The torch landed with a thud, illuminating the full platform as the carpet I was on rose again. There wasn't enough space. I would definitely have my work cut out for me.

As the carpet descended, I prepared myself for the running sprint. I was on the edge opposite the handle, and as soon as the ascent started, I took off, hoping the extra elevation would give me the little oomph needed to jump. I flailed through the air and barely caught the edge with my fingertips. I slammed against the platform wall, terrified I would fall back into the abyss, but my fingers somehow held up, and I managed to pull myself onto the carpet platform.

Inventory

Death Boons: 2

Djinn Lamp *(Relic)*: 3 of 3

- **Effect:** Congratulations, you have completed the set and have the key to defeating the Djinn.

- **Description:** Rub the lamp in the Djinn's presence, and you will have one wish. Terms and conditions apply but are not valid in the state of Utah.

Phenomenal cosmic powers! Itty bitty living space!

The lamp handle was a godsend as I reached out my hand to its magical presence. "Finally," I breathed, "the Djinn Lamp Handle."

A little inventory message popped up; one Elizabeth hadn't shown in a while because of all the Aerlyntiums and item harvesting I did in my last run.

"What's a Utah?"

[Oh, that's not important, but there is one thing you can easily do to fix this situation. You can wish yourself out of here. Back to life.]

"I could do what?"

[Think about it. You have a wish that you can freely use—one time. Sure, you can use it to fix this broken hell of an afterlife *or* save yourself. Wish yourself out of Penance and be alive again—what everyone in here is always dreaming about.]

"But at what cost?"

[What do you mean?] Crystal asked innocently, but I could tell there was something in her tone.

"What I mean is that I use the wish to bring myself back home, then I abandon you, Thomas, Klericho and all the people stuck here. They will never be able to get through the Djinn's magic. I wouldn't betray everyone like that." I paused, waiting for Crystal to respond, but she didn't.

"Look, I know I made some bad choices that messed things up—sometimes on purpose, but I never meant to hurt anyone. Recalling my scattered memories, the one thing that stood out to me was that I never wanted to be the kind that hurt people. Sure, I helped destroy that zoo and probably got caught trying to kill the king. I guess I stole, too, but that was always from people who had more than enough or wouldn't miss a meal over what was lost.

[Stealing is still...]

I cut her off. "Is it worse than the theft they already do from everybody else? I know it is still wrong and evil, but I'm not defending my actions. I'm just saying that even alive, I wasn't entirely the person I've been here, and if I use that wish that way, I won't be the person I want to be. Besides, there's no way I can wish for that, or the gods would have appeared the second I grabbed the last piece. No, there is only one way for the wish to work: if I use the magic on the Djinn itself."

[What are you gonna do with that wish, then?]

"I don't know, but I'll figure it out. Is it a wish?"

[Yes.]

"Like infinite lives, money, becoming a god, those kinds of wishes? From the stories?"

[Affirmative.]

"Then I guess it depends on how the fight goes or what limitations exist for that wish. This could be an easier fight than our friends let on. They were wrong about everything else. I mean, why would they never try anything other than the suicidal charges they kept attempting? It doesn't make any sense. What if there is some stupidly obvious mechanic to the fight, and they never even tried it."[Good for you, Rod.]

"What do you mean?"

[You are changing. The wish didn't even tempt you, and you're questioning whether what someone told you is true.]

I shook my head and paused. *Why wasn't I being greedy? A few runs ago, I would have been all about a wish that gave me everything I wanted and let me escape.*

"Maybe I am, but it's a moot point. We're trapped here unless you can levitate me, too."

Dwelling on the mystery of the wish wouldn't do me any good when I had to figure out a way out of my current predicament. I stared at the carpets, too far away for me to reach them unaided.

[I'm going to try to be nice today, even though I already helped earlier. There are quite a few solutions to your problem. You could wish your way out, remove the platforms you used up above, or try placing Aerlyntium pieces down as well. There are so many choices.]

I frowned. That was a pretty smart idea.

My current platform and the few I had built likely would need something more to make a bridge to the other platforms. But if I started building more, I could eventually spread the material enough to reach the two crates, chests, or anything glinting in the darkness.

The laziness in me wanted nothing more than to ignore the items in the room and get up, but I knew I could barely afford any more mistakes when it came to laziness. What was it that Rellum had said? That our sins aren't often the problem? But rather our perception of those sins and the harms they do to others?" It felt cryptic then, but the thought still lingered in my mind.

As I gathered more materials from my inventory, I fashioned them into boards and managed to force them together; it didn't feel very stable, but what would I do? Sprout wings and fly? I laughed and got back to work.

At the end of about 30 minutes, I had fashioned something that managed to reach the other platform and felt stable enough to climb out over it. As I moved out onto the makeshift bridge, things felt mostly stable until, about halfway through, a piece of metal attached to the bridge fell away. I shuddered in fear, thinking the bridge would collapse as it started to bobble. I would hate to have to restart, I muttered, but I didn't stop moving. The shaking got worse and worse and worse until I got to the chest and realized it wasn't the bridge shaking at all, but instead, it was me.

Slowly, I breathed in and out, intending to calm down. It took a minute, but eventually, I stopped shivering and felt my breathing return to normal. I was afraid of heights now. That's good to know. Next time, Klericho or Thomas could handle this room, and I would just make my way to the end and wait.

Chapter Eighty-Nine
Demon Bodies

I opened the rare chest, anticipation thrumming through my veins, only to be met with a wave of disappointment. The chest creaked open, revealing a small pile of gold coins and a worn leather armor piece, the same as the four others I had already collected. I let out a heavy sigh, the air escaping my lungs in a frustrated huff. Sweat trickled down my forehead, stinging my eyes, and I wiped it away with the back of my hand. My muscles were sore from the constant strain, and my fingers throbbed from the countless battles. It was not worth it.

With a resigned shake of my head, I lifted my bridge, feeling the weight of it settle in my grasp. My enhanced strength, courtesy of the ridiculously powerful ring I wore, made the task feel almost effortless, though my muscles continued to protest.

I aimed for the remaining chest, determination hardening my resolve. This time, I wedged the bridge up against the chest. My heart raced, pounding in my chest like a war drum, as I took off like a bullet, not at all afraid of death.

Nope, no, sir. I was not afraid at all. This wouldn't be the end of the run; I knew it deep in my bones. The end of this floor was within reach. Third floor. Third floor. I repeated it like a mantra, a lifeline to cling to as I pressed forward.

I stared at the carpet moving in the distance, a seemingly endless expanse of rich, woven patterns that stretched out before me. The intricate designs seemed to shift and pulse with a life of their own, a mesmerizing dance that almost lulled me into a trance. But I couldn't afford to lose focus. The air was thick with the musty scent of old fabric and the faint, metallic tang of blood. My leather armor clung to my skin, damp with sweat, and the room's oppressive heat made every breath feel heavy.

I had a loose plan forming, a spark of hope amidst the chaos. I surveyed my surroundings while mentally cataloging the materials I had. The biggest problem getting to the carpet wasn't even the distance; it was the height. The drop was intimidating—a yawning chasm, ready to swallow me whole. My stomach churned with a mix of anxiety and adrenaline as I began to construct a new staircase. Each piece fell into place with a resounding thud, the wooden planks creaking under their weight.

It took me around an hour to make the new staircase appropriately. Every muscle ached from the exertion, and my remaining hand was raw and blistered. I needed room for a running start and enough elevation to cross the gap. I stood back and admired my handiwork as soon as I was done. The staircase stretched skyward, a precarious structure that looked like it could collapse at any moment. The thought sent a shiver down my spine, and I tried to ignore the dread that gnawed at my insides. I focused on the carpet, watching it move downwards, knowing I needed to go now.

My worst fear was realized when I crossed the halfway mark of the staircase. I felt the support slowly giving way, the wood groaning under the strain. Panic surged through me, and I put on a burst of speed, my legs burning with the effort. I leaped before I even realized what I was doing, the world blurring around me. The staircase crumbled behind me, disappearing into the void, and for a heart-stopping moment, I was weightless, suspended in mid-air.

I grabbed for the corner tassel, my fingers scrabbling for purchase. My grip slipped—and for a split second, I was sure I'd plummet into the abyss. But then, miraculously, I managed to swing up and hook my arm—my only good arm—over the flat surface of the carpet. I was left dangling like a fish on a line. My arms trembled with the effort and a bead of sweat trickled down my temple. I felt helpless and tired; every ounce of strength drained from my body. But I couldn't give up. I gritted my teeth and pulled myself onto the carpet, breathing in ragged gasps.

I had done it. The last item I needed to clear this cursed floor was within my grasp. The thought of fixing everything with a wish crossed my mind, but a nagging doubt held me back.

Who knew what ramifications that would have? The lamp in my inventory felt heavy, a constant reminder of its power.

But could I trust that power? I banished the thought, refusing to entertain the possibility of another shortcut. I started toward the door I had never gone through, the promise of the third floor urging me forward.

From how the floor worked, I knew the Goblin King's room was just opposite where I had initially entered. The air grew colder as I approached, a chill seeping into my bones. I took the lamp out of my bag, the cold metal pressing against my palm.

Then the same floating demon ate me approached, I saw a gleam in its eyes, a ravenous hunger that made my blood run cold. Its gaze locked onto the lamp, and I immediately hid it back in my inventory, heart pounding.

"Mine!" the demon snarled, its guttural voice sending shivers down my spine. The air around us seemed to thicken with tension, and I forced myself to meet its gaze, my fear bubbling beneath the surface.

"Look," I said, my voice steady despite the turmoil inside me. "I know you can't do anything against the Djinn or whatever, but you can let me go through that door, and I can clear this floor. I know I can't stand against you, but if I die, that's it. The lamp is gone. You can't access my corpse, and I won't leave the first floor again if I do. You'll be stuck here forever without hope."

My words felt like a desperate gamble, but I stood my ground, refusing to show weakness.

The demon hovered in the air, its orange fur and bold eyes a constant contrast to the danger I felt. It seemed to consider my words, its malevolent gaze boring into me. I could feel the sweat trickling down my back, the cool air chilling the moisture on my skin. My heart raced, every beat echoing in my ears.

"You didn't have to go so hard. I promise I only eat things once, and you weren't so tasty that I feel the need to break that rule again," it said, its voice oozing with sinister glee. My stomach twisted at the implication, confusion flickering across my face.

"Wait, what do you mean again?" I asked, my voice barely above a whisper. But before he could respond, all of the demons vanished instantly, leaving me blinking in the sudden brightness.

The room transformed, light and color flooding back into the space. It looked nice and cozy, like an oasis amidst the chaos. The Aerlyntium hung in the air, a tantalizing prize just out of reach. But as I placed my hand on the orb, an infuriating message appeared before my eyes.

[Insufficient organic material.]

The words felt like a punch to the gut, and I racked my brain, trying to find a solution. My mind raced, but no matter how hard I thought, I couldn't find a source of corpses for the material. The floor was almost cleared.

Laughter filled the room as I almost curled into a ball again.

Frustration bubbled inside me, a boiling rage that threatened to spill over; I bit my tongue to stop the emotion. And then, Rellum was here.

The god's appearance was sudden, his presence overwhelming yet strangely comforting. I shook my head, not wanting the false emotions. He held his hands up in a placating gesture, his voice calm and soothing.

"I come in peace," he said, and I felt a flicker of that false hope.

"If you're here in peace, then stop with the false emotions. I already have enough trouble keeping myself in check here." All at once, the emotions, calm, and anger ceased. I was left with a muddling hollowness. "Why are you here by yourself?"

"Sometimes, there are no good options. Sometimes, it is okay to be upset at the circumstances we find ourselves in. While we must be slow to anger, it is not the anger itself that is the sin; it's how we direct it. Striking out in anger, attacking, or yelling at others, and blaming others for our failures all come from the sin of Wrath."

His words struck a chord.

"But what am I supposed to do?" I demanded, my voice cracking. "I'm stuck here with no way out and no way forward. How am I supposed to fix this?"

The god sighed, his eyes filled with compassion. "You must find another way. Look deeper within yourself. Sometimes, the answers we seek are not in the obvious places."

I took a deep breath, trying to steady myself. The air felt heavy as I inhaled, each breath a struggle against the suffocating pressure.

"But I've searched everywhere. There has to be a way out of this mess." My voice was barely above a whisper, the words laced with desperation.

"Patience, everything will be fine." the god advised softly. "Oh, and I have a little gift for you waiting in one of the final rooms."

"Just remember. Sometimes, there are no good options. So you have to pick the one that does the most good. Monsters aren't the only thing that respawns in this dungeon." The god replied solemnly. His words hung in the air, heavy with implication. He vanished, leaving me alone with the weight of his message.

As I picked myself off the ground, I looked around at the room's pristine condition. All of the blood, all of the demon bodies, and gore piles had evaporated. It was all gone, leaving the room eerily clean. I knew what the god wanted me to do. I needed to go back to the entrance.

Chapter Ninety
Lightning Slam

I'd stopped by the Mini Djinni to reclaim Grendel. He was waiting, eyes sharp and hunger satiated. He fell in beside me without hesitation.

"Grendel, follow me," I commanded, my voice steady despite the turmoil.

We trekked back through the various rooms until we came to the entrance. If I were to turn the guards into a bunch of werewolves, I would do this right and evacuate as many people as possible first.

I had three ideas, but my first one worked perfectly. I put the torch back into my inventory and told Grendel to stay in front of Klericho's house.

I constructed a box-like platform in the town square and started yelling, "The werewolves are coming! The werewolves are coming!"

[Hide yo kids, hide yo wife!] Crystal helpfully added, her voice tinged with a mix of urgency and humor.

After my proclamation, a crowd started to gather. I was concerned for a second that they were about to drive me out of town, but instead, a voice shouted from the crowd, "What do you mean?"

"The night is going to finally come again. The curse will be lifted today, but before it is, the night shall fall," I explained, trying to keep my expression grim and my words serious, but I had a little trouble at the end as I heard Crystal snicker.

"Are we going to die?" a frightened voice asked, the fear palpable in its tone.

"No, everyone remain calm. No one will die. I can defeat the werewolf scourge, but everyone should go to their homes and barricade themselves. The werewolves will go for the obvious remaining prey," I reassured them, trying to project confidence and calm.

The crowd murmured, the tension thick in the air. One courageous voice shouted, "Why should we believe you?"

I couldn't have asked for a better opening. I held my hand up and used the scroll of darkness. Slowly, night descended on the city. First, one voice joined in, then more joined in, screaming and gasping at the sudden twilight. And then, like a dam breaking, the crowd dispersed. People rushed home to safety.

As the last of the villagers disappeared into their homes, I climbed down from the platform, my heart pounding with adrenaline. "Grendelkin, stay close," I whispered, the darkness around us feeling more oppressive than ever.

I took a deep breath, trying to steady my nerves. "Crystal, do you think this will work?"

[It's a good plan,] Crystal replied, her voice soothing. [You've done well to prepare.]

I nodded, feeling a bit more confident. "Alright. Let's get this over with."

We moved quietly through the darkened streets, the silence only broken by the occasional rustle of leaves or distant murmur of a villager securing their home. I could feel the weight of the night pressing down on me, the responsibility of what I was about to do heavy on my shoulders.

As we approached the guards, I could see their eyes glinting in the dark, wary and alert. "This has to be perfect," I muttered, taking another deep breath.

With a swift motion, I raised my hand and cast the spell to transform them into werewolves. The air crackled with magic, and the guards began to change, their bodies contorting and morphing into monstrous shapes.

I watched a mix of horror and fascination in my heart. The guards—now werewolves—snarled and growled, their eyes glowing with a feral light. I had to act quickly.

"Grendel, go!" I shouted, pointing towards the transformed guards. Grendelkin lunged forward, fiercely engaging the werewolves.

I focused on maintaining the spell, my mind racing with the need to control the situation. "This has to work," I whispered, the mantra repeating like a desperate prayer.

As the battle raged on, I felt a surge of energy and hope. Maybe, just maybe, we could survive this night and emerge stronger on the other side.

"Stay strong, Grendel!" I called out, my voice echoing through the night. "We can do this!"

And with that, I threw myself into the fray, ready to face whatever came next with determination and courage.

The howls began in earnest, and I felt a thrill of fear go up my spine as they got closer and closer. Time froze. There were twelve of them, and they looked bigger than I remembered. I thought: *now that I had Malikap's powers, did he replace the fourth spell with what it should have originally been?*

"Crystal, what's my full spell list?" I asked with a hint of urgency.

[Your complete spell list is as follows: **Fireball**, Malikap's **dual Fireball**, **Ice Breath**, Malikap's **Ice Beam**, **Mana Drain**, **Mana Battery**, **Lightning Glove**, and Malikap's **Lightning Slam**.]

"**Lightning Glove? Lightning Slam?**" I echoed, excitement bubbling beneath my fear. Each spell sounded awesome, but I also felt a trickle of anger. "Malikap, you've given me great boons but keep interfering beyond the rules."

Grendelkin charged forward to act as a shield. I was still unsure of the consequences of using **Lightning Slam**, but I knew I needed whatever extra power it offered. Unlike previous spells, I felt the electricity radiating from my feet and hands and flowing inward to my core. Power curled inside me, and before I knew it, I took off like a falcon, speeding straight for the cluster of werewolves. I slammed down onto the ground, and all of the stored electricity arced around me, clinging to the fur of the werewolves and making their hair spike out.

[You have used Malikap's **Lightning Slam**, You have dealt 67, 89, 43, 66, 99, 91, and 55 damage to the werewolves.]

I looked at the move counter, and despite its power and the fact that it allowed me to move, it only cost one move. My body shook in tremors; my hand and my left stump felt as if I had been struck by lightning, which I essentially had. I wouldn't let a little pain get in the way of victory, though, and I reared up for a second **Lightning Slam**. This time, since I was near the targets, the force of the lightning power lifted me into the air before slamming me down onto the earth and releasing the pent-up energy directly onto a target before radiating out further.

[You have used Malikap's **Lightning Slam**. You have dealt 67, 89, 43, 66, 99, 91, and 55 damage to the werewolves.]

I waved away the death notifications because the second group was a bit further away and visibly spread out. It would be risky, but I hedged my bets and ended my turn without taking the second round. The werewolves rushed forward, snarling and snapping, anger coursing through their eyes at their dead compatriots. I still had plenty of mana but was running out of health. After the battle, I could regenerate through the moonlight constantly shining down on my face, but until then, I could only afford to get attacked a few times.

The first werewolf to approach had wild, crazy eyes that flickered between Grendelkin and me. Its huge tongue slicked out, but instead of biting me, it wrapped around me, constricting my movements while its friends came closer. Their turn ended, and I started to panic. "One false move, and I'll be wolf food," I muttered.

I didn't trust the **Lightning Slam** with how little HP I had left, but I needed to get the monster off me somehow. I remembered fire being effective, but I definitely wasn't going to use the **Dual Fireball** at such a close range either. Instead, I shouted my spell, making sure to be very specific.

"Normal **Fireball**! Definitely not the bad one that ate my hand!" I yelled, desperation clear in my voice.

The fire came forth and ate through the tongue of the werewolf. It fell backward, screaming a strangled cry before the flames spread throughout its entire body, crisping it to ashes. I facepalmed. "Great for getting me out of my situation," I muttered, "but I needed the corpses."

I checked my mana and noticed I had burned through all but ten. I hated to have to use a move on it, but I reached toward Grendel and cast **Mana Drain**, hoping the spell could be used at a distance. To my relief, it was possible.

A large, constant stream of visible mana flowed from the giant form of Grendelkin and through my only hand. I felt the energy surge through me, revitalizing my depleted reserves. Then I curled up electricity, knowing it was the only way to end this battle. Blue bolts arced around my skin, and the pain dimmed as adrenaline coursed through me. I charged forward and slammed down into the remaining crowd of werewolves.

[You have used Malikap's **Lightning Slam**. You have dealt 72, 84, 47, 63, 94, and 87 damage to the remaining werewolves.]

As soon as the bolt dissipated, I glanced at my 10 health and charged again. This time, I floated higher into the air as if the magic sensed my desperation to end the battle here.

[You have used Malikap's Lightning Slam. You have dealt 67, 89, 43, 66, 99, and 91 damage. Critical hit! All damage doubled!]

I collapsed to the ground, unmoving, all the nerves in my body radiating pain. As the dust from the fight settled, I lay there hoping my amulet would heal me quickly. Unlike my previous fights in the dungeon, the lightning attacks drained my stamina and most of my little health, and of course, it drained my mana, too. These spells ate resources like Grendelkin and GluttyKnee ate corpses. I probably had to stop Grendelkin from eating the corpses, but I didn't have the energy.

"Crystal," I gasped, trying to focus through the pain, "how much health do I have left?"

[You have 5 health remaining,] Crystal responded, her voice tinged with concern. [You need to rest and recover.]

I blacked out, my body succumbing to my exhaustion.

Chapter Ninety-One
A Slight Change of Plans

A s I got to my feet, I finally noticed it. My lightning attacks had vanquished the werewolves and nearly depleted my mana battery. The giant creature looked up at me with wide, pleading eyes.

"HUNGRY!" he whined, his voice carrying a desperate edge. I felt a pang of guilt; he'd been instrumental in the fight, and now he was suffering for it. But I couldn't feed him until I reached the other room.

"Great," I muttered, feeling the weight of my mistakes settle heavily on my shoulders. The exhaustion was overwhelming; I didn't even have the energy to facepalm. Slowly, I shuffled towards the tavern. My limbs felt like lead, and every muscle ached from the strain. I knocked on the door, the sound echoing hollowly in the silence, signaling everyone inside that it was safe.

The door creaked open, revealing the villagers peering cautiously, their faces mixed with fear and hope. The tension in the air was palpable, thick enough to cut with a knife.

"Is it over?" One of them asked, their voice trembling with relief and disbelief.

"Yes," I replied, my voice barely above a whisper, the weight of the night's events pressing down on me. "The werewolves are gone. You can come out now."

The villagers hesitated for a moment before slowly emerging, their eyes widening in awe as they took in the aftermath of the battle. The ground was scorched where the lightning had struck, and the air still carried the acrid scent of burnt fur and ozone.

I sank into a chair, feeling the weight of my body sink into the worn wood. The relief was immediate, the pressure lifting off my aching feet. "Crystal," I murmured, my voice barely audible, "let's hope the next battle isn't this tough."

[Agreed,] Crystal replied, her voice a soft murmur in my mind, soothing and comforting. [For now, rest and recover. You've done well.] Her words felt like a gentle caress, easing the tension in my chest. I closed my eyes, the villagers' celebrations fading into the background. A sense of peace washed over me for the first time in a long while. Together, we faced the darkness and emerged victorious. And with that comforting thought, I allowed myself to drift into a well-deserved sleep.

~ A While Later ~

This was it. I had one, maybe two rooms left, and then I would face the Djinn. Alone. The thought sent a shiver down my spine, but I pushed it aside. No shields to get in the way this time. Just me, my wish, and whatever resolve I could muster. I could feel it intrinsically like I felt mana flow through my veins, that the wish wouldn't be enough to kill the Djinn outright. The magic came from him, so it probably had some safeguards. But if I could word it right, I could figure out a way to end him before he could kill me. This was my one chance to end this, to make the second floor the second floor again.

As my mana slowly replenished, I took a quick bite to eat, feeling the energy seep back into my body. The stale bread and dried meat did little to satisfy my hunger, but it was enough to keep me going.

I returned to the Goblin King's throne room, my mind racing with strategies and plans. If my guesses were correct, I had the Oasis Room and the Djinn's room left. This dungeon floor was already absurdly large, and I couldn't afford to overlook any new threats.

Just before entering the Goblin King's room, a realization hit me like a ton of bricks.

I turned on my heel and rushed back to the entrance, my heart pounding. I gathered the corpses that the citizens hadn't even cared about. The stench of death clung to the air, a ghastly reminder of the chaos and destruction that had unfolded.

I was so used to whatever was wrong with my brain getting in the way of doing things right the first time that I didn't even let this lapse of judgment phase me. I was honestly relieved that the corpses were still there.

Back in the king's room, I placed my hand on the Aerlyntium, feeling relief as it swirled to gather the corpses and everything else I had laid out. The orb's soft glow illuminated the room, casting long shadows on the walls. I watched in fascination as it absorbed the materials, the air buzzing with energy. I was glad I had the foresight to throw out some wood and metal, noting how the Aerlyntium picked those up, too.

All in all, I removed about half of what I had gathered from the entire floor, an insane amount of materials that made my head spin. A notification flashed before my eyes, the text bright and crisp against the dim background.

I waved it away before it even formed. And pulled up my list of people to place. At the top of the list was a name I didn't expect at all.

"Thumbs?" I repeated a mix of disbelief and hope flooding my voice. My heart raced as the diminutive goblin materialized before me, and without thinking, I scooped him up in a giant hug. "Oh, Thumbs, I am so sorry I let you get hurt." The goblin squirmed in my arms, but I held him close, feeling the warmth of his small body against mine. I let him go after a minute.

"Yes, yes, I's Thumbs!" He did the little jump thing where he stuck out his thumbs in a pose, his face beaming with pride. It was him. Relief and joy washed over me, the emotions overwhelming in their intensity. I felt my eyes well up with tears, and I blinked them away, not wanting to cry in front of him.

"You are?" I asked, my voice trembling with emotion. "It's me. Rod. I'm your master, remember?" Thumbs nodded vigorously, his eyes shining with excitement. "Yes, Master Rod! Thumbs remember! Thumbs remember!"

I felt a wave of relief and joy wash over me. "I thought I'd lost you," I admitted, my voice breaking. "I thought I'd never see you again." The emotions were too much, and I felt a lump in my throat. I swallowed hard, trying to keep my composure.

I placed Thomas and then Klericho on the ground, breathing a long sigh of relief as they blinked into existence. Their presence reminded me that I wasn't alone in this fight. I had missed them, especially given how often I had become a god's plaything when they weren't around.

"What, how? Where are the demons?" Thomas's gaze was a bit bloodshot, and he looked rather confused. Klericho seemed scared, darting glances into the room's corners like he wasn't sure if everything was safe. We had been eaten by demons, after all.

"It's fine, Klericho. You're safe. I gave the demons something they wanted, and then a god vanished them." I explained, trying to calm him. The relief in his eyes was evident, but there was still a hint of wariness. Overall, my situation was great now. I had two powerful allies, a minion, and a few spells. I didn't have a way to recover mana, but luckily, I expressed this out loud, and Klericho spoke up.

"Oh, they sell those in the market, and unlike health potions, you can chug those all day. This is great since you finally got the mage build you've wanted," Klericho said, his voice tinged with excitement. The prospect of easily accessible mana recovery was a game-changer. I had been so excited for actual magic my entire time through the second floor, but when I finally had it, I didn't even have time to react the way I should have because I was so focused on what Malikap did to me and then on making sure I got the pieces I needed to clear out the Djinn.

This reminded me. I pulled out the Djinn Lamp and showed it to Klericho and Thomas. The sparkle in their eyes was unmistakable. It was the same hunger I had seen countless times before—a thirst for power, for control. They wanted the Djinn Lamp to serve their interests instead of the good of everyone. The realization made my stomach churn. The glint in their eyes was why I had always ignored religion. Rellum seemed great, but everyone who served him seemed just as self-serving as I was. I sighed, feeling a heavy weight settle in my chest. I didn't want to be that person who judged everyone when I knew just how well perceptions could alter one's opinion of anything, most definitely on matters of judgment and morality.

"Look, I know this lamp is powerful," I began, my voice steady. "But we have to use it wisely. This isn't just about us. It's about everyone trapped here." My words hung in the air, a solemn reminder of the gravity of our situation.

Thomas nodded slowly, though I could still see the hunger in his eyes. "I understand," he said, but his voice lacked conviction. There was a hesitation in his gaze, a conflict of interests that made me uneasy.

Klericho, on the other hand, seemed more earnest. "We need to be careful. The Djinn is powerful, and if we misuse this wish, we could end up worse off than before."

"Exactly," I agreed, the gravity of the situation weighing heavily on my shoulders. "We have to think this through. No rash decisions. Agreed?"

"Agreed," Klericho said firmly, while Thomas reluctantly nodded. The tension in the room was palpable, a quiet storm brewing beneath the surface.

I turned to Thumbs, who had been listening quietly. "Thumbs, we're going to free you from Kingsley, and defeat the Djinn, but we need to work together." The little goblin nodded, his eyes shining with determination.

Instead of letting my anger rise or getting mad at their looks of jealousy, I rushed forward and hugged my friends. "I'm sorry for how I've treated you all here. I promise I'll do better." The words felt heavy with sincerity, a promise to myself as much as to them.

Thomas nodded, a small smile tugging at the corners of his lips, but Klericho stiffened when I touched him. The cleric's reaction was unsurprising; we had never been close. But it wasn't worth the energy to dwell on it. He didn't have to like me, but as long as his god did, I knew he would accept me for who I was.

Eying the final name on my list, I said something to my friends. "So guys, before we head to kill the Djinn, there's a slight change of plans."

Chapter Ninety-Two
Never Done This Before

Klericho looked ready to pounce on me, but Thomas held up a hand to control his companion. I wondered how Thomas had been the one to summon Malikap instead of Klericho. Klericho was constantly arguing. How did he not gain wrath points? Was it because he didn't feel bad? Because he didn't act on that anger? I wished I had more time to think, but Thomas spoke.

"I'm sorry. Can you repeat that, please?" Thomas shook his head, looking confused.

"I said, 'What do you mean?' I'm not in a rush, but what's the change of plans? How many rooms do we have left?"

"Oh, only around two to four, depending on how many rooms this floor typically generates," I replied quickly.

"Around fourteen," Thomas mused. "Honestly, not that many more than the first floor."

"Alright then, the change of plans is that we will bring out Kingsley from the Aerlyntium and fight him. Afterward, we can heal up and go back to the entrance, get some grub, and fight the Djinn, who is also fully healed."

"And why are we fighting the Goblin King?" Klericho asked, suspicion evident in his tone.

"I made a promise to Thumbs," I explained, gesturing to the goblin with my right thumb, snickering to myself.

"Whoa, Thumbs is back. How did that happen? I thought Malikap ate Thumbs or something," Thomas exclaimed, his eyes wide with surprise.

"I managed to get him back through the Aerlyn Orb," I said, smiling down at Thumbs. "He's been through a lot, and I promised him I'd help free him from Kingsley."

Thumbs did his signature pose, sticking out his thumbs proudly. "Thumbs fight! Thumbs free!"

"I think minions respawn," I said, glancing at Thomas. "Unfortunately, he has no memory of my earlier runs with him, but he still wants to be free of Kingsley's control. He says he will join us if we free him."

Thomas nodded, his expression determined. "That's worth it. I died last time the guy got himself killed, running head-first into a mob."

A chill ran down my spine at the memory. "Add a blurb about the turn-based mode being turned off in the king room."

We decided to each take flanking positions while Thomas faced the goblin. Turning the turn-based mode off would be an adjustment; I hadn't had a real-time battle since my run as the Archer ended. And never with magic. I was worried about the wind-up that spells had. It was a definite disadvantage that I couldn't overcharge spells in this fight. If things went awry, I decided to play it safe and only use the Aurentum-aligned spells. It wouldn't do to double over in pain after failing to turn the Goblin King into a battery.

As soon as Kingsley appeared, chaos erupted. The Goblin King didn't even wait to talk, apparently taking our flanking positions as a threat. He immediately burst into action, thrusting a staff towards Thomas's face and casting a blank fire spell.

"Watch out!" I yelled, heart pounding.

I had often encountered mages in boss fights, and this one was no different. I shook my head and charged a **Fireball** at his head. The dice rolled, and I appreciated that I could freely flank him as the boss turned toward Klericho. I cast another **Fireball** as Thomas lunged with his sword. He only managed one swing before the Goblin King reset his counter.

"I realized I hadn't cast **Scan** yet!" I shouted over the din. I immediately incanted the spell, hoping it would give us the needed edge.

The information unfurled in front of me: [Kingsley. Eldest son of Grendel. Betrayer of the Grendelkin. Enslaver of goblin kind. This is a group-level boss. It is highly recommended that you take this on with peers. The minimum group recommended is 5+. This boss has 999 HP, the maximum encountered on Floors 1 and 2 except by secret bosses.]

I stared long and hard at the paper as it curled to the floor, but I didn't dawdle long. As soon as it fell, I tossed a potion to Klericho. "I only have 2 left. Ration where you can, and save some for Thomas. Our only hope is that he can build up damage on his sword. Just like the other Grendelkin, he's tough."

Klericho caught the potion and pocketed it, giving me a curt nod. My potion bag jostled. It was a little lighter but worth the purchase. I cast **Mana Drain** on the goblin, hoping to score enough to continuously cast **Ice Breath**. The ice beam would do more damage, but we really needed the ability to distract the Goblin King.

As my breath connected with the Goblin King's neck, I could smell his rank odor, almost faltering in my step. The sewer was a bouquet compared to the stench of death radiating from the 'king.'

I did my best to ignore the overpowering stench while I cast my spell, but as soon as it was done, I knew I'd have to inhale a mouthful of him. I pinched my nose and jumped away, but the smell still sent me to the floor, gagging.

Kingsley laughed, his voice echoing through the chamber. He turned to face me, a cruel smile spreading across his grotesque face. "You think your tiny little spells are magic?" He laughed again, the sound grating on my nerves. Meanwhile, Thomas didn't waste the opportunity of Kingsley's turned back and started hacking away at the dense fur of the Goblin King. I lost count of how many strikes he landed, but Kingsley didn't flinch. Instead, he laughed again and said, "This is magic."

A fireball launched from his staff, and I went for broke. I fired off an **Ice Beam** to counter it. I could feel my teeth cracking in the cold, but I held the beam with as much will as I could muster. The **Ice Beam** obliterated the fireball and continued forward, shattering the orb atop Kingsley's staff. I grimaced, wishing the staff would drop. Instead, it disintegrated before my eyes.

I smiled, defiant. "What was that about real magic?"

Kingsley's eyes narrowed in anger. I was sure I was about to lose more teeth, but I cast an **Ice Breath** again, aiming for the Goblin King's giant-pawed hands. I only managed to freeze one, and the excruciating pain cost me four teeth. I spit them out, the metallic taste of blood filling my mouth, and charged forward through the agony, casting **Ice Breath** again. The pain intensified, but I could see it working as the other paw became more vulnerable and easier to dodge.

Meanwhile, Thomas had been tirelessly swinging his sword, striking repeatedly. Chunks of hair and blood flew from the Goblin King as a golden shield appeared around Klericho and me. Thomas's shield thankfully still held. The timing was almost too perfect, as if rehearsed, just as the Goblin King let out an unearthly roar that kicked us all back 20 feet. I hit the ground hard, the wind knocked out of me.

The Goblin King immediately bounded on all fours and ran, shedding his front paws as he moved faster than lightning. Before we knew it, he had burst through the door and into the oasis. Without hesitation, we ran after him, plans to heal be damned.

"Don't let him get away!" Thomas shouted, his voice filled with urgency.

I struggled to my feet, every muscle aching, and followed. The sight of the oasis was almost surreal, a stark contrast to the dank chamber we had just left. The Goblin King was already at the far end, his monstrous form silhouetted against the shimmering water.

"Cut him off!" Klericho yelled, his voice hoarse from the exertion.

I nodded, my resolve hardening. There was no turning back now. We had to finish this, no matter the cost. As I prepared another spell, I could feel the last reserves of my strength draining. But the sight of Kingsley, now visibly wounded, gave me a surge of determination.

"This ends now," I muttered, pushing through the pain, ready to give everything I had to bring the Goblin King down.

The worst part about his entering was that the accessible spots had already been compromised. Panic clawed at my mind, but I forced it back. I wasn't sure if my companions had done the same. Driven by pain, I ran faster than I ever had before. We would each need to move in different directions to navigate the room safely. Somehow, the doors didn't drop. I didn't have time to ponder why, so I immediately ran to my left.

I was determined to end this run on floor three and not fail at the finish line. I was hurt, bleeding, and weary, but Kingsley and the Djinn were going down. "What's the plan, guys?" My speech was chopped and stilted. It hurt to talk, but I projected as loudly as possible while waiting for Klericho or Thomas's response.

"I don't know! Kingsley has never done this before!" Klericho's voice was tinged with desperation.

"Just keep chasing him. If I can get a couple more hits on him, he should be easy to take down. But he's headed for the Djinn room," Thomas replied, his tone grim but focused.

My grin faltered, and I almost stumbled, but I managed to regain my footing as I ran straight for the door. The Goblin King had already left the room.

Chapter Ninety-Three
The Djinn of Aerlyn, Part 1 of 6

I could have waited, maybe should have waited, but as soon as the door closed behind me, Kingsley turned around and swung his paw. Time seemed to slow down as I barely managed to duck, feeling the rush of air from his massive paw just inches above me.

The room was dimly lit, the flickering torchlight casting eerie shadows on the cold terracotta walls. My heart pounded in my chest, the adrenaline coursing through my veins like wildfire. Sweat beaded on my forehead, stinging my eyes. My breath came in ragged gasps, the air heavy with the scent of damp stone and burning wood.

In a split second, I retaliated with a point-blank **Fireball**, the heat searing the space between us. The flames roared to life, illuminating the room with a blinding light. Kingsley snarled, recoiling from the attack, and quickly backed away as Thomas burst into the room, sword drawn and ready for battle.

Without hesitation, Kingsley turned tail and bolted, his heavy footsteps echoing through the chamber. My eyes darted around, quickly taking stock of the room. It was then that a chilling realization hit me—I had overlooked a crucial detail.

Kingsley's roar shattered the brief moment of clarity, and I watched in horror as eight goblins materialized, their forms twisting and warping into grotesque, hulking figures. Their skin was a sickly green, and their eyes glowed with a sinister red light. The air filled with the acrid scent of molten metal as they brandished red-hot swords, their edges glowing with intense heat. They carried buckets of bubbling lava, the liquid sloshing and hissing as it splashed onto the stone floor.

"Here they come!" I shouted, my voice bouncing off the cold stone walls. The sound was almost drowned out by the clamor of the goblins charging forward, their eyes glowing with malevolent intent. The heat from their swords and lava buckets was palpable, making the air thick and stifling.

As the first goblin closed in, time seemed to freeze as turn-based mode, silently thanking whatever luck had decided to favor us. My breath was ragged, and I could feel the weight of the situation pressing down on me. The pressure was suffocating, every second stretching into an eternity. But I couldn't afford to hesitate.

I charged forward, channeling my energy into a series of **Ice Breath** spells. The cold magic flowed through me, and I cast the spell three times in rapid succession. The temperature in the room dropped sharply, a biting cold permeating the air. Frost spread across the ground, creeping up the walls and encasing the goblins' monstrous forms in ice. Their growls turned to shrieks of agony as the cold bit into their flesh.

Thomas appeared beside me, his sword flashing through the air with deadly precision. He moved like a dancer, each movement fluid and calculated.

His blade cut down the frozen goblins one by one, each strike clean and efficient. Despite the chaos, I wasn't overly worried about being killed; the furthest goblins were still a safe distance away, enough that they'd only get one or two hits in before I could freeze them again. The cold air burned in my lungs, and every breath was a struggle as the frost spread.

A soft glow surrounded me as I started to feel the weight of the approaching goblins. Klericho's ward had activated, casting a protective barrier around me. The warmth of the ward contrasted with the cold of the ice, creating a comforting sensation that bolstered my resolve. I smiled, feeling a surge of gratitude. It was a rare moment of camaraderie amidst the madness. My muscles ached from the strain, my body trembling with exhaustion, but I pushed through the fatigue.

A goblin lunged at me, swinging its red-hot sword with a menacing growl. The blade crashed down, but the ward held strong. The sword shattered on impact, the brittle metal breaking into pieces. I couldn't help but laugh, the relief washing over me like a wave. The rest of the goblins paused, clearly intimidated by the display of power. Their hesitation was palpable, the air thick with their fear.

Grinning, I prepared for my attack. With the enemies within striking distance, I quickly grabbed a mana potion from the bag Klericho gave me in the previous run. The liquid was cold and invigorating, sending a rush of energy through my body.

"Time to chill," I muttered, unleashing two consecutive **Ice Breath** attacks. The temperature in the room plummeted, and the air filled with the crackling sound of ice forming. The goblins were quickly encased in thick layers of frost; their movements slowed to a crawl. I didn't have time to question my insane luck, so I brushed the errant thought aside.

Thomas, moving with the speed and precision of a seasoned warrior, dispatched the remaining goblins. His blade cut through them with lethal efficiency, leaving nothing but shattered ice and defeated enemies in his wake.

I dropped to the floor in exhaustion.

If I'm this tired now, how am I going to face two bosses?

There was no need to expend more mana or energy; the battle was over, and we had won. My body felt heavy, and the adrenaline crash left me drained.

As soon as I recovered, I gathered the corpses, carefully saving the organic material for future runs. Every bit counted, and I wasn't about to let anything go to waste. The room was silent now, the echoes of battle fading into the distance. The air was cold, the frost from my spells still lingering. With the immediate threat neutralized, we sprinted after the Goblin King, the urgency of our mission driving us forward. The stone floor was slick with ice, and we moved quickly, our breath visible in the chilly air.

As we ran, my mind raced. The encounter with the goblins had been a diversion, a distraction from the real challenge ahead. The magic lamp weighed heavily in my thoughts. I still didn't have a concrete plan for dealing with it or the Djinn. The rules were clear—I couldn't directly harm the Djinn. But perhaps there was a way to wish for the fight to be easier or end quickly. The thought was tempting, but I knew it was too vague. The Djinn was notorious for twisting wishes, and a careless request could spell disaster.

Frustration gnawed at me, a bitter reminder of my inadequacies. "I wish I had done better in school," I muttered under my breath, the words tinged with regret. Maybe then I'd have been smart enough to devise a real plan, something foolproof that could guarantee our victory. But there was no time for self-pity. My legs burned from the exertion, my muscles screaming in protest.

We burst into the final room of the floor, the air thick with an oppressive energy. The atmosphere was stifling, the weight of the magic in the air pressing down on us like a physical force. The room was vast, almost rivaling the entrance in size. The Djinn floated casually in the air, cyan wisps of smoke radiating from his arms and legs, the magic reflecting his power. His skin was a deep blue, and his eyes gleamed with malevolence. He held a spear in one hand and a fireball in the other. His expression was one of cruel amusement, a smile playing on his lips.

Funnily enough, two more lamps were in the room, guarded by pillars of golden wards. Cyan smoke rose from the lamps, lazily drifting toward the Djinn as it vanished. I used **Scan** immediately.

Secret Boss Entry 0002: The Djinn of Aerlyn

This Djinn has been ravaging the city of Aerlyn for ages, taking away the hopes and dreams of any Penitent trying to reach the 3rd floor. This secret boss was unleashed by Thomas's and Klericho's meddling. This would never have happened if they had simply not poked into a room they weren't ready for. Let that be a lesson to you, Rod.

Stat:Level: ???**Effect**:

Health: ????/????This boss monster is currently invisible and immune to damage.

I stared at the space where the invisible monster used to be as the king cackled in the background. The air was thick with tension, every sound amplified in the silence. A double-boss fight had nothing on the four-boss gauntlet the first floor had become, but an invisible boss seemed insurmountable. My palms were sweaty, the lamp in my hand slippery with moisture.

"I know what my wish needs to do," I thought, "I just need to figure out how to make it." Discreetly rubbing the lamp hanging at my side, I whispered my wish. Nothing happened. The silence was deafening, my heart pounding in my ears.

"Hey guys, how do I activate the lamp?" I asked, my voice tinged with frustration and desperation. The air was thick with the scent of burning, the smoke from the Djinn's fireball hanging heavy in the air.

"Give it to me," Thomas said, an unusual anger glinting in his usually calm eyes. His face was flushed, a bead of sweat trickling down his temple.

"What, no? Crystal just said you were the reason this mess even happened!" I snapped, my voice louder than intended. Anger flared within me, burning hot and fierce. The gods wouldn't have meddled this much if there hadn't been so much chaos on this floor. My hands shook, the lamp rattling in my grip.

Thomas's expression hardened, and for a moment, I saw a flicker of something dark in his eyes. "We don't have time for this, Rod. Just give it to me!" His voice was sharp, edged with desperation and urgency. His jaw was clenched, his knuckles white as he gripped his sword.

"No!" I clutched the lamp tightly, my knuckles white. "We'll figure this out together. I'm not letting you make things worse." My heart pounded; a mix of fear and determination drove me. My mouth was dry, my throat tight with anxiety.

Klericho stepped between us, his eyes darting nervously between me and Thomas. "Rod's right. We need to think this through. Fighting among ourselves won't help." His voice was calm, but I could see the tension in his posture, his hands clenched at his sides. His face was pale, a sheen of sweat glistening on his forehead.

Thomas let out a frustrated growl but backed down, the tension in the room palpable. The Djinn watched us with amusement, his eyes glowing with dark energy, an evil smile playing on his lips. His laughter echoed in the chamber, a haunting sound that sent chills down my spine.

I took a deep breath, trying to calm my racing heart. "Okay, we need a plan. The Djinn is now invisible, so we need to make him visible. We can worry about hurting him later." The words felt heavy, each one a struggle to get out.

Klericho nodded, his brow furrowed in concentration. "Maybe we can disrupt the flow of energy from the lamps. If we can cut off his power source, he might become tangible." His voice was steady, but I could see the worry in his eyes.

Thomas's anger seemed to subside, replaced by a steely determination. "I'll take out the guards around the lamps. Rod, you focus on keeping the Djinn distracted. Klericho, see if you can weaken the wards." His voice was firm, his eyes locked on the Djinn.

"I got it," I said, my grip tightening on my staff. Let's do this." The air was electric with anticipation, the weight of the coming battle pressing down on us. We were in for the fight of our lives, but I was ready. The sweat dripped down my back, the adrenaline surging through my veins. This was it. No turning back.

Chapter Ninety-Four
The Djinn of Aerlyn, Part 2 of 6

With a nod, we sprang into action, each determined to end this battle and the Djinn's reign of terror. The fate of our mission depended on it, and failure was not an option.

Of course, the Djinn threw the first fireball in the middle of our arguing. The explosion sent us rocketing backward, the force of the blast rattling my bones. My vision blurred for a moment, and the heat singed my skin. I could feel the scorch marks on my arms, the pain sharp and searing. As soon as I recovered, I sprinted to my feet and let out a scream. "This reign of terror ends now!" I shouted, my voice echoing in the vast chamber, reverberating off the stone walls. The air was thick with smoke, and the acrid smell of burnt hair filled my nostrils.

I pulled out the lamp, my hands trembling with a mix of fear and adrenaline. I didn't think—I just wished. The barriers blocking the lamps shattered into a pile of sand with a deafening crash, and my lamp floated out of my hands. Inky cyan smoke flowed from the Djinn as he grabbed the lamp back, the tendrils of smoke wrapping around it like claws. The temperature in the room seemed to drop, the cold air prickling my skin.

"Foolish mortals, you can't defeat me," the Djinn taunted, his voice dripping with contempt. His laughter echoed, a sinister sound that sent chills down my spine.

I groaned at how cliché the Djinn sounded—like every villain from a Shooksword play.

"Seriously? Foolish mortals? That's what you're going with?" I taunted back, trying to mask my fear with bravado. The effort to maintain my composure was palpable, every word feeling like a lifeline in the midst of chaos.

[He sounds like a comic book supervillain,] Crystal laughed in my mind. I had half a mind to ask her what a comic book was, but another fireball came hurtling toward me, forcing me to leap to the side. I could feel the heat of the blast singe my hair, the acrid smell of burnt fabric stinging my nose. My heart raced, each beat pounding in my ears.

He was still invisible, cradling the lamps in a pile of smoke. Meanwhile, I heard a scream as the Goblin King reared up on his hind legs and attacked Klericho. Panic surged through me as I realized things were spiraling out of control. If we didn't do something to change the situation soon, we would have to restart. There was no way for me to revive my friends; there wasn't any Aerlyntium in the room. My hands shook, the weight of the situation pressing down on me like a vice.

I glanced at Thomas, who was fiercely fighting off the goblin boss. His movements were swift and precise, every swing of his sword a calculated strike.

"Rod, we need to make him visible now!" Thomas said to me.

"Any ideas?" I yelled, desperation creeping into my voice. My throat felt tight, the words barely escaping my lips.

"I'm working on it!" Thomas shouted back, his voice strained with effort. His sword flashed in the dim light, cutting through the guards with deadly accuracy. Sweat dripped down his face, his breathing heavy and labored. He didn't look like he'd have a chance to help.

Klericho, struggling against the Goblin King, cast a spell that weakened the wards around one of the lamps. It was odd, because it was a spell

I'd never seen him use before. His hands moved in intricate patterns, the magic flowing from him in shimmering waves.

"Hurry, Rod!" he called out, his voice a strained whisper. The effort of the spell was evident in his trembling hands and pale complexion. I rushed forward to grab a lamp and tried making another wish.

But nothing happened.

"What are you doing?" Thomas shouted, frustration in his voice. "Those lamps aren't real."

He was right, it felt odd in my hands like a cheap recreation. I turned to face where the Djinn had last cast an attack but I knew it was the wrong location.

I wasn't sure what they wanted me to do. I had no way to make him visible. Nothing in the room seemed like it could help. Suddenly, Klericho went down.

I rushed forward to him kicking up a cloud of dust from the sand as I went. By the time I got to him he was casting a **Heal** spell.

He shoved me off and said, "I'm fine, do your job."

I looked around the room uncertain what we were supposed to do, when I spotted it. The pile of sand. It felt silly, but I rushed forward and grabbed handfuls of the sand. I waited for the Djinn to attack, hoping that my standing around like an idiot wasn't about to backfire.

He sent out a beam attack at Thomas, and I knew where the Djinn was.

I rushed forward sand spilling from my hands and threw the dust at the Djinn. He shrieked as if I had stabbed him with a sword, the sand causing red welts to appear and his invisibility to vanish.

"There! He's visible!" I cried out, hope rekindling within me. The sight of him sent a thrill of fear down my spine, but I pushed it aside, focusing on the task at hand.

He was unlike anything I had ever seen. He appeared human, but his skin was a translucent shade of shimmering blue. His torso ended in a tornado of blue smoke. The red welts vanished almost immediately but he continued floating in the room smoke wafting off him now like a dying fire.

With the Djinn now vulnerable, we launched our final assault, each fighting with everything we had. The room was a blur of motion, the clash of weapons and spells echoing in the chamber. The battle raged on, but we no longer fought in the dark. Together, we had a chance to end this once and for all. My body ached, every muscle straining with exertion, but I refused to let up.

I rushed forward, reveling in the freedom of not being stuck in turn-based mode. The sensation of real-time action was exhilarating, the adrenaline pumping through my veins like fire. I dived into the inky cyan smoke, grabbing another one of the lamps.

The glass was cold under my fingers, and I could feel the power thrumming within it. This one was real. With a decisive motion, I smashed it against the ground. It shattered into a thousand tiny pieces, the sound ringing out like a death knell.

"You dare destroy my lamps? You'll pay for this!" The Djinn roared, his voice seething with rage. His eyes blazed with fury, and the air around him crackled with dark energy.

"Again, man, what is with the lines?" I retorted, rolling my eyes. My voice was shaky, betraying the fear lurking beneath my bravado. Crystal snickered, her amusement a strange comfort amidst the chaos.

[Are you trying to be a Spiderman villain? C'mon, stop bantering and kick this guy to the curb!] Her voice echoed in my mind, tinged with exasperation.

I couldn't help myself. "Spiderman? That sounds incredibly creepy," I muttered, shuddering.

I hate spiders. The thought of a spider-themed hero was unsettling, and I pushed the image from my mind. The Djinn was incensed now, launching fireball after fireball in volleys aimed at me. The heat was intense, the flames licking at my skin. My breath came in ragged gasps, the air thick with smoke and the smell of burning.

I ran to see if Thomas and Klericho were okay, but the relentless onslaught forced me to focus on avoiding the fireballs. My muscles screamed in protest, each dodge a struggle against fatigue. The heat seared my skin, and my heart pounded in my chest like a drum.

"I need a little help here, guys! I can't do anything with him targeting me like this!" Klericho shouted, desperation creeping into his voice. His voice was strained, and I could hear the fear in his words.

I kept running, not waiting to see if Thomas would do anything to help. Instead, I focused on keeping my feet out of the fire. Then, I felt the glow surrounding me, and I knew what I needed to do to relieve the pressure on us all. The warmth of the golden shield was a welcome relief, a barrier against the relentless heat.

Thomas was dominating the Goblin King, his movements precise and controlled. He didn't step in to help Klericho, so I needed to run interference on the Djinn. With the golden shield around me, I changed tactics. I kept running but angled myself and started to run toward the boss. My heart pounded in my chest, the thrill of the chase coursing through me.

He kept launching fireballs, but as I dodged side to side, I could see uncertainty on his face. The Djinn's confidence seemed to waver, the anger in his eyes flickering with doubt. When I thought he would keep throwing fireballs, he changed tactics and vanished, taking the lamps with him. The room plunged into an eerie silence, the absence of the Djinn's presence palpable.

I couldn't quite tell what he was up to in the dim light of the room. Suddenly, he reappeared and slammed a fireball into Klericho's face, downing the Cleric. The blast sent Klericho crashing to the ground, his body limp and motionless. His face charred beyond recognition.

"No!!! Klericho!" I shouted, my voice cracking with panic. The sight of him lying there, unmoving, sent a surge of terror through me. My chest tightened, and I struggled to breathe.

I was shocked that Klericho went down so quickly, but I had no time to react as the two bosses changed their targets. The Djinn focused on Thomas, his eyes blazing with malice, while the Goblin King turned his gaze on me. His massive form loomed over me, his eyes burning with rage.

Panic surged through me, but I forced myself to focus. The Goblin King's presence was overwhelming, his sheer size and strength intimidating. Knowing I wasn't a physical match for the King, I backpedaled, launching fireballs as quickly as I could. The spells were draining, the effort leaving me breathless. The pain was almost blinding, the strain of casting taking its toll on my body.

I'm not sure if my aim was better or if the Goblin King is weaker and slower, but either way, more of my attacks are connecting than I expected, I thought, adrenaline coursing through my veins. Each successful hit felt like a victory, a small triumph in the midst of chaos. Then, because I hadn't been paying attention to my feet, I tripped over the small altar the lamps had been placed on. The cold stone scraped against my skin, and I stumbled, my heart racing.

The Goblin King reared back and pounced for me, his massive form a shadow in the dim light. His claws gleamed, and his eyes burned with a fierce intensity. In that split second, I made a decision that likely changed everything. The weight of it settled in my chest, heavy and suffocating.

Chapter Ninety-Five
The Djinn of Aerlyn, Part 3 of 6

I knew I shouldn't have done it, considering how painful it had been the last few times, including the second time when I passed out. But I cast **Mana Battery**, and things got crazy real fast. The spell surged through me, a rush of energy that made my head spin. The world around me blurred, the sounds and sights merging into a dizzying haze.

[What are you doing? You can't turn a boss into a minion! That will upset some powerful people that you don't want to be on the wrong side of...] Crystal's voice rang out in my mind, filled with alarm. Her words barely registered, the intensity of the spell overwhelming my senses. "W hat do you mean? Who is more powerful than the gods? Didn't I already upset..."

And that's when I blacked out as a Memory Core suddenly overtook me. The world faded away; the battle, pain, and fear all disappeared into darkness. My last thought was a prayer that we would somehow make it through this. That we would survive.

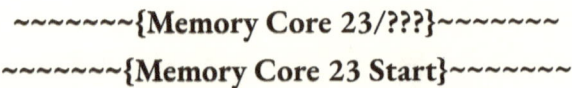

~~~~~~~{Memory Core 23/???}~~~~~~~
~~~~~~~{Memory Core 23 Start}~~~~~~~

When I came to, it wasn't reality. I stood in a dirty and battered alleyway, the walls around me crumbling and covered in grime. The ground was littered with refuse, and the stench of decay filled the air, thick and nauseating. Peckolin stood before me, wearing his distinctive blue and gold wizard's robes, the vibrant colors now stained with blood where a dagger jutted out from his chest. His eyes, usually sharp and full of life, were now clouded with pain and confusion. He gave me a betrayed look, tears brimming in his eyes, reflecting the dim, flickering light of a nearby streetlamp. The light cast eerie shadows on the alley walls, making the scene feel even more surreal.

I didn't understand the scene. I kept looking around for the inky mist that usually accompanied the false memories, but I didn't see any. The alley felt too real, the cold, hard cobblestones beneath us, grounding me in the moment. The air was cold, and a shiver ran down my spine as the reality of the situation set in.

"No, I... I didn't mean to," I stammered, my voice trembling. Peckolin fell to the ground, his knees buckling as he crumpled in a heap. Blood seeped from his wound, pooling on the dirty stones beneath him. The sound of his labored breathing filled the air, each gasp growing weaker.

"First Candor, and now me? Why? All we ever did was..." he trailed off as he died, the light leaving his eyes. His words hung in the air, heavy with accusation and sorrow.

"This can't be real. I can't have murdered Peck," I thought, a knot forming in my stomach. The scene felt too vivid, too raw to be just another hallucination. Peckolin was my one real friend, and here I was, standing above him, the dagger in his chest a stark reminder of my actions. The sight was too much; bile rose in my throat, and I threw up, the sour taste burning my mouth. I wasn't sure if it was reality or the vision making me sick.

~~~~~~~{**Memory Core 23 End**}~~~~~~~

As I cleared my vision of the memory, I shrugged away the pain. The scene shifted, and I found myself back in the battle, the echoes of the vision still lingering in my mind. The words flowed from my mouth as if they had a mind of their own.

"I already have a god-shaped target on my back. What's one more enemy going to do? Besides, it's one more battle, and the floor is over. It's not like I can retain him through runs, and he probably can't even come with me to the next floor," I muttered, trying to push the haunting memory aside. My voice was strained, the weight of the memory pressing down on me.

Elizabeth, surprisingly silent, seemed to understand the gravity of the situation. Her usual quips were absent, leaving an uncomfortable silence in my mind. I laughed, a bitter, hollow sound that lingered a second too long in the air, and Crystal screamed in frustration.

The Goblin King didn't have the same calm face as the other minions. Instead, he glared at me, his eyes burning with fury. But the compulsion of the spell forced him to follow my command. The dim, torch-lit chamber around us was filled with the echoes of our footsteps and the distant sounds of battle. The air was thick with tension, each breath a struggle.

"Go attack the lamps. We need to destroy them both," I ordered, my voice steady despite the fear gnawing at my insides. The King turned, screaming in frustration, his voice a guttural roar. The new commands forced on him were a nice bit of irony; the former slave owner was now a slave. His muscles bulged as he struggled against the magic's hold.

[Congratulations. You have unlocked the secret minion, Kingsley, the Goblin King (**Mana Battery**), level 10]

I grinned at the success—a small comfort amidst the ongoing boss fight. I couldn't believe that had worked. The insane amount of pain had been worth it. But my grin faltered as the memory of the vision clung to me, a shadow in the back of my mind. I hadn't believed I deserved

Penance until I saw it. Out of context, it made no sense. I had no idea If it was even real or one of the many fake ones. But the lack of inky smoke in the memory had me doubting myself.

But now wasn't the time to dwell on thoughts. Lately, it was never the time, but whatever. I ran after my new minion, a **Fireball** on my lips, ready to give the Djinn a taste of its own medicine.

My feet carried me fast, and I spotted an opening, so I took it, launching an **Ice Beam**; but before my spell went off, several things happened at once. Thomas raised his sword above his head and phased quickly through the intangible boss. Just as I thought something terrible would happen to Thomas, my new pet jumped into the air, claws swiping as they aimed for one of the few remaining floating lamps.

The lamp flew, spinning through the air, as little strands of inky black smoke fell like water through a sieve. The room was filled with the sound of crackling energy as the magic in the lamps began to dissipate.

Before the Djinn could react, my **Ice Breath** hit the final lamp. The cold, icy bright blue blast contrasted sharply with the dim blue radiating from the Djinn. The air around me crackled with the sudden drop in temperature. While a **Fireball** would've been safer and less painful, I noted as another tooth fell out, followed by a wave of pain, the **Ice Breath** was the best option because it physically moved things. The spell collided with the last lamp, shattering it with a resounding crash. The room was filled with the sound of breaking glass and the hiss of escaping magic. I collapsed as the pain in my mouth worsened, my vision blurring from the intensity. I was frustrated that these spells were so powerful but exacted such an excruciating cost.

I sighed, fighting back tears as my tongue slipped over the gums, the pain was like nothing I had ever remembered experiencing before. The battle raged around me, the Djinn's evil laughter echoing through the chamber. His voice was a haunting melody that sent chills down my spine. The fate of our mission depended on our next moves, and failure was not an option. The air was thick with tension, the weight of the situation pressing down on me.

As I racked my brain trying to figure out how to get through this situation, I remembered what the mini-Djinni had said: "Oh, my father can't be killed. He can only be overthrown and trapped like in those Aerlyntiums." The words echoed in my mind, a reminder of the Djinn's power and the futility of our struggle. But then I spotted it. Underneath where the Djinn had been the entire time was an eerie blue lamp, the same shade as the Djinn. There was an obvious answer. I just needed to trap the Djinn using its own lamp. The realization hit me like a bolt of lightning, and I felt a surge of determination.

I rushed forward and dived underneath the Djinn. The lamp was cold in my hands, the metal smooth against my skin. The room seemed to hold its breath as the words left my lips. The magic in the air seemed to pulse with anticipation. The lamp glowed brightly, and a blinding light filled the chamber. I felt a surge of power coursing through me, the energy almost overwhelming. But instead of solving our problem, things went from bad to worse.

Chapter Ninety-Six
The Djinn of Aerlyn, Part 4 of 6

As I held the lamp above my head, my voice trembled with desperation as I shouted, "I wish the Djinn was trapped in the lamp!" The words seemed to echo in the oppressive silence, each syllable charged with the weight of my fear and determination. The room held its breath as if the very air was waiting for what would come next.

The same cyan mist that had poured out earlier now enveloped the Djinn, beginning to flow back into the lamp. It snaked around the room in questing, searching tendrils, seeking out its prey like a serpent hunting mice. When it grabbed the Djinn, he laughed—a sound that grated on my ears and made me scream in pain. The laughter reverberated through the room, mocking and cruel, slicing through my resolve. The mist wrapped around me like a liquid shroud, lifting me into the air. The sensation was disorienting, and my heart raced as the ground disappeared beneath me. In a dizzying whirl, the mist pulled me, Thomas, Kingsley, and the Djinn into the lamp, spiraling us through a vortex of cyan smoke.

~Run 7, The Lamp, Floor 2, The Fallen Merchant City of Aerlyn~

I awoke in a strange, otherworldly place. Everything felt unnaturally large: chairs too big, torches the size of humans, a table meant for giants. The scale was unsettling, like being trapped in a giant's playroom. The cyan smoke permeated the room, a hazy fog that blurred the edges of reality. For a second, I almost felt like I was back in the perfumed prison room. The air was thick with an oppressive sense of magic and confinement, making it hard to breathe. Each inhale felt like drawing in a thick, heavy substance, weighing me down.

The Djinn, now also trapped, appeared before us, laughing maniacally at our shared fate. His laughter echoed ominously, bouncing off the unseen walls of this mystical prison. "Welcome to your new home!" he jeered, his form flickering like a disturbed flame. His eyes burned with evil glee as he relished in our mutual imprisonment. "Escape if you can," he taunted, his voice dripping with malicious amusement. Then, just as suddenly as he had appeared, he vanished, leaving Thomas and me to our fate.

Thomas's scream echoed through the cavernous room as he slammed his fist into the giant table. The sound was a dull thud, swallowed by the oppressive atmosphere. "This is all your fault. If you had just given me the lamp, I could have fixed things," he spat, his face twisted with rage. His eyes blazed with anger, the intensity of his emotions palpable.

"Sure, like I knew he would trap us inside of here," I retorted, my voice rising in response. The defensive anger surged within me, a desperate need to shift the blame and protect myself. The tension between us crackled in the air, thick and suffocating.

"This is why I never wanted to work with you," Thomas snarled, his eyes flashing with a mix of anger and past grievances. "Ever since Klericho…" He paused, frowning as if struggling with his emotions. Then, he turned away, the fire in his eyes dimming. His anger seemed to deflate, replaced by a weary resignation. "It's a moot point, and this arguing gets us nowhere." He walked forward, placing his hand on the wall, just as I had taught him, searching for a way out.

We navigated the perimeter of the vast room for what felt like an eternity. The silence between us was heavy, filled with unspoken tensions and the weight of our predicament. As we moved, a faint whirring noise caught our attention. The sound grew louder with each step, soon accompanied by a whooshing noise and distant screams. The atmosphere grew tense, and our shared silence was filled with unspoken fears and anxieties.

We both paused, looking at each other. "What do you think that is?" I asked, dread creeping into my voice. My heart pounded in my chest, each beat a reminder of the unknown dangers lurking ahead. The air felt thick with anticipation, every nerve on edge.

Thomas's face hardened. "I'm not sure, but considering how much the Djinn changed the second floor, I'd bet my entire inventory that it's a trap or something," he said, his voice shaky with uncertainty. Despite his words, there was a flicker of determination in his eyes, a resolve to face whatever lay ahead. The uncertainty gnawed at us, but there was no other choice.

"The only way to find out is to charge ahead," Thomas replied, determination hardening his features. His jaw was set, and his eyes burned with a mix of fear and resolve. The resolve in his voice was almost reassuring, a strange comfort amidst the chaos.

~Run 7, Guillotine Room, Floor 2, The Fallen Merchant City of Aerlyn~

The next room was bizarre. A singular, rickety wooden suspension bridge, held up by magic, joined two clay platforms, each holding a door. The bridge swayed ominously with every gust of wind; each creak was a harbinger of potential doom. Halfway down the bridge was a platform with an all-too-familiar altar. On that altar sat a carbon copy of the Djinn's lamp—the one we were trapped in now. The sight of it sent a chill down my spine, the implications clear.

Then I heard the noise again. Giant axes and three guillotines descended from the sky, slicing through the gaps between the bridge's planks at different intervals. The sharp, metallic sound was accompanied by a low hum, like the distant growl of a beast. At the other end, a literal horde of bizarre creatures awaited us. Their faces were contorted into angular shapes atop beanpole bodies, their limbs little more than hands and feet jutting out at odd angles. As they noticed us, they screeched and started crossing the bridge, three, four, five at a time. Their shrill cries filled the air, a cacophony of terror that sent shivers down my spine.

As they made their way down, the axes and guillotines descended from the sky. It was a slaughterhouse. Creature after creature was sawed in half, cut off at odd angles. The sight was gruesome, a macabre dance of death. The screeching was a horrifying, gut-wrenching sound like a toddler being ripped apart. The sight of their twisted bodies being severed sent waves of nausea through me, but I couldn't tear my eyes away. The blood splattered across the bridge, the metallic scent filling the air.

I glanced at Thomas, his face pale but determined. "We have to get across," he said, his voice steady despite the chaos around us. His expression was grim, a stark contrast to the panic rising within me. I nodded, swallowing hard as we prepared to face the deadly gauntlet ahead. The bridge seemed to stretch out infinitely before us, a narrow path lined with deadly traps.

My heart shattered at the sound of the creatures' screams, and then things got worse. The parts of the creatures that didn't fall off the bridge bubbled, jerked, and then morphed into more of the creatures, leaving behind almost a gallon of blood each time. The air was thick with the stench of blood and decay. If we didn't hurry, the room was going to overflow with their grotesque forms. The sight of the multiplying abominations, drenched in blood, filled me with a deep, primal fear. Their numbers grew with each passing moment, a relentless tide of horror inching closer and closer to us, blocking the only path forward.

The fear clawed at my chest, threatening to overwhelm me. But I forced it down, steeling myself for the ordeal ahead. We had no choice but to cross the bridge and face whatever awaited us. The thought of failure was unbearable, the consequences too dire to contemplate. With a deep breath, I took the first step onto the creaking, swaying bridge, the weight of the situation pressing down on me like a physical force. The air was thick with the promise of danger, and I could only hope we would survive what lay ahead.

The air was thick with the acrid stench of sweat and fear. My shirt clung to my back, drenched with the exertion and terror of the situation. Every breath felt like inhaling hot coals, and my muscles screamed in protest as I forced them to move.

"What are we supposed to do against that?" I screamed, my voice raw. The horde of abominations surged forward, their grotesque forms multiplying with each slash of a blade. Panic twisted my gut into knots, and I felt a cold sweat bead on my forehead, mixing with the grime and blood that coated my skin.

Thomas, ever the calm in the storm, glanced at me with a steady gaze. "Maybe they are weak to magic since physical damage isn't working. Maybe try using **Scan**," he suggested his voice a lifeline of rationality amidst the chaos. His eyes were sharp and focused, contrasting with the frantic energy that coursed through me.

"**Scan!**" I shouted, the word tearing from my throat as the creatures drew closer. Their bodies were a nightmarish amalgamation of twisted limbs and bubbling flesh, each more hideous than the last. The bestiary entry appeared before me, the text clear but offering little comfort:

Enemy Entry 0030: Abomination (Djinn) *(Level: 4)*
The abominations are beings created by the wild, disruptive magic of the Djinn. Unlike most other abominations in Penance, these creatures

are laughably weak. However, physical attacks that rend the flesh will separate the creature into two or more pieces, forcing the remaining pieces to regenerate into increasingly grotesque forms. The longer the torso, the more times the creature has regenerated. The progenitor is the only creature that can truly die. To find it, look for the smallest abomination.

Weaknesses: Lightning
Strengths: Everything else; physical damage absorption

Stats

- **Level:** ???

- **Health:** 10/10

Loot

- No loot unless you want limbs that will reform into a new abomination and buckets of blood.

Chapter Ninety-Seven
The Djinn of Aerlyn, Part 5 of 6

I stared at the entry, my mind racing. The description was a cruel joke, offering a glimmer of hope only to snatch it away. The bridge beneath us seemed to groan under the weight of our impending doom, the cold stone slick with blood and ichor. Thomas's face was set in grim determination, his jaw clenched.

Without warning, he charged forward, a blur of motion. His sword sliced through the monsters, but instead of stopping them, they split, regenerating into more horrid forms.

His movements were precise, almost mechanical, as he threw the pieces over the edge. For a moment, I stood frozen, my heart pounding in my chest. And then I realized what he did.

The pit wasn't a pit—it was a rising lake of blood, fed by the endless tide of abominations, already filling with the guillotined monsters.

I forced myself to move, jumping into the pool below. The blood was thick and viscous, clinging to my skin like a second layer. The metallic tang filled my nostrils, making bile rise to my throat, but I pushed forward.

The creatures flailed wildly, their limbs thrashing as they struggled against the viscous, dark-red liquid that clung to them like a sticky web. Their distorted faces were locked in expressions of silent agony, eyes wide with terror, mouths open in soundless screams. The thick, syrupy substance proved too resistant for them to advance, trapping them in place.

Desperation surged through me as I realized the creatures were too numerous to bypass. Gritting my teeth, I did the only thing I could think of. "**Lightning Slam**!" I shouted.

Raising my arms to the sky, I felt the crackling energy surge from within, radiating from every pore. Lightning arced and danced around me like an explosion of raw power, illuminating the dim chamber in brilliant, blinding light. With a fierce cry, I brought my hands down, slamming them into the bloody pool.

Bolts of electricity cascaded outward, snaking through the crimson liquid and striking each monster with lethal precision. The creatures convulsed, their bodies jolting violently as the lightning coursed through them. The stench of burning flesh filled the air, mingling with the metallic tang of blood.

Panting heavily, my body trembling from the exertion, I forced myself to move in the brief respite. Blood dripped from countless wounds, mingling with tears that streaked down my face. The overwhelming pain and exhaustion threatened to overwhelm me, but I couldn't afford to stop.

I stumbled forward, pushing through the temporary lull, and found myself below the platform. The dim light above cast long, sinister shadows, and the air was thick with the stench of blood and ozone.

I clawed my way up to the platform, my fingers slippery and numb. I managed to get my leg over and rolled onto my back. The lamp, our only hope, was just within reach. But as my hand closed around it, it vanished, slipping through my grasp like water.

"No!" My scream was torn from my throat, raw and desperate. Thomas's scream told me he saw the whole thing.

The Djinn appeared, mocking us with a twisted grin; the lamp held aloft like a trophy. His laughter was a dagger, twisting in the wound of our hopelessness.

The room seemed to close in around us, the walls pulsating with the eerie glow of the Djinn's magic. Thomas's eyes were locked on the creature, his expression a mask of defiance.

"Don't give in to this monster. We'll beat him," he said, his voice a steady anchor in the chaos. "We fight with everything we've got."

The chase that followed was a blur of motion and noise. Thomas leaped over the abominations with practiced ease, his movements fluid and precise. I plunged back into the blood, swimming through the tide of monsters, my muscles burning with exertion. But just as I pulled myself up onto the other side of the bridge, the door slammed shut behind Thomas, leaving me alone with the horrors of the pit.

I pounded on the door, my fists aching with the effort. The blood continued to rise, inching closer to the platforms. The abominations flailed as the axes continued cutting the ceaselessly multiplying monsters, their cries a cacophony of pain and despair. I hugged my knees to my chest; the cold seeped into my bones. The nightmare seemed endless, an inescapable loop of terror and hopelessness.

Crystal's voice cut through the haze of my thoughts, sharp and scathing. [Are you seriously giving up just like that?]

"What can I do? The door won't budge!" My voice was barely a whisper, choked with exhaustion and fear.

[If I had a body, I would throttle you. Do you see your friendly neighborhood boss over there, munching happily away on abominations?]

"Yes?" I glanced over; the sight almost comical in its absurdity. My goblin king was feasting on the endless supply of monsters, seemingly oblivious to the chaos around it.

[Why don't you have him knock on the door before giving up?]

I blinked. It was obvious that knocking on the door was one of my only ways forward, especially considering how low on mana I was after using **Lightning Slam**. The thick, acrid air filled my lungs as I struggled to regain my breath, the room's continuous flooding adding to the growing tension.

It took a while to coax him over to my side. The creatures' grotesque forms still thrashed in the bloody sludge, making every moment feel like an eternity. The air was heavy with the stench of ozone and blood. When he finally reached the door, I asked him to knock it down, hoping against hope. He threw his weight against it, but the door didn't budge. The sound of his futile attempts echoed in the chamber, a cruel reminder of our predicament.

"Ahhh!" I screamed in frustration, the sound reverberating off the walls.

[Use your overpowered magical spells, or try anything other than immediately giving up?]

C'mon, Rod, get it together. I know you can beat this; I chided myself.

The words were a spark, igniting a fire in my chest. My breath came in ragged gasps, but I forced myself to my feet, the weight of my exhaustion bearing down on me. The former boss goblin was within reach, and I had to push through. Summoning the last vestiges of my strength, I cast **Mana Drain** on him.

Mana Drain was a spell of dark elegance, pulling the shimmering essence of mana from a target and channeling it into the caster. As I focused, my hands glowed with an eerie blue light, and I felt the cold, hungry tendrils of the spell extending toward the goblin. His eyes widened in panic as the magical energy left his body, flowing into me as he died. The rush of stolen power was intoxicating, filling me with renewed vigor and strength.

With my mana reserves replenished, I prepared to cast again. I closed my eyes, focusing on the familiar pull of power within me. The room seemed to shrink away as I delved deep into the blistering heat at my core, drawing out the threads of magic. "**Fireball**!" I shouted, releasing the spell. The fiery orb shot from my hands and splashed harmlessly against the wall, leaving only a scorch mark.

"**Ice Beam**!" The spell left a small hole, barely a pinprick, but it was enough. I felt the magic drain from me, the cold seeping into my veins. My vision blurred, and my head swam, but I held on, pushing the spell further. The pain was a constant, throbbing ache, but I ignored it, focusing on the task at hand.

Finally, the hole was big enough. I collapsed, my body trembling with exhaustion. My HP was dangerously low, the bar flashing red in the corner of my vision. I fumbled for a potion, the cool liquid a balm against the burning in my throat. As my health was restored, I grabbed my bag, stuffing it with the rest of the mana potions, and tied it to my belt. I was ready.

As soon as I crawled into the new room, the stifling air hit me, thick with the scent of sulfur and burning wood. Sweat clung to my skin, dripping down my face and stinging my eyes. I had to dodge as the Djinn sent spell after spell in my direction, the air crackling with raw energy. I barely had time to catch my breath before retaliating, launching a couple of **Fireballs** that exploded in a blaze of orange and red, illuminating the room in a fiery glow. The heat from the flames washed over me, mixing with the adrenaline coursing through my veins.

Chapter Ninety-Eight
The Djinn of Aerlyn, Part 6 of 6

Thomas, undeterred by the barrage of magic, charged in with a fierce battle cry, his blade gleaming in the dim light. His face was set in a grim expression, eyes narrowed with determination. He swung with all his might, and to my surprise, his blade cut through the air and made contact, drawing a thin line of crimson from the Djinn's arm. The metallic scent of blood mixed with the smoky air was a stark reminder of the life-or-death stakes of this battle.

The Djinn snarled, its eyes narrowing with a mix of anger and amusement. It raised a hand to its wound, fingers brushing against the cut. Thomas pulled back, his chest heaving with exertion, readying himself for another attack. The Djinn, however, was quick to recover. It unleashed a burst of wind, a powerful gust that sent Thomas staggering backward, nearly knocking him off his feet. His boots scraped against the rough stone floor as he struggled to maintain his balance.

Not wasting any time, I focused my energy and conjured a bolt of lightning. The air hummed with electricity, and I felt the familiar tingle in my fingertips as the spell charged. I sent it crackling through the air toward the Djinn. The electricity danced along its form, causing it to shudder for a brief moment, the smell of ozone filling the room.

Thomas regained his footing and charged again, his sword aimed for the Djinn's heart. Sweat glistened on his brow, his breath coming in ragged gasps. This time, the Djinn anticipated the move and vanished in a burst of light, reappearing behind him. Before Thomas could react, the Djinn swung its staff, knocking him off balance. Thomas let out a grunt of pain as he hit the ground, the impact echoing through the room.

I quickly conjured another **Fireball**, the heat searing my palms. The Djinn warped again, avoiding the spell with a smug grin and reappearing closer to me. It grinned wickedly, its eyes gleaming with malice, and unleashed a dark bolt of energy. The spell struck me square in the chest, pain shooting through me like a thousand needles piercing my skin. My muscles seized up, and I could barely move, the world around me blurring. My breath hitched, and I felt the cold sweat of fear trickle down my spine.

The Djinn took advantage of my stunned state, warping across the room to unleash another spell. A dark wave of energy erupted from its hands, sweeping toward Thomas. He tried to dodge, but the spell hit him, and he cried out as he was thrown off his feet, landing hard on the ground. The room seemed to spin, the edges of my vision darkening as the spell's effect wore off. I struggled to regain my bearings, the pain in my chest still throbbing.

My vision cleared just in time to see Thomas getting up, his face pale and drawn, but the Djinn was faster. It warped again, appearing directly in front of me. Its eyes were like burning coals, full of contempt. It sent a shockwave of energy at my feet, causing the ground to ripple and buckle. I stumbled, trying to keep my balance, but the floor gave way beneath me, and I fell to my knees. The cold, hard stone bit into my skin, and I gritted my teeth against the pain.

Thomas, too, was caught in the Djinn's trap. The ground beneath him surged upward, tripping him and sending him crashing to the ground. We were both vulnerable, struggling to regain our footing as the Djinn hovered above us, its eyes glowing with triumph. It raised its hands, gathering energy for another attack, the room crackling with power. The air was thick with the scent of magic and battle, and the atmosphere was charged with tension.

But I knew we couldn't give up now. With a surge of determination, I pushed myself up, my hands trembling with the effort. Electricity crackled around my fingers, the familiar sensation grounding me. With a shout, I released a **Lightning Slam** toward the Djinn. The spell shot forward, lightning arcing through the air. At the same moment, Thomas rose to his feet, his sword at the ready. The Djinn tried to warp away, but my spell hit it just as it began to fade, disrupting its teleportation.

Thomas took the opportunity to charge, his blade cutting through the air with deadly precision. The Djinn let out a howl of pain, staggering back as blood seeped from its wounds. The metallic tang mixed with the acrid scent of burning magic created a nauseating combination. Thomas and I stood side by side, panting and battered but ready to finish the fight. The room crackled with energy, the air thick with the scent of magic and battle. My heart pounded in my chest, each beat echoing the urgency of the moment.

"Keep at it, Thomas!" I shouted, launching another **Fireball**. My voice was hoarse, the words barely carrying over the chaos. Thomas kept swinging away with his sword, his face a mask of grim determination. "I won't stop until this thing is down!" he yelled back, his voice barely audible over the din of battle. His hands were clenched around the hilt of his sword, knuckles white with tension.

I threw **Fireball** after **Fireball** at the Djinn, my hands shaking from exhaustion and the strain of constant spellcasting. The heat from the flames scorched my skin, and my throat burned from the acrid smoke that filled the room. I drank potion after potion, the cool liquid soothing my throat and replenishing my dwindling reserves of health and mana. Just as I was about to cast another spell, a voice spoke into my mind.

{There's no rule about taming a secret boss either. Now's your chance.}

Without hesitating or even wondering where the familiar voice came from, I threw out my hand and cast a **Mana Battery**. The force of the spell was immense, and I felt myself being thrown to the ground like discarded trash. Pain exploded in every part of my body as if every bone had shattered at once. My vision blurred, and I gasped for breath, the agony almost unbearable.

A small lamp burned onto my arm next to the crown for Kingsley and the thumbs up for Thumbs. The heat was intense, searing my skin, and I clenched my teeth against the pain. The lamp's glow was eerie, casting a strange light over the room.

[Congratulations! You have tamed Djinn, the secret boss. (**Mana Battery**)]

Suddenly, like a veil had been lifted, the foggy remains of Djinn's lamp vanished, and we were back in the boss room. I laughed, a bitter sound that echoed in the silence that followed. I looked around at the chaos and destruction the fight had caused. The room was filled with smoke and ash, the remnants of our battle scattered everywhere. Blood pooled on the ground, both mine and Thomas's, as well as a dark, spreading stain around Klericho's body. Unlike past attempts, his body hadn't evaporated into an Aerlyn orb.

I sighed as I walked forward to Thomas, feeling the exhaustion in my bones. My muscles ached, and my wounds throbbed with a dull, persistent pain. Just as I was about to clap my hand on his shoulder, he turned around and thrust the sword into my gut. The pain was immediate and overwhelming, a fiery lance through my abdomen. I let out a bloody gasp, my vision darkening at the edges.

"You—what—?" I stammered, the words barely escaping my lips. Pain and shock overwhelmed me, the betrayal cutting deeper than the blade.

"All this time, practically years pretending to be something I'm not, well, no more," Thomas hissed, his eyes cold and filled with fury. As he snapped his fingers, a flood of demons entered the room, their eyes glowing with malevolence. A gauntlet formed around Thomas's hand, hovering over the tattoos on my left arm. Inky blue magic, similar to the Djinn's, flowed from the tattoo as it vanished off my arm, receding into the gauntlet. The Aerlyn orb had vanished off my arm, leaving a dull ache in its place.

"What—what did you do?" I struggled to speak through my broken mouth and mortal wounds, tears rolling down my face, unbidden.

"There is more to this dungeon than your pitiful gods—real, ancient power. And it thirsts for an ancient vengeance that can no longer be held back."

Thomas pulled the sword the rest of the way out of my slowly fading body. The pain was excruciating, a burning agony that spread from my gut to every part of my being. I assumed I still had a single point of health left, or the run would have ended, but I had no energy to move and little more to speak. My vision blurred, and I felt the cold hand of death closing in.

"For years, Rellum has abandoned me to this horrid place as a guard. No promise of advancement, making a name, or even attaining *salvation*." He spat at the ground as he said the word 'salvation,' his voice dripping with contempt. "What *she* has promised has already been delivered. Powerful weapons. Freedom. The chance of ascending to the top. And without the Aerlyn orb, that horrid excuse for a man over there will never return." He glanced at Klericho's lifeless body with disdain. "I got myself killed to get away from him the first time. Imagine my shock that a fourth full year had passed before someone was worthy of Penance." He laughed bitterly, the sound grating against the eerie silence that had settled over the room. "I will surely see you again, but it will be in your power, not Malikap's. Any last words?"

Pain seared through my body, my vision fading in and out. I knew I had only moments left. With the last of my strength, I managed to choke out, "**Ice Beam**, bitch." The words were barely a whisper, but the spell surged from my mouth, and a blast of cold energy shot toward Thomas. The surprise on his face was the last thing I saw before my mouth exploded in a red mist, and everything went dark.

As I lost consciousness, the cold of the spell was the only sensation I felt, the icy power contrasting with the burning pain of my wounds. I heard Elizabeth's voice, distant and cold, intone,

[You have died. End of Run 7. Due to the destructive power of whatever Thomas did, your corpse has been obliterated, destroying all of the items on your person.]

The world went dark, and I was left with nothing but the lingering echoes of betrayal and the bitter taste of failure.

Chapter Ninety-Nine
Jamie, Run 2, Part 4

I stood among the remains of the shattered chapel. Its once majestic stained-glass windows were now broken and scattered across the cold stone floor. The sight filled me with a deep, aching sadness, a stark reminder of the sanctuary this place had once been. The air was thick with the scent of decay and lingering magic. It felt more like a graveyard than sacred ground.

A lump formed in my throat as I recalled the warmth and light that used to fill this space. Now, only darkness and desolation remained. The dim, flickering torchlight barely illuminated the eerie scene, casting long, ghostly shadows that danced along the walls. The corpses of my father's guards lay scattered across the floor. Their bodies were frozen in grotesque poses, locked in eternal agony.

Despite the passage of time, they remained unclaimed by decay. Their armor rusted but intact. The sight was a macabre tableau. I couldn't shake the feeling that they might suddenly rise and attack, their hollow eyes filled with some unfathomable malice. A cold shiver ran down my spine. My skin prickled with unease.

Hovering above me was Malice: the floating, talking crystal that embodied all things malevolent. His dark, smoky core pulsated with a dark purple glow, contrasting sharply against its polished, reflective surface. He bobbed slightly in the air, exuding an aura of sardonic amusement. His voice, cold and mocking, filled the air with an unsettling presence.

[Killing family guards? That's almost like killing a brother. You're moving up in the world. I am so beyond proud of you; it brings tears to my eyes,] he laughed, a sound of distorted joy.

I felt angry at his words, my hands clenching into fists. The crystal's twisted sense of humor always grated on my nerves. This time, it felt like a knife twisting in an open wound. The guilt and horror of what I had done were still raw. Malice's callousness only deepened my shame.

A shiver ran down my spine. The weight of the situation pressed heavily on my shoulders. Once a place of reverence and sanctity, the chapel now felt like a twisted parody of itself. It was a place of death and decay. My heart ached with the loss of its former beauty. I wasn't sure how I had ended up in this cursed place, but being trapped with Malice for eternity seemed like a fate worse than death. I needed to focus on the task at hand—collecting loot. Malice insisted it was essential to gather enough resources on this floor to stand a chance against the looming threat of the big boss.

"If I get all the loot on this floor," I muttered, trying to muster some semblance of resolve, "I'll have a better shot at beating whatever's waiting for me." My voice sounded hollow, even to my ears. The words were meant to be reassuring but felt like a flimsy shield against the overwhelming dread looming over me.

Malice's tone turned sharp, a dangerous edge to his words. [Listen here, Missy. We had a deal. Get all the loot on this floor and then face the boss. Otherwise, I'll make your life even more miserable than it already is.] The threat hung in the air, heavy and suffocating. I felt a knot of fear tighten in my chest, the reality of my predicament settling in with a cold, hard clarity. Arguing with a floating crystal felt absurd, yet it was my reality.

Hours passed as we scoured the rooms I had initially skipped in my haste. The cold stone corridors echoed with our footsteps. Each step felt like a step further into the abyss. The oppressive silence amplified the weight of the situation. We collected over 200 coins and two armor pieces—copper and iron. Though old and slightly dented, the armor still held a certain weight of craftsmanship. Malice claimed this would make our journey to the next floor easier if we encountered any merchants. To me, 200 coins seemed pitiful in the grand scheme of things. A sense of futility crept in, the thought of facing the unknown with so little at my disposal gnawing at my confidence.

"Malice, can you pull up your map?" I asked, the need for a plan growing in my chest. The crystal flickered, and a sprawling palace map materialized before me. It was detailed, with colored dots marking the rooms I'd visited and those I hadn't. The map even highlighted potential secret locations, eerily mirroring the secret passageways of my palace in real life. Despite the chaotic rearrangement, only a few rooms were left.

An unsettling quietness settled over the hallways as we approached the next room. The door was slightly ajar, and a chill ran down my spine as I pushed it open. My fingers tightened around the shaft of my halberd. The room beyond was dimly lit, cluttered with overturned furniture and scattered debris. It looked like a storage area, though nothing was ever as it seemed in this place.

Malice hovered beside me. His core pulsated with a faint, eerie light. He radiated a smug satisfaction, as if he knew something I didn't. [You know,] he began, his voice dripping with sarcasm, [I never tire of these charming little surprises this place offers. It's like a never-ending treasure hunt, but with more death and decay.]

Ignoring Malice's taunts, I scanned the room for signs of danger. My eyes landed on a figure slumped in the far corner. At first, it looked like another corpse, one of many we had encountered. As I stepped closer, the figure moved. Its head snapped up to reveal a gaunt, decayed face. It was a zombie. Its eyes were hollow and lifeless, yet filled with a mindless hunger.

I felt a surge of adrenaline as the zombie began to rise, its movements jerky and unnatural. My grip tightened on the halberd, and I braced myself. The creature lunged at me, its rotting hands reaching out. I was faster. With a swift motion, I swung the halberd, the blade slicing cleanly through the air. The impact was jarring but satisfying as the blade bit into the zombie's neck, severing its head in one clean strike.

The head rolled across the floor, stopping at Malice's base. The crystal bobbed in the air, a chuckle emanating from his core. [Well, that was disappointingly quick. I was hoping for more of a struggle. But then again, you have a knack for getting straight to the point.]

I ignored Malice's jibes, focusing instead on the task at hand. Kneeling beside the now-lifeless body, I rifled through its tattered clothing. My fingers found a small pouch of coins and a few tarnished jewelry pieces. It wasn't much, but every bit counted in this cursed place. I pocketed the items and stood, my gaze sweeping the room for anything else of value.

The room was filled with broken shelves and ancient artifacts, most too damaged to be of use. Still, I couldn't shake the feeling that something important was hidden among the rubble. I continued to search, my movements quick and efficient. We needed to gather as much as we could before moving on.

Malice floated closer, his voice low and mocking. [Ah, the noble quest for loot. It's almost touching. Like a band of merry adventurers on a grand quest, only with more blood and less heroism.]

I shot the crystal a glare, my patience wearing thin. "If you're not going to help, at least don't distract me," I snapped, my voice tight with irritation. Malice's constant commentary was grating, but I couldn't afford to let it get under my skin. Not now, with so much at stake.

After what felt like hours, we finally gathered everything of value. I straightened, feeling a mix of relief and exhaustion. The zombie had been a minor threat, easily dealt with, but it was a reminder of the dangers that lurked around every corner. We couldn't afford to let our guard down for a moment.

As we left the room, I glanced back one last time. The zombie's headless body lay sprawled on the floor, a grim testament to the twisted reality of this place. I turned away, my mind already on the next challenge. We had to keep moving, keep collecting, and keep fighting. It was the only way to survive.

A knot of anxiety tightened in my stomach as I realized that it would likely be the boss's room. The possibility of facing my father filled me with a mixture of dread and confusion. What would I do if it was him? The thought sent a chill through me, the image of my father's stern face flashing in my mind. The man who had always been a pillar of strength and authority was now a potential enemy. The thought was almost too much to bear.

The massive, ornately detailed door loomed before us as we approached the throne room. It was a masterpiece of craftsmanship, installed shortly after my mother's death. The door, crafted from rich rosewood, was inlaid with intricate patterns of gold leaf, depicting scenes of royal grandeur. Silver metal handles, polished to a gleaming finish, reflected the dim light. My father's new family emblem was emblazoned prominently, a symbol of his vanity and obsession with appearances. The irony wasn't lost on me; more money had been spent on this door than my coronation. If my father had cared as much for the people as he did for his luxuries, perhaps our country wouldn't be in its current state. A wave of bitterness washed over me, the memories of my father's neglect and indifference resurfacing.

The door was a testament to his misplaced priorities, a painful reminder of the rift between us. My thoughts were abruptly cut off as we stepped inside. The throne room, once a symbol of power and authority, was now a mockery of itself. Instead of the expected treasures or fearsome monsters, the room was filled with mundane items—mops, buckets, and other cleaning supplies. It was a stark contrast to the grandeur of the rest of the palace, an anticlimactic and almost absurd discovery.

"Malice, can you confirm if we've cleared everything?" I asked, frustration bubbling up within me. The scene felt like a cruel joke, the disparity between expectation and reality striking a raw nerve.

Malice's voice was cold and detached. [The floor is empty. Now, we head to the throne room.] There was a finality to his words, a sense of inevitability that made my heart race. The weight of the impending confrontation loomed large, the uncertainty of what lay ahead gnawing at my resolve.

I paused, staring at the imposing door that led to the throne room, and took a deep breath. This was the culmination of everything we had worked towards on this floor. The air was thick with anticipation, and I knew that whatever awaited us would be a turning point. My eyes scanned the room one last time, a mixture of relief and trepidation coursing through me. I couldn't make any mistakes; the next step was crucial. With a final nod, I pushed open the door, ready to face whatever lay ahead. The moment felt monumental, the world's weight pressing on my shoulders. Whatever happened next, it would change everything.

I should have expected it, but I was unprepared for the words that met my ears.

"Hello, Jamie."

END OF BOOK ONE

Thank you

Thank you for sharing this adventure with me.

If you have enjoyed this story, I'd be truly grateful if you'd leave a review on Amazon.com. It helps a metric ton!

And, for updates and more adventures, you're invited to join my mailing list at ShadowLightPress.com/penance

Come hang out with me and other authors on our discord at Immersive Ink.

Acknowledgements

I did it. I wrote a book! My God, my God, I did it!

You'll never understand just how much work goes into writing a novel until you complete your first one, and there's no way an author can do it 100% alone. I have so very many, many people to thank for this novel finally being in your hands.

First, my wife, who from day one has tirelessly supported my new hobby. She has believed in me every step of the way, and this story would not exist without her pushing me on the days I just didn't want to write. I am so grateful for her never-ending support. Love you, boo!

Next, my friend Blue—without whom this project would never have made it past the idea phase, let alone secured the publishing deal it did. Everyone needs a Blue in their life. I'm lucky to have mine.

Third, to the YouTube musician VectorU—I don't know what it is about his music, but it gets my writing juices flowing and keeps me focused like nothing else.

Then there are the wonderful Trailblazing Authors who shouted out my tiny story during its initial launch and helped it flourish: Juggernaut, Bainan, Reecebrooks, SAH, and quite a few others. Thank y'all so much!

Next, my publishing company, Shadow Light Press—Fobywoby, MisfitMonkey, Niinawo, Anajade, and the rest of the gang took my hobbling, disfigured monster of a book and turned it into the wonderful manuscript you've (hopefully!) just given five stars.

718 PENANCE: BOOK ONE

Then there's the whole Immersive Ink gang, which grows by the day and continues to inspire me and keep me rooted: Emrys, Foby, Dom, Grey, Popo, Rook, Madfire, Erebus, Weaver, and the 1,800 other members of the Discord (as of publication). Y'all inspire me every day to improve and become the writer I've always wanted to be.

And finally, you—the reader. The reason this book exists. Most especially, a few fans who've given me the special joy that only a writer will ever know: the joy of someone taking a look at your story and genuinely getting something out of it. It's the greatest feeling in the world.

Special thanks to: Malus Michael (the OG Penance fan), Rhod Briar (the second-ever Fan of the Month!), Softcorebash, KateSpell, Lorddarkrai, Catstrike, CGicognito, and the dozens of others who've commented on my story throughout the past year. Every single comment made my day, and I will cherish y'all forever.

A Bit About The Author

JF Lingsch is a middle school teacher from San Antonio, Texas, where he lives with his wife and two dogs. In his free time, he enjoys watching movies of any genre, reading books, and playing video games, particularly RTS, RPG, and Zelda games.

Penance is a passion project that he spent way too many days dreaming about and too many more writing. But he is forever grateful that he can tell his 12-year-old self that he did become the published author he dreamed of when writing the first ever Avatar: The Last Airbender fanfiction published on the net. And umm for a quote maybe, "Life is a Struggle Between Good and Evil, Those who create and those who destroy.

You may also like...

For more Penance and pre-published words by Fiddlesoup, you can read ahead on **Novelizing.com** and **RoyalRoad.com**

If you enjoyed this book, you might also enjoy:

Terra Mythica: A LitRPG Epic Adventure by John Stax, available now on Amazon.

The world is dying, and everyone knows it. But is the alternative worse?

In rust-choked streets and hollowed-out cities, there is only one way out—Terra Mythica, a virtual world so immersive that time warps, hunger vanishes, and even the most broken can live like kings.

Jace wasn't supposed to make it in. He cheated death, and now it's catching up to him. As the reluctant protégé of Hades, Jace finds himself thrust into Mount Olympus University, where gods manipulate Travelers, and the line between real and digital blurs with every step.

Rise of The Infernal Paladin: A LitRPG Apocalypse by Emrys Ambrosius, available now on Amazon.

They took everything from him. Now, he will take their world.

When the System integrated his universe, Ambrose Severen lost every-thing -his world, his loved ones, his very purpose.

Now, all he has left is revenge.

With nothing to lose, Ambrose embarks on a ruthless quest for power, determined to tear down everything the First

Forerunner has built.

No price is too high, no challenge too great, as he fights to carve a path of retribution through a shattered world.

Return of the Wing Mage by Dominick Ruiz, available now on Amazon.

What would you do if you had the chance to rewrite your greatest failures?

After eight years of brutal war, victory is finally in sight.

The forces of North America stand united, one final enemy stronghold left to conquer.

Santiago Silva - Santi to those who know him - leads the charge, his magic commanding the winds.

But just as the end seems near, a desperate enemy ritual goes awry, flinging Santi back in time.

Find more at ShadowLightPress.com

Groups and Communities

Join the newsletter at Shadow Light Press
Hang out with us on Discord at Immersive Ink
Author Facebook group at Immersive Ink
LitRPG Facebook group by Magic Dome Books
Hang out with us on Facebook at Shadow Light Press